MERIDIAN

c. j. **YEE**

Book One in the **MERIDIAN** SERIES

For Courtney.

SOUTH CONTINENT

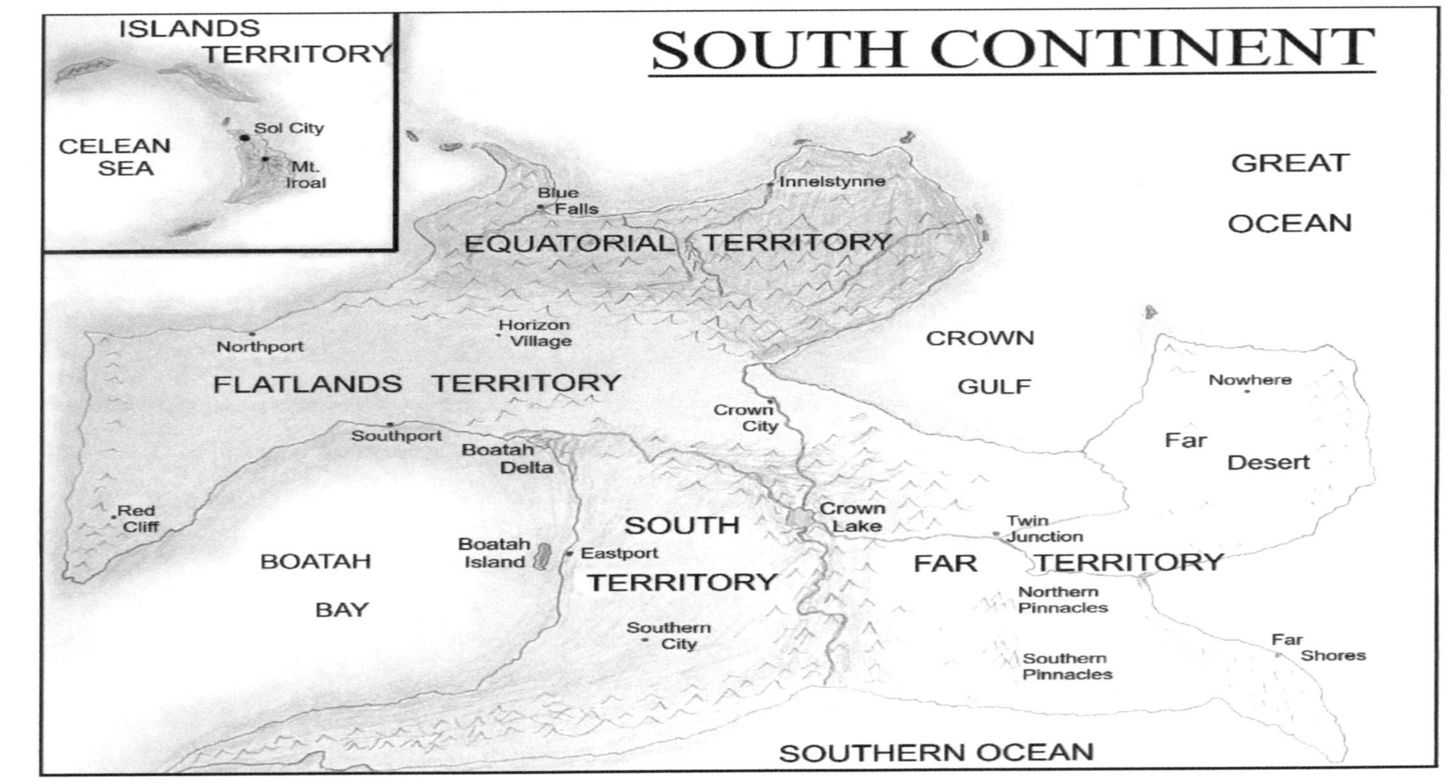

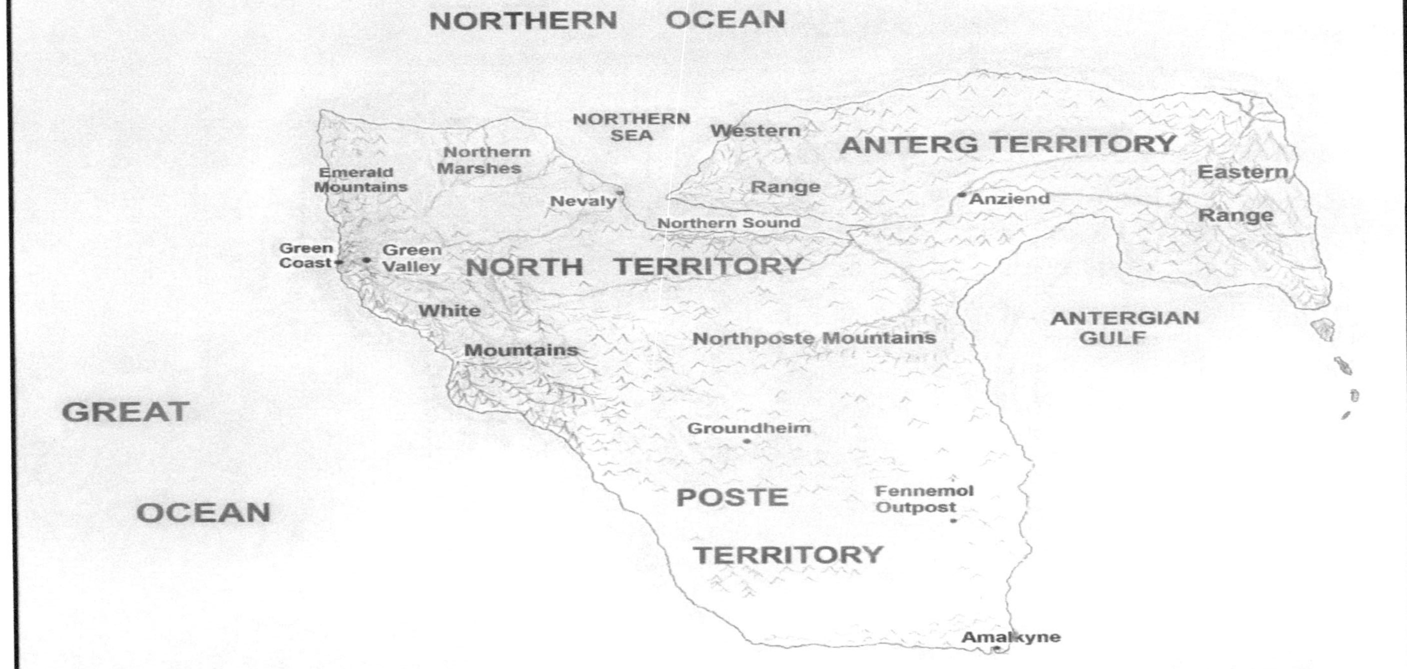

NORTH CONTINENT
NORTHERN OCEAN
GREAT OCEAN
CELEAN SEA
ANTERGIAN GULF
NORTHERN SEA
Emerald Mountains
Northern Marshes
Nevaly
Green Coast
Green Valley
White Mountains
NORTH TERRITORY
Western
Range
Northern Sound
ANTERG TERRITORY
Eastern Range
Anziend
Northposte Mountains
Groundheim
POSTE TERRITORY
Fennemol Outpost
Amalkyne

TABLE OF CONTENTS

The Machine

WHAT *are we even doing here?* Kezane thought to himself. He knew that this was absolutely ridiculous that they would risk so much on a mission that would yield so little in return. Even if they retrieved the data, it was guaranteed there would be nothing of use on it.

It's not like the Machine would know this was their sector even if it did find the *Marina*. As far as it was concerned, the vessel was just a long-abandoned relic of a bygone civilization. Nothing out of the ordinary compared to the thousands of others it would have overrun in the last 60,000 years. There was no way it would know the difference, considering the *Marina's* sole purpose after the Scuttling should have been to intentionally transmit aimless electromagnetic signals. However, if the Machine found the *Duskletter* on the other hand…

Kezane shuddered at the thought. High Command had not heeded his many objections. 'Get in. Get out. Retrieve anything that the engineers can use,' were what his orders had read. Short and to the point, at least, but there would almost certainly be no useful Nel-Mara tech on board. Any lay person in the Empire could tell you that was all long gone many thousands of years ago.

Kezane was fed up with High Command. The fact that they

demanded this farce of a mission only affirmed his lack of faith in their judgment. Something had shifted in recent years, and not just because of the growing divide between Ramen and the Tricouncil. Something much deeper had been feeling very off lately, and he was far from the only Valanse to sense it. Though he would have to admit that he was perhaps becoming too outspoken on those matters…

Kezane was well aware that he was once the spoiled golden boy of the Meridians — he had enjoyed all the political perks that come when High Command grooms you to be a future leader. He was the most naturally powerful Valanse the Meridian Empire had seen in an age, and he inevitably developed a swagger complex that made it easy for him to speak his mind without compunction. That had started to land him in trouble on more than one occasion recently. He'd never been one to shy away from speaking his mind, but lately it seemed there was corruption and hypocrisy lurking around every corner, and Kezane was not afraid to call it out. Rank or political station did not matter to him when it came to ethics.

He figured this whole mission was a punishment of sorts for his most recent run-in with High Command. Emperor Ramen himself had tasked him with investigating reports of the Valanse Academy facilitating a potential Shatter Industries takeover of the facilities on Mareia. One does not refuse a request from the Emperor, so Kezane did his duty. During his investigation, he discovered that a contingent of Valanses under the direction of High Commander Silvane had indeed been orchestrating a deal.

He also found evidence of a Shatter subsidiary running operations on an off-limits system, but before he could investigate that lead further, High Command found out he was snooping around behind their backs and reprimanded him quite thoroughly. Had they known that he already informed the Emperor of these dealings, this mission might have been the least of his punishments. Emperor Ramen had promised to keep their whole exchange confidential, so Kezane just had to accept the consequences, whatever they were going to be.

Though he was glad to know Silvane's true colors, his big regret was that he and his entire crew would be gone from Meridian systems for no fewer than seven years on this mission. Ever since travel outside of the Local Sector was banned millennia ago, a mission of this scale was almost unheard of. Even pushing well beyond the accepted velocity limits of thirty percent, it still took them over three years to arrive at their destination. Now that they were here, they would do *maybe* one day of work, then make the long trek back home.

Such a waste.

At least most of the time on the trip would be spent in the liquid suspension pods, which Kezane thought were rather comfortable. Besides, seven years wouldn't even scratch the surface of the long lives Valanses led. He was mostly upset that he wouldn't be able to see his loved ones back home for many years, and as long as it would be for him, it would be even longer for them.

Punishment or no, a mission like this would normally never be dispatched. In recent years, though, High Command had been pushing to salvage any Nel-Mara technology they could. They were worried about the increasing signs of odd solar activity in nearby systems — and rightfully so — but even if this trip were to be commissioned, it should have been conducted by an automated drone scout. Of course, remote warfare had been banned long ago, but this was not warfare.

There was only one reason Kezane could think of where it could make even the smallest shred of sense to send a full company under the command of an elite Meridian Valanse — and that was if they were worried that there was a good chance the *Marina* had information aboard that compromised the Empire.

Maybe it did, but he still thought it far more likely that the *Duskletter* being there was a much riskier play than leaving the *Marina* well alone. The nearby solar oddities only meant one thing as far as he was concerned, so time and care was of the essence. What made things even worse was that the *Marina* had briefly stopped transmitting altogether while the *Duskletter* was en route.

He didn't want to think about what it was that could possibly stop and re-start transmissions on a long-forsaken Nel-Mara vessel. The only thought Kezane could summon to ease his mind was that maybe the disruption was from some illegal salvage operation. That was extremely unlikely, though, as the *Marina* was so far from any settled system. No salvagers would have the resources available to pull off a long-range mission such as this. His rational mind knew this had become a near worst-case scenario, and he was highly unsettled that they were out here at all. They were risking so much!

Kezane did have to admit, though, that despite all his reservations, he'd been slightly intrigued to board the *Marina*. Even though it figured to be a potentially dangerous mission, and was certainly a wasteful one, Nel-Mara technology had always fascinated him. Nobody had seen any firsthand for thousands of years, aside from what the Meridians already possessed, of course. Kezane fancied himself a self-taught engineer and loved to get his hands on any tech he could...

Trailing from his thoughts, he refocused on the moment, looking up as the airlock hummed when the pressure evened out. The four Valanses he had just scouted the *Marina* with — Masa, Nolane, Ritose, and Falare — were now crossing back over to the *Duskletter*. The five of them had painstakingly cleared the massive, wheel-like vessel room by room, hallway by hallway. At first, he was disappointed to have his normal team reassigned, but he had to admit this new outfit was very good. They all communicated with such ease, working fluidly and silently. They had been assigned to his command just before this mission, no doubt some ploy by High Command to mess with his head.

Kezane refused to let it get to him, and they'd cleared the entire vessel quite quickly considering the size of the place. But as they all searched through the *Marina*, the anxious thoughts of the other four Valanses mirrored his own. By the end, all five of them were plagued with deep pangs of unease.

While they were sweeping through the *Marina*, Kezane observed some signs of destruction throughout. It was a weird sort of damage that he'd never seen before, one that almost seemed... *self*-inflicted, as if the place was trying to salvage its own constitution.

Huge red flag.

Of course, his first inclination was that the Machine had already happened upon the discarded vessel, but truthfully, he would have no idea what that would even look like. Everyone had grown up with stories of the Machine, but it was always something that was portrayed as so far away, whispers of a ghost from another lifetime. At the most, it was something for a future generation to deal with. There were many who didn't even believe it was real, though Kezane knew better. He was too well-educated and too well-informed of the evidence for its existence.

Even if this wasn't the Machine's doing, though, all the signs indicated that *something* had infiltrated the vessel. The hallways should have been clean and tidy, but there was this sort of metallic dust all over the ground, as if someone had been drilling into the walls. Kezane was just glad that whatever caused this didn't seem to be around at the moment.

Nevertheless, he ordered the Valanses back to the *Duskletter* as the engineering teams completed their work. He would remain on board to watch over them, but he wanted as few people as possible aboard the *Marina* in case they found any trouble and needed a quick exit.

Just a few more minutes... he told himself, suppressing the screaming in his gut to get everyone out of there now.

The sooner the engineering teams retrieved everything they could use, the sooner they could leave. Only then could he return back to the Capital system and repair his good standing with High Command. He tried to distract himself with the pleasant fantasy of reverse engineering some of the Nel-Mara tech on his own, but nothing could quell his uneasiness, which was becoming worse and worse with each passing moment, a rising tide that could not be stopped.

Kezane just shook his head and subdued his misgivings with all of his will.

Command doesn't have to know if a schematic or two goes missing... he thought to himself, forcing the distraction to the forefront of his mind. He breezed over to the nearest room from the airlock, stepping up to the center console to connect his own Utility Machine, or Ut. There would be plenty downtime on the voyage back, so studying some new tech was a great way to kill time.

In the split second that he connected his Ut, an intense burning sensation flooded through his mind. He barely had a chance to react, but he managed to throw his Ut to the ground, drawing his handgun and disintegrating the thing in an instant, severing the mental connection.

"STOP!" Kezane shouted through the room to all the engineers working. "BACK TO THE SHIP NOW!"

He urgently reached for his other Valanses.

It's here! Turn on the shields! NOW! To the Hole with this mission!

He sprinted to the airlock bridge, colliding with one of the engineers — Kezane was pretty certain his name was Firsin — and hauled him back to his feet with a single motion.

"Wait!" Firsin cried. He'd dropped his Ut and started back for it, but Kezane turned around and destroyed it as he had his own. Firsin gaped at him with a look of incredulity, but Kezane paid the engineer no mind, grabbing him with one arm as he barreled back to the *Duskletter*.

"BACK TO THE SHIP! DON'T ASK QUESTIONS!"

As the words were leaving his mouth, his entire reality started playing in slow motion, as Valanse training allows for. He knew *something* was on that vessel behind him, but he could not describe it, nor did he have time to.

It was a *feeling…* one that gripped his entire consciousness. It was everything — everywhere around him, like water is when one is submerged. Freezing, painful water.

He would normally have gone back for everyone behind him, but he knew with all of his instinct that there was no time. There was a more important necessity at hand, as horrible as it sounded. Where the other engineers stood, they would no longer in mere seconds. As he hurled Firsin into the airlock bridge, he lost the mental connection to his crew aboard the *Marina*, just as he'd feared.

They were gone.

All of them.

Just… *gone*. Only he and Firsin remained. It had to be the Uts. Somehow, the thing had turned their own machines against them — and lethally. What manner of intelligence could do that so quickly?

Firsin groaned in pain from being shoved to the ground with excessive force, but Kezane knew he'd thank him for it later. He then vaulted himself into the airlock with Firsin. Something burned on the back of his leg, but his only focus was on hitting the override button to close the connecting door to the *Marina*.

The bright flash behind him barely even registered.

HOLD ON! He had to yell to Firsin through his thoughts because no sound would come out at this point. He didn't even have time to turn his mask back on and reached for the nearest edge he could grip.

The air got unbelievably cold and there was no sound at all. The feeling was a strange one, but one he had felt before during his training. There was an intensely strong pull that only lasted seconds, but it felt like an eternity. Soon after, he heard a hissing noise that turned to a hum. He was able to function once again.

His lungs burned and no voice would come out, but he screamed to everyone around him with his mind. *WE NEED TO*

GET OUT OF HERE! NOW!!

He turned to help Firsin up, but the engineer was gasping and stumbling. Already full of rage and guilt over the loss of the other engineers, Kezane had but a split second to scold himself. He needed to be in the moment for Firsin's sake.

For all their sakes.

He draped Firsin's arm over his shoulder to help him to the med bay. He'd be fine, but Kezane needed to get him there fast. However, just as soon as he darted from the airlock with Firsin in hand, time slowed for him once more.

He was not confused; he only reacted instinctively, ducking and dodging the assault as he slid low and to the right. The wall behind him sparked from the impact of the shots that had just missed him. He pulled out his blade in one hand and his sidearm in the other. In one moment that seemed to defy time, he sliced with his blade and fired from his gun, dropping two targets immediately. He ducked around the corner for cover, but instead of staying there, he leapt upward as high as he could, putting himself in line of sight once again. His unexpected and immediate counterattack surprised the remaining two opponents and he quickly neutralized them.

He landed hard on the ground, agonizing pain still squeezing his lungs from the pressure drop when the airlock had been damaged. Although he needed to desperately get to the bridge, all he could do was stare at the scene of what had just transpired. In the chaos, he had no time to process any of it.

Coming to awareness, he looked to the ground by the airlock, where lay the lifeless body of Firsin, along with his four Valanse colleagues, whom he had just dispatched.

Why...?

His head was sent spinning.

Why would they do this?? And right now of all times?!

The sudden coughing of blood startled him.

Nolane.

At least he wasn't dead, but one look told Kezane that he didn't have long for this life. Masa, Ritose, and Falare, on the other hand, were quite dead. Kezane knelt down beside the duplicitous wretch and touched his head. In Nolane's weakened state, he was so vulnerable to Intrusion, and Kezane was able to see exactly why they had done what they'd done.

Silvane.

Red-hot anger swept through him. He should have known from the short-term roster change to his crew right before departure... He vowed that he'd expose that man as soon as he got back. *If* he got back.

Kezane could not dwell on his anger a split second longer and dutifully snapped himself out of his stupor. Leaving Nolane to his fate, he sprinted through the halls and up the stairs to the bridge.

"Get this ship out of here! NOW!!" he bellowed as he entered the bridge.

The room was already quite bustling when Kezane burst in, but surprised heads swung in his direction and silence ensued. He pushed one of the flight engineers aside from his post to complete his checklist for him. Kezane couldn't exactly blame the man for freezing up, but he should have been able to stick to his training. This was no time to gawk!

"You heard him!" First Officer Galen Anstraes roared in support for his commander, which seemed to spur the crew into action. In a mad scramble, everyone on the bridge scurried to their stations and set to prepare for departure. "Masks on, find a seat, strap in!"

Suddenly, the entire room was enveloped in a brilliant aurora that shone as bright as Providence. In any other situation Kezane might have appreciated its beauty, but he knew what it was. A timeless moment of quiet stilled the air on the bridge as an invisible shockwave raced through the darkness toward the *Duskletter*.

Less than a moment later, the ship shuddered from the impact. Before Kezane could even find his own seat, the world seemed to flip upside down. A massive impact had completely severed the docking connection from the *Duskletter* to the *Marina* and the room was sent into weightlessness. Everyone that had not secured themselves went flying, hitting the low ceiling with force. Panic immediately abounded, but he could hear Anstraes still delivering orders.

A fine officer, Kezane thought, just before he slammed into what must have been the ceiling. The whole bridge seemed upside down, consoles and seats now above him. It was as if the decks were Switched like during the halfway points of space journeys, but an instant later, his world reversed and he was returned to right-side up, albeit in a daze.

After a few seconds of disorienting confusion, Kezane found

his bearings, and was more than grateful to be alive and conscious. Through the din of shouting voices and crashing bodies, he knew that the *Duskletter* had almost immediately self-corrected to resume the circular trajectory that it kept during its docking.

Thank the Mara for Meridian engineering! he thought.

As people scrambled to their feet from the floor, flashing lights and a warning siren filled him with dread once again. He knew that siren — it was the one that would signal excessive levels of radiation on the exterior of the ship. He sprinted to a screen and pulled up the real-time schematics of the *Duskletter*, immediately understanding why that aurora that surrounded them was so radiant. The ship wouldn't be able to withstand that much gamma radiation forever...

"Destroy the *Marina*," Kezane commanded calmly.

At this point, survival was paramount to worrying about facing whatever the consequences for losing the *Marina* would be. It was already lost. Besides, this was Command's own fault for sending them on this mission in the first place. He *knew* this would happen. He knew it in his gut. And he had *told* them. There was no time for contempt right now, though. Only action.

"Commander?" Anstraes looked at Kezane questioningly.

"Four Mark III's. Destroy it NOW and get us into SGL away from this place!" Kezane yelled more urgently. "Everyone hold on to something! Strap up if you're able!"

Anstraes gave him a curt nod, then executed a series of commands on his console before the ship aggressively turned away. Kezane gripped hard onto the railing with his hands while wedging his legs under his seat. He didn't see the missiles on their flight path through space — only the bright flash of the subsequent explosion outside.

There was a brief silence as everyone held their breath in waiting.

An instant later, those not fortunate to be strapped in were sent crashing into the walls as all manner of chaos broke out. Kezane was supremely focused on the moment and was able to keep his balance, but nobody else seemed so fortunate as the trained Valanse. He tried desperately to grab onto whoever he could, but it was too tall an order. As soon as he would stabilize one person, a sharp jerking motion would send them flying right back where they came from. Arms, legs, and even necks were snapping from the repeated impacts with the cascading debris from the *Marina*. Blood pooled into floating droplets and was sent splashing across the room in all manner of directions, some even onto his face.

The screams of the unfortunate pierced Kezane's very soul, but he had to steel his nerve. He loved these people and was responsible for their safety, but he *had* to make that judgment call. If the *Marina* had not been destroyed, the *Duskletter* surely would have been.

Whatever it was — the Machine, he presumed — had been bombarding them with the highest levels of gamma radiation he'd ever seen. Although this ship was equipped with the very best long-range radiation shielding, they weren't going to last much longer. Seconds, maybe. Had he not acted, none of them would have made it out. This was not a time to go down with the ship because they *had* to transmit the emergency warning to the Empire. They *had* to.

Fortunately, the aurora cocooning the *Duskletter* was no longer, which meant that the radiation bombardment had subsided. Now, he just needed to hope that his crew was able to hold on for dear life as they were pinballed through the wreckage of the *Marina*. Just before the explosion, Anstraes had managed to send the ship into standard gravity level acceleration, but the turbulence was still enough to send those not buckled in hurtling across the bridge.

After a particularly severe collision sent Anstraes himself sailing overhead, Kezane abandoned the safety of his refuge and hurled himself through the air, grabbing hold of the unconscious officer with a tackling motion. Just before the two landed in a manner he was expecting, another jerk of the ship accelerated the wall unexpectedly toward them. Kezane reactively turned his body to cushion the impact for the two. As if adding insult to injury, they dropped from the wall and hit the floor hard. After struggling to his feet, Kezane used the break in action, however long it would be, to rush Anstraes over to a chair, strapping both of them in together. There was nothing else he could have done for the others.

Another collision rocked the ship, and Kezane held Anstraes' head tightly with his arms while bracing himself by wrapping his legs around the base of the seat, once again becoming aware of the jarring pain that shot from his lower leg. He must have injured it worse than he thought when he first escaped from the *Marina* to the *Duskletter* with Firsin. It was of no matter, though — he would have to bury this pain and focus on the moment. His life depended on it.

All their lives depended on it. They needed to send the transmission.

After enduring a seemingly endless minute of battering, Kezane was much relieved when the periodicity and intensity of the impacts finally waned. The spinning Shell had done its job well enough because the ship still stood intact. No radiation bombardments, no hull breaches, and no engine failure.

Thank the Mara, he sighed.

His gratitude faltered, however, when he was finally able to survey the human cost. He looked around the room, utterly horrified to see most of his crew lying twisted and broken on the floor. Each violent impact with the debris had produced havoc too unpredictable for most people to react to. Kezane, of course, had years of intense mental conditioning, but the rest of his crew was not so lucky. The knowledge that he made the right call did little to soothe the guilt and sorrow he felt over their deaths.

"Anstraes!" he hissed.

No response.

"Anstraes!"

Kezane adjusted his hands and felt for a pulse. He was alive, thank the Mara.

When he pushed the First Officer away from his body, though, he clearly saw the side of his head slicked with blood. Anstraes must have hit his head hard during one of the collisions. Kezane knew he needed to get him to the med bay, but he was nervous to unstrap in case there were any more pieces of the *Marina* on a collision course with the *Duskletter*.

"Mose! Aragase!" he shouted.

"Commander!" both of them returned. At least someone was still alive. Second Officer Michele Aragase and Flight Deck Engineer Noralie Mose both seemed alert and coherent. Good.

"What do the schematics say? Are we clear of debris?" Kezane asked them.

The two set to work, performing a series of swipes on the screens before responding.

"Yes, Commander, it looks like we are clear," Mose replied with an audible exhale of relief.

"Okay. We need to get people to the med bay, now," he said sharply. "Mose, come with me. Aragase, run all the diagnostics to be sure we are good. And make sure AutoNav is working correctly. Then come help us."

"Yes, Commander," they both replied.

He finally unstrapped himself, straining to keep Anstraes' unconscious body from slumping to the ground. There was no backboard on the bridge, so they'd have to carry him by arms and legs to the med bay. Luckily, it was only one level down from the bridge.

"Grab his legs," he instructed Mose.

She obeyed and the two of them hauled Anstraes' dead weight across the room. Kezane gritted his teeth as they stepped over dead bodies, most of them grotesquely twisted into contortions that were beyond what was compatible for life. Mose's breathing became shaky as they clambered over more and more of their fallen crewmates. Kezane saw the panic rising in her and knew he needed to distract her.

"Focus on Anstraes. Once we get him to a station, find a backboard."

"Yes, Commander." Her voice wavered, but she knew the duty she needed to perform.

As they left the bridge and climbed down to the med bay, Kezane remembered he had destroyed his Ut back on the *Marina* during his escape. Not having a Ut connected was going to be annoying for so many little things — like not being able to open doors.

"Can you open it?" he asked Mose. "My Ut is fried."

Mose nodded and the med bay doors slid open to reveal a bright, spotless room, even whiter than the rest of the ship. The two of them waddled Anstraes over to the nearest station and heaved him up onto the platform. Kezane swung the monitors over him and tried to connect his Ut to the machines.

Ugh! he thought once more. This was going to be even more annoying than he thought. He knew he was attached to that tiny piece of machinery, but it seemed as if every little thing he wanted to do was dependent on it. He swore that when he was out of this mess, he would eliminate his dependency on the damn thing! Everyone should. After all, Uts could now be used as a weapon against them by the Machine...

Still, he needed one now.

"You need the Ut for this too..." he said to Mose, rolling his eyes. "Can you set him up on the machines? I'll go take the backboard and go get more people."

"Of course," she replied.

Frustrated anew, he unfolded a backboard from the wall and glided it back up to the bridge, setting about the grim task of corpse recovery.

After several minutes, the unpleasant business was completed. He stepped back onto the bridge, his mood gruff after finding no one else alive. His right calf was burning worse and worse, but he'd only check himself into the med bay after all tasks were completed.

"Commander, we are on course for Trevi Nali," Aragase announced. "Diagnostics are clean. There was some damage to the starboard crew decks, but those have been sealed off and adjustments have been made to the trajectory."

"Very good," Kezane absently replied.

"Would you like me to send the transmission?" she asked.

"I will send it, thank you," he replied calmly.

He nodded to her, then stepped up to the console. He was annoyed at himself for nearly forgetting about the damn transmission! Losing focus, even for a moment, was very unlike him. And this wasn't just any task! It was to send the most important message in the history of the Meridian Empire — and it needed to be sent immediately.

He knew they were lucky to even have the chance. The mission had come dangerously close to total failure. This *had* to be the Machine. It *had* to be. There was so much evidence starting to pile up at home in favor of its existence, and this encounter would confirm the worst fears of it being hostile. It had tried to kill them.

No, not tried...

It *did* kill them. Most of them at least. All of the engineers aboard the *Marina*, and now most of his flight crew during their escape.

And it had all happened *so* fast. This wasn't at all how the Machine had been depicted in the Legends, where brave defenders battled massive hordes of mechanical legions. The real thing was much more effective than anyone realized. More silent. More invisible. It was so terrifyingly efficient in its assault, and Kezane figured the only reason any of them survived was because of the *Duskletter's* significant radiation barriers.

Worse, he suspected that this wasn't even the tiniest fraction of what it was capable of. They were so far from any star system that whatever energy it could access out here had to be only a sliver of what it might wield closer to a power source. What had attacked them was likely nothing more than a meager scouting filament.

He thought of all the star systems that were experiencing solar oddities… there were millions, possibly even *billions*… How would they even stand a chance?

The absolute scariest part was that it now *knew* they were in this sector. Kezane was thoroughly terrified at how smart it was, and reflected solemnly on how it behaved.

The way it repurposed the *Marina's* reactor…

The way it knew exactly how to defeat them once it learned of the Ut…

The way it bombarded their ship with the most focused levels of gamma radiation he'd ever seen…

And the way it waited patiently for its ambush…

Basically, the Meridians were in trouble. That much was clear. There was no way that level of intelligence had not sent transmissions of their whereabouts back to the rest of… itself.

Judging by the proximity of star systems exhibiting solar anomalies, a realistic estimate placed a full-scale Machine incursion into Meridian space within a decade. Twelve years at the most, if those systems were its point of origin. This was bad. *Very* bad.

Kezane would warn the Meridians about everything he saw, but would they even listen? All parties in charge would need to cooperate to the fullest, and cooperation wasn't something the Meridian leadership had been proficient at in recent years. That revelation now worried Kezane more than ever.

He was beyond furious with Silvane for the assassination attempt, but the Empire could *not* afford division — not now. Whatever Silvane had done, he was vital to their survival. The man was an exceptionally strong leader and commanded much respect among the people. Realistically, Kezane knew the only chance they had was with Silvane and Ramen working together. Against his deep personal wishes, he supposed that no, he would not deliver the scathing report of High Command they so deserved. This wasn't the time for vengeance.

Swallowing his pride, he began the transmission and delivered a very carefully worded message. He omitted everything about the Valanses that had tried to kill him, but reported on every other event in detail. He warned Command of all the specifics he experienced from their encounter with the Machine — everything from its ambush tactics to the electromagnetic bombardment. He delivered the unfortunate news of casualties, which had turned out to be everyone besides himself, Mose, Aragase, and Anstraes. Lastly, he gave a few suggestions.

Chief among them: begin construction on a gamma-ray shield. Immediately.

After ending the transmission, he collapsed into the back of his seat and sighed, allowing himself a moment to catch his breath. His leg still burned, but he suddenly paused in thought, distracting himself with something he remembered from long ago. Something he had learned from the An-Mara, of all people.

The Prophecy of the Stewards.

It had always been a joking matter to the Meridians. Kezane himself thought the An-Mara were nothing more than self-righteous clowns who preached down their noses with a holier-than-thou attitude. Making claims about a prophecy was so on-brand for them. But suddenly it now seemed so... *hopeful*.

There was something about this Prophecy of the Stewards that suddenly sparked intrigue within Kezane. When he was very young, An-Mara zealots had approached his family, claiming that *he* was the candidate of this prophecy, the one they called the Child of the Nel-Mara. He was well aware that he was the most powerful Valanse in an age, but Kezane knew deep down that he was not this prophesized Child of the Nel-Mara.

He always thought prophecy was such a ridiculous notion, but what if it was actually real? Could this be the key to defending their sector? If the Machine was as infinite as the evidence in the galaxy suggested, all the might and technology of the Meridians would not save them from an onslaught. They needed something more than they had.

A Child of the Nel-Mara would be a start, if this individual existed. Though he was not this Child himself, Kezane decided that it would be prudent to devote his abilities to finding them.

Yes, that is what he'd do.

Besides, High Command had just proven that they did *not* deserve his talents any longer. Even if he did go back, he didn't have to be a Valanse to know that they'd lay the blame on him for everything: for the destruction of the *Marina*, for the lives lost, even for leading the Machine to their sector. He'd be their scapegoat, perfect and complete. Silvane would see to that quite thoroughly.

No, he would not be going back to them. Not just yet, at least.

"Commander?"

Kezane was still leaned back in his seat and barely noticed Mose and Aragase trying to get his attention.

"Apologies," he said, snapping back to the moment. "Correct the trajectory to the An-Terino system. I will be departing upon our arrival at An-Terino. You two will then continue en route to Trevi Nali."

Both Mose and Aragase looked very confused, wrinkled eyebrows and all.

"I have business I must conduct before returning," he added, deliberately being as vague as possible. High Command wouldn't reprimand those two so long as they were not aware of his intentions.

"At Alashadar?" Aragase seemed very hesitant, and rightly so. That place was not traditionally very welcoming to Meridians. Or anyone, for that matter...

"Yes," Kezane responded. "Mose, you and I will prep the suspension pods. We should aim to transition into the Greater Acceleration as soon as possible. And don't worry, this detour will only tick off a few months."

Aragase and Mose reluctantly nodded and set off about their tasks. They no doubt had many questions, but Kezane didn't let them see his own apprehension about any of this. This had to be the most awful day of their lives — the least he could do was give them a commander who was confident in his plans.

Internally, though, questions abounded in his mind.

First and foremost was that of his family. Would they be persecuted if he was seen as a deserter and a traitor?

Kezane Pfase — the one who led the Machine to the Local Sector, then fled like a coward.

He knew that's the reputation he would be branded with, but he'd never been one to concern himself with the judgment of others. Knowing his true worth had always been enough, and right now he knew he was doing everything in his power to save their civilization.

However, he would not stand idly by while his family was punished as some political collateral on his account. He needed a way to keep them safe from afar, as he was steadfast in his resolve to find this Child of the Nel-Mara before returning home.

Hmmm. He would have to devise a plan to satisfy these worries of his...

Fortunately for him, he had no shortage of time to do so.

Kezane glanced at the AutoNav calculation and sighed to himself. This was going to be a *very* long four years with only this skeleton crew for company…

Before getting up to prepare for the Greater Acceleration, he allowed himself one more moment of deep thought, overwhelmed by the existential fear that now hunted at the back of his mind.

———————

PART ONE

The Green Coast

1

Homecomings

THE trees went by, some starting to become studded with blossoms and fruits, but most others wrapped only in thick foliage. The occasional farms and fields along the side of the road were carpeted with pristine grasses that glimmered of recent rain. They were quiet today — it was still early in the spring season, but soon all the farms would be humming with activity.

On both sides of the road, all shades of green were blurred with gold as Niko Ryen stared out the window into dimmed, low angle sol-rays. She had always appreciated the scenery on this stretch of highway, especially on days like today where broken sol-light would illuminate the hills in patches. The drive reminded her of trips her family would take when she was young, though they would usually go later in the year when the weather was more pleasant.

Good memories.

It rained many days out of the year up on the Green Coast, but even in the early spring one could catch a few minutes of sol-light here and there. That year-round rain, along with the cold and snowy winters, kept the area to a lower, rural population. Niko didn't hate the small town she grew up in, but lately she'd been feeling an itch to get out and experience the wider world. Luckily for her, she recently had the opportunity to do just that.

In fact, she was currently on her way back from the airport in Green Valley, the only nearby city that could pass for the term. About two hours inland from her home by car, Niko had always thought of Green Valley as a huge city, growing up on the Green Coast and all. However, seeing the great Sol City in person had put everything into perspective.

A continent away, the capital of the Islands Territory was an actual megalopolis of what seemed to be a hundred times the size of Green Valley, and Niko had just spent the last week there. The place was nothing like how it looked in pictures... The way the skyline remained stationary as they sped by on the city's high-speed rail made the towers seem more as mountains than manmade structures. The railways themselves were an architectural feat of strength — the way they intertwined with the buildings and the sky, reaching nearly half the height of some of the skyscrapers!

The Islanders of Sol City were just as much a wonder to her as the architecture was, if not more. Beautiful, regal — always gliding around with their signature golden blond hair and shimmering dark skin, their colored eyes seemingly glowing in the shade of their sharp features.

Niko had always been a little envious of them, although perhaps the whole world was. The Islands were the richest and most powerful of the Territories, and their people the best looking.

If only I could have that golden hair... she wished to herself. *Or the perfect dark skin... Why can't I be like Riesen?*

Thinking of Riesen made Niko pause. Thoughts of him always brought her mixed feelings. She loved her brother dearly, but success came way too easily to him, and that was so infuriating. She laughed inwardly at the foolishness of her jealousy, not bothering to hide the smug smile that spread across her slender face. In truth, she was exceedingly proud of Riesen.

"Whatchu smiling at?"

Niko lifted her head up from against the window, startled by the broken silence.

"Ah nothing," she replied, that same uncontrollable smile swelling even more. "Just thinking of the other day."

Keran turned his eyes back to the road, and Niko saw that same infectious pride that she was feeling sweep over him, also. This had been going on the entire two hours they'd been in the car. It was impossible to think about the other day *without* smiling.

I can't believe we won! Niko thought, almost breaking into a laugh. It really was almost too good to be true.

The largest sporting event in the world, the Field World Championships, was held each year to commemorate the Anniversary of Arrival, the day when the world changed forever, or so the old people said. Niko was much too young to know the difference. The world had been a stable place her entire life, and the Arrival was just a chapter in the history books. That, and a week of never-ending parties…

This year, her hometown had even more reason to celebrate than most — it just so happened that the star player for North Territory was none other than Riesen Ryen, the wonder boy from the Green Coast. He was only seventeen, barely a year older than Niko herself, and not only was he one of the best Fielders in the world, but he was recently crowned world champion Slider. As if that wasn't enough, he had also just recently graduated Primary School rank number one in all of the territories. Just a single one of those accomplishments alone would turn someone into a star. Notching all three under your belt… Well, he was now a world superstar, plain and simple.

Niko thought that she'd always wanted to be a star herself, to be striking and beautiful and influential, but there was no chance she'd ever be any of those things. Besides, seeing the subtle changes to Riesen over the past year had made her think twice. She knew the real Riesen, and it seemed like he was changing from a nice, shy kid into a more confident man, almost borderline cocky, which was a lot different than he'd ever been.

Why can't boys grow up nice?? She sighed to herself.

Although, she maybe should give him a small break… After all, he played no small part in winning the World Championships for the Northerners. And besides, he was coming home tonight instead of joining the great parades they were sure to have in Nevaly. That decision must have required at least *some* degree of loyalty to his hometown.

"You're still smiling."

"So are you!" Niko protested, making a face at Keran.

Keran smirked back, and with one arm draped over the wheel, he proceeded to poke Niko with the other. Would he ever grow out of his big brother phase?

Forget 'nice'... Boys don't grow up all! she thought wryly.

Niko didn't usually mind the banter, though; it almost made her feel accepted in an odd sort of way. She'd become accustomed to that sort of teasing her entire life, being the little sister and all.

Of course, the two siblings did not resemble a shred of the other. Even sitting in this truck, Keran towered fifteen centimeters over her, his shaggy blonde hair brushing the ceiling. Niko was sometimes complimented by adults for being cute as a kid, but she always felt so tiny and simple next to the rest of her family. To be fair, it wasn't her biological family, but it was who she lived with, and it was hard being so plain in comparison.

Niko had been adopted by the Ryen family, but at least she wasn't the only one, and that always gave her a sense of reassurance and belonging. Riesen was also adopted by the Ryens, and it was obvious that he was no Northerner by blood because he was a spitting image of the Islanders, if only a little paler from his time way up north out of the sol.

Niko just continued to smile and shrugged off her brother's poking barrage as she settled back into her seat. They were just now rounding the long corner where the highway turned south along the hillside.

Lit by the sol-light that was now facing them, the full Green Coast came into view. The road would eventually wind itself down the slope and the view would become partially obscured by trees and hills. For a few moments, though, the panorama had to be one of the best views in the world.

Saturated clouds still choked out much of the sol-light, but it was a relatively clear afternoon for the Green Coast. The visibility was always best right after the rains had stopped. Today, the whole Coast seemed like the embodiment of natural splendor, especially now that an unreal rainbow hung over a fertile, green valley floor.

Niko Looked further south toward the mountains looming high in the distance and noticed them covered in what looked like fresh snow. "Been storming a lot this week, I guess?" she commented.

"Yeah," Keran replied, gesturing out toward the west over the ocean. He was ever the weather expert. "A pretty big storm set up earlier and camped us all week. Snow was pretty low. Even got some back home. The wind was supposedly crazy, too."

"Wow, I bet," Niko remarked as she noticed a few piles of leftover slush on the side of the road.

There was always year-round snow on the peaks of the White Mountains to the south — the ones that her friends Cryo and Ravenna invited her to climb with them last year — but it usually didn't snow on the valley floor of the Green Coast itself this late in the season. Maybe two or three times a year after the winter season had ended would they actually get light drifts in town.

"It actually warmed up the last couple days," Keran added, "except it's supposed to storm again tomorrow night."

"Hmm, that's what I heard. Stuff still on for tonight then?"

"Should be," Keran replied hesitantly, with an almost undetectable smile at the corner of his mouth. Niko had been around her brother enough to see the tell — he was *definitely* trying to keep something from her.

"Okay, what is it?" Niko asked, smiling.

"Oh nothing. Tyson just called me earlier saying that cleanup at the Farm was almost done, so I'd assume it's all still on," Keran continued on, attempting to hide his little slip.

Interesting, Niko thought. If Tyson was in town, then maybe Jen would be around also? And if Jen was back, maybe Kate also?

It was a long shot, but she missed her big sister ever since she'd departed for her service with the Meridians last fall. Niko got along with her whole family really well, but she was closest with Kate. The sisters shared a room and had spent countless nights talking and talking and talking.

It was always Kate who would soothe Niko whenever she had one of her *dreams*. Those things were scary — different from regular nightmares. They had a strange haze about them, an element of reality that made them hard to shake. They often featured people she knew, but in places or situations that made no sense, and they felt way too real to be brushed off as nothing...

She stared out the window as the truck crept along the wet highway, thinking about the *dream* she had two nights ago in Sol City. She'd awakened in a cold sweat after dreaming of people jumping off a huge, burning bridge. Two of the people she didn't know, but two she did: Riesen and Nico...

Wait! Ughh! Niko became frustrated after calling Nicodaren Nico... She'd already resolved to start calling him Daren because Niko was *her* name!

She shook her head, but resumed her thoughts, telling herself the bridge was only a dream. Of course it was only a dream. Why would *anyone* jump off a bridge that high otherwise? She would've told her sister of it, but unfortunately she wasn't due to be back in town for another three months.

Leaving for service to the Meridians was not a matter of choice, but one of duty after graduating Primary School. However, it wasn't so much seen as an obligation as it was an exciting rite of passage into adulthood. Besides, from what some of the older folks said, the Meridians were far more relaxed than some of the preexisting militaries of times before the Arrival. The Meridians were highly regarded now, and it was no secret they'd brought a sense of standard and order to a very confusing and chaotic episode in time.

Niko, now thinking about the Meridians, had half a mind to press Keran about what he knew of life beyond Arhanda, but she decided to let it be. He'd probably just respond how he always did — with all that 'small steps' nonsense everyone spewed. Plus, they were almost home now, anyway.

She looked out the window as they passed the Green Coast city limit sign. Population 912...

"Feels good to be back," Keran sighed in relief.

"Tell me about it. Almost forgot how gnarly our town was," Niko joked sarcastically, though she was happy to be back.

The town's 'skyline' sprang into view as they passed the last grove of apple trees before turning onto Main Street. It wasn't quite as grand as she'd once thought, but driving down Main Street was a refreshing feeling. The road was barely wide enough to be considered two lanes, and almost every building on either side was only one or two stories. The tallest structure in town was a tower for an old bell that hung above the Collection center, but even that was overshadowed by some of the Northern firs that dotted the town. How had she gotten so used to Sol City so quickly?

"Aw c'mon, you gotta love it here," Keran prodded. "Tomorrow morning's supposed to be prime at the Farm. Think we're all going out. You should go."

But it's so cold here... she complained to herself.

Niko loved Sliding, but she'd been spoiled last week. The sport's stereotype was of a hot, sandy beach and thousands of tanned spectators laying out and enjoying the spectacle — which was exactly how it had been at the Islands. Niko was always amused by the contrast between that image and the reality of the sport on the Green Coast, which was a few friends in the freezing cold water with one or two people bundled in jackets watching from the cliffs above a narrow, rocky shoreline.

"Yeah, I'll go out tomorrow," Niko replied absently.

"Good, cuz we're not taking no for an answer," Keran said, smiling as he turned the truck onto a narrow dirt road.

After topping a small hill, he pulled into a gravel driveway lined with apple trees on one side and a grassy field on the other. The driveway wrapped around the field and led to home sweet home, a modest one-story house that meshed well with the landscape.

The buildings were so small here! Niko couldn't believe how quickly her mind had adapted to life in the city. Still, there was something to be said about home and she was all too happy to be back, if for no other reason than to get out of her cramped seat.

As soon as Keran parked his truck along a row of trees, Niko tumbled out and immediately set about stretching her legs. She'd spent six hours of the day on an aircraft and two in a car, neither of which seemed designed for comfort. She reached into the back to grab some of her luggage, then headed up the cobblestone path that led to the front door.

The path was enclosed on both sides by a lush yard full of all kinds of assorted plants. Niko's mother, Trienne, had imparted a thorough gardening education on her when she was young. Niko had taken to it quite industriously and naturally had a very keen eye for detail. The arbor that hung over the path was still dripping from the rains, but the weather had been getting warmer overall. Hints of budding flowers of all colors climbed both sides of the arbor, with more already bloomed near the fence by the field. Soon enough, overflowing grasses would carpet the yard, meaning she'd have some work to do.

She would also need to recoat the fences and gates with sealant. Niko doubted that her younger brother Mack had seen to it while she was away. Sure enough, the wood at the base of the gate looked like it was already becoming warped. Too many exchanges between wet and dry would do that.

"I told him to recoat the gates," Niko complained out loud.

Keran seemed confused as to what Niko was talking about, but after Niko pointed toward the warped wood, he just shrugged and replied, "hmm, well, you know Mack."

Niko just shook her head. Her younger brother was so stubborn sometimes. He was probably too busy reading his books or playing

VR. How could anyone go through life spending as much time indoors as that kid did? Perhaps it was because he was so much younger than the rest of them and had nobody to play with?

Niko made her way up the porch, still intently scanning the garden, making mental notes of what needed tending to. All of a sudden, the front door to the house burst open, and she found herself blindsided by multiple people. Like in a brawl from a cartoon, luggage was sent flying and bodies somersaulting. It seemed that the rest of the Ryen family had been lying in wait for her and Keran. They were a very physical and affectionate family, and Niko was too tired and her legs too stiff to stand her ground this time.

Untangling herself from the pile, the first faces she discerned were the characteristic brown-haired, brown-eyed family members of Mack and her father Jame. Her mother Trienne and Riesen also joined the fray, their Islander characteristics unmistakable. Although her mother was an Islander expatriate, she was so Northerner in spirit that it never occurred to anyone that the family should even resemble Islanders. They were Northerner through and through and that's all there was to it.

"Welcome back, kid," her father greeted.

Niko's nickname in the Ryen family had always been 'kid', which had grown increasingly annoying as she grew older. Even more annoying was that they called Nicodaren *Nico*…

His name is Daren, and I will die on that hill, she promised herself.

"Missed you guys!" she exclaimed.

"I know! I wish we were able to stay for the last game and meet up," her mother said. "You'll have to tell us all about your trip with your team, though! Three weeks with them — I'm sure you have some great stories. And Keran, how was the drive?"

Her mother turned to greet her older brother, and the next face Niko saw sent her reeling — but in a good way.

"Kate!! I knew it!!" she exclaimed. "…But your hair!"

She didn't notice her big sister immediately because her signature wild golden hair was dyed black, cut shorter, and straightened. Strange that it should look so natural on her either way she wore it. She loved her big sister too much to be truly jealous, but at the same time she always had to admit how beautiful Kate was in comparison to herself.

The girl had perfectly smooth features, glowing eyes, and a fit, feminine figure that Niko wished she had. Sure, her sister would constantly remind her that she was still young and would turn into a beautiful woman in time, but Niko doubted that she would ever hold a candle to Kate. That was just the big sister reassuring the little sister that all was well, even if it wasn't.

Niko sighed inwardly. It wasn't as if she was exceptionally ugly. She just felt that she had no shape that she wanted. She felt like a little kid compared to her sister, and even to her friends her own age, for that matter. Thinking about how she got confused for a boy by some random lady a few months ago still infuriated her!

"I know! Funny story, but the hair accidentally caught on fire during our training, so I decided to just cut it and dye it all! It was time for a change, y'know," she laughed. Leave it to Kate to catch it on fire and still turn it into something that looked good.

"Well, it looks great," Niko said in truth, as the two Ryen girls embraced in a forever hug. "I want to tell you so much! I can't wait to catch up with you!"

The smell of dinner was starting to linger from the open door, though, so she promptly finished hugging her sister. As she did, she noticed the entire Jenaei family waiting their turns to greet the homecomers.

"Jen Jen! I missed you, too!"

Niko embraced Kate's best friend, who was by default one of her closest friends also. Jen Jenaei had practically grown up with the Ryens, and the three of them had spent many a girls' time out together.

"Hey, kid," Jen replied. "Missed you, too!"

As Niko finished hugging her, she caught sight of Jen's younger brother Brandon, who happened to be Riesen's best friend. Her heart always seemed to stop when she caught sight of him, for she had always had quite an unmentioned crush on him. Of course, she would never ever admit that to anyone else, but he was just so... His green eyes were so... And his hair...

Snap yourself out of it, she scolded herself. *C'mon, pull yourself together, girl!*

"Hi... Brandon," Niko started.

Why did she just stutter? The butterflies came immediately, and as she started forward, she second guessed herself and didn't know if she should hug him. Instead, she just awkwardly stood to the side and waved, internally cursing her ineptitude.

"Hey, kid. How was the trip?" he casually replied.

Every time he called her 'kid', it killed her inside a little bit. Did Brandon really see her as a little kid? He wasn't even a year older than her!

"It was good!" she exclaimed.

Ugh, calm down. You do *sound like an excited little kid...*

"I'll tell you guys all about it at dinner, although Riesen's stories are probably more interesting." Niko laughed nervously, rolling her eyes.

"Nah, we'll hear yours. Riesen's insufferably cocky now. He'll probably tell us this story of being World Champs for the rest of our lives," Brandon replied, playfully elbowing his friend in the arm.

"You know it," Riesen shot back, grinning with what Niko could only pinpoint as a newfound swagger at his friend. She was fairly certain that he didn't have that same demeanor a few months back.

She was excited that Brandon said he'd rather hear her stories over Riesen's, though. *Did that mean anything?* Probably not... She shouldn't get her hopes up for that kind of thing. She'd certainly *never* live it down if word got out that she had a huge crush on Brandon.

Sighing to herself, she decided to congratulate Riesen again. She gave her brother a big hug and added a little sucker punch to his gut.

"Ouch, thanks for the love," he complained.

"That's for ditching me for those girls after the game." Niko made sure to level her best glare at him.

"Ooooh, what's this now, Riesen?" Kate chimed in.

"They were reporters!"

"Sure they were..." Kate teased.

"I can't say no to interviews after the game, you know," he pleaded.

"Not the reporters!" Niko playfully hissed. "After, when I was waiting in the lobby for you!"

Riesen's face grew a little heated. It was subtle, something only a sister would notice, but she knew it got to him. Maddeningly, he played it off so cool, like he did everything else in life.

"Oh, those were girls I knew from School. They were in the program with me."

Niko continued to play her best stern face, but knew she

shouldn't expect her seventeen-year-old brother to spot her in a busy lobby while he was surrounded by girls, as annoying as it was…

Both the Ryen parents and the Jenaei parents laughed, probably thinking the same thing.

"Well, dinner is almost ready," Trienne announced, diffusing Niko's attempted scolding of Riesen. "Keran and Niko, go ahead and get cleaned up if you want."

That was music to her ears. An entire day of traveling would have anyone longing for a nice shower. Besides, she was writhing on the inside for looking like this in front of Brandon. She spared a glance in his direction as he headed into the house with Riesen, no doubt congratulating him on those girls he 'knew from School'.

Ugh! Boys... They were the worst!

As everyone else headed back into the house, Niko went back to the truck to grab the rest of her luggage. Mack was still rolling around on the ground so Niko pulled him up and matted his shaggy brown hair. He was young, only eight still, and only came up to his sister's shoulders. At least she could play big sister to somebody.

"What happened to recoating the gates, dude?"

Mack only looked away and sheepishly grinned. *Oh, blazes. I shouldn't make the poor kid feel bad,* Niko thought.

"It's alright, we need to replace that fence anyway," she added, barely suppressing a wince. That was a chore she was not looking forward to. "Missed you though, bud."

He smiled up at her and darted back into the house. He was an odd one, Mack. He never seemed to talk much to anyone. Except to Kyler. Maybe it was the love of machines they both shared.

Shaking her head and smiling to herself, she grabbed her last two suitcases out of Keran's truck and paused to enjoy the last few minutes of sol-light before heading inside. Even though she'd become quite enamored by life in the outside world, there was something about this place.

Okay, it's nice to be back, she admitted to herself.

Her attention was drawn back to the house, where she could hear the sounds of dinner. She was also starting to smell the meal from out front — definitely tomato soup, probably with some sort of meat and spiced with all kinds of herbs the way her mother was fond of. She thought she could smell some home baked bread, as well. Her stomach growled, and she suddenly realized how hungry the day of travel had made her. She hadn't eaten a single thing, other than the light breakfast early in the morning. That thought alone spurred her on toward the house.

As she walked along the pathway to the front door, she could make out the hills that dropped straight down to the ocean beyond the trees to the west. Right over the crest of those hills was the Farm, which at the moment was being prepped for the big gathering tonight.

CHAPTER TWO

2

The Farm

THE fire crackled and pitched, trying to fix itself up into the bonfire it had been earlier. That battle was long over, though. Niko's halfhearted last ditch efforts to keep the fire alive only succeeded in sending it into its death throes. Most of the dry wood had already been used, and she was now tossing in pieces that were still damp. Maybe she should just hold off; most people had gone inside anyway. To be sure, loud music and sounds of jollity drifted down to the beach from the house that was just up the hill.

The night wasn't even half over, but it had gotten chilly quite rapidly over the past half hour or so. Niko would have headed in long ago had she not been engaged in conversation with her friends. Kate and Jen kept shivering and rubbing their arms to keep warm, but Daren — *NOT Nico*, she thought irritably — never seemed to notice discomforts, the cold least of all. He was the quietest person she knew, and she didn't think she had ever heard him complain about anything in his life.

Niko just stood with her hands in her pockets to stay warm, not yet about to show how cold she really was. The four of them were the only ones still down on the beach, and she enjoyed talking to her friends in small groups rather than among a mob, which would be the case if she headed back up to the house.

They had been talking for quite some time, first about Kate's new hair style, then about style in general. The Sol City Collections were nothing short of amazing and Niko had plenty to share with Kate and Jen.

Maybe Green Valley has some of those? Niko thought. *We gotta go Collecting one of these days, before Kate and Jen have to leave again.*

Ever since her sister and Jen had left for the service, Niko always found herself hanging out with the boys. It's not that hanging out with the boys was unenjoyable, but sometimes she just really wanted to feel like a girl. Her Field team was all girls of course, but usually when she was with them it was all grind, all work. All of those girls lived two hours away in Green Valley anyway, so she never really got the chance to bond that closely with them.

The conversation slowly switched to Field and all the fun they had playing when they were younger. That led into the World Championships and Riesen, of course, and now they were talking about Sliding. It seemed most chats with her Green Coast friends had to do with one of those few topics: Field, Sliding, or Riesen.

Case in point: she had to endure an entire night's worth of her hometown friends glorifying her brother for the accolades he'd racked up over the months. A small amount would've been alright — after all, he deserved some praise for what he'd accomplished. But all night?.. *Seriously??* It wasn't unexpected, though, especially after more than a few of the locals got too much drink into them.

Niko was more of an introverted type, like Daren. The vast majority of the Green Coasters she was raised with, though, seemed to love the big social atmosphere, which was psychotic to her. Even Daren didn't seem to squirm in large gatherings the way she did. But if there was one thing she hated more than being in the middle of a big crowd, it was being treated like a little kid.

Why should everyone else be allowed to drink the Anniversary Ale and not her? She hated always being the youngest one! Her dad let her try some of the brew last year and she absolutely detested it, but it was the principle that mattered! Riesen wasn't of drinking age yet, either, but nobody seemed to care about that. She wasn't even a year younger than him, and everyone treated him like an adult and her a little kid.

Small things, she tried to reassure herself as she took a deep, cleansing breath. These were only small things.

The night had been fun, though — more exciting than she thought it would be. Niko had vaguely suspected that Daren and Kyler might be back in town, but she didn't expect her sister and Jen to be around until Keran slipped up in the car. Even more surprising was that Cryo and Ravenna were back also. She had thought they were supposed to be climbing the mountains in eastern Anterg, the highest in the world.

Having Cryo and Ravenna back in town made her heart leap almost as much as having Kate back. Those two were possibly her biggest role models growing up. They were adventurers, pure and simple. She hadn't seen them since last summer when they had taken her along on one of their climbing expeditions in the White Mountains, the ones that loomed just to the south over Green Coast. Remembering that trip brought good memories. That was some of the most fun she'd ever had in her entire life, even if it was challenging.

"...and I was like, 'That's what's gonna happen sometimes.' I mean, what a joke," she heard Jen say.

She had been telling a story, but Niko was only half listening. Something about how she'd been harassed by some guys during her training, and then beat them up. Or something like that. Niko had her reservations of Jen's take on the encounter. Jen was a great friend, but Niko had grown up hearing many a wild tale from her. Besides, she was way too sweet to actually beat someone up. Not to mention, Niko doubted Jen was even capable of it — she was rail-thin and never liked to do anything physical.

Niko found herself laughing, nevertheless. Daren just smirked and stared into the fire. What was left of the fire, anyway. He usually had that stoic expression on his face. He was fairly short of stature, but carried himself with this manner of self-confidence that could be quite intimidating. He reminded Niko of one of those forest cats, sleek and athletic.

He was four years older than Niko and nearing the end of his service to the Meridians, who apparently thought him to be a pretty big deal. It wasn't surprising, considering he had enjoyed similar success to Riesen when he was younger. After all, he was on the North Territories national Field team for several years. The guy was an all-around prodigy, even if a lesser sort than Riesen.

Come to think of it, part of the reason Riesen was becoming

such a big star now was because a spotlight had already shifted over to the Green Coast a little bit. Ever since this place was put on the map through the sport of Sliding, and after Daren had graduated from Primary School rank three, the Meridians had been very interested. The world had been interested, for that matter. Still, their little corner was well off the beaten path, and it wasn't often that outsiders would go out of their way to visit the quiet town.

Sooo far off the beaten path... Niko laughed to herself as her thoughts wandered to how remote her hometown was.

Tonight though, there was this stranger who had shown up to their very party. Niko figured her to be a Meridian official of some sort. Daren seemed to know her and defer to her, much like she imagined he would to a superior in the Meridian service. Whoever she was, she was definitely no Northerner.

Well, at least she won't take interest in me, Niko thought. *I'm about as normal as can be compared to Riesen, and Daren, and Kate, and Cryo, and Ravenna, and...*

She sighed to herself, as that list would go on and on before she would find anybody that she was as impressive as.

"Anyway, why are we still out here, again?" Jen cracked first and asked the question that the others were sure to be thinking. You could always count on Jen to tell it how it was. "It's blazes freezing out here."

"Yeah, another storm's supposed to come in," Niko remarked, thinking about how it sure *was* getting blazes freezing outside.

She peered westward into the pitch black. Neither of the two moons were out tonight, but the clouds were so thick it wouldn't have mattered. Of course, she didn't have the crazy blue Islander eyes that were said to be able to see in the dark, but she knew she was staring in the direction of the galactic Dark Patch.

Niko had taken an interest in astronomy for several years, encouraged by her father. That's how she knew where all the stars would be even when the view was blocked by the clouds. The galactic Dark Patch was particularly interesting to her because the reason for its existence was still an unsolved mystery waiting to be discovered. Maybe she would go into that field and be the first to uncover the secret to why one half of the galaxy had so much more interstellar dust than the other half...

She had recently decided on pursuing it for a career, but was becoming increasingly scared of the amount of math involved...

Niko was not a fan of that subject.

"Well then, I'm heading in," Jen declared, brushing a strand of white-blonde hair out of her face. "Been fun, girls, but it's too cold for me!" Laughing, she hurried up the rocky trail to the house.

Kate and Daren just grinned and shook their heads.

"Well okay then," Daren said.

"Guess I'm gonna head up as well. Someone needs to chaperone that girl," Kate said, moving to cover the fire with piles of mud.

"Don't worry about it, I'll get the fire," Daren said, shooing Kate away. "I'm gonna hang out here for a few more minutes, anyway."

"Alright then, thanks," Kate said, shrugging as she turned to go. "Come on Niko, let's go."

The two sisters made their way up the path, steep stone stairs forming a few switchbacks. With the Northern pines and ferns cluttered on either side, it was more reminiscent of a mountain forest trail than a beach path. It was very dark out and hard to see, but as they rounded one of the switchbacks near the top, Niko noticed someone else coming down. The figure neared and Niko realized it was the stranger she had just been thinking about.

"Ah, Kate Ryen. I thought I might find you out here." The lady spoke in a very paced and formal, yet pleasant tone. The way she softly enunciated her words made Niko think of the way an old poet might recite their works to an audience.

"Yes, here I am." Kate offered her a respectful smile.

"Your friends think very highly of your brother," the stranger said.

"Yeah, they haven't let me forget about it. Tonight, at least." Kate laughed, most likely thinking of how insufferable some of them had been. The sisters looked at each other and rolled their eyes, as Niko recalled Tyson Ander grabbing a microphone, climbing on top of the house, and teasing Riesen by singing him a love song. Of course, Cryo only made it more hysterical, egging Tyson on by improvising an instrumental accompaniment to that farce.

"They are good friends, though. You all seem very... loyal to each other," the stranger continued, her eyes now scanning over to Niko. "It is rare that I see such devotion. And this must be your sister Niko, who you were telling me about?"

It was not a question; it seemed obvious she knew very well

who Niko was.

Why would Kate tell her about me? Niko wondered.

"Yes," Niko timidly answered. She hated conversations with people she didn't know. She had gone outside and down to the beach to be away from this kind of interaction, go figure. What was she supposed to say right now? How was she supposed to address this person? "Ma'am."

"No need to call me ma'am," the stranger offered as she lightly chuckled. "My name is Ajane Solase."

She extended her hand and Niko shook it, and thought she felt a sweeping sensation come over her, but only attributed it to her overwhelming nervousness in the face of meeting someone new.

Her words seemed soft and kindly, but Niko was not expecting to be made the center of attention right now. This Ajane Solase's gaze made her feel very nervous. It was almost... *knowing*... much like how Niko would expect being put on the spot in a queen's court would feel.

Whatever that's like... They don't even have queens anymore, she reminded herself, becoming frustrated at her lack of focus.

At any rate, Ajane had this regality about her that Niko likened to what a queen might have been like a hundred years ago. She was very slight of build, but possessed this sort of unseen strength to her. She was definitely old, probably older than her own grandparents, but Niko thought her to be very beautiful despite her age. She had unusually smooth skin and hair, and these gleaming grey eyes that seemed to dig holes into Niko. Yes, she was certainly quite striking.

"My little sister," Kate said, beaming as she hugged Niko with one arm. Normally, that kind of thing was what bothered Niko — how people would treat her like a little kid — but this time she was only grateful that it took some of the heat off of her.

"You two are quite lovely," Ajane said, smiling gently. "Actually, I was wanting to speak with Niko about her dreams you were telling me about earlier?"

"Yeah, absolutely," Kate replied, nodding in respect. There was not even a slight hint of hesitation to her acquiescence. She had to have sensed Niko's glare, though. "I'll be up at the house, kid. See you in a bit!"

Kate playfully nudged Niko with her elbow, and Niko angrily watched her sister disappear off up into the trail.

That little...! Niko thought heatedly. The dreams were not for

Kate to go blabbering around to any random stranger! *Ugh! I'm going to kill her!*

Niko was so shocked that her sister would tell this *stranger* about her dreams that she didn't hear the question that Ajane had asked. She just stood there gaping, as if a bear had descended onto the path in front of her. Realizing that she was being rude, she tried to form sentences, but had tried to combine too many thoughts at once. What resulted was only one jumble that made no sense whatsoever.

"Uhh… what? I mean… sorry," Niko sheepishly corrected, her face growing red.

"I make you nervous. I do apologize." Ajane smiled reassuringly at her. "How could I be so rude? I should explain why I am here. I teach at an academy near Sol City and several of your friends from this town have gone through my school."

"I'm sorry. I don't mean to sound nervous," Niko said, laughing embarrassedly.

"Not to worry!" Ajane gave her a sympathetic look. "Now, Kate has told me that you have been having some realistic dreams?"

"Oh," Niko replied, not sure exactly what she should say. "I mean, I guess?"

"In my line of study, dreams are of great interest," Ajane said. "What can you tell me about yours?

"Umm," Niko hesitated. "I don't know…"

What do I even say? Niko panicked. It was bad enough Kate told her whatever she did, but she was *not* about to elaborate on them to some random stranger.

"It's okay," Ajane coaxed. "I would very much like to hear the one about your brother that Kate told me about. The one where you saved him?"

Kate told her about *that*?! Niko shuddered. She didn't like to think about that memory at all. She wished she could think of happier dreams, like maybe one with Brandon in them or something.

No, that would actually be highly embarrassing! she thought, her face again turning red and quickly snapped that out of her own mind. *Definitely not those…*

"Umm, what do you want to know about it?" Niko cautiously offered, refocusing on Ajane's question.

"I would like to hear your experience with it," she replied, her words as kindly as ever. "Where were you when it happened?"

"Well, it was when I was at Green Lake with my family a few years ago. The Ryens, that is. I'm adopted."

"Oh yes, so I have heard. They are absolutely your family, though," Ajane encouraged, smiling.

"Oh, I know, I know!" Niko scolded herself for implying otherwise. "I just meant... I mean... I don't know."

"So you were at the lake, then what happened?"

"Well, we were at the lake, and I had a dream that my dad ran into the water and pulled Riesen out. It was so real, and it was pretty scary."

She couldn't believe she was actually telling this stranger about it, but Kate had already done that anyway. What choice did she have but to continue? She couldn't lie at this point. There was also something about this lady that made it feel like she couldn't lie even if she wanted to.

"As one would imagine," Ajane said. "After you had the dream, Kate says you woke her up and were shouting?"

Niko shrugged, her arms hugging herself for warmth.

"I guess. She didn't believe me and told me it was just a dream. Riesen was one of the best swimmers we knew. At least she talked with me until I fell back asleep." Niko paused before continuing.

"And this dream came true, didn't it?" Ajane asked. Her lack of surprise was unsettling.

"Ummm, yeah," Niko said.

Ajane looked at her expectantly. Was she supposed to tell her the whole story of how it happened? Niko sighed to herself, but continued.

"The next day, I saw the front doors opened exactly how they were in my dream. Even though I wasn't even near the water, I yelled at my dad to get Riesen out. My dad just looked at me for a second, not understanding what I was yelling about, but then he saw Riesen just floating there and ran outside and pulled him out of the water. Apparently, he hit his head on a rock diving in from the cliffs. Thirty more seconds and he could've died."

Just thinking of what happened sent shivers down Niko's spine, and not only because Riesen almost died. A short silence followed as Ajane looked off into the distance, her eyes even more alive, if that was possible.

"I don't like thinking about that," Niko said, finding more confidence in her voice. "It was just so scary, and even scarier thinking that what I dreamed came true. Like… I know it's stupid, but I always thought that somehow I caused it."

"No," Ajane responded, returning her gaze to Niko. "Not to worry, you did not cause that. How many dreams have you had that came true like this one?"

"Well, there are little ones that sometimes feel like they come true. Something small, like going to the store, or a rainstorm coming, or… I don't know, things like that. Nothing big."

"Very interesting," Ajane paused in contemplation. "Have any other people around you experienced any other life and death situations that you had dreamt of?"

"Well…" Niko started, not sure if she should tell her about the latest dream. She hadn't even told Kate about that one. "I've had a few other dreams like that one that just seemed so real. None of them have come true though. I didn't even recognize any of the places in them."

"Was anyone you know in any of your other dreams?" Ajane asked.

"Yeah, I guess so," Niko replied, thoughtfully recalling her dreams. "Riesen has been in a few…"

"You've had one recently, haven't you?"

"Well…" Niko hesitated.

"That's okay if you don't want to talk about it," Ajane offered. Her grey eyes were ablaze, though, and she looked eager for Niko to continue.

"Well, I'm sure it doesn't mean anything," Niko said, looking down toward the ground.

Blazes, this is completely crazy.

"Believe me, you are not crazy, if that's what you are worried about," Ajane coaxed.

Niko's eyes snapped back to Ajane. *Did she just…*

"I have been studying this kind of thing for a very long time," Ajane added quickly.

"Well, okayyy. If you say so…"

"It is alright if you do not want to share what happened, Niko," Ajane offered. "I completely understand."

Niko felt bad that she was being so shifty about it. She might as well just tell the lady. Kate had already done all the damage anyway…

"No, I'm sorry," Niko reluctantly continued. "The one a few

nights ago, I don't remember much, but I think I remember Riesen and Daren jumping off this really big bridge or something. There were a couple other people I didn't know, too. It sounds dumb, I know, but I just like panicked when I woke up. It felt *so* real."

"Who is Daren?" Ajane asked curiously.

"Oh, sorry," Niko sheepishly apologized. "Nicodaren. I just started calling him Daren from now on because everyone calls him Nico and that's my only name."

Both Niko and Ajane laughed.

"You know, I support that one-hundred percent, young lady. I will start calling him Daren also," Ajane declared with a smile.

At least there's one person out there who won't call me 'kid', Niko thought wryly.

"A bridge, you say, though?" Ajane continued. "Do you remember what it looked like?"

As Niko recalled the bridge, Ajane's eyes seemed to dig into her brain. Niko felt as if she didn't even need to describe it, as if Ajane already knew exactly what it looked like.

"I wonder if…" Ajane quietly said to herself.

"Hmm?" asked Niko. She was very confused now. Should she know this bridge? Was this a real place?

"Oh, nothing. My apologies," Ajane said, obviously lost in deep thought.

Niko hesitated, briefly thinking of the ridiculous possibility that Ajane had read her thoughts about what the bridge looked like. That wasn't possible, was it? She hoped not, for all her childish thoughts about queens, and for thinking about her dreams with Brandon. She laughed on the inside about this nonsensical thought. *How embarrassing would that be?*

"No problem," said Niko as she laughed nervously. She was just starting to get more relaxed talking with this stranger, but she suddenly felt much more insecure again. An awkward silence followed until Ajane spoke up.

"I was also very interested in your scan results from two months ago."

Niko just stood there, unable to respond once again. Everyone takes the scan at the end of their tenth School year to monitor their health, but nobody hears back about those. Thinking of how her biological grandmother died of a brain tumor, she began to panic.

"Was something wrong with it?!" Niko didn't bother to hide

the panic that was surely written all over her face.

"No, nothing like that," Ajane assured her with a smile. "It was actually the activity in the region of the brain associated with dreams. I have never seen such concentrated activity."

"Oh. Hmm, okay," was all Niko could muster in response. She was glad to hear it wasn't a tumor or anything. Maybe this would explain why she was always lost in daydreams?

"I would like for you to have the chance to undergo further testing and training, if that would be okay with you?" Ajane announced.

Niko thought that this was less of an invitation and more of a request.

"I have also had the chance to speak to your brother Riesen today. He is quite remarkable. The two of you could be Inducted into our program early. I could get the process started, if you are willing?"

"Riesen is pretty incredible," Niko confessed, irritated that the revelation of her being special in some way was interrupted by proclamations of Riesen's greatness once again. "He will definitely be a good student for you, if you're instructing him also. He's the best at whatever he does."

Niko rolled her eyes on the inside because it was so true.

"What, umm, would we be instructed in? Or tested in?" Niko asked.

"Oh, mostly similar to what you already do in your School," Ajane said. "But also mental exercises. My general area of expertise is in improved use of the brain, if you will."

What in the blazes is that even supposed to mean? Niko thought. She should've been feeling excited, but she was more worried that they were going to put her through some awful mental conditioning. Would it *hurt*?

Ajane seemed to pick up on Niko's uneasiness.

"Don't you worry," she said. "It will be just like School, just in a different setting with different people."

"When would this all happen?"

"I would get the process started tonight," she replied, "and we could have you out to Sol City in a week or two."

A week or two? Sol City??

"Ummm…" Niko stammered, desperately searching for an excuse that would save her. "What about my family? Or my friends at School? Or my Field team?"

"You would be able to see them every week," Ajane replied, as if that were any consolation.

Once per *week*?!

"We would fly you back and forth," Ajane continued. "This would be a huge change, to be sure, but you would still be able to lead your life. And besides, you would be with others your age who are going through the same thing. I have met some of them already and they are very nice young men and women."

Niko wasn't quite convinced that this was something she wanted. Sol City, though… she could get used to living there. "I'd need to talk to my parents about it."

"Of course, of course," Ajane replied.

"When would you need to know by?"

"Well, you could ask them tonight? And you could all discuss and reach back out to me in a day or two."

Niko had her reservations, but maybe this was an exciting opportunity after all. She did want the chance to prove herself special, and this sounded like the one.

"I'll ask them either tonight or tomorrow," Niko agreed.

"Excellent," Ajane replied with a smile. "Well, you must be quite cold, young lady."

Niko simply shivered and nodded, forcing a smile.

"There is a storm coming, to be sure," Ajane added, staring off into the black of night toward the ocean, as if she could actually see the clouds building or stars rising.

Niko glanced off into the distance, pretending she could also see the storm or stars or whatever the blazes she was looking at. It was pitch black, there were clouds everywhere, and even if there were no clouds, it was dark that way anyway because of the galactic Dark Patch.

What could she possibly be looking at?

"Well, not exactly that one, though that does look like a nasty little tempest," Ajane laughed. "No, what I refer to is a metaphorical storm, you could say. 'A storm is coming' is what *Meridians* say when they get those feelings of some impending change."

Niko just continued to stare, feeling more and more uneasy by the second. What impending change did Ajane speak of? And the way she rolled the word *Meridians* off her tongue made it seem like there was a slight hint of tension. It was only just barely detectable, but definitely there.

Ajane resumed her pleasant smile. "But Niko Ryen, I do not mean to spoil your night! A good change is what I am hopeful for."

Niko laughed. Boy, did this woman have a cruel sense of humor.

"Well, I think that once I go back up, some of my friends will spoil it for me," Niko said, wincing at the prospect of extreme socialization.

The music was getting even louder — if that was even possible — and she could hear Tyson and Kyler shouting something, even from way down on the beach path. They were probably getting some chant started or something ridiculous like that. They *loved* doing that sort of thing. Typical boys...

"Yes, your friends are very energetic tonight, indeed," Ajane commented with a grin. "I do apologize if I gave you too much to think about. Talk to your parents, but don't worry yourself too much about it. It was very nice to meet you, Niko Ryen, and I very much appreciate you opening up to me about your dreams. I look forward to seeing you again in the future, if I should be so honored."

Niko took her hand politely, and as they shook hands, that same strange flooding feeling flowed through her once again. She couldn't describe it — only that for a moment it felt like a brief sensation of understanding streamed through her. It was strangely pleasant, but also incredibly unsettling, as it had been before.

This meeting was too bizarre for Niko's liking. Just ten minutes ago, her biggest worries in life had to do with there being too many people to socialize with, or people calling her a little kid. Now she would welcome that sort of treatment rather than having to worry about uprooting her entire life.

Shivering, Niko slowly headed up to the top of the path. Ajane glided off in the opposite direction with a smile on her face. She was probably going down to talk to Daren, who was still on the beach. Niko would have to ask Kate more about Ajane later tonight, right after she was done giving her a piece of her mind for outing her dreams to a complete stranger! For now, she would head back in, but not before she took a moment to recuperate her spirit.

―――――――

The house was so loud. Speakers in the living room were blaring with music, though John Maksolhoff had put on something a bit softer than the driving beats that were booming earlier. After all, it was his house; he could put on whatever music he wanted. Most of the noise, though, came from the continuous chatter, laughter, and shouting from the dozens of guests inside. To be heard above the din, they each had to speak louder and louder. It was not anything out of the ordinary, though. Gatherings at the Farm were always quite raucous.

The Farm, as it was called, was only one of many farms on the Green Coast, but this particular one had become a haven for Niko and many of her friends in recent years. John Maksolhoff had been one of the driving forces behind the sport of Sliding and had encouraged the kids to give it a shot at the beach on his property. After his wife had passed away seven years ago, getting the kids and their families together to go Sliding had become a passion for him. Before long, the Farm was one of the Green Coast's premier hang out spots.

The rooms were well lit and very spacious, perfect for these kinds of get-togethers. There were no other homes nearby for kilometers, so there was really no limit to how loud people could get here. More than a few guests were content to push that to the extremes.

"RIESENNNNN! SPEEEECH!" Tyson stood atop a chair in the middle of the room, calling across to Riesen with cupped hands. The whole house abounded with noise, but the demand was clear enough to turn heads throughout the room.

More people joined in, "Speech! Speech! Speech!"

Niko just chuckled and shook her head. *Just what I needed to clear my head,* she thought sarcastically.

"Riesen, I see you! Get up here you little chum!" Tyson joked as he hopped down to drag Riesen to the makeshift pedestal. As strong as Riesen was, it was probably not worth struggling; Tyson had that same strong, lean physique that Riesen had anyway.

He actually resembled Riesen far more than Niko did. He had Islander blood in him on his mother's side, and had the characteristic windswept blonde hair and tanned skin. Everyone used to joke that Riesen was actually a long lost member of Tyson's family.

Riesen, like Niko, was adopted by the Ryens, but the manner of his adoption was so mysterious. Apparently he was found abandoned as a baby, and the Ryens took him in as their own. It was assumed he had mostly Islander blood in him, though, so he never looked out of place in the Ryen family like Niko did.

"Been trying to hide this whole time, huh boy?" Tyson playfully accused Riesen.

Riesen only smiled and shrugged. You just had to play along with Tyson. Resisting only made it worse, and that had been learned by everybody a dozen times over. He wasn't ever nasty or vengeful, but he would embarrass you more and more until you went along with whatever he had in store. He was a joker, through and through. Niko winced at all the times he had embarrassed her in public.

The worst was when, for no reason at all, he told a bunch of people in a group — *including Brandon* — that Niko had a crush on John Maksolhoff's grandson. That kid was only *thirteen* years old! She was so mad. Of course it wasn't true, but she still had to scramble to convince everyone that Tyson was making things up. At least that was easy enough for everyone to buy. But still, she was mortified that Brandon had to hear that. The worst thing about it was that Brandon seemed indifferent to it all. She still hadn't completely forgiven Tyson for that.

"LET'S GOOOOO!" Tyson bellowed as he thrust Riesen onto the chair. "Riesen's gonna give us a SPEECH!"

There were already about thirty people packed into the living room, but upon hearing this proclamation, more came flooding in. The living room wasn't small — this was one of the biggest houses on the Coast — but there were so many people crammed in that it seemed tiny. People even stood in the kitchen and on the stairs to listen to Riesen's coerced 'speech', which was probably his fourth or fifth of the night.

There were easily over a hundred people in attendance. Parents, kids, and the whole spectrum came out to enjoy each other's company on this last night of the Anniversary celebrations. This night was always a big event, but tonight was also a special party thrown for Riesen. Everyone expected a speech now that Tyson had them all riled up. Nevermind that it had already happened several times throughout the night… Everyone was so tipsy that most had probably forgotten any of the previous 'speeches'. Niko rolled her eyes at the thought.

"Okay, okay, *eeeasy*," he urged to Tyson, who was still pushing him up onto the chair. Both Tyson and Riesen already had quite a bit of the homemade Anniversary Ale that the Ryens had brought, and Niko was nervous that he was going to knock the chair over while Riesen stood on it. As much as she was annoyed with Riesen tonight, she still felt protective of her brother. But Riesen didn't seem the least bit worried and raised his hands, acknowledging the crowd that had gathered.

"Just for Tyson, I'll give the lamest speech I can muster," he began with a huge smile.

Everyone in the crowd laughed, booed, and cheered all at once.

"Sooo, let me start by thanking everyone for coming back into town. It means a lot, to be back here with friends..."

Oh blazes, isn't this the corniest thing I've ever heard, Niko thought to herself, rolling her eyes as she buried her face in her palms.

"Awww, c'mon, Riesen. Booooo!" she heard people jeering from the kitchen.

But Riesen just pointed at them and blew them a kiss. He always had an answer for everything. He was so cool under pressure in all situations. Even *social* situations. Especially social situations. This was just another one of his many talents. He was so infuriating!

"Alright, alright," he yielded. "You guys over there can go to blazes, and the rest of you... Leave a poor kid alone! How's that for a speech?"

Cheers and laughter erupted as Riesen hopped down from the chair and tackled Tyson, who was heckling him from behind. The two went sprawling across the floor and knocked over three chairs on their way down.

Boys! Niko thought. Would they not ever grow up? At least they preferred humor to that nauseating moment of corniness.

Riesen offered a hand to Tyson after he pulled himself from the floor. Tyson might have trouble getting up on his own at this point in the night after the amount of Anniversary Ale he'd consumed. They gave each other a hearty hand clap, and Tyson moved to join the group in the kitchen, probably to go make some more noise. That was his specialty.

As Niko watched Tyson stumble his way to the kitchen, a pat on her shoulder redirected her attention. She turned, and standing there was Cryo Siriar. A complete contrast from Tyson, Cryo was probably the calmest and most under-control person she knew. Sure, he would crack his fair share of jokes just like any Green Coaster, but he always seemed so… *normal.*

Plain as he may be, Niko had to admit that he was very attractive. Not that she had anything for him. After all, he was like an older brother to her. But she still could admit that, couldn't she? It was nothing like she had a crush on him or anything — it was more that she admired him as a role model and wanted to be like him.

Slightly blushing, she silenced any thoughts of the sort. He was Cryo, and that was that. Besides, the liking she had was for Brandon anyway. After all, Brandon was much closer to her own age. Talking to Cryo always made her feel very comfortable, though, and a chat with him right now would be quite welcome after her strange encounter with Ajane.

"So, Ajane talked to you?" Cryo asked in a lower voice, nodding as if he already knew the answer.

"Yeah. She was so… mysterious," Niko replied. "She made me so nervous!"

Cryo laughed. "Yeah, I remember when she first talked to me. Me and Ven both, actually. We were off on a mission on Boatah Island, and she was just kinda there. Really weird. I actually had a dream about it beforehand."

That's right, Cryo has these weird dreams also, she remembered. Niko had wanted to tell Cryo about her dreams for some time, but hadn't had the opportunity because he'd been gone for so long. She might've told him now, after having just told a complete stranger about them, but she wanted to hear the rest of his story.

"We were crouching in these bushes, and Ven flipped," Cryo continued with a smirk. "She thought it was one of our buddies at first."

Niko could picture that. Ravenna hated being caught off guard. Not that she had seen her caught off guard many times, but there was the time when Tyson and Kyler dumped cold water on her when she was watching Cryo doing some Sliding out at the Farm. They had tried to run away, but Ravenna had caught both of them before they got to the top of the hill, then proceeded to beat on them. She was actually quite vicious and Niko admired the blazes out of her for it.

"Ven whirled around ready to kill, and there Ajane was," Cryo continued. "Just standing there all creepy like."

"Well, at least I got to see her coming, I guess," Niko admitted. "I even got introduced. Kind of."

"You'll get used to her," Cryo insisted, laughing.

"Who is she, exactly?" Niko asked, not sure if she really wanted to know the answer.

"Well, for one, she's my boss," Cryo replied. "Our boss. Kyler, Ven, and I work for her. Nico and Kate also, although nobody is really supposed to know about that." He paused and shrugged. "What did she tell you?"

"She didn't tell me much," Niko replied truthfully. "She asked about my own dreams, which I've been meaning to talk to you about. I've been having some like yours and I wanted to ask you about them."

Cryo lifted his eyebrows. "Oh?"

"Yeah," Niko said. She shrugged, not sure what else to say.

"Wow, I'm glad I'm not the only one having them," Cryo said.

"You're not the only one," Niko echoed with a nod. "But Ajane said she wants to study them. She wants to have Riesen and I Inducted into the program early and train and test down at Sol City."

"You and Riesen both, huh?" he asked.

"Yeah, that's what she said," Niko shrugged. "Did you ever have to do training because of them when you were..." Niko was interrupted before she could finish.

"CRYOOOOO!" The familiar shout signaled that Tyson had returned to the room and had his sights set on his friend on the other side.

"Well, looks like we aren't gonna be able to finish this little chat here," Cryo said, rolling his eyes. "We should talk later, though."

Niko only nodded before Cryo was whisked away. She stood there for a few moments, smoldering in her frustration. She had just worked up the nerve to ask Cryo about the dreams, only to have Tyson ruin it all.

Ugh! she thought. *That guy is the literal worst!*

It was strange that Cryo and Tyson were such good friends, being complete opposites and all. Even weirder was the addition of Kyler to that friend group, who was now helping Tyson corral Cryo into the kitchen. The interaction between those three was always downright hilarious.

Kyler was loud and blunt also, but lacked the sort of coolness that Tyson had. He was athletic and lean of build, but he worked as a machine scientist and was so pale that he looked like he never saw the light of day. On top of that, he had an unfortunate case of pimples on his face and a mouth that looked too small for his head. Kyler was a quintessential nerd that somehow ended up being in high social circles. Thinking of Kyler's fortunes always puzzled Niko.

How is it that he is more popular than me?? He's one of the most annoying, nerdiest guys I know…

To be fair, Kyler was on the receiving end of a lot of jokes, although Niko couldn't exactly feel too sorry for him because she thought he brought a lot of that on himself. He was not one for subtlety and would dish grief out to everyone without prejudice, occasionally pushing it too far. He used to be quiet and mild mannered, but he developed this warped sort of cocky complex in recent years. Maybe it was just further evidence of Niko's suspicions that all boys turned rotten at some point or another.

After watching the three disappear into the kitchen, she decided to go find Kate and see if perhaps she would be able to shed any light on the Ajane situation. She also needed to give her big sister a thorough drumming for going and blabbing her secrets to utter strangers. There were so many people in here, though, that finding Kate was going to be a chore.

She'd only been back inside the house for an hour and she already wanted to leave. Moving from room to room in here was almost as bad as it had been fighting the crowds at the Field stadium in Sol City.

And what was this music?! Couldn't they play anything good?

"So, where have you been all night?" asked a familiar voice from behind. She spun around and there was Riesen, looking smug as always.

"Hey, *kid*," Niko said, emphasizing the word as her frustration boiled over. "Just listening to stories of you over and over and over."

"Tell me about it," Riesen winced. "I'm so over this."

Maybe Niko was being too harsh on him. After all, he didn't ask for all this glorification; he just kind of earned it through being good at everything. Why wouldn't he try to be good at everything?

"Yeah. But it's nice that they let you drink up all you want now that you're the big star around here." Her bitterness wasn't completely gone.

"What's up with you?" Riesen just smirked and narrowed his eyes, sensing her frustrations.

"Nothing," Niko sighed. She was *not* about to tell him about her conversation with Ajane. "You know I hate these things."

"Well, hang in there, kid."

There it was again. *Kid.* Unbelievable.

Letting it go seemed to take all the strength she could gather, but she did. Why was she so frustrated tonight? She took a deep breath as he clapped her shoulder and patted her hair, turning to go.

"Wait, have you seen Kate around?" she asked.

"No," he replied. "I think she and Jen might've gone into town to grab some stuff."

"Great," she muttered under her breath, as Riesen headed off into another mob of people.

Niko wished she could just go to sleep right now, but it was far too loud. Most people stayed the night here at the Farm for the Anniversary, but they wouldn't be going to sleep for another couple of hours.

Stewing in her own antisocial misery, Niko grabbed her jacket and headed back outside into the cold. At least it was quieter. Mentally and emotionally exhausted, she collapsed down on the stone bench at the top of the cliffs and stared out at the ocean. Of course, she couldn't see a thing, but she could hear the waves rolling onto the rocks down below. Just for fun, she tried to envision the coming storm the way Ajane had seemed to, but to no avail.

I'm hopeless, she thought.

Kate would always tell her not to compare herself to anyone, but she couldn't help it. Everyone around her seemed to do anything and everything better than her. She felt so ugly and plain when she'd hang out with Kate and her friends, so shy and awkward when she'd hang out with Riesen and the boys, and so unimportant when she was with adults. She wished Cryo and Ravenna would take her on a climbing trip or something again. She could actually relate to them, even if they were older.

Niko sighed.

Maybe all she needed to feel better was some rest and relaxation for a few days… As fun as it had been, she'd been on the go for three weeks straight! She was tired.

She settled back onto the bench and recalled some of her better memories from her trip. Those soothed her just enough for her to fall asleep, but not quite enough to keep her from another one of her restless *dreams*.

CHAPTER THREE

3

News in the Morning

WAKING to the pitter-patter of rain seemed commonplace here on the Green Coast. The light murmur of raindrops was usually quite comforting… if one was not waking up outside, soaking wet, freezing cold. How she didn't wake up earlier, Niko did not know. *What time was it?*

Opening her eyes to blurry vision, she could see that daylight was attempting to creep through, but the clouds were thick. '*A storm is coming*', she remembered the lady saying in her dream. Was that a dream? Niko blinked water out of her eyes and forced herself to sit up.

Wait, was *that a dream?* The grogginess of waking accentuated her confusion, and she had no idea what was dream and what was real. *Did* she have another one of the *dreams* again?

Ajane Solase. That was her name. Was that real? she asked herself, trying hard to recall last night's events. Putting her hands to her face to wipe the water off, she realized she couldn't feel her skin at all. She looked around and saw that she was sitting on that stone bench atop the cliffs at the Farm, the same one she had sat down on last night.

Blazes! Did I sleep outside all night? Simple instinct told her that she was quite cold and that she better get inside and warm up. Maybe the fire was still going...

Upon standing up, she nearly toppled right back over, her feet only responding to her wishes as much as blocks of ice would. She shook her head at her own idiocy for falling asleep in the rain and stumbled along the narrow dirt path to the house. It was all muddy now, so she hugged the grassy edges, praying she didn't slip. She was still half asleep and her balance wasn't fantastic at the moment, so she ended up stepping into the mud anyway.

There was smoke rising from both of the chimneys, though, which was a welcome sight. She would park herself right in front of the fireplace all morning, right after she grabbed some towels first and dried off so she didn't track a river of mud indoors. How did she not wake up when the rain started? It must've been raining for hours — she wouldn't have been any wetter if she had jumped into the ocean! Or any colder for that matter.

As she neared the house, she became a little more awake and alert, at least more than she had been a few moments earlier. Her head was still quite foggy, but she had it sorted out that Riesen and Daren jumping off that bridge again had indeed been a dream, but that the conversation with Ajane had definitely been real. Neither comforted her in the slightest. The dream with Riesen and Daren was now recurring, and she remembered how her first dream came true all too well.

What does this dream mean? Is that bridge real?

Ajane seemed highly interested in her dream and that put Niko a little on edge. She didn't like the thought of her friends jumping off a bridge, if it were to come true. There could be nothing good about that. Indeed, the setting of the whole dream did seem to be a hectic situation. New this time was all the yelling and explosion noises in the dream. The whole thing just didn't sit well with her at all.

Sighing, Niko shook some loose water off of her hair and clothes, then entered the house. She looked around the room, her bearings mostly recovered. The floor was littered with the sleeping bodies of Green Coast revelers from the previous night.

Blazes, how many people fell asleep in this one room? Almost everyone celebrating the last night of the Anniversary at the Farm would usually stay the nights, but this seemed like more than normal.

How nice they have it to be dry, Niko thought bitterly. *And sleeping so peacefully...*

Snapping herself out of her frustration, she scolded herself. She knew that it wasn't any of their faults. They were just living their lives. She carefully stepped across to the hallway so as not to drip water on any of her friends, and found the cupboard that John Maksolhoff kept towels in.

I must look like a drowned field mouse, she thought sullenly, just as she glanced at a sleeping Jen Jenaei, who looked pretty even in her sleep.

She was so exasperated at her own discontent lately, but it was just so unfair that those around her should always look so good. At least for the past few weeks, she felt a little better being away with her Field team. Nobody cared how they looked when they were sprinting all over the field. Although, they did spend the last few days in Sol City, and seeing the Islander women in person really made her wish she had that dark skin and flowing blonde hair. *So unfair!*

Frustrated anew, she grabbed the towels and dried herself off before too large a puddle settled on the floor. She backtracked from where she came, wiping dry her trail of water and mud, then headed into the back room with the fireplace. There would be fewer people in that room, hopefully.

As she rounded the corner in the hall, she thought she heard soft voices coming from the kitchen. She peeked across the living room and saw Daren and Ravenna not in the kitchen, but standing outside on the path in front of the window. Niko peered closer and thought it looked like they were arguing about something.

Eavesdropping was such a guilty pleasure for her; she was curious by nature. Niko realized her stomach had been growling, and grabbing something to eat from the kitchen would be an excellent excuse for her to see if she could hear what was going on. John Maksolhoff usually had his kitchen well stocked and always encouraged everyone to help themselves to whatever they felt like. Oatmeal sounded good this morning. Maybe some tea, as well. Something to warm her up since she was still numb from the cold.

She placed some water into the tea machine and waited, trying to catch what the fuss outside was about. As she listened, it started to seem less like an argument to her, but Daren and Ravenna were nevertheless discussing something quite animatedly. As Niko watched them intently, she thought they might actually be agreeing with each other, nodding and the whole like, but they definitely were upset about something.

Niko immediately felt a pang of worry, seeing them in a stir like this. True, Ravenna was temperamental and moody at times, but never in a state of alarm like it seemed right now. Something about the way her brows were furled seemed *off* to Niko. Even Daren's characteristically calm stare seemed shifted as his eyes darted between Ravenna and the ground.

Niko had been watching them so intently that she became startled when the beeper for her tea sounded. She turned around quickly to shut it off before it woke anyone up. Too quickly, though, for her head throbbed when she did. At least some feeling was coming back, but she did not want to deal with a headache today. Unfortunately, raging headaches often accompanied her dreams. All she could do was pause all motion, brace herself against the counter, and squeeze her eyes shut to let her head settle.

After the throbbing of her head subsided a little, she poured her tea into a cup and the leftover hot water into her oatmeal. She gobbled her breakfast down so quickly that her mouth and throat burned. She squeezed her eyes shut once more at the pain, but she was still more worried about what this conversation between Daren and Ravenna was all about. When she opened her eyes again, both of them were gone.

What the blazes? Where'd they go?

Just then, however, she heard the door open, and she saw Ravenna storm over to where Riesen lay in the back living room and shake him.

"Riesen, wake up," she said quietly but sharply. "Riesen!"

Riesen sat halfway up, but when he looked around and saw Ravenna, he turned back over and pulled a blanket over his face, grumbling something unintelligible.

"Riesen, you need to get up!" she hissed.

"Blazes! Stop, girl. Let me sleep!" he pleaded, his voice muffled by blankets and a pillow.

"You need to see this. Like now." Ravenna's voice was stern, as was her body language. Her arms were now folded across her chest, which indicated she meant business. "And where's Niko?"

"What's wrong?" Niko blurted out. Daren and Ravenna whirled around to face Niko, probably startled that she was standing right there. Riesen seized upon the distraction to bury himself further into the couch.

"Your brother needs to wake up is what's wrong," Ravenna replied, turning back to Riesen and pulling off all his blankets. He was still wearing jeans, a t-shirt, and even shoes. He had probably fallen right to sleep after collapsing on the couch last night.

"Alright, alright," Riesen yielded. Stretching with a big yawn, he looked up at Ravenna and Daren. "What am I getting up for?"

"Because this." Ravenna pulled out her Ut, turning the projection toward Riesen. Without asking, Niko scooted around behind the couch to watch. Magistrate Andersane was giving some address, and as she listened, her bad vibes increased twofold:

Early this morning, explosions erupted at the Trans-Antergian Highway just outside the Minedyne station at Anziend. This was the work of An-Mara TERRORISTS. Make no mistake, we will not stand for this TREACHERY. All of those responsible will be held accountable and...

Disbelief was the only thing that flooded her mind. Niko looked to Ravenna and Daren. No wonder the solemn faces. The An-Mara had come to Arhanda years ago when she was young. Although the Meridians left them well enough alone in Poste Territory, rumor had it that they were a mercenary army seeking recruitment to whatever their cause was. Everything was so cryptic when it came to these damn Meridians. In any case, it seemed ridiculous that the An-Mara would attack a Meridian base. They'd always been at peace with each other, even if they didn't necessarily like each other.

"Why would they do that?" Niko asked out loud.

"We don't really know much of anything right now," Ravenna replied.

"So, what is this? War?" Niko immediately felt worried for her brother, as well as her sister. All her friends in the Meridian service for that matter. If it was war, did that mean they would have to fight? Something had to be wrong; war was a thing of the past. There hadn't been any wars since before the time of the Arrival!

"It's a possibility," Daren replied, shaking his head. "The Meridians aren't wasting any time rounding up everyone on leave. Just now got a message that we are supposed to report to Green Valley this afternoon."

Unbelievable. Just as I get everyone back in town, now they all have to leave again... Niko thought disappointedly. And this time it would be for something way more uncertain and scary than just leaving for jobs or school.

"Is Ajane still here?" Niko asked. "What does she say about all this?"

"Cryo went to go talk to her," Ravenna replied, eyeing Niko with a sort of surprise in her eyes. She was surely wondering how Niko knew Ajane. Before she got a chance to ask, Riesen spoke up first.

"Well, until Cryo gets back I'm just gonna catch another couple minutes of sleep," he yawned.

His hair was comically matted and he looked like he was still in a state of bewilderment from his sudden awakening. How he wasn't alarmed to the max was beyond comprehension. Did he not hear the word 'war'?

"No, I think you've had enough sleep," Ravenna scolded as she grabbed him by an arm and effortlessly yanked him to his feet, giving him a light, playful slap to the face. Riesen groaned, rubbing his eyes, but to his credit he didn't slump back down into the couch.

Just then, Cryo walked in the door wearing an unreadable expression. Ravenna reached out and touched his arm, offering him a questioning look. A lot of the communication between those two was often nonverbal. They'd grown extremely close throughout the years, Cryo being more or less adopted by Ravenna's father Abel when he was a baby.

"Ajane's on a call, but she'll be over in a few minutes," Cryo announced. "She said we should get packed while we wait, though."

"Packed?" Riesen asked. "We going somewhere?"

"Yeah, all of us plus you and Niko," Cryo responded.

"Me?!" Niko was taken aback by the invitation. To possibly go on some adventure with Cryo and Ravenna was exactly what she wanted, but not under these circumstances.

"Yes," he replied simply.

"Wait, did you meet Ajane last night?" asked Ravenna. She eyed Niko with what looked like a sort of respect. "What'd she want with you?"

"Well, she asked me about dreams," Niko responded warily. She didn't know if she wanted to talk about them just now, especially since Daren and Riesen were present. "Then she told me a *storm* was coming."

"Hah! She's been saying that ever since I've met her," Ravenna scoffed, grunting a half laugh. She turned and looked at Cryo, raising an eyebrow, then quickly turned back to Niko. "Alright, well you should get packed also."

"Umm… alright. I need to tell my parents first, though. Riesen does also."

Niko shot Riesen a firm glance because he was so bad about telling their parents anything. He would *always* disappear without telling them where he was going. Even worse, he would never get in trouble for it! The one time she did the same thing, she got grounded, and that wasn't even her fault! The double standard was so unfair.

She also still needed to ask her parents about the possibility of her and Riesen leaving early for Ajane's academy in Sol City. She doubted this would be a good time to ask them about it, though; that seemed like it would require a much longer discussion.

"Okay," Ravenna said nonchalantly. "Kate is out right now. Tell her to grab you some dry clothes. Why the blazes *are* you soaking wet anyway?"

"I… fell asleep outside," Niko said sheepishly, her face growing red.

"Good one, kid," Riesen began to ridicule, shaking his head. Niko narrowed her eyes at him and opened her mouth to speak, but he changed the subject and turned toward Cryo and Ravenna before she could defend herself. "Where are we going, though? And when are we leaving?"

"I don't know yet, Ajane just said for us to get packed." Cryo shrugged as if the request was the most commonplace thing in the world.

As Niko was sending the message to Kate to bring her some clothes, she realized that she still was numb from the cold. The tea and oatmeal had at least satisfied her hunger slightly, but they had not done the trick in warming her up.

"I'm going to go make up some breakfast right now, anybody want some?" Ravenna asked.

"No thanks, I just ate," Niko replied. Her throat was still burning anyway, the only part of her body that wasn't freezing cold. "I might get some water, though."

"Okay," Ravenna shrugged. "You should take a warm shower or go sit by the fire for a few minutes while you wait for Kate to bring you some dry clothes. You look like a frozen, drowned rat."

"Thanks," Niko replied dryly, rolling her eyes.

A frozen, drowned rat. Awesome.

Well, in any case, it was a good idea. She dragged herself over to the washroom and was all too happy to get out of her wet clothes. She felt so much lighter; her clothes were incredibly heavy from being soaked with all that water. She wrung out what felt like several buckets' worth of water into the tub, then laid her clothes on the rack to dry as she turned on the shower all the way to hot.

She let the shower heat up for only a minute, and without thinking, she plunged in with full commitment. A wordless gasp escaped her lungs — the instant burning sensation was not what she expected. It was just like her throat experienced a few minutes earlier, but this time her entire body screamed. It took all the self-control she had to not yell out loud. She practically levitated right back out the way she came as she turned the temperature down a bit, but the brief seconds she was in had turned her entire body pink-red.

OWWWW! she yelled silently. *What the blazes!*

The day had only just begun, but it was starting off very poorly. Reaching back in to test the temperature, she felt lukewarm water rushing over her hand and eased back in slowly this time. She would've preferred to soak in comfortable warmth, but she could only handle cooler water because her skin was already sensitive from the newfound burns. Feeling started to return to her extremities, though, which was much better than the numbing cold from before. After a few minutes, her Ut alerted her to new messages from her sister.

'*Got you two sets, back in a few,*' the message read. She quickly finished up and dried her hair vigorously, then scooped up her wet clothes and wrapped herself in a towel. She went back into the living room and sat next to the fireplace to bask in the heat while she waited for Kate to arrive with her clothes. The warmth of fire felt so good, but she started to feel awkward sitting there in nothing but a towel.

She was very self-conscious, due in no small part to everyone always making fun of her for being too scrawny. Her mind wandered back to when that random lady confused her for a boy a few weeks earlier. She knew it was ridiculous and that she shouldn't care, but it still wasn't anything a sixteen-year-old girl wanted to hear.

"Ugh", she grumbled under her breath, as if conversing with the fire. Riesen could lounge around in his underwear and not make it awkward at all. Why must she hoard all the awkwardness of her family?

As she stared into the flames, images of her earlier dream occupied her mind once again. Why was it so real seeming?

The smell of the dust.

The sounds of the explosions.

The urgency of her friends.

It was almost as if she was there in that dream, except she wasn't. It was a weird feeling, like she was some invisible observer and had no way to interact with anything that was happening. There was no way she could explain it to anyone; they wouldn't understand. She'd already told Ajane about it, and almost told Cryo, but how could they understand? They must think of her just as a dumb little kid.

A dumb little 'boy', that's all I am. She forced a laugh as she tried turning it into a joke for herself, but it didn't quite land right.

At least she was starting to feel a little warmer and more comfortable. Her hair was still damp, however, when Kate and Kyler walked through the door. She instantly wished she had more than a towel on. The rest of them didn't make her feel uncomfortable, but Kyler always seemed to be looking for insults to dish out, so she ducked low, praying that he didn't notice her by the fire. She tried to make eye contact with her sister, but to no avail.

"Kate!" she hissed urgently from across the room. "Clothes!"

"Blazes, kid! What are you doing?! You trying to act like Riesen now?" Kyler prodded her, smirking his maddening little smirk. The dig hit as intended because Niko always thought it was so tacky how Riesen liked to show off his body. She sure hated being likened to him now...

Niko's face instantly turned red. She wished so badly that she could just punch Kyler in the face! Why did he have to be such a jerk all the time? Being the good older sister, Kate elbowed him in the gut on her way across the room to hand Niko her clothes. He simply laughed and scurried away with a snicker.

"Don't worry about him," Kate laughed, rolling her eyes. "Ravenna will put him in his place before too long."

Niko simply took the clothes and darted back into the washroom. If Ravenna didn't 'put him in his place', then Niko vowed that when she got older, she would punch him in the face herself. That was a fantasy that brought her a satisfying smile.

She was also happy to see Kate brought some of her favorite clothes: comfortable blue sweatpants and a loose-fitting long-sleeve top, along with her puffy black jacket. Putting on her clothes was now painful, though, due to her foolish battle with the scalding hot water. Her skin definitely was quite pink and tender, especially on her shoulders and back where most of the water made initial contact.

Oh well, she thought. What else was there to do except deal with it? She would rather have dry clothes than still be in her wet ones, even if she now had burns.

I should say something to John about his water temp, though...

She didn't want others to make the same mistake she had. Maybe it was something with the water heater in the garage? She'd have to check on that today when everyone was awake. Although, if they were supposed to be packing, would they even be around later today? What about Sliding? The prospect of Sliding this morning had excited her and she was looking forward to it.

A knock on the door startled her.

"Yes?" she shouted back, still agitated by Kyler's taunts.

"Everything okay in there?" Kate asked.

"Yeah, I'll be out in one second!"

"Okay, just checking! Looks like Ajane is heading in now."

Niko realized she was drifting, lost in thought as often happened. Many people over the years had made it clear that was one of her faults — being a perpetual daydreamer — but her father had always reassured her that her deep thinking was one of her blessings.

She adored her father greatly. He was often her champion when she was not even her own. He encouraged all her hobbies, as weird as some of them were. She didn't do as well in School as her older siblings did, but her father once told her that she was the smartest of all the Ryen kids — that it was the system in place that was at fault for her poorer scores. She didn't know if that was exactly true, but she always kept that compliment with her wherever she went.

There I go, getting sidetracked again...

She rushed to get dressed and hoped to be back out in the living room before anyone could give her any grief. When she emerged from the hall, she immediately spotted Ajane standing with the group, who all seemed fixed in stunned silence. Even Riesen seemed to be one hundred percent awake now and practically standing at attention.

What a goody goody... Niko thought derisively. So what if she was still annoyed from all the attention he'd been getting...

"Good morning, Niko." Ajane spoke in that same pleasant tone from the night before. "I was just getting ready to explain the plan for today."

It seemed as if she was waiting for Niko to get there, which was weird. Niko was so accustomed to constantly being out of the loop for everything, so it was nice to feel important and needed for a change.

"Good morning!" Niko leveled her the brightest greeting she could, but she wasn't sure she hid all of her apprehension well enough.

"I'm sure you saw the news about the Minedyne station in Anterg?" Ajane asked.

Niko nodded in reply.

"Well unfortunately, just a few minutes ago, several other Minedyne stations were also attacked," Ajane announced. "Including the one in Green Valley."

4

Rest and Relaxation?

NIKO'S head was sent spinning. No wonder the others were standing in stunned silence. Green Valley?!? That was so… local. Even though it was a several-hour drive from the Green Coast, Green Valley was a sort of second home to all of them. Everyone saw it as part of their off-the-beaten-path corner of the world. It was where her Field team was from! Why would the An-Mara attack Green Valley? What could possibly be the reason?

"What?!" Niko exclaimed as she reeled back in disbelief. "Why?"

"Is it really the An-Mara?" Ricsen asked, his eyes narrowed in an expression of what looked like deep consideration. As much of a meathead as he was, he really was super intelligent deep down.

Ajane paused before answering, seeming to weigh her response carefully. "It was. But the situation is a little more complex than what it seems."

Niko looked around the room and tried to read the emotions of her friends, but there were only blank stares. Apparently she wasn't the only one who needed answers.

"As you know, Minedyne is where the Meridians conduct business related to certain technologies," Ajane continued. There it was again. The way she said 'Meridians' carried the ever so slightest hint of disdain.

"The An-Mara have been on to Minedyne ever since they landed here. In fact, that's the reason they came in the first place. One of the reasons," she added, glancing across toward Riesen for the smallest fraction of a second. "The Meridians have known about the An-Mara, but they have been very reluctant to engage in open conflict with them."

Although this was a lot to take in, it all made perfect sense. It wasn't like this was some huge revelation that shocked her foundation to the core. The An-Mara, like the Meridians, came from the stars to settle on Arhanda. However, the An-Mara only came within the last fifteen years, whereas the Meridians had been here for over sixty years. Everyone knew the two factions didn't see eye to eye on everything; they obviously had a history back wherever they all called home.

The An-Mara were people just like Meridians and Arhandans, but their culture just felt... different. Sure, they spoke the same Universal Common just like everyone else, but their accents were so strange. They talked slowly with a drawl, and always added weird inflections at the end of their sentences. Niko thought pretty much everything about them was weird, but she had to admit no one really knew all that much about them. Nobody even knew how many of them there actually were on Arhanda. They all settled in Poste Territory, so unless you were from there, you probably weren't crossing paths with them.

Niko could've asked a million questions just about the An-Mara alone, but she realized a more prudent question had been steadily burning inside her, and it finally boiled up to the surface.

"Will this affect training for Riesen and me?" Niko blurted out. "If there is war, won't we be too young to join?"

"Perhaps," Ajane said. "But also perhaps not. It is too early to tell."

This was not exactly the answer she was hoping for. Although it was sort of exciting to feel included, she really had been yearning for some rest and relaxation upon her return from her trip. She needed some time to recharge before being whisked away to be Inducted early into the service to the Meridians.

"I understand why Riesen's here, but why is *she* here?" Kyler asked bluntly, gesturing dismissively toward Niko.

"She is here because of the dreams," Ajane replied, less than amused at his attitude.

Wow... Niko thought as blood rushed to her face. First Kate blabbed to Ajane about the dreams — now Ajane outed her to everyone! *What the blazes?!* Before Niko had a chance to get too mad, Ajane continued, turning back to Niko and softening her tone.

"The dreams have to do with psychic potential, something we are very much interested in. It's a lot to explain right now, but it will be explained in time. For now, we need to get you to one of our stations for a test."

Niko blinked. It was well known that psychic potential was a thing that was being studied at the Meridian academies, but what sent her into a tailspin was the thought that maybe *she* could play a part in that world.

There's no way, she thought. *There's nothing special about me ever.*

Was that a tinge of... *excitement*... that she just felt?

"They're just dreams," she tried to reason to herself as much as to the others. The more she thought about it, the more she was convinced that there wasn't anything uncommon about them. Everybody dreams. "It could just be a coincidence the one about Riesen came true."

Riesen raised his eyebrows. He had no idea about the dream that Niko had about him drowning when they were younger. She'd never told him.

Ajane shook her head. "There was no coincidence. I would need some tests from you to be sure, but this seems as clear as day to me." Ajane's eyes held no jest in them.

Niko stepped back as if hit with a ton of bricks, too much in shock to even react when Kate walked up behind her and draped both arms over her shoulders, regardless of the sensitive skin from her burns.

Psychic potential...

"What kind of psychic potential?" Niko asked hesitantly. "What does that even really mean?"

"Oh, I wouldn't overly concern yourself with that," Ajane attempted to reassure her. "You need years of training to reveal the extent, but ninety-nine percent of cases end up very mild. Being able to sense a future event, or sensing an intention from someone near them, for example."

"What about the other one percent?" Niko asked skeptically.

"Well, since I have been on Arhanda, the most major abilities that I have seen are slightly more extensive thought-reading abilities."

Normally Niko wouldn't have pried, but the way Ajane was answering without hesitation gave Niko the confidence to continue asking questions.

"What about, you know… *Meridians*? *An-Mara*? People from beyond Arhanda. Whatever other people there are…" Niko hesitated to ask, but she figured they had to be way more advanced than the people here on Arhanda. The Meridians did, after all, introduce many revolutionary technologies to the planet. Computing machines, vaccines, city cleaners, and Uts were just an immediate few that came to Niko's mind. Not to mention that they were capable of *space travel*…

"Small steps," Ajane responded in a reassuring tone that did anything but reassure her. "You will all learn about the wider worlds in due time."

As disconcerting as all this was, Niko was comforted in the sense that she felt like an important part of the discussion. She was slightly disappointed that she was not getting answers to all her questions, though. She wanted to know now! To the blazes with waiting!

"The whole reason for training psychic potential is to improve communication. Profound communication is the most important element for progressing a society," Ajane added.

Hmph, Niko thought to herself. It was funny that communication be considered so important to these Meridians, yet they were always the ones so cryptic about everything. If Ajane was even Meridian at all… Niko was beginning to have questions about that because every time she mentioned the word 'Meridian', it oozed with a tinge of disapproval.

"So nobody has crazy powers where they can shoot lightning or fire out of their hands?" Niko asked. The question was intended as a joke, but she was curious about the limits of this psychic potential Ajane spoke of.

The way her friends chuckled seemed to answer the question for her, but Ajane simply shook her head lightly as if that wasn't such a crazy question after all.

"Trust me, if I could shoot lightning and fire, Kyler would not still be standing here," Ravenna joked, leveling a not-so-joking glare toward him. He must've just done something else to earn her ire. Nothing new there. Kyler just played the innocent card, shrugging his shoulders and spreading his hands like he had no idea why she would say such a thing.

"Hmmm, I could do with some fire-slinging abilities," Kate mused.

"Same here," Riesen added. Something told Niko that if anyone could learn that, it would be Riesen.

"You guys can take the fire, but I'll take the lightning," Kyler quipped. "And if we could do all that, I could think of better powers to have anyway."

"There will be plenty of time to play pretend later, but for now the reason I'm here is to take you seven to a station we have hidden down south in the White Mountains," Ajane announced. She seemed half amused at the banter, but also half annoyed, as if she were a mother forest cat in a hurry to herd her unruly cubs. "Green Valley is not very far from here, and if whoever attacked the station learns that several of those in Minedyne's employ live out here, they could come looking for you. And we are on a very short timetable with the accelerating political landscape as of this morning."

Well, that's just great, Niko thought. Anxiety gnawed at the pit of her stomach. War coming to the Green Coast? The idea was laughable, yet anything seemed possible given the chaotic news from this morning.

"The one we've been to?" Cryo asked, motioning toward Ravenna.

Ajane nodded once in reply.

"Okay, so we leave now, then?" he asked.

"Yes," Ajane replied, "and we don't plan to be there too long, but it is a bit of a hike for those of you who haven't been. Grab what gear you need and let's meet back in fifteen minutes."

With that, Ajane turned around and glided out the door without saying anything else. The whole thing made no sense to Niko. Why would they make a Minedyne station accessible through a route only available through a hike from the Green Coast?

I hope everything will be explained on the way, Niko thought. She was starting to feel awkward for asking so many questions, so she decided just to play along. Would her parents even let her go, though? Youth on the Green Coast were very independent compared to the rest of the world, but still… if Kate, Riesen, and Niko all just up and disappeared, their parents might be a little worried at least.

"Shouldn't we ask Mom and Dad?" Niko asked Kate as people got up and started heading out.

"I already told them you, me, and Riesen were going on a hike with Cryo, Ven, Nico, and Kyler," Kate responded. "They're cool with it."

"Do they even know what's going on at Green Valley?" Niko asked, giving Kate her best look of disapproval. There's no way they would approve of their youngest daughter going out on an excursion when there was just an attack not too far away at Green Valley.

Kate shrugged. Niko loved her older sister dearly, but this would not be the first time Kate had ever tried to hide things from their parents. In fact, all of her siblings would do that. Niko was the rule-follower of the family, through and through.

"I just… I'm kind of worried about this to be honest," Niko confessed her reservations to her sister. "Cryo says he trusts her completely — and I guess I trust his word completely — but I only met this lady last night."

"Well, to be honest, I haven't worked with her very long, either. But like you said, I trust Cryo, too. And besides, all my dealings with Ajane have been super positive and eye-opening so far."

"Okay, well if we don't make it, I'm putting this on you," Niko laughed and gave her sister a hug. "Wait, you didn't grab any of our snow gear before you came, did you?"

"No, I should have. Let's make this fast," Kate grimaced through her teeth. "Riesen! We're going to the house to grab our stuff, c'mon!"

Thirty minutes later, Niko quietly shut the door so as not to wake the denizens still sleeping on the floor in John Maksolhoff's house. She then headed to the driveway where Cryo's car and Daren's truck were loaded with hiking gear, backpacks, and skis. Kate, Kyler, and Riesen were already packing into the truck and seemed ready to go.

"Is she actually going with us?" Kyler sneered loudly, seeing

Niko emerge from the house.

"Yes, she is," Kate replied firmly, directing a don't-mess-with-me stare at him.

"Can she even keep up, though? I mean, we're used to going pretty fast…"

"Kyler, we are bringing *you*. It's not Niko who's gonna be slowing us down," Ravenna retorted. Niko smiled inwardly at that dig and saw Kate smile outwardly. She even thought she saw a small hint of amusement cross Cryo's face, as well. At least they were all on her side. "Niko, you're riding with us. All your stuff is already in the back."

"Okay," Niko replied, noticing that she'd called her *Niko* instead of *kid*. Still, she wasn't totally sure of whether or not she was completely welcome. She didn't want anyone to think she was a burden, not even Kyler.

"Don't listen to Kyler. You'll be fine," Ravenna added, seeing the uncertainty on Niko's face. "You have no say in the matter, anyway. Ajane says you need to come with us, so you come with us. You're a part of this."

The word '*need*' didn't exactly make Niko feel comfortable with this trip they were taking, but maybe she would get an adventure out of it. She'd always loved adventures of the sort since she was a little kid. As long as she didn't think about the part where there was a possible war going on, she thought she might even have fun.

"How far is this place we're going, anyway?" she asked Ravenna.

"Back a ways kinda by where we went last year, but not up so high," Ravenna replied, packing two more bags into the back of Cryo's car. The place they'd climbed in the mountains together last year wasn't too far away. Niko could see those peaks from the north end of the Green Coast.

"Okay, that's it then? That's all we need?" Niko liked to have everything in order. She probably forgot something, but everyone seemed in a hurry. She doubted that they would allow her to double check at this point.

"That's it," Ravenna said. "You can hop in if you want."

Niko grimaced as she peeked in the back. There was barely room for someone to sit between all the bags, even for someone as narrow as herself. She squeezed into a thin gap between the driver's seat and a backpack, and it felt as if someone was giving her a bear hug. Even still, she would want a car like this when she was older. It was a white model, flat and fast, but with four-wheel drive and big enough tires to get around the back roads of the Green Coast. Almost everyone preferred trucks, but she'd always been a car person.

Just as she settled in, a startling crash sounded from near the house, and she swung her head to see Tyson stumbling into some trash cans next to the back door. He looked as if he'd seen quite a night. His long, blonde hair was disheveled and all over the place, and he squinted as if the sol was shining directly into his eyes, even though it was all cloudy out right now.

"What in the blazes are you guys doing?!" he half yelled, picking himself up.

"Tyson! Shhh!" Ravenna hissed back, shaking her head and rolling her eyes. She turned to Cryo. "He better not wake anyone else up."

"Well, that's rich of you to say! I woke up because y'all were making so much noise."

"Cryo, go deal with him, please," Ravenna groaned.

Cryo gladly heeded the call and was able to quiet him down a bit. Tyson had made it clear last night that they would all go Sliding together later this morning. She couldn't hear what they were saying, but Niko guessed that Cryo made some sort of deal with him about that, because after about a minute, Tyson just jokingly blew a kiss to the group outside and headed back in the house with a combination of a smile and a wince. He was probably still mostly asleep anyway and wouldn't remember this in a few hours.

"He'll be cool?" Ravenna asked Cryo, looking skeptical.

"Yep," Cryo replied as he returned to fastening ropes on the gear. Ravenna stared at him with what looked like suspicion for a second before leaving to speak with Daren.

Niko wondered what that was about. Why did they not want Tyson to come with them? And why was he not supposed to know they were leaving? Were they worried about him having too much to drink last night? These internal questions were only making Niko feel stressed out, so she took a deep breath and thought about the mountains. The first thirty minutes of her morning had started off horribly; she was determined to make the rest of her day a good one.

"Sorry about the tight fit," Cryo said to her, shooting her a sympathetic smile as he got in. "We won't be in here that long."

"It's okay," Niko replied. "Us small folk are always used to being crammed into the tight spots." Indeed, when she took trips with the Ryen family, she and Mack would always have to sit in the back with all the gear.

"Well, if they'd hurry up over there, we could be on our way," he joked.

Just then, Ravenna and Daren looked as if they'd finished whatever conversation they were having. Ravenna walked over and hopped into the passenger seat, which looked quite spacious.

"We all set?" Cryo asked.

"Good to go," Ravenna replied, clicking her seat belt shut. "Daren thinks Ajane will meet us there."

"Got it," Cryo nodded, then pulled around and zipped out of the driveway. His car was so plain and unassuming that it seemed at odds with how fast and smooth it actually was.

I definitely want a car like this, Niko thought again. *Except more spacious in the back, maybe.*

Niko turned to look out at the ocean between all the bags. It looked peaceful, despite the waves from the storm that was surely rolling in. She had finally just come home yesterday for some rest and relaxation, only to be thrown in the midst of some goosechase that she did not completely understand. Sliding now seemed awfully tempting... She needed something fun and low stress to decompress. The view of the ocean disappeared shortly after they embarked, however, so any notions of Sliding would have to wait.

The drive was mostly uneventful, except for the forest cat they had to slow down for. The magnificent animal had crossed the road right in front of them, its shaggy grey and white fur glistening from the broken sol-rays attempting to shine through. It was always such a beautiful drive, but today it was even more so after the recent rains and snows. The combination of greens of the foliage and whites of the mountains made for a stunning image.

After what seemed to be only a few minutes, the road deadended and they pulled off into the brush. They drove for about fifty more meters through dense cover, finally coming to a stop in what looked like a makeshift garage that was half buried in the ground and covered with several fallen trees.

"What... we're not gonna drive all the way through the mountains?" Niko asked, trying her best to crack a joke.

"If you wanna stay crammed in the back there, I can try to drive up the cliffs for you," Cryo replied, smirking as he finally put the car into park. "Go ahead and grab your stuff. Your skis are in Nico's truck. I'm gonna take a look at the trail for a second."

Niko was only too happy to get out of the cramped back seat. She'd only been in the car for a few minutes, but her legs were already starting to cramp. As she grabbed her pack from the trunk, she took a peek through the trees back at the Green Coast. It was quite a view from here and would only get better as they climbed higher. Even when cloudy, the visibility was always very good right after a rainstorm.

At the far corner of the Coast, where the highway to Green Valley rounded the bend, Niko thought she could make out a line of traffic.

"Why is there traffic on a day like today?" she asked Ravenna, motioning over to the highway.

Ravenna turned to look, her hawkish eyes scanning deep and hard. Her brows furled up as an intense look of concentration settled over her face.

Well, that's not at all worrisome... Niko thought sarcastically.

"Hey guys..." Ravenna called out to the others. "We might wanna speed up the timetable of our little trip!"

5

Skis

NO sooner had they collected all their gear when the party of seven was off and away up what looked to be a very well-hidden trail. 'Trail' was a generous term, as they had to step through fresh snow and push back low hanging branches every step of the way. There was no choice but to march in single file because the path was so narrow, and all of them were hit with the recoil from the branches as soon as the person in front of them stopped pushing the brush away.

Cryo led the way, followed by Riesen, Daren, Kate, and Kyler. Niko trailed sixth and the group was rounded out with Ravenna in the back. Ravenna kept intently looking back toward the coastline where the line of traffic steadily rode closer and closer to the town. She had these intense, hawklike eyes that Niko imagined could see like binoculars. They definitely announced her as not of pure northern blood. It seemed like half of her friend group was part Islander or Southlander or something foreign.

Apparently Ravenna's mother was from somewhere on the South Continent, but she had died when Ravenna was very young. Niko had seen a Memory of her, though, and she looked a lot like Ravenna, only with the darker features and a softer face characteristic of the Southlanders. Her father, however, was through and through Antergian, with his stout muscular build and chiseled facial features, strong jaw and all. How Ravenna's parents ended up together in the first place was always a curiosity because the Southlanders and Antergians traditionally did not like each other at all. Each were known for their distinctive appearances, but Niko thought the combination manifested in Ravenna surely had to be the most exotically beautiful in the world.

In addition to having the bright purple Southlander eyes and perfect skin, her hair was a strange, natural blend of blonde, brown, and red, reminiscent of those calico cats the Meridians always kept with them. She was short in stature from her Antergian bloodline, but nevertheless was strong and lean. Her features were sharp and stern, and she carried herself with such poise and coordination. However, as much as anyone would admit that Ravenna had supermodel good looks, the running joke was that her brusque personality was often quite a deterrent from any romantic interests ever pursuing her.

She had a quick and fiery temper and would not take any grief from anyone. Kyler and Tyson were often on the receiving end of that, as were many boys who would get too rowdy. She was *very* serious for a Green Coaster. It didn't seem like she smiled or joked around like the others very often, but considering what happened to her family, it wasn't surprising. Not that she was overly nasty and mean — she was just antisocial to a point. Niko always had such an admiration for Ravenna's independent spirit, and if there was one person she could be like when she was older, it was her. Or Cryo. Either of them.

"Can you see who it is?" Niko asked.

Ravenna shook her head. Well, maybe her eyes weren't superhuman after all. "I think it has to be the Meridians. Hopefully it's them. Most likely they're securing the roadways from Green Valley."

"Why'd we need to hurry and get away from them then?" Niko asked.

"Well, if they met up with us, we would at the very least be stopped for procedure and questions. They might've even loaded us up for active duty right then and there. Ajane told us she'd take care of everything and that we need to get to the station as soon as possible. Like before noon."

"Oh," Niko replied. "What's so urgent about all this?"

Ravenna shrugged. "It's gotta be because of everything that happened with the An-Mara this morning. There's a console at the station that we need to get Kyler to asap, and then the rest of us need to input some data for Ajane, also."

The hike was getting steeper, each step climbing up footholds that almost felt like stairs. The snow would only get deeper and deeper the further they went, and it was already getting harder to talk while breathing. Still, this was her first real chance to get some answers about what the blazes was going on.

"So what exactly happened?" Niko asked. "I've been so confused about everything."

"You know about as much as I do, unfortunately," Ravenna responded, shaking her head. "The An-Mara have always known about the Minedyne sites, but they've never shown any aggression toward Minedyne, the Meridians, or anyone."

"It just seems like I'm missing something," Niko admitted, breathing more heavily from the increasingly steep hiking. "One day everything's fine, and the next I'm waking up finding out we might be at war. I don't get it at all."

"You and me both," Ravenna said, pausing in thought. "I mean…"

Ravenna's pause made Niko suspect that there really was something she was missing.

"The Meridians aren't this perfect little organization like you're led to believe, I guess," Ravenna admitted. "I don't exactly know why we were attacked today, but I guess it doesn't surprise me that some people aren't happy with the way things are being run, especially with the Minedyne sites."

Niko's curiosity was brimming, but her eyes remained focused on the path ahead, which was flanked by a stream on one side and a steep, fifty-meter cliff on the other.

"I can see what you mean, if my dealings with Ajane so far are any indication," Niko said smirking.

"Oh believe me," Ravenna responded, "compared to the rest of the Meridians, she's about as plain speaking as they come. You have to get to know her a little bit, but you can count on her."

"Sorry," Niko winced in reply. "I didn't mean to diss her."

"No, no," Ravenna assured her, "I know what you meant. I was more talking about the other Meridians and how there's just so much shady secrecy all the time. Fortunately, Cryo, Kyler, and I are privy to a lot. But there are still things they don't tell us."

Niko wondered what type of things exactly, but it was starting to get hard to think about how to carefully phrase questions while keeping up with the quick pace they were setting at the same time. Even though she was in good fitness from all the Field she'd been playing, hiking through the snow in full gear was a different sort of fitness.

Blazes, I forgot how tough this is!

As they rounded the corner past a large rock face, Niko saw what she assumed was the trail leading up to a pass a couple hundred meters ahead. None of this looked familiar, though. It was hard to remember specifics from her trip with Cryo and Ravenna last year, but she thought they might've been a little farther inland today. She remembered being able to see the ocean the whole time last year, plus she didn't remember that spot they parked the cars today. This had to be a different route.

"What I do know is that once we get inside the station, we'll be able to access a lot more information on what exactly is going on," Ravenna continued. "The ports they have in there will put us on their network and we can see all the orders going out."

This sounded very appealing to Niko because she was eager to learn a little bit more about the goings on of the Meridian service. As the students her year were getting closer to joining up, nerves were starting to increase. Nobody knew what to expect.

Now that it was very possible that she'd be Inducted soon, she was even more nervous, but maybe this would give her an edge on her peers? She'd been dying to feel more confident about *something*, but she never quite could. Her mind was often her own worst enemy, keeping her trapped in a vicious cycle.

"Oh, that's good," Niko responded in labored breaths. How was Ravenna not even breathing hard??

Well, I guess she and Cryo do *climb the highest mountains in the world for fun*, she remembered, answering her own question.

As if reading her mind, Ravenna smiled up at Niko. "You got this! We're almost to the top, then we get to ski for a bit."

Niko just responded with a hopeful grunt. *Almost there.* Looking ahead though, it didn't look like they were almost there at all. They had at least several hundred meters left to climb…

She tried to wish away her negative thoughts and summon

positive ones to carry her up to the top. *It's all mental...* That's always what Cryo was saying, and Niko supposed it was true.

Almost there, she repeated to herself, this time convincing herself a little more.

After what turned out to be *not* almost there, the group finally crested the top of the pass. Niko wanted to collapse onto a rock, but the rest of the group was already almost done putting on their skis. Niko did like to ski, but was not particularly good at it. She preferred the sensation of sliding on her front and back like they do when they go Sliding in the ocean. As she halfheartedly set to work putting her skis on, she turned around to take in the view, which was magnificent mountain peaks and beautiful green valleys as far as the eye could see. The Green Coast was now completely out of sight, though, so it was impossible to know what ever happened with that line of traffic.

Hopefully Ajane cleared everything up with them and we aren't in some big trouble, Niko nervously thought. Even though she was not part of the Meridian service yet, she was starting to feel connected to it all. Or at least she thought that's what she was feeling. Speaking of, where was Ajane?

"Do we know for sure if Ajane meeting us at the place? Like will she already be there?" Niko asked the group, still out of breath from the steep hike up to the top of the pass.

"I don't know," Daren responded with a shrug. "All she said was that she had something to take care of real quick and that she'd meet us when she could."

"I guess we'll find out soon," Cryo said. He pointed over to the left down to a beautiful snow-covered slope, even if it was a bit steep for Niko's liking. She hadn't skied in years, so she was probably very rusty. "That's where we're headed. The station is just down the hill off that way. If you get lost from the group, just find the two mountains that look like cat ears and it's between those two. See you guys down there in a minute!" With that, he was off and away.

Riesen did not even hesitate two seconds and followed with a grace and speed that made Niko frustrated anew. *Of course he would be good at skiing also…* Why was he so good at literally *everything*? Just watching him glide over the snow like a winter fox made Niko feel even more self-conscious about her skiing ability, or lack thereof. She just shook her head and reminded herself that this was not a competition; they were just using it to get from point A to point B.

A few seconds after Cryo and Riesen took off, the rest of them followed one by one, Niko being the last. She wanted to give herself some space, but didn't want to get too far behind also. She didn't like how Cryo even made mention of getting lost. Was that a possibility? Leave it to her to be the one that gets lost…

She pushed off and within only a few seconds she quickly picked up speed. The rush was otherworldly as wind ripped at her face. A panorama of white and blue was her entire awareness as the ground streaked by. She immediately questioned herself as to why she didn't do this more often as she dug in for her turns. This was so fun! There were trees to avoid on either side, but the clearing was plenty wide enough to get going pretty fast. She looked ahead to make sure the cat ear mountains were on either side of the clearing she was headed for, then crouched down in a streamlined position to pick up some real speed.

She flew over a small dip, then noticed a blind bump in the slope ahead where all her friends disappeared from view. She didn't see any of them slow down beforehand, so she assumed it was fine to maintain her speed. Only a couple seconds passed after she went over that hump until she was able to see the entire valley below. The route opened up into a very steep final slope, but she was already going too fast to second guess her descent. Two figures were already stopped way down at the bottom, too small to tell who they were. It had to be Cryo and Riesen since they took off first.

Wow, they got down there fast, she thought. *I guess here I go!*

The rest of her companions also dotted the hillside, some getting close to making it down all the way. She didn't want to wipe out, but she did need to hurry because most of them were so far down already. At least there was still someone right here with her.

Is that Kyler? Why was he moving right in front of her?…

"KYLER!" Niko yelled, bracing for the impact.

It all happened in a split second. One moment she was enjoying the view and embracing the rush, the next she was flying through the air, unsure of which way was up and which way was down. It seemed like an eternity floating weightless in midair, but as soon as she made contact with the ground all she saw was snow and sky, sky and snow. She tumbled once. Twice. Three times. When would this stop?

She landed hard on her side multiple times and the air was completely knocked out of her. She finally settled on her back, but she didn't slow. If anything, it seemed like she was picking up more speed as she kept sliding down the steep hill. She then began to spin in a circle, one second flying headfirst and the next second feetfirst. Instead of snow and sky, sky and snow, she was now seeing the trees rotate dangerously near.

Just as she started to really panic, she skidded to a halt, thanking her lucky stars. Nothing felt broken. Right? Her breath was still knocked out from the impact on her back, but that was about it.

That could've been a lot worse... she persuaded herself, half dazed and half relieved.

After a few timeless seconds, though, all the pain started to flood her body at once. She couldn't tell exactly where the pain was coming from, but whatever it was, it was most likely going to leave a significant bruise. Still, nothing felt broken at least. She'd broken bones several times before — mostly when playing Field — so she knew what that felt like. If something was fractured, she would have felt it by now.

After a few seconds lying there in bewilderment, she sat up and looked around. Kate and Riesen were running over to her. From the looks of it she made it down the hill. In style.

What happened...?

To answer her own internal question, Kyler was sprawled out about twenty meters off to her right, looking hilariously ruffled and shaking unreasonable amounts of snow off of himself.

"Niko! Are you okay?!" Kate exclaimed as she gave her sister a very careful hug, searching her body for signs of injury. "What happened?!"

"What happened is she tried to kill us!" Kyler loudly complained as he stood up, skis nowhere to be found. "What the actual blazes! What were you thinking?! *Kid.*" The way *kid* oozed off his tongue made Niko's blood boil. "I told you we shouldn't have taken her with us!"

I swear, that's the last time he calls me kid, Niko fumed as her teeth clenched and fists curled up into balls. Her vision turned red with rage as tears of frustration welled up. *How could he possibly blame me for that?? He cut me off and there was nothing I could do to react!!*

"Dude Kyler, I watched the whole thing. You literally veered in front of her and cut her off at the worst possible moment," Riesen defended his sister. "You can't blame that on her."

"Are you kidding me?!" Kyler exclaimed. "She's the most terrible skier I've ever seen! That's on her one-hundred percent!"

It was too much. Niko burst into tears and wished she could disappear. She didn't know if she was crying because she was angry at the unfairness, in pain from the fall, or emotional because her brother just stood up for her. Whatever the reason, crying in front of people was one thing she did *not* want to ever be caught dead doing. Especially in front of people like Cryo and Ravenna. Or even Kyler.

How embarrassing is this?! The more she thought about it, the worse it got though. She just turned away, curled her knees up and buried her head, pretending no one could see her.

"I'm fine, I just need a second." A warm, tight hug signaled that her sister had rushed in, but right now she didn't want to be touched by anyone. "Please just leave me alone."

"You okay for real?" Kate asked, taking a step back. She attempted to sooth Niko by running her fingers through her hair.

Niko just nodded in return, head still between her hands and knees.

"Oh, blazes. So are we just going to have to sit here and play babysitter until she feels all better?" Kyler sneered.

"KYLER. Shut. Up!" Kate challenged.

"Oh come on, look at me," he pleaded. "I took the same fall she did and no one is babying me making sure I'm okay. And whattaya know, I'm perfectly fine."

Kate stepped forward toward him with fists clenched, but Riesen put one hand on her shoulder to hold her back.

"Apologize, Kyler," Riesen said quietly. It was a pure demand; there was no question in his voice. "Now."

Niko had never seen this protective side of Riesen on such brilliant display. All the annoyance and jealousy of him that she'd been feeling over the last few days instantly faded away. This was the sweetest thing she'd ever seen, even if he looked utterly terrifying. Terrifying on her behalf was okay.

Kyler threw up his hands and sighed in exasperation. "I have to apologize to her, but she doesn't have to apologize to me?"

"Yes," Riesen said. "You have to apologize for being an ass."

"Kyler," Cryo said softly, leveling him a simple no-nonsense expression.

Kyler looked back and forth between Cryo and Riesen and eventually gave up. Apparently the look from Cryo was what did it.

"Look, *kid*, I'm sorry. I didn't think anyone was right behind me." It wasn't much, but it was something. Except there was that *kid* again.

"Stop calling me kid," Niko said quietly.

"What was that?" Kyler asked, leaning closer.

"Stop calling me kid," she repeated.

Kyler looked around and shook his head exasperatedly. "Is there a mouse somewhere? I can't even hear her. Can anyone else?"

"STOP CALLING ME KID!" She exploded this time, but she didn't care. "Thank you for apologizing, but I really wish you would stop calling me *kid*. I wish *ALL* of you would stop calling me kid. My name is Niko!" Her frustration was now directed at everyone, even though the only one she was mad at was Kyler. "And you can call Nico '*Daren*' because my name is Niko and I only have the one name!"

With that she stood up and went to look for her skis, too agitated to be bothered by the obvious open-mouthed stares from behind her back. Thankfully, she quickly spotted them sticking out of the snow close by. As she reached down to grab them, she noticed Kyler's skis nearby as well.

He can go grab his own, Niko thought bitterly.

She was about to turn around and walk back, but paused. After second thought, she sighed and picked up his skis also. Some good will was in order, whether he deserved it or not. Niko had never been one to hold an outward grudge for too long.

With both pairs of skis in hand, she turned around and stormed back to the group. If she wasn't in such a mood, she might've been amused to see everyone still gawking at her. As soon as she started back, though, they all quickly turned away to avert her gaze. Everyone except Ravenna, who was off to the side leaning up against a tree with arms folded, the ever-so-slightest hint of a smile etched onto the corner of her mouth. If Niko wasn't imagining things, that was a look of pride if she'd ever seen it.

Niko marched back over to Kyler, curtly handed him his skis, and moved on. The look on Kyler's face was priceless. He had to have felt like the biggest clown on the planet. As well he should.

For what felt like the first time in her life, Niko actually felt *powerful*. She just brought a group of overachieving superstars, all of them older than her, to speechlessness.

CHAPTER SIX

6

The Station

THE station wasn't far from where Niko and Kyler had just recovered from their wipeout. After reaching the bottom of a well tucked-in valley, the group was able to continue on skis cross-country style for about another kilometer — if even that — when a small wooden door became visible on a dug-out hole on the hillside.

"Is that the station?" Niko asked, eager to be done with the trek. It was only a relatively short excursion, but her body was aching all over, nonetheless. Even though Ajane was still nowhere to be found, all Niko felt was the relief to be done with all the walking and skiing.

She'd had quite the morning so far: she woke up with borderline hypothermia, scalded her back and shoulders under a hot shower, learned of a possible war, trekked up the side of a mountain, and took a high-speed wipeout on that last steep slope. Even if the wipeout was Kyler's fault — *it was*, Niko affirmed to herself — she felt sheepish for feeling so sore when everyone else seemed like it was just business as usual.

"Sure is," Ravenna replied. "In we go."

At first glance it looked to be nothing more than a flimsy wooden closet. The edges were warped from the exposure, just like the fence back home that Mack never coated. How many years had this even been here for? It could've easily just been an old storage shed for skiers or mountaineers. Cryo struggled to open the door, wriggling the edges free with his boot. Once liberated, the door swung open to reveal a set of concrete stairs that descended for a couple meters. At the end of the stairs, there appeared to be a vertical tunnel with a ladder.

"Alright," he said. "You can leave all the gear off to the side here." He swung off his pack and discarded his skis against the wall. Everyone else did the same, so Niko followed suit.

As she got closer to the edge, she peered down into the dark. It didn't look too far down, maybe another five or six meters. That was a relief. She was worried she was going to have to climb down a thousand rungs! She wasn't exactly scared of heights, but she wasn't fond of them either when she didn't have to be. Cryo climbed down first and jumped the last few rungs, landing onto the ground with a small splash. Of course there would be a puddle down there... The others followed quickly, though, as did she.

Once at the bottom, she tiptoed around the water, avoiding it altogether like a cat would, then turned to face a much sturdier door. This one was heavy and round with a complicated-looking locking mechanism overlaid on the sides. This was more of what she was expecting for some secret station; she was so underwhelmed by the wooden dummy door on the outside.

Cryo opened a panel on the wall and typed in some code. Almost immediately, an unlocking sound reverberated through the door. From the sound of it, Niko figured this door had to be at least a meter thick!

"Wow, this door is heavy duty," Riesen remarked, mirroring her own thoughts.

"It really is," Kate agreed, laughing.

"It's like the ones at the Green Valley station," Daren added thoughtfully.

That's right, he's never seen this place either, Niko reminded herself. He hadn't really said much the whole trip, so it just seemed like he knew what he was doing the whole time. Daren was probably the quietest one in the group, though, so him not saying anything was nothing out of the ordinary.

Cryo nodded. "This is a satellite station for Green Valley. Each of the major stations has at least several of these. They're not on the main schematics on display in the big stations, but we can still plug into the system and access the tunnels."

"What are the tunnels?" Riesen asked before Niko even got the chance to. She was thankful someone else was doing the asking this time.

"All the stations around the world are connected by an underground rail system run by Minedyne. It's one of those things they don't want us talking about, so if you tell anyone, I'll have to kill you," Cryo joked. Riesen just flashed his cocky smirk back. "But seriously, you and Niko aren't supposed to know. So if you can, don't tell anyone or we could take some heat."

He called me Niko!

Riesen crossed his heart in a playful gesture. "I will carry it to the grave, my captain!" He bowed to Cryo and blew him a kiss. Kyler took this opportunity to exaggerate the role-play, kneeling to Cryo and bowing in fake reverence.

Boys are sooo stupid, Niko thought once again, rolling her eyes. She and Kate shared the eye roll at each other, but then Kate laughed and joined in also. *How fake.*

"Lead the way, o'captain!" she exclaimed.

Before Niko could get too annoyed, the door finished humming and slowly pressed open, revealing a space about twice the size of their living room back home. It was decently lit, which was surprising to Niko considering just outside it looked like a shack that had been abandoned in the frozen mountains for centuries. There was a table in the middle with two machine consoles on top. In the center, overhanging the tables from the ceiling, was a glass screen with gridlines on one side. Along the edges of the room was more tabletop space, furnished with more consoles.

Is that all that's in this place? Just machines? She didn't know exactly what she was expecting, but it was something different than what she was seeing. She thought there would be more rooms. On the other side, however, there was another door. Maybe they were going through that?

"Okay, Kyler, log in and see what's up with Green Valley," Cryo said, motioning to the console in the center of the room. "Nic...Daren...," he paused, obviously making an honest effort to respect Niko's wishes, "you and Kate can log in on those ones over there. Can you get Riesen and Niko set up? Ven and I will see what's up with Ajane."

Wow, he actually called me Niko AND Daren 'Daren'!

"Her World Test right?" Kate asked.

"Yeah, they need to take it and we need to submit the results to Ajane asap," Ravenna replied.

What the blazes is the World Test? Niko wondered. She did not like tests. They made her jittery and she wasn't very good at them. She glanced over to Riesen, who didn't seem fazed in the least. How infuriating. She admitted that his life had become so extraordinary that something like this would be pretty low stakes and mundane for him.

"Alright," Kate replied. "Over here guys." She motioned over toward two consoles on the side wall. Daren was already there typing something into both of them, swiping all over the screen until a program loaded up that read 'World Test'.

"Okay, Niko you can sit here, and Riesen you got that one," Daren announced. "Time is a factor with this one. She wants it timed and you can't talk once you start it. It's fast, though, I promise." He offered his most reassuring smile.

How wonderful! The reward for enduring everything from today is me getting to take a test, Niko thought wryly.

"Let's get this over with," she said to her brother as she sat down on the slightly uncomfortable seat that was in front of the console screen.

"No talking," he reminded her sarcastically, one side of his smug grin tugged up. She just made a face at him in return.

Focusing her attention to the screen, she saw a single option to begin the test. She clicked on it and the screen swapped to a picture of some mountains. Was it stuck? She tapped the monitor and the picture changed to a lake. What was going on? She tapped it again and this time a picture of sand dunes from the desert on South Continent popped up. She was just about to ask Daren what was going on when the screen shifted once more.

The next image was of a street scene, but this time a single prompt popped up and asked, 'Where is this?' There were no hints other than the picture, but fortunately she'd seen this place before. This was easy; it was the Fraton Quarter of Sol City. She was just there! She went to type in her answer of 'Sol City' in the response box, but only a single word was eligible to be typed.

Hmmm, she thought. Well this was frustrating. She knew the answer, but now she didn't even know what to put in. Should she type in 'SolCity' with no spaces? Should she type in 'Islands'?

Should she type in 'Fraton'? She looked over at Riesen and he looked as cool under pressure as ever, like this was the easiest test in the world for him. Of course it was. This should be easy for her too, but she had no idea what this question wanted from her.

Glancing around the room was her nervous habit whenever she was stumped during tests, as if any of her surroundings would give her the answer. They never did. Making matters worse, she was also starting to become distracted because she could hear Cryo, Ravenna, and Kyler all whispering animatedly to each other.

What are they up to? she wondered. Maybe she could rush through the test as quickly as possible and then join the discussion. It was nice being included in so much today, so now she didn't want to miss out on anything ever again. Returning her attention to the test, she just typed in 'SolCity' with no spaces and moved on. *Close enough*, she thought.

After submitting her answer, another image popped up on the screen. It was just a bunch of trees with no prompt, so Niko tapped on the screen. This time, the image stayed. She tapped again, this time a little bit harder, but it still didn't change.

"What the blazes," she said out loud.

"Shhhh!" Riesen taunted her. She didn't even give him the satisfaction of looking over at him.

She tapped the screen once more, and luckily a new prompt showed up. The question read, 'What color do you see?' The box was flashing all the colors of the rainbow switching from each through a continuous gradient, over and over and over. When she went to input an explanation that it was the whole spectrum of colors switching, she realized the response box would again only let her input a single word.

Hmm, maybe the word 'all'? she asked herself. She tried to type in the word 'all', and it prompted her that only numbers were allowed for this answer.

Numbers only?? Are you kidding me? How the blazes am I supposed to answer this? she asked herself, her frustration once again visible. She sighed deeply and sat back in her chair. Riesen chuckled at her display of frustration, which made it even worse for her. *Not everyone is Mr. Genius over there like you*, she imagined telling him.

Once again she looked around the room. Kyler was trying to be quiet, but his arms and hands were flailing all over the place as he was whispering something to Cryo and Ravenna. That made Niko giggle on the inside. He was always so dramatic! It was probably something so simple he was talking about, too. Definitely not anything to be so excited over. On the other side of the room, Daren and Kate were minding their own business on their own separate consoles. They seemed to be oblivious to Kyler's antics.

Focusing back on her own screen once again, Niko just typed in the number '1' for her response, for absolutely no reason at all besides to hurry the test up. Next question.

"Explain how to tie your shoes."

What in the world are these questions??? Niko angrily thought to herself, now beginning to feel like this was all a waste of time. Just earlier, Ajane had been talking to her about psychic potential. What did any of this have to do with that? At least there was no image of landscapes this time. She figured she would repay the test for wasting her time by responding with a mock answer in turn.

Taking out my revenge against an inanimate machine — that will show them. Niko sighed at her own foolishness, but this was starting to become very frustrating indeed.

'Don't tie your shoes. Just get the ones that slip on', she answered. She smiled, satisfied at her snarky response. At least this question let her type in actual multiple words. Next.

"If you could go anywhere in the world, where would you go and why?"

These were the lamest questions she'd ever seen on a test! How would the assessor even determine anything from these? What was there to be measured? She'd been expecting some math, or history, or geology, or…*anything* besides these ridiculous questions she was being asked. At least this question had something to do with the world, since it was called the World Test and all. She rubbed her temples and squeezed her eyes shut before attempting to answer this one legitimately.

'*I would go to Sol City because it has everything: Field, Sliding, Collecting, perfect weather…*' This was all true. If she could go anywhere in the world, she probably *would* go to Sol City again. Submitted. Next.

"Assessment complete."

Wait. That was it??

Daren wasn't lying, that *was* fast. Niko breathed a sigh of relief to be done with that ridiculousness, but also started to worry that she did very poorly on it. What *was* being assessed? That test was nothing but insanity. She looked over to see how Riesen was doing, but he wasn't even at his console.

What?? When did he finish!?

"What're we supposed to do now?" she heard Riesen asking. He had joined the discussion with Cryo, Kyler, and Ravenna, as had Kate and Daren. All of them seemed quite agitated about something.

"What's going on?" Niko asked, walking over to the group, upset at herself for once again being left out of a discussion.

"Ajane was arrested and brought to Green Valley," Riesen replied.

Ummm, excuse me?? The news hit her in the gut.

"Arrested?.." Niko managed to croak. It felt like the air had been taken from her lungs, just as it had when she fell on the slope earlier. What were they to do now? This whole time everyone was just waiting for Ajane to tell them what to do next.

Aside from the stupid test, she was just starting to feel comfortable with everything that was going on. Well, not exactly comfortable considering there was possible war brewing in the wider world, but she was getting comfortable being in everyone's company here. What were they to do now? Suddenly everything felt out of place and wrong all over again.

"We don't know all the details. Kyler's trying to look for more," Ravenna said, turning to face Niko. "It looks like that line of traffic was in fact the Meridians coming to Green Coast. But they were coming to look for her."

"Are they looking for you guys too?" Niko asked, suddenly worried for her friends. It felt as if all the blood drained from her face, making her even more pale than she normally was.

"Not because of association with Ajane, but they are looking for us because we're supposed to report to Green Valley," she said. Seeing Niko's worried expression, she added, "Everyone's supposed to be reporting right now, so it's nothing specific to us. We're fine."

"I'm not seeing any of her correspondences or anything," Kyler said. "Nothing that I can find where I won't get tracked, that is. I'd need way more time to set some programs up if I wanna be able to sneak around."

Niko did have to admit that it was impressive seeing Kyler in his element, furiously typing into the console. She knew he was an expert machine tinkerer, but she'd never seen anyone type that fast. She didn't even recognize half of the symbols that were flying across the screen. It was like he spoke a completely different language, and an insanely complex one at that. He might be an ass, but he did have quite a talent.

"I noticed when I was talking with Ajane last night, she seemed like she wasn't exactly a fan of the Meridians," Niko remarked. "Does that have something to do with this?"

The others looked around at each other, but no one immediately spoke up. They had to know something.

"Well, she's skeptical about some of their Minedyne operations," Kyler started cautiously.

"Let's wait until she can tell us more herself," Kate interrupted. The others were quick to nod in agreement. They definitely knew something Niko didn't.

Whatever, Niko thought, trying her best to let it go. *Maybe they were sworn to secrecy or something.*

"Alright, well… what do we do now?" Riesen asked.

"Hmm." Cryo furrowed his brows in thought. "I really don't know. We might wanna get back as soon as possible. What do you guys think?

"I agree," Riesen said without any hesitation at all. Of course — he didn't want to run afoul of the Meridians before he was even Inducted. Neither did Niko.

"I just… I don't know," Cryo said, shaking his head. "Something isn't right."

"I feel like we need to have a plan if we do go back," Ravenna said. "They obviously don't like something about Ajane, and we're completely in league with her. If they find out about our work, we could be in trouble also."

What work? Why would that land them in trouble? Niko wondered to herself. Just when it felt like she was getting answers, she suddenly realized she knew absolutely nothing about what was going on.

"Well, I'm doing the best I can trying to get information for everybody," Kyler said in an exasperated tone. He was probably still grumpy from getting shut down by Niko earlier in the day. That memory made Niko smile on the inside.

"Riesen and Niko haven't had time to do any work for Ajane, and the Meridians and everybody would know that," Kate spoke up.

"Let's at least get them back so they can report in." There were murmurs of agreement all around in support of that proposal.

"OH!" Kyler squealed in his nerdy delight, startling everyone. "I just found something! Ooohhh, very weird."

He swiped a couple times and then some sort of schematic popped up on the big glass screen, overlaid onto a map of the area. It looked to be of some huge structure that was buried deep in the ground. Maybe the rail system they were talking about?

"Is that a well?" Riesen asked.

"Or the rail system?" Niko chimed in.

As Kyler zoomed out, it definitely looked more like a well. He zoomed out to see the entire Green Coast, and it was revealed to be this huge vertical structure that continued to stretch on and on below the frame. It was enormous, larger than the size of the whole town.

"Is this real?" Kate asked Cryo and Ravenna. Those two had been in the know with the Meridians the longest and would have the best idea as to what this was.

Both Cryo and Ravenna seemed as unsure as everyone else, though. They had the most solemn, concentrated looks on their faces. They gave each other a glance that seemed like it was an extensive conversation between them, but it held no meaning for anyone else.

"It's not the rail," Cryo said. "See right here is the rail." He pointed to a much narrower tunnel that ran horizontally from the east and then shot off to the south. It looked like it ran right through this station.

"Wait, does the rail go through here?" Riesen asked, once again before Niko got the chance.

"Yeah, except this door's been sealed shut," Cryo responded. "Kyler tried opening it from the console already and it looks to have been physically sealed shut. We can't open it. Which is another weird thing going on here…"

"Lame, I was hoping to catch the train back to town," Niko joked, but no one laughed except Riesen. The rest were all buried in deep thought, looking at the map.

At least I made Riesen laugh.

"Wait, zoom out, Kyler," Ravenna commanded, leaning forward.

Kyler did just that without any complaints, probably because he was thinking the same exact thing. Upon zooming out, the well

— or whatever it was — showed no signs of stopping. It stretched on for several kilometers deep at least! And he continued to zoom, and continued to zoom, and continued to zoom. The well structure kept extending down into the interior of the planet, and soon, Green Valley entered the frame. As it did, a second well structure became visible.

"What the blazes are these things?!" Kyler asked in exclamation. In dramatic fashion, he leaned back in his chair, putting his feet on the desk and his hands on his head. "Did any of you know they were there?" Everyone shook their heads, clearly just as confused as the next person.

"Are they actually there, though?" Kate asked. "How do we know they aren't just plans? It seems like we would've known if something this big was being built. There would be so much commotion and mining and…"

"The info on the schematic I pulled up says this is a real time interaction," Kyler interrupted, shaking his head. "Look, if I zoom in you can see the train moving here." He zoomed in and pointed to a train clearly moving along the rail between Green Valley and Nevaly.

"They could've been built a long time ago?" Ravenna suggested.

"Must have been," Cryo agreed.

Kyler still leaning back in his chair, zoomed out with one hand, this time even farther. What he saw probably shocked him so much that he lost his balance, slamming his feet on the table and smacking the sides of his chair with his arms.

It was hard to fault him for the surprise, though — he had zoomed out far enough to where most of the entire North Territory was now visible, along with what looked like dozens of these well structures. Even more jaw-dropping than the number of them was just how deep they all went. Every single one of them looked like it went so far down that they had to extend past the crust and into the mantle.

That's what they called those layers of the planet in School, right? Niko didn't even know that it was possible for any structures to be that deep. Wouldn't they melt? From what she remembered of her instruction in geology, any structure that deep underground would surely be melted.

Every single person in the room seemed puzzled beyond words.

Niko had so many questions spinning around in her mind. How did they make these? Where did they get the materials to make them? Why did they make them? Who made them? What are these things for, and why are they at every single station? Surely for some huge geology program. All Niko knew was that the big company Minedyne was tied in with the Meridians, and that their focus was on developing new technologies through the production of specialized minerals.

"Are these things all Minedyne mines?" Niko asked.

"I honestly have no idea," Cryo said, obviously dumbfounded just as much as everyone else. "All of Minedyne's production I know about doesn't need nearly this much material. Besides, we would see some major atmospheric side effects with this much mining."

"I'm calling it right now," Kyler declared, "this is some sort of spaceport or something to do with space travel for when we make contact with the rest of the Meridians." It wasn't a half-bad conjecture, even if he was only geeking out to his fantasy of space travel, which he did quite often.

Cryo shook his head, though. "I don't think so. *Mayyybe* mining for the fuel?"

"Is it like this all around the planet?" Kate asked.

Kyler zoomed out completely and sure enough, these well structures dotted the entire planet. Arhanda looked like a pincushion. There were even wells in the ocean. Many of them. *How did they even build those??*

"Blazes!" Kyler half-yelled, startling everyone. He kicked himself back into a seated position on his chair with lightning speed and started typing up a storm at the console.

"What?" Ravenna asked sternly.

He ignored her for a few more seconds as he unleashed an ungodly whirlwind of the fastest typing and swiping Niko had ever seen. In a split second, the entire schematic was deleted off the screen and he sat at the ready, looking very tense.

"Someone tried to hack in and track me," he responded, breathing heavily.

"Ummm, okay… what does that mean?" Riesen asked.

"Did they see you?" Ravenna asked at the same time. "Did they know it was our station?"

"I… I don't know," Kyler stammered. "I don't think so."

"Well, they already arrested Ajane, for whatever reason," Ravenna said cautiously. "It makes sense that they're trying to retrace her steps."

Kyler nodded in agreement.

"I think we're fine," he said, not quite reassuring Niko that things were indeed fine.

"Okay, well," Cryo started, "I think we've overstayed our welcome as it is. Let's head back to town. At least to get Riesen and Niko back like we talked about."

The group all nodded in agreement and nobody needed a second reminder to make a move to leave.

"Don't forget all your gear up top," Cryo continued. "If you need a snack, I have some in my bag. It's going to be a lot more walking on the way back since we can't ski down anything."

Niko's initial reaction was disappointment since it was already such a grueling hike out here, but she was also glad to not have to deal with more downhill skiing. Although it started out fun, it ultimately ended up causing her a lot of pain, misery, and embarrassment.

"You can go ahead, I'll close up here," Ravenna told her. "I also need to load your test results onto my Ut since I can't send anything over to Ajane for the time being."

"Okay, see you up top," Niko replied with a shrug. She headed out the door as Ravenna stopped to load up the results from the console. She climbed the ladder up and grabbed her pack and skis, putting them on with haste. At least this first flat section would be cross-country on the skis. After that would be the long climb back to the top of the pass that Niko was not looking forward to.

Niko collapsed onto her bed after Cryo and Ravenna dropped her off. Daren had to make a stop at the Farm when they got into town, so Riesen and Kate would be home shortly. No one else was home, though, and it was nice to have a few minutes of quiet to herself. She hoped Riesen and Kate would take a long time because she didn't want to talk to anyone right now. It had been decided that they would head to Green Valley with all the rest of the townspeople as soon as they got back, but she was so exhausted and just wanted some time to rest.

Her entire body screamed. The burns on her shoulders and back were even more tender than they had been earlier. Her pack had been digging into her sensitive skin every step of the hike. She also felt massive bruises starting to develop on her left hip and tailbone from her wipeout earlier. Also, even comfortably home, every one of her muscles still quivered from carrying all that gear up and down those endless elevation gains. Furthermore, it started raining and even snowing toward the end of the trip, making the going even slower. Kate had offered to carry some of Niko's gear, but she would absolutely *not* be letting anyone think she was so weak as to need help with that.

Niko tenderly rolled over to her back and suddenly felt that she also had a massive headache. She realized how dehydrated she must have been, so she reached for her water bottle and gulped the entire thing down, water trickling down the sides of her face and all. She did not care one bit. That was the best tasting water she'd ever had.

She set her bottle down and closed her eyes, recalling her conversation with Riesen on the way back. She hadn't had a chance to ask him about his opinions of the test while they were at the station, which was fair because they were so preoccupied with the other business. Once they had crested the high pass on the way back, though, she settled in line next to him and they discussed their responses.

She was very disappointed with her answers indeed. First, there was the question about the picture of Sol City. The question read, 'where is this place?' She had typed in 'SolCity', one word, no spaces. Riesen said he answered with the word 'here'. It was a riddle, he said, and the answer to 'where is this place?' is 'here'. *So obvious, ugh!*

The next question about the changing colors was a machine question. Niko had no idea what to answer so she typed in a random answer. Riesen said he answered with '11111111', the machine code for the color white, because all colors of light combined produce white light, he had said. Of course he would answer with something so clever. He said he was debating typing in all 0's, the machine code for black, because all colors of pigment combined will yield black. But since the colors were displayed due to the light emitted from the screen, he opted to answer with all 1's.

How am I supposed to know any of that? Niko thought to herself, trying to rationalize her poor answer in her own head. *Oh, well.*

When she asked him how he answered the question about how to tie your shoes, he just shrugged and said he gave his best, clearest step-by-step instructions on how to do it. At least Niko felt like her answer was the clever one this time. She was proud of her snarky response to that ridiculous prompt, even though she knew it was probably incorrect.

The last one about where you would want to be in the world if you could be anywhere seemed like it had no right or wrong answer. Both Ryen kids had answered the same — they would most want to be at Sol City. Niko felt that probably most people in the world would want to be in Sol City. It was a very desirable locale — why wouldn't anyone want to be there?

Both Riesen and Niko thought the test overall was kind of a joke. Niko was glad to hear that Riesen's test had the same malfunctions that hers did where the images were getting stuck on the screen. When she asked what they were even testing for, though, Riesen said that they were probably monitoring response time for all the questions. Niko admitted that made sense because it seemed like there was nothing to assess otherwise. Those questions were so bogus! Thinking about the test was starting to make her headache worse, though, so she changed the subject in her own mind.

She instead focused on the sound of the increasingly steady rain outside. That sound was so soothing sometimes. A couple more seconds of this and she could fall asleep...

Just then, she heard her front door burst open. Kate and Riesen were back, much to her dismay. All she wanted to do was sleep, just for a few minutes at least!

Ugh, she thought. *That was a fast trip to the Farm...*

"Niko! You home?!" Kate called, knocking on her door.

"Yes."

Kate softly opened the door, seeing the pathetic sight of Niko sprawled out on her bed, snow clothes still on and her pack and skis still draped over one arm. She had no energy to bother getting comfortable before lying down. Kate smiled at her sister.

"You know, you could've at least dumped your stuff onto the floor."

"Too far," Niko replied, attempting humor but without changing her facial expressions. She was too tired for that also. Kate laughed, at least.

"Well, you'll probably be glad to hear that we can't make it out to Green Valley today," Kate said. "The weather got really bad and I guess there was a rockslide across the highway a couple of k's outside of town."

Niko let out a sigh of relief.

"I know that's supposed to be bad news, but for me that's the only *good* news I've heard all day."

Kate grinned. "Yeah, me too," she replied, lying down next to Niko and snuggling up against her sister. "I think we plan on leaving first thing in the morning. For now, I could use a nap also."

It was still only the afternoon, but Niko was too tired to fight the likelihood that this might end up being a deeper slumber than just a mere nap.

7

Floating

A bright yellow hue flooded her vision. Blinking her eyes was about all she could do. There was a dusty tinge to the atmosphere, but that did little to block out the blinding sol-light that beat down on the sandy rocks all around her. She had her goggles with her, but what happened to them?? It was so hard to see, even with a squint. She turned to look in the other direction, but moving was so difficult. It was as if her body was glued to the ground she was lying on.

Wait.

Why *was* she lying down right now? She took a deep breath before trying to stand up, but that was only accompanied by a sharp pain in her lungs.

What was going on?? Where was she? She tried breathing again.

The same sharp pain. It was bearable, but the thick layer of sand swirling around in the air didn't make it any easier. Wait, was it snowing? Is that why it was so quiet? Dust that might have resembled snow swirled through the air.

She blinked again. Was that someone talking to her? Riesen? Her vision was blurry so it was hard to tell for sure.

The thick air muffled the sound of someone shouting back. She could see him leaning over her, but what was he saying? Was that the dust muffling the sound? It couldn't be snowing — the rocks all around were yellow, bare, and dry. Not a snowflake on them.

With all the concentration she could summon, she tried sitting up but her whole abdomen protested against the motion. As she finally positioned herself up, the background noise steadily increased in volume — along with a ringing in her ears and a throbbing in her head. She leaned against the stone, or whatever it was behind her, and felt a warm trickle run down the side of her face. She wiped away what she assumed to be sweat and looked at the smear of red on her hand. That wasn't sweat. Was it blood? She tried to stand up but was *so* dizzy.

Why is this so hard!? Why do I have no control over my body? she wondered.

A bright but silent flash to her left sent shards and dust raining into the air. She saw Riesen stumbling away from her on all fours, struggling to gain traction. Why was he carrying a rifle?

The confusion was too much right now. She had no clue what was going on, but one thing was perfectly clear — she had to get out of here. Now.

She closed her eyes tight and gritted her teeth. With every bit of willpower she could muster, she tried to get up. She *was* going to get up. It seemed like she was making progress at first, but after only budging a couple of centimeters, it ultimately felt like she had no strength in her abdomen whatsoever. There was no way she would let this stop her, though. There was *no* way. She *had* to get up.

Another try.

As she labored to stand, she realized that both sound and comprehension were returning slowly. It was like whoever was in charge of the volume had muted it completely and then was carefully turning it back up one level at a time. After what felt like an eternity of pulling herself up, she became discouraged to recognize she was still slumped against the same debris she had been all along.

What the blazes??! she thought angrily. What is wrong with me?? And where am I!?

In all directions, the ground was littered with crushed rock and stone. What once looked to be some sort of structure was now barely more than a pile of rubble. There was a tower with cables running overhead still standing to the left, though. And there was a doorway. Maybe she should get up and get over there; she felt very exposed where she was.

Just then, another bright flash, this time accompanied by a distinct cracking noise, came from the tower. One of the overhead cables she'd just noticed cracked through the air with a wicked hiss, and the ground she was sitting on seemed to heave with ungodly force. That was it — she *was* getting up this time.

She leaned to the side, hoping the leverage of the roll would help her to her feet. As she leaned forward, she looked down and saw something metallic sitting on her chest. It was tiny — there was no way that *this* was weighing her down. She reached down with shaking hands to push it off, but it did not budge the way she wanted. Instead, a searing pain shot through her body, one even stronger than what she felt with every breath she took. A warm trickle rolled from the object down her belly.

This wasn't real. It couldn't be. There was no way she was stabbed by this… well, whatever this thing was. Sure, she was in a fair amount of pain, but surely she would feel worse agony than this if she were actually stabbed.

Something reminded her of her training — she knew she wasn't supposed to remove the object in the case that it was stymying the blood flow. Looking up, she let out a cry of frustration. It sounded funny to her, like it was not her own voice, but she didn't care. She just wanted out of this place.

She looked down again to assess her wound. She couldn't tell how deep the object had punctured, but she knew she needed to wrap it in something. She looked around for anything that would suffice, but it was only rocks and rubble and dust that surrounded her. She looked over to where Riesen was scrambling and tried to call out for help from him. He was facing away, though, and he was busy dodging fair-sized chunks of falling stone.

Cracks started to run up the tower to the left and dust was shaking free from everywhere. She thought she saw the ground start to twist ahead in the distance and at this point she knew she must be hallucinating something fierce. Maybe if she rolled out of here? On second thought, she figured that might be difficult with this thing sticking out of her chest.

Suddenly, she realized just how loud everything was around her. There were clear voices shouting at each other now, as people were struggling to stand on the shaky ground. Riesen and another guy with blonde hair that she didn't recognize were helping some other guy to his feet in the distance. She didn't recognize that guy, either. He had a dark complexion and a ragged beard, but maybe wasn't that much older than herself. The three staggered forward until their legs found traction, at which point they started sprinting.

There was another guy shouting at her from her left, over by the tower. It was Daren. He was ducked underneath the doorway, sheltered from the pieces of the tower that were falling all around him. She could hear him yelling, but she couldn't make out what he was saying because there was an increasingly deafening roar all around her. The cracking noise from the tower was now coming from the ground. She yelled for help and reached out her arm in his direction.

He cupped his hands to yell something back to her, but everything else was much too loud to understand anything he said. He then shifted his poring gaze behind her to the right. She tried to turn to see what it was, but she couldn't move without feeling that same immobilizing pain that had her pinned to the ground. Daren gave a thumbs up and nodded to whoever it was, but the nod looked more like a question than anything. He looked upward, waiting for a break in the rainstorm of stone above him. He seemed to find it, because he darted out in the attempt to make it to where Riesen and the two others were waiting.

It was a few tense moments of Daren scrambling to the left, darting to the right, avoiding falling rubble, but he was nimble and quick. He looked like a Field attacker streaking down the line, dodging defenders left and right. He quickly made it to Riesen and the others and they all huddled together under a protruding corner that protected them from raining debris.

She leaned her head back in relief, but no sooner had she felt any when the ground dipped violently. All four of the guys got up and sprinted off the edge of the bridge, just in time to avoid the smashing of the tower that had stood to her left.

She was on a bridge.

And her friends jumped off.

A few moments of stunned confusion was followed by… what *was* this feeling? Was she starting to *cry*? Was this defeat? As in a cruel joke, her vision started to fade and the pain started to numb.

This is not right, she pleaded, as if someone would be listening to her.

This had to be a dream. It couldn't be ending like this. Was she *actually* dying? How did she even get here? There was nothing right about any of this at all. She closed her eyes in a desperate attempt to wake up.

The pain came sharply as her body was jerked forward, one arm scooping under her armpit to hold her up as a strip of cloth was wrapped around her abdomen and cinched tight with unbelievable quickness. She was too immobile to protest when another arm scooped under her legs and elevated her in an instant. She looked up to see who this mysterious benefactor was, but her vision was way too cloudy now that tears were flowing. As soon as he had grabbed her, though, she knew who it was.

Cryo. It was like his touch had communicated with her. She held tightly around his neck with her arms, her grip feeling stronger than it ever had in her life, even though she was in a more weakened state than she had ever been in.

Weird.

It had to be the adrenaline. She could barely see a thing at this point, but she felt as if she was floating. Nevermind the ground was erupting wildly all around her. The bridge was even tilted to the point where she could see the dark blue of water down below. Of all the things that didn't make sense, though, she actually started to smile. It was kind of a fun feeling, floating.

Floating toward the edge.

The edge.

They were airborne in an instant and hurtling toward the water below.

PART TWO

War Against the An-Mara

8

The Highway to Green Valley

NIKO threw her arms out to the side for balance as if that would stop her fall. She let out a shriek and opened her eyes. She could see.

Bewildered, she realized she was not falling. She was not on the bridge. She wasn't even outside. She was in her room, half buried under her covers. She wiped away the blood from her face, and realized it wasn't blood at all — it was only a combination of sweat and tears. In a panic, she looked down at her chest and sure enough, no protruding object. She breathed the deepest, most genuine sigh of relief in her life. It didn't even hurt to breathe! No air had ever felt sweeter. *Thank the heavens!*

What time is it? What day *is it? Am I actually in my room?* A period of questioning her very existence usually followed a sudden awakening from a deep slumber. She needed a few seconds to catch her bearings and gather herself. Was that all really just a dream?? It was so real.

The *dream*.

Blazes! A gnawing sense of dread washed over her. Although insanely relieved that monstrosity of a nightmare was *not* in fact real, her mind was far from being at ease. Her recurring dream had now escalated to her… *dying*? Was that what *dying* felt like? That was the most awful thing she'd ever experienced! She'd already had an almost identical dream where Riesen, Daren, and those two other guys jumped off the bridge, but now she'd seen herself as part of the same dream, and not in a good way…

She suddenly remembered that Ajane was missing. Ajane was the one link that would have helped Niko understand all of this. Or was that a dream also?

No, that was real, she concluded with disappointment. She desperately wished she could rewind time to a few weeks ago. No war, no dying dreams, and no uprooting of her life. The only thing she wanted to worry about was when her next Field game would be.

She turned to her side to face where Kate was sleeping, but her sister wasn't there. What time was it? She mentally reached out through her Ut for the time. *03:46*. Okay, so it was the next morning already. How had she fallen asleep for so long? Her stomach was growling, reminding her that yes, she did indeed miss dinner last night. She must've slept for at least twelve hours!

She pulled herself out of her covers and stood up to stretch. Blazes, was she sore! It was nice to be able to stand up without effort, though. Without *dying*. The way she wasn't able to move in her dream was horrible. Niko winced at the thought. She would just have to try to put that out of her mind. That dream would *not* come to pass. Niko would make sure of it.

One easy way is to never go near a bridge. Ever… Niko thought to herself. *No thank you.*

If she ever saw *anything* that even resembled that place in her life, she would just turn around and run the other way. Perfect solution.

As she slowly reached for the ceiling to stretch, she realized just how much she was actually hurting. Her skin was still sensitive from the burns, her core was feeling every small motion she made, and her calves felt like they were about to cramp if she moved them even the slightest. But the real tenderness was from her left leg. Even brushing against it hurt. Looking down, she could even see a nice dark bruise setting in. It was enormous! It was sticking out from below her shorts and she could feel it run all the way up to her hips.

She'd fallen asleep in full snow gear, but she had no recollection of getting dressed, so Kate must have dressed her into her sleepshorts while she was out cold. She smiled in fondness thinking of her sister. She was so happy to have her back in town, even if it would turn out to be short-lived. It was too early to go thank Kate now, but she would when she woke up. Who knows how long that would be, though, because Kate had always been notorious for sleeping in late.

She finished a side-to-side stretching motion, then waddled her way out into the hallway and over to the kitchen to get something to eat, using the walls as a crutch to help her walk. She chuckled to herself because she knew she looked absurd. At least she finally caught her breath after waking in a panic, even if she was still breathing more heavily than normal.

When she emerged into the living room, she was startled to see that Riesen and Kate were already awake.

"Good morning, sleepyhead," Kate chided affectionately.

"Why are you guys up this early?" Niko asked in surprise.

"Kate got a call from Mom and Dad last night and they said we needed to meet them in Green Valley by…" Riesen paused abruptly. "Are you okay??"

"Yes," Niko replied, smirking to herself on the inside. *I must look ridiculous, all out of breath and limping and everything.*

Riesen narrowed his eyebrows in a look of doubt.

"Yes, I promise I'm fine." It was a complete lie, because the truth of the matter was that she wasn't fine. The dream had rattled her to the core. She wasn't about to tell Riesen and Kate about it, though — she doubted they would understand. She knew one-hundred percent that they would just tell her it was only a dream and not to worry about it. It wasn't worth being treated like a little kid right now. Maybe later.

What she really wanted was to tell Ajane about the dream. She would know what to do. Funny how the other day she was so hesitant to tell this lady anything, and now the only thing she wanted was advice from her. Only she couldn't talk to Ajane because she was *arrested* and nobody had heard a thing from her. On the hike back yesterday, she'd tried to eavesdrop on Ravenna and Cryo about it, but caught almost nothing. All she gathered was that no one had heard from Ajane and there was no way to reach her.

There was nothing to do for her right now, at least not for Niko. Maybe she could tell Cryo about the dream? If anyone would understand, it would be him. Although, she would be a little hesitant because he was now a part of the dream also.

"You're soaking wet," Kate said, a look of worry crossing her face. "Are you ill?"

"Oh, I just woke up super warm is all," Niko lied again. Well, that part wasn't exactly a lie. She did wake up feeling very hot under the covers. She must've been completely drenched in sweat in order for Kate and Riesen to notice from across the room.

"Lemme make sure you don't have a fever or something," Kate pushed, that annoying motherly concern starting to cross her face. "We were outside in the snow all day yesterday after all..." Kate jumped up and rushed over to Niko, putting a hand on her forehead.

"No, no, I promise I'm fine," Niko protested, lightly trying to push her hands away. "You don't get sick from the cold anyway."

Kate just shot a disapproving look at her, but seemed to at least rule out fever.

"What were you saying about Mom and Dad?" Niko changed the subject, turning to Riesen.

"Oh yeah, they're already in Green Valley," he responded. "They want us to meet them there by 07:00 this morning."

"Why so early?" Niko groaned. It wasn't as though she needed more sleep, but she did want some time to just relax. Her life had been go, go, go for the last several weeks now. The last few days were supposed to be her chance to rest, but instead they were probably the *least* restful of all of them. "I just want to stay home and do nothing today."

"Ummm..." Riesen said as he shared a glance with Kate.

"I mean, I just want a day to myself..." Niko said with a sigh.

"Did you forget everything that happened yesterday?" Riesen asked with a hint of sarcasm. "Are you sure you're feeling okay?"

"Oh the blazes!" Niko replied in exasperation. "I *know* what happened, thank you very much. I just don't want to have to keep trekking around the world. I just want a day off."

"Hiking a few k's is not what I'd call trekking around the world," Riesen scoffed quietly under his breath.

"Why are you being such an ass?" Niko shot back. She already took a bunch of grief from Kyler yesterday; she was not about to take some from her brother now. He was even the one who stood up for her against Kyler!

An intense, fiery look came over Riesen's expressions as if he was more than ready to duel wits with her. Niko was in a no-nonsense mood, though, and was all too ready to battle back. Fortunately, Kate was there to play mediator.

"Riesen, it's fine," Kate interceded, shaking her head. "She just woke up and is clearly hurting. Maybe give her a break."

Niko knew she should be grateful for her sister running interference on her behalf, but what she said somehow made her even more frustrated. She wished she could mask her pain a little better. Riesen and Kate were the golden children of the Ryen family, and nothing made Niko angrier than when they pointed out her weaknesses as something to feel sorry for.

"I'm fine!" Niko angrily sighed out loud, flinging her arms to the side in frustration.

"Kid, you're obviously not fine," Kate responded bluntly. She probably felt Niko's burning glare and seemed to immediately realize her mistake. "Niko, I mean…"

Niko just shook her head. She was not in the mood to deal with this right now. Maybe she was extra touchy because of the dream she just woke up from — and everything else that was going on for that matter. To be fair, she did have reason to be cranky.

"Ughhh! I just… I'll get packed I guess," she growled without turning around as she stormed back into her room, doing her absolute best to hide her limp.

She knew she shouldn't get so angry. There was no reason for her to be upset with her siblings. It was the dream. It was the news of the war. It was the soreness. It was the burns. It was the weeks on end with not a single day of rest. It was all just so much. She sank down into her pillow and let the tears flow. She would have screamed if no one was home, but the last thing she wanted was for Kate and Riesen to hear her make any more of a scene than she already had.

After a couple minutes of cathartic release, she wiped her face and pulled herself up to get dressed and start packing.

Again.

Packing was all she seemed to be doing lately. She'd only just unpacked from her long trip to Sol City two days ago, then again for another trip yesterday, and now she had to pack again…

Do I really need any extra clothes? How long will we be gone?

Wherever they were going, she was sure they'd have clothes and stuff there for them. She was fairly convinced it would just be a day trip, so she only packed the bare minimum. She desperately wanted a shower, but the burns from yesterday's scalding made her skin way too sensitive.

I'll just go stinky and I don't even care at this point, she indignantly thought to herself. If she smelled bad, then that was Riesen and Kate's problem.

04:12 her Ut read. It was still mostly dark, but the first hint of light was starting to peek through the shades on her window. The storm from yesterday must have mostly passed because the only way any light made it through this early was if there were no clouds. Niko checked the weather forecast, and indeed, a sol-bright day was called for.

At least there's that, she admitted to herself, already so over these storms. She was ready for Islands weather. *As if we would ever get weather that nice on the Green Coast...*

She barely looked up as a light knock tapped on her door. "Niko?"

"You can come in," Niko sighed in relent. She was feeling a little better after dumping her feelings into her pillow. A *little* better.

Kate smiled as she cautiously squeezed through the door. "You okay?"

"I'm fine," Niko responded, not bothering to look up at her sister as she was finishing packing some personal items into a bag.

"I'm sorry about that back there."

Niko just shook her head. "No, I'm sorry. Don't know why I flipped out."

"You asked us yesterday to call you Niko, and I already relapsed," Kate apologized. "We've been calling you 'kid' your whole life, so we might slip up every now and then. But I promise I will try to call you Niko like you asked."

Why was she being so infuriatingly nice?

"It's okay, I get it. Do you know how long we're gonna be gone?" Niko asked, changing the subject.

Kate looked at Niko and sighed. Niko knew her sister had come into her room to get her to open up, but she just wanted to move on. She didn't want to talk about any of that right now.

"I assume it's just for the day?" Niko asked again.

"I'm not sure. But I think so, just for the day," Kate replied with another sigh, not attempting to hide her disappointment in her younger sister's unwillingness to open up.

This bothered Niko because Kate would always use this tactic of outwardly projecting her disappointment as an attempt to manipulate Niko into talking to her. With steadfast resolve, Niko was determined that it wasn't going to work this time. She had too much on her mind that her sister couldn't help her with right now.

"Are Keran and Mack already over there also?" Niko asked, not acknowledging Kate's longing expression.

"Yep. Everyone is."

Niko paused. "Everyone?"

"The whole town. The Meridians came yesterday and provided an escort to get everyone over there safely. They drove whoever attacked the station in Green Valley away, so now they want to account for everyone," Kate said, shrugging.

"I'm so confused," Niko confessed, shaking her head.

"I know. Riesen and I just got some more updates while you were snoozing away your beauty sleep. We'll fill you in when we're on our way."

Niko nodded, doing her best to ignore the dig about her *beauty sleep*. Kate wouldn't have understood anyway. Besides, Niko was intrigued about what new information they learned.

"I'll let you get ready, but we're gonna leave in about thirty minutes," Kate said as she stood up. Before leaving though, she walked over and gave Niko a tight hug.

Niko felt an intense feeling of guilt wash over her. As much as she was annoyed with her sister, she really did love her. At the end of the day, all of Kate's overprotectiveness was only because she wanted the best for her sister. Niko wanted to just break down right then and tell Kate everything about the dream, but she couldn't bring herself to do it. She simply settled for a nice hug. After the two embraced for longer than several seconds, Kate got up and headed over to the door.

"Oh, and no offense... but take a shower. It smells like something died in here," Kate said before ducking out of the room.

———————

Niko had ridden on the highway from Green Coast to Green Valley countless times, but it seemed entirely different being stopped on the side of the road. It really was beautiful, she had to admit. On one side of the road ran a river... Well, not really a river, but more of a healthy stream. The road and stream were both flanked by towering hillsides. Until the other week, the hills were starting to become mostly green, but the recent snows had turned them white again. Looking down the road, Niko imagined seeing Green Valley. She couldn't see the city yet — they weren't even halfway — but once this narrow canyon opened up into the wider valley, she'd be able to see it since it was a clear day.

The same seven who made the trek to the hidden station in the White Mountains yesterday were the same who were caravaning together today. The plan was to check in with the Meridians when they got into the city, then they were going to meet up for lunch with the rest of the Ryens, the Jenaeis, and the Amibars. Even if there was an aura of uncertainty in the air, it would be nice to get out and go to lunch with her family and friends. And Brandon would be there… Dare she even hope that today would be that restful day she'd been yearning for?

It wasn't a great start, if she had to be honest. Yesterday's storm had sent a rockslide sprawling across the road about fifty k's outside of town, so they all had to get out to try to clear some of the rocks, at least enough for the vehicles to pass. Riesen, Daren, Ravenna, and Cryo did most of the heavy lifting, while Kate was pulling the largest rocks with her truck. Niko and Kyler were left standing around without a job at all. Niko was actually so upset to not be helping. She had felt so included in the group's affairs yesterday, but today she was just the seventh wheel.

It was Kate that convinced the group that Niko was hurting too much to help with the moving of the rocks and that she should wait in the warm car. Niko tried to protest, but her sister was adamant that she 'take care of herself'. This frustrated Niko, but it wasn't worth dealing with Kate playing the victim if Niko pushed back too hard. In her own small way of defiance, she was determined to *not* sit in the car while everyone else was outside laboring. The least she could do was be out there with everybody. Even if it was uncomfortably cold…

Niko was used to being treated like a little kid and left out of adult stuff, but she did find it somewhat amusing to see Kyler in her situation. Although, it was slightly disappointing to see that he didn't care. He even seemed rather happy that he didn't have to help. Not that it surprised her — Kyler was always the one trying to get out of any responsibilities. That was yet another thing that bothered her about him. He was all talk, but when it came down to it, he was one of the most unhelpful people she knew.

"No, not those! I think we need to move from that other spot over there," Kyler shouted, attempting to direct the group lifting the rocks. "If you take too much from that spot, more rocks are just gonna come right back down."

Ravenna paused in the middle of rolling a massive rock through the mud. She said nothing with her words — only gave him a glare that said all it needed to.

"Hey, I'm serious! Don't listen to me if you don't want, but I for one wanna get out of the cold and back on the road," he said, feigning virtue as if his contributions were the greatest of all of them.

"Who votes to leave Kyler out here once we're done?" Ravenna proposed, raising her hand. The entire group raised their hands, even Niko. The only one to abstain was Cryo, who had both hands full because he was walking over to dump an armful of medium sized boulders off to the side. He wasn't even that big — how the blazes was he so strong? They all were so strong. Riesen had just finished dumping a load of rocks even bigger than Cryo's. Even Ravenna was hauling massive boulders, and she wasn't much bigger than Niko herself.

"I vote no," Kyler snickered. "You need a one-hundred percent majority to pass the vote. Sorryyy suckers, looks like I'm here to stay!"

"If I drag you out of the car and leave you in the mud before anyone notices, then what are you gonna do about it?" Ravenna challenged him. Niko didn't know if she was entirely joking or not.

Kyler just smirked back at her, apparently not honoring the fact that this was an actual possibility.

"You know, you could help haul some rocks away, you lazyass," Riesen said.

"Nah, you guys got this," Kyler replied. "Looks like you're almost done anyway."

"Oh, *now* we're almost done?" Ravenna deadpanned. "Just two seconds ago you were telling us how we had it all wrong."

"You guys listened to me and got the right spot," Kyler said, grinning back. He thought he was so slick, but in reality he was just annoying. And everyone knew it.

Cryo just laughed and shook his head. He was such good friends with Kyler so the two of them never argued, but Kyler probably argued with every other person alive. He would even get in huge fights with random people on his Ut. It was unbelievable; he was supposed to be an adult.

"Kyler's right," Cryo said. "I think if we just clear out this section over here it's good enough to get by." He pointed past where they had just cleared, over to a few medium sized boulders.

Wow, they *were* almost done. That didn't take long at all.

"See! I told y'all. That section over there," Kyler beamed at Ravenna, so proud of himself to have Cryo's endorsement.

Ravenna just shook her head, refusing to do word battle with him anymore.

"Kate, you wanna see if you can squeeze the truck through here in a second?" she asked.

"Yeah, let's do it," Kate agreed, pulling the truck up to the narrow opening between giant boulders.

As soon as Daren and Riesen had moved the last big rocks out of the way, Kate pulled through slowly. Niko thought that they'd maybe have to clear out a little bit more, but she was thoroughly impressed when Kate made it through without so much as scratching the side. The group cheered because that meant they could get out of the cold and back onto the road.

It was a frigid morning, but at least the sol was starting to crest the tops of the mountains to the southeast. Almost all of the clouds had moved on, but the storm had dumped a lot of snow and rain the day before. The ground was covered with a dirty slush of mud and snow, and Niko was all too happy to get back into the car. The others seemed relieved also, but the mood had been a little somber this morning nonetheless.

On the car ride up to this point, Niko had learned that the Meridians had declared a global lockdown and imposed martial law. This was the most extreme situation she'd ever experienced in her life. The last time this happened was in the early days of the Arrival, when the entire world was engulfed in a world war.

From what she remembered in history classes, the Meridians arrived out of nowhere sixty-three years ago and effectively ended the conflict almost overnight. Martial law followed for several years, lasting until Meridian institutions were fully established. After that, order and peace reigned over the world and that was all most people alive had ever known.

Of course, not everyone was happy, as Arhanda was abound

with many distinct cultures before the time of the Meridians. The older folks always complained that the Meridians had taken away so much culture in their normalization of the whole planet. Many of them still got especially upset about all the old languages being eradicated. Certain old words were still sprinkled in here and there with certain names of places or streets, but Niko was never allowed to learn any of the languages properly. It seemed weird to her that before the Meridians came, Universal Common didn't even exist for the peoples of Arhanda; now it's the only language she and all her friends have ever spoken. As far as Niko was concerned though, if the clash of cultures led to apocalyptic world wars, then she was more than happy to pay the cost of culture normalization to avoid that.

No one seemed to know how long this current episode between the Meridians and the An-Mara would last. Hopefully it was already over, truth be told. Apparently, what had happened was the An-Mara from Poste Territory had blitzed many of the Minedyne stations all over the world in a coordinated strike. They simply infiltrated the stations, then retreated just as quickly. Their motive was a complete mystery, at least to Niko and her friends. They had to be after something, though.

Ajane would probably know, but she was still missing and nobody knew how to reach her. Cryo and Ravenna tried asking the Meridians about her when they contacted them yesterday, but got no answers. It seemed like very peculiar timing that these strikes were launched just yesterday, and then Ajane was arrested on the very same day. Why would they arrest her? She was a Meridian. She was one of them… wasn't she? Or was she a part of the plot? An insider? A *traitor*?

Niko tried to shove that last thought away. It was brought up in the group's discussions, but everyone seemed to think that there was no way she was a traitor. They were convinced that there was some unseen political maneuvering, particularly by Magistrate Andersane, the prime Meridian administrator on Arhanda. Cryo and Ravenna had insinuated that he and Ajane were not on good terms. Most of it went over Niko's head, but the bottom line was that Ajane was now arrested and that made the Green Coast crew look bad for their association with her.

At this point, Niko had no idea who the good guys were and who the bad guys were in this whole situation. She'd always grown up learning that the An-Mara were self-righteous zealots who thought they were better than everybody. They shut themselves away with most of the rest of Poste Territory and no one really knew all that much about them.

She'd actually just seen some of them in-person for the first time ever on her trip to Sol City for the Field World Championships. The first thing she noticed was their odd style of dress. They wore these heavy tan or grey robes, and sandals with crisscrossing straps that went up the length of their calves. It looked so formal and ancient at the same time! Many of the men had full beards, and many of the women wore silver or gold headbands. Their facial expressions were terribly serious, as if they weren't enjoying the spectacle one bit. She didn't recall that she saw *any* of the An-Mara smile, not even once.

But as odd as they were, it seemed a far stretch to assume that these were simply evil people with evil intentions. There had never been any indication about conflict between the Meridians and the An-Mara before, so why now?

After considering this thought for a moment, she clambered over the rocks they'd just cleared and hopped into Kate's truck. Cryo and Ravenna were already in Cryo's car, and Daren, Riesen, and Kyler were loading into Daren's truck.

She barely settled into her seat when she saw the shadows of two huge birds imprinted onto the far canyon wall. Except these birds were *way* larger than any that she knew existed on Arhanda — even larger than Antergian condors. The shadows moved rapidly their way and had soon completely overtaken the group stalled at the rockslide. Niko looked out the other window where the sol was blocked out.

These were no birds at all. They were aircraft.

9

Child of the Nel-Mara

NIKO hadn't seen anything like these ever in her life. They looked like they shouldn't be airworthy, but they moved with surprising grace. Their exterior was of a dull metallic finish and it looked like there were no windows anywhere on them. They seemed to float silently, but as they got closer, a loud tornado of gushing wind suddenly enveloped the ground as the two craft swooped down to land. Before Niko had a chance to wonder about their inner workings, doors slid open on the sides and a dozen armed people clad in a loose-fitting, hooded outfit burst onto the ground.

"STOP WHERE YOU ARE!" a strange, loud voice boomed, echoing against the valley walls. "OUT OF THE VEHICLES. HANDS WHERE WE CAN SEE THEM."

Was this for real? This was starting to become too much for Niko's brain to handle. One dream was already too much. Two dreams on the same day was simply outrageous. She needed to wake up. *Now.*

She shut her eyes as if that would do the trick, but when she opened them, she saw Kate outside of the truck kneeling on the ground, hands spread wide.

"OUT OF THE VEHICLES AND ONTO THE GROUND.

HANDS WHERE WE CAN SEE THEM."

Was this actually real? This seemed a lot different from her dream last night. Although there was a considerable amount of confusion in both situations, Niko seemed to at least know who she was right now. She could *feel* who she was at her core, something she didn't feel during her last dream. That didn't stop the whirlwind of questions that was swarming around in her brain, though. Most of her questions could just be summed up as '*what the blazes is going on?*'.

Realizing she was still sitting in the truck dumbfounded, she leapt to action. Something told her that she didn't want to have these people ask a third time.

"SLOWLY! NO QUICK MOTIONS. EXIT THE VEHICLE. ON YOUR KNEES. HANDS WHERE WE CAN SEE THEM."

Niko did just that, making sure to clearly show her hands. Once outside, she flinched and turned away, curling up defensively in pure instinct. Without the cover of the truck, she suddenly felt very exposed with all these weapons pointed at her. She'd never had a firearm pointed at her in her life, and her heart dropped at the sudden rush of fear. She'd always wondered what her response would be in a traumatic experience. Was she fight, flight, or freeze?

Apparently I'm duck and cover and curl into a little ball, she thought ashamedly.

The armed figures approached cautiously, stopping first at Kate. One of them grabbed her arms and bound them behind her back in cuffs. Two figures then approached Niko, one of them clearly a woman, and did the same. Niko involuntarily let out a chirp from the pain of the forcefulness of the motion. Her skin was still so tender and her body so sore, but these people paid no mind to her misfortunes.

As soon as she was bound, they dragged her over to where Kate was kneeling and moved on. Four men with rifles stood over them in guard, although their posture was more relaxed at this point. They probably realized that the two Ryen girls were no threat, but even relaxed as they were, they still looked quite deadly to Niko.

"Niko! Blazes, are you okay??!" Kate asked worriedly. Niko was quite certain that if she were free to do so, her sister would have pulled her into the tightest embrace imaginable. She was a hugger, Kate was.

All Niko could do was nod back, eyes wide in panic. She started shaking so badly that no words would come out at this point.

"NO talking," one of the men guarding them instructed. "Not until we get you sorted out."

A couple seconds later, Cryo and Ravenna were dragged over to the same location with Niko and Kate. They seemed strangely calm, as if perhaps they were used to this sort of thing in Meridian training.

"You okay?" Ravenna asked Niko as she was thrust down next to her.

"NO TALKING," the man said again, this time in a much more intimidating tone. Ravenna hadn't been there for his first instruction, but he seemed annoyed that he had to repeat himself nevertheless.

Ravenna just glared at him without blinking. The guard responded by pointing his weapon straight at her, to which she didn't even flinch.

Please just stop, Niko silently pleaded to Ravenna in desperation. She had no idea who this guard was or how unstable he was.

"Do not test me, little girl," he sneered, moving one step closer to Ravenna.

Niko stared in disbelief. She'd never heard anyone talk down to Ravenna like this. Not even Kyler. Nobody dared to. The one or two times she saw Tyson or Kyler get too disrespectful toward her, Ravenna had made sure they immediately regretted their actions. Her viciousness was legendary. If Ravenna ever got out of this situation, she was genuinely worried for the guy. Ravenna would *kill* him.

Before the situation got any more tense, however, Kyler could be heard clearly making quite a fuss back by Daren's truck. He started to engage in his typical trash-talk, but these were the wrong people to mess with. She heard three muffled grunts and a short while after that, Riesen, Daren, and Kyler were dragged to the front to join the rest of them.

Kyler was doubled over, wheezing for air. Niko would have normally reveled in the event of Kyler getting put in his place, but the only thing that came over her was anger. Kyler was part of *her* group. *They* weren't allowed to do that to him. Only she was. Or Ravenna. This whole situation was just so unfair!

Who do these people think they are that they can treat us like this? We haven't done anything!

Feeling red-hot anger creeping under her skin, she came to the realization that she was oddly coherent if this was a dream. *This must be real. This must be happening*, she decided.

As the Green Coast crew looked around to make sure their companions were okay, a man stepped forward, removing his hood. He seemed to be the leader of the squad, but looked young, maybe only a couple years older than Niko. He was tall and wiry with dark skin, black hair, and a full beard. He looked strangely familiar.

Wait. It can't be...

"I would convey an apology for the forcefulness of our actions," he drawled, glancing toward Kyler, "but we needed to be sure that you were not an active threat."

Kyler, still trying to catch his breath, peered up with a sour, vengeful look on his face. Much to his credit, he wisely refrained from anymore sarcastic remarks. Niko had rarely known Kyler to display intelligent restraint, but he really had no choice at the moment.

"I know several of you serve under the... *Meridians*... so we had to be sure," he continued. His accent was strange, but the way he let the word 'Meridians' slide off his tongue was reminiscent of the way Ajane had done yesterday. "You will not be reporting back to them, however. You would do well to answer our questions so you can go back to your families and loved ones at some point."

At some point?? That sounded a lot like a threat, one that made Niko's stomach churn.

"Why even waste your time with us?" Ravenna asked boldly. "We're just trying to join our families now. Don't you have bigger fish to fry?"

"Or perhaps you are scouts attempting a rendezvous with your command," the man shot back, his gaze flittering to each of the captives, eventually settling on Riesen. A look that came over his face when he recognized Riesen was the first chink in the armor of an otherwise indomitable expression. The man appeared... conflicted.

"Riesen Ryen?" he asked, although he clearly knew the answer.

Riesen nodded in return, chin held high in defiance as if he would fight them right alongside Ravenna when given the chance.

"Excuse me one minute," the man said, walking over to one of the two craft with one of his associates. The other armed figures were all whispering to each other at this point.

The Green Coast crew exchanged confused glances with each other, unsure of what the significance of Riesen being there was. Nobody spoke though, deciding that wouldn't be in their best interest. Niko was glad of it, because she did not enjoy the consequences of the confrontational attitudes of Ravenna and Kyler.

She felt bad for Kyler, who was clearly still in pain from what she assumed was being punched in the stomach. He could be quite an ass, but she didn't like seeing him in a state of such defeat. Was that... *protectiveness*... that she felt? Surely not over Kyler. He'd been her biggest nemesis over the last couple days, that's for sure.

The mixed feelings of frustration and loyalty toward Kyler were too confusing on the brain right now. All she cared to focus on was not doing anything that would upset these people more. She *needed* to get out of this situation. She *needed* to be back with her family. Although, she wasn't sure if playing along would even help. From what the bearded man had said, it sounded like they might not be released anytime soon...

After remaining with his associate inside one of the craft for a couple of minutes, the man returned to the group.

"I would convey an apology, but you are all going to come with us," he announced.

"The blazes we will!" Kyler blurted out. So much for the nonconfrontational attitude...

What an idiot, thought Niko. He just could not help himself. He *always* had to have the last word, no matter the consequences.

"Wait, we need to know who you are," Cryo spoke up quickly, before they had a chance to beat Kyler into submission yet again. "And why exactly do we need to go with you?"

"Seeing as though you are bound and we are the ones with all the weapons, you do not have much of a choice," the man replied. His response left little room to argue, although he lightened his tone somewhat, as if in a show of good faith. "We are the An-Mara. And I am the one called Riiz Alke-Tani."

It *was* him. The guy from her dream that was with Riesen and Daren when they jumped off the bridge. Niko felt a strange blend of dread and relief. In the dream, he seemed like a friend — which was odd, considering he currently held them all at gunpoint. Maybe the dream wasn't entirely accurate? Maybe they wouldn't have to jump off after all? Maybe she wouldn't need to *die*... Maybe the whole point of the dream was that she was simply meant to meet this Riiz

Alke-Tani guy. Whatever the excuse would be, she refused to let herself believe that the bridge scenario would come to pass.

I need to get to Ajane, Niko yearned. *She can tell me what this all means.*

"We aren't going anywhere until you tell us why," Cryo stood his ground. "You're obviously not going to kill us, so at least just tell us. We'll freely go with you if you just tell us why."

Riiz Alke-Tani sized up Cryo with an unreadable expression for a few seconds, and then looked over at Riesen again. "This is Riesen Ryen, the Child of the Nel-Mara."

The what???

Everyone else must've had the same internal reaction that Niko did, because every single one of them wore the most puzzled look on their faces. Riesen and Daren shared a glance with each other and began to snicker. The man looked expectantly at the group for some sort of acknowledgement.

"The Child of the Nel-Mara? The Return of the Nel-Mara? You have not heard of the Prophecy of the Stewards?" Riiz asked, as if that should have been a household term.

Oh, great. These guys are blazes insane. Actual madmen and madwomen.

"What the *blazes* are you talking about?" Kyler blurted out, a hilarious expression of perplexity written on his face. You could always count on Kyler to say it how it was, and at the moment, his question was not out of line.

"You are telling me you have never heard of the Prophecy of the Stewards?" Riiz Alke-Tani looked shocked.

Kyler shrugged his shoulders and scrunched up his face in complete confusion. "And what the *blazes* is that?! You act like we should know."

"Never??" Riiz asked with incredulity once more, as if they would suddenly remember.

The Green Coast captives replied with nothing except blank stares.

"The Nel-Mara?"

Same thing — blank looks, some shaking heads.

"Look what they are teaching their people," another of the An-Mara remarked to Riiz. "They hide the truth from everyone!"

"They do," the woman who had bound Niko agreed. "How are we ever going to get these people to leave this place? They are completely brainwashed."

"No matter," Riiz said. "We will spread the truth if they will not."

"Can you *pleeeease* tell us what's going on?" Riesen begged, his amusement starting to run thin. "What the blazes is the Prophecy of the Stewards? You claim that the Meridians hide the truth from everyone. So *you* tell us the truth."

It was a reasonable request. Riiz sized up Riesen with obvious respect before answering.

"Very well," he said. "I will start with the Nel-Mara, since none of you appears to know who they are."

What ensued was the wildest tale Niko had ever heard in her life. It was hard not to laugh. According to Riiz, the Nel-Mara were mythical omnipotent beings of the past that presided over the *entire galaxy* — which was crazy talk because for one, space travel was limited by speed and distance. Anyone who knew astronomy would know this. Two, magic was not real. Sure, she wished it was, but it wasn't. And three, just how many worlds were there in the galaxy? Too many for one civilization to shepherd, that's how many. Not feasible. This was absolute crazy talk.

But Riiz continued on in the most serious of tones. Niko was starting to think that these An-Mara didn't have a sense of humor at all, unless they were all pulling some elaborate prank on them. According to Riiz's story, the Nel-Mara disappeared *sixty-thousand* years ago, but there was one last remaining Nel-Mara after the rest had disappeared. That last Nel-Mara — who Riiz called Beriph Nel-Arana — had a *human* baby that was jettisoned off to a distant world. And that distant world just so happened to be *Arhanda??* And that baby was *Riesen??*

It took all the self-control Niko ever possessed to not laugh out loud. But Riiz was not done there. He then went on and on about the Meridian Empire and the An-Mara, about how they split up thousands of years ago after the disappearance of the Nel-Mara. The An-Mara were the loyal peoples awaiting the return of the Nel-Mara. Meanwhile, the Meridians had given up and created their own empire. He claimed the Meridians were nothing but colonizers who only cared for their own expansion, and that they were attempting to colonize Arhanda for all its resources. That's why the An-Mara infiltrated Minedyne sites, he said. They needed evidence of the Meridians' intentions before exposing them to the masses.

Niko was honestly surprised her friends even let him go on long enough to finish. Kyler looked like he was about to crack off some wise-guy comment for about half the story, but he never did. The fact that the An-Mara still had the guns, and Kyler had gotten gut-punched for his insolence earlier probably played no small role in his silence.

"So there is your truth," Riiz said, finished with his story for now. Niko figured that he probably could have kept going, that this was just the abridged version. "Now it is time for you to hold up your end of the deal and come with us peacefully."

The Green Coast friends just stared in complete disbelief, clearly unable to process what they had just been told. The first one to laugh was Riesen.

"So you're telling me I am *thousands* of years old?!" he wheezed through fits of laughter. Kyler and Kate joined in, only egging Riesen on harder. Even Daren was smirking on the far end of the line.

Riiz and the other An-Mara did not look amused. They simply waited silently until the laughter died down. These people looked like they didn't know how to have fun if it smacked them in the face. They were so serious! The way they spoke in their slow pace, measured and proper, only added to that certainty for Niko.

"They are a waste of time," the woman captor nearest to Niko said to Riiz. "This whole planet is a waste of time. Let us just take the Child and leave the rest of them to their fate."

"We gave you our word," Cryo responded, shooting his friends a look that shut the laughter down immediately. "We'll come with you freely."

"Excellent," Riiz said. "I would convey deepest apologies, but you have to understand that we must keep you restrained until we arrive at Groundheim."

Niko thought that the An-Mara were not so apologetic about that at all. They seemed very upset that the Green Coast crew didn't believe their story. Even worse, they'd been mocked. The woman standing near Niko was practically shaking in anger. Niko was glad that she herself didn't join in the laughter, even though she was very close to doing so. She didn't want to seem more like an enemy than she already did. All that mattered now was getting out of this mess, and that meant convincing the An-Mara that she wasn't a threat.

"What of our cars?" Daren asked. He hadn't said a word in a

long time, but he treasured that truck of his. This was something worth speaking up for. "Can we at least pull them off to the side of the road?"

Riiz looked back over at the cars and shook his head. "You will not need them anymore."

———

Although her arms were still bound behind her back and cuffed to a rail along a bench, the flight was surprisingly comfortable. Also, much to her surprise, she could see out the sides of the craft. The entire wall served as a window of sorts, which was an interesting effect because it had looked like a solid, opaque surface from the outside. Under different circumstances, Niko might've even enjoyed this flight.

They were headed south into Poste Territory, crossing over the White Mountains at a pace that was much faster than it felt like they were going. Niko had never been able to see the White Mountains from this view, and it was spectacular. Peaks upon peaks covered in brilliant white snow ran as far as the eye could see to the south. Their little excursion the other day only scratched the surface of how extensive this mountain range really was. To the west lie the ocean and Green Coast, her home that she was starting to miss very much. To the east she saw the mountains drop down into a low valley with a river, several lakes, and... oh, that tiny, silvery shimmer must be Green Valley way off in the distance.

She immediately felt a pang of homesickness wash over her. She missed her parents a lot. She'd only just arrived home for one day from her big trip across the world to Sol City, and then now they were already separated again. Who knew when she would be able to see them next. There was no way to contact them, either — the An-Mara had disconnected all their Uts right before they were loaded onto the craft. They wouldn't even be able to be tracked.

The one time Niko had spoken up during this whole ordeal, she asked if they would be able to contact their parents. The response was a resounding no, although she did get a look of sympathy from an An-Mara woman while being loaded into the craft — the same woman she was now seated beside.

"Is that your home?" the lady suddenly asked, seeing the obvious look of longing as Niko gazed across the plains to Green Valley.

Niko shook her head. "No, Green Coast is that way," she replied, nodding to the west. "That's where I'm from."

The woman looked to the west and nodded back. "This is a nice place. Very green. My home is a desert."

"I'm Niko." Niko seized the opportunity to make a connection and nervously introduced herself with a smile.

"Kira-Tharn," the woman responded casually, still looking out toward the west. "I am the one called Kira-Tharn."

She was of medium height and build with jet-black hair that was cut just above her shoulders. She couldn't have been much older than mid-twenties, but her skin looked weathered from the sol beyond her years. The most noticeable features that stood out to Niko, though, were her strong, protruding nose and beady black eyes that reminded Niko of a raven. She was pretty in her own way, but definitely strayed from the beauty standards set by Sol City.

She did not strike Niko as overly friendly, but to be fair none of the An-Mara did. They were the most serious people Niko had met in her entire life. She hadn't seen any of them smile a single time since she had encountered them, not even when Riesen tried cracking a joke to them. At least this Kira-Tharn had showed a small sign of humanity by talking about her home, even if it was the briefest of remarks.

Maybe I am *getting somewhere*, Niko thought to herself. She was determined to get this Kira-Tharn lady to like her.

"How far is Groundheim?" Niko asked.

"About twenty minutes," Kira-Tharn responded.

Twenty minutes?! Groundheim had to be close to a thousand kilometers away. How would they get there in twenty minutes? Kira-Tharn's expression did not waver at all, though. She must be serious. Indeed, they were moving very fast from what it looked like. Much faster than the flight Niko had taken from Sol City last week.

"I've never been to Poste Territory before," Niko remarked, trying to keep the conversation alive.

"It is not much," Kira-Tharn responded bluntly. "Just many mountains and many rocks."

"Is it true that most of the buildings are built into the

mountains?" Niko asked. "That everyone lives underground?"

Kira-Tharn shrugged. "I suppose many of the buildings are underground. Moreso than in your territory."

Poste Territory had been an enigma to most of the world. Though the Meridians governed it just like they did all the territories, it had been notorious for resisting the Meridian encroachment more than any of the others. The only time Posters ventured out of their territory was for large events like the Field World Championships. They also rarely engaged in global media, which is why they were such a mystery to the rest of the world.

Niko stared out the window for several minutes, attempting to observe any landmarks she could discern from the great height at which they flew. She figured they had to be at least 20,000 meters up, although she doubted she would be able to tell the difference between 15,000 and 20,000, or even 30,000 meters for that matter. All she knew was that her previous flight to and from Sol City flew at 10,000 meters, or at least she thought that's what the pilot had said. This flight seemed much, much higher. She looked around for any hints of what she could determine to be Groundheim, but all she saw was the continuous expanse of the White Mountains.

"Once we get to Groundheim, where do we go then?" Niko asked in curiosity, attempting to spark up conversation once more after having been silent for a few minutes.

"The Mainquarters, I would assume. I do not know the specifics of the orders concerning your people, but upon arrival you will need to be processed for questioning."

That did not sound reassuring.

"Processed? Questioning?" Niko asked timidly.

"To determine your intentions," Kira-Tharn clarified. Upon seeing the look of terror on Niko's face, she added, "do not worry, we do not torture."

"Oh, good," Niko exhaled. She hadn't even entertained that idea, but was glad it was off the table all the same. Even so, she still felt very uncomfortable. "I don't think I'm gonna be much help. I promise I don't know anything at all."

"I believe you, Niko," Kira-Tharn said with a shrug, "but that is not for me to decide. The Heads of Knowledge will need to make that determination."

"The Heads of Knowledge?" Niko asked. "Who are they? Like police investigators?"

"Not exactly. They are the ones with the most knowledge in order to make the best decisions for the whole."

Kira-Tharn was being awfully patient with Niko, which Niko was very thankful for. She could've been seated next to the man that threatened Ravenna earlier. That man seemed to have a major issue with all of the Green Coast crew. He still had his gun in his hand just for show, even though all of Niko's companions were clearly bound to the rail along the bench.

"Wait, so if these Heads of Knowledge decide they don't like someone, then they can just condemn them?" Niko asked skeptically. This was sounding a little bit like authoritarianism to Niko. She'd recently been educated on the world wars before the time of the Arrival in her history classes, and she'd learned that the authoritarianism of Old Anterg was one of the main reasons for the conflict in the first place.

"They would not make a decision to condemn anyone just on the basis of dislike," Kira-Tharn explained. "They take into account all knowledge and are able to assess a fair and impartial resolution."

"How can you be sure? What if there was a Head of Knowledge who was corrupt?" Niko was not convinced that this was a good system in the slightest.

"That would not be our way," Kira-Tharn responded, as if there was no chance corruption was a possibility. "A Head of Knowledge would not make it into that position if they had such character."

Although Niko had serious misgivings about this process, she would wait to save judgment for when she met these Heads of Knowledge. She was beginning to feel very nervous about this impending interrogation, but she very much hoped it was as Kira-Tharn described. If they made a fair and impartial decision, then they would surely return Niko and her friends back to their families.

"I have to be honest," Niko started, "your ways confuse me a little bit. I don't mean to be rude, they just seem very… different."

Kira-Tharn looked at her quizzically. "How do you mean?"

"Well, for one, I never see any of you smile or laugh," Niko replied honestly.

"We do not laugh," the woman stated matter-of-factly. "Laughing is an honor sacred to the Tel-Mara. Until we become Tel-Mara again, the An-Mara refuse to partake."

Niko just stared back at the woman, unsure if what she said was only a joke. Talk about a buzzkill! How do you go through life without laughing?? She tried to find a response, but only stuttered with a short, nervous laugh instead. It was probably not the response she should have given because Kira-Tharn showed a hint of annoyance for the first time in this conversation.

"All you people want to do is laugh, but none of us are Tel-Mara, so it is an affront to all who respect the Time. Although I suppose you lot are the closest thing to the Tel-Mara, being left on your own for so long. But until *we* become Tel-Mara again, all An-Mara refuse to partake in laughter. That is how it has always been. That is our way."

Niko was so confused on many levels. For one, all these names were getting confusing. "I'm sorry. What's the difference between all these different Mara you're talking about? Tel-Mara, Nel-Mara, An-Mara… Well, I know you are the An-Mara."

Kira-Tharn narrowed her eyes at Niko, but at least she responded. "Like the one called Riiz Alke-Tani explained earlier, the Nel-Mara were the presiders of the galaxy many millennia ago. The Tel-Mara were their subjects — the humans they genetically engineered from their own biological history billions of years ago."

"Ummm, okay." Niko stifled a laugh, attempting her best to play along with the An-Mara story, as if their tale couldn't get any wilder. "And you think you are going to become the Tel-Mara someday if you don't laugh?"

"We respect the Time," Kira-Tharn said coldly. "So yes, *someday.*"

"I'm… sorry," Niko apologized. She really didn't mean to offend these people. She just had a hard time believing that someone could go through life without laughing. No wonder they really didn't like the Green Coast crew. They were on the absolute other extreme of the spectrum when it came to laughing and having a good time. "I didn't mean to offend. What's the Time, though? I've never heard of that before."

"Of course you have not," Kira-Tharn responded with a small hint of disappointment, barely holding back a sigh. "You were never told anything of substance by your precious *Meridians.*"

"How is that our fault?" Niko shot back. It was not fair that Kira-Tharn was making it sound as if Niko were to blame.

"It is not," Kira-Tharn admitted, but she still irritably shook her head. "It is just that our way is all about respect. The Meridians go wherever they want and take whatever they want. There are some that are more honorable than others, true enough, but the ones that come to Arhanda only seek to exploit and brainwash."

Niko thought that the only brainwashing here was that done to this woman. To all these An-Mara. How do you go through life without *laughing*?? That's not living...

"How have they brainwashed us, exactly?" Niko asked, curious to hear Kira-Tharn's point of view.

"Well, none of you knew anything about what we had to tell you earlier," Kira-Tharn replied. "Nothing about the Nel-Mara, nothing about the Prophecy of the Stewards, nothing about the Time, nothing about the star systems beyond your own. I would conjecture that they have not even told you where they were from."

"They have told us about that," Niko protested. "Well, sort of. They just say that small steps are necessary for our cultures being able to come together."

Kira-Tharn just shook her head. "They say small steps are necessary because that buys them the time it takes for them to colonize you."

"If they were trying to colonize us, I think it could've been done a lot faster when they first came here. We were helpless compared to them."

"No, it has nothing to do with technological superiority," Kira-Tharn responded. "It has to do with the time it takes to get the Engines up and running."

"The Engines?" Niko asked, shaking her head in confusion.

"I imagine they never told you about the Engines either?" Kira-Tharn scoffed.

"Umm, no," Niko admitted, bowing her head. She doubted there was some nefarious plot the Meridians were exacting upon the people of Arhanda, but she did have to admit that this woman was right about the Meridians keeping the people in the dark about certain things.

"Hmph, that figures," she said with a grunt.

"Well, what are the Engines?" Niko asked.

"The Engines," Kira-Tharn responded, "are why we infiltrated all the Minedyne sites."

"That doesn't explain what they are," Niko pressed. She was starting to become very confident in speaking with Kira-Tharn. Even though she'd only just met her a matter of minutes ago, she was beginning to respect this woman. At least Kira-Tharn told her what she thought to be the truth. Whether it was the actual truth or not was another story...

"They are the mechanisms which..."

"We will be landing in about five minutes!" Riiz Alke-Tani loudly announced from the front. It was unfortunate that he'd interrupted Kira-Tharn, but Niko was glad to be out of the craft soon. Sitting with her hands bound behind her back was starting to become unpleasant. "Once we have landed we will be taking you to more comfortable quarters."

Niko appreciated that Kira-Tharn was going to explain what the Engines were without hesitation, but she realized the more important thing to ask about was what to expect when they landed. She had been momentarily distracted from her anxiety about the coming interrogation, and she really wanted to know what she was walking into.

"So, do I just tell the Heads of Knowledge everything that happened to us?" Niko asked, changing the subject. "I'm sure they'll let us go once they realize we're innocent."

"Yes, they will ask you the questions and you will answer," Kira-Tharn said. "They will know the truth."

"Great," Niko responded. She desperately wanted to get back home.

"If you look outside, you can see we are now in Poste Territory," Kira-Tharn told her. "Since you appeared so interested to look out the windows earlier."

Niko looked out and sure enough, the terrain had shifted without her noticing. Instead of the snow-covered peaks of the White Mountains, she saw an endless expanse of grey, rocky landscape. It was very rugged and mountainous, but there was no snow. Niko didn't expect to see much water in Poste Territory since it was technically a desert, but down below she saw there were many rivers snaking their way through the rocks. She also thought she saw what looked to be a city to the east. Well, not a city exactly, but a settlement. She couldn't see the architecture from where they were, but it was most definitely built low to the ground.

"I have to admit, this was the fastest flight I've ever been on," Niko said. "What makes this thing so fast? And how does it fly so quietly?"

"I am not an engineer," Kira-Tharn replied. "You would have to ask them."

"Oh," Niko said. "I've just never flown in anything like this. It's interesting."

Kira-Tharn shrugged. "I suppose I have never given it much thought. We have *much* faster ships than this."

Niko was officially very intrigued. She'd never shown a predisposition to math, so she never truly considered a career path in engineering, but that didn't mean she couldn't be fascinated by how things worked. Her father Jame *was* an engineer and he had nurtured her interest in such things. The two of them would spend hours together in the project room where they'd take things apart, then he'd show her how to put them back together.

Niko remembered this time together fondly, and it was a great challenge to suppress the wave of emotion that followed. She wanted so badly to be back home. Whatever she needed to do to convince these Heads of Knowledge to return her home, she would do it.

The craft had now slowed and descended, moving much closer to the ground. As they swung dangerously low around an outcropping of silvery rocks, a noticeable city emerged into view. There were no skyscrapers or towers, but Niko could tell it was a much larger city than Green Valley, possibly one rivaling Nevaly. It was hard to tell the size, though, because buildings were built into the terrain just like she'd heard about this place. It seemed like there might be just as much underground as above ground, if not more. There roads, packed with moving vehicles, were only semi visible, as they were woven seamlessly throughout tunnels cut into the rocks. It was an architectural style she'd never seen in her life and she was very much in awe. It must've taken forever to construct this place!

They passed over the city for several k's until it became clear they were headed into the largest cavern Niko had ever seen in her life. It was crazy to think a place like this existed on Arhanda, and after comfortably ducking inside, the cavern seemed to expand even more, if that was possible.

Niko leaned forward to get a better look, immediately feeling the butterflies in her stomach as they sped straight toward a huge hourglass structure that spanned from the ground to the ceiling in the distance, nestled right in the middle of a city center that sprang into view.

Their craft glided silently toward the tower, then reared back to further reduce speed just in time to avoid slamming into the walls. The sound got louder, as she expected, when reverse thrusters completely halted their forward motion, setting them down onto a platform. It only took a matter of seconds before the entire landing process was complete.

"Welcome to Groundheim," Riiz said.

10

The Heads of Knowledge

THE city was larger than Niko had suspected at first glance. Much larger. She and her friends were transported along a highway that wound its way in and out of grottos and tunnels that were elegantly carved into the rock, revealing an incredible subterranean metropolis. She had just learned a few minutes ago that the entire city had been originally built underground. The parts of the city that were exposed to the surface had only been built post-Arrival.

The history buff he was, Cryo had been explaining to the others that Groundheim was built during the days of the world wars. Its fortification among the rocks, he said, was a great strategic defense from the aerial bombardments of the Antergians. Of course, now that defense was obsolete, but it still made for impressive architectural splendor.

As they moved deeper into the city, it was clear that the vast majority was hidden from outside view. When the highway ducked underground, the real city came to life. Multiple caverns, some of them hundreds of meters high, were connected by an intricate labyrinth of roads and walkways. Homes, parking structures, Collection centers, and every manner of eatery Niko could think of lined the sides of the tunnels. In addition to the cars, countless pedestrians bustled along fancy paths that crossed over and under the streets. This city was definitely larger than any that Niko had seen, with the exception of Sol City of course, which was still much larger.

Niko was surprised that it wasn't dark or gloomy when they went underground, yet rather the opposite. The lighting was mostly artificial, but each large chamber sported giant shafts that looked like they were designed to collect, amplify, and redistribute the sol-light in all manner of directions. The cars didn't even need to drive with their headlights on!

This city was very much alive, which was a little strange to Niko considering the events of the past twenty-four hours. There were no hints that this city was under martial law like the rest of the world was supposed to be.

Where were the Meridians?!

She knew that Poste Territory had always been the rebellious province, but she figured that Meridian presence would still be more than evident in a large city such as Groundheim, especially right now. She was tempted to ask Kira-Tharn why that was, but thought twice. The Meridians were a touchy subject for the An-Mara, and she didn't want to offend them further.

Their transport, which reminded Niko of one of the buses that she rode on in Sol City, took an exit that was clearly labeled '←......An-Mara Mainquarters......1 km'. The exit curved up into a narrow tunnel, carved delicately through streaking silver stone, then emerged onto the open surface once again. Rock columns lined the sides of the road, which eventually dead-ended into a large building that seemed to camouflage into the silvery terrain. The building was low to the ground, flat and wide with no doors. Instead, an open ground level floor dotted with pillars allowed access into the building's interior.

Upon pulling adjacent to the building, the transport screeched to halt. Niko winced as the force of the abrupt stop tugged on all the sore spots on her body, which were still plenty tender. She rolled her shoulder to stretch her torso and looked outside. A line of guards dressed in those same hooded uniforms that her captors wore stood in formation, as if they were expecting the arrival.

Riiz was the first one out, and he performed a half-kneeling gesture in deference to one of the men outside. Niko could see them conversing quietly for a few short moments before the man walked over to the transport.

"Welcome to our An-Mara Mainquarters," the man said. "I am the one called Var Ashal-Han. I would convey an apology for the inconvenience."

Inconvenience? Niko snorted to herself. *An inconvenience is when you're late to an appointment, not when you kidnap someone and drag them a thousand k's away...*

He shot a look her way, as if she'd said that out loud. Her face went frozen in sheepish embarrassment, even though it wasn't as if he could actually hear her.

"We will be taking you to more comfortable quarters, but first you must understand that we require determination of your intentions," he continued. "Please follow me."

Why are they so obsessed with our intentions? Niko wondered. *Isn't it obvious that all we mean to do is get back home?*

Var Ashal-Han swung his robes over his shoulder in what struck Niko as a very pretentious move, as if to tell everyone that he was the one in charge without explicitly saying it. He then marched across the open courtyard to a gap in the columns that led to a stairway. The Green Coast crew followed, flanked on either side by dozens of armed An-Mara.

They had to walk quickly to keep up with this Var Ashal-Han, and Niko's legs were screaming inside. She did her best to hide her limp, but she was in quite a bit of pain from the ever-continuous mixture of the bruises she suffered from the fall and the overall soreness she acquired from the climb. Stepping down the stairs without showing weakness was exceptionally difficult.

How many stairs could there possibly be in this blazes place?

After descending what seemed like the longest stairwell in her life, Niko stepped into a large, open antechamber. The air shifted to a cooler, staler texture, and her eyes adjusted to the muted yellow-brown walls. There were no decorations or furnishings, only rows of columns and arches.

At the far end, a wide archway revealed a second chamber buzzing with activity. As the group was marched straight through the middle, conversations quieted and heads turned in their direction. They weren't malicious stares by any means — the watchers seemed curious, if anything. They were probably wondering who Niko and her friends were and why they were there.

Why ARE we here anyway? Niko wondered, her mood

becoming more negative by the minute. She just wanted to be home.

Var Ashal-Han stopped at a closed door built entirely out of stone. He placed his hand against the wall and the door opened up, admitting passage to a small, plain room. The group was directed to wait while Var Ashal-Han spoke to someone through a device that seemed very similar to a Ut.

"Sit here," Kira-Tharn commanded Niko, gesturing toward a metallic bench that lined one side of the room. She'd been right behind her this whole time; Niko didn't even notice. She took a seat on the cold, smooth bench and waited for Var Ashal-Han to deliver further instructions.

"Are we going to see the Heads of Knowledge right now?" Niko asked Kira-Tharn.

"No talking. I can answer your questions if I see you later."

Niko was annoyed, but she heeded Kira-Tharn's orders. She did not like this whole situation because it really made her feel like she wasn't in control of her life. She was completely at the mercy of these An-Mara. They could do whatever they wanted to their prisoners and Niko was powerless to do anything about it. She supposed it could've been worse, though; she should feel grateful that they'd been quite humane so far.

Kyler might've felt otherwise. She spared a glance toward him, and saw he still wore that same bitter look of contempt from this morning. He was probably plotting how he would repay the An-Mara for his treatment. She thought it to be a little comical because unless he had a machine to hack into their systems, there was nothing he was capable of doing to these people. She was quite sure they would beat him back into submission as easily as nonchalantly batting away an annoying fly.

Ravenna on the other hand... She had clearly not forgiven the one guard for belittling her. She was one to hold a grudge, Ravenna was. Even though she was not nearly as strong as that guard appeared to be, she possessed a viciousness and resourcefulness that Niko had witnessed firsthand on several occasions. She was legitimately worried for that man if he ever found himself alone with a freed Ravenna.

"The processing rooms are ready," Var Ashal-Han announced. "This way."

He performed the same ridiculous swing of his robes over his shoulders and marched into an adjoining hallway. Niko was pulled to her feet and the group followed him through the corridor, which turned a darker shade of blue-grey as they traversed deeper into the building. After a couple of right and left turns, he stopped.

"You, in here," he motioned to Daren, who had been at the front of the line. "And you, this room. And you, this next room. And you…"

Each of the Green Coast prisoners was shown to a separate chamber. Niko was hoping that they would all be interrogated together, but she'd already assumed otherwise in her mind. It was best to keep expectations low so there would be no unpleasant surprises.

Her heart was pounding at this point. Even though Kira-Tharn had told her she wouldn't be tortured, she was still half-expecting some manner of ugly business. Upon entering the room with two guards behind her, her gaze was drawn to the lone chair in the center. There appeared to be nothing else in the room. No windows, no interrogators, no Heads of Knowledge.

Up to this point, she hadn't been separated from her friends. Now she was alone, and every fiber of her being was screaming to get out of this situation. She just felt so trapped. So isolated.

"You may sit," Kira-Tharn commanded. Niko felt strangely soothed hearing her voice. It was one source of familiarity in an otherwise alien environment, even if she'd only just met the lady this morning.

Niko obeyed and sat down. Although her hands were still bound behind her back, no other clamps or binding mechanisms sprouted out of the chair like she was half-expecting. Niko breathed a sigh of relief to herself. At least it seemed what Kira-Tharn had said would hold true. There were no torture devices or anything of the like.

After waiting on the cold chair for what seemed to be no longer than a few minutes, a mysterious voice filled the room.

"What are you called?" it said.

Where was this voice coming from? Niko looked all around, but she had no idea where the source was. Other than the two silent An-Mara guards behind her, there was nothing in this room besides four blank stone walls. The manner of projection had to be similar to the technique used by the announcers at the great stadium in Sol City for the Field World Championships.

"What are you called?" the voice repeated.

"Niko." She blushed, embarrassed for trailing off in thought.

"Full name please."

"Ryen. Sorry… Niko Ryen."

"What is your age?"

"Sixteen."

"Where are you from?"

"I'm from Green Coast. It's a small town about a hundred k's west of…"

"Are you here with any companions?" the voice interrupted.

"Umm, yes..?"

What a stupid question, Niko thought. *Of course I'm here with others. Do they think those people I came with were just random strangers I've never met in my life?*

"What are your companions called?"

"Ummm… Well there's my brother Riesen, my sister Kate, and…"

"Full names please."

"Sorry. Riesen Ryen, Kate Ryen, umm… Ravenna Night, annnnd… Cryo Siriar, and Daren… err… Nicodaren Amibar, sorry. And… and Kyler Pierson. I think that's all of them. That was seven, right? Including me."

"What is your purpose here?"

"Uhhhh…" Niko didn't know how to answer that question. "I have no purpose. I was kidnapped against my will…"

"What was your purpose before you were apprehended?"

"Well…" Niko started, "my friends and I were trying to get to Green Valley to meet up with our families."

The voice didn't say anything, as if expecting a more thorough answer.

"That was our purpose," Niko said flatly. She was trying to be as polite as possible, but these questions had her feeling a little defiant.

"Do you have any ties to the Meridians?"

"I mean… We all have ties. How could we not have ties? They govern the entire planet. I'm expected be Inducted into their service soon, but I'm not currently in their service."

"Are any of your companions currently in their service?"

"Mmm, yes," Niko replied honestly. She didn't want to lie; honesty was probably the best course of action.

"Which of your companions is currently in their service?"

"Well," she replied hesitantly, "all of them besides me and Riesen. Riesen Ryen, that is."

"Do you know of any intentions they may have that would place the An-Mara at risk?"

"No, of course not."

There was an extended pause of silence. Did she answer incorrectly? She just realized that Ravenna and Kyler may have held ill intentions, but that was only in response to misconduct from the captors. It was their own fault. They wouldn't have those intentions if they'd never been set upon in the first place. And it wasn't like they were plotting some elaborate form of sabotage.

I'm sure it's fine, Niko reassured herself.

"That is all. You may exit," the voice said after the pause.

That's it? Niko was surprised. *That was quick.*

"You may come with us," Kira-Tharn said.

"Wait, that was it?" Niko asked her. "That wasn't the Heads of Knowledge, right?"

"No," Kira-Tharn responded. "You will encounter them later. Those were the processing questions."

Oh blazes, Niko thought. It's what she had figured, but she was also hoping that maybe, just maybe, their questioning was over and done with.

"Come with us," Kira-Tharn instructed again.

Niko stood up from the chair and followed her out of the room and into the hallway. All her companions were already outside of their own processing rooms. There was Riesen, Cryo, Ravenna, Daren, and Kate...

Where was Kyler?

They all waited in the hallway for a few minutes when Kyler finally emerged from his interrogation looking very agitated and shaking his head. No doubt he was wasting time being argumentative and difficult. Niko gritted her teeth in anxiety. She wanted this all to go smoothly so that they could be freed.

Her parents must be worried out of their minds. She hadn't been able to contact them at all the whole day. Between the seven of them, someone must've surely been looking for them by now. As far as anyone knew, though, they were still at the location of the rockslide. There was no possible way for anybody to know that they'd been taken to Groundheim by the An-Mara. All Niko could do was just let this situation play itself out.

All the cinematics she'd ever seen or stories she'd ever read always had the hero finding a way to escape a situation like this, but Niko had no thoughts of doing anything like that. She'd sometimes daydreamed of doing something heroic in a dire situation when she was younger, but something like that seemed unnecessarily risky being here now. She felt ashamed thinking about how she flinched and cowered when the An-Mara first pointed weapons at her. But what was the point in being brave there? Kyler had resisted, and look where that got him. Besides, this didn't seem like such a dire situation that they needed to antagonize the An-Mara around them. At least not yet. She wondered if anyone else in the group was thinking of a plan to escape. She certainly hoped not, because that didn't seem like the best idea.

The best way to get through this, she thought, *is to tell them what they want to hear and then they'll let us be on our way.*

"Your processing is complete," Var Ashal-Han announced to the group, his disapproving gaze settling on Kyler. "You may now follow me to more comfortable quarters."

Comfortable quarters sounded nice, but Niko wasn't very confident that they would actually be comfortable. 'Comfortable quarters' was probably just a fancy euphemism for a prison cell. She just hoped that she wasn't placed in solitary confinement away from her friends.

Var Ashal-Han led the group deeper into the building, navigating through unfamiliar corridors instead of the ones they'd used to arrive. After a few turns, they came to a bank of three elevator lifts set into a flat wall of the same dull stone. At this point, the group was split among the three, with Niko and Kyler ushered into one with six silent guards.

The doors closed, and for a moment, the only sound was the low hum of ascent. Kyler stood slumped with a very unpleasant look on his face, so Niko decided not to say anything to him. She only spared him a sympathetic smile, which to her relief he returned, even if it was halfhearted. She may have been feuding fiercely with him yesterday, but today they were on the same side, simply companions and friends thrust into an unfair situation together.

As the smooth lift eased to a halt, Niko, Kyler, and the six guards filed out, as did her friends in the other two lifts. The procession continued silently down the hallway for about a minute before Var Ashal-Han raised his hand in showy fashion, signaling the group to stop. He placed his hand on the wall just as he had done before, and a set of doors Niko hadn't noticed opened up.

The inside of this next room was spacious and well-lit. There were no windows, but it strangely felt like real sol-light was streaming through, warming the sides of her face and everything. They had to be close to the surface.

To Niko's surprise, the room was filled with furnishings, something she hadn't seen in any of the other rooms in this whole building. There were several comfortable looking chairs and benches. On the side, a short hallway led to what appeared to be washrooms and even bedrooms.

Thank the heavens! Niko exclaimed to herself. This was like a sort of suite.

"Here are your quarters for the moment," Var Ashal-Han announced. "You will be meeting with the Heads of Knowledge tonight, but until then, you may be comfortable here. You may not leave, but if you require any assistance there is a communicator right here."

He walked over to a flat object on one of the tables. He pressed a button on the side and it lit up, then dimmed when he released it.

"We will be bringing you meals in thirty minutes," he added. A meal sounded very nice, considering Niko hadn't eaten much of anything this morning. "If you would turn around, we will now undo your restraints."

She was all too happy to comply, and her arms felt refreshing freedom when she heard the click of the release. She was already quite sore beforehand, but now that her arms had been bound behind her back for so long, she was surprised she could even move any part of her body at all.

"We will be in further communication about when you may expect to meet with the Heads of Knowledge," he said.

With that, he flourished his robes in the same absurd fashion once more and marched out of sight. The guards all followed and the door was shut behind them, leaving the Green Coast crew locked in this place. If they had to be locked anywhere, Niko had to admit this was ideal. It was much more comfortable than their experience so far, that was for sure.

"And who the blazes are the Heads of Knowledge?!" Kyler blurted out as soon as the doors had shut. Everyone just shrugged in response, obviously as clueless as he was. "They expect us to know everything about them."

"I was talking to Kira-Tharn, one of the guards," Niko said proudly. She felt special that she knew something relevant to their predicament that none of the others knew. "The Heads of Knowledge are like their sort of judges. She says that they take all things into consideration and make their determination. They'll be responsible for what happens to us."

"That sure sounds like a lot of power for one person," Kate pondered. "Shouldn't we have a representative or a jury or something?"

"So they just decide whatever they want to do with us?" Kyler asked. "Like if they don't like us then they can just keep us prisoner? Or *execute* us?"

"That's what I said!" Niko agreed excitedly. "It sounds kinda like Old Antergian authoritarianism. She seemed convinced that the Heads of Knowledge were very fair, though."

"I don't buy it," Kyler muttered, shaking his head. "I *know* they don't like me. I'm screwed."

"Kyler, nobody likes you," Ravenna teased. "Yet we all still keep you around. I'm sure they won't execute you. They'd probably just rather keep you around to torture you for fun instead."

Everyone laughed, but nobody seemed quite convinced that this wasn't a possibility.

"Well," Niko stated after they were done laughing, "at least Kira-Tharn was dead serious when she told me they don't torture people. So there's that."

"How much did you talk to this Kira-Tharn lady?" Riesen asked. "When did you even have time?"

"We talked on the flight over," Niko responded. "She was actually kind of nice, in her own way. These people are weird..."

She then recounted the whole conversation with Kira-Tharn to her friends. She told them all about their refusal to laugh, their system with the Heads of Knowledge, all the Nel-Mara nonsense, the Time, and even about the mysterious Engines she wasn't able to learn about.

"The Engines..." Cryo seemed lost in thought. Of all the things she told them, he was most interested in the Engines? "I wonder if that has anything to do with those huge wells we saw on the schematics?"

Niko had to admit that he may have been on to something. What *would* those huge structures be? The group considered what he said, but before they could discuss the Engines, he changed his own subject.

"We should really have a plan," he said, "for when we talk to the Heads of Knowledge. That way we don't contradict each other." Everyone nodded.

"I think we should just tell the truth about what we know," Niko chimed in. "Kira-Tharn said they'll know the truth if we tell it."

"Yes, but some of us know secrets that we can't reveal," Ravenna said. "We can't betray our own."

Niko was silent; she knew Ravenna was right. She hadn't been privy to the type of information that the others were, so she had it easy.

"I think we just need to go over scenarios of possible questions they ask, and how we're gonna answer as a group," Cryo said. "They said we were going to all be together when we meet the Heads, so let's just go over this and come up with something. Then we can all take naps or relax or whatever."

Although Niko was supremely exhausted, she did *not* want to take the chance on having another dream right now. The others could take a nap, but she vowed to stay awake no matter what. There was plenty on her mind to keep her occupied anyway.

———

More than a couple hours later, the Green Coast friends were gathered in the main room of what might've passed for a cozy lounge, if not for the locked doors that kept them imprisoned. The remains of lunch sat scattered on the low table before them, while some of Niko's friends had started to put on a show parodying their An-Mara captors.

"You may now come with me," Kyler droned in a voice mocking the slow, proper pace of the An-Mara. He swung a towel that was draped over his shoulders. "I am the one that is called Vashalashalaran."

"Yes, my master," Riesen said as he sarcastically performed a curtsey.

"No," Kate joined in. "You are the master, Riesen Ryen, Child of the Nel-Mara."

She performed an elaborate bow, and the others joined in mock reverence to Riesen.

"They're on their way now!" Niko protested. Although it was funny, she didn't want the An-Mara to walk in to the group making fun of them. They'd already been touchy enough at something as innocent as *laughing*. "You better hope they don't see you guys."

"Oh, what are they gonna do?" Kyler said. "Kidnap us? Oh wait…"

Everyone laughed, even Niko.

"I really don't like these pretentious asses," Ravenna said. "Especially Var Ashal-Han and the one guard, Setten-Lo I think his name is."

"Was that the guy that called you a little girl?" Kate asked Ravenna.

"Yep," she replied, her face not hiding that truth that she was dead set on exacting her revenge upon him. Someday.

"I couldn't believe that," Kate whistled. "I wanted to throttle that guy for you. Not that you'd have any problem doing it yourself."

"I was definitely seeing red a little bit," Ravenna laughed.

"You guys weren't even the ones who got punched! Just think how I feel," Kyler said. He always found a way to make it about him, but he did have a point.

"Awww poor baby, your little boo-boo okay?" Ravenna taunted him.

He made a face at her in return, but just then, some shuffling could be heard outside the door. Everyone scrambled to the chairs to pretend as if they hadn't just been making fun of the An-Mara. The doors swung open and Var Ashal-Han entered the room with unnecessary show.

"I hope you have all had the opportunity to rest comfortably? I would convey an apology about your confinement, but this is all just temporary. Necessary, I am afraid, but temporary nonetheless."

It better be temporary, Niko thought to herself. She had just sat awake in that room for hours now and she wanted out. She wanted out of this whole place, away from these people.

Var Ashal-Han rubbed her the wrong way from the beginning. He just seemed so… *fake*. He displayed this outward sense of self-importance, but she got the feeling that the other An-Mara didn't necessarily like him from the way they reacted around him. Nothing major or disrespectful — it was only tiny glances here and there.

He was tall and sturdy with dark features, like many of the other An-Mara. Niko thought he wasn't that old — maybe somewhere in his thirties — but his beard was slightly graying. He had strong-looking hands and Niko imagined he could carry himself well in a fight. All these An-Mara looked like they could.

"You will come with me at this time," he said. "Please follow me."

Everyone stood up to follow without saying a word. The group was now silent, as if they weren't all being rowdy just a minute ago. Hopefully none of the An-Mara had heard them…

Instead of leading them toward the lifts they'd taken earlier, Var Ashal-Han turned the other direction. He strode silently down the unfamiliar hallway with the rest of the group in tow until they all arrived at a single lift. This one fit the entire group of seven plus the An-Mara.

Their entourage was much smaller this time. The An-Mara must have determined that they were not a threat from the interrogations earlier, so that was a good sign. They were even still free of their restraints!

The lift hummed as it made its descent, carrying them far underground, judging from the amount of time they were in there. When the doors opened, they stepped into what looked like a waiting area: square walls, low lighting, and a scattering of wide archways along the perimeter. Without pausing, Var Ashal-Han crossed to the far end, placed his hand on the wall, and a set of doors opened up to reveal a large chamber beyond.

Like the rest of the An-Mara Mainquarters, it was plain with no furnishings, though there were the trademark columns and grand archways cut into the stone. The one thing different about this room was that it was very dark, illuminated only to the point of twilight. Squinting through the darkness, Niko could clearly make out a raised platform with five shadowy figures facing the room, seated behind a long desk. None of their faces were visible at all; their silhouettes were the only thing Niko could make out with any sort of detail.

These have got to be the Heads of Knowledge, she thought.

"You may sit here in this row," Var Ashal-Han instructed the group. The row of seats they would sit on was much lower than the level of the five shadowy figures, which made Niko uneasy. The way they put these Heads of Knowledge on a raised platform seemed symbolic in a way that felt wrong to her.

"Are these the Heads of Knowledge?" Niko asked one of the guards quietly.

There were only two guards with them, besides Var Ashal-Han. She would've felt much more comfortable if Kira-Tharn was there, or even Riiz Alke-Tani, but surely this guard would answer her questions. Niko remembered her name to be Mora Nant-Zern; she had delivered food to the group earlier and seemed pleasant enough then. She simply glared back at her now, though, without saying a word.

Well, okay then... Niko thought irritably, rolling her eyes. These people were such a mystery!

"I now take my leave," Var Ashal-Han announced in a statement, as if what he had to say was the most important thing in the world. He turned to Riesen, who was seated at the far end of their row closest to the edge. "I shall be seeing more of you in the days to come, Riesen Ryen."

Well, that didn't sound ominous at all... Niko thought sarcastically to herself. Why were these people so obsessed with Riesen? Sure, he was a wonder kid who was pretty much the best at everything he did, but the chosen one?? What did they call it?... The Child of the Nel-Mara? It all seemed way too far-fetched. Whatever they had in store for him didn't make her feel comfortable one bit.

As soon as the doors closed behind Var Ashal-Han, the Green Coast crew was left alone in this large room with only the two An-Mara guards and the five shadowy figures that loomed over them.

"Welcome to the Hall of Knowledge," the central shadowy figure announced in a male voice. "We are the five Heads of Knowledge for the An-Mara here on Arhanda."

"We were able to review your case and have found fit to make judgment upon your circumstance," a female figure next to him continued. "In light of your statements and intentions..."

"Wait, just like that?" Kyler interrupted. "You don't want to hear from us at all?"

For the love of the heavens, please shut up, Kyler, Niko pleaded in her mind.

"You must refrain from speaking out of turn," the figure cooly responded back. They were obviously not accustomed to being interrupted. "We did hear from you. You each gave statements at your processing. Your intentions were quite clear, and we have found reason to release you to your people."

Niko exhaled breath that had been waiting to escape the entire day. This was one of the greatest feelings of relief she'd ever felt in her entire life — right up there with waking up this morning realizing her dream was only a dream. Her entire soul screamed in hope.

"But..." the figure continued.

The word 'but' stopped all that joy in its tracks.

"We do have a few questions."

What questions? What did we do wrong? Did someone say something wrong? It wasn't me...? It couldn't have been me... Kyler! It had to have been Kyler. I swear, I'm going to...

"In particular," a different female voice started, "we had concerns about the intentions of two individuals among you. Kyler Pierson and Ravenna Night. We were able to sense a great deal of resentment and animosity toward the An-Mara as a people. We would seek clarity and reconciliation on the matter, if at all possible."

Kyler was unsuccessful in suppressing a snort. "Well, it's not that hard to..."

He barely stopped short as he sensed a glare from Cryo. They had gone over the plan for what to say quite thoroughly while they were shut away in their suite, but Kyler was about ready to throw it all out the window because he had zero self-control. He *had* to have the last word, no matter what kind of trouble it landed him or anyone else in.

"I mean," he continued, reminded by Cryo's glare to keep his cool, "I was upset because I felt like I was unfairly treated by your goons... errr, forces... as we were taken."

"I see. Please explain," the figure requested.

"Well, we were on our way to meet up with our friends and families when we were ambushed by your people," Ravenna took over. "We surrendered quite peacefully, but Kyler had said... something. He posed no threat, though, and was physically beaten into submission anyway. As for myself, I merely went to check on Niko here because she seemed injured and hurting. Instead of simply asking me not to talk, the guard shoved his firearm into my face and taunted me, calling me a little girl. I took offense to that disrespect."

Even though she couldn't see their faces, Niko could *feel* the Heads of Knowledge peering at them with such intensity that they could probably burrow tunnels with their eyes. After a couple seconds of silence, the central voice spoke up again.

"You are correct," he said. "This was not proper conduct and those responsible will be delivering an apology to you."

Wow, Niko thought. Was she hearing this correctly? The An-Mara were *apologizing* to them? Kira-Tharn had told her that these Heads of Knowledge would be fair, but she didn't actually believe that they were going to receive vindication of this level.

"Thank you," Ravenna said. Kyler just stared at them, but at least his face softened from the perpetual pout he wore all day.

"Now our next question," another male voice spoke up, "is how do you know the one called Ajane Solase?"

The Green Coast friends looked around, stunned in silence as they no doubt wondered how these people knew about Ajane. This was something that they had all vowed that they were *not* going to say anything about. Were they listening in on their conversations at the suite? They had to have been, although Niko thought she remembered that nobody actually mentioned her full name. Nobody replied for what felt like a minute, but Kate spoke up first.

"Who?" she said, shaking her head in feigned ignorance.

"Can you repeat the name?" Kyler asked. "I don't recognize that one."

The others, including Niko, just shook their heads and displayed intentional confused stares to maintain the act.

"It is not wise to lie to the Heads of Knowledge," another figure warned them.

"We are familiar with the one called Ajane Solase, and we do know that you are familiar with her, as well," the central figure added.

The group was silent for several long seconds before Cryo of all people broke first.

"How do you know that we know her?" he asked.

"We are the Heads of Knowledge." It was a simple reply, but it gave all the information it needed to.

Cryo paused in hesitation, peering up at the shadowy figures for a few moments before continuing.

"Fine. We know her," he admitted. "We know her because we work for her."

Cryo had been the one that urged the group to *not* bring her up. Why would he be telling them this now? Maybe he was trying to manage the situation through damage control?

"In what capacity do you work for her?"

Cryo sighed, but continued nonetheless.

"She runs a program that investigates Minedyne activity at all the stations," he replied. "We are tasked with uncovering this material without the Meridian Command knowing."

What the blazes?

Niko was aghast at the admission. She had so many questions about all of it the other day, but no one gave her any answers. They all just told her they didn't know anything about what was going on, but they obviously did. She was a little offended that they didn't entrust that information to her — but yet they would tell these random An-Mara kidnappers about it?

She looked across to her companions, and they all had mixed feelings stamped on their faces. Riesen seemed shocked, so Niko was sure that he had no idea about any of it, just like her. The others seemed to be embarrassed, though, like they were children who got caught sneaking cookies by their parents. They weren't surprised like she and Riesen had been.

They knew.

Had they all been keeping this from her?!

The feelings of relief and joy just a few minutes ago had now turned to betrayal and resentment. Why would her friends keep this from her? Even *Kate* had been lying! After the initial confusion wore off, Niko felt tears of frustration begin to well up. She summoned every bit of nerve she possessed just to prevent the tears from boiling to the surface.

"And what were your findings?" the figure asked.

"We... don't exactly know," Cryo responded hesitantly. "But we do know they've started expanding their mining operations."

Why is he telling them this? Isn't this borderline treason? Niko wondered worriedly. If the Meridians found out Cryo had been telling their secrets, he could be in real trouble. Could *she* be in real trouble by association? Niko started to panic as her mind went to the worst places.

"Excuse us for a moment," the central figure among the Heads of Knowledge said. All five of them floated to the back of their raised platform to converse.

Niko was still too much in shock to really wonder what they were talking about. She was more concerned about why Cryo was telling the An-Mara their secrets, and why he *didn't* tell her or Riesen anything.

"Cryo, what the blazes?" Riesen hissed over at him, clearly echoing Niko's sentiments.

"It's fine, Riesen," Cryo replied. "It's... nevermind. I'll tell you after."

Riesen shook his head, obviously a little angry for being left out. Before any more discussion could get going, though, the Heads of Knowledge returned to address the group.

"We are currently seeking corroboration on your account," the central figure announced. "In the meantime, can you please provide us with her whereabouts?"

Cryo shook his head. "We don't know where she is. She was arrested yesterday and we have absolutely no information about where she is."

"I see," the central figure replied.

"Would you happen to know when and where she was arrested?" one of the other Heads of Knowledge asked. "And by whom?"

"Well, she was arrested yesterday morning by the Meridians," Cryo replied. "We don't know exactly where, but we assume in our town of Green Coast."

The Heads of Knowledge looked at each other through the shadows once more. Niko was beginning to think they had to be using some unseen and unheard form of communication. She had no idea how, but she remembered Ajane talking about psychic potential. After a short pause, they turned back to Cryo.

"Are you then also familiar with the one called Callum Sehs?" one of the Heads asked.

"I know of the name," Cryo responded warily. "None of us has ever met him."

Niko had never heard of a Callum Sehs before. Should she have?

"We do appreciate your truthfulness in this Hall," the central figure declared.

It seemed like they were satisfied with the truths Cryo was telling. Maybe this would be enough for them to finally let them go? Cryo's plan seemed to have paid off.

"May I ask a question?" Cryo asked boldly. "Your people speak about the great honesty of the An-Mara versus the cryptic nature of the Meridians. I would be honored to experience it firsthand."

Ooooh, smart, Niko thought. It seemed like he learned that manipulation from Riesen's tactics earlier.

"Very well," the central figure allowed. "Speak it."

"What is the An-Mara interest in the mines?" asked Cryo. "I assume you infiltrated them for a reason?"

The Heads of Knowledge shared a glance with each other for a few seconds before the central figure responded.

"Your planet is rich in certain rare elements," he said. "Meridian corporations have become quick to colonize lesser peoples in search of such materials. Our directive is to evaluate the scale of their intentions."

"And what of the Engines?" Cryo asked. "What's your interest in those?"

This question completely caught Niko by surprise. There was no way he knew what they were. She had only mentioned the Engines once to Cryo, and she hadn't been able to explain anything about them. Kira-Tharn never finished telling her what they were. Did Cryo figure out their purpose? He had obviously been doing a lot of thinking. Cryo *was* really smart, after all.

The question had also taken the Heads of Knowledge by surprise. This was the first time Niko observed them to be unsure of how to proceed. Cryo must have really stumbled onto something major here. Niko should've felt satisfaction from one of her friends stumping these Heads of Knowledge into hesitation, but the truth was that it made her feel very uneasy. There was just this feeling of... *wrongness*... about this whole situation. The Heads looked back and forth to each other, but no one gave a quick answer.

Before they could give an answer, all attention was drawn to a rattling noise along the bench. The rattling was soon accompanied by a subtle tremor. A *groundquake*? As soon as the shaking had started, however, it stopped.

*Well, that was weird...*Niko thought. She'd already stood halfway up in panic as her first instincts told her it might be an actual groundquake. She was the only one to react like that, though. The rest of her friends and the An-Mara alike had just merely looked around. Had her brain had time to think, she would've remembered that there were hardly ever groundquakes in Poste Territory. *It* *must've been something else.*

"You asked about our interest in the Engines?" the central Head of Knowledge asked, doing his best to ignore the quick tremble that had just rattled the room.

Cryo nodded. "Yes."

"What is your background knowledge in such matters of the Engines?" the central figure asked.

"Mmm, well we don't really know anything at all," Cryo responded truthfully. "We just know that they exist and that they're all over the planet."

"I see," the central figure said. It was too dark for Niko to see any of their eyes, but she was certain that they were intensely fixated upon Cryo. "There is not a brief answer to give to someone without a background knowledge of the inner workings of the Engines."

"Is there a short answer?" Cryo was not backing down.

The Heads of Knowledge looked back and forth at each other once more.

"The Engines are related to the mines. They are…"

The Head of Knowledge stopped in the middle of his sentence as the room was rattled once more. This time, the shaking was far less subtle. A loud noise accompanied a sharp jolt and Niko gasped out loud. This had to be a groundquake.

"Should we get to cover?" she asked, her eyes wide in alert.

"Yeah, shouldn't we?" agreed Kate.

The other Green Coast friends started to stand up in alarm as Niko had earlier.

The Heads of Knowledge whispered to each other, but didn't immediately make a move to run for cover.

"We would convey an apology," the central figure announced, "but this session will require a brief pause. Please wait here for a moment."

The Heads of Knowledge then proceeded to glide out a back door that was up on their platform. Niko and her friends were left alone with the two An-Mara guards to panic at the unfolding situation, as another sharp tremor rocked the room.

11

Meridian or 'Meridian'?

WHAT the blazes is going on out there? Niko asked herself. Groundquakes didn't strike like this.

"Soooo…" Kyler started. "They just leave us in an underground room while a groundquake destroys the whole facility around us. Nice."

Although his statement was slightly dramatic, Niko was definitely thinking the same thing. Why would they all just leave them in here by themselves? What was going on?

"The situation is being evaluated," one of the guards said. Niko thought his name was Shol Vera-Nim. Both Shol Vera-Nim and Mora Nant-Zern, the two guards with them now, were the ones who brought them food earlier in the day. "The Heads of Knowledge will return shortly to deliver their assessment."

Their calmness was reassuring to Niko, but that didn't mean her nerves would be magically soothed. Only after a few minutes went by without any more tremors did concern slowly die down. As it did, Riesen turned to Cryo to question him.

"Cryo! Why tell them all this?" he whispered angrily. "You never told me *any* of it!"

"They knew," Cryo responded with a simple shrug. "I don't

know how, but they knew that we work with Ajane. We had no choice but to tell the truth."

Riesen just looked to the floor and shook his head. "Are you *really* investigating the Meridians behind their backs?"

Ravenna spoke up, answering for Cryo. "We all are, because the attention the Meridians are giving to the Minedyne sites isn't adding up with all their other policies. If we could somehow talk to Ajane, she has a lot of evidence that would all make perfect sense for you."

"I hope so," said Kyler. "To be honest, you're not alone, Riesen. I'm also confused as blazes with what's going on right now."

Before anyone could discuss the matter further, the Heads of Knowledge returned from whatever business they were conducting outside the room.

"We would convey an apology for the interruption," the central figure said after they took their seats once more. "We do have an assessment for the current situation, which has been complicated by an incident that we have..."

"Is it safe for us to be sitting here?" Kyler demanded. "Are there gonna be more groundquakes?"

The Heads of Knowledge did not look pleased that Kyler continued to interrupt them out of turn.

"There was an assault on our facility just now, but the situation has been cleared of danger. You must please refrain from interruptions while we are speaking."

An assault!?

It just now dawned on Niko that the groundquakes were not in fact groundquakes, but instead strikes over their very heads, probably from the Meridians. It seemed that they actually might be at war after all. She desperately wanted it all to be over with. Something — probably anxiety — burned in the pit of her stomach. Whereas the experience from their capture in the morning had been extremely unpleasant, this was somehow a lot worse. She *should* be happy the Meridians were here, but all she felt was a deep fear, similar to the feeling from the dream last night.

These Heads of Knowledge claimed that there was no more danger, though — did that mean that Meridians were killed? Or were they remote missile strikes? Niko was pretty sure that remote warfare was a permanently banned practice. Either way, what if the

Meridians sent more attacks? Was there a bunker or something that could keep them safe? Was there any way to somehow let the Meridians know that they were in the building?

So many questions went flying through Niko's head, but the central Head of Knowledge continued in his same, calm-as-ever voice.

"We have communicated your status with a Meridian delegation and they have agreed to halt attacks in order to transfer you back to their charge, immediately," he said.

Thank the heavens! she proclaimed in her head. This whole day had been the most insane emotional roller coaster, and now maybe — just *maybe* — they'd be getting out after all! The Meridians were coming for them! Dare she hope? Or was this too good to be true?

"We had already found fit to make the judgment that you be returned to your people," one of the Heads added. "We would ask that you deliver an honest assessment of your treatment here upon your return."

Whatever it is they want us to do, I'll do it, Niko promised herself. *As long as we get out of here.*

Another Head spoke next. "Furthermore, we have three individuals here to deliver an official statement to you before you take leave."

Three shadowy figures then entered from a door below the raised platform, level with where the Green Coast captives all sat now. One of them stepped forward, head bowed.

"On behalf of my people, I convey a deep and honest apology for your treatment during your capture." The familiar voice of Riiz Alke-Tani rung throughout the Hall.

Niko grinned as he stepped back. She was surprised that they actually held true to their word to deliver their apology. Good for them.

Another figure stepped forward. "I would address the one called Kyler Pierson, and would convey a very deep apology for the unnecessary physical mistreatment against you in the morning."

Kyler snorted audibly.

Why, for the love of the heavens, could he not just show goodwill and accept the blazes apology?! They were almost out of here... If he did anything to jeopardize this opportunity, Niko would never forgive him.

Fortunately, the man did not react to Kyler's derision and

stepped back in line, his head still bowed, as the third figure stepped forward.

"I would convey a very deep regret for the unnecessary disrespect to the one called Ravenna Night. Please accept my apology." The shadowy figure of Setten-Lo stepped back with the others.

Niko looked over and noticed Ravenna slightly nod her head in acknowledgement of the concession. She doubted that Ravenna forgave the man entirely, but it was a start.

"On behalf of the entirety of the An-Mara contingent," the central Head spoke up, "we would convey a deep apology for the confusion and inconvenience of your detention. The one called Riiz Alke-Tani, with whom you are familiar, will now escort you to the Meridian delegation we have been in contact with. This is our directive. We do appreciate your truthfulness and we wish you well."

Without further ceremony, the Heads of Knowledge then stood up and filed out through the door up on their platform.

Well, that was sure fast, Niko thought. One second they were delivering their directives, and the next they were just gone. After they had all exited, Riiz Alke-Tani stepped forward once more and ushered the group to him.

"We have a transport waiting for you," he said. "Please follow me."

He wasted no time walking across the room and out the doors. Niko and her friends scrambled to their feet as they hustled to follow him, footsteps hushed as they scurried out of the dark, stone theater. Everything seemed so rushed right now, but Niko was fine with that, as long as her legs could keep up, belligerent as they were. The sooner she could get out of this place the better.

As she left the Hall of Knowledge, she instinctively turned toward the lift they'd arrived on, but Riiz instead strode over to a different hallway.

"We use the stairs on the side," he said, noticing that some of them had already started toward the lift.

Great, more stairs, Niko silently groaned as she scrambled back over to where Riiz was headed. Her soreness had been steadily rising as the day went on and was only going to get worse.

The stairwell was darker than the rest of the building, with the exception of the Hall of Knowledge, of course. It spiraled upward in sharp right-angle turns, and when she peered up over the railing in the center, she saw it stretched into the distance farther than she could see. How far underground were they?!

She steeled herself for a tough climb, but was deeply relieved when the group stopped after only a few flights. She had assumed the transport was waiting at surface level, but it turned out that there was an underground tunnel system that the transports use. She should have known… she was in Groundheim after all.

The tunnel they emerged onto was wide and tall. Part of the cavern was bounded by constructed walls, but the ceiling looked like it was natural, adorned with hanging stalactites and all. The air felt damp and thick, and Niko could see small trickles of water running down the side of the opposite end of the cavern. They were so deep that it would've certainly been pitch black if it weren't for all the artificial lighting illuminating the entire room. There were several transports waiting on the sides, all very similar to the one she'd ridden in on. At the far end of the massive hollow, where the road disappeared down smaller tunnels, she saw Kira-Tharn waiting outside one of the shuttles.

"Over this way," Riiz said as he strode over to where Kira-Tharn and two other An-Mara were waiting.

As soon as they saw Riiz walking toward them with everyone in tow, they opened the door to the transport and disappeared inside. Niko heard the vehicle turn on, immensely glad that they weren't waiting for anything. They were actually getting out of this place! Butterflies flurried in her stomach, and her heart jumped with hope.

Niko smiled at Kira-Tharn, forgetting that smiling at an An-Mara was not the kind gesture that it meant to her. Kira-Tharn just nodded with a solemn, unreadable look in return. Niko would never understand these An-Mara…

As she pulled herself aboard and took a seat, she looked around at her surroundings. The first thing she noticed was that Riiz did not have his whole crew with him this time. There was Kira-Tharn, Setten-Lo, and the one who had punched Kyler — she wasn't sure of his name — but it was only those three from his original crew from earlier. In addition to those three, there were four newcomers — two that she'd never seen, and then also Mora Nant-Zern and Shol Vera-Nim, the two guards that had sat with them in the Hall of Knowledge.

"Do you know where we're going?" Niko asked Kira-Tharn.

"Yes, we are transporting you to Fennemol Outpost, where you will be transferred to the Meridian delegation."

"Hmm, I've never heard of that place. Is it far?"

Kira-Tharn shrugged. "You will likely consider it far."

"Well, how far are we talking?" Niko asked. "Like how long will we be in here?"

"Probably about ten hours, maybe a little more."

"Ten hours?!" Niko exclaimed. "What time even is it now?"

"Just past 21:00," Kira-Tharn replied.

"Why can't we fly where we're going?"

"It is not safe to be flying right now," Kira-Tharn responded nonchalantly.

"Why not?" Niko asked.

"There is currently hostile traffic in the air between here and the Islands."

"Oh," Niko sighed. She was so happy to be returning to her parents that she didn't even take the time to fully process what was going on outside. She'd even heard the explosions when they were in the Hall of Knowledge, but it somehow didn't register that this was a very dangerous time to be out and about.

Kira-Tharn must have picked up on Niko's worry. "The Meridian delegation is very aware of your transfer to Fennemol Outpost. I consider it very unlikely that they would do anything to jeopardize your safety. You will be fine."

"I hope so," Niko replied. She felt strangely soothed that Kira-Tharn went out of her way to make her feel better.

"I know so," Kira-Tharn encouraged. "Now, perhaps you could get some rest tonight. The duration of this trip should allow for that. My attention is required at the front, so I must take my leave."

Niko wished she had time to continue their earlier conversation and ask her more about the Engines, but that would have to wait. Maybe she could ask Cryo what he knew of them? She was, after all, quite curious about his exchange with the Heads of Knowledge...

She looked around to find him and saw everyone at the back of the transport together. She moved over to join them, and found that they were already discussing the encounter.

"But I don't get why you wouldn't just *tell me* that you were working with her against the Meridians," Riesen said, obviously in the middle of grilling the rest of them.

"We aren't working against them," Kate contended. "It's complicated."

"This was highly classified, and you weren't given clearance, Riesen," Ravenna added plainly.

"I get that, but I would say things have been a little different the last two days. Wouldn't you?" Riesen countered. Noticing Niko creep up and take a seat near them, he motioned to her. "Both of us deserve to know the truth, since we're risking the same as you in all of this. Blazes, she's just a kid and was taken prisoner at gunpoint by the enemy!!"

That was enough to bring heat to Niko's face.

"First off," she started angrily at Riesen, "I told you to stop calling me kid. I literally am less than a year younger than you. Second, I think we need to all talk to Ajane before we start throwing blame around."

"*Thank* you, Niko," Kate said. "That's what I've been saying!"

"That doesn't mean I'm not upset for being left in the dark," Niko continued. "Riesen is right. We were practically *begging* you guys for information on what the blazes was going on yesterday. And you lied to us."

"We didn't lie to you," Kate protested. "Everything we said was the truth. We're confused about a lot, just like you. We don't know what the Engines are. We don't know where Ajane is. And we still don't know why the An-Mara attacked the stations."

"Well, tell me what you do know, then" Riesen challenged. "And please don't lie to me."

"What do you want to know that you don't already know?" Ravenna asked him bluntly. She was leaned back in her seat, arms folded. She looked very dangerous when she was angry.

"You can start by telling me why you're part of some secret operation to investigate Minedyne," Riesen demanded.

"Fair enough," Cryo said, seizing upon a small silence to speak. He took a deep breath before continuing. "But it's kind of a long story."

"I don't need the long version of the story, I just want to know why you're working against the Meridians."

"Riesen, blazes!" Kyler pushed back. "We aren't working *against* the Meridians. Just shut up and let Cryo talk."

Niko was floored. It seemed like that was one of the first reasonable things that had come out of Kyler's mouth in a long time.

Maybe ever.

Riesen just spread his arms. "Fine, go ahead."

"Well, the short of it is that the Meridians aren't actually..." Cryo hesitated, "well... *Meridians.*"

"What the blazes does that mean?" Riesen asked in the same flustered tone.

Niko herself was left wondering what Cryo meant by this. What did he mean that the Meridians weren't Meridians??

"I mean, they *are* Meridians, but..."

"Just tell him how you got involved in the first place, Cryo," Kyler said. "It'd make more sense."

Cryo sighed, but continued.

"Fine. Abel — Ven's dad — was working with the Meridians a long time ago to get mining operations started at the Anziend Station in Anterg. I guess he found a huge shipment of uncatalogued minerals that were being sent off-world, so he started to investigate."

Riesen leaned back to stretch, breaking out in the most exaggerated yawn that Niko had ever seen.

"You don't want to hear it? Fine by me," Ravenna said. "Just don't complain to us when you get burned by them."

"No, no," Riesen said, finishing his yawn. "Go ahead."

"Riesen!" Kate scolded, hitting him hard on the arm. "Don't be an ass!"

"Okay, okay!" Riesen relented. "Sorry, Cryo. Weird shipment?"

Cryo looked annoyed, but he resumed his telling, lowering his voice.

"Okay, yeah, so something was off. Abel was about to report it, and that's when Ajane and this other dude, Callum Sehs, reached out to him."

"Wait," Riesen interjected at Cryo's slightest pause. "I heard those An-Mara ask about that name... Callum Sehs? What's his deal? Where's he at?"

Cryo shook his head. "I don't know. He went off planet years ago, and that's all I know. Anyway, he and Ajane said they were officially from a '*Meridian Empire*', which was different from the group that calls themselves the Meridians here. Well... not different exactly, but the group here is some sort of an offshoot or something that's on an unsanctioned mission. Weird, right?"

"Uhh sure, I guess," Riesen said. "But how do you know

Ajane's not just full of it? She seemed pretty sketchy to me…"

"She's not sketchy," Ravenna defended, simply glaring across the aisle at Riesen, who had the gall — and foolishness — to roll his eyes at her.

"I'm getting there, just hang on," Cryo continued, diffusing any altercation between Riesen and Ravenna. "So onto the 'Meridians', or whatever you want to call them… Ajane and Callum were able to work their way into their organization because the 'Meridians' were scared of them."

Riesen was about to open his mouth, but Cryo held up a hand and continued before he could interrupt again.

"The way I know it," he continued, "the 'Meridians' were threatened because Ajane and Callum *were* official or whatever. From what I was told, the 'Meridians' had no choice but to accept them because they didn't want the full force of the *actual* Meridian Empire to come and interfere with whatever they were doing here. Something like that. It's all kinda confusing, even still."

"Mmmm, I'm sorry but I don't know if I buy any of it," Riesen hawed. He was skeptical, and rightly so. Niko always believed Cryo's word on everything, but this seemed a little far-fetched. Not as far-fetched as that insane An-Mara tale about all that Nel-Mara nonsense, but she still needed to hear more of what Cryo was going to say before she passed judgment.

"Just let him finish, Riesen," Kate spoke up. "Please."

"Okay, fine. Sorry Cryo, go on," Riesen mocked disingenuously. Niko didn't like how rude he was being to Cryo. Cryo was one of the nicest people she knew! He didn't deserve this.

Cryo simply sighed, only the tiniest hint of frustration crossing his voice. He had to be the most patient person Niko knew.

"Okay, so Ajane's goal when they first worked their way into the 'Meridian' service was to try to force them off planet, but because the 'Meridians' had already been well established on Arhanda — and since they did more good than bad for the people here — it wasn't worth running them out. Instead, Ajane and Callum adjusted their goal to keeping tabs on them and keeping them honest."

"So, that's it?" Riesen asked. "You've been working for her doing *that* ever since? Keeping them honest? What even is there to keep them honest about?"

"Well, hang on, there's this one more thing. I promise I'm

almost done," Cryo said, reading the rising impatience on Riesen's face. "After Ajane recruited Abel to help her with her mission, somebody must've found out. Abel's family — Ven's mom and sister — were murdered in a home invasion gone bad. It was made to look that way at least, but Ajane always said that it was a message. The same thing happened to two other people Ajane recruited."

Woah... Niko looked over to Ravenna.

This would make sense as to why she was always so hardened to emotion. If it was true, that was absolutely one of the most terrible things she'd ever heard. Her family was *murdered* as a *message*? She'd always known Abel was killed a few years back, but she didn't know that happened to the rest of Ravenna's family, also.

"That was when Ven and I were really young. We were brought up in all of this and had no choice. I get it now — why Abel was always so driven and angry all the time. We worked with him and Ajane for a long time trying to figure out what the Meridians want."

"And what *do* you think they want?" Riesen asked. His tone still sounded a little sarcastic, but at least he was letting Cryo speak.

"So far, it turns out to be pretty consistent with what the An-Mara said about them just wanting to use this place for mining. Everyone who's Inducted into the Meridian service is basically just a body to help them with their operations. They keep us distracted with things like the Anniversary, and Field, and all that stuff."

Riesen was silent, but Niko was sure he was only thinking of some smart remark to fire back. She was pretty certain that he didn't buy any of what Cryo said. To be fair, it was a lot for her to process, as well. All of it sounded like it could *mayyybe* be plausible to her, but she also didn't want to believe that the Meridians — the people running the entire planet — were crooks. Even Cryo said they did a lot of good for the planet. They stopped all the world wars after all! They brought peace and order to the most chaotic epoch in Arhandan history.

"So now you understand why I care so much about it," Ravenna said, still leaning back, looking as dangerous as ever.

"And why we have to keep that secret," Daren added. This was the first Niko had heard from him in hours. He didn't speak often, so his words carried a lot of value when he did. "They will come after us if they know somebody's snooping around. They will come after our *families*."

"Neither of you can ever say anything, to anyone, under any

circumstance," Ravenna confronted both Niko and Riesen. Her expression told Niko that she was not messing around. It was actually quite terrifying. She wouldn't want Ravenna as an enemy.

Niko nodded, eyes wide and mouth shut.

"I'd need to see stuff to believe it," Riesen said.

What an ass. Even if he didn't believe any of it, the least he could've done was be more tactful with his wording. After all, Ravenna's family had been murdered, and she just had to relive it all right now.

"And what about these guys? What about the An-Mara? Where do they fit in all of this?" he asked.

Cryo shook his head.

"I honestly don't know. They've been pretty secretive since they've been here. Niko probably knows more than any of us," he replied, shooting a smirk to Niko. "She made fast friends with that Kira-Tharn."

Niko pursed her lips, trying to downplay the pride that surged within her. She got the feeling that Cryo really respected the way she was able to make friends with one of the An-Mara.

"I already told you guys about everything we talked about," Niko said. "But I actually was going to ask you, Cryo, how you knew about the Engines? Or how you knew that the Heads of Knowledge would react the way they did when you mentioned the Engines?"

Cryo shrugged. "It was a hunch. I guessed that what we found in the station was what they called the Engines, so I asked them about it. We still haven't gotten an answer, though. This will be something that we'll have to ask Ajane when we see her."

"Hmph, *if* we see her," Kyler corrected.

"True," Kate agreed. "I wish we knew where she was at the very least."

"Yep. I think that's the first thing we need to focus on when we get back," Cryo said.

"What does that mean for me and Riesen?" Niko asked. "Ajane asked to have us in her program early, but I assume the Meridians don't want to do that anymore?"

"Since all this happened, I have no idea," he said, shaking his head. "Going back to the An-Mara, one thing I do know about them is that there are way more of *them* than there are Meridians. If we are actually going to war with them, then all tenth years and above will probably be Inducted very soon."

"Yeah, unfortunately," Daren agreed. "We haven't had any communications, so we just don't know. But it's probably an all-hands-on-deck situation."

The feeling of dread that plagued Niko all day hadn't quite gone away, but if it had retreated slightly, it was now back with full-force, as if swallowing her whole. Would that mean *she* is going to war?

Please, no, she begged. She was not ready for this. Would this be how her dream came true?? With everything else going on, this was just too much. Tears started to well up in her eyes once more. Kate seemed to notice and scooted next to her, wrapping an arm around her tightly.

She looked over to Riesen and had no idea how this information didn't even faze him. He wore a completely calm and stoic expression, but he surely was terrified just like Niko. Right? He was usually good at hiding emotions, but there was no way he wasn't scared out of his mind.

Was this what happened to boys as they got older? Did they just stop showing emotion? She thought that was the stupidest thing ever. It wasn't like showing emotion made someone weak... There was nothing wrong with it.

Was there?

Now Niko was second guessing herself. She *hated* when she did this, because now she worried she might be showing too much emotion, even though it was perfectly rationalized in her head. This was all so stressful! She was scared. Actually, truly scared.

Nobody would understand how she felt anyway. The dream made all of this a hundred times worse, and there was no way she could tell any of them about it. The only person she would tell at this point would be Ajane, and no one had any clue as to how they were going to find her.

The long hug with her sister was only interrupted by the slowing down of the transport, as well as the chatter among the An-Mara up at the front.

Oh, come on... What now? Kira-Tharn said the trip would take ten hours, but they had only been traveling for a couple minutes it seemed. What could possibly be going on?

"Oh good! Finally we're here!" Kyler said as he stood up to get off.

Ravenna pulled him back down.

"You idiot!" she hissed. "We are not *here*."

"Oh," he said. "Flat tire?"

Ravenna just rolled her eyes, not even bothering to dignify his foolishness with a reply.

Niko looked out the window to get a better view of what was going on and saw the same beautiful characteristics of the caverns she'd become familiar with. On the left side, a magnificent waterfall cascaded down the side of the cavern, illuminated by the blue and green lights of the roadway. Up ahead, though, she saw what looked like a blockade of vehicles, along with several armed troops. They completely had the tunnel roadblocked.

Unfortunately, it looked like the An-Mara, and not the Meridians she was hoping for. Or had been hoping for before Cryo's story about who they actually were…

As their transport came to a halt, Kira-Tharn turned to address the Green Coast friends. "Wait here. Do not move," she instructed, as she, Riiz, and two others exited the vehicle.

Niko and her friends all shared a look with each other for not even two seconds before all clambering to scoot a little bit closer to the door. They all wanted to hear what was going on out there, of course, although the splashing of the waterfall made it difficult.

As she peered across the half-lit roadway, Niko saw Riiz walk forward, then a man from the other side of the blockade did the same.

It was Var Ashal-Han.

How did that guy get here so fast? she wondered. *What is actually going on?*

"You have the one called Riesen Ryen with you," she thought she could hear Var say without any pleasantries. Not that the An-Mara spoke with many pleasantries anyway…

"We do," Riiz replied. "The Heads of Knowledge arranged the exchange of these Arhandans to the Meridian delegation with whom they have been in contact."

"I see," Var responded.

"Yes," Riiz said. "They are expecting us at Fennemol Outpost at 06:00 sharp, so we must be on our way without delay."

"I would be happy to send you all on your way, but we first require Riesen Ryen to come with us."

All heads turned to Riesen. Was this about the Child of the Nel-Mara or whatever they'd been prattling on about earlier? Riesen just shrugged back at everyone, clearly just as confused as anyone else.

"Negative," Riiz replied. "The directive was clear. All names are on the Record, including the one called Riesen Ryen. You may check for yourself."

"I would, except that I do not have access to the Record at the moment. I am the senior commander and my orders are for you to hand over the one called Riesen Ryen to my charge," Var pushed.

"You are the senior commander, so you must have access to the Record at all times," Riiz countered, his eyes narrowing in defiance.

"I do not currently," Var said without any explanation. "Please hand over the one called Riesen Ryen to me so I can let you pass."

"I will not disobey a directive from the Heads of Knowledge," Riiz responded, standing his ground.

"You will hand him over if you intend to complete your delivery on time." The insistence of Var was starting to sound rather terrifying. What would he do if Riiz kept refusing?

"I will not," Riiz replied. He was not budging. "Kira-Tharn, please open a channel to the Mainquarters and inform them of the situation."

Kira-Tharn nodded and pulled out a device. It looked a little bit different from a Ut, but it most likely served the same purpose. Before she could do anything with it, though, Var Ashal-Han drew his sidearm and pointed it straight at Kira-Tharn. The other soldiers that formed the blockade alongside him all followed suit, raising their weapons in tandem.

12

Handoff Standoff

NIKO'S blood froze at the unfolding series of events. Even though the weapons weren't pointed at her, she suffered that same involuntary twitch of fear from earlier when they had been. As if the day couldn't get any worse…

"You will not open the channel," Var sneered. "I am the senior commander and you will obey my orders over those of the one called Riiz Alke-Tani."

Kira-Tharn froze and looked worriedly between Riiz and Var.

Riiz nodded to her and calmly pushed her arm down, removing the device from her hand.

"My orders come from the Heads of Knowledge, which eclipse yours, senior commander," Riiz said plainly. Niko couldn't believe how fearless he was in the face of all that firepower staring him down. She would've admired his bravery if she wasn't so utterly terrified that his actions were going to get all of them killed.

He then pressed the button on the device.

Kira-Tharn!! Niko closed her eyes, fully expecting Var and his troops to start firing.

To her great relief, the sound of shots never commenced, and she slowly opened her eyes. It looked like Riiz had opened a communication video link back to the Mainquarters before Var gave a command to fire. He must've feared the Heads of Knowledge to some degree, enough to stay his trigger finger at least.

"As you can see, we have a conflict here," Riiz said to whoever was on the other line of the communication. "The senior commander does not have access to the Record, and does not trust my word that all seven Arhandans are to be transferred to Fennemol Outpost immediately. This was the directive, was it not?"

"This was the directive," the voice on the other end of the line said. It was difficult to hear with the waterfall in the background, but it sounded like the central Head of Knowledge himself. "If there is a challenge to the directive that the one called Var Ashal-Han would desire to propose, it must be brought to the Hall of Knowledge."

"There would be a challenge," Var interjected. "I would propose that the Heads of Knowledge adjust their directive to allow six of the seven Arhandans to be transferred to Fennemol Outpost, and the one called Riesen Ryen to be maintained under An-Mara charge."

A ton of bricks hit Niko in the gut.

Please, please, pleeeease don't let them take Riesen, she pleaded. She couldn't take another blow at this point. The rest of her friends looked just as worried as her. They wouldn't actually let Var keep Riesen, would they?

"The Heads of Knowledge are not in a position to be assembled at this moment," the Head of Knowledge said. "Due to the time sensitive nature of the arrangement with the Meridian delegation, all seven of the Arhandans must be present at the exchange scheduled for 06:00 at Fennemol Outpost."

"I respect the judgment of the Heads of Knowledge," Var relented.

His words were respectful, but the look on his face was anything but. He started to turn around, as if to order his troops back, but stopped short.

"If I may present one more case to my…"

"You may not." The Head of Knowledge cut him short.

"With complete respect for the Time, I must protest," Var pushed. "For the sake of the…"

"Furthermore," the Head of Knowledge interrupted, "because you do not have access to the Record, the one called Riiz Alke-Tani is temporarily promoted to acting senior commander in your stead.

You will be escorted by the acting senior commander back to the Mainquarters immediately. Upon your return and clearance by the Heads of Knowledge, you will be reinstated to senior commander only when you regain access to the Record."

Wowww. Niko's mouth was surely wide open. *Var just got completely owned!*

"I would address the one called Riiz Alke-Tani," the Head of Knowledge continued. "You are to escort the one called Var Ashal-Han and his charges back to the Mainquarters. Select three of your own charges to accompany your escort back. The other three of your charges will continue with the exchange of the Arhandans at Fennemol Outpost. That is all."

The video link went dead immediately. The Head of Knowledge was short and to the point, and made it clear that all of Var's authority had now been transferred to Riiz. Var had struck Niko as someone who was insecure about his power, and it seemed that her intuition proved correct. This must have been the worst blow imaginable for him.

Indeed, his dark face had turned red with anger. His fists had clenched and his jaw was quivering. Niko wasn't so sure that he wouldn't just shoot Riiz right then and there. After a few seconds, though, he simply turned around and ordered his troops back into their vehicles, much to Niko's relief.

Riiz simply marched back to the transport with the others. There was no emotion printed on any of their faces, though Niko thought she might have noticed a small hint of relief at the corner of Kira-Tharn's eyes.

"You seven will stay on board," Riiz said to the Green Coast friends as he stepped back onto the transport. "I am required to travel back to Groundheim. The ones called Kira-Tharn, Setten-Lo, and Breva Taxa-Lon will accompany me. The ones called Mora Nant-Zern, Shol Vera-Nim, and Den-So will continue with you on to Fennemol Outpost. You must depart immediately. We have already wasted too much time. I wish you well."

Right before leaving the transport, he turned to Riesen and added, "I would warn you that the one called Var Ashal-Han is not done with you yet. Tread carefully in his presence."

With that final message, he stormed off the transport and strode over toward Var and his troops with Kira-Tharn, Setten-Lo, and Breva Taxa-Lon close behind. Niko hoped that they would never have to worry about that warning. If she could have it her way, she would never be in Var's presence ever again. Surely her friends felt the exact same way.

She was all too happy to get out of this place as quickly as possible, but as she watched Kira-Tharn board one of Var's vehicles, a strange and conflicted feeling came over her. Not only was Niko sad to not have Kira-Tharn with her for the reminder of the trip, but she was also worried for her well-being. What if Var tried to take revenge upon them on their way back to Groundheim? She could only hope that his fear of the Heads of Knowledge was able to keep him in check from attempting something like that…

"Let us be on our way," Den-So announced to Niko and her friends, wasting no time. He was the one who had punched Kyler earlier. Niko never quite caught his name then. "It will be about nine and a half hours until we reach our destination. Make yourselves comfortable."

He made the quick announcement, then disappeared to the front with Mora and Shol. Niko's cheeks were still damp from the tears earlier, but she didn't know what to feel anymore. She realized that her hands were shaking, but it wasn't from straight fear. Maybe this was the adrenaline people talk about when someone is placed in a high-stress situation. Before she could think too much about it, Kyler interrupted the silence.

"What the actual blazes just happened right there?!" he exclaimed with a huge grin. "Riiz is a blazes badass!"

"That was crazy," Daren agreed, also smiling. "I thought Riesen was for sure a goner."

"Can't touch me," Riesen smirked.

Kate reached over and hugged Riesen with a smile of her own. Even Cryo started laughing with all of them. How were they all smiling and joking around right now? Did they not just realize they all could've just died?? Niko was completely drained of emotions at this point. She wasn't going to cry anymore, but she also had no energy to join in the laughter. She was just so exhausted.

Aside from Niko, Ravenna was the only other one of them not smiling. She just sat there off to the side, staring out the window with arms and legs folded up.

"Wake up!" she heard her sister saying. The command was accompanied by the shaking of her shoulders. "Niko! Wake up."

"I'm up, I'm up!" Niko responded frantically.

She jolted upright and looked around, attempting to catch her bearings as quickly as possible. She was still on the transport, and all her friends were still there, half of them asleep.

Good.

Did she dream? It didn't seem like it. She couldn't remember any dreams at least.

Thank the heavens, she thought gratefully.

"You started to toss, so I woke you up like you asked me to," Kate said.

"Oh, thank you," Niko expressed wholeheartedly. She really was so grateful. "How long was I out?"

"I don't know. A couple of hours maybe."

Niko leaned back and took a deep breath of relief. Kate looked at her quizzically.

"What's up? You seem like something's bothering you," she prodded Niko.

Niko firmly ran her fingers through her hair, her head spinning from waking up too quickly, probably.

"Something bothering me?" she responded with a hint of incredulity. "I mean, yes, there's a lot bothering me. Are there not a million things also bothering you?"

"Fair point," Kate winced. "But did you want to talk about why you're terrified to fall asleep? And why I have to stop you from tossing and turning?"

"Not really," Niko muttered honestly as she looked down. "No offense. I just don't want to talk about it is all."

Kate sighed. There she went again, doing that same thing that drove Niko insane where she would play the victim in order to get Niko to open up.

"Please don't try to pull it out of me," Niko insisted. "You're trying to make me feel bad for not opening up to you, but it's just something I *really* don't want to talk about right now. I wish you'd respect that. And I promise I don't mean to make you feel bad."

No matter Niko's intentions, Kate looked supremely offended at what she just said.

Oh blazes, that wasn't too harsh. Was it? Niko started to second guess herself. Was she being too mean to her sister? After all, she did the nice thing by waking her up when she asked her to.

"I'm sorry, Kate," Niko sighed. "It's just that... I... I've been having these dreams again. Like the one with Riesen. And I just don't really want to think about them right now."

"What'd you dream?" Kate pushed.

Niko shot her sister a glare.

Did she not just hear me that I don't want to think about them? Is that too hard for her to understand?

"I'm just trying to help, Niko," Kate said in recoil as if Niko had punched her. She was really starting to play the victim card and Niko was over it.

"Last time I told you about my dreams, you went and blabbered them to a complete *stranger* without my permission, if I recall," Niko challenged.

"Oh, you can't be upset about that," Kate replied defensively. "I did that to *help* you with them! Ajane is there to help, you know. That's one of the main things she does — help people with dreams."

"It's not about whether she can help or not," Niko shot back. "It's about you taking what I told you in *confidence* and spreading it to someone I didn't even know, *without* my permission!"

"Well, you're gonna have to just get over that," Kate said plainly with a shrug.

Ohhh, she did not just say that...

Niko didn't even reply. She was fuming with frustration and had to turn away before she said something she regretted.

"Maybe next time I just won't wake you up?" Kate continued.

"Good!" Niko started to shout back. "Don't!"

"The blazes is going on over there?!" Kyler sat up from a nap of his own. "Do you guys mind?"

"Kyler! SHUT. UP!" both Ryen sisters snapped almost simultaneously.

"Yowsers!" he responded as he laid back down, eyes wide in shock.

It would've been funny if Niko was in the mood, but she was far from it. She sighed and turned back to Kate.

"I'm sorry for snapping, but I really don't appreciate you

pressing me on something that I *asked* you to not press me about," Niko insisted, lowering her volume.

"I'm sorry, too, but I really think you'd be better off if you told someone."

"Yeah, well, maybe I would, maybe I wouldn't. I don't know. All I know is that I've had way too much going on the last few days and I just want some of it off my brain."

"I know," Kate said. "Which is why I push for you to open up. I only want to *help* you with getting it off your brain."

Kate reached over to hug Niko. A hug wasn't what she wanted right now, but if she refused, it would only trigger Kate further and that was the last thing she wanted to deal with.

"This all just needs to end," Niko grumbled. "It's like one thing happens, then when I think it can't get any worse, it does."

"I know," Kate said. "We're almost home, though. It will all be over soon."

"Yeah, until we are then drafted into a war," Niko muttered.

"Well, we don't know what's going on for sure," Kate tried to reassure her. "Who knows, maybe it's all over by the time we get back. It was probably all a big miscommunication and things are gonna go back to normal."

It was wishful thinking, but Niko admitted that was probably the best way to look at things right now. She even said it herself, this was all too much and she just needed it to end. Maybe she could at least make it end in her own mind for the remainder of the travel. There was nothing they could do right now anyway.

"I might try to go to sleep again," Niko told Kate. "I'm so exhausted. I haven't had good sleep in days."

"I'll wake you up if I see you tossing and turning," Kate offered.

"No, it's okay," Niko said. "I'll be fine. I feel better."

Kate looked at her questioningly, but she probably knew better than to keep the argument going.

"How much longer do we have anyway?" Niko asked.

"I think around five hours," Kate answered.

"Okay, well, wake me up if I'm still asleep when we get to the place."

"I will if I'm awake," Kate agreed. "I might try to catch some sleep of my own."

"Sweet dreams," Niko said sarcastically, forcing a smile for her sister's sake.

"You too." Kate returned the smile back.

As she leaned back, she tried to will away her frustrations. Why did they have to get into that pointless spat of an argument? She wished her sister would just, for once, listen to her. With everything else to worry about, dealing with Kate's passive-aggressive nonsense was something she didn't need to add to the list.

Her mind started to race, and she prayed desperately that she wouldn't slip into that dream of the bridge again. Any dream except that one would be fine with her. She tried flooding her mind with thoughts of good things in her life. Green Coast. Her friends. Her parents. Brandon. Field. Sliding…

Niko's eyes slowly opened as she felt the transport slow down. No one woke her up this time; she did that on her own, which was a good sign. She didn't feel rested, but at least she wasn't in a frenzy of panic from a bad dream. True, she'd only been able to force herself into a half-sleep, but it was nice to at least close her eyes for a while.

As she caught her senses, she was suddenly aware of the bright light that shone all around. She peered out the windows and saw silvery mountains contrasting with the yellow-blue of the morning sky.

They had emerged onto the surface.

How long ago did that happen? Niko just assumed the tunnels ran the entire way to this Fennemol Outpost where they were going, but they clearly did not. She sat up, twisting her body to stretch her core, looking across to the window on the other side.

Barren desert. As far as the eye could see.

They must be right on the edge of the Great Poste Flats. She remembered learning about this place in her geology classes. They mined something important here, but she didn't remember what it was.

School seemed like something from another lifetime. After all, she'd been on vacation for several weeks for the Anniversary of

Arrival. That extended break, combined with everything else that was currently happening, completely upended her internal sense of time. School was always such a hassle for her, but after what she'd been through over the last few days, she was all too happy to get back into the classroom.

As she was gazing out the windows and letting her face take in the sol-rays, she felt movement. There was a tingle in her legs as she realized her circulation was being restricted by Kate's head, which was draped over her lap for who knew how long. Kate began to shift as she awakened, and she moved just enough for Niko to take the opportunity to slide out from under her. Blood and fresh air rushed to her legs as she attempted to straighten them.

Blazes! She was still quite sore, to no surprise. It was likely she would be sore like this for several days yet. What she really needed was a day off. Or an ice bath. Or both.

Niko shifted, becoming aware of the others reacting to the slowing of the transport, also. Kyler and Riesen sat up with the same bewildered eyes that Niko surely had. Cryo and Daren hadn't been lying down — they were only leaned back in their seats — but they had soft, sleepy eyes as if they had been dozing off also.

Ravenna was still sitting by herself off to the side, looking out the same window and wearing the same grim expression from earlier. She must not have slept at all. Niko felt bad for how she had to relive her childhood trauma last night when Cryo was explaining why they don't completely trust the Meridians.

It was awful what had happened to her family, but Niko still wanted to give the Meridians the benefit of the doubt. Even if it was Minedyne related, surely it wasn't the Meridians who killed her family. There was no way. Everyone, even the older folks, always spoke of the Meridians with such high regard. If it weren't for them, the whole world might still be plunged into savagery. Maybe there wouldn't even be a world without them! If the Meridians' intentions were so nefarious, they wouldn't have gone out of their way to save everyone. Besides, they were there to save Niko and all six of her friends from An-Mara clutches now. She was glad to be rid of the An-Mara, even if they had been strangely kind and reasonable.

The bright sky disappeared once more as the transport pulled into a large hangar bay. Niko could see a few Meridian military vehicles on the open side with several dozen forces waiting outside. She was suddenly more wary of these forces than she ever had been.

Normally, they would've given her the sensation of hope and security. She hoped Cryo's story didn't ruin her image of them... She wanted to be able to trust these people like she always had.

In order to trick her mind into feeling that sense of hope, she envisioned all these forces escorting her back to her family in a big parade with celebrations. She imagined her mom, her dad, Mack, Keran, Brandon, Jen, and even Tyson, all among a crowd cheering as the soldiers reunited the families. It would be daytime... and warm... and perfect, as she would embrace all of them in a great group hug.

Her mind snapped back to reality as she heard Den-So address them from the front of the transport.

"Are all individuals awakened back there?" he asked loudly.

"Awake and ready, good sir," Kyler teased from his seat sarcastically. "Is it time for our morning beatings?"

Den-So looked as if he was searching for something to say, but he only looked back at Kyler with a straight face of disapproval.

"We have arrived at Fennemol Outpost," he announced, keeping things professional and civil. "Once the vehicle comes to a stop, we will be handing you over to the Meridian delegation that is already there."

"About damn time..." Kyler huffed.

There was a murmur of agreement

"I do convey a deepest apology once more for... all that has happened," Den-So offered with a bow.

Niko found it to be very genuine and was a little irritated when Kyler just scoffed in return. She thought he really needed to just forgive and forget...

The transport came to a complete stop and the door slid open. The three An-Mara stepped out first, motioning for Niko and her friends to follow. As they filed out, the first thing Niko noticed was that the assembly of Meridian troops was armed to the teeth and had now surrounded the transport. They were obviously quite on edge, which made sense if the Meridians and An-Mara were embroiled in a war between each other. Every soldier looked ready to pull the trigger at any given second, which made her that much more nervous.

At the center of them all stood a recognizable figure. He was tall and imposing, and wore a harsh expression on his weathered face. Niko immediately recognized him as none other than

Magistrate Andersane, the prime Meridian official on Arhanda! Just seeing him in person had her completely starstruck. She was most surprised that he would be at this exchange. Their capture must have been a lot higher profile than she thought. He stepped forward two paces, arms behind his back.

"You are late," he said sternly. "The deal was that the hostages be returned no later than 06:00."

"We would convey a deep apology," Den-So offered with a bow. "We were delayed by… an incident."

"Incident or no, you have broken your terms. I have conferred with your general Ashal-Han and he assures me that your actions have jeopardized fragile peace."

That's not how it was at all! Niko protested in her mind. That little weasel Var Ashal-Han…

"If I may present case," Den-So started, "the senior commander was…"

Andersane sharply raised a hand to silence the argument.

"Seize these An-Mara oath-breakers," he commanded sharply.

Niko was still in the process of waking up, so it happened all so quickly. The three An-Mara were no doubt caught off guard, as well. They were fairly relaxed and at ease one second, and then in the next they were swept up by a dozen armed Meridian troops. They had no choice but to surrender without resistance.

A day ago, Niko would've loved to have seen this sight; the tables were completely turned from their capture yesterday morning. All three An-Mara were now kneeling on the ground, arms bound behind their backs, just as the seven Green Coast friends had been when they were taken. However, they had been treated well during their ordeal and Niko didn't wish any of them ill will. She preferred to have all this just put behind them.

Niko looked wide-eyed around to her friends. If none of them were going to speak up on the An-Mara's behalf, then maybe she should. She thought at the very least Magistrate Andersane should be aware that Var Ashal-Han could not be trusted. Before she could say anything, Mora Nant-Zern protested on her own behalf.

"That is not how the events transpired," she objected, her head bowed in respect. "If you would let us contact our commander, we would…"

A single shot of Andersane's pistol cut her plea short as she slumped to the ground.

A collective gasp rung out from Niko and her friends. Shol Vera-Nim and Den-So shifted their weight, as if they were both on the precipice of rushing forward to their friend, but they ultimately both stayed put. They were still bound and probably too shocked to make any sudden moves.

Panic raced through Niko once more. Her thoughts immediately strayed to Cryo's assertion that the Meridians were not to be trusted. She'd never before observed this level of unfairness perpetrated by the Meridians herself. This was new. She'd also never seen anyone die in front of her before. She instinctively took a step back and turned away, clutching the hand of whoever it was who stood beside her.

Magistrate Andersane paced forward to approach the remaining two An-Mara. Niko waited for him to say something, to make some sort of proclamation or even a demand. But when he walked over to Shol Vera-Nim and placed his weapon to his head without saying a word, time stopped for her all over again.

She didn't even hear the shot because anxiety was already ringing out of control in her ears. She was about to plead for Andersane to stop, but an arm crossed over in front of her chest.

"No," Ravenna whispered to her with a look that said all it needed to. Of all people, Ravenna had reason to hate these Meridians, but her eyes told Niko that this was not the time for action.

Den-So, on the other hand, leaped up to exact retribution for his fallen friends. He charged forward with an unintelligible wail and got no more than a fraction of a meter before the four soldiers behind him cut him down with their rifles.

———

13

Amalkyne

NIKO closed her eyes, the image of the three An-Mara lying lifeless on the ground still burned into her vision. These people had been... *nice*... to her. They didn't deserve this. *Why* would the Meridians do this? Why wouldn't they listen to what the An-Mara were going to tell them? Wouldn't *this*, of all things, jeopardize the peace??? She needed no more convincing — these Meridians were no longer the good guys in her mind that she once thought.

This realization brought even more fear to her mind. Would they be able to know that Niko knew who they really were? Did they have... what was it Ajane called it?... *psychic potential*? Andersane had no problems executing these An-Mara — would he also execute Niko and her friends? Her lower lip quivered and tears of desperation started to well in her eyes when Ravenna stepped in front of her and shoved her behind.

Ravenna then fell to her knees in front of all of them, drawing their attention. Niko was convinced that they would turn their weapons on Ravenna, but right before she turned away in case that happened, Ravenna raised her hands to the sky toward the Meridians. The gesture looked as if she was praising them with... *worship*? And *thanks*?

What the blazes?

"Oh, thank you! Thank you! Thank the heavens!" Ravenna exclaimed, her voice wavering in a pitch much higher than Niko had ever heard from her. And was she… *crying*? Niko didn't even know crying was in Ravenna's biology. "You are all just in time! They meant to kill us!"

She scampered forward and threw herself around the neck of the nearest soldier, burying her head into his chest with deep sobs that shook her body uncontrollably. Niko was beyond confused.

"Wait," Magistrate Andersane commanded dangerously, weapon still in hand. "Step back."

"I'm sorry! I'm sorry!" Ravenna wailed as she complied. Were those *real* tears? What in the blazes was happening?

"General Var Ashal-Han accused you seven for being in league with the An-Mara seeking to cause sabotage," Andersane stated. His voice boomed with thunderous authority. The man was quite intimidating.

"What?! No! No!" Ravenna pleaded, back on her knees. "That's how they made it look! They tried to set us up! I promise!"

"Explain," he requested.

"The man, Vashalarasharan, tried to stop them from taking us, but *that* one," she said as she pointed to the corpse of Den-So, "…that one beat up Kyler right in front of all of us and forced us to stay quiet. Tell them Kyler!"

Kyler looked surprised, but he went along with it.

"It's true. When I resisted them, that scum hit me and threatened to kill me in front of the others," he said as he spat on the ground in Den-So's direction for good effect.

It started to dawn on Niko what this was. This was an act. They were no doubt going to be interrogated upon their return from An-Mara custody, and this must be a ploy to convince the Meridians of their innocence. Especially if the Meridians were already swayed by Var Ashal-Han's sneaky manipulations.

"And Niko!" Ravenna sobbed, rising to her feet and staggering over to Niko. "Poor Niko is barely a teenager, and she was taken violently against her will and made to think that she was going to be tortured and executed the *entire* time. Just look at the poor thing. She's *still* in tears!"

Sure enough, Niko's tears were still streaking down her face. Little did they know her tears were from the fear of the Meridians, not for the reasons that Ravenna was spinning.

Wow, Niko thought. *She is GOOD.*

She'd never seen this side of Ravenna before. It was impressive, but also quite frightening. She thought she knew Ravenna well, but she started to realize she might not even know her at all...

"We just want to get to our families," Ravenna pleaded.

Niko was shocked to see the hard expression of Andersane had softened a little bit. Was he buying this? It *was* pretty convincing, Niko had to admit.

"We are glad that you are no longer in peril," he said. "But our question for you was why you weren't with the others from your hometown when we recalled everyone?"

"Oh! Well, we were probably out Sliding," Ravenna responded with complete naivety, puppy-dog eyes and all, as if Sliding was a perfectly obvious excuse to Andersane.

"Sliding?" he asked, eyes narrowing.

"Yes, of course," Ravenna said, shrugging her arms in innocence. "We always go Sliding the morning after the Anniversary celebrations."

"I do not know what that means," he said flatly.

One of Andersane's officers beside him spoke up.

"It's a sport, Magistrate," he said. "One that's becoming popular with the youngsters. Troublemakers, in particular."

Troublemakers? Niko thought indignantly. *Well excuse you, but I'm no troublemaker.*

"I see."

Andersane paused, raking over Ravenna with intense scrutiny. He was no doubt deliberating in his head about what to do with the Green Coast crew.

"Well, we don't want to put you through anymore trauma. Let's get you loaded up and back to your families," he proclaimed.

The emotional roller coaster had been raging inside Niko the entire past two days, but this was probably the most hopeful she had felt. With the Magistrate himself intending to escort them to their families, a huge weight lifted off her heart. She inhaled a deep breath of sweet air as if she hadn't taken a breath for several minutes, which maybe she hadn't.

"I would expect one as accomplished as Riesen Ryen to display much better judgment in the future," Andersane added, his eyes scanning over to Riesen in disapproval.

"I'm sorry, Magistrate," Riesen said with a bowed head. "It will not happen again."

"See that it won't," he said softly. "You have too bright a future ahead of you to waste on such foolishness as… *Sliding*."

Riesen stepped back and looked sideways at Ravenna with what Niko thought to be malice. How could he possibly be upset at her?? She just saved all of them. If not their lives, she at least saved them from who knows what manner of interrogations and unpleasantness. Niko just shook her head at her brother's stubbornness.

Blazes, Ravenna's a downright genius! Niko thought. Riesen should be grateful! Using Sliding to portray them as innocent youngsters who got themselves into trouble was brilliant. It was much better to be thought a troublemaker than an enemy to the Meridians.

"Let's load up, people!" Andersane shouted the command, before turning to the Green Coast friends. "I believe you are due to Green Valley?"

"Yes! We are!" Ravenna gushed. "Thank you so much for coming for us. Thank you so much!"

She raced forward to give him a hug for extra effect.

Andersane just patted her back, nodding regally as he looked ahead with a smug expression of pride. No doubt he thought himself powerful for saving these helpless youngsters from a nasty fate at the hands of these evil An-Mara.

"We will be traveling south to our station at Amalkyne," he said. "From there, we will see what we can do about transferring you to Green Valley."

Ravenna released the hug and beamed back at him. He smiled kindly back, as if he hadn't just murdered three unarmed people a few minutes ago.

"You seven will ride in this transport over this way," he said as he led them over to one of the vehicles. "It's not comfortable, but at least you aren't prisoners any longer."

"Magistrate?" Niko found the courage to ask, though her voice sounded rather meek. "How long is the journey to… ummm… what's the place we're going again?"

"Amalkyne," he repeated. "The new capital of Poste Territory as of yesterday after Groundheim was rightfully declared a hotbed of violent extremism. It is about seven hours by road."

———————

Niko had gone inside, but she was still sweating. She'd been to the Islands only recently, so she thought she knew what hot weather was. This heat was next-level, though. She originally wanted to go outside and lounge around in the sol-rays, seeing as though she'd been stuffed inside for the better part of the last several days, but she had quickly changed her mind after sitting out on the terrace for only a couple minutes.

Back inside their quarters, the machine-cooled room was the exact opposite. It made a winter day on the Green Coast feel like an oven in comparison. As soon as she stopped sweating, she'd probably go right back outside. Why couldn't the temperature be a happy medium? She just wanted to find one place where she could relax comfortably until they were due to leave for Green Valley.

Unfortunately, they weren't able to be transferred back home immediately and would have to spend the rest of the day in Amalkyne. Not that it was a bad place or anything. It was actually quite nice. Niko had no idea this place even existed. It was probably only slightly larger than Green Valley, but it reminded her of a miniature version of Sol City. Luxurious resorts lined the cliffs all the way down from the top, and the harbor in the middle boasted what normally would be a lively market. Of course, everything was on lockdown right now, but this place seemed very pretty. The only downside was the oppressive heat.

It was only just past 15:00 and they weren't leaving until early tomorrow morning, so they had some time to kill. Kyler, Kate, Riesen, Daren, and Cryo were still not back from going swimming in the bay. The Meridians had told them to stay in their quarters for the time being, but her friends argued that no one would care and that they weren't going far. Even if they weren't afraid to break the Meridians' rules, weren't they worried about an An-Mara attack or something? Thinking about the whole conflict between the Meridians and the An-Mara put Niko in no mood to celebrate.

It appeared that Ravenna shared Niko's somber sentiment at least. She'd been looking glum since even before their awful encounter this morning. She was still just sitting on the couch inside their temporary accommodations, wrapped in a thick Northern blanket and staring at the wall. She looked… off. Niko was still a little terrified of the way she flipped her personality on a switch earlier. She dared not talk to her yet, though it was more that she just didn't know the right thing to say to her. What *would* she even say after learning about what happened to her family?

Maybe I should have gone swimming with the others, Niko thought. The water sure would have felt good…

She just about had enough of the freezing indoor temperature and decided to head back into the heat to go watch her friends swimming from the terrace. Just as she opened the door, however, she became startled at the broken silence.

"Why is it like this?" she heard Ravenna croak from the couch.

"Hmm?" Niko asked, confused if the question was directed at her or not.

"Why is this world so completely messed up?" Ravenna asked, now making direct eye contact with Niko.

"Ummm," Niko stuttered. She had no answer. "I… I don't know. I mean, it's not all bad, right? We could be dead."

It was a half-joke, but neither Niko nor Ravenna so much as cracked a smile.

"Also, just think, we're gonna be back with our families and friends in a couple hours," Niko offered.

"Hmph, families." Ravenna snorted quietly.

Niko realized bringing up family to Ravenna was absolutely the worst thing she could've done.

"I'm sorry, I didn't mean to…" she started.

"It's fine. Don't worry about it," Ravenna said. "I've dealt with not having a family for most of my life."

"No, Ravenna, I feel really bad about what happened to them," Niko tried to console her. She was not the type of person that needed consolation, though, so there really was nothing that Niko could say to make things right.

"Yeah, well, they're gone and it's up to me to just live my life."

"Yeah, but you're allowed to be sad. I'm sorry."

"You know, I don't even get sad anymore," Ravenna said, deep in thought. "I can barely even picture them. It's like they're too far removed or something. How messed up is that?"

"I mean, I don't know."

Niko thought it was a little weird she wasn't even sad for her family anymore, but what was she supposed to say? It was absolutely awful with what happened to them. Heavens forbid if something like that ever happened to Niko — she didn't even know how she would react. She couldn't even imagine. Who was anyone to judge how Ravenna felt?

"But you're still alive," Niko added. "You get to carry on their legacy."

Ravenna shrugged with what looked like it might have been slight agreement. Or Niko was just hoping it was.

"And you need to live your life to the fullest. Come on, let's go outside," Niko urged.

For a second, she thought Ravenna would take the offer. She budged, but then paused and looked off to the distance at nothing in particular.

"I *almost* killed him today," Ravenna whispered.

Niko was at first confused, but then it dawned on her.

"Setten-Lo?" Niko asked.

Ravenna looked back and cocked her head to the side in confusion.

"Setten-Lo?" she echoed. "Oh, the An-Mara? No, not that clown. He's not worth my time."

"Wait, who are you talking about?" Niko was convinced Ravenna wanted to kill Setten-Lo ever since yesterday, but now she had no idea who she was talking about.

"Him," Ravenna replied, as if the answer was obvious.

Should I know who 'him' is? Niko wondered. She had no clue who this 'him' was, if it wasn't Setten-Lo. *Maybe Var Ashal-Han?*

"The Magistrate," Ravenna corrected after seeing Niko's thoroughly blank stare.

"Huh?? The Magistrate?? Why?" Niko did not have to accentuate her confusion or bewilderment.

"Because he killed my dad. And had my mom and sister killed."

After hearing about the rest of her family last night, Niko had wondered if her dad's killing also had something to do with the Meridians.

"I... uh...," Niko sputtered. "I... heard what happened to your dad. But I didn't know it was that. I'm so sorry."

Ravenna just shook her head and Niko looked away for a few long seconds.

"How do you know?" she finally asked. "I mean how do you know it was him?"

"It was him," Ravenna replied, as if that reason alone left no room for argument.

Niko wondered if there was any chance that it wasn't him. She didn't want it to be true. The Meridians *had* to be the good guys. It would turn her world upside down if this actually was the full truth. After what she'd witnessed this morning, though, it seemed like a distinct possibility. Andersane was a killer and there was no doubt about it.

"I'm really sorry, Ravenna," Niko offered. "I heard you and Cryo were there, but that's all I knew."

"We were," Ravenna said quietly. "And Jack."

"Jack?" Niko asked. She had never heard of a Jack before.

"Just a friend. We were all together when it happened."

"Oh," was all Niko could say. "Well, I'm really sorry. I don't mean to invade your business on any of this."

"It's okay, you're not," Ravenna replied. Her expression softened just a little.

Niko thought it was odd that Ravenna was opening up to her so much right now, but it wasn't unwelcome for her. Maybe Kate was right. If people bottled too much up, eventually it would need to get to the surface.

"Well, if it makes you feel any better," Niko said, "I hope the Magistrate gets what's coming to him."

She offered an encouraging smile, but Ravenna just looked down and shook her head.

"I almost did it," she said in a barely audible whisper.

She must have been talking about killing Magistrate Andersane today.

"How did you…" Niko started, not exactly sure how to phrase her question delicately. "You know… I mean… I mean you were like… *hugging* him. How did you do that if he was the one to kill your family?"

"I had to," Ravenna replied. "I had to for Cryo. I had to for all of you."

Niko reeled back. She had only ever known the Ravenna with steel emotions. This was something special, a different version of her that she'd never seen. Putting on an act and hugging a man that she wanted to kill must've been impossibly difficult for her. Niko had no idea what to say back to her.

"Well, I'm glad you didn't kill him, because they would've probably killed you," she said, willing more tears to stop before they surfaced. She didn't want to get all sappy. She knew Ravenna would not appreciate that.

"Wait, but how did he not recognize you?" Niko added. She just realized that if she and Cryo were there when Magistrate Andersane killed her father, how did he not recognize them today?

"He never saw us," Ravenna shrugged. "I don't even know if he knows we exist."

This was strange. Niko had always thought the Meridians kept super detailed databases of all Arhandan citizens. He would definitely know who she was.

"Don't they know everybody who exists?" Niko asked with a nervous laugh.

"The Meridians act like they know everything and everyone, but really we all just slip through their cracks," Ravenna said plainly. "They know Riesen because he is Mr. Famous-boy, but all the rest of us they couldn't give two blazes about. Their whole organization is such a joke. They act like their military is so organized, but they promote officers like handing out candy. Ajane always complains about how they've made a mockery of the true Meridian military."

"Hmmm, well, what about all the tests we take?" Niko asked. "And school and everything? And being Inducted?"

"Oh, they have the data, but they don't do anything of use with it. Arhandans do the bulk of the heavy lifting with everything. That's why our work with Ajane is so easy."

This didn't make sense to Niko. It felt as if her advancement through school was monitored so closely. Her parents knew *everything* about her progress and would receive reports weekly.

"I'd like to be able to slip through the cracks now that they're probably gonna be recruiting everyone for war," Niko said dryly.

"You never know, you just might."

It sounded like a joke, but it didn't look to Niko as if Ravenna was joking.

"Anyway, I've been a grouch long enough," Ravenna suddenly changed the subject. "I think I hear the others coming up now."

Niko wished she could ask Ravenna a few more questions — when would she ever be this open again? But Ravenna suddenly spang up off the couch with graceful quickness and walked over to the terrace outside. Her naturally multicolored hair glowed brilliantly through the sol-rays as she gazed across the bay.

"Oh yeah, there they are," Ravenna noted, pointing at the path down below.

A mass of superheated air, thick with salt, blasted Niko in the face as she followed over to join her at the edge. Sure enough, five figures were heading up the path leading to them now. They'd probably be up in no more than a minute or two.

"One other thing, Niko," Ravenna said, as the two were perched over the balcony looking out across the bay.

"Yes?"

"Don't ever forget that men will always underestimate a vulnerable woman. Don't overplay it, but you have that card for when you need it."

The Sol had finally just set, but it had only gotten hotter over the last couple of hours, however that was possible. Riesen, Kate, and Ravenna had been arguing to keep the door open, while Kyler wanted it shut. Niko would have preferred it shut also, but she didn't feel like butting into another argument, nor did she feel like publicly siding with Kyler. Cryo and Daren were always the neutral parties who didn't seem to care, and she would rather follow their example.

"Why don't we prop it open just a tiny bit?" Cryo suggested, probably fed up with the pointlessness of the dispute. "Like this."

He walked over to the door and opened it just enough to let some of the heat in, but not enough to blast the room.

"How hard was that?" Daren muttered from his seat. "Everybody happy?"

Nobody protested immediately, so it seemed like the crisis was averted.

"But it's the principle…" Kyler started after a few seconds.

"Kyler, deal with it," Cryo said. "I swear, nobody better argue over one more single thing tonight."

He was in rare form to lose patience like this. Although this would be the tamest blowup from anybody else, the fact that Cryo was starting to get snappy told everybody to just drop it. He never, ever got mad… but when he did, you knew that everyone had messed up.

The group sat quietly for several minutes, probably dwelling on the foolishness of their argument. After all, they just finished getting rescued from a harrowing several days together. Niko thought that should have bonded them to the point where they wouldn't ever need to argue about anything. But then again, these people all grew up together and knew how to get under each other's nerves.

"Soooo, who wants to talk about Ravenna putting on the plays earlier?" Kyler said, startling the silence.

"Not me," Ravenna said quickly, making it clear that was off limits. "And not anyone."

Just as he always did, Kyler did not take the hint.

"I thought she was gonna kiss Andersane!" he continued.

Niko thought the guy must have a death wish. Ravenna just looked calmly at him, but didn't move to strike.

Yet.

She was probably plotting the attack in her head.

"I was so glad that you asked me to join in!" he said excitedly to her. "I didn't even have to act when you talked about Den-So. I'm so glad that little chum got what was coming to him."

"They all definitely got what was coming to them," Riesen agreed. His expression was cold and held no emotion, which made Niko a little worried.

"They didn't deserve to die," Niko said, unable to hold back from joining the conversation any longer. She didn't want for it to be an argument, but she did not appreciate the way Den-So and the other An-Mara were being talked about. "I'm happy we're away from them, but I thought they treated us okay, all things considered. I think it's awful they're dead, and I'm more worried than ever being around these Meridians."

"You didn't experience it like we did," Kyler retorted. "You got the royal treatment from your little An-Mara friend."

"Are you kidding me, Kyler?" Niko raised her voice in defense. "It was your own damn fault you got beat up like you did. I would've done the same thing to you if I were them!"

"Nice to know who you consider your real friends to be," he jeered. "Maybe you should go back and become one of them."

"No, I just have a sense of humanity about me that *you* seem to lack," Niko fired back. "You're seriously telling me you are *glad* that those unarmed An-Mara were shot… and killed… right in front of us?!"

He just shrugged in response, which made Niko fume. How could he be so cold to not care? They were people and had lives, just like themselves. Even if they weren't allowed to smile or laugh, they still probably had families and friends. They were probably even friends of Kira-Tharn — who she now felt an affinity for. Thinking of her, Niko became even more emotional. What if it had been Kira-Tharn who was killed?

"Didn't we just talk about not arguing?" Kate interjected before Niko could respond.

Niko opened her mouth to say something nasty to Kate, but she thought twice before continuing. Kate was right, they needed to stop this. Why were they all fighting about everything??

"Hey, I'm not the one doing the arguing!" Kyler said, feigning innocence. "I was just defending myself."

"You are *always* the one doing the arguing, Kyler!" Ravenna backed Niko up. "Every single time you open your mouth."

"What?! I am *not*!" he responded as his voice cracked with a high pitch squeak.

"I am *not* arguing!" Kate imitated his squeak as she pounded her fists like a toddler.

The group broke off in laughter and that seemed to diffuse tensions for the moment. Even Kyler started laughing.

Niko was still quite heated, though. She was upset that some of them would be so callous to those people dying in front of them earlier, but nothing she was going to say right now was going to change their minds.

Their laughter trailed off as a knock sounded from the door.

"What the blazes now?" Kyler said as he got up to answer it.

When he opened the door, Niko froze as her gaze fell upon two Meridian soldiers. One or both of them must have been an officer because Kate and Daren hopped to their feet and stood at attention.

"Good evening," the officer greeted. "You may relax. I am Major Willer Brooks of Amalkyne command. How are things tonight?"

"Oh, you know," Kyler smirked, "just all getting along nice and dandy."

Major Brooks looked slightly confused, as any stranger would be at that comment.

"We're good, Major. Thank you," Kate responded, seizing control of the conversation from Kyler.

"Wonderful to hear. If you need anything else, please let us know."

"Yes, Major. Thank you very much."

"Of course. I come with some news that might be important for y'all, seeing as though your Uts are… gone."

Niko winced. She didn't feel like a prisoner anymore, but they were all in the dark without their Uts. Being without hers was torture for Niko, especially right now. The Meridians had notified her parents that she was okay, but she still hadn't been able to talk with them herself. Their Uts hadn't been replaced, nor were they given access to any machines that would keep them connected with what was going on in the world. It was quite frustrating.

Major Brooks continued. "Today at 16:07, we launched a retaliatory strike against An-Mara forces near Groundheim. At 18:10, they launched their own counterattack against several of our stations."

He paused before continuing.

"Green Valley was one of the stations they hit."

A collective gasp rang throughout the room, but Brooks quickly continued speaking.

"Don't worry, though — your families are accounted for. That was one of items of information that Magistrate Andersane first requested."

"What about the residents?!" Niko blurted out. The debilitating anxiety that flooded her system entirely too many times over the last couple days struck again. She was very grateful to hear her family was okay, but she knew so many people from Green Valley. Her Field teammates all lived there! She really hoped they were all okay.

"There were no civilian casualties as far as we know. Most of the damage was limited to the station itself. Unfortunately, several troops were killed. Furthermore, several prisoners were able to escape."

Okay, well that's good news, she thought to herself. Not for the troops that were killed, obviously. Or for the prisoners that escaped. She didn't want anyone to die. Seeing three people die was enough to last a lifetime for her. The *good news* was meant for the fact that no civilians were killed.

"What does this mean for our transfer back to Green Valley?" Riesen asked.

Major Brooks scanned his eyes over to Riesen with an expression on his face that Niko couldn't quite read. The other soldier with Brooks had the same look on his face. Perhaps they were upset that their teams got beat by Riesen in the Field World Championships recently? Niko only let that thought pass through her mind as a joke, but maybe there was some truth to it.

"You will not be transferred to Green Valley at this time," Brooks announced. "We were not convinced of Green Valley's security, nor anywhere in North Territory. We will be consolidating our power further south. That being said, your family is being transported to Amalkyne as we speak. They should arrive in the morning."

Niko looked around the room and saw her friends were all exchanging looks with each other, also. She was so glad that she would get to see her family in the morning, but she was worried what all this meant about the war. It seemed like things were escalating.

"Barring some further drastic news, I will leave you all to your quarters for the night," Brooks continued. "At 07:00 I will return with an update on the situation."

"Are you able to give us temporary Uts?" Kyler asked. "Or any machine of some kind?"

Of course Kyler had to ask about access to a machine, but Niko couldn't knock him for that. She, too, wanted some sort of access to a machine, even if it wasn't her Ut.

"I regret not," Brooks replied. "Seeing as though not all of you are adults, Magistrate Andersane requested that be a matter handled by your families upon your return."

"And what of those of us that are?" Kyler replied with attitude. He wasn't going to take no for an answer easily.

"I'm sorry, those were my orders from the Magistrate himself."

"Can we speak to *him* then?" Kyler kept pushing.

Niko was starting to feel uncomfortable at his insistence. She didn't want to make enemies with anyone at this point. She saw what the Meridians were capable of earlier. Kyler had made too many situations worse for no reason at all over the last few days; he needed to just stop.

"Unfortunately, he was required to return to the Islands for briefing," Brooks said, shaking his head but keeping remarkably calm.

Niko was glad to hear that man was nowhere near them anymore, but she thought she might've noticed Ravenna exhale in disappointment at that admission. Ravenna did want to kill the man after all…

"But he did ask for me to extend you his best wishes," the Major continued. "I would stay to answer all the questions you have, which I'm sure you have a lot of, but I fear I am needed elsewhere at the moment. Good night to you all."

Before Kyler could argue his point further, Brooks nodded to the group, clicked his heels, and whirled around. Neither he nor the other solider looked back as they disappeared into the dark across the courtyard. Kate and Daren stood at attention once more until the door shut.

"Sometimes I hate how cocky those Southerners act," Kyler commented. Niko was worried that Major Brooks wasn't even out of earshot, but she couldn't disagree. He definitely seemed like he was looking down his nose at the Northerners the entire time.

The Major was definitely not an actual Meridian, but almost certainly an officer from somewhere on South Continent. The Meridians had a very characteristic look and Brooks didn't have it. Most of the people in the Meridian military were in fact Arhandans, so that was nothing out of the ordinary.

"They think they're better than everyone just because they have cool-colored eyes," Kyler continued.

Ravenna shot him a look that told him to shut up. Her brilliant purple eyes were from her mother's Southern blood after all, and she took exception when anyone would speak poorly about her mother.

"Not that Southerners are bad…" Kyler tried to backtrack after seeing her frown. "Just this guy seemed cocky is all."

"He was probably just upset that we beat them in the World Championships," Kate said with a smirk.

"I thought the *same* thing!" Niko agreed with a laugh. "He definitely gave a look when he saw Riesen. Anybody else would be asking for an autograph, but this guy looked jealous."

"Eh," Riesen said. "I didn't get that. I thought he was alright."

"No way!" Niko laughed again. "He was definitely jealous."

"I don't know, kid," Riesen said. "I think y'all have been smoking the twig or something."

Did he really *just call me 'kid' again?* Niko's mood had been feeling better, but she was instantly thrust back down into crankiness with that errant 'kid' from her brother. Before she could say anything, Kyler interjected and made it a thousand times worse.

"Oh yeah, kid, that reminds me," he started, "did that one An-Mara friend of yours give you any hints that they were going to attack more stations?"

"Two things, Kyler..." Niko said, trying her very best to maintain her composure. "And Riesen. What did I ask you to *not* call me?"

"Oh shoot, Niko, my bad!" Kyler exclaimed facetiously. "I forgot you are renaming poor Nico over here. Errr what's his new name? Daren?"

"Kyler, just let her have it..." Daren spoke up. "She did ask all of us, and it makes sense. If I can call her Niko, then so can you."

Niko felt bad for Daren. She just kind of took over the name without asking him his feelings on the matter. If he actually did feel *renamed* by her, then that wouldn't be okay. Why did he have to be so nice about everything?! It would've made it so much easier if he had Kyler's attitude.

"Whatever you want, my man," Kyler said with a shrug and wide eyes. "You said you have a second thing, though ki... err Niko?"

Niko ignored the obvious bait.

"Yes, the 'An-Mara friend' you talk about has a name — *Kira-Tharn*," she asserted. "And just because I was talking to her the other day doesn't mean that she would tell me about An-Mara plans. She probably has no idea! You know as well as I that those either come from the Heads of Knowledge or that Var Ashal-Han chum. Stop trying to get a reaction from me. I'm seriously so over it."

"Okay, okay... Sheesh, I'm sorry!" he replied. He staggered backwards as if he'd been slapped, then slumped down in a chair on the opposite side of the room from Niko.

He turned toward Riesen for one last dig, speaking low, but loud enough for Niko to hear.

"Teenage girls, am I right?"

This was too much for Niko. She wouldn't give him the satisfaction of a blowup, but she also wasn't going to stick around and take this any longer. She'd argued with Kate, argued with Riesen, and argued with Kyler far too much over the last few days. *Everyone* had been doing way too much arguing. Enough was enough. It was time for bed.

14

The Proclamations

NIKO smiled. This was shaping up to be a good day. Or at least a better day than the ones she'd been having recently. For one, this was now several sleeps in a row where she didn't have that awful dream. Two, her parents were due in a few hours. And three, none of the Green Coast friends had argued this morning. Yet, at least. Granted, she hadn't spoken one word to Kyler, but she was still hopeful that the day was going to be a good one.

She was currently out on the terrace, basking in the morning sol-rays. It was still not even 07:00 yet, so she feared it might get unbearably hot later, but right now the temperature was perfect. Niko had just been thinking about her reunion with her parents and how badly she'd been wanting it, and she had planned out exactly what she'd say for the better part of the last hour.

She also resolved that she would rush over to Brandon and give him the biggest hug she could. She was even contemplating telling Kate about her crush on him. The last several days had given her a newfound boldness, a clarity that life was too short — if she never got the chance to see Brandon again, then she would have regretted at least not trying to pursue a relationship with him. Just as she made up her mind, Kate of all people opened the door to join her out on the balcony. Niko immediately chickened out.

"Good morning," her sister greeted as she smiled at Niko.

"Hey." Niko smiled back.

"Sleep well?" Kate asked.

"Yeah. No bad dreams."

"That's a plus."

"Sure is," Niko replied with full, affirmative expression. "How about you? How'd you sleep?"

"Great," Kate responded. "These beds are so comfortable."

"Really? I thought they were a bit too soft."

"Oh yeah, I forgot you like to sleep on rocks," Kate said, rolling her eyes.

"Pfft, I just don't like to sink down through all the covers and everything is all," Niko protested.

"Oh please, you don't weigh enough for that," Kate teased. "You would probably float if you tried to sleep on top of a cloud."

"I wish," Niko said. She thought that would be fun to try to sleep on the top of a cloud, to use its wisps as blankets and pillows. Although, she remembered her brother Keran imparting a thorough education of cloud densities upon her when she was younger, being the meteorology nerd that he was. 'It would be impossible to step onto a cloud,' he had said, destroying her fantasies when she was only five years old.

Kate draped an arm over her shoulder and stared out at the bay with her. It was so beautiful right now. Jagged cliffs tumbled down to the water's edge, their rugged white faces interrupted by elegant architecture that blended seamlessly into the landscape. The water below was still and glassy, the way Niko and other Sliders appreciated, and beyond the edge of the cliffs, the bay opened up into the greater Celean Sea, where to the southeast beyond the horizon lie the Islands.

"I didn't even know this city existed," Niko admitted to her sister. "I could definitely live here if it wasn't hot as blazes during the afternoons. It's not even summer yet!"

"This place is nice," Kate agreed. "I just wish we could visit when we weren't on lockdown."

The morning was so blissful that Niko almost forgot that they were still in the middle of a burgeoning war.

"Do you think we're in any danger here?" she asked her sister. "Like from an attack?"

"Well," Kate said, "they haven't attacked actual cities yet, from what I know. It's just been the stations they're attacking."

"How far is the station from here?" Niko asked. "Was that where we came in from with the Meridians?"

"Mmmm," Kate hummed, "I don't think so actually. I think the Amalkyne station is a ways out of town. Kinda by those mountains to the north."

"Oh, Niko responded. "Well, that's good. I hope that's true about them attacking stations only and not cities."

Kate must've sensed Niko's apprehension because she tugged her in tighter and rubbed the outside of her arm.

"We're gonna be fine, I promise" she said, her perfectly white teeth on display in that lovely smile that always infuriated the blazes out of Niko.

"Yeah, I know," Niko said as she returned the squeeze. "I just miss Mom and Dad so much. I know it's only been a few days, but still."

"They'll be here soon, don't worry."

"At this point, I just don't wanna get my hopes up too much," Niko laughed. "Every time I do, something takes a turn for the worst."

"Hah!" Kate responded. "Tell me about it."

Niko stopped laughing and turned to a more serious note.

"Do you think we're safe with these Meridians around?" she asked quietly. "They're not going anywhere, and it's just... I mean, is it really as bad as Cryo was saying?"

"Well," Kate hesitated, "not all Meridians are bad. We just have to remember all the good things that they do."

"Yeah, I guess," Niko acknowledged. "But the Magistrate scares me to death."

"I don't know, he's not all that bad, I don't think. Maybe from his perspective he thought those An-Mara were actually gonna kill us," Kate suggested. "We have to remember, that Var Ashal-Han guy kinda manipulated him. Now *that* guy scares me."

"True. But they were in the middle of trying to explain what happened, and he just... *shot* them."

Just saying the words suddenly brought tears to Niko's eyes. She tried to pretend that the bright sol-light from the east was to blame, but Kate knew her sister too well.

"Oh, Niko," she said as she enveloped her into a great bear hug.

"I'm so sorry you had to see that."

"And not only that, but he killed Ravenna's family too!"

Kate released the hug for a moment, which was uncharacteristic. She looked at Niko quizzically.

"The Magistrate, he killed Ravenna's parents," Niko repeated. "You knew that, right?"

"Ummm… no," Kate said. "Magistrate Andersane? Killed Ravenna's parents himself?"

"Yeah…" Niko squeaked sheepishly. "Pleeeeease don't tell anyone. I thought you already knew."

"No, I didn't know that. What did she tell you exactly?"

"Just that he killed her dad, and that he also had her mom and sister killed."

"How does she know it was him?"

"I don't know, she didn't tell me. I asked the same thing."

"Hmm, well that changes things if it's true."

Well, blazes, Niko thought. She didn't like how subdued her sister had become in an instant. She wished she had said nothing at all. Instead of incessant hugging, Kate was now just brooding and staring out at the water.

"Just please don't say anything?" Niko asked once more.

"I won't," Kate promised.

Niko wasn't too sure that she wouldn't, though. Kate had one of the biggest mouths she knew — like how she'd told Ajane about Niko's dreams without her permission. If she told anyone that Niko was blabbing about Ravenna's family…

Niko shuddered at the thought of Ravenna being upset with her. She would probably be the worst person imaginable to have on your bad side.

"We should get some breakfast," Niko scrambled to change the subject.

"Oh, yeah, good idea," Kate agreed. She took the bait, but still wasn't quite as cheery as she had been a minute ago. "I'm starving."

"I saw a bunch of stuff in the kitchen," Niko said as she stepped back inside the room.

Blazes was it freezing! Even the heavy aroma of salt that she could taste on the air seemed to vanish as she passed through the threshold.

"I'm feeling pancakes today," Kate said. It looked to Niko like her sister was doing her best to try to repair the mood. She probably thought that she needed to be strong for Niko's sake. She always would try to act like the mother field hen to Niko, which was ridiculous because she felt that Kate was probably emotionally weaker than she was.

"I agree, today is a pancake day," Niko concurred.

As the two sisters walked over to the kitchen to begin their hunt for pancake materials, a knock at the door startled them.

"Oh that's right, it's already 07:00! Major Brooks said he would be back," Kate said. "I'll get it."

She strode over to the door and opened it. It was not Major Brooks this time, but rather the soldier who was with him last night. Kate still saluted and stood at attention, so this must also have been some sort of officer.

"Ryen," he greeted curtly as he handed her some sort of object. He obviously knew who she was. "I was to deliver this. You all are ordered to tune into a broadcast from Major Brooks in five minutes. Wake the others up if they aren't already awake."

"Yes, sir," Kate said as she took the device.

He clicked his heels like Brooks had done last night and Kate stood at attention until he turned around and left. As soon as he had, she relaxed her posture and made a face.

"You know that guy?" Niko asked Kate.

"It's a long story," she said and rolled her eyes.

Niko perked up and shot her sister a questioning look.

"His name is Brody Felleter," Kate reluctantly continued, seeing that her sister would probably not have let it go at just that response. "*Second Officer* Brody Felleter."

The way she said 'second officer' with such sarcasm intrigued Niko more.

"Do tell."

"Pfft," Kate responded. "Just a guy that tried to make a move on Jen when we were new into the service. She declined and he made things very awkward for us. A truly awful person."

"Oh," Niko said. "What a jerk."

"Yep," Kate said. "I'll tell you more later, but we have to wake everyone up now or else we're going to be late for this broadcast, whatever it's about."

They set to work fetching everyone, and luckily the others were all awake already — everyone except for Kyler. Waking him up entailed Riesen dumping water on him, much to Niko's amusement.

Kyler deserved a little bit of misery today as far as she was concerned.

Upon receiving a full bucket of water to the face, he jumped up in a fury and had now proceeded to chase Riesen around the rooms. The water seemed to do the trick because he was very much awake now.

Niko worked with Cryo in the main room to set up the device that Brody Felleter had dropped off for them, which turned out to be a projector. Why wouldn't they just give them all Uts instead? Niko imagined it would've been just as easy... Plus, she was still very much longing to talk to her parents.

Just a few more hours. I can make it.

"Alright, let's get everyone out here," Cryo said.

As soon as Niko and Cryo finished setting the projector up, they flipped the 'on' switch and the projection lit up the nearby wall.

"Riesen! Kyler!" Niko yelled. "Where'd they go?"

Just then, she saw two blurs streak by outside the window. It appeared that Kyler was still chasing Riesen, his own bottle of water in his hand.

"Get those two clowns inside," Ravenna told Kate, who was standing at the door watching the spectacle.

"Hey! Boys! Get inside! Andersane's asking where you are!"

"Oh blazes!" Kyler squealed. He immediately stopped and raced back inside. "I'm here, I'm here!"

He looked around the room frantically, but upon realizing that Kate had duped him, he just made a face at her.

"You little cheat!"

"Awww poor Kyler," she responded with a grin, pretending to blow him a kiss. "But the broadcast is starting right now and you weren't about to come in."

"Okay, okay," he said, still out of breath from chasing Riesen all around. "But I get to throttle Riesen after the..."

"Kyler, shut up. No talking," Ravenna snapped.

Just as Kyler was about to squabble back at Ravenna, the shape of Major Brooks flickered onto the wall from the projector machine.

"A projector?!" Kyler exclaimed. "Why didn't you say we had one of those?!"

"We literally did, Kyler," Kate jumped in, rolling her eyes. "You were too busy playing tag with Riesen."

"We could totally hack this thing!" he said.

"Later, Kyler," Cryo said. "Let's just hear what they have to say."

"I could do it real quick! I promise! I think it can just…"

Kyler trailed off as Major Brooks started speaking.

"Good morning, Amalkyne," his voice said in a much warmer tone than he had displayed last night. "There is an important broadcast directly from Magistrate Andersane himself that everyone needs to hear. The information is crucial, so please listen carefully. If you miss anything, not to worry — it will be posted afterward. Thank you."

As the projection of Brooks faded, another familiar figure took his place. Niko thought that Magistrate Andersane looked intimidating even on a projection. His booming voice instantly brought back bad vibes from yesterday. She couldn't shake the image of those poor An-Mara lying dead on the floor. Even though he was kind to her and her friends, she did not like this man one bit.

"Citizens of Arhanda, there are some major updates in our current conflict with the An-Mara terrorists. I regret to announce that the peace that was restored between us two days ago has failed. Their aggressive surprise attacks against our stations… against *your* stations… gave us no choice but to declare war upon their ranks. We must defend our world against the relentless violence of these fanatics. They seek to threaten not only you, but your families, your homes, and your way of life. It tells us all that we need to know about them that they would choose to attack us on the heels of the most sacred of all our holidays."

So there it was. *Full war*.

This was going to be difficult for Niko to listen to. The way he spoke made it seem like the An-Mara were these vicious, mindless brutes, and that the Meridians were righteous defenders of the peace. If only the citizens could see how he murdered unarmed prisoners…

"In order to best accommodate our defenses," he continued, "there will need to be some concessions made by all of us. I thank you all in advance for what will need to be done for the collective good."

"The first proclamation, as had been discussed as a possibility, is that we must expand our position with numbers. All tenth years and above will be Inducted into the Meridian service immediately. Furthermore, all current Candidates can expect to be given station assignments by the afternoon. Not to worry, these new recruits will not be used for infantry, but instead for critical logistical tasks. In addition, all reserves will be called into active duty over the next forty-eight hours. All active-duty personnel currently on leave will also be recalled immediately."

Niko's heart froze once more. They had talked about this when they were on the transport to Fennemol Outpost, but this proclamation made it so final.

She was going to war.

It can't be any worse than it has already been the last couple days, though, she encouraged herself. *Can it?*

Surely she experienced the worst of it already, especially if she wasn't going to be on the front lines like he said. Her mind was drawn back to the dream, though. She had been *dying* in that dream, and it seemed to be during some sort of battle that was more and more likely to take place now that she was going to war. Before she could spend time pleading for her safety in her own mind, Andersane continued.

"The second proclamation is that martial law has been extended. Our previous final date has been eliminated. Seeing as though we don't know how long this conflict will last, we must remove that restriction. I am deeply regretful of this turn of events, and I sympathize with you all. Again, this is being done for the safety of all citizens. So far, this policy has protected everyone — no civilians have been killed thus far. We are all in this together, and together, we will defeat these terrorists!"

Niko thought she heard cheers from around the city. True, it was great that no civilians had been killed, but she thought that was more because of An-Mara choosing rather than the Meridians' martial law.

"The third proclamation is that all remote communication will unfortunately be limited to local access only. Transmissions will be restricted to within city limits of designated Territories municipalities. As of the end of this broadcast, all Uts have been reconfigured to reflect these restrictions. We cannot risk An-Mara terrorists intercepting valuable communications."

"We do apologize for all the hardships these proclamations cause for all peoples of the Territories. Our hope is that this conflict comes to a swift and peaceful end. In accordance with our continued transparency over all matters, we will be broadcasting daily at this same hour to keep everybody duly informed. The Territories of

Arhanda will be victorious!"

Well, wasn't that just the biggest load of propaganda I've ever seen, Niko thought as her head was left spinning. She couldn't believe that she heard *cheering* coming from outside. Loud cheering. As if the entire city was *happy* they were in this situation. She felt like she was living in a crazy dream.

Should I be happy with any of this?

There was no way. The An-Mara weren't savage terrorists. At least she didn't think they were. Most of them seemed nice and civil. Granted, she had no idea what their deep intentions were, but it didn't seem to her like they were after death and destruction.

"What the blazes has this world come to?" Ravenna muttered.

"This is ridiculous," Kate agreed. "Why are they suddenly making this a military state? The next step is we lose the right to representatives."

"They do have a point though," Riesen said. "I mean if our stations are just being attacked left and right, we need to stop this somehow. We can't just roll over and let them do whatever they want."

Nobody could argue with that. Why *were* the An-Mara attacking the stations? They were such a mystery to Niko. They seemed like straight shooters in some regards, but then in others she had no idea what went through their minds. Anybody that couldn't laugh probably shouldn't be entirely trusted. She could trust Kira-Tharn though, couldn't she? She would have loved to talk to her right about now.

Hopefully she's okay... Niko thought.

"Well, what's done is done for now," Cryo said. "Kyler, maybe you can mess with this thing and see if you can hack into the database. We still need to find out where Ajane is."

"Don't have to ask me twice," Kyler responded as he leapt forward to mess with the projector machine they'd been delivered. Just as he grabbed the device, though, the figure of Brooks was projected onto the wall once more, causing Kyler to jump backwards.

"Good morning. I take it you all saw the proclamations from the Magistrate?" he asked.

"Yes, we did, sir," Kate responded in salute, prompting Daren to also jump to attention.

"You may relax," he told them. "I have news about your

families."

Niko perked up. This is what she had been waiting for.

"Some of it is good news, but some of it is bad news unfortunately. Which would you prefer to hear first?"

"Good news," Kyler said without consulting the rest. Niko would have preferred to get the bad news out of the way.

"The good news is that there are two full planes from Green Valley arriving here in a few hours," Brooks declared. "We do not know who is on the planes, but we will be transporting you over to the airport in any case."

"And the bad news?" Riesen asked crossly. He was probably just as fed up as Niko was with all the bad news they'd been given over the last few days.

"One of the three planes bound for Amalkyne from Green Valley has been diverted to the Islands instead. It was a materials decision made by command. Those planes carried items that needed delivering at Sol City. Again, we do not know which families were on which plane."

"Really?" Kyler complained out loud. "Why is everything so disorganized?"

Major Brooks seemed to ignore Kyler's complaints and continued straight to the point with his message.

"We will be escorting you to the airport at 11:00, so be ready to leave by then, please. Any questions?"

"No, sir," Kate saluted before Kyler could make any other smart remarks.

"Good, we will see you then," he said as the transmission immediately faded.

The Green Coast crew was left looking at each other silently. Niko had been punched in the gut with bad news too many times. Her family had *better* be at the airport today. She didn't know if she could deal with anymore nonsense. There was a two-thirds chance that they'd be there.

Better than half! They'd be there. They *had* to be there.

———————

Unlike during their ride to Amalkyne, when they had traveled together on one large transport, the Green Coast friends were split into three smaller groups for the drive to the airport. *Second Officer* Brody Felleter was driving the car Niko was in, and she was beginning to see exactly why Kate did not like him.

He'd made it plenty clear that he was an officer in the Meridian service and that Niko must treat him with respect. She hadn't even been Inducted yet, but since the proclamations declared that she would be Inducted soon, he demanded that she salute him and address him as either 'sir' or 'second officer'. What a clown this guy was…

Luckily, Cryo was there with her. Apparently, he had also risen to officer status when he was with the service. She never knew that about him, although it wasn't exactly surprising to her since he was always so humble and quiet. The great part about it was that Cryo's ranking had technically been higher than Felleter's, so when Felleter tried pulling rank on Niko, Cryo pulled it on him in return.

"You are no longer active in the service, so I don't need to exercise proper decorum in this situation," Felleter argued.

"That's fair," Cryo admitted. "Anyone not currently sworn into the service should be exempt from that decorum."

"Exactly," Felleter said triumphantly, as if he had won some duel of wits with Cryo.

"So, for example, if there was a tenth year who hasn't been sworn in yet," Cryo said, gesturing toward Niko, "they would not need to salute any officer until they are."

"Yes… I mean… no… uhhhh…" Felleter stumbled over his words. He realized Cryo had him there.

How fragile is this guy's ego? Niko wondered amazedly. He needed a sixteen-year-old to salute him properly, but then refused to salute someone else with the same logic. Niko couldn't wait to trash-talk this guy with Kate later.

"She's going to have to learn sooner or later, so she might as well get started now," Felleter defended his position. "You could say that I am helping her."

"I think she has plenty on her mind right now," Cryo said. "I would imagine she'd want to try to push all that stuff back until it's forced upon her."

Niko nodded her head and mouthed a silent 'thank you' to Cryo.

"Hmph. In any case, what I was saying," Felleter said as he changed the subject back to what he was talking about before, "was that you must wait until after the passengers are processed through the airport to greet your families. Security is a little heightened right now, which goes without explaining."

Neither Cryo nor Niko responded. This had already been explained to them in detail by Major Brooks. Felleter was just talking now because he liked to hear his own voice. He waited for confirmation of some sort from either of them, and got visibly agitated when it never came. Niko didn't care though. Her mind had already wandered back to her parents.

She'd been thinking a lot about them this whole morning and was starting to get butterflies in her stomach. Knowing her luck, her parents would probably be on the flight that got diverted to the Islands. Along with her friends. And Brandon.

Speaking of Brandon, she had already planned out what she was going to say to him when she saw him. Nothing too over-the-top gushy. She didn't want to appear as some desperate, lovesick little girl. She wanted to play it cool, but still be affectionate nonetheless. She'd already chickened out once today, though, when it came to telling her sister about her crush on him. She hoped she would have the courage to do so at some point.

As the car pulled off into the turnout for the airport, Niko was all too thankful that the rest of the drive had been completed in silence. It wasn't a long drive — maybe only five minutes — but she still let her mind wander anyway. Her thoughts had just shifted to Kira-Tharn and the An-Mara when Felleter pulled their car through a security checkpoint. The guards there saw the three vehicles in the convoy and let them pass into the plaza beyond.

The plaza square was wide and open, probably a few hundred meters across, with some white geometric sculpture that was the centerpiece for a fountain in the middle of the square. The airport buildings had the same architectural scheme, which she noticed to be the same theme common to much of the city they had just driven through. She really did like Amalkyne's style.

They drove past the center of the plaza and toward a spot designated for military personnel. As soon as they parked, Niko did not wait for permission and hopped out of the car. It was starting to get hot, and she much preferred the machine-cooled climate inside the car, but she wasn't about to wait for Felleter to make some grand decree about how she had to follow behind him, or any other drivel of the like. She immediately walked over to her sister.

"Hey, ki… Niko," Kate said, catching her near slip-up and putting up her hands in apology. "I'm sorry, I'm sorry! I've been trying to remember, I promise!"

Niko just smirked and play punched her sister in her arm. She wasn't about to start drama. Not right now.

"So what are the odds you think Mom and Dad are on these two flights?" she asked.

"Two-thirds, give or take," Kate responded sarcastically.

"Well I know *that*." Niko rolled her eyes. "I guess we'll find out in a few minutes."

"GREEEEEN COOOOOAST!" Their quiet side conversation was startled by a thunderous bellow. That could only have been one person that Niko knew, although his characteristic long, blonde hair had been cut shorter, revealing an uncanny resemblance to Riesen.

"Tyson!" Niko never knew that she could be so excited to see that guy. "And Jen Jen!"

The two were standing over by the entrance holding hands. Niko was happy they were back together; she always thought they were so cute. Tyson was sometimes annoying, but she had to admit that he did have a good heart, at least.

Niko rushed over to greet them, but Kate was faster. She ran over and enveloped both of them into a group hug.

"You guys had quite the weekend, huh?" Tyson said. "That's what happens when you let Cryo lead the way."

"Thank you for the vote of confidence, brother," Cryo said dryly, as the friends hand clapped and hugged.

"So what happened to you guys?!" Tyson asked. "We heard some crazy stories."

Niko stepped back, giving the older friends space to reconnect. Her gaze drifted past them as she searched for her parents, but the crowd made it nearly impossible to pick out any familiar faces. She tried to listen to the lady on the loudspeaker, but the hundreds of people that bustled about in front of the exit doors caused too much of a racket to distinguish what was being announced. Felleter had warned them they might have to wait up to an hour, yet it seemed like all the passengers had already finished whatever processing was required.

She did notice a couple members of her Field team, which made her heart leap a little bit. She would've gone over to talk to them if she wasn't intent on finding her parents first. There was plenty of time later in the day to connect with some of her friends. They didn't notice her from afar anyway, so she just stayed quiet and kept searching for her parents.

"Niko!" she heard Kate call to her.

"Yeah?"

"Jen says Mom and Dad weren't on their flight, but she's not sure if they were on the other one that came here, or the one that got sent to the Islands. Nobody can call them because of the stupid communications block they just enacted."

"Hey, kid," Jen greeted Niko with a smile and a hug. She obviously hadn't been around for all the name drama over the last several days, so Niko would give her a pass.

"Hey," she responded warmly. It was nice to see her again.

"She's going strictly by Niko now," Kate laughed. She probably felt guilty for slipping on her name a few minutes ago. "And we're calling Nico *Daren*. Long story."

"Oh?" Jen said, tilting her head.

"Wait, so you haven't been able to reach my parents?" Niko asked Jen, not wanting to make a big deal over the 'Niko' versus 'kid' situation.

"No. Unfortunately not."

"If we can't reach them, doesn't that mean they aren't within the city limits?" Niko asked, a wave of disappointment threatening to wash over her.

"Oh, yeah…" Kate ruminated.

"I'm sorry," Jen said apologetically. "Those are cute shorts, though, Niko."

"Oh, thanks," she responded as she struck a pose with hands on hips. Jen's were probably cuter than hers, though. Or she made them look better, which she always did. "The perks of Amalkyne hospitality. I like yours, too."

It was hard to hide the letdown from her voice. For several days, all she wanted was to see her parents again, but the homesickness kept perpetuating with no end in sight. When would her parents be redirected back to Amalkyne with the rest of them? And when would they actually get to go back to Green Coast to just live their lives?

"Maybe they're here and communications just aren't working

at the airport?" Kate suggested. It was a possibility, but Niko was exhausted from having her hopes tugged all over the place.

"Hmm, maybe. Where are the city limits anyway?" Niko asked. "Do they end right at the airport?"

"I'm not sure, to be honest," Kate replied.

"Can you try them again, Jen?" Niko asked. "We don't have Uts anymore."

"Sure."

Jen tried contacting the Ryens again, but to no avail. Niko had resigned herself to the fact that she might not be seeing her parents today after all. She tried her best to put on a cheerful front for her sister and Jen, but she really just wanted to be by herself right now. She started to cave in on her own thoughts, and barely noticed that the rest of the Jenaeis had shown up.

Even seeing Brandon off to the side talking with Riesen didn't lift her spirits like it should have. She no longer wanted to see him now that she wasn't feeling her best. She had spent so much time imagining their reunion, but now, the weight of her disappointment made it impossible to think about anything else.

"Oh, Niko!" a friendly voice said from behind her.

"Hi Lizzy," she returned the greeting, faking her best smile. "Hi Roger."

She gave both the Jenaei parents a warm hug, praying that the despondency on her face was not as visible as she thought it might be.

"We were so worried about you!" Lizzy said as she brushed her long, blonde hair out of her face. She was a spitting image of Jen, only older. "Are you all alright?"

"Yes," Niko responded, forcing a laugh as Lizzy tenderly held her face in her hands like a worried mother would do. She was a sort of second mom to Niko, so it did give her a little bit of comfort. "It was stressful at times, but yes, we are okay!"

"Your parents have been worried to death," Lizzy said. "They are going to be over the moons when they see you."

"Did you happen to see which plane they got onto by any chance?" Niko asked, still hopeful there was a small chance they'd arrive today.

"We didn't," Roger replied, shaking his head. "I think they said they were going to be traveling with the Piersons and the Amibars, though."

"I tried contacting them, but nothing is going through," Jen said.

"Yeah, since they barred communications outside of city limits now, we're thinking they might be on the plane that went to Sol City," Kate added.

"Kyler and Daren can't get ahold of their families either," Tyson chipped in.

"Hmm, that sounds like they're probably headed to Sol City, then," Roger confirmed. "If there's anything you girls need until they get here, we got you covered."

"Thank you," the Ryen sisters said together. Niko was devastated that her parents weren't there, but she was so glad that at least the Jenaeis were.

"Now where did Brandon go off to? Did he find Riesen?" Lizzy asked no one in particular as she scanned around to find her son. "Oh, there they are. Brandon! Riesen!"

Niko looked over toward the two boys, who now started to walk over toward their group. Brandon sure was nice to look at…

Except…

Who is that girl? Niko thought in alarm.

Brandon had his arm draped around some girl, and she was holding *his* arm with *hers*. Niko did not recognize her at all. She was very pretty, and from the way her hair was unnaturally curled and glossed, Niko figured she must have spent an inordinate amount of time dolling herself up. This was not good. Not good at all.

Just as Riesen, Brandon, and this new girl made their way to where the group had assembled, the girl stood up on her tip toes, nuzzled her nose up to Brandon's, and kissed him.

Niko's heart froze.

She couldn't believe what she was seeing. It was as if someone had stabbed her in the gut with an icy, jagged blade and twisted it. She was already feeling miserable from the fact that her parents were not here; now she was entirely broken. She knew this was not a dream, but it felt almost as cruel as the one where she was dying on the bridge.

This is just my life now. Just when it can't get worse, it does…

Niko clenched her jaw to hide the immense devastation from her face. She knew that somehow this was her fault. A thousand reasons why this was happening ran through her head: she wasn't pretty enough, she wasn't smart enough, she wasn't social enough, she wasn't confident enough, she waited too long to tell someone… the list went on and on and on.

The Jenaeis were in the middle of greeting Riesen, but Lizzy must have noticed Niko staring with her mouth wide open because she made a point to introduce Niko to this newcomer.

"Niko!" she said. "You remember Brynne, right?"

Brynne? Brynne Delilah?? Niko was aghast. *This was Brynne!?*

She looked completely different than Niko remembered. Brynne Delilah had been on her Field team when she was younger, but she hadn't seen the girl in several years since her family had moved away from the Green Coast. Niko never got along with her, nor did anyone, really. That girl had the most rotten attitude ever since Niko had known her. She was more or less the reason why Niko switched teams to play with the girls from Green Valley. One time, during an awards ceremony for Niko's team, Brynne threw a massive tantrum because she didn't get the award she wanted. At least the other girls on Niko's team knew her true colors. Brandon hadn't seemed to receive the memo, though.

"Hey, kid," Brynne said without completely making eye contact. She was still too busy laying smooches onto Brandon's cheek.

"Hey Brynne," Niko greeted back in as polite a manner as she could. "Been a long time."

She was *not* about to get into a fight with Brynne right now over her name. She was above the antics. But who did this girl think she was to call her '*kid*'?! She was literally the same exact age as Niko. And what the *blazes* was Brandon doing with her!? It was one thing if she was never able to be with Brandon herself, but for heaven's sake, why would he ever get together with Brynne?! How disappointing.

"Brynne and Brandon reconnected a few weeks ago, and now we're all here together in Amalkyne!" Lizzy beamed to Niko.

Niko returned the best smile she could. She couldn't fault Lizzy — she was super nice to everyone, just like Jen was. But blazes was it hard to fake happiness right now. She just wanted to curl into a ball and sleep for the next month. As long as she didn't have to dream, that is.

"Where are Mom and Dad?" Niko heard Riesen ask Kate.

"They aren't coming," Niko jumped into the conversation

bluntly. At least her parents not being here was a good enough excuse for her to appear upset, which she very much was at this point.

"Yeah, we're pretty sure their plane was the one that got sent to Sol City," Kate said.

"Oh," Riesen replied. He looked as if he couldn't care less. She knew deep down that he loved their parents just as much as she did, but his cool cucumber attitude really irked her right now.

Niko wished she could just relax like Riesen, but nothing was going to calm her down at this point. She needed to get out of here. She needed to just find somewhere alone and lie down. The airport was still bustling with hundreds of people, so this was not the environment she wanted. She sauntered a couple of meters off to the side, pretending to move so she could sit in the shade.

"We'll wait here until it clears out a little, but if the Ryens, Amibars, and Piersons aren't coming, then we should probably head over to where we are staying," Roger said to the group. "It's very hot out."

"Yeah, that sounds like a plan," Lizzy agreed. "Where're the shuttles at?"

"Oh, they said they'd be across from here," Kate answered, pointing to the opposite end of the plaza from where they were now. A few shuttles were clearly visible among the throng of people hurrying about. "Over there."

"Oh, I see them. Do some of us want to start heading over that way now?" Lizzy suggested as she bent down to pick up her luggage.

"I'll take that," Tyson offered as he swooped up her bags.

"Oh, you're a sweetheart, Tyson," Lizzy beamed at him.

What a complete goody-goody, Niko thought in irritation.

"Yeah, some of you head over now so you can get us all a shuttle," Roger said.

"Are we all staying near each other?" Brandon asked the group.

"Yes," Ravenna replied. She, Cryo, Daren, and Kyler had appeared out of nowhere. They must've been checking the arrivals kiosk.

"Oh, hey guys," Brandon said. "Are the places nice?"

"Oh, yeah," Kyler responded with enthusiasm. "Dude, they have these balconies that open out into the bay! And the water is blazes warm."

"Sweeeeet," Brandon remarked. He looked over at Brynne. "Did you want to hang out with us today, babe?"

Babe?? UGH!! Niko screamed internally. She thought she might vomit right there on the spot.

"I'm not sure if today is a day for hanging out," Roger said. "Y'all heard the proclamations from earlier. It would probably be best just to get to our accommodations in case they need to do a check-in for all the arrivals."

There was a murmur of assent from everyone around.

"You're always welcome to spend time with us, Brynne," he added with a smile. "But because of the proclamations, you might want to be with your family for today."

Thank the heavens, Niko thought. She would not have been able to stand being in that girl's presence for the rest of the day.

"Oh, you're absolutely right, Mr. Jenaei," she gushed.

"No, no," Roger laughed. "I've told you so many times, call me Roger!"

"Right, I'm sorry, Roger," she fell about with the fakest laugh Niko had ever heard.

Niko turned away from the group because there was no way she could control the involuntary eyeroll that ensued.

"Alright, well I'm gonna head off to my family, then. Good to see everyone!"

Brynne went around giving everyone farewell hugs, and Niko was fortunate to be far enough off to the side from the group that she was skipped over. She would've much rather given Brynne a swift shove to the ground instead of a hug, but she was glad enough to do neither.

"Bye, Sweety-B. Love you," she said as she pulled Brandon in for an exceptionally tight hug and a kiss.

Sweety-B!? Are you kidding me!?

As soon as she walked away, Kyler wasted no time to heckle Brandon. It was in that guy's DNA to make a mockery of everything.

"Do you want me to get your bags, Sweety-B?" Kyler teased.

For once in her life, she was grateful for Kyler's ruthless attitude. It was only right that Brandon should feel embarrassment for taking up with *that* girl.

"Yes please," Brandon joked back. "Thank you."

"Aww, too late, I'm sorry. Too far away now. Love you, though, Sweety-B."

Kyler playfully pretended to kiss Brandon, then scampered over to where Tyson was heading with a bunch of luggage. Everyone just laughed at the exchange, even the Jenaei parents. Niko enjoyed the moment of justice, but she was in no mood to laugh with the others. She was so disappointed on so many levels, and her mood was completely shot. She just sat there in silence, lost in thought, as everyone got up to follow Tyson and Kyler over to the shuttles.

"You okay?" Cryo asked after everyone else had already walked ahead, interrupting her from her thoughts.

"Oh, yeah, sorry. Just wish my parents would have been here, y'know?"

Cryo nodded, offering her a sympathetic smile and a light pat on the shoulder. Unlike the majority of Green Coasters, he wasn't particularly affectionate, so even that small gesture meant a lot to Niko. It was nice that he made the effort to stop for her, but the thing Niko was most grateful for was that he didn't press her to open up like Kate would have. He just let her know that someone cared and then gave her space.

Thank the heavens for people like Cryo, she thought.

She took a deep breath, gathered her composure, and went to follow Cryo over toward the others. But as soon as she rose to her feet, a booming voice echoed across the open square.

"Attention all citizens of Amalkyne. In accordance with the first proclamation declared this morning, all active-duty personnel currently on leave are recalled immediately. Please report to Amalkyne Airport by 14:00. From there, you will be transported to the Meridian Complex at the Islands. All persons affected have been notified through Uts."

Wonderful, Niko thought. *Just wonderful.*

This announcement meant that Kate, Daren, and Jen would be leaving in a couple hours. Bad news had been chewing her up and spitting her out ever since she got back from her trip to Sol City. She had been on top of the world last week, traveling the world and watching her brother win the Field World Championships — now, she had witnessed murders, been kidnapped, held prisoner, and was on the verge of being sent to war.

She shuffled over to wait with the others, sulking in her sour mood. Riesen and Brandon seemed as chipper as ever, laughing animatedly about something, but Kate and Daren were talking to each other solemnly, and Jen had her head buried in Tyson's chest.

It was obviously starting to dawn on them that they were being summoned for war.

Niko suddenly felt very scared for them. During Andersane's proclamations earlier this morning, he had assured everyone that the younger people being Inducted into the service wouldn't be seeing the front lines. That didn't offer any protections for people like Kate, Daren, or Jen, though, since they were already in active Meridian duty. Would they be sent into combat??

A stray thought struck Niko about the religions of the peoples prior to the Arrival. Of course, religions were abolished and banned since they were deemed to be major underlying culprits behind the world wars, but she remembered learning that in these religions, people would pray to certain deities. If there were actually deities out there, she thought she might pray to them now to keep all of her friends and family safe. She needed something — anything — bigger than herself to scoop her out of this calamity.

As Roger hailed a transport and gathered the group to board, Niko suddenly found it very difficult to breathe. Her legs were still sore from the other day, but her lungs had been fine for the most part. What was happening right now?? After a few seconds, it felt like her heart was racing and the world was closing in around her.

Blazes, she thought. *Can this please STOP!?*

She tried to will herself to breathe normally, but it felt like the more she thought about it, the worse it got. Her chest tightened, and each breath felt too short. The noises around her faded, leaving only the pounding of her own heartbeat in her ears. She started to cry, which was the only other sound that registered in her brain.

Whyyyyy!? This is soooo stupid!

She felt an arm wrap around her, but she didn't know or care whose it was. Her sobs were now compounded with shortness of breath, and the resulting feedback loop was making the whole thing way worse. Trying to breathe was all that was on her mind now. What the actual blazes was going on???

"It's okay, Niko," she heard Kate repeating. She didn't know how long it had been going on for, but she suspected it was probably longer than she thought, although she couldn't really think rationally about anything. Time seemed like something so far away. After what seemed like at least several minutes, she thought that maybe whatever was happening was easing up. As soon as she caught a small break, however, she choked on more tears, sending her back into a breathless frenzy.

This was the most embarrassing thing that had ever happened to her. She still had her eyes closed, but she could just *feel* all the stares on her. There were so many people that must've been watching. Most of her friends. All of her role models. Everyone except her parents.

My parents.

Thinking of them only made her fit worse, and she spiraled further into her misery. She tried taking deep breaths, but it was noisy, ugly, and difficult. Kate's hand streaking through her hair was the only thing that offered her any relief from the onslaught.

"Shhhhhh," she heard her sister attempting to soothe her. She didn't know when she had become draped over Kate's lap, but she didn't care. She buried herself deeper into her sister's embrace and tried to ride out whatever this was.

She tried taking deep breaths in a rhythm, forming a sort of song to them. After settling to that rhythm for what seemed like an eternity, she realized that whatever this was might be finally fading away. She still had moments where her control would waver, but eventually she did rejoin reality on planet Arhanda.

"Oh the blazes," she whispered to Kate in oscillation. "I don't even know what happened. This is so embarrassing."

"Shhhh," Kate continued to soothe. "It's okay, Niko. This has been a lot for you."

When she finally opened her eyes, she saw her sister aggressively mouthing some words to everyone else, and they all turned around. Even Kyler remained silent.

You know it's bad when even Kyler won't talk trash, she laughed to herself.

A few minutes ago, she would have been absolutely mortified if Brandon were to ever see her like this, but now she could care less. He could go hang out with however many Brynnes his heart desired for all she cared. Thinking about that turn of events almost sent her back into turmoil, but luckily she held onto sanity by a thread and remained calm.

"I'm so sorry, I'm so sorry," she kept whispering through labored breaths to Kate. "I don't even know what happened."

"It's okay," Kate continued to soothe. "That was a panic attack, girl. I don't blame you. I feel the same way."

So that's what a panic attack feels like. She'd always heard of them, but had never experienced anything like this.

"Yeah, but you're not a blubbering mess in front of all your friends and everybody," Niko replied with strenuous huffs.

"Nobody thinks less of you, Niko," Kate said with a laugh. "I promise. I've been there before."

"You have? When?" Niko asked. She found it hard to believe that Kate had ever lost it like this.

"A couple years ago," Kate answered. "Mom had to calm me down. It was after Grandma died, and that combined with school being really stressful was just too much. She said that you gotta let it out every now and then. You can't bottle it up forever."

Kate was right — she shouldn't just be bottling up her feelings. Maybe this was the release that she needed. She was still breathing heavily, and her nose was now completely stuffed up, but she somehow felt a little better knowing this had also happened to Kate.

She guessed that she looked absolutely horrendous, though. Her face was completely flushed, and she could feel the sticky remnants of tears that had been streaming down her face. She felt bad that she'd dumped them all into Kate's lap, but that was Kate's choice.

Bless her soul, Niko thanked her imaginary deity. That made her laugh out loud.

She then used her own shirt to wipe away the remaining dampness on her face and sat up. Her head spun and her vision became spotted when she did, so she squeezed her eyes shut once more.

"You okay, honey?" she heard Lizzy say as she felt another set of arms close in around her.

"Yes, I'm so sorry!" Niko stammered, her voice still a little shaky. "I don't know why this just came over me all of a sudden."

That wasn't entirely true because she could name ten reasons in an instant, but it was true in the sense that she didn't know why she collapsed into a full-blown panic attack.

"Your mom and dad are coming soon, I'm sure," she coaxed. "We're here for whatever you need until they get here."

"Thank you," Niko replied.

New tears queued their way to the surface, but it didn't feel like she was melting back down. These were probably just the result of Lizzy being so sweet.

"We're almost back to where we're staying," Lizzy said.

"We'll get you the most comfortable bed and you can just lie down and close your eyes for a while."

Blazes!

She hadn't even realized that they'd boarded one of the shuttles, let alone noticed that they'd been moving. She would be all too happy to never experience another panic attack ever again.

"Thank you," Niko said to Lizzy. "That would be nice."

CHAPTER FIFTEEN

15

No Ordinary Dream

A bright yellow hue flooded her vision. Blinking her eyes was about all she could do. There was a dusty tinge to the atmosphere, but that did little to block out the blinding sol-light that beat down on the sandy rocks all around her. She had her goggles with her, but what happened to them?? It was so hard to see, even with a squint. She turned to look in the other direction, but moving was so difficult. It was as if her body was glued to the ground she was lying on.

Wait.

Why *was* she lying down right now? She took a deep breath before trying to stand up, but that was only accompanied by a sharp pain in her lungs.

NO... she demanded. *This is a dream and I WILL wake up.*

She looked around, but she remained in her surroundings.

For the love of Arhanda, please wake up.

She closed her eyes and thought hard about something she knew to be real. Her home. Her room. Her bed. She opened her eyes once more, but she remained on that heavens-forsaken bridge.

This was different than her last dream, though. She was so... *aware*. She knew this was a dream. She almost had control over her actions, although she still couldn't get up, and it still hurt to breathe.

She looked down and saw that same piece of metal protruding from her chest.

Damn!

She leaned her head back in frustration and didn't move a muscle. What good was it to fight against this dream? She'd already experienced it several times over now; she might as well just ride it out until she woke up. This hurt like the blazes, though!

As she tried leaning to the side, she could've sworn that she heard a voice on the wind around her. She even thought she saw an image of a robed figure standing in front of her, blurry as it was.

What's going on now? she wondered, slightly frustrated. This was new.

"Niko."

Who said that?

"Niko, try to listen."

She couldn't respond out loud because she was in too much pain. What did this new voice expect from her?

"You can hear me, Niko."

Yes, I can, she thought irritably, *but I'm a little busy DYING right at the moment.*

"Focus on me."

This was ridiculous. She couldn't even breathe — how was she supposed to focus on anything besides the pain??

Who am I even talking to? An imaginary blur in a blazes-accursed dream?

"You can hear me, Niko."

WHERE ARE YOU? I CAN'T EVEN SEE YOU. I CAN'T SEE ANYTHING.

"Focus on me, Niko."

This was actually starting to trigger Niko considerably. She was in so much pain, couldn't see, couldn't move, and couldn't talk. Seriously, what did this voice expect from her?

"Niko."

WHAT???

"Try to focus on my voice, Niko."

"BLAZES! WHAT DO YOU WANT!?" she screamed.

She... *screamed*? How?

As soon as the realization hit her, she found herself not on the bridge, but up on the cliffs by the Farm on a clear Green Coast night. She wasn't lying down anymore; she was standing, and she could move! She looked down and saw no protruding object from her abdomen. There was no blood, no dust, and no deafening explosions. She knew that the cold of night should have chilled her, but this felt strange, like there was no temperature. The last time she'd been here, she was talking to Ajane, in the flesh.

Ajane. That's who was standing in front of her now.

"Ajane?" Niko asked, finding her voice yet again.

"Very good!" Ajane congratulated her in that pleasant tone that she'd almost forgotten about.

"How? How is this possible?" she asked. "I feel like I'm still in a dream."

"You are!" Ajane responded. She seemed so proud of Niko.

"I don't get it. Can I just wake up already?"

Ajane chuckled softly. "You are in a dream and I can communicate with you quite clearly. This is very impressive!"

Niko didn't respond, but instead walked over to the path that led up to John Maksolhoff's house. She was in a dream. She could do whatever she wanted and it wouldn't matter in real life, right? She stepped off the path into some bushes, but the twigs did not snap. Instead, they fluttered softly, like pieces of grass on a breezy evening.

"Niko," Ajane said once more. "You are wandering."

"I'm in a dream," she said matter-of-factly. "That's what dreams are for."

This was crazy. Who was she even talking to? Ajane? Herself? *Who does one even talk to in a dream anyway?*

"Yes, yes. But you are communing with *me* in this dream!" Ajane said. "And so soon in your journey. This is incredible!"

Niko just shook her head and laughed to herself. This was such a crazy dream, but it was actually kind of cool. It wasn't dangerous like the bridge one had been. She reached out to touch a tree on the path up to the house. It had a strange texture, not like a real tree. It almost felt... *smooth*. Yes, that was the best word to describe it.

"Niko," Ajane said again. "I do have a message for you, and I cannot stay long with you now."

"Okay, okay," Niko relented. "What's the message?"

She decided it might be best to indulge this figment of her imagination, if that's what Ajane even was right now. Maybe it would say its piece, then leave Niko to explore the dream on her own.

"I need for you to gather Cryo, Ravenna, Kyler, and Riesen. Tell them that tonight, just after the blue of twilight has faded, all five of you must swim out past the edge of the bay to the east. From there, one of my company will bring you to where I am."

Now this is more like a dream, Niko thought. A chance at adventure and instructions that made no sense whatsoever — those were some of the main tenets of a dream.

"Can you relay this message to them?" Ajane asked, looking quite intent.

"Sure, sure," Niko replied absently. She was now distracted by a glowing butterfly that glided over her head before stopping on one of the fronds of the palm tree.

The *palm* tree?

There were no palms on the Green Coast. She looked around at her surroundings. They must have changed without her even knowing! Rows of palms lined the terrace of a great cliff, and down below lie a steep cut bay. She knew this place. Amalkyne. This was where she was now, in the real world. Right?

"I must leave you now." Ajane's voice echoed against the soft fabric of the dream as she faded from view. "Remember, past the edge of the bay to the east, just after the blue of twilight has faded into black."

"Wait!" Niko tried to call out to her, but she was already gone. She knew it was only an imagined specter of her dream, but she still had unfinished business.

Blazes, how did I forget to ask her all of those questions!?

A few seconds ago, she hadn't even remembered any of that. Only now that she was gone did Niko remember about all that she needed to discuss with Ajane.

Oh well, it's not like some character in my dream is gonna answer anything for real, she thought rationally.

As Niko scolded herself for no reason, the gradient of her dream faded into something else entirely. Sol-light streaked through a window, bathing the side of her face in blissful warmth, the other half of which was fully buried into the depths of a pillow. The rest of her body, however, was exposed to wintery cold.

The covers were only halfway over her, prompting Niko to immediately reach for them. The machine-cooler in the room had turned her living quarters into an icebox! She grabbed the covers and rolled back over, huddling her limbs against each other to trap some of her body heat.

In a split second, though, Niko shot up vertically in her bed. Had she just been dreaming again? She put a hand to her forehead and opened her eyes wide. She was in a state of bewilderment, which wasn't exactly uncommon after waking up suddenly from a dream — except that this was no ordinary dream. It felt so... *real*. Even more so than the dream on the bridge had felt.

Blazes! She *had* dreamt of the bridge just now! That heavens-accursed dream would never leave her be! Except that it *had* this time — it disappeared completely and transformed into something else entirely.

It all came back to her at once. She remembered Ajane. She remembered being on the Green Coast. She remembered Amalkyne. And she remembered some 'message' that she was supposed to deliver to her friends.

She also remembered everything that had happened over the last few days. She let herself fall onto her back, sinking once more into the covers in disappointment as she recalled all her woes.

There was a war on outside... Her parents were still gone... Brandon had found himself a *girlfriend*... She was being Inducted into the service... The Meridians were not to be trusted...

Niko sighed.

Whatever energy graced her upon awakening was now fleeting. These were going to be a long few days without her parents, especially now that her sister was gone, also. Kate had been summoned back to the Islands yesterday along with Daren, Jen, and hundreds of other young adults from Amalkyne.

Seeing her off had been an awful experience. Niko had just recovered from her panic attack when it was time for Kate to leave. She tried to stop from crying — she knew that she'd done enough of that for two lifetimes during her breakdown — but everyone had already seen her at her worst, so what more was there to lose?

When she returned back to her quarters, Niko just went to her room and stayed there the entire remainder of the day and night. Lizzy was nice enough to come in and check on her from time to time, but Niko had fallen asleep early. She missed dinner, and it was evident because her stomach was growling now.

"Good morning." Ravenna stood in the doorway, dressed in her typical combination of relaxed pants and a tight shirt.

"Hey," Niko grunted back as she sat up. "What time is it?"

"A little past 10:00."

"Oh blazes," she muttered, falling right back onto her pillow.

"There's a bunch of fruit and veggies out in the kitchen if you wanted some," Ravenna said.

Great, Niko complained to herself. *Fruits and veggies are all that girl ever eats.*

If Niko was going to get up and eat something, she wished it would be something a little more substantial. Or sweet. She probably should go out and eat *something* though. Even Ravenna had heard her stomach growling from across the room, and shot Niko a look when it did.

"Thanks," she said. "I might wash up and head out in a second."

"We're all going swimming in a few minutes. You should come with," Ravenna invited.

"I'll think about it," Niko said. "Even you?"

"Yeah," Ravenna responded.

Maybe Niko would go after all. Ravenna *rarely* went swimming with any of them. She was very outdoorsy and active, but she seemed to hate the water. Niko always likened her to a forest cat, too prissy to ever get near the water.

"Come out here really quick, though," Ravenna added. "Kyler was able to rig the projector they gave us."

"No way?" Niko said. Of course he did. Give him a machine and that guy could do anything with it.

"Yeah, come on."

It wasn't a request, so Niko sighed one last time before pulling herself out of bed. She opened the drawer and sifted through the clothes provided by the Meridians, trying to find an outfit that wouldn't be too hot or too cold. She settled on some leggings and a loose t-shirt, an outfit she commonly donned. She threw the clothes on in a whirl and rushed out to follow where Ravenna had gone.

When she emerged into the main room, she was glad to see Kyler busy working. She really wasn't in the mood to hear some snide comment about how she slept in late. Her attention drifted to the makeshift station that was sprawled all over the table. Was all of *that* the projector from yesterday?

"I didn't find anything there," he said.

"What about the section down here?" Cryo asked, reaching over to swipe to a jumble of numbers and letters that Niko couldn't make any sense of.

"I already went through those lines."

"Oh," Cryo responded. "Well I don't know then. Maybe central comms really did get shut down."

"That's what I've been trying to say this whole time!"

Niko had no clue what they were talking about, but it sounded like they were looking for something.

"Are you able to use that to track our parents, by any chance?" she butted in.

"We already did that," Kyler responded without looking up.

"And…?" Niko asked, after he didn't elaborate. The guy was so rude sometimes. And clueless.

"They're keeping them in Sol City," he said.

What does 'keeping them' mean? Niko wondered to herself. She hoped it didn't mean anything long-term.

"Yeah, unfortunately all transportation is locked down right now," Cryo elaborated. "They're trying to keep the traffic around the Islands clear, now that they've recalled all the active-duty people."

"Oh." Niko was so callous to bad news at this point that she didn't even react. She'd already dumped all her emotions out yesterday; she only felt numbness today.

"Yeah, sorry," he winced. It had to have been obvious how badly she wanted to see her parents.

"What're you guys trying to find now?" she asked.

"Well," Kyler said, "we were trying to datamine their logs for incarceration inventories, but we keep running into stonewalls on the lines that…"

"We were trying to find Ajane," Ravenna cut him off, no doubt saving Niko from all of his machine jargon.

"Yeah, that," he said sheepishly.

"Oh, weirdest thing," Niko recalled, "she was just in my dream last night."

The others stopped and looked at her.

"That's weird," Cryo said. "She was in mine, too…"

"And mine…" Ravenna slowly added.

"Wait, what the blazes?" Riesen said from the kitchen. Niko didn't even know he was there. "You guys all had dreams with Ajane in them?"

"Not me. I slept as hard as a rock," Kyler announced, but then looked around at all his friends. "Wait, you guys *all* dreamt of

Ajane?"

The friends looked around and nodded warily. This was weird. Too weird.

"*All* of you?? What was she doing in your dreams?" Kyler asked, now completely abandoning his focus on his new tinkering project.

Nobody spoke at once. They all just continued to look around at each other. Niko did not want to share first. Her dream had been way too bizarre, and there was no way she was about to share that 'message' with them all. This all just had to be a huge coincidence.

"In my dream, she just appeared out of nowhere and told me that Niko or Cryo had a message for me," Riesen said laughing. "Then I woke up. Blazes if I knew what brought that about."

The friends just stood there looking at each other for a few seconds. Niko thought that this all had to be a huge prank they were pulling on her. But how would they know she had a dream about Ajane in the first place?

"Ummm, that was my same exact dream too," Ravenna said after the pause. "Cryo? Niko?"

Niko and Cryo just looked at each other. This was an eerie feeling, even more chilling than her dream about Riesen drowning a few years ago. Maybe not more dire, but the idea that she was *communicating* in a dream felt a little too weird. She knew that psychic potential was a thing, but this was a little much. It should be completely against all the laws of nature!

"I dreamt she had a message for me," Cryo said. "You too, Niko?"

Niko nodded, her nerves too wracked to form a sentence just yet.

"Sheeeesh," Kyler exhaled, leaning back from where he was sitting. "You guys sure you're not all ganged up trying to prank me?"

"I wish," Cryo said. "Niko, what was your message?"

"Ummm…" She stumbled as she tried to craft a semblance of coherence. "Well, it was that we were supposed to go and swim around the bay and meet up with people. Or something like that."

Cryo nodded as she finished what she was saying. "Tonight, after the blue of twilight has faded? Is that what she said to you also?"

Niko nodded.

Well, this sure throws a wrench into the day, Niko thought. *Now I'm a blazes psychic freak.*

At least Cryo had the same thing happen to him. And Riesen and Ravenna for that matter. Did that mean all of them had psychic potential?

"Wait, wait, wait," Riesen pleaded, his normally cool gaze disrupted with surprise for once. He probably noticed Niko's genuine apprehension. "Nobody's messing around?"

"I think this was real," Cryo responded calmly.

"Wait, so why didn't I get the dream?" Kyler asked.

"I guess you just don't have the psychic potential," Ravenna said with a smirk. "Brainpower is too low maybe?"

"Haw. Haw," he said as he made a face at her. "But seriously. I want to know why the blazes that is!"

"Something we can ask Ajane when we see her," Cryo said in all seriousness.

"I think it's safe to say that she escaped from prison or wherever she was," Riesen remarked. "Did you guys notice the other day when Andersane said prisoners had escaped when they attacked the station at Green Valley?"

Oh yeahhhhh! Niko thought. That made all the sense in the world. How did she not put that together?

"Yep, I had a good feeling that was her," Ravenna said.

"When the Heads of Knowledge asked about her the other day, part of me wondered if she was actually in league with them," Riesen suggested.

"She's not in league with the Heads of Knowledge," Cryo said, shaking his head.

"How can you be so sure?" Riesen asked, tilting his head to the side.

"We work with her, remember?" Ravenna said. "We would know if she was in league with the An-Mara."

"I guess so," Riesen acknowledged. "Just seems very weird timing to me is all."

"Everything about everything is weird," Niko muttered under her breath.

"So, what does all this even mean?" Kyler asked, still looking comically bewildered. "What did you say we're supposed to do? Errr, what did *she* say we're supposed to do? In the *dream*."

"Swim out past the bay tonight," Cryo said with a shrug. "She said there'd be someone meeting us. That's what you got too, right Niko?"

Niko nodded. That was *exactly* what Ajane had told her in the dream.

"After the blue of twilight has faded into black."

"So it's decided," Ravenna announced. "We leave tonight after dinner."

CHAPTER SIXTEEN

16

A Nice Evening in the Bay

DINNER was an awkward occasion for more than one reason. Not only had the Green Coast friends sat mostly in silence after much of the day had been spent bickering, once again, but to make matters worse, *Brynne* was in attendance. Niko was at her wits' end after being forced to watch her and Brandon canoodling the entire time. She had even been accidentally *kicked* under the table by Brynne when Brandon had been tickling her. It took everything she had to stay calm and quiet. Her only moment of vindication had come when Lizzy snapped at Brandon to 'behave appropriately' at the dinner table.

As soon as the dinner was over, Niko had quickly volunteered to do the dishes just so she didn't have to see any more of that. Never mind that dishes were her least favorite chore — it still beat having to spend one more second being surrounded by that disgusting display of public affection. She'd been having serious reservations about leaving with the others to meet up with Ajane, but after seeing Brandon with Brynne, she was more than happy to go.

As far as their supposed rendezvous with Ajane went, there was still much disagreement with how to proceed, if they should even go at all. Riesen was fervently against the idea, whereas Cryo and

Ravenna insisted that it was necessary. Kyler didn't have the dream like the rest of them, so he'd been less vocal in the debate — for once in his life. In the end, Niko figured he would do whatever Cryo and Ravenna said.

Everyone had dispersed from the dinner table a good thirty minutes ago, and given how awkward it had been, everyone naturally drifted off to do their own thing. Roger and Lizzy went out to the terrace to enjoy the night air, Brandon and Tyson were listening to music in the other room, and — thank the heavens — Brynne had returned home. That left Niko, Riesen, Cryo, Ravenna, and Kyler to resume their discussion from earlier.

They had better make a decision soon, Niko thought.

The day had almost completely turned to dark, and this was the hour that Ajane had requested they made their move. It was still so odd to Niko how she had *actually* communicated with all of them through a dream. It shouldn't have been possible, and was now just one more thing to add to the growing list of questions she had for that woman.

"I just can't leave, not right now," Riesen pushed. "We don't even know how long it will be for. If the Meridians list us as AWOL, then we can be sure that…"

"I doubt they even will," Ravenna interrupted. "Not for a while at least. They're actually so disorganized compared to how they portray themselves."

"But they will!" Riesen pushed back. "I can't go *anywhere* these days without somebody paying attention to me."

He had a point, Niko admitted. Much to her occasional annoyance, he was now a world-famous star and attracted attention wherever he went.

"True," said Cryo. "But you can't deny it's pretty important that we go. She wouldn't have gone to those lengths to reveal herself in a damn dream if it wasn't super important."

He also had a point.

"We told you exactly what we do and who the Meridians are, Riesen," Ravenna lectured. "I would say it's as plain as Flatlands that we need to go. And soon."

"It's not that I don't trust you guys, but I haven't seen any reason to doubt the Meridians so far," Riesen said.

"No reason??" Niko blurted out.

She couldn't hold back from joining the conversation any

longer. She was very hesitant to go, but she also thought it was utterly insane to say that the Meridians gave no reasons to doubt them.

"How about that their *leader* killed three people in cold blood right in front of us?" she argued. "Or that they're enacting all these... *totalitarian* policies out of nowhere for a war we know nothing about? Or that they won't even tell us where mom and dad are? Or that they have never told us *anything* our entire lives??"

"I think you've been smoking the twig with that An-Mara friend of yours a bit too much," Riesen returned sarcastically.

"You don't get to do that, Riesen," Niko said calmly, refusing to take the bait. "Not this time. Don't treat me like a little kid. You can't deny what I say makes sense."

He took a deep breath, probably having thought better after searching for something clever to say. "I just... I can't leave. If you guys want to leave, then fine. But I can't give up my entire future for some *dream* we had. Even if it was real, I'm staying. That's my final decision."

"She said you had to come, too," Ravenna insisted, arms crossed with a stern look on her face that said she wasn't accepting his decision.

Riesen shook his head. "I *can't* leave. What are Brandon and Tyson gonna think? And Roger and Lizzy? We can't just bail on them. Not to mention this whole plan is borderline treason!"

"I get it," Cryo admitted. "I really do. But we have to go. You had the dream. You know about the war."

"Exactly!" Riesen exclaimed. "The war is going on right this very minute! They're counting on all of us to help fight!"

"Niko's right that you don't even know what they're fighting for," Ravenna said. "You don't know like I do..."

"Oh, and what makes you so all-knowing about this?" Riesen rebutted.

Ravenna glared at him, but didn't say anything. Niko took the opportunity to defend her.

"Did you not hear anything they said on the transport the other day?" she asked him. "Her family was *killed* by them."

"Oh, please," Riesen scoffed. "You don't know that. I feel so bad for what happened to your family, but you can't possibly believe the people who *saved* our planet are suddenly killing people off."

"I was there," Ravenna spoke up.

"We both were," Cryo joined in.

Riesen just stared at them for a second, not completely understanding what they meant. Or pretending to not understand.

"And what does that mean? There for what?"

"We were there when he killed Ven's dad," Cryo responded flatly. "Andersane killed him. He walked straight up to him while he was wounded, pulled out his gun, and shot him in the head right in front of us. And before he did, he taunted Abel, telling him how he killed the rest of her family. Heard it with our own ears, saw it with our own eyes. We only escaped because Abel made us promise to stay hidden."

"You can believe us or not, I don't care," Ravenna asserted, malice barely hidden behind her violet eyes. "But don't ever say we didn't tell you."

Nobody spoke for several seconds afterward. No wonder Ravenna hated Andersane so much. It was one thing if he killed her dad, but it was another thing entirely if he taunted him about murdering her whole family also. Andersane surely had to be one of the most terrible people in the world if this was true. After what Niko witnessed the other day, she had to admit that this was plausible, as much as she didn't want to believe it.

After staring at the floor with eyebrows raised for several long seconds, Riesen blew his breath out in a long sigh. "I just... I *can't* leave all our people right now. I'm sorry."

If he wasn't convinced that he needed to leave with them by now, he was never going to be. Niko knew exactly how pigheaded her brother could be. He surely thought he was being some noble defender of the people, but really he was just being a stubborn teenage boy.

"So, you're really not coming?" Kyler asked him.

"I can't," Riesen said, shaking his head as he leaned forward into a slump. "I just can't. I'm sorry."

"Fine," Cryo said. "But you cannot, under any circumstances, tell anyone about this. About where we're going, about the dream, about what they did to Ven's dad... nothing about any of it. Not to the Jenaeis, not to your parents, not to Tyson. Nobody."

"Yeah, yeah, of course," he said, avoiding eye contact.

"Got it, Riesen?" Ravenna said sternly, backing Cryo up with daggers for eyes until Riesen met her gaze.

"Yes, yes, fine. I got it," he said. "But what do I even say if someone asks where you guys went?"

"You don't say anything," she said. "Just say you have no idea. Easy as that. It's not like you've never lied before."

Riesen just shook his head and rolled his eyes.

"So, the rest of you are actually going?" he asked. "Even you, Niko?"

She nodded. "We can't trust these people, Riesen. Mom and Dad aren't even coming here anymore, and we have no idea if we're safe here anyway. From anyone. An-Mara or Meridians. We just have no idea what's going on. Ajane can tell us."

Riesen chuckled.

"What's funny?" Niko asked, recoiling in perplexity. She was slightly irritated that he was laughing at her now.

"Oh, just that I never thought I'd see the day where I'm the one following the rules and you're the one breaking them," he said.

Blazes, I am *breaking the rules, aren't I?*

"Well, I'd say these are extreme circumstances, wouldn't you? Doesn't *any* of this scare you about the Meridians?"

"The An-Mara scare me a lot more," he responded. "They were the ones who started this war. They are the ones attacking stations now."

He did have a point. If the An-Mara hadn't launched their assaults in the first place, they wouldn't even be in this mess.

"All the more reason to talk to Ajane and see what the blazes is going on, in my opinion," Kyler said.

Niko was very unsettled by the fact that Kyler was being so rational and reasonable about all of this. He was even on her side! What was this world coming to?

"He's not gonna change his mind," Ravenna said irritably, facing toward everyone except Riesen. "Let's just go." She stood up to walk away.

"I don't think it's fair that I'm portrayed as the bad guy here," Riesen insisted before she could walk away entirely. "I wish you'd respect my decision. I'm doing it for our friends and families."

"See. We're not changing his mind," Ravenna said again, even more visibly exasperated this time.

"We're not trying to make you feel bad, Riesen," Cryo mediated in a lighter tone. "We just think that getting to Ajane is what needs to be done. But I get it. I get that you're staying for the people. That's your call."

Ravenna just shook her head and walked out of the room. Everyone watched her go for a second without saying anything. Niko was feeling quite uncomfortable from all the tension between everyone the last few days.

"As your friend, we do respect your decision," Cryo added, turning back to Riesen.

"Thanks," Riesen said, his argumentative demeanor easing.

"But as our friend, you can't tell anyone where we went. We do need to get going right now, but we will be back soon, hopefully."

He walked over to Riesen and gave him a hand clap and a hug, and Kyler did the same. Even though they had just been arguing a second ago, Niko suddenly felt sad all over again. This was too much loss for one day. No one died of course, but she was still losing people left and right — her parents, Kate, Jen, Daren, Brandon… and now Riesen. She waited for Cryo and Kyler to leave, then approached her brother.

"I'm sorry, but I have to go with them," she said as she gave him a hug.

"It's okay, I get it," he said. That was strangely reasonable of him, considering he'd just been arguing with all of them with such flawed logic.

"If Mom and Dad get here before I'm back, just tell them…" She paused. What *did* she want him to tell them? Not where she went, obviously. "Just tell them I'm okay."

"Alright," he said. "Just get back as soon as you can. Right after you guys meet up with Ajane, if possible. I don't want to have to answer too many questions about you."

"We'll be back soon," she promised. She gave him one last squeeze, then left the room without looking back.

The would-be group of five was now cut down to four as they made their way down to the water. It still felt weird for Niko to acknowledge that she was given instructions from a damn dream. According to the dream version of Ajane, they had to swim out past the edge of the bay, which seemed like a decently far swim — maybe a kilometer or so. At least they were all strong swimmers. Well, except for Ravenna. Niko didn't actually know how strong of a swimmer Ravenna was because she'd never actually seen her in the water before. She never went Sliding with the others, instead preferring to just watch from the cliffs. Hopefully she was a good enough swimmer…

As they headed down the path, Niko's heart felt like it was going to beat out of her chest. She knew she had to do this, but that didn't quell her creeping apprehension. There were too many questions swirling around in her mind. Was the dream real? Would Ajane actually be there? Who was her associate that was to meet them? Would they be caught? Could they get in trouble? How much trouble? What would the Jenaeis think?

And what in the blazes were they supposed to wear!? Up on the Green Coast, she would wear her full-body watersuit, which kept her warm and buoyant in the cold ocean. She obviously didn't have one with her now. Even if she wasn't whisked away from her home without having time to prepare, the water here was way too hot for a full-suit. Luckily, her quarters had been stocked with swimwear, but she felt uncomfortably exposed when she put on that… *thing*. She decided to wear shorts and a shirt over the top. Hopefully it wouldn't be too much drag for her.

"Do we swim all the way around the bay from here?" she asked Cryo as they reached the water's edge from the path.

"I guess so?" he seemed just as unsure as she did, which was not comforting, since he was always the one who knew everything. "She said around the edge of the bay to the east, right?"

Niko shrugged. "Yeah, that's what I remember."

"Alright, I guess let's get this over with before people realize we're gone," he said, forcing a laugh.

It was very dark, but even still, Niko could see his physique rippling with muscles as he took off his shirt to ease into the water. He was always so modest and humble, so it was weird that he should actually be so gorgeously fit. Most every other guy she knew loved to show off their muscles. Sure, she never minded the sight, but she actually thought it was so embarrassing how much most boys loved their own muscles. Very cringeworthy.

Kyler and Ravenna followed suit, discarding their clothes over their swimwear. Kyler, although lean and fit, looked a little awkward. Something about the dimensions of his physique just didn't quite add up. Niko sighed to herself, though, because Ravenna made her suit look so good. Niko wanted to fit in, but she still didn't feel comfortable wearing nothing but that tiny piece of cloth that passed for swimwear here in Amalkyne. The thing was so outrageous that she would've felt even less exposed had she stripped down to her normal underwear to go swimming. Before she had too much time to second guess her decision, Kyler disturbed the stillness with a less than graceful flop into the water, making more noise than any of them would have preferred.

"Oww!!" His shout was muffled as he partially submerged beneath the glassy surface.

"Kyler! What the blazes?!" Ravenna hissed from the shallows. "Shhhhh!"

"Sorry!"

Niko did have to admit that flop probably hurt. She looked to Ravenna, who was shaking her head.

"Let's just get this over with," Ravenna said to her. "Are you going in your clothes??"

"Mmm," Niko hesitated. "I'm not a huge fan of the suits."

"I'd way rather have a full-suit right now, also," Ravenna said, "but the bay is kind of long and it will probably be wayyy easier without the drag of those things."

Niko sighed. Ravenna was right. She'd tried to swim in her clothes once before and it was way, way more difficult than she thought it would be.

"You guys are going swimming now?!" a familiar voice called, startling the silence once more. "Wait up!!"

Before her eyes had time to register, Tyson sprinted past where she and Ravenna were standing and leaped into the water with a flip, followed by a thunderous cannonball splash. Ravenna was frozen in place, no doubt panicking about how they were going to get rid of him.

Tyson surfaced and immediately shouted, "Why didn't you guys tell me you were going swimming?!"

"Tyson! Shhhhh," Cryo urged him. "We're not supposed to be in here. Curfew, remember? They'll kick us out if they hear us!"

"Didn't figure you guys for the rule breaking types," Tyson said, looking around at who all was present. "What're you guys doing out here?"

"Just enjoying a nice evening in the bay," Kyler wisecracked with his usual sarcasm, his voice still way too loud.

"How are we gonna get him to go back?" Niko whispered to Ravenna.

"No idea," she sighed, as Tyson ducked down and broke into a sprint out into the deeper water.

"Wait, Tyson, get over here!" Cryo tried to get his attention quietly, as if that would even be possible.

"What?!" he yelled back. "You guys need to lighten up. What's the worst they do? Kick us out and make us go back?"

Ravenna then jumped into the deep water and slid over to Cryo.

"What do we do?" she whispered urgently.

"I don't know," he said. "Kyler, any ideas?"

Kyler laughed. "I guess he's coming with us. There's no way he's getting out and going back inside now."

It was the truth. Once Tyson committed to something, there was no stopping him. How were they going to explain the whole Ajane thing to him, though? Did they even need to explain it to him? Or should they just let him figure it all out later?

"Honestly, that's so true," Cryo said with a laugh. "I think the goal now is to just get him to shut up."

Tyson was now about fifty meters away from everyone, and shouted even louder. "What're you guys waiting for?! It's so warm!"

"Let's go," said Cryo. "We'll figure it out."

He, Kyler, and Ravenna broke off in a swim to follow Tyson, leaving Niko standing by herself on the shore. She did *not* want to have to sprint to catch up to them, so she frantically ditched her clothes to the side, donning that miserable piece of a half-suit as she dove into the water.

The usual, cold rush of an ocean plunge never washed over her, which was surprising. She knew it would be warm, but she didn't expect it to be *this* warm. Not that she was complaining... she hated cold water, so this was amazing. It might even end up being a bit too warm, considering they were going to have to swim at least a kilometer to get where they needed.

She put her head down, kicked her legs narrowly, and paddled with all her strength to catch up to the others. As she did so, her eyes immediately stung, so she lifted her head up as she continued to swim.

Why is the water so salty here!? she wondered, pausing briefly to wipe the water out of her eyes.

Swimming head up wasn't going to be practical if she wanted to sprint for any amount of distance, so she buried her head once more and kept her eyes shut. She could taste the salt in her throat and feel it burning in her nose. *Ughh!!*

Niko had always been comfortable with the ocean, but it was a little eerie swimming in strange waters in the dark. She did not want to think about what was lurking beneath her. That stray thought itself was motivation enough to catch up to everyone else.

Safety in numbers, she supposed, sprinting to catch up.

After a few minutes of rhythmic paddling, she found herself next to Ravenna, who was just calmly stroking along. Usually, people who didn't swim often looked very awkward in the water, but Ravenna wasn't half bad. Niko figured she must've spent some time swimming in her past.

Just ahead of her were Tyson, Cryo, and Kyler. True to the form of boys never growing up, all three were dunking each other while sprinting back and forth. What a waste of energy. Did they not know they had to swim all the way around the bay? This foolishness was not uncharacteristic of Kyler and Tyson, but she was a little surprised to see Cryo engaging with them like this. At least they weren't shouting too loudly…

Whatever, Niko thought. *When they get tired, they'll regret it then.*

Niko just comfortably settled next to Ravenna and matched her constant pace. They continued like this for about twenty minutes, and Niko let her mind wander during that time. She thought about the war, the Meridians, Ravenna's family, the An-Mara and Kira-Tharn, Brandon and Brynne, her parents, Kate, Keran, Mack...

Most of what she was dwelling on had been stressing her out, so she switched her thoughts to Ajane and what that reunion might look like. She had quite the list of things she needed to talk to her about: her dreams and what they meant, the test she and Riesen had to take, the Engines, the Prophecy of the Stewards, the An-Mara, the Meridians… Blazes, there was so much she was confused about right now! Hopefully Ajane would have the answers…

Soon, the city lights began to disappear around the edge of an outcropping of rocks. They must've made it to the edge of the bay. Good. The burning in her shoulders told her that she was getting pretty fatigued. The water was very hot, and it was a longer swim than she'd been anticipating. At least she wasn't as sore as she had been a few days ago. She would definitely feel it in her arms tomorrow, though.

Without the city lights illuminating their waters anymore, it was incredibly dark out. Fortunately, the sky was clear, and the mountains stood silhouetted against the faint glow from the city and the distant shimmer of stars. This time of year, the sky was darker, with the bright side of the galaxy hidden on the far side of the sol. Luckily, there was just enough starlight to guide their way.

Where were they supposed to meet, though? Niko picked her head up to see if she could get Ravenna's attention, but she was breathing to the other side. She stopped swimming for a second to scan her surroundings, but she couldn't see anything that stood out. It didn't even look like there was any space available beneath the cliffs to meet. It was hard to tell, but it looked to Niko like the cliffs were completely vertical and ran all the way down to the water. How were they even going to get out of the water? She tried feebly to reach out to Ajane with her mind, as if she could possibly hear her. That was a ridiculous notion. To be fair, though, so was communicating in a dream.

"Niko! What d'you see?" she heard Cryo call to her.

"Oh, nothing!" she answered back through heavy breaths as she swam to catch up with the group, who had now stopped. "Just trying to see where we're supposed to meet!"

"I think it's going to be a ways ahead still," he said.

"Oh, she told me that it was around the edge of the bay to the east," Niko said.

"Well, technically, this is still in the bay," Cryo said. "The east side kind of opens up before rounding a sharper corner another k or so ahead."

"Another k!?" She thought they had to be almost done…

"Now, Niko, I don't wanna hear anymore complaining from you," Kyler chided her.

"Shut up, Kyler," was all Niko said back. She was too out of breath to get into an argument with him right now. At least he called her Niko.

"What the blazes are y'all talking about?!" Tyson spoke up. "We're meeting someone?"

"Yes," Ravenna said. "We tried to tell you to go back, but you were not gonna listen to anyone."

"You were trying to get rid of me?!" he exclaimed. "Why?!"

"We were supposed to meet Ajane tonight," Cryo said. "But since you're here now, you can either come with us or go back."

"Go back?! No way I'm going back now!" he said. Niko had to imagine the grin he surely sported; it was much too dark to actually see it. "You think you can get rid of me that easy?"

"Alright perfect. Let's keep going," Ravenna said in her usual, stern manner.

"Yep, let's go," Cryo agreed as he started off once more.

The others followed suit, as did Niko. She settled into her rhythm, humming a song in her head to the beat of each stroke in order to mask the fatigue. She couldn't believe they were only halfway to the edge of the bay. She knew the pain was all mental, but it was hard to regain her motivation after she'd already convinced herself that they were almost done. The others didn't seem to be struggling, though, so she just fed off their energy and hoped it would be enough to carry her along.

Another thirty minutes had gone by, according to Ravenna, who she had briefly conversed with a few minutes ago. Niko had been letting her mind wander again. That seemed to be the trick to make it go by faster — other than when she started thinking about what creatures might be cruising around underneath them. She thought she remembered learning that there weren't any dangerous sharks in Poste Territory, but she couldn't be sure. She really hoped so, because these were unfamiliar waters and she really had no idea *what* was there. She didn't even know how deep it was.

Just as she let her mind resume back to that worrisome thought, something *grabbed* her leg from beneath the surface. She practically jumped halfway out of the water and let out a short yelp, thrashing her arms and legs.

"Easy, girl!" Ravenna said. "Just trying to point you in the right direction."

"Oh!" Niko squealed embarrassedly, laughing to cover up her moment of terror. "Sorry! Thank you."

She put her head underwater and yelled at herself for being so unaware, but she did have to admit she was grateful it was only Ravenna who grabbed her and not some creature.

Her attention was drawn to the side, where it appeared that several of her friends were being hauled onto a small dinghy. How had she not seen this? Thank the heavens Ravenna stopped her, or else she might still be swimming away on her own.

"Grab my hand," she heard a familiar voice say. "There is no need for panic."

"Oh, I wasn't panicking," she defended herself. "I just got surprised by Ravenna is all."

"I see," the familiar voice said.

Niko knew this voice. *Who was it?*

As she took the man's hand, the water rushed off her in a torrent as she practically took flight into the boat. Blazes this man was strong! Niko knew that it was hardly cool outside, but the water had gotten so hot that the night air felt very refreshing in contrast. It was almost *cold* in comparison. She suddenly felt very exposed again, as she was wearing nothing but that ridiculously undersized excuse for what those damn Amalkyners called swimwear. Luckily it was still quite dark out. She simply huddled up, took a seat on the edge of the dinghy, and dug her feet into the holds.

"Grab my hand," Niko heard the man with the familiar voice offer to Ravenna, but it looked like she just ignored him and effortlessly pulled herself out of the water, taking a seat next to Niko.

"This is all of your company, is it not?" the man asked.

"That's it," Cryo responded. "We're good to go."

The man nodded through the dark and accelerated the craft without warning. Niko gasped — she would've for sure fallen out if she hadn't dug in with her feet beforehand. She was only able to breathe again once the craft eased its acceleration after a few seconds, at which point she was able to enjoy the cool ocean air blowing against her flushed skin. It actually felt *amazing* since she was so overheated from the hour of intensive swimming. She figured they'd at least gone close to three kilometers, which was more swimming than she had done in a very long time. Maybe ever. It was a bumpy ride on the dinghy, but she was so relieved to be able to sit down and rest.

How far were they going, though? And who was this man?! She knew his voice. His accent almost seemed... *An-Mara*??? Her heart rate spiked at the thought. He couldn't be An-Mara. Ajane said it would be her associate. She tried to peer through the darkness at him, but it was far too dark to tell who it was. Should she say anything?

"Thank you for picking us up," Niko said meekly, though she had to speak loudly enough to be heard above the rushing wind and the droning of the boat's motor. The man only replied with a grunt and what looked to be an ever-so-slight nod of his head. His indifferent response now had her worrying that what she said was stupid.

She would have asked Ravenna if she was supposed to know this man, but it wasn't worth yelling. They all just sat silently as they skimmed across the water, each bump of the waves pounding the bow like a drum. The glow of city lights grew dimmer and dimmer as they made their way further from the bay. At some point they must have turned around a sharp cape, because that glow now shone from their left.

She heard Tyson yelling something to Cryo, but she couldn't decipher what he was saying exactly. He was no doubt still wondering what the blazes they were all doing and why. The fact that he just went along with all of this astounded Niko. If their roles were reversed, there would be no way that she would've been a good sport about it. As it was, she wasn't quite sure that she should be there, anyway.

After way too long a time spent on the dinghy — she guessed at least thirty minutes or more — the boat dug in and took a sharp turn toward the shore, threatening to dump her back into the ocean. The cliffs here dipped into a 'V' shape and she thought she could see something on the shore. Was there actually a beach here? It was all just cliffs the entire way up to this point.

As the dinghy slowed down to a glide, Niko could see that there definitely was a beach, and on the beach was an aircraft. It looked very similar to…

No.

Niko knew that craft — it was the very same that the An-Mara had abducted them with. She involuntarily panicked inside. Were they being captured again? Even her friends started to shift in alarm.

"What in the blazes?" she heard Tyson say.

"I thought we were meeting Ajane," Kyler added, a light hint of worry crossing his normally sarcastic tone. "What is this??"

"You are meeting the one called Ajane Solase," the man with

the familiar voice said. "We must transport you by aircraft from here."

The dinghy skidded to a stop as it grounded itself on the beach. The familiar man, whose identity Niko was desperately trying to figure out, stepped to the front and hopped off.

"Let us go," he said.

As Niko and her friends followed, she turned to Ravenna.

"Who is that??" she whispered.

"The one called Setten-Lo," she sneered back, her voice dripping with sarcasm.

Blazes! Of course! Niko thought to herself. How did she not pick that up immediately? She should've known just by the way Ravenna ignored his help onto the dinghy in the first place. That would have been a rude gesture to anyone else, but Setten-Lo deserved it from the way he treated Ravenna several days ago. At least he apologized, even if he was forced by the Heads of Knowledge. The big question that was now swirling around in Niko's mind was why Ajane was in league with Setten-Lo?

"Do we go with him?" Niko asked apprehensively, unsure if this was the best idea anymore. Why were the An-Mara here? Wouldn't Ajane have warned them that it was An-Mara picking them up if that were the case?

Ravenna shrugged. "We don't really have a choice at this point. What else do we do? Walk back in these blazes-accursed half-suits?"

It was a fair point; there was really nothing else they could do right now.

"At least you look good in yours," Niko attempted to joke.

Ravenna just snorted in reply.

"Why are the An-Mara here?" Tyson asked, but nobody immediately replied.

"I swear, Ajane better be on that ship," Kyler demanded loudly before anyone had a chance to answer Tyson's question.

"If you would only be patient," Setten-Lo started, "you will see that..."

The door to the aircraft slid open in the middle of Setten-Lo's sentence, prompting him to stop. As it opened, a bright light illuminated the sand around them. Niko's eyes only took a second to adjust before she recognized the slight figure of Ajane step out in front of the craft, accompanied by Riiz Alke-Tani.

Niko heard a collective exhale from her friends, and her own heart jumped for what seemed to be the first time in an eternity. She didn't even know this lady a full week ago, but now she was as happy as if it were her own parents that emerged from that craft.

"Hello," Ajane addressed the friends from across the beach with a warm smile. "It is good to see you all. I am so glad that you were able to get the message."

"Oh, we got the message," Kyler said. "Everyone but me…"

Ravenna elbowed him to shut him up.

"Thank you for coming for us," Cryo said.

"Of course. We have a lot to discuss, so let's get you on board and comfortable."

Her pleasant hum was music to Niko's ears, and it didn't take anyone to ask twice before she hurried forward to the aircraft. As she did, a random pang of hunger had her wondering if they would maybe have some snacks aboard? Even though she'd only eaten dinner a few hours ago, a long session in the ocean always made her ravenously starving.

"The Meridians have increased their patrols along this coastline, so we need to head out immediately," Ajane said.

She scanned over the Green Coast friends as they boarded, pausing in thought. Confusion with a slight hint of disapproval was written all over her distinguished face as her gaze settled on Tyson. "Who is this?"

17

Reunion

"I'M Tyson!"

Ajane peered studiously at him while Riiz and Setten-Lo looked back and forth confusedly. No doubt they'd mistaken Tyson for Riesen. Niko couldn't exactly blame them for making that mistake — now that he had recently cut his hair, Tyson did look a lot like Riesen in a certain light. He had similar height, build, coloration, and he even walked like him. It even took Ajane a minute before she actually noticed that this wasn't Riesen.

"Tyson Ander!" he repeated his name, beaming in mischief.

He reached out to shake Ajane's hand, which she took slowly. Niko was nervous that she was going to be mad at all of them for bringing Tyson along. Or that she was going to be mad at them for *not* bringing Riesen. Or both.

"Tyson Ander," she repeated slowly, cautiously sizing him up and down with her sharp grey eyes.

"Yes, ma'am," he said respectfully. He was doing his best to suck up to her, just like Niko saw him doing with Jen's parents the other day.

Ajane looked over towards Cryo, who just turned his palms outward in a small sort of shrug, his nonverbal way of an apology.

"I tagged along," Tyson said, sensing the tension. This was a rare moment to see his normally lively ego so subdued. "I'm sorry if I messed anything up. I don't need to know what's going on with all of this, if it's secret or anything. I just saw my friends going swimming and wanted to go with them."

"Not to worry. It is quite alright," she assured him, then turned toward Cryo, Ravenna, and Kyler. "He is okay to come with us?"

"Yes."

"Yeah, I guess so."

"Mmm hmm."

All three of them replied with affirmatives, and that seemed good enough for Ajane, who resumed her typical, pleasant smile after a few seconds of deliberation.

"Wonderful! Welcome to our little soiree," she said. "We will catch you up with everything that is going on in due time."

"Thank you, ma'am," Tyson said in the meekest, most polite tone he could muster. Niko stifled a chuckle because she knew Ajane would learn soon enough of Tyson's boisterous nature.

"Of course. I look forward to working with you, Tyson Ander," she responded. She then scanned over the Green Coast crew once more. "Now I notice Riesen Ryen is not here?"

"He wouldn't come," Ravenna said. "Believe me, we tried…"

"That boy is more stubborn than Niko on a bad day," Kyler quipped.

I am NOT stubborn, Niko mentally scoffed, scrunching her face up as she looked over at Kyler.

A dozen worries shot through her mind as she now started to wonder what she did to come across as stubborn. She never thought she was. In fact, she always wished she could've been more assertive, like Riesen was. When had she been too stubborn? Was it recently? Had Kate ever tried to tell her?

Ravenna elbowed Kyler in the gut hard enough to force a wheeze out of him, which was almost enough to bring a satisfied grin to Niko's face. Ajane just lightly chuckled at the horseplay.

"Now, now, be nice, you two," she light-heartedly chided the friends, as if she were their mother.

"Yes, be nice," Tyson repeated to them with a mischievous smirk. He was never one to pass up an opportunity to seize the moral high ground. Ravenna glared at him as if he were next on her list of people to punish.

"Was there any reason that Riesen gave for not coming along?" Ajane guided the conversation back on track before the Green Coast friends could derail it with too much goofing off. "I was quite sure that he was going to be one to sense that dream."

"Oh, he did," Ravenna said. "He still didn't want to come. He has this ridiculous sense of obligation to the Meridians, or whatever."

"Hmmm. Well, that's disappointing," she confessed. "No matter, we must be on our way all the same. Let's all get on board and we can talk en route."

"Where are we going, ma'am?" Tyson inquired. "If I may ask?"

"We are going to a complex in the Northposte Mountains," she replied. "There is a setup there that will provide ample respite for everyone."

A respite sounded nice to Niko, but this made it sound like they would be gone for longer than she'd expected. She hadn't mentally planned for a long trip; couldn't they just figure out what was going on here and now? That way they could get back to Amalkyne before anyone noticed they were gone. Ajane didn't elaborate any further, though. She simply whirled around and disappeared into the craft. The others looked around at each other for no more than mere seconds before following her without question. It seemed like they really did trust her implicitly.

"Are we not going back to Amalkyne tonight?" Niko asked Ravenna as she scurried up the ramp after her.

"I don't know, it doesn't look like it," Ravenna responded indifferently. Seeing the concern written on Niko's face, she added, "don't worry, Ajane will have all of this under control."

Niko wasn't exactly sure that was the truth, though. If she had everything under control, she wouldn't have been arrested the other day. If she had everything under control, Niko and her friends wouldn't have been abducted by An-Mara. If she had everything under control, they wouldn't be stuck in the middle of a war. If she had everything under control…

Niko needed to chill out. There was nothing to be done right now. At the very least, they were reunited with Ajane, and she was there to answer questions that had been burning for some time.

As they all boarded the craft, Niko looked around for any sign of Kira-Tharn. If Riiz and Setten-Lo were here, maybe she would be here also? She looked to both ends of the craft, but it only seemed to be those two An-Mara in Ajane's company. Niko had strangely been missing Kira-Tharn. Even though she wouldn't have complained if she never had to meet another An-Mara for the rest of her life, there was a sort of affinity for the woman that she'd developed. Kira-Tharn seemed very... *genuine* to Niko, although the tale about Riesen being that Child of the Nel-Mara — or whatever it was called — still seemed very far-fetched. She'd have to ask Ajane about that. She doubted that any of it was real, but maybe there was *some* element of truth to what they told them? Heavens knew she couldn't trust anything the Meridians told her now.

As she shuffled to the back and took her seat, she realized she was still wearing nothing but that outrageous half-suit. It wasn't particularly cold on the craft, but she still curled up and folded her arms around her knees anyway. As if the universe answered her wishes, Riiz came from the front and tossed all of the Green Coast friends a pile of blankets without saying a word.

Thank the heavens! she exclaimed in thought as she scurried over and wrapped herself in the biggest blanket she could find. The warm evening air had already blasted them dry in the time since they were plucked from the ocean, but even still, a blanket was exactly what she wanted. Aside from actual clothes...

Now wrapped up comfortably, she sat back in her seat and let her thoughts drift to her parents. Maybe it was from flashbacks of her last trip in a craft like this, but another pang of homesickness hit her hard. When *would* she be seeing her parents again? She thought it to be silly because she'd just spent three weeks without them and felt completely fine. Maybe she felt a *little* homesick then, but nothing even close compared to what she was feeling now.

It was more than just her parents weighing on her mind, though. Everything compounded on top of another was definitely getting hard to take. She should have been most upset about the war that was breaking out — or seeing an actual killing in front of her very eyes — but one of the things weighing heaviest upon her was seeing Brandon with *Brynne*. Logically, she knew this was petty and juvenile, but she couldn't shake the feeling. She hoped they would break up soon. Maybe then she would grow enough guts to actually let people know how she felt. Except...

No! I am not going to stoop down to that little... Ughh! If that's what Brandon's taste in women is, then I'm glad to never date that guy!

Niko felt very satisfied proclaiming this in her head, but deep down she thought she'd probably say yes even if he asked her out this very moment. His beautiful green eyes were so…

Stop it, Niko! she scolded herself. *Ughh!!!*

"You okay?" Ravenna asked. She must have noticed Niko visibly shifting in her seat with irritation.

"Yeah, I just…" Niko hesitated with a sigh, scrambling to tell her anything besides the Brandon thing. "I just miss my parents."

"We'll see them soon," Ravenna replied.

"I know, I'm sorry."

Niko cursed herself. Of all the people she could've complained to about not seeing her parents, she had to complain to the one person whose parents had both been *murdered*… At least it beat telling Ravenna the truth about Brandon, though. Nobody would understand that one. Niko herself didn't even understand that one anymore!

As her thoughts drifted from topic to topic, she realized that she hadn't even noticed the craft take off. It was such a smooth vehicle, and it didn't even require a runway to accelerate. Niko was fascinated by those maneuverable engines that allowed the craft to hover upon takeoff and landing. If only her father was here… She would have loved to dissect the craft's engineering with him.

It was way more comfortable now than her first ride on one of these a few days ago, when she'd been handcuffed to a rail and forced to sit sideways. This time, she was curled cozily in a blanket and even had room to lean back. The inside lights were dimmed, and Niko was sort of able to make out the terrain visible from the window, even though it was very dark outside. It must have been getting very late because she looked to the east and could make out the corner of a big fuzzy patch starting to rise in the night sky. Some of the elderly people who remembered things from before the Arrival had called it the Great Halo. It was usually very dim, but on a clear night it would appear as a large, glowing fuzzball, much the same texture as their own galaxy appeared. During the autumn months, it would take up most of the sky, but tonight only the corner would be visible.

The Meridians called it the Andromeda Galaxy, but Niko had now come to question everything she'd ever learned underneath them. However, as much as she was now beginning to distrust the

Meridians, it was so strange that Ajane had allied herself with the An-Mara. Niko had to admit that they were the ones who appeared to be the aggressors in this conflict, considering their attacks on the stations and everything.

It was curious, though, that it was only Riiz and Setten-Lo with her. Where were the rest of them? Pretending to shift into a more comfortable position, Niko inched a little closer to Ajane and Riiz in the attempt to eavesdrop better.

"We must depart immediately," she heard Riiz say. "We cannot stay."

"I understand," Ajane responded. "But we must know this information. Much depends on it."

"I know what it is you seek and for what reason, but I cannot be the one to deliver this for you," Riiz replied as he shook his head. "Not at the moment."

"Any small bit of information would be better than none," Ajane prodded. Niko wondered what information it was that she was so desperate for.

"I do not have this information you seek," Riiz responded firmly. "I am not made aware of those operations through the Record. That one fool called Var Ashal-Han has opened an official inquiry upon me, and I would be Recycled if I were to pry into matters of the Heads of Knowledge without proper approval. This flight is all that I can endeavor without garnering further scrutiny upon me."

Ajane paused before responding, not bothering to hide the disappointment from her face.

"I am sorry to put this pressure upon you," she said. "And I am quite grateful for all that you have already done. We just *must* know what direction the An-Mara are going with this."

"I have come to agree with you, Ajane Solase. You know this," Riiz said. "It just cannot be through me in which you learn of their intentions."

"Very well," Ajane said after a short pause. "I will think on the matter and come up with a solution. Don't think that I don't appreciate all you have done for me."

"I do know that," Riiz said. "And if I can help, I will. Any directives that promote mass killing of innocents are antithesis to the Time. Whispers of the Machine should not sway our people from that path."

"Absolutely," Ajane agreed. "Let me converse with our friends in the back and then we can resume this conversation later, if need be."

Riiz nodded and returned to the cockpit with Setten-Lo. Niko pretended to be dozing off as Ajane got up and walked over to the back. Even more thoughts churned in her mind now. What information was Ajane seeking? It was probably dangerous if Riiz couldn't risk searching for it. Much of what they were talking about was confusing, but she remembered hearing some of these strange words before.

The Record. The Time.

Oh... what is the Machine??

She'd never heard of that term before. Maybe the Machine had something to do with the Engines? Blazes, there was so much to be confused about...

"I'm sorry I was not able to greet you all properly before," Ajane said to the group as she sat down in between Niko and Ravenna. "How have you been?"

Niko faked waking up with a yawn, smiling and nodding in response.

"So glad to see you," Ravenna said. "We've had quite the exciting few days."

"So I've heard," Ajane clucked. "I do apologize that I was not able to meet you as we planned. I've had quite the exciting few days myself."

"We tried to find any trace of you, but we found nothing," Cryo said. "The Meridians were pretty hush-hush about it. What all happened?"

"Well," Ajane began, "the Meridians suspected that I was working with the An-Mara who attacked the stations, which I was not of course. They came to question me, and I thought it best to limit my association with you all, so I allowed them to take me into custody."

"What *is* your association with the An-Mara?" Ravenna asked Ajane levelly.

"Riiz Alke-Tani and Setten-Lo are my inside eyes and ears into the An-Mara organization," she responded. "That is the extent of my association with them. The An-Mara have been very secretive and exclusive. A tough nut to crack, certainly."

"When did this happen?" Ravenna asked, narrowing her eyes.

"Alke-Tani and Setten-Lo were the ones who captured us and took us away in the first place."

"Yes, I did know that," Ajane admitted with a wince. "It was for optics. Both the Meridians and the An-Mara needed to believe that you were just innocents in this conflict."

"Are we *not* just innocents?" Niko spoke up. She would feel very uncomfortable if she were being used as a pawn.

"Oh, yes, you are," Ajane corrected, looking pointedly at Niko and Tyson. "The others have some extra information that you don't have yet."

"I found out some… stuff… the last few days," Niko said. "It wasn't a fun time…"

"I do apologize," Ajane offered. "I so very much wish that I had time to explain more to you before we were all separated. That was the plan."

"It's okay," Niko said. "I suppose nowhere is really safe from danger anymore these days."

"I didn't intend for you to endure any hardships," Ajane said. "The An-Mara are quite humane in their treatment of prisoners. You were never in any danger."

"Hmph," Kyler grunted. "They must not have got the memo on that one."

Ajane looked confused while Niko and some of the others rolled their eyes. Kyler was going to play the victim card for as long as he could get away with.

"Were they not gentle?" Ajane asked.

"They just beat up Kyler a little bit when they took us," Ravenna said. She shifted her gaze to the front where Setten-Lo sat. "And they were a little disrespectful."

"Oh, I am sorry to hear that," she said, offering Kyler a sympathetic look. "Your capture needed to appear genuine, but I was sure they would have been temperate."

"He's fine. He deserved it anyway," Ravenna said shortly as Kyler shot her a look of incredulity. "I think the main concern we all have now is that the An-Mara are blazes insane. They have some crazy religious prophecy or whatever and they think Riesen's some sort of chosen one. It's ridiculous, and they're dead set on getting to him. There was one An-Mara in particular that seems like he isn't gonna stop until he gets his clutches on Riesen."

"Var Ashal-Han?" Ajane asked.

"Yes," Ravenna answered. "You know him?"

"I know of him," Ajane said. "Riiz has spoken of him before. I'm trying to learn more about that situation, but we will speak more of that once we land and get comfortable."

"How long are we gonna be gone?" Niko seized the opportunity to ask. "I think all of our friends and families expect us to be back before morning."

"Hmmm," Ajane mused, "I think it would be best if you all stayed until we sorted out what's what in this conflict. The Meridians do not know what the intentions of the An-Mara are. Most An-Mara don't even know. Only the high-ranking administration within the An-Mara knows, which is what we need to find out."

"Is there no way to tell anyone we're okay?" Niko asked. Lizzy and Roger would be worried sick about them missing!

"I regret not," Ajane said softly. "The Meridians put a communications ban in place, so you would not be able to communicate anyway."

"Yeah, we know," Cryo said. "We were there for all their proclamations. Niko and Riesen were going to be Inducted into the service, also."

"Yes, one more reason to remain away from them," Ajane said. "I do think that it's best this way. I wish things were playing out differently."

Niko was bitterly disappointed to hear that they weren't going to be able to contact anyone, but she wasn't able to dwell too long on her thoughts as they were cut short with a question from Ajane.

"Now, Niko, you mentioned that you have learned some things?" Ajane asked.

"Well, yes, I did," she answered earnestly. "Some things about the Meridians."

"She knows some, but we haven't told Tyson anything about them," Ravenna added.

"What?!" Tyson exclaimed, putting his hands out to the side pretending to be hurt. It was all in playful jest, though. He never took anything too seriously.

"I see," Ajane said. "Well, we shall catch you up, Tyson."

Tyson gave her a polite smile and a nod, then turned to his friends and made some sort of face that was supposed to draw laughs. Nobody did, though, whether it was because everyone was too tired from the swim, or because they just weren't in a laughing mood.

"We will be landing in about ten minutes!" Riiz yelled from the front, startling Niko.

She was surprised yet again at how fast this ship was. She didn't know exactly how far the flight was, but she did know that Amalkyne was on the farthest southern tip of the continent, and the Northposte Mountains were on the northern border of Poste Territory. Maybe it was a thousand k's away? She would love to know what allowed this craft to travel so fast compared to the planes she was used to.

"Okay, well maybe we can catch you up once we get settled at the complex," Ajane said. "There are quarters for everyone there, and they are fully stocked. I'm sorry you all had to swim to where we met up. I'm sure you understand the situation with the lockdown and all. The roads leading away from the city were out of the question."

The swimming had been the least of Niko's hardships. After her adventures from the past week, she was becoming accustomed to being whisked around on a whim.

"I am so glad to see everyone again," Ajane continued as her characteristically calm smile returned to her face. "We will have plenty of time to get back to work, and hopefully this conflict runs its course and settles down in the meantime."

Niko, now sporting dark sweatpants and a sweatshirt, left her room as she headed to where Ajane had asked to meet her. They had landed only an hour ago, but she wasted no time getting to her room so she could ditch that absurd half-suit.

She was comfortable now, and supremely relieved that this place was nice. Very nice. The bedroom quarters each had their own washrooms, and the showers were stocked with all sorts of cleaning products. Niko took full advantage of that since her hair had felt so horribly thick from their swim in the salty waters of Amalkyne Bay. Recalling the swim, she noted how much different it felt than being in the ocean back home on the Green Coast. She liked the temperature of the Celean Sea, but she much preferred the feel of her familiar Northern waters.

As she walked through the hallways, she tried to recite all the questions she had. Her mind was still wandering, though, this time drawn to the facility's construction. The hallways were molded from the terrain and lined with ducts and pipes, just as she expected from an underground compound. Concrete floors were lined with metal grating, just like at the station they'd visited in the White Mountains a few days ago. The two facilities were actually quite similar, though this one was much larger and more extensive. There were likely twenty or more bedrooms similar to the one she'd been given, along with a spacious kitchen and dining commons, though the whole place was empty except for her company.

As for her company, no one was in sight anywhere right now. It didn't surprise Niko, though — everyone was probably sleeping. She was exhausted and might've done the same, if not for her upcoming meeting with Ajane. The anticipation of the conversation overshadowed any weariness from the long swim. She turned right around one more corner, then descended a short metallic staircase that led to a secluded room cut into the stone. Ajane and Cryo stood at the far end.

"Ah, Niko, come in," she said in her familiarly pleasant tune. "Sit down, make yourself comfortable."

Niko obliged, settling onto a cushioned couch along one wall. She leaned back, already aware that her shoulders were definitely going to be sore from the swim. At least her legs had mostly recovered from her adventure in the mountains. Even the bruise she'd suffered from her fall while skiing seemed to be fading.

"Hey, Niko," Cryo said, interrupting his own conversation with Ajane.

"Hey." She didn't know why, but she suddenly felt a strong warmth inside. She was so very glad to have Cryo as a friend. She never felt like a burden to him like she did to others sometimes.

"I'll tell them, then," Cryo said, turning back to Ajane.

"Thank you," she said. "I will meet with you guys before you leave."

Niko wasn't sure what they were discussing, but she didn't like the word 'leave'. She loved a good eavesdrop, but it was too late in their conversation to pick up what was going on, anyway. Besides, she still had her own questions to rehearse in her mind. The dream. The Meridians. The An-Mara. The test. The prophecy. The Engines.

The Machine.

Blazes! There were *sooo* many questions.

"See you, Niko," Cryo said as he walked out of the room.

"Wait, where're you going?" she asked.

"Nowhere just this second," he assured her, picking up on her obvious concern. "We'll be here when you're done with your meeting."

He simply offered her a sympathetic smile, continued on out of the room, and disappeared around the hallway. Niko really hoped that he and whoever else, probably Ravenna and Kyler, weren't going to be gone for long. Well, it might be nice to have Kyler out of the way for a while, but not the others. Niko swiveled her head back around as she heard Ajane speak up.

"Don't worry," she reassured Niko. "You'll have a chance to talk with them before they leave."

"Where're they going?" Niko asked. Her inquisitive nature was persistent of late.

"Well, I probably shouldn't tell you that one," Ajane hummed. "That information is a little bit sensitive."

Niko was more than disappointed by that response. She had come here for answers and transparency from Ajane, not to be kept further in the dark. She was trying to form an appropriate sentence to convey her feelings, but Ajane continued too quickly for Niko to spill her thoughts.

"I know you must have many questions about what is going on," Ajane announced. "I promise I will do my best to fill you in. I believe we were discussing your dreams the last time we spoke?"

Niko nodded, still thinking about her friends having to leave. *Focus, Niko. Focus.*

"Have you had any others since then?" Ajane asked. Niko had forgotten how intense the gaze from Ajane's soft grey eyes could actually be. "Besides the recent dream where we communicated. Which I was intending to discuss with you tonight, by the way."

"Oh, yeah," Niko said without hesitation. "I have, actually. I've been really wanting to ask you about it all."

"Oh? Anything different this time?"

Niko nodded. "Yeah, well, kind of. It was the same dream, but way more intense, and it felt like I was there."

Ajane nodded in acknowledgement but stayed silent, clearly waiting for Niko to continue.

"It was so real," Niko explained as she lowered her voice. "And I think I was… I think I was… *dying*."

Ajane's gaze narrowed, but she never blinked once, keeping her eyes set upon Niko's.

"Please explain," she said.

"Well, I was on that bridge just like last time. But this time I couldn't move, and I felt the worst pain in my chest. When I looked down, there was this piece of metal or something sticking out of me. Blood was getting everywhere, and then my vision went blurry and everything got all fuzzy. I think Cryo was there, and he picked me up and we had to jump off the bridge also."

Ajane stayed quiet for a moment, but then straightened up in her seat.

"These dreams can be quite frightening, Niko," she said. "One thing I can tell you is that just because you have the dream, it doesn't necessarily mean it happens the way you think. This may come to pass, or it may not. In my experience, every time I've known someone to have a dream where they are terrified of their ending, it has *never* come to pass. The dreams instead have all sorts of meanings. Hopefully that helps?"

This wasn't a very clear explanation to Niko, but the mere suggestion that it may not come to pass made her feel *way* better. She nodded back to Ajane.

"Besides Cryo, were there any other new people that you recognized?" Ajane asked. "You said before that it was Riesen and Daren there, correct?"

"Yeah Riesen and Daren," Niko affirmed. "And yeah, I know one of the other people in the dream now… It was Riiz Alke-Tani. The other guy I still don't know."

"Interesting," Ajane mused. "And you didn't meet him until after you had the dream?"

"Nope," Niko shook her head.

"I see," Ajane said. "I still stand by what I said about not worrying about the dreams too much. Any other small details you can remember that were new?"

Niko shook her head. "Not really. Just everything seemed more real. The towers falling and everything. The sounds, the colors, the smells. I don't know, stuff like that."

"Well, we will keep in touch daily about this," Ajane said. "It's good to monitor, but for now, like I said, I wouldn't worry too much about it."

"Thank you." Niko was glad to hear all this, but she still wanted to know why *she* got the dreams. What made all of this happen? Not to mention, she wanted to know how the dream worked where Ajane had appeared to her.

"Have you been scared to sleep?" Ajane added before Niko could ask anything.

Niko widened her eyes in emphasis and nodded.

"That is only natural," Ajane chuckled. "I can assure you the dreams are a great gift and you shouldn't be worried at all. None of them are going to cause anything. They are only a reflection of possibilities that can happen around you. If you are really struggling to sleep, I have some medication that can help."

"I'll be okay," Niko said. "But thank you."

"Of course, of course," Ajane replied.

"I was wondering how the dreams work, though?" Niko asked. "Especially the one we just had where you *appeared* to us — how is that even possible?"

"That is the question of the ages," Ajane said with a soft laugh. "We know a little bit about how they work, but we don't know everything. We kind of know why they affect some people more than others, but not entirely. I wish I had better answers. If we are able to better integrate *Meridian* society with the people of Arhanda, the context will make all of this much clearer."

There it was again. The same barely-detectable emphasis on the word 'Meridian'.

"I would explain more about that right now, but it would be best not to overload you with too much information about societies beyond your own. Not right now, at least. There are just thousands and thousands of years of history that you need to be instructed in, but that is out of the question with our current accommodations. There are technologies that assist in the acquisition of knowledge that we do not currently possess here on Arhanda. I hope you can understand."

Niko was a little dissatisfied, but at least Ajane sounded like she was making an honest attempt to enlighten Niko.

"Well," Niko said, attempting to hide her disappointment, "there's so much I want to ask about that, but it's okay."

"I do apologize." Ajane wrinkled her brows with a look that appeared genuinely regretful, which Niko appreciated. "Was there anything else you wished to discuss?"

"There was, but now I'm spacing..." Niko laughed.

Ajane smiled and was about to say something when Niko remembered one of the things she was going to ask Ajane about.

"Oh!" she exclaimed. "Riesen and I took some test at that station that we had to hike to. The 'World Test'? Did you know anything about that? That thing had me so confused."

"Oh, yes," Ajane said. "And that also reminds me — I have your Ut."

She reached under the table and opened some compartment, pulling out a few Uts. Sure enough, Niko's was right at the top of the pile. She pointed to it and Ajane slid it across to her.

"Thank you!" Niko said excitedly. She had felt incomplete without this thing, as much as she hated to admit it. It seemed like the whole world was addicted to their Uts, so she figured it was probably good that the Meridians strictly regulated those things. She wanted to connect it to her chip right then and there, but she thought it would be rude if she did that while she was in the middle of a conversation with someone.

"You're welcome," Ajane said warmly. "Riiz Alke-Tani was in possession of them and was able to deliver them to me. So about your test... Yes, I was able to analyze the results."

"Was that the right test that I did?" Niko asked. "I was so confused. Riesen and I both were confused. It felt so... pointless."

Ajane laughed. "The questions are intentionally very odd, and the point of that test is to assess a few things — primarily response time and processing methods when you are confused. It tracks your eye movement, heart rate, and metabolic functions, and combines all of those with your actual responses. Then, they are all thrown into a complex algorithm that gives assessors insight into your cognitive potential."

Niko just stared back at Ajane, nodding and pretending she understood half of what she just said.

"Don't worry about the inner workings of the test," Ajane laughed, correctly aware that Niko probably confused.

"Okay, well... how'd I do?" Niko asked.

"It's not exactly a test where you get a high score or a low score," Ajane said. "But as far as my expertise is concerned, your results have confirmed that you are likely on the high end of the psychic potential spectrum. I suspected as much from my interactions with you so far, but this test just confirms that."

Niko didn't know whether to feel elated or scared. On one hand, she'd never been on the high end of any spectrum in her life. She was always in the shadows of her friends and family, so this was kind of exciting. On the other hand, she didn't want to end up being a test subject. Was this something they would use as an excuse to put her through more tests?

Of course, things were all in limbo as it was. She assumed she wouldn't be Inducted into the Meridian service at this point, not until things were cleared up at least. Even if she hadn't run afoul of the Meridians, would this war even be over anytime soon?

"So what does that mean for me?" Niko asked.

"Well, things are a little different now with the current political climate," Ajane answered, seeming to know exactly what she was asking. "But I will be teaching you on my own how to hone your interactions in your dreams. For the time being, of course."

"What type of training will I have to do?" Niko asked nervously. "Is it hard? How long will it take?"

"Well," Ajane started, "this training is something that will never be complete. It's something that you will progress throughout your entire life. But it's no harder than doing anything else, really. You will be able to lead a normal life in every sense. This is just extra. Think of it as playing a sport. It's something you do and progress, and you always get better and better at it. But it's not something that prevents you from living the rest of your life."

Niko wasn't exactly sure that was the best analogy. Her Field training had taken up a significant portion of her life. She and her teammates always complained that they never had time to do anything social outside of Field.

At least Field was fun, though. This didn't seem fun in the slightest if involved having more dreams. Although, that last one where she was able to control herself was kind of fun, in a weird sort of way. Maybe she would learn how to do that in every dream? Niko was very curious to learn more, but she suddenly remembered she had so many more questions to ask.

One last question on the dreams, then I'll move on.

"When do I start?" she asked.

"I think you've had quite a busy day — quite a few busy days, actually — so nothing more for tonight or tomorrow. I'll have you start the next day. Deal?"

"Sure, sounds good," Niko agreed. *Thank the heavens I get a day off.*

"Excellent," Ajane responded. "Now did you have any other questions I could answer?"

"Uhhh, yeah I did," Niko said, searching through the annals of her brain for any one of the thousand questions she'd planned on asking. Now that she was on the spot, though, it was so hard to remember them!

"Oh! Yeah, I was curious about a couple things the An-Mara said when I was with them. Actually, a bunch of things about the An-Mara."

"Of course. I will certainly answer what I can."

Niko frantically cycled through her mental list of things the An-Mara said, just so happening to land on the Engines. Maybe it was a little out of order, but she'd get to everything eventually. She was indeed curious about the Engines ever since Kira-Tharn had mentioned them, and her interest was piqued even more when Cryo and the Heads of Knowledge began to discuss them the other day.

"Well, when I was talking to Kira-Tharn — one of the An-Mara I met — she mentioned something about the Engines. Do you know what she was talking about?" Niko prayed Ajane would answer about the An-Mara more thoroughly than she had about the dreams.

"Hmmm, the Engines..." Ajane contemplated with a long pause. "The Engines... Well, they are why a few of your friends need to be gone for a couple of days."

———————————

Niko rubbed her arms instinctively as she started shivering. She was so warm earlier that she didn't even notice how cold this place actually was. Why couldn't any of the buildings just be a normal, neutral temperature? Still, it wasn't enough to distract her from how unsettling that meeting had just been. Was she sure she wasn't dreaming?

Head still spinning, she walked through the halls back to her quarters. She hoped this meeting would give her the peace of mind she'd been desperately longing for, but it was not to be. Even though she was grateful that Ajane was able to shed so much light on some of what the An-Mara said, her mind was far from feeling at ease. She half-expected that some of it would be true to a point, but she wasn't expecting Ajane to full on corroborate almost all of what they said. Especially the part about Riesen.

'He checks all the boxes', was all Ajane had to say about that when Niko asked her why the An-Mara thought him to be some prophesized being. Then she proceeded to double down and say that 'indeed it is well-conjectured that there is some lost progeny of the Nel-Mara, likely in human form somewhere'. Niko was still not entirely sure who these Nel-Mara were, and she wasn't sure she wished to know any more about them at the moment.

All this was a bit too much for her brain right now. It was like everything she'd ever known was kind of chopped up, thrown into a blender, and mixed around indiscriminately. She took back the way she felt earlier when she was disappointed that Ajane wasn't able to reveal everything about psychic potential and the dreams — a big part of her now wished she knew less. Ignorance was bliss, right?

The one thing she still needed to know, though, was why all the people were kept in the dark for so long. Why would the Meridians do this to them? Even if they were only using Arhanda for resources — which Niko still wasn't one hundred percent sure was the case — the Meridians had given the people so much. Wouldn't they just rather assimilate everybody into their society completely?

Ajane did admit that the Meridians were not who they appeared to be. Niko was slightly amused when Ajane set to bashing their whole hierarchy and military system. She said something about how they treated it like a joke here on Arhanda, and how it was nothing like the honorable, structured system they had back home. This reminded Niko of how Ravenna had said similar things about the lack of organization in the Meridian service.

Thinking of the whole conversation, Niko just shook her head, staring at the floor as she rounded the corner, when she almost crashed directly into someone walking the opposite way.

"Oh! Sorry!" she squealed, looking up to recognize a few familiar faces.

"You're good!" Cryo responded, laughing. He was walking with Ravenna and some other guy that Niko had never seen before.

…Or had she? She did a double take, thinking he might've looked a little familiar. She gave him a closer look and…

Blazes was he beautiful… His messy blonde hair was threaded with natural ringlets, and his green eyes were sharp and vibrant, a little bit darker than Brandon's. They oozed of what Niko imagined to be intelligence, as if you could see that as an outward trait. He wasn't particularly tall, but he looked quite muscular even underneath his unassuming, loose-fitting shirt. He had light skin and a strong jaw, complete with a cleft chin signature of Antergian bloodlines. He looked to be not that much older than herself, if at all, but she never was great at guessing people's ages.

Ravenna must have seen her staring at this guy because she nudged her arm with a smirk and introduced their new friend.

"Niko, this is Jack," she said. "Jack, Niko."

He held out his hand while he locked his sharp eyes directly onto hers without so much as a twitch.

"Jack Sehs," he said as he grasped her hand firmly. "Nice to meet you."

"Niko Ryen," she said, returning the pleasantries. A wave of butterflies slammed against her stomach hard. "Nice to meet you."

Why did I just say the exact same thing he did? Should I have said something else? Why do I have to be so awkward all *the time???*

She wished she could be natural and clever and, at the very least, socially acceptable. Especially in front of a boy so utterly attractive. This was so stupid, though. She was *not* some boy crazy flirt — why was she being so weird about it right now?

"Ryen," he repeated, his green eyes narrowing. "Related to Riesen Ryen?"

"Yes," she blushed. "He's my brother. Well, adopted brother. We don't share the same blood, obviously, since we don't look a thing alike. But we are brother and sister, anyway. I was adopted when…"

She trailed off, realizing that she was already starting to ramble nervously. This guy didn't need to know her entire life story. She only just met him!

Please shut up, Niko.

"Quite the famous brother you have," he said with a half-grin. "How's *that* like to live with?"

"Oh, well, you know," she answered timidly. "It's okay. He's just still the same old brother I've always known. Only people recognize him everywhere we go now."

"I bet," he said. "That sounds annoying if you ask me."

This guy gets it, Niko thought to herself. *Beautiful and smart. Ugh! Snap out of it, kid, before you weird him out!*

Did she just call herself *kid*? Her brain was officially a bona fide mess. She needed to get out of here right now, before she made a fool of herself any more in front of this Jack Sehs. She just simply nodded and shrugged, hesitant to open her mouth again.

"How'd your meeting go?" Cryo asked, saving her from the awkward silence that was sure to ensue.

"It was good," she half-lied. It *had* been a good meeting, but she was also thrown thorough a massive loop after some of what Ajane had told her. "I get to start training."

"Very cool!" Cryo remarked.

"Yeah, starting in two days," Niko said, still undecided if the training was going to be a good thing or a bad thing. "Are you guys leaving somewhere?"

Cryo nodded.

"We are. Sorry, we aren't trying to bail on you on purpose," he grimaced. He had to have known that all the splitting up of friends was taking an emotional toll on her.

"It's okay," she assured him. "It sounds important, whatever it's for."

"Yeahhh…" he said, still looking guilty. "It is."

"We can't tell you what it's about," Ravenna added bluntly. "Sorry."

"Oh, no no no," Niko said, trying to hide any hint of disappointment. She did *not* want to pull a Kate and guilt trip her friends into telling her everything. That was not her style. "It's totally okay! Ajane told me it was super sensitive. I get it."

"Hopefully we'll be back soon," Cryo said.

"You guys leaving tonight?" Niko asked.

All three nodded.

"We're meeting with Ajane right now and then heading out right after," Cryo said.

"Oh." Niko was certain that she was showing crestfallen spirits, but it was too difficult to hide. She really wished her friends were staying at least through the night. "Well, safe travels I guess."

She rushed forward to hug Ravenna and Cryo in farewells. Neither of them was physically affectionate like her own family was, but so many years of growing up in the Ryen family made it almost second nature for her to automatically hug people upon greetings or departures. She made sure not to overdo it, only giving each of them light, brief pats on the back. Then she found herself standing face to face with Jack Sehs. Without thinking, she reached forward to hug him, as well.

She made sure to stay as far as possible so as not to make it weird, but because of that, she lost her balance and fell in anyway. Heat rushed to her face as she immediately felt his muscles through the embrace, which she released at breakneck speed to prevent from drawing any attention to her embarrassment.

Blazes!

"Nice to meet you, Niko," he said politely as she stepped back.

"You, too," she croaked, the intense sparkly sensation still washing over her. She quickly turned away from him and toward the others. "I guess that's bye to everyone then."

"See you later," Ravenna and Cryo both said in echo.

Niko smiled, gave one awkward wave, then immediately turned around in humiliation and walked at a brisk pace back to her quarters. She couldn't believe she actually just collapsed into that guy. Surely, he thought she was the most awkward girl on the planet.

Ugh!! she groaned.

She knew she should just relax. 'You're never as awkward as you think you are,' Kate had told her on so many occasions. It was good philosophical advice, but she just didn't trust her mentality right now. She already had too much on her mind. All of the other stuff combined with feeling giddy over a boy was too much to think about. Although, maybe thinking about this guy was a good way to get over her scuttled feelings for Brandon?

She sighed, scurrying around one more corner and down the underground hallway that led to her quarters. Once she burst into her room, she immediately flung herself onto the bed and sprawled out, staring at the concrete ceiling. Although she was supremely tired, there was way too much on her mind right now to fall asleep. At least she wasn't scared to dream anymore, though.

If one good thing came from her meeting with Ajane, it was that she'd been assured there was nothing wrong with falling asleep. Knowing that Ajane was right here in the complex with her, just in case anything went awry, made her feel that much better.

She started to wonder about the training and what it was going to be like. Would it be physically tough? Mentally tough? Boring? Exciting? Her intuition told her mentally tough and boring. Before they parted from their meeting, she had asked Ajane about it, but she had just laughed and told Niko to relax and enjoy her day off. She would just have to wait and see.

She willed any further thoughts of her training away in the hopes that her mind would wander to something else. There was so much to think about, but for some reason, the only other thing on her mind right now was this new guy Jack Sehs. Sure, he was cute — gorgeous, even — but there was something more about him that Niko couldn't quite put her finger on. Cryo or Ravenna might have mentioned his name once or twice before, but it was more than that. She felt like she knew him from somewhere. Or that he was an acquaintance… Except that he wasn't. She was sure she'd know if she'd met him before.

As Niko racked her brain, it came to her all of a sudden. She knew where she'd seen him before! She practically levitated as she shot out of her bed, thinking that she should go straight away to talk to Ajane, but she thought twice.

The soreness was already setting in and her body begged her to stay down. Besides, Ajane would be there in the morning; she could tell her tomorrow just fine. It wasn't like this was some huge emergency or something. Ajane was probably still talking to Cryo, Ravenna, and Jack anyway.

She freely sunk back down into her bed, this time pulling the covers over her. It was a little cold in her room, but she wasn't about to get back up and make the effort to reconnect her Ut just to adjust the thermostat. She could do that in the morning also. She was happy to have her Ut back, but it was going to be a hassle to set everything up again.

She took a deep breath, and drowsiness soon crept in, lapping like gentle waves on a shore. It was funny how that worked — only mere seconds ago she was beyond energized, her mind tugged in a thousand different directions. All she needed to do was come to the realization that she could just push all her worries off to tomorrow.

Her eyelids became heavier, and she didn't fight it. After a few more seconds, her mind started to fade into fuzziness as she thought about Jack. She couldn't believe she didn't connect him to the dream earlier than she did.

Blazes, that was him!

She now knew all the people from that dream: Jack, Riiz, Cryo, Daren, and Riesen.

Riesen... Ugh that little...!

The thought of missing her brother was the last conscious one she had before she slipped into the deepest, most comfortable sleep in what felt like a lifetime.

271

PART THREE

Induction

CHAPTER EIGHTEEN

18

Training Day

THREE weeks had gone by since the regrettable parting with the others. Riesen still thought about his friends every day, but he'd been growing increasingly frustrated with how stubborn they all had been. Particularly Niko. She was his little sister and he had always felt a bit protective over her. There was no way he could protect her now from whatever she'd gotten herself into. All of them were now wanted as potential traitors, and the Meridians were hungry for any information from him. He wasn't about to serve his friends and little sister up on a platter for punishment, but he also wasn't going to risk his own skin for their pointless notions at whatever they thought they were doing. They all acted so arrogant in their assumptions about the Meridians that they didn't even stop to think what the An-Mara were doing and why. Just thinking of their foolishness and stubbornness really had Riesen heated.

Luckily, ever since Induction, the Meridians were lagging on his own training, so they had paid him little mind. Of course, he was still right in the beating heart of Meridian operations since he'd been posted at the headquarters here outside Sol City. Andersane himself had requested that Riesen be Inducted as a Candidate into Meridian High Command under his authority.

This was a great honor for Riesen, but sometimes he really wished he could just be like the rest of his friends and fly under the radar. He had the feeling that some of them, especially Niko, were a little envious of his newfound fame. They had no idea what it was really like, though. If they only knew how tiresome it was to always be noticed everywhere… Honestly, most days he would give anything just to go back to being normal. It felt like he was being observed and judged every hour of every day. It was like his life wasn't his anymore.

He took a deep, cleansing breath as he stretched out on the relaxing pad. This was actually one of the rare moments he had to himself. Luckily, Brandon was his only roommate, and he was currently out with Brynne. Those two were irritatingly tied at the waist. Riesen wasn't much a fan of Brynne — he found her to be somewhat annoying and shallow. She was also kind of a jerk to Niko, so he always held a quiet disdain for her. He did have to admit she had gotten very pretty since he last saw her a few years ago, though.

Good for Brandon, I guess.

Riesen figured they would be back in an hour or so, but until they got back, he was just going to enjoy the solitude. Things had quieted down the past few days, both on the war front and in training. There hadn't been any more attacks on stations in over a week now, and that brought him some relief. Fortunately, he'd been able to pull enough influence to keep Kate stationed here in Sol City, but Daren and Jen were deployed abroad. It made him nervous that his friends were out and potentially in harm's way. He knew that this was important work and that they all needed to do their part for the success of the people, but he still got bad feelings when his friends were out there. No one knew when or where those damned An-Mara were going to strike next.

For better or worse, Riesen had spent the better part of this past week just lounging around. Part of him was itching to finish his training so he could become a valuable member of the war effort, but the downtime did have its perks. Yesterday, there had been enough swell for him and Brandon to go out Sliding. The only downside was that a huge crowd had assembled to watch him Slide within only a few minutes of him being out there. That had been annoying, although he was getting better at ignoring stuff like that. Still, it was nice to have a day like today where he was able to enjoy nobody's company but his own.

His quarters were square and boxy, and they had that monochromatic Islander vibe to them, which he would always associate fondly with his time here during the World Championships. It was usually quite an easy place to relax on demand, but just as he closed his eyes for what was going to be his second nap of the day, he snapped to attention as his Ut alerted him to a message from Major Commander Daaz:

Riesen Ryen,
Please report to the eastern wing of the upper training grounds at 15:00.
MC Daaz

Riesen liked Major Commander Williame Daaz well enough. He was much more tolerable than those pretentious clowns he had to travel with from Amalkyne, particularly Brooks and Felleter. Major Brooks seemed to harbor a deep-seated resentment against him for some unknown reason. His friends had joked that it was because North Territories won the World Championships last month. Who knows, maybe it was? Riesen was pretty sure Major Brooks was a Southlander, and it was no secret that North Territory had a particularly violent game against South Territory in the semifinals. Who actually knew what that guy's deal was, though…

But as poorly as Brooks had acted toward him, he didn't find him nearly as bad as *Second Officer* Brody Felleter. That guy was such a tool! He was obsessed with his rank, as if he was above everyone in the entire world. He had even forced Riesen to salute him before he was even Inducted! Riesen swore that as soon as he outranked that guy, he was going to find him and force him to salute just for fun.

With the trajectory he was on, it wouldn't be long before Riesen achieved Second Officer status. A matter of weeks, probably. Not only was he on a fast track to High Command, but training and promotions were also being expedited because of the war. This prospect was encouraging to Riesen, so he had no problems in finding the motivation to head over to the eastern wing. As eager as he had been for his nap, he was all too happy to report for training duty. He always preferred to be out and about, anyway.

Heart pounding and soaked with sweat, Riesen lay on his back with his eyes closed, taking in the surroundings with his other senses instead. He could smell the rocks of the Islands, feel the ruthless beating of the sol-light, hear the congratulations of other people, and taste the blood in his mouth. After a few seconds of internal silence, he rolled over and dragged himself from the grassy field over to the shade by the benches. The tall, white walls that flanked the sides of the training field provided some protection from the sol-light that beat down at an angle this afternoon. It was starting to get very hot this time of the year — it was even considerably warmer now than it had been last month during the Championships. This weather was what Riesen usually considered to be perfect, but not when one is trying to fly all over the field at full speed for an hour straight.

"To the victors go the spoils!" Major Commander Daaz announced. "The winning team is excused. Losing team must complete the circuits before partaking in recovery. Thank you all for a great show."

"Yes, Commander!" all the participants saluted in synchronous harmony, including Riesen.

This was ridiculous, though. There was no way this was anything besides the most obvious attempt to screw him over. When Major Brooks had picked the teams for this game, he put Riesen with the worst seven players out there. He even put all four *girls* on his team. Some of them looked like they had never played Field before in their lives! Meanwhile, the other team was stacked with everyone that could play. And it wasn't like he was playing against mediocre players, either — Rangar Thomson and Rush Fils, who both played in the Field World Championships last month, were on that team. Riesen knew he was the best player out there, but there was still no way he was going to carry a team that barely knew how to play against a stacked team of veterans.

The worst part about it was that Brody Felleter had been put on the other team. He was probably the worst player on that team, but that didn't stop him from gloating and taking full credit for beating Riesen after the final bell sounded.

"Thanks for the easy win, Candidate," he snidely jeered as he walked past Riesen. "You're not so great without the rest of your Territory to carry you."

Riesen didn't even give Felleter the satisfaction of acknowledging him. He was beneath him, like an insect compared to a giant. He just sat there, still too irritated from losing, but Felleter didn't move on. Finally, Riesen looked up at him.

"Stand at attention, Candidate," Felleter demanded.

Since they were all in the presence of High Command, Riesen reluctantly got up and saluted the pompous ass. He made sure to move so casually slow, though, so as not to make Felleter feel important. He still didn't even meet him with eye contact.

"You may be a big shot where you're from, but you will learn your place here, Candidate," Felleter sneered.

He stood at least fifteen centimeters shorter than Riesen, and didn't have much of an athletic build. There was something about his round face that suggested to Riesen that he was probably bullied as a kid. Riesen just summoned patience and did not engage in any insubordination with this guy right now. He just reminded himself that he would outrank Felleter in due time and just went with it. Part of him actually felt bad for the guy. Why was he so desperate to express dominance over Riesen? No doubt he was compensating for his lack of real-life superiority.

As he stood at attention, Riesen maintained complete stoicism, the only exception being the small gleam of a smirk, which probably angered Felleter even more. The second officer just huffed and turned around, storming off to the buildings with his nose turned up to the air in a comical show of self-importance.

After he disappeared from view, Riesen just shook his head and smiled to himself. That guy was too much. Something like that might make most people mad, but Riesen only found it to be pathetic. It even succeeded in soothing some of his grumpiness from losing the Field match a few minutes ago. Not entirely, though, because as Riesen turned toward the sidelines, his sour mood returned in full as he watched some of his teammates from the losing team heading over to the circuits.

He puffed his cheeks out and exhaled an audible sigh of despair as he trudged over to join them. It had been asserted that immediately after the game, the losing team was to perform ten full-ups and one lap around the circuit for every point they got scored against them. Once Riesen knew they had no chance to win, he changed tactics for his team and had them play a packed-defense strategy. There was no way he could win with that strategy, but at least they would limit the number of points that were scored against them.

In theory.

As it was, some of his teammates still couldn't follow simple directions and they ended giving up twenty-one points! Twenty-one! That meant two-hundred and ten full-ups and twenty-one laps. This was going to take hours.

I'm so above this, he thought bitterly. *All I needed was one more player that knew how to play and we would've easily won.*

Riesen was so mad. What's worse was that everyone from the winning team was hanging out on the sides as if they had just won the World Championships. At least he had a *real* World Championships gold medal. And a World Championships MVP trophy to boot. Something none of them would ever have in their wildest dreams. Thinking of that brought him a small sense of consolation.

"Let's step to it, Ryen," Major Brooks prodded. "This was part of the deal."

"Yes, Major," Riesen replied, masking all semblances of emotion. That guy could torment him all he wanted; Riesen was not going to show any of his irritations.

Riesen stepped underneath the bar and immediately set to work. The less time he gave himself to think of how unpleasant this was going to be, the better. He dropped to the ground, pushed up, then jumped up to the bar in one smooth motion. He pulled himself up with enough acceleration to where his entire torso was all the way above the bar, then let gravity do the work to take him down to the ground for the next repetition. And the next. And the next. And the next…

After completing ten repetitions, he set off onto his lap around the circuit. He was relatively used to this type of training; this would be a normal conditioning workout with his national Field team. Although today, the heat was a major factor in making it a lot worse, not to mention he was only minutes past just having to play a full game of Field. Nevertheless, he was determined to maintain a quick pace on his laps. He could feel High Command watching him closely, as well as some random spectators who were allowed access to watch the game. He would show them all that he was indestructible. Very conscious of the eyes upon him, he kept an unrealistically quick pace as he zipped around the circuit.

One mental trick he always found helpful when completing laps was to treat everything like a continuous math problem, always calculating how much farther he had to go. Since he had twenty-one laps today, that meant that he would have ten and a half kilometers total. He just passed the halfway mark of this first lap, so that meant he had ten and a quarter kilometers left to run. As soon as he reached this next marker up ahead, he would only have ten and an eighth kilometers left.

This back stretch was way nicer, also. It was covered from the shade of the walls, plus he could see the skyline of Sol City in the distance to the east, along with the towering volcano to its right. He didn't have much time to take in the view, though, because he rounded the corner soon enough, emerging back into the beating sol-light. He sprinted back to the full-up bars, where he was somewhat amused to see a few of his unfortunate teammates still struggling with the first round of full-ups. They were even using the pull-up assists. Poor souls.

After cranking out all ten of his full-ups, he set off on lap number two. Those last few reps felt a little difficult, but he wasn't about to show any weakness. Considering he had nineteen more sets, though, it would be foolish to think he wouldn't show struggle at some point.

"You're insane, Riesen," one of his teammates said. He only knew her as Pira, and had just met her today. She was another Candidate assigned to High Command, and she wasn't particularly good at Field. At least she'd attempted to follow his game plan from earlier.

He didn't know how to respond, so he just laughed and said, "this *sucks*. We've got this, though."

She had just started on her first lap when he started on his second. He didn't want to be rude, but he also wanted to get this blazes punishment done, so he accelerated off and didn't wait up for her.

Nine and fifteen-sixteenths k's left.
Nine and seven-eighths left.
Nine and thirteen-sixteenths.
Nine and three quarters.

Nine and eleven-sixteenths.
Nine and five-eighths.
Nine and nine-sixteenths.
Nine and a half.

He rattled off his counts as he sped around the circuit. He didn't make direct eye contact with any of the commanders watching, but he was very aware of their scrutiny. Andersane wasn't there, nor were any of the vice magistrates, but there were several Major Commanders besides Daaz. He'd already lapped five of his seven teammates, and he used that as motivation to push himself faster and faster. He would have to be careful to not tire himself out too fast, but he thought this was a pace he could probably hold for the entire time.

It was blazes hot outside, though. The fact that they weren't allowed any water until they were finished was insanity to Riesen. He understood that it was all about mental toughness, but in this heat, it could get dangerous for some of the less capable conscripts.

Riesen stepped up to the full-up bar for his third set of ten full-ups. There was one other person at the bars right now, a guy Riesen knew only as Bryce, but it looked like that guy was finishing his last rep. No matter, Riesen would lap him soon enough. At least he had good full-up form, even if he did look like he was struggling.

Riesen chugged through his full-ups and raced off after Bryce, eager to try to catch him during this lap.

Nine and seven-sixteenths.
Nine and three-eighths.
Nine and five-sixteenths.
Nine and a quarter.
Nine and three-sixteenths.
Nine and an eighth.

"Try-hard," he heard Bryce say as he whooshed past him on the outside.

Riesen didn't know if Bryce was joking with him or if he was actually upset about something Riesen did. Bryce was one of the people Riesen was most frustrated with for not following the game plan. He had told him to play in the center right by the goal box so many times, but Bryce kept coming out, and then they'd get scored on. Maybe Riesen was a little bossy, and maybe he did snap at him one of the times they gave up a goal, but still… They would've probably had to do at least five to ten fewer laps right now if it weren't for Bryce's rogue actions during the game. Riesen just ignored him as he cruised into the sol-light and over to the full-up bars.

Riesen chose the farthest bar from the circuit just so he wouldn't have to interact with Bryce, just in case he actually was upset with Riesen. He rushed through the full-ups and headed back to round number four on the circuit.

"Try-hard," he heard Bryce say again.

Riesen just offered him the Meridian Crescent 'C' sign with his right hand, as if to say 'it's all good', as he glided by without looking back. He definitely wasn't going to stoop down to this guy's level and argue with him right now. He and Brody Felleter must have been smoking the same twig today. What was with them?!

Onto the circuit once more, he settled right back into his zone, resuming his countdown for every sixteenth of a kilometer he clocked. He cleared his mind of Felleter and Bryce, instead focusing on catching the last person he still needed to lap. If he didn't catch them this lap, it would for sure be on the next one.

Riesen just about collapsed after his last lap was completed. That had been way more difficult than he thought it would be. Instead of getting cooler as the sol dropped, it only seemed to get hotter and hotter. He was able to hold the pace he set on his early laps around the circuit at least, but the full-ups were what got him. He struggled on his last several rounds. At least he didn't have to use the assist. That would've been humiliating, even though all the commanders had left even before Riesen was at the halfway point. That in itself irritated him. What was the point of him doing this if they weren't even monitoring? However, nothing topped the irritation he felt when Major Brooks sounded the bell immediately after he completed that twenty-first lap.

"That will be enough for today," he announced over the sound enhancer. "Take your recovery before reporting for evening duty tonight. You will meet at 21:00 at the northern wing of the upper training grounds."

Are you kidding me!? Riesen thought. *Everyone else gets to finish, too? Even though they aren't even close to being done!?*

He lapped the next fastest person, who ended up being Pira, six times! And what was the deal with evening duties? He thought he was done for the day.

Whatever, he thought indignantly. *It better not be physical training, that's all I can say.*

After lying flat on his back for a few minutes in exhaustion, he got up and staggered over to the side where he set his water bottle. He furiously gulped down half of it before pouring the rest all over himself. He was already completely drenched in sweat, so he wasn't any wetter now than he had been before. He walked over to the towel dispenser and grabbed two towels, draping one over his head and wiping himself off with the other.

He didn't bother staying to socialize with any of the others, nor was he going to give Major Brooks or the other officers any opportunity to stop him for such nonsense right now. Brooks said they were excused, so he was going to excuse himself.

Riesen walked through the large doors and into the building that connected to the dormitories. The rush of machine-cooled air that splashed over him upon entry was much needed relief from the brutal heat outside. The ceiling was high in this great hall, probably at least fifteen or twenty meters. On one side was the dining commons, where hundreds of soldiers bustled about. On the other side was a series of hallways that spidered outwardly, connecting to separate buildings. He took the third hallway from the right and walked down the long set of stairs. This one would eventually lead to his quarters, but he had to descend about a hundred meters worth of steps first.

The whole complex was built on the slopes at the base of Mt. Iroal, the towering symbol of the Islands. The hillside setting made for spectacular architecture, but right now he was annoyed that he had to traverse so many stairs just to get back to his quarters. He then would only have a few minutes to unwind before having to climb all the way back up to report for his evening duties. Just as he was wondering about said evening duties, his Ut alerted him to just that:

Riesen Ryen,
Report to the northern wing of the upper training grounds at 21:00.

Do not be late.
Major Brooks

The tone of the message seemed menacing to Riesen. To an impartial observer, Books was a fairly effective leader and treated everyone under his command well. Everyone except for Riesen, that was. Every time he interacted with Riesen, he would always add a little something extra. Something like giving Riesen less rest during a training set, or giving him last choice on duties, or like this last example of putting him on a team that had no chance to win the Field game. It was difficult sometimes, but Riesen did his best not to pay it much mind. Most people in command were very flowery towards him, especially those that actually mattered in High Command. He hoped whatever was in store for him tonight was not run by Brooks.

The northern wing, though — that made him a little nervous. That place was notorious for being reserved as a physical training venue for the lower ranks, and Brooks was a common sight on those grounds.

Whatever, it will be what it will be.

Riesen prided himself on being very go-with-the-flow. There was nothing he could do to change the outcome now — the only thing he could control was his own mindset about it.

He turned a few corners and arrived at his quarters on the first floor. When he opened the door, the first thing that came to sight was Brandon lounged on the relaxing pad with Brynne's head sprawled across his chest. Riesen's arrival obviously startled the pair, who looked like they'd fallen asleep while watching something on their Ut projectors.

"Blazes, what happened to you?" Brandon asked Riesen, raising his head from the cushion.

Riesen looked into the mirror in the entryway and realized he was quite the sight. A substantial bloodstain ran down his chin and onto his shirt, which was soaking wet from the combination of sweat and the water he dumped all over himself. His left arm was red with grassburns and his right middle finger was already swollen from the jam he suffered during the game. Nothing out of the ordinary after a Field game, though.

"They had a game at the training grounds today," Riesen shrugged.

"No way, and you didn't even tell me?" Brandon said in what

Riesen thought to be an attempt to downplay his enthusiasm for Brynne's sake. "I would've gone for sure."

"Trust me, you're glad you didn't."

"Hey, Riesen," Brynne said softly, smiling tenderly up at Riesen, stretching her arms as she lifted her head from Brandon's chest.

A small part of Riesen felt very uncomfortable around her at times — sometimes he could swear that she was trying to flirt with him, even though she was together with his best friend. At least Brandon never seemed to notice, though. Riesen just tried to ignore Brynne as much as possible, so he just nodded back at her now, barely acknowledging her presence.

"Did you guys get summons for evening duties tonight?" Riesen asked.

They both shook their heads.

"Hmmm, I did," Riesen said. "I have to report to northern wing in like an hour."

"Ooof," said Brandon. "Northern wing? Why? I thought we already finished basic physical."

"I thought so, too," Riesen agreed, frowning.

"I brought some extra soup up if you want any before you have to leave, Riesen," Brynne offered.

"Oh, thanks," he said, as he took a huge swig of his water bottle. At least that was a nice gesture from her. Maybe he should start being a little more pleasant to her...

"You should take those clothes off first, though," she suggested with what looked like a half-smirk. "You look so dirty."

Riesen nearly choked on his water, slamming his bottle onto the counter beside him.

There she goes again, he thought to himself, unable to prevent from narrowing his eyes. Who says it like that!? She could've just been like 'Oh, go wash off' or something. What the actual blazes was wrong with this girl?

"You do look pretty destroyed," Brandon added, seemingly unbothered by what Brynne had just said. Maybe Riesen was thinking too much into it.

Simply offering an unintelligible grunt in response, he had to admit it wasn't a bad idea. He felt absolutely disgusting now that his body had cooled off. His dried sweat and blood had become sticky, and he surely smelled the part. Besides, his shirt was completely destroyed, torn to shreds and stained with blood. He had no idea he even had a nosebleed until a few seconds ago. Sometimes, that was just what happened when you played Field.

He turned around and strutted down the hall to wash off, if for no other reason than to just get away from Brynne. The last thing he wanted was for her to say something inappropriate too overtly. Then Brandon might feel jealous or whatever and that was something Riesen could do without.

He turned on the shower to cold as he entered the washroom, sliding the door shut behind him and scraping off the workout clothes that were now pasted to his skin like adhesives. He could definitely feel the grassburns, and would likely be feeling them tomorrow, too. He'd tried so hard to win today! Well, maybe not win, but he sure tried hard to not let the other team score so many points. Shaking his head, he jumped in for the shortest shower of his life. There were no locks on the washroom door and he didn't exactly trust Brynne to not come barging in.

Thankfully she didn't, however. He figured she probably only flirted with him just enough to make him feel uncomfortable. She was an opportunistic bully like that, always searching for what bothered people the most, and having no qualms about pushing those buttons. Tyson would also do that, but his version was funny and good-natured; hers was not.

Thinking of Tyson brought him a new frustration, though. Riesen couldn't believe that Tyson, of all people, had abandoned them back in Amalkyne. It made absolutely no sense at all to him! He involuntarily clenched his fists in agitation before snapping back to reality. The trail of dirt and blood that washed down the drain had faded to normal water, so he briskly finished up his shower. He needed to relax.

After drying off, he grabbed a clean version of the same workout outfit he was already wearing. All the clothes for the Meridian service were the same, which he appreciated. He never had to think about what he was going to wear; it was already chosen for him. He threw his dirty clothes into the laundry chute, then headed back out to grab some of that soup they brought him.

"Wow, that was fast," Brynne remarked as Riesen emerged from the washroom all freshened up.

"Uh huh," he said indifferently as he walked over to the bar and took a seat. "Thanks for the soup."

"Of course," she responded. She'd now sat up to face Riesen, looking as if she was searching for some way to torment him further. Thankfully, she just stayed quiet. Was she waiting for him to say something else?

Riesen just set about eating his soup silently, and blazes, was it good. Most food from the dining commons was. He especially enjoyed the combination of potatoes and venison, which were two of his favorite foods on their own.

"How'd the game go?" Brandon asked.

"Lost," Riesen said. "Brooks fixed it. So ridiculous."

"Hah," Brandon snorted. "Sounds about right."

"Guy's an ass for sure. Probably gonna have to deal with him some more tonight. Whatever."

Brandon clicked his tongue. "Yeah, what can you do," he shrugged.

Riesen just nodded, still focused on the soup. What could you do, indeed. For now, he would just sit back and enjoy his meal. Afterward, though, he should probably lay out and massage his muscles before they tightened up too much. He didn't really feel like doing that, but he knew it was the smart thing to do. In a few hours, his body would surely be grateful for it.

"What do you think you're gonna have to do tonight?" Brynne asked him curiously. "Is it supposed to be a long session?"

"I don't know," Riesen said with a shrug in between gulps. "Guess I'll find out in an hour."

———

19

Training Day, Again

RIESEN opened his eyes as consciousness settled into place. Radiant sol-light streamed in from the east and now tumbled across his face. What time was it? What *day* was it? He lay on his back and stared at the plain white ceiling without blinking for several seconds.

That was weird, he thought, recalling his dream from moments earlier. He was entirely sure that he'd been dreaming about something else before *she* appeared. He couldn't quite remember what it was, though. The only bits that came to him were fleeting images of Mt. Iroal — or rather a dream version of a mountain that resembled Mt. Iroal — and then also the dining commons here at the training complex. He was there with… well, now he couldn't even remember who he was there with. The only thing he remembered now was Niko flickering in and out of the dream. Except he was pretty sure that she *wasn't* part of the dream he'd been having before. It was like she was some sort of intrusion on his preexisting dream.

It was strangely reminiscent of that one dream from last month where Ajane had appeared to all of them. This one was different, though, because Niko was never really that clear. She never even said anything. It was more like a fuzzy feeling of her being there rather than an actual image. Very strange.

He blinked his eyes several times just to make sure he was fully coherent, then sat up. Upon moving, he was painfully reminded of yesterday's events. The soreness pressed against every centimeter of his body like a cold-water full-suit was trying to squeeze the life out of him. He scooted slowly to the edge of the bed, then tenderly eased one foot after the other onto the white tile floor. Before standing up straight, he reached down toward his feet to stretch his hamstrings. Blazes, even his toes were a mess! Half of his nails were black and blue, and one looked like it would surely fall off today.

That's what happens when you run about fifty k's, he sarcastically thought to himself as he suppressed a grimace. He had to have run at least that far yesterday, not to mention the twenty-one laps he ran the day before, plus the Field game. And not only was there an inordinate amount of running, but he endured what had to have been thousands of jumps, push-ups, pull-ups, full-ups, crawls, wrestling matches, and more. The last two days had been nothing but a diabolical attempt to break him and the other Candidates in his squad.

What made it so much worse is that he had allowed himself to succumb to sloth in the days leading up to this training session from the blazes. He got lazy and comfortable, two traits that didn't mesh with toughness. Then, without warning, he was slammed with the most difficult physical training he'd ever experienced. Of course, he was used to tough workouts, being on the national Field team and all, but this was beyond physical. After the first hour or two, it became all mental.

All things considered, he actually thought he did a pretty good job handling that session. Much better than the rest of his squad-mates, at least. Out of the whole squad, he and Pira were the only ones to make it through without giving up. Of course, she was not able to complete nearly as many repetitions on any of the activities as he was, but he did admire her for plugging through the entire twenty-four hours without giving up. The instructors had been taunting the Candidates the whole time, telling them it could all be over whenever they wanted. All they had to do was walk up to the commander and announce their submission.

He did have to admit, there were a couple times he was severely tempted to quit. All he had to do to resist, though, was imagine the shame he would feel if he submitted. He was Riesen Ryen — there was no way he was going to give up. The whole world would know about it if he did. He would never be able to look any of his friends or family in the eye if he failed like that.

Swinging his thoughts back to the present, he gritted his teeth thinking about how he'd have to summon that same inner strength again today. The instructors seemed very eager to break both him and Pira. They were nothing but a bunch of sadists if you asked Riesen. Because he survived part one, he was rewarded by being thrown into another physical training today. This time, he would be included with a fresh squad of reserve duty troops that were being recalled to the war effort. Rush Fils and Rangar Thomson, two of his nemeses from the Field World Championships, would be part of this squad. There was no way he would be able to compete with them physically today, so his entire goal was just to endure mentally.

If he did manage to survive today, though, he would be commissioned as an officer in the Meridian service. From what Kate told him last night, normally the process to becoming an officer would take months, even years sometimes. Now though, the Meridians were so desperate for capable bodies in their service that they offered this accelerated option. Granted, he already completed several weeks of advanced training, along with the months of pre-training he went through over the course of the past year. This was just the final test.

Exhaling carefully so as not to agitate his bruised ribs, he eased into a completely upright position. He moved tenderly from side to side to loosen his core and shoulders, then reached up to the doorframe to pull his arms taut, feeling just how tight they were. This was going to be a truly awful day. He really should've taken the time to sit in an ice bath last night, but he was too exhausted to do anything besides throw his clothes off and collapse straight into bed. He finished stretching with a yawn, rubbed his eyes, and walked out into the living room. Brandon was already out there doing some sort of reading and paperwork.

"No Brynne today?" Riesen asked.

"Nah," responded Brandon. "She had training this morning at 06:00."

"Hah," Riesen grunted. "I'm sure she was thrilled about that."

"Tell me about it. The only thing I heard from her all last night was a bunch of complaining." Brandon rolled his eyes. Riesen was well aware that when Brynne complained, it was a nonstop affair, potentially for hours. He had been there before.

"Well, I'll try not to complain also, then," Riesen grumbled.

"Rough day?"

Riesen just puffed his cheeks out and slowly blew the air out to emphasize his current mood. "Probably the roughest workout I've ever had. Absolutely brutal."

"Wow," Brandon remarked. He obviously knew Riesen worked out like a madman, so he surely knew that when Riesen said something was difficult, he meant the truth. "You do look pretty jacked today."

Riesen smirked. He supposed the silver lining was that the workouts from the past two days made him look exceptionally muscular. He walked over to the mirror and flexed. He *did* look jacked.

"Well, round two today," he said, still staring at the mirror as he shifted his pose.

"Seriously?" said Brandon. "I can't believe you're not done with it yet. I thought for sure they would've at least stationed you to High Command by now. Pretty crazy if you ask me."

"Kate said this is the last day. If I make it through today, then I pretty much have passed everything to get my commission."

"Hah!" Brandon snickered. "You say 'if' as if you aren't gonna pass."

Riesen shook his head. "Dude, it was rough yesterday. I swear I almost quit."

"Nah, there's no way golden boy Riesen Ryen would ever quit," Brandon teased. "But damn, they're already commissioning you, huh? That was honestly really fast."

"Tell me about it," Riesen agreed. "I'll take it, though. Definitely not complaining."

Brandon nodded. "For sure."

"So, what're you doing today?" Riesen asked.

"Umm, I have a test at 12:00. I'm trying to get some studying in now."

"Oh nice, good luck," Riesen offered.

"Thanks," Brandon accepted with a grimace. "I think it might be tougher than I thought it would be. I swear I don't know any of this stuff I'm reading."

"What is it?" Riesen asked.

"Reactions mostly. Lots of stuff on explosive properties or

something," Brandon responded. "If I have to hear the word hydrogen one more time after this test is over, I'm gonna lose it."

Riesen nodded, forcing a slight grin. He remembered all of his chemistry courses very well. He thought it was really easy stuff, but Brandon also wasn't as good a student as he was. He figured Brandon would probably do just fine, though. He was just being dramatic.

"Brynne and I are going to the beach after I get out," Brandon said. "Wanna come with? If you're done by then, obviously."

"I doubt I'll be done then," Riesen responded with a frown. "And even if I am, I think I'm just gonna sleep for the next hundred days."

"Fair enough," Brandon shrugged. "What time do you leave?"

"In about thirty minutes."

"Oof," Brandon replied. "Brynne left some of the breakfast over if you wanted."

"Oh, nice," said Riesen. "I might grab some for sure. Thanks."

"Help yourself. It's eggwraps and protein biscuits."

"Nice." Riesen walked over to the bar and grabbed three of each, immediately setting to devouring them. He knew he probably shouldn't eat so much, considering he was going to be working out in less than an hour now. He didn't care, though; he was entirely ravenous.

"Sheesh, don't forget to take a breath, brother," Brandon chided.

Riesen just ignored him, reaching for his water after inhaling two eggwraps and a biscuit in what he imagined to be world record eating pace. He barely took one gulp of water, then pounded the rest of his food down in a second go. He considered grabbing one more eggwrap, but thought better. The three wraps and biscuits would tide him over for now.

"I'm gonna wash up, brother," Riesen said as he wiped clean the mess he made with the biscuits. "Be back in a few."

"Cool, you can help me study for a few minutes before you leave."

Riesen casually flashed Brandon the Crescent 'C' without looking back. He would definitely help Brandon out before he left. That might even redirect his thoughts away from the impending agony he was about to suffer. He summoned a blank expression for his own sake, but allowed himself a few more negative thoughts before trying to put it all out of his mind. The best he could do was enjoy these next thirty minutes of peace before he was thrown back into the blazes.

The air was thick with humidity, but at least the sol-light that relentlessly beat down all day had disappeared. Nighttime had arrived, but the training had migrated to the indoor facility anyway. Riesen swore he could smell the sweat mixed into the stone. He even thought he could practically taste it. It was quite disgusting in there, but he had no ability to care about that right now.

He looked to his right, and then to his left. Everything hurt so bad, but he wasn't about ready to drop. Not when almost everyone else still kept going. He *would* be the last one still going at the end. He clenched his jaw… his fists… anything to try to release some of the pain writhing through every fiber of his being. He couldn't control the shaking of his legs, not even a little bit. They screamed at him to stop. He even let his face show weakness, something he very rarely did. But he was not going to drop. After what felt like an eternity, he saw Rush Fils slide down the wall into a slump, sucking air through gritted teeth as he did.

"Fifteen minutes and forty-two seconds!" he heard Kate announce. His sister, of all people, had been assigned to administer this last portion of the training. He never knew she could be so cruel and harsh. He might've even thought it was awesome — if he wasn't on the receiving end of it, that was. "I know how bad it hurts. Fils here just dropped. No shame now for anyone. If you continue, you better keep your legs ninety degrees, though!" As she walked by Riesen, she slapped the top of his thighs hard.

There was no way he was dropping, even though he sensed several others give up in the ensuing seconds. Like Kate had said, Rush Fils — one of the stars of the Islands national Field team — had already given up. She said there was no shame, but that was only a ploy to get more people to give up. He refused to fall for it.

One by one, though, more and more people fell from their holds. It was like Rush dropping had split open a reservoir dam and the whole lake came crashing through at once. He looked to his sides once again. There were only five people still going at this point.

Now four.

Just a little bit longer, he promised himself. *You have to do this. Don't even think about giving up...*

Three.

Come on, come on, come on! He wanted to stop so badly, even though he knew it was all mental. Holding his form just got infinitely harder, and at the same time, his vision started to become starry. This had to be because of the simple thought that he was almost done. It was weird how that worked. That revelation didn't make it any easier, though. This was *so* painful. He wished the others would just give up already.

He glanced to his left to see who they were. He was not surprised to see Rangar Thomson, another star from the Islands national Field team. That guy was an animal. The other brave soul holding on was Pira. There was no way she wasn't in the same pain that Riesen was, but her face looked way too serene right now. He had developed an insane respect for her after seeing how gracefully she handled all of this misery over the past few days, but respect or no, he was *not* going to allow her to beat him now.

He faced forward and squeezed his eyes shut, not caring that his face was probably twisted around in some ugly contortion. He breathed quickly and loudly through puffed cheeks. He *was* going to win. He heard Rangar doing the same breathing pattern that he was doing himself, so that comforted him. He already beat this guy in the World Championships, so there was no way he would lose to him now. *No way.*

The other trainees who'd already given up started to recover from their own pain and cheered the remaining three survivors on. It was becoming increasingly loud and that only seemed to make things more difficult. Riesen tried to stay as calm as possible, hoping that this raucous attention they were getting from their peers would affect the other two more negatively than it affected him. He had to maintain for just a little bit longer now...

Kate was saying something, but he paid it no mind. She was probably taunting them or something. Anything to make them give up sooner. He opened his eyes again and stared straight ahead to the ceiling, continuing to puff his cheeks in and out. In and out. In and out. In and out. He tried to allow the repetition to put him into an automated trance, but the burning sensation was too strong.

When he looked to the left again, he met Pira's gaze. She was definitely struggling. Her face was involuntarily twitching and her legs were shaking so badly that he didn't know how it was possible that she still held her position. Riesen offered her a nod, but she closed her eyes and allowed her face to warp into a grimace. There was no way she was going to last much longer. Just then, he heard Rangar let out a long howl, mixed in with labored breaths. He had to have been searching for the last vestiges of effort that he had left. Riesen was going to win if he just held on a little longer…

"Twenty minutes!" Kate yelled.

It was as if Kate had swept all their legs out herself with her words. All three of them dropped to the floor in sync, although Riesen thought he might've lasted a second longer than either of them before dropping himself.

The cheers from the others continued to ring throughout the room as they rushed in to congratulate the victors. Riesen clutched his legs as he kicked them straight out in front of him. They continued to burn even worse than they had when he was holding the wall sit. This was awful! He was still even seeing stars in his peripheral vision.

Aghhhhhhhh! he screamed internally. It was the only thought his brain could process. He had to squeeze his eyes shut and turn his face directly up towards the ceiling.

Finally, after way too long, the burning subsided. He managed to crawl over and grasp hands with both Rangar and Pira, and the three of them shared a bonding moment. A few seconds ago, they were nothing but opponents that he would beat at all costs. Now, he held utmost respect for them that they were able to withstand that same pain that he did.

"Well done!" Kate congratulated them. "Great job."

"Thank you, Second Officer," Pira accepted gratefully, sweat pouring down her face.

Riesen wasn't used to hearing 'Second Officer' used to address Kate. He kept forgetting that just this morning, widespread promotions had been issued all across the service. She had been a Third Officer, but now she was Second Officer. Riesen was very happy for his sister; she deserved it.

"Everyone may take a moment of respite before we wrap up for the night with conclusions for the commanders. Three minutes," she announced.

Riesen was utterly parched, so he squatted himself up despite the protests from his quadriceps. He reached out hands to Pira and Rangar and pulled them to their feet before heading outside to where the water was. The still air was quite warm, even though the sol had set several hours ago. The temperature had made things difficult today, but much worse to Riesen was the humidity. That made it feel way hotter than it actually was, and it made it harder to catch his breath when he strained.

As he doused himself with cool water, he noticed a familiar sight stroll into the training room. Brody Felleter. That guy was such a joke, but at least he hadn't been present for the majority of the training the last few days. Riesen watched him out of the corner of his eye, and it looked like he was making a beeline right for Kate. Riesen set his water down after he had plenty enough and walked back to the room, keeping his eye on Felleter.

His blood froze when he saw Felleter prowl right up next to Kate, brushing his hand inappropriately over hers. Kate appeared blindsided by his onset and recoiled from the touch. Before she pulled away too far, he grasped her hand and pulled her back toward him, reaching around her waist with his other hand. As she was reeled in, she held him at arms length with her other hand and arched her head and neck away from him.

What the blazes does that chum think he's doing?!

Riesen immediately felt the urge to rush over there to make sure everything was okay, but Kate seemed to have it under control. She wrung her hand free of his and then pushed him away with both arms, but stood her ground, not even slightly backing up herself. By this point, Riesen was close enough to hear the exchange.

"…it was not at all," he heard her say. "I'm dead serious. You will *not* do that to me."

Good for her, Riesen thought as pride swelled over him.

"Address me correctly," Felleter replied with a sneer, pointing to the emblem on his chest.

Riesen realized that although Kate had been promoted to *Second* Officer, Felleter had now been promoted to *First* Officer. He immediately became defensive for his sister. He was not going to let this chum bully his own family, but he knew he couldn't embarrass Kate by improperly intervening and jeopardizing his own progress.

Kate made a halfhearted attempt to salute Felleter properly.

"First Officer," she said curtly, then strode to the other side of the room in an apparent attempt to diffuse the situation. "One minute left!" she shouted to the trainees that were finishing their break.

Everyone who was outside shuffled back into the room and started to organize for Kate's conclusion. A few more minutes of standing at attention and Riesen would be done with this wretched training. After Kate finished up, they would all file outside and assemble for the conclusions with the commanders, then that was it!

Thank the heavens, Riesen sighed. He had made it. His body would hate him for a few days, but he had made it.

"Reserves and Candidates," Kate said formally as soon as all the trainees were arranged in a formation in front of her.

"Second Officer," the whole group said in reply.

"We are concluded for our tra…" Kate started to say as she was cut off.

"Hold on one second," Felleter butted in sharply. "The salute should be to the ranking officer in presence. You all know better. Assume plank positions, hands on ground."

Riesen couldn't believe it. There was no way Felleter was going to make them all do more push-ups. Riesen had already done thousands over the last two days. The others seemed to not even hesitate, however, so he dropped to the ground without a second thought.

"Down and hold," Felleter commanded.

Riesen and the others dropped low and held the position ten centimeters from the ground.

"You, as well, Second Officer," Felleter ordered Kate. "Down and hold."

Kate looked at him with daggers in her eyes, but she obeyed. The commanders were already starting to assemble outside, and she knew better than to openly defy a superior officer, especially in their presence.

"Now, our esteemed Second Officer here has a history of forgetfulness," Felleter said with a hint of scorn, "but I would expect the rest of you to know the difference between a First Officer and a Second Officer. Up."

Kate and the trainees silently pushed up.

"Down and hold," Felleter commanded again. "This open disregard of rank is a dangerous thing to play around with. All of you, including insubordinate officers such as Ryen here, will learn proper respect."

He could humiliate Kate in front of the trainees, but Riesen was amused that Felleter could not even bring himself to even look Kate in the eye. That showed Riesen just how weak and pathetic of a chum this man actually was.

"Up," Felleter said after leaving the trainees down for about thirty more seconds. "Down and hold."

He was silent this round, as were all the trainees, although some of them were starting to breathe heavily under the strain. Riesen's arms were so incredibly tired, but his anger toward Felleter seemed to provide him extra strength.

"Up."

Everyone pushed up, though more people were struggling this time. Even Pira had dipped a knee to press up.

"Down and hold. Not you, Second Officer. You will stand up at attention." Felleter snapped the command at Kate, but still did not meet her eyes.

Kate obeyed and stood up.

"All of you right now have this inept officer to thank. All the responsibility of subordinates' actions falls to their commanding officer. In the field, there is no room for mistakes. Or poor leadership."

This was ridiculous on so many levels. First, Felleter had not ever been in the field. What did he think he was talking about? Second, even if there had been a breach of conduct — which there wasn't — then by his own logic wouldn't *he* be the commanding officer that should assume all responsibility? Third, Riesen knew that this was all just retaliation for Kate refusing Felleter's inappropriate advances. This guy was too much. Riesen would most certainly be reporting this incident to Major Commander Daaz after they were all finished tonight.

"Up."

Just then, two of the commanders walked in.

"Good evening, Lieutenant Commanders," Felleter announced in flowery salute. "I am just educating these Reserves in proper decorum. Down and hold."

The Lieutenant Commanders — Riesen forgot both their names — simply smiled and stood off to the side to observe. Felleter must have sensed that the commanders were eager to get the conclusions started, though, so he wrapped up their torment with one last repetition. He made sure to leave them down struggling for an exceptionally long time before bringing them back up.

"Reserves and Candidates," he said, testing their responses. He was no doubt fishing for any excuse to punish them further.

"First Officer!" the room rang out in chorus. Nobody was eager to perform any more isometrics.

"Please assemble outside for the final conclusions with the commanders," Felleter requested loudly and formally.

"Very good, First Officer," one of the Lieutenant Commanders congratulated him. "You clearly have a great command over your trainees."

This irked Riesen because this was Kate's command for the night. Felleter had just arrived out of nowhere, harassing his sister and then assuming all credit for her command. He couldn't wait to report this guy for this ridiculous behavior. All of the rest of the trainees looked just as angry as Riesen, but no one dared say anything with so many commanders around.

Riesen supposed Felleter was digging his own grave, though. Did he not realize that half of these people would outrank him in a few months' time? That guy was going to have so many enemies. Riesen would have felt bad for the guy if not for the way he treated his sister...

"Second Officer!" Riesen heard Felleter call out to Kate as the commanders filed out of the building and over to the field where the rest were already assembled. "Stand at attention."

He was too far to hear what they said, but from his angle, he could see inside the building where Kate stood in front of Felleter. To Riesen's horror, he saw Felleter make the same move as before, grabbing Kate's hand and pulling her in by the waist. Kate struggled free once more and stormed out, but Riesen was seeing red at this point and had to turn away. Before he had too much chance to imagine himself pummeling Felleter, though, Major Commander Daaz started the conclusions.

"Reserves and Candidates," he called out, his voice projected with the sound enhancer.

"Major Commander!"

"Well done completing a difficult day of training. I was very pleased to monitor your progress today. Thank you to all commanders and officers who participated. Stay alert and expect further commands for tomorrow. I wish you all a good night." The trainees all held up their 'C' signs to their chests as Daaz stepped off the platform and exited the field. The rest of the commanders filed out after him, and only then were the trainees able to stand at ease.

Without thinking, Riesen turned to leave. He was all too happy to get back to his quarters, but first he would stop by Daaz's office to submit a formal complaint about what had just happened. Before he took three steps, though, he heard that same nasal whine from Felleter once more.

"Riesen Ryen, is there some reason that you already forgot your lesson in properly addressing a superior officer before departure? Is there something wrong with the mental capacity in your family?"

Riesen turned around slowly, trying his very best to stay calm and professional. He halfheartedly saluted Felleter with the Crescent 'C' to appease the nasty buffoon.

Almost done, he reminded himself. *Stay calm, you're almost done. Then you're free to report this pompous chum.*

"Drop down on the floor, Ryen," Felleter commanded.

"Why?" Riesen asked calmly. Even as tired as he was, he summoned enough strength to stand up at his full height, towering over the First Officer. "I saluted properly, as you requested."

"You do *not* question a superior officer in public!" Felleter snarled. "You are in direct violation of rank, *Candidate*. You *will* drop down into plank position."

Riesen had half a mind to disobey, but out of the corner of his eyes he noticed one of the commanders glancing over his shoulder at them, surely wondering what the fuss was about. He begrudgingly dropped to the floor and suffered through several minutes of an unjust onslaught of push-ups. After Riesen could barely support his own weight any longer, Felleter decided he had enough.

"Let's try this again," he jeered loudly as Riesen barely scraped himself up from the grass. At this point, more of the commanders had turned around to see what the commotion was. "*Candidate.*"

"First Officer," Riesen said clearly enough for the commanders to hear the respect, saluting with a 'C' once again. Before stepping away, though, he lowered his voice to a volume none of the commanders would be able to hear.

"I will not forget this," said Riesen. He knew his tone was threatening; that was his intent. He held his gaze without blinking, and Felleter immediately looked away. Only then did Riesen turn around and walk away, ever more irritated about how things all went down tonight.

"Your sister's body felt nice in my hands," he heard Felleter say from behind him.

It was as clear as the Celean Sea for Riesen, but unfortunately too quiet for the commanders to hear. It was too much, though. Instinct took over, and before Riesen had any chance to think twice about the consequences of his actions, Brody Felleter was sent stumbling dizzily to the ground from the powerful left hook that Riesen delivered to the side of his face.

20

High Command

THE skyline crept ever closer, small details etched into the architecture starting to come into focus. The clouds glowed pink against the rising sol to the east, casting multicolored shadows against the towering buildings. The whole scene looked fake, like it was something ripped straight out of a painting. Even though he'd spent the better part of the past two months in Sol City, Riesen was still only getting used to its magnificence.

He rode on the central-eastern rail now, one of the particularly busy networks that ran from the Meridian Training Complex to the government headquarters in downtown Sol City. The track climbed in altitude as they neared the city center where all the skyscrapers were clustered. As it did, the rail smoothly banked to the left, encircling an outcropping of the first tall buildings. After making a quick stop at a station nestled halfway to the top, the train resumed its journey, sweeping up to the right as it split the gap between even higher towers.

Despite whipping around corners at high speeds, the ride was unbelievably smooth. Even as they accelerated into and out of stations, passengers were left with the sensation that they were relatively unmoving. Meridian engineering was something to marvel at. His father, Jame, worked as an engineer, and Riesen was pretty sure he was involved in some sort of rail construction. Or something. Niko would know. She knew a lot more about their dad's profession than Riesen did.

As he thought about his sister, he was reminded of how badly he wished she didn't run off last month. He worried for her. Was she even still alive?? He didn't want to contemplate such grim possibilities right now. As it was, he only spared her a fleeting thought because his mind was otherwise completely preoccupied with the upcoming meeting that loomed over him.

He instead refocused his thoughts to the myriad ways it could go. Not that he didn't already have plenty time to stew over the last five days… In his more extreme moments of paranoia, Riesen feared that his friends or family would be punished for his actions. His rational judgment told him there was no way that would happen, but his mind went to some pretty dark places while he was shut away from the world.

He had always heard of confinement as a punishment, but he never really paid it that much mind. It never seemed nearly as bad as some of the pre-Arrival punishments of Arhanda's barbaric past. Maybe it still wasn't, but he could definitely feel his sanity slipping a little when the only time he saw light was twice a day when they brought him meals. At least he was able to walk around now, but he still suffered from some of the after-effects, such as the annoying readjustment of his vision to the outside world. The sol wasn't even completely risen and he had to squint to not be overwhelmed by the brightness of everything.

In any case, he was out now. That's what counted. But he didn't consider himself lucky just yet — he was on his way to report for an interview about the incident with some of the members of High Command. He didn't bother pleading his case when he first was arrested because he knew it didn't matter. He had struck a superior officer, and that was that. He even did so in the presence of several commanders. There was no excuse that would have exonerated him from his stint in confinement. He accepted the punishment for what it was. His only regret was that he didn't hit Felleter harder. Although, watching that chum stumble around, desperate for balance as he faceplanted into the grass, was highly satisfying.

"This way, Ryen," he heard Major Brooks say.

Riesen snapped out of his daydream and back to reality. The

train had stopped, and as he exited the cabin, he spared a glance over the edge. A hundred meters below, thousands of cars and pedestrians bustled about their business, the gleaming silvery-white roads and walkways stretching for several kilometers in every direction. He'd already grown accustomed to the sounds of the city and found it all to be quite soothing.

He took a deep breath and followed Books across the platform up to where the extravagantly large doors that led into the headquarters of Meridian Command stood. The building wasn't the tallest one in Sol City — many others that surrounded this building were taller — but it was up there. It was by far, however, the biggest building by sheer volume, spanning at least a hundred meters across on every side. Some of the taller buildings tapered out in sharp spires, but the Meridian headquarters was topped out by an impressive pyramid. Huge square columns protruded from the platform on which he stood right now, rising to support the giant, triangular monolith. Below, the walls of the tower were adorned with an alternating pattern of glass windows and grand stone slabs that ran hundreds of meters all the way down to the ground.

Upon passing through the massive entryway, the typical monochromatic, white décor of Meridian buildings dominated the setting. In the middle of the great room was a central terminal of desks, behind which several large hallways disappeared into the depths of the headquarters. If you asked most Arhandans, Meridian architecture and interior design was a little austere, but Riesen always admired it. Ever since he was young, he always imagined what their buildings back home looked like. If this is what they were able to build in just a few years after arriving here, what must their actual homeworld look like? It was crazy to think about.

"Third Officer," Brooks addressed a kiosk attendant as they marched up to one of the desks in the center.

"Major," she saluted in reply. Her eyes drifted to Riesen, widening in recognition of who he was. "Candidate."

"Third Officer," he saluted. Although he didn't even hold any fancy rank, Riesen sometimes felt like some of these people he was saluting were so starstruck by his celebrity status that it felt like they were the ones deferring to him. It was quite annoying, actually. He was just another person after all...

"Major Commander Daaz is expecting us," Brooks said.

"One moment," the Third Officer replied. She appeared

focused in concentration, staring blankly into the distance as she was probably cycling through order logs on her Ut. "You are cleared to proceed," she announced after a few seconds. "You know the way?"

"Yes," Brooks said. "Thank you."

All three saluted each other with the Crescent 'C', then Riesen and Brooks continued into one of the hallways. After taking an elevator up a few floors, they emerged onto what Riesen noticed was an exceptionally busy and hectic scene. Officers and civilian workers together seemed quite worked up into a frenzy. There were even people *running* back and forth between machines. He wondered if anything special was going on.

"Did I miss something that happened the last few days, Major?" Riesen asked Brooks. He made sure to emphasize the word 'Major'. He did not find Brooks to be as petty as Felleter, but the guy still seemed to have something against Riesen for whatever reason. He wasn't going to take any chances and find himself back in confinement.

Brooks shrugged. "An-Mara attacked another couple stations two days ago, but other than that, nothing."

So, nothing super out of the ordinary, Riesen thought to himself. All this rushing around must just be typical wartime administration.

Those damned An-Mara, though! What in the blazes did they want? Why were they being so aggressive? As far as Riesen was concerned, they were mindless goons who could not be reasoned with. Even before he was locked away for five days, there had been no successful communication between Meridians and An-Mara. They simply were attacking stations for no other reason than to sow terror around the world. Riesen really wanted to get out there and do his part to fight them off. After all, he still held a grudge from when they kidnapped them all last month. He *knew* he would be able to make a difference out there.

"In here," Brooks said, stepping aside as he opened a dark, wooden door for Riesen. "Good luck, Candidate."

"Major," Riesen nodded at the gesture and saluted. Maybe Brooks wasn't so bad. Compared to Felleter, he was a blazes angel. Compared to Felleter, anyone was an angel…

As he stepped through the door, he saw three men conversing in the office. Major Commander Daaz sat behind a large, stone desk, his dark brown hair parted neatly at the middle. Two other commanders that looked familiar to Riesen sat in chairs on the sides of the room. Based on their appearance, which slightly resembled Andersane himself, Riesen had them pegged for actual Meridians. A lone, empty chair stood in the center of the room facing the desk. The room was well-lit, thanks to a full-length window spanning the back wall, offering a sweeping panorama of Sol City and the ocean beyond. Riesen did not enjoy the view as much as he normally might have, though. The sol-rays from the east mercilessly reflected off one of the buildings in the background, and since his vision was still adjusting, he had to squint upon entering the room.

"Ah, Candidate Ryen, come in," Daaz requested warmly.

"Major Commander," Riesen saluted as he entered the room. He turned respectfully to the others. "Commanders."

"This is Major Commander Zazise and Vice Magistrate Ralane."

"Candidate," they both said, offering him smiles. They didn't seem stern or upset, and furthermore he was surprised that a vice magistrate would be part of this interview. This seemed promising.

"Major Commander. Vice Magistrate." Riesen saluted both of them, making sure to accentuate his respect.

"Please, sit down," said Daaz.

Riesen obediently took his seat, still maintaining the upright posture customary when sitting at attention.

"I imagine you know what this is all about," Daaz started. "I hope you are well enough, all things considered?"

"Yes, Major Commander," Riesen replied with a formal nod. His legs were still so tight, and he had a raging headache from the brightness of everything, but he was not about to complain about how awful sitting in that tiny cell had been. It was his own damned fault he landed in that predicament.

"Very good," said Daaz. "The five day confinement was standard protocol, I'm sure you understand. Striking any fellow colleague, especially a superior officer, is a grave offense. We cannot afford dissent and chaos, especially in a time of conflict. The whole system runs off smooth interactions and thorough communication between members of the service."

Riesen nodded. "Absolutely, Major Commander. It will not happen again."

"Mmhmm, I have no doubts," Daaz said, not once taking his dark, beady eyes off of Riesen. "However, we would be very eager to hear of the whole ordeal from your perspective. Someone as esteemed as yourself, someone who I know to be of impeccable character, would surely not act out in a manner without sufficient provocation."

"Well…" Riesen started, "… I do take full responsibility for my actions. I understand it was completely out of line and never an acceptable course to take. I have no excuses."

Daaz smiled as he glanced to the other Major Commander and the Vice Magistrate. "You may speak freely in here, Riesen Ryen. We appreciate the accountability that you have taken. Your confinement term is over, and we only want insight on what made you do what you did."

"It is perfectly acceptable to speak the truth, Candidate," Vice Magistrate Ralane assured him. "This is more an informal inquiry, as it be."

"Ummm…" Riesen began, "… well, I had plenty time to reflect on my actions and would not repeat them. But thinking back several days ago, I suppose I was… defending my family."

"Explain?" Daaz entreated, tilting his head to the side in question.

"Well, Second Officer Bro… sorry, *First* Officer Brody Felleter had made inappropriate advances toward my sister, who also happens to be an officer in the Meridian service. He repeatedly made unwanted physical contact toward her, then proceeded to unjustly humiliate her in front of a squad of reserves and Candidates that she was training, all because she refused his advances. You may ask any of the reserves that were present — they can corroborate the unjustness of the punishment he administered toward her."

"Do you have names of those reserves?" Daaz asked, leaning forward.

"Yes, certainly."

"Send them to me via Ut," he requested.

"Yes, Major Commander," Riesen responded, cycling through his Ut and recalling the names of all the other trainees that were present during that incident. "I don't think any of them witnessed the inappropriate advances he made toward my sister, but they did experience his improper abuse of power afterward."

"I see," Daaz said, peering at Riesen with scrutiny. "How certain are you that Officer Felleter was making these… advances… toward Second Officer Ryen?"

"Undeniably certain, Major Commander," Riesen confirmed. "He grabbed her hand, pulled her in, and wrapped his arms around her waist. He did this on two occasions, and she resisted twice. I know for a fact that they have no romantic history, because she despises him, so this was one hundred percent harassment from a superior officer."

"Well, Ryen," Daaz said calmly. "Thank you for the report."

Riesen wanted to tell him about the comment that Felleter made just before Riesen pummeled him, but he wasn't sure if it would appear like too much of a fabricated accusation.

"Was there anything more to this incident?" Daaz asked, sensing Riesen might be withholding more of the story.

"Well," Riesen hesitated. "Actually, yes, Major Commander. I believe Felleter targeted me after he harassed my sister. He intentionally drew attention from the commanders, then taunted me and unfairly accused me of violating rank. After I obliged every one of his instructions, he then lowered his voice and told me that he liked how my sister felt with his hands. I know there is no excuse for my actions, but I was so exhausted from the training and already so angry at him for accosting my sister that I lost control at that point. That's when I struck him."

Daaz, Zazise, and Ralane looked at each other for a few moments, almost as if they were conversing silently, then turned back to Riesen.

"Your sister has denied any wrongdoing by First Officer Felleter," said Daaz.

What?!? Riesen was dumbfounded. There was no way Kate would deny that Felleter wasn't completely out of line. He had been *sooo* awful to her. *What in the blazes?!* Riesen just simply puffed his cheeks out and shook his head, exhaling slowly.

"I... I..." Riesen stuttered. He suddenly became very angry at Kate. If she didn't want to tell the truth, then fine. But he wasn't going to sit here and pretend what happened didn't happen. "I don't know why she would say that. It's what happened."

Riesen could feel the intensity of the poring gazes of the two commanders and the vice magistrate. They stared at him in silent appraisal for several seconds before any of them said anything.

"We do know your character, Riesen Ryen, and we do believe what you say is the truth," Daaz declared. "If you'll wait outside for five minutes, we need to follow up with others that were present.

We'll call you back in when we are ready."

"Yes, Major Commanders. Vice Magistrate." Riesen saluted all three before exiting the room, where Major Brooks was waiting casually against the wall.

"All done?" Brooks asked.

"Not yet, Major. They just need a few minutes to check on something."

"Got it," Brooks said. He looked like he wanted to say more to Riesen, but refrained.

The two just stood quietly outside the doors, which Riesen much preferred. He couldn't hear anything from inside the room, though. No doubt it was sound proofed for security reasons. Good. That meant Brooks wouldn't have heard any of the dirt about his sister.

As he thought about Kate, Riesen wondered why in the blazes she wouldn't report Felleter's misconduct. He was so mad at her right now! He just told his truth — the real truth! — to the commanders, and now it was completely at odds with her testimony. They would surely determine that she was lying after checking in with the trainees that experienced Felleter's ridiculousness firsthand. What would they do to her? Could she be demoted for lying?

Hmph, he grumbled to himself, *she probably* should *be demoted for being so stupid as to lie about that!*

Riesen just stood there with his own heated thoughts swirling around in his head for what had to be at least ten minutes. He was so embroiled in his irritation that he became startled when the door to Daaz's office finally cracked open.

"Candidate Ryen? You may come back in."

Riesen didn't hesitate. He marched in, saluting all three commanders once more as he took his seat in the center.

"We were able to contact and interview multiple others present for your events," Daaz announced. "We have also conferred with Magistrate Andersane on the matter and have made a decision on your status."

Riesen nodded, his heart suddenly beating much faster from the anticipation. He knew the decision was coming, but he'd been successful in distracting himself with frustration toward his sister. And why had they brought Magistrate Andersane in on this drama?!

"We find your testimony to be genuine and thorough,"

proclaimed Daaz. "You are cleared of any wrongdoing."

Riesen exhaled the breath he realized he'd been holding this whole time. *Thank the heavens.*

"Thank you, Major Commander," he said.

"Your character continues to shine though, Riesen Ryen," Daaz continued. "And I am very pleased to have the honor to announce that you are no longer to be referred to as Candidate Ryen. Magistrate Andersane himself has signed your commission, and you are hereby to be addressed as Third Officer Riesen Ryen. Congratulations."

Riesen was floored. He was pretty certain they wouldn't expel him from the service, but he came in here half- expecting to be sent back to the beginning of his training. He definitely didn't expect to be fast-tracked into an officer's commission straight out of this.

"Thank you, Major Commander," Riesen said, summoning the most stoic expression he was capable of.

"Congratulations, Third Officer." Major Commander Zazise and Vice Magistrate Ralane also extended their regards. He stood up and formally grasped forearms with all three as he allowed himself a polite smile.

He was mostly glad that he didn't have to go through the training again. The more he thought about it, though, he knew it was only fair that he did receive the commission. Had he not done what he did to Felleter, he would've been commissioned as an officer in an outdoor ceremony at the Meridian Training Complex a few days ago. He knew that he completed the training with flying colors. Out of the ninety-six Candidates that began the training alongside him, it was only him and Pira that earned officer's qualification. He did want to offer her congratulations in person, but surely she was given placement and likely long gone already. Riesen wondered where she was to be stationed. Probably somewhere on South Continent — Crown Lake maybe? He also wondered where *he* was to be stationed, for that matter.

"Thank you, Major Commander. Thank you, Vice Magistrate," he thanked the Meridians. "I am curious... where am I to be stationed?"

"Ah, yes," said Daaz. "Magistrate Andersane himself personally requested that you are to serve under his direction right here at the headquarters. He tasked me to direct you to report to his office at 12:00."

It was as if a hand just wrenched his heart from out his chest, but he did well to not allow his countenance to display such feelings. He was beyond disappointed, though. He'd been yearning to get into the fight against the An-Mara ever since they had abducted him last month, but now all those hopes were dashed with... *office work*?

"Will do, Major Commander," he saluted properly, his emotion well-hidden.

"You have greatness in the future ahead of you, Riesen Ryen," Vice Magistrate Ralane assured him. "You may think you want to get out there and fight these dirty An-Mara on the ground, but I assure you the work you will be doing here will be the biggest weapon against them."

Riesen nodded, not sure that was the truth. "Thank you all for this opportunity," he saluted once more.

"May you fare well, Third Officer," Daaz said once more as Riesen made his way over to the door.

"You as well, Major Commander." Just before exiting, though, Riesen paused.

"Is there something else, Ryen?"

"If I may I ask," Riesen humbly requested, "what will become of First Officer Felleter? Or my sister?"

"First Officer Brody Felleter will now be *Third Officer* Brody Felleter," Daaz said with a smug huff. "As will Kate Ryen, I regret."

Riesen stepped with a newfound lightness through the halls, all too happy to be rid of his escort. It was a relaxing change of pace from the humiliating trek through the training complex this morning. True, even that beat sitting in the darkness cooped up in a tiny cell, but he had been escorted by the arms, still in cuffs, right through the middle of everyone. Heads had turned from all directions as everyone clambered to get a look at the famous Riesen Ryen being marched across the grounds.

Riesen had been so embarrassed, but it was somewhat vindicating when he heard cheers erupt from trainees throughout his procession. Everyone had to have heard what happened last week.

There was no way they didn't know at least most of the story. Rumors spread quickly by nature, and the others surely told a story favorable of Riesen. Nobody liked Felleter, so Riesen had probably become some sort of martyr to all the trainees for what he did. He was not convinced he would do the same 'heroic' thing again, though. His stint in confinement was not a fun time.

None of that mattered anymore, though. Riesen was exonerated and Felleter was demoted. The funny part about it now was that both of them were the same exact rank. Felleter wouldn't be able to pull his nonsense any longer. Furthermore, Riesen would probably be promoted much more quickly than Felleter would be since everyone in High Command seemed to love him. Once he outranked that little chum, he would go find him and force him to stand at attention. Maybe he would even throw in a few push-ups for old-times' sake. He figured that he probably shouldn't do that last part, but it was fun to think about.

He smiled to himself as he emerged into the rising Islands sollight after exiting the headquarters. He closed his eyes as he took a moment to bask in the warmth, although he was fine keeping them open now since his vision had mostly readjusted to the daylight. He strolled down the stairs that led to the rail station, then glanced to the side where he spotted Kate walking up to the entrance. He immediately alerted her on his Ut and told her to turn around. He *had* to know what the blazes she was thinking by lying to the commanders. She whirled around and immediately met his gaze, a no-nonsense frown etched across her face. He jogged over to his sister to greet her, but was only met with a closed fist to his shoulder when he arrived.

"You idiot!" she scolded.

"Wha..." Riesen started.

"You never use that brain of yours!" she interrupted, smacking him on the side of his head.

"I..."

"So what is it they did to you?" she interrupted again, her hands now crossly on her hips.

"They..."

"You have to start training over?" she continued.

"Nah, I..."

"Confinement?"

"I..."

"Or kicked out entirely?"

"Blazes, girl!" Riesen managed to blurt out exasperatedly. "If I could get a word in…"

Kate just stared back at Riesen silently this time, her expression locked in fierce, big-sister anger.

"Five days in confinement," he stated bluntly.

"Pfft," she hissed, blinking in obvious annoyance. "I could've told you that's what would happen."

"But then I got promoted," Riesen added, pointing to the updated design on his emblem. He waited for her to respond, but she just stared back at him, her mouth slightly ajar in an expression that Riesen thought was either surprise or doubt.

"I'm actually serious," he said. "They cleared me of the whole thing. I'm being stationed here at the headquarters."

"Wow…" she uttered. "Whaaa…"

"Yeah, tell me about it," he responded. "The bigger issue, though, is why did you *lie* to the blazes commanders? I saw what Felleter did to you."

Kate's tanned face went aghast at the admission. She obviously didn't expect that he knew that she'd been harassed, much less that she had concealed that from the commanders. She rolled her eyes and stepped back, throwing her arms to her sides in indignation.

"You didn't tell them, did you?" she demanded.

"Well yeah… I had to, Kate," Riesen said, throwing his own arms to the side. "Why didn't you?!"

Kate just shook her head and turned around. He could see her curling her hands up into closed fists, certain that she was going to lash out once more. He instinctively got ready to deflect any punches, but they never came.

"You don't understand," she said when she finally turned back around. "You couldn't understand."

"What do you mean I don't understand?" Riesen asked incredulously. "What is there not to understand? Felleter was a complete ass to you. You report him. Simple as that."

Kate shook her head, tears of frustration barely restrained behind the corners of her eyes. "You don't get it," she said.

Riesen scoffed in return, shaking his head with a laugh. *Blazes, what is her deal?*

"You don't know what it's like!" she said, shoving him with both hands. He barely even moved backwards, thanks to his muscular frame. "You have no idea what it's like to be a girl!"

"A *girl*...? What does that have *anything* to do with you telling the damn truth?" Riesen asked, still laughing and shaking his head.

"You're so clueless!" she practically shouted. At this point, heads turned from passersby that happened to walk too closely.

"Then enlighten me," Riesen laughed.

"You're being a condescending ass," Kate challenged.

"I really am not," Riesen shot back. "I'm just trying to know why you would openly lie to the commanders. To protect Brody *blazes* Felleter of all people!"

"You *are* being an ass," Kate said, thankfully lowering her voice again. "And it wasn't to protect Brody *blazes* Felleter."

"Then *why*?" Riesen begged. "Why did you lie to them?"

"Because if I go and report that to Command," she said, "then my whole fitness to lead is in question. If I can't even do my job without having to go tattle on someone for harassing me, then it appears that I can't handle myself."

"What?" Riesen stuttered. He thought that was preposterous. It made no sense at all. "What are you talking about? Nobody would think lesser of you. Everyone knows Felleter was in the wrong. You have *so* many people that could've vouched for you!"

"No, Riesen," Kate said, shaking her head. "You don't get it. That's not how it is for us girls."

"It has nothing to do with gender," Riesen rebutted.

"It has everything to do with gender!" she cried. "You don't see it because you live your sheltered little life where you're just the golden boy this, golden boy that. Everywhere in the world, society treats boys as stronger, better leaders, smarter, more dominant — the list goes on and on. A guy who's harassed can stand up for himself — maybe even knock the guy out — and they are celebrated."

"Is that supposed to be a dig?" Riesen asked, narrowing his eyes.

"No, it's not," she replied sternly. "It means a girl who stands up for herself, a girl who is strong, a girl who's dominant... she's not celebrated the same way. She's seen as a squawk."

"No she's not!" Riesen said. "I think it would have been awesome if you knocked that guy out!"

"Oh yeah? So I could join you in confinement? That's the typical, brainless boy thing to do."

"Maybe you should have," he shrugged. "I ended up getting promoted, and you're getting *demoted*."

He immediately regretted uttering those words. He should have waited to let the commanders deliver the news. Kate visibly deflated upon hearing it, and that was probably the one thing that could have tugged on Riesen's heartstrings right now. He much preferred fiery, feisty Kate over sad, dejected Kate.

"I… I'm actually getting *demoted*?" she stammered quietly.

"I'm sorry," Riesen sighed. "I should've let them be the ones to tell you."

Her eyes glazed over, but to her credit, the floodgates never opened.

"And this is why it sucks to be a girl," she said softly.

Riesen still thought this had nothing to do with being a boy or a girl. It had everything to do with him telling the truth to the commanders and taking accountability, versus her lying to them. He was not about to argue further, though. Not now that he'd already kicked her while she was down by telling her she was getting demoted.

"I guess I shouldn't have outright lied," she surprisingly admitted after breaking a short silence between the two. "But seriously, Riesen. You have no idea what it's like. I wish you could live one week in our shoes."

He didn't know how to respond without triggering her. He fundamentally disagreed with what she was saying. She claimed the world was being so sexist against girls, but by her creating the issue, he knew she was being the sexist one...

"I guess we can just be glad we don't live like pre-Arrival anymore," he joked, attempting to lighten the mood. "Girls had a grand total of zero rights then."

"Tell me about it," she muttered. Riesen thought she still hadn't let go of the argument, so he tried to deflect the conversation further.

"Well," he said, "I think we can both agree that Felleter can go to blazes."

"Yes," Kate agreed firmly, her eyes reigniting with fire. "Yes, he can."

"I know I shouldn't have hit him," Riesen said, "but he just made me so mad. I was so tired, and then he purposely got the commanders' attention after all his weaseling was done. And trust me, you don't even want to know what he said about you."

"He is a weasel," Kate said. "He's always been like that. He's really good at taking the first shot, then getting people caught when they retaliate. He sure played you."

Riesen thought he saw a hint of a smirk on the corner of Kate's mouth. This was good news, even if it was at his expense. Although… she was right. Felleter *did* play him.

Never again, Riesen promised himself.

"Yeah, maybe he did," Riesen said. "But I'm not gonna lie, it was satisfying to see him go down after I hit him only once."

Kate smirked back at him, widening her eyes and nodding. Riesen was then caught by surprise when she stepped forward and slung her arms around him, clutching tight and not letting go. He couldn't be too surprised though — Kate was ever the hugger.

"I love you, Riesen," she said. "Thank you for always sticking up for me. Even when I don't need it."

"Of course," he responded, returning her hug. "Love you, too."

"I'm super glad they're stationing you here," she said, still holding her brother tightly.

"Meh," Riesen mumbled. He was still upset about not being sent to go fight the An-Mara. "At least there's Sliding. And you guys."

"Oh, hey!" Kate exclaimed, finally letting go. "If you're free, I'm going over to visit Mom and Dad tonight. Wanna come with?"

"Sure," Riesen said with a shrug. That actually sounded nice to him. He hadn't seen them since several days before his confinement. Sure, he might have to endure a little bit of a scolding from them, but they might also be proud of his promotion. "If I'm free. I'm reporting in at 12:00, so I'll let you know when I know."

"Cool," she said. "Well, I guess I'm off to go face my doom," she added with a wince.

"I'm sorry about that," Riesen said, mirroring her wince. "You don't deserve it. But at least you'll be happy to know that Felleter is getting demoted all the way to Third Officer."

Of course there's an antechamber, Riesen remarked to himself. He thought the hallways leading to Major Commander Daaz's office were impressive, but they paled in comparison to the Magistrate's wing. The hallway that led into this antechamber was huge, and the antechamber itself was even bigger! How did all of this even fit onto one floor?

What he was most surprised about was the number of staff bustling about whatever duties they were all performing. Did the Magistrate really have this many people working for him? Is this the work *he* would be doing? It looked so… *boring*. He had been dwelling all morning on the fact that he was not to be stationed out in the field, something he'd really wanted for a long time. Vice Magistrate Ralane had told him the work at the headquarters was so important, but all Riesen saw was a bunch of people running back and forth between machines or speaking through Uts.

Ugh, office work…

He strode across the floor, barely dodging an older man that was carrying a box of something across the room in the opposite direction. He followed the man with his eyes, curious to see where he was going, but then almost crashed into a lady carrying another box the other way. He had to weave through several more people, each on a mission of their own, before finally escaping to the hall where Andersane's office would be. This place was absolute chaos!

After ducking into the hallway, he rounded a corner where the din of the activity in the antechamber oddly faded away. Meridian sound technology had always been an enigma to him. The transitions were soft, seamless, and effective. As he continued to the end of the hallway in peaceful quiet, he saw two black doors, stark against the pale paneling. The Magistrate's office.

One of the doors was slightly cracked open, signaling to Riesen that he was expected and welcome to enter. He stepped closer to push the door open, but stopped when he heard voices discussing something inside. Was he not supposed to enter just yet? He didn't want to barge in on any meetings Andersane was having. He wanted to make a good impression when he met the Magistrate.

Technically, he'd already met the man last month when the Meridians had rescued him and his friends from the An-Mara, but that introduction was something he'd rather forget. Ravenna had put on some sort of a show and humiliated the blazes out of him. Because of her, Andersane thought that he was just some hooligan messing around, and that's why he got into the mess he did.

Thinking about that still made Riesen so mad. Thinking about all of them made him so mad. He still couldn't believe that they'd abandoned all their people right during the most important moment of their lives. The Meridians needed everyone to fight against the An-Mara right now! How did they not see that?

"I assure you, I have been hearing what you are saying," he overheard Andersane say as he willed thoughts of his friends out of his mind. "You've said they are convinced about the Machine three times now."

"Then I trust you will do the right thing?" a lady asked back. Her voice sounded extremely familiar.

"You can always trust that I'll do the right thing," Andersane responded bluntly in his deep, resonant voice. He sounded like he was not in a mood to be trifled with.

The lady... *chuckled*?

Wow, Riesen thought. She was either really brave or really foolish to scoff at the Magistrate. Who was she? He felt like he knew her.

"I... regret that we've had the dealings that we have." Andersane sounded like he stopped just short of apologizing. "Rest assured, this is very critical information and I will be convening with my generals. We always knew this was something that could be coming."

"Yes, we did," she agreed. "Then we are in understanding?"

Wait a second, Riesen thought as it dawned on him. He carefully peered through the crack between the doors, widening his eyes in surprise at what he saw. He had to do a double take, but it *was* her.

Indeed, displayed onto the wall was a Ut projection of none other than Ajane Solase. A thousand different thoughts and emotions flooded through him all at once. What was *she* doing conversing with Andersane? Wasn't she a criminal and a fugitive? To be fair, he still wasn't completely sure who she was or what she wanted. His friends said one thing, but the Meridians said another. He definitely leaned more to the side of the Meridians — they had a way better grasp of what was going on in the world, after all — but she was still a complete mystery. Especially after that dream that they all had...

Seeing her now made his heart leap because he associated her with his sister and his friends. He hadn't heard from any of them since they all left that one night, but now he wondered if there was a way to get in contact with them? He wished they would all just come back. Of course, they couldn't just simply stroll into Sol City like nothing happened. They were all wanted by the Meridians for desertion. But maybe — just maybe — this discussion between Andersane and Ajane was a good sign that they'd find some clemency if they returned.

"We are in understanding," Andersane confirmed. "I will be in touch after I discuss the matter with counsel."

He didn't wait for any fancy farewells; he simply turned the projection off and turned to the other man standing in his office. Riesen recognized him as General Maxime Oto, the highest ranking general in the Meridian High Command.

"We should never have allowed them to settle," Andersane growled.

"We were under strict orders not to engage until they did," Oto replied. "Our hands were completely tied."

"Sometimes I swear they're out of touch back there," Andersane continued to rant.

"Sometimes," Oto agreed. "But I would trust he knows what he's doing. His designs have never failed us yet."

"Yes, I suppose so," Andersane grunted in reply. "But that delay is so vexatious. *So* vexatious…"

"It is," Oto agreed. "So much can change in that amount of time. But again, his designs have been flawless so far."

What the blazes are they talking about? Riesen wondered. He did not want to be caught dead eavesdropping on this conversation, though. It sounded very classified. Should he enter now and incur their suspicions of him overhearing something he wasn't supposed to? Or should he wait for them to finish and then pretend he was just arriving?

His Ut told him it was 11:59 now, so he figured he probably should just 'arrive' now and knock on the door. He did just that, and the conversation between the two men inside abruptly concluded.

"Ah, Riesen Ryen," Andersane shifted his tone to a more pleasant manner. "Come in, come in."

"Magistrate," he saluted. He turned to General Oto, feigning surprise as if he had no idea he was in there. "General."

The room was similar to Daaz's office, although the window was blacked out with a holographic cover. Riesen was sure it would've been a spectacular view — they were on one of the highest floors in the whole tower. There was a long, wooden table in the middle with tall seats arranged around its perimeter, but neither the Magistrate nor the general offered for Riesen to take a seat. He just stood at attention about two meters past the entryway.

"Your meeting with Major Commander Daaz was a good one, I hope?" Andersane asked Riesen.

"Yes, Magistrate," he replied.

"I was briefed on the matter of your... altercation," Andersane said. "I do not condone your actions, and I don't think I need to tell you that is not something that can ever happen again."

"No, magistrate," Riesen affirmed. "It will not."

"Good," Andersane said sharply. "Now onto other matters, I wanted to discuss your station here. Your commanders told me that you have been keen to be deployed to fight the An-Mara on the front lines. I completely understand — I too want to be there in person to fight those damned zealots — but I can assure you that the work we do here is equally as important as fighting them in the field. More important, I would say."

"Yes, Magistrate."

"Now, for your work here, there will not be much of a training phase. You will be thrown into the middle of it, more or less, but we are supremely confident about your ability to learn quickly. Essentially, what you will be doing is working with information and communications."

"Broadcasts and news, in particular," Oto interjected, seeing the obvious look of doubt on Riesen's face. "Your considerable public presence is something that will help galvanize the entire war effort."

"Don't get us wrong, you will likely see action in the field before the conflict is over," Andersane added. "But at this early stage, your celebrity will help spur the effort in the right direction. There are some pockets where the war effort, is... less than popular. We obviously can't afford that, so we think we can encourage some more support by having you be a face for our efforts."

So they wanted him to be the *posterboy* of their campaign? His first instinct was to protest. First, he would feel like a complete imposter if he was paraded as the face of the war effort, where other soldiers were out there fighting and dying and doing the real work. Second, he *hated* being in the limelight. He never asked to be some big star. It just kind of happened. This decision was out of his hands, though, and it wasn't as if he could just say 'no thanks' to the Magistrate.

"Understood." Riesen allowed no emotion to cross his face as he continued to stand at attention.

"Very good," Andersane smiled. "I knew we could count on you. We are also keeping you close by so that you can learn the operations of command. We all see big potential in you, Riesen Ryen. We want you to learn how to command. Here, you will be able to see the day-to-day operations from ground zero."

Riesen had his doubts. He thought the best way to command was by setting a good example to those underneath him. If he was hiding behind the safety net of Sol City the entire time, nobody underneath him would ever respect him. He could feel himself getting slightly perturbed, but he wasn't about to argue his points. The decision had been made. The only thing that he would do now was make the best of the circumstances, as he always did.

"So where do I report to first, Magistrate?" he asked.

"You will report to the Communications office as soon as you leave here," Andersane instructed. "From there, you will report to Lieutenant Commander Anson Fils. He will fill you in on your duties."

"Understood," Riesen confirmed once more. That name sounded familiar. Anson Fils.

"Good," Andersane said. "I'm quite sure you will enjoy the freedoms that come with this post. Congratulations on your promotion, Third Officer."

"Thank you, Magistrate."

"Now if you will excuse us, the general and I have some matters to discuss on our own," Andersane said, dismissing Riesen from the office. "Will you shut the door on your way out?"

Riesen nodded and saluted properly before turning around and departing from the office, shutting the door behind him as he did. His head was spinning in circles as he walked back through the hall and into the bustling antechamber. He was so preoccupied with his thoughts that he paid little mind to the clamor of the chaos around him.

He really didn't want to be some public figure. He much preferred to fly under the radar and do his own thing, although it seemed people already recognized him everywhere he went now. He wondered what he was going to have to do for this new post, though. Would he just be appearing on announcements, making grand remarks for the troops? He did remember seeing Rush Fils appear on several advertisements a few months ago… Would those advertisements be what he was going to do, only for the war effort? That would be so embarrassing! He and his friends always ripped on Rush for doing that. It was even one of the things his team used for motivation when they beat the Islands in the World Championships. He prayed that he wouldn't have to be some tool used for show like that.

He continued to subconsciously navigate through the building to the Communications office, still quite bothered by the discussion Andersane and Oto were having with Ajane *blazes* Solase. Why were they talking with her all of the sudden? *How* were they talking with her all of the sudden? Wasn't there a block on Ut transmissions? Had they been in cahoots this whole time? He vowed to find answers — for the sake of his lost sister and friends — but he would need to be sneaky about it. He most definitely was not meant to hear what he did. As his brain cycled through stray thoughts, he was suddenly jolted back to the present as he stood before a tall metal desk at the front of the Communications office.

"Third Officer," he heard the lady say. He was warily aware that she seemed very eager to meet him. Of course she would be, he was Riesen *blazes* Ryen.

"First Officer," he responded neutrally, barely preventing himself from rolling his eyes in annoyance of his fame. "I'm here to report to Lieutenant Commander Anson Fils?"

"One moment," she said as she cycled through her order logs. "Ah yes, Ryen? Riesen Ryen?"

As if she doesn't know who I am.

"Yes."

"You may proceed down this hall," she gestured. "Lieutenant Commander Fils' office is the last door to the right."

"Thank you," Riesen said, saluting her as he walked over to the hallway that she pointed to.

Seemingly like everywhere else in this building, the Communications office was buzzing with activity, if only a little less than the Magistrate's wing. The room was much smaller, as was the hallway he was directed to. Most of the rooms had windows facing inward, allowing Riesen to see in as he traversed across the floor.

He could see into several conferences, but none of the participants paid him any mind as he walked by. Only one of the rooms had the curtains drawn to prevent anyone from looking in, which just so happened to be Anson Fils' office. He tapped on the door lightly, and it opened with a click.

"Riesen Ryen," a gruff voice announced from inside. "Come in."

"Lieutenant Commander," Riesen saluted properly.

Fils lazily returned the salute, still busy working on whatever he was doing before Riesen arrived.

"I was just notified by Andersane this morning that you're to be joining us," he said. "Have you been briefed on the matter?"

"Only that I'm to be working with communications and information to be used to increase morale in the war effort," Riesen replied with a shrug. Indeed, that was pretty much all he knew about his supposed duties.

"Hmph," Fils grunted. "Did they tell you what we're working on today, at least?"

"No, Lieutenant Commander," he responded truthfully. "They did not."

"Of course not," he muttered.

"I'm sorry, Lieutenant Commander," Riesen started.

"What are you sorry for?" Fils replied sharply. "That wasn't your doing. And I swear I'm going to lose it if you call me Lieutenant Commander every time you open your mouth."

"Yes... sir?" Riesen corrected hesitatingly.

"Just call me Fils," he sighed, looking up from his machine console and pausing whatever work he was doing. "I apologize, it's been quite a morning."

Riesen didn't reply. He just nodded, waiting for Fils to fill him in on what exactly he was supposed to be doing.

"So," Fils began, "you are the vaunted Riesen Ryen. I have heard a lot about you. I believe you know my son? Rush Fils?"

"Yes, I do, Lieu..." Riesen caught himself before finishing the words, drawing a raised eyebrow from Fils. "Yes, I do."

"We were all quite disappointed to lose that final against you," he said to Riesen, almost directing an accusatory tone toward him. "But what a game that was. You're an incredible player, and your team was on point," he added, morphing his accusatory tone to a gracious one.

"Thank you," Riesen said, releasing a small smile. He was relieved that this Anson Fils didn't in fact bear him any ill will.

"Now let's see," he said, turning his console screen to where Riesen could see. "What Andersane asked for me to do with you today was create the Daily Update."

Riesen blinked in surprise. *The* Daily Update? He was going to be creating *the* Daily Update?? Andersane surely did place a lot of trust in him if he was entrusting the creation of the Update to him.

"Do we... have a template or something to go off?" Riesen asked. "I always thought the Magistrate himself does the Updates."

"Hah!" Fils laughed. "As if the Magistrate has any time for that."

Of course that was a foolish notion. Andersane had way too many responsibilities for that. Now looking back, it made sense that he delegated its drafting to assistants. Andersane must've only been responsible for reading the thing.

"But yes," Fils continued. "We do have a template. If you look at my screen here, this is what we need to put in the Update. Our job is to hit the four main Tenets of Broadcast Information: optimize the audience, simplicity and repetition, activate emotion, and demonize the opposition."

Riesen looked over the screen at some of the information. It looked like there was a map of the stations that were recently attacked. Two in Equatorial Territory, one in southern Anterg, and one in Flatlands Territory. Good. He didn't know anyone stationed at any of those. None of his friends that he knew of, at least. There were also two halfway completed obituaries from soldiers that were killed in the fighting from the other day. Was this all of the information they were supposed to provide in the Daily Update?

"So let's start with this map here," Fils said, pulling up some sort of geographic information systems program. "What we need to do is think of a way to show this map, but hit all four Tenets."

"Do you have an example from yesterday's Update at all?" Riesen asked, as an idea suddenly popped up in his head. He needed an example to see if he was on the right track.

"I do," responded Fils. "Good idea. Let me find it."

He swiped around on his screen and then produced two things: a completed copy of yesterday's Update, and then the source material, much like he had on his screen a minute ago. Riesen looked back and forth, studying everything carefully for a few minutes.

After sifting through what he was shown, he thought he could see Fils' thought process. As arrogant as it sounded in his own head, he thought he could see an even better way to present what was published.

"Okay," Riesen said. "I think I see how to do this. Can you go back to today's? I might have an idea."

Fils obliged his request and swiped back over to the source material for today's Update. Riesen stood up and moved over to the screen with confidence.

"So for this map," he began, "I was thinking we show this first one, then overlay it with maps of all previously attacked stations in the whole world. It's kind of overwhelming, which is the idea, right? We can say the An-Mara have attacked x amount of stations and then cut to an image of the destruction like you have over here." He reached over to an image of Anziend Station, the first one attacked last month. "Hammer home the destruction. Second Tenet: simplicity and repetition. It'll sound really good with the Magistrate reading in the background. Third Tenet: activate emotion."

"I like it!" remarked Fils. "Except one thing. Andersane said that *you* are to be the one reading the Update today."

"Me??" Riesen asked surprisedly. "He wants *me* to read the Daily Update??"

"He does," Fils confirmed. "He sounded very convinced that you'd be good at it. First Tenet: optimize the audience. Your word carries a lot of weight these days."

Riesen was taken aback by his new directive. The Daily Update was something that every citizen on Arhanda was required to tune into. He was already famous for Field and Sliding — there was definitely no going back to obscurity if he did the Daily Update. He sighed and realized the only way out was forward. He definitely didn't want to mess this up.

"Let's make the thing first," Fils suggested. "Then we can worry about the delivery."

"Okay," Riesen said. "Ummm, so what I was thinking was that we can then transition into the obituaries for the lost soldiers. Afterward, I can say something about the An-Mara and how we need to…"

"The An-Mara savages," Fils corrected. "Fourth Tenet: demonize the opposition."

"Well, yeah," Riesen said. "I hate those guys anyway, so I

won't need to exaggerate in order to sell it. It's not difficult to demonize actual demons."

Fils looked amused. "Very good. Andersane was right. You are a natural at this."

"I don't know about that," Riesen said humbly. "I just saw a direction for it and went with it."

"It's a good direction," Fils encouraged.

The two set to work for a few hours, Riesen detailing the plan he envisioned, while Fils provided some critique and guidance, such as showing Riesen things like how to incorporate sounds and music to the greatest effect, or how to manipulate statistics to his benefit. Once the piece was all finished, Riesen looked over it in review and was pleasantly surprised with how it turned out. It was short and to the point, but Riesen felt confident that it would be engaging for all the citizens across Arhanda. He hoped that it would motivate them to continue their support of the war effort. That was the whole goal, after all.

He finally sat back and was able to take his first breather since starting that marathon session to complete the Update. Just this morning, he had been so upset about his placement at the headquarters, but looking back, he realized that he'd rather enjoyed his time today. He still was slightly disappointed about being cooped up away from the front lines, but all things considered, he thought this work with information and communications might be something that he'd be okay with.

Daily Update complete! he thought proudly to himself. *Now all I have to do is present it to the world...*

CHAPTER TWENTY-ONE

21

Embarkments

THE sand was getting quite hot, but Riesen was much too comfortable to get up and move. Besides, he was exhausted from the four hours he spent in the water this morning. He supposed he could've asked Brandon or Brynne to go get a shade when they picked up lunch, but he was still cool enough from the water at that point and didn't think about it.

It wasn't even officially the hot season yet, but it was a beautiful day nonetheless, just like nearly every day at the Islands. Patchy clouds dotted a deep, endless blue sky. Below, where the air met the ocean, crystal-clear water shimmered with bands of emerald where vibrant coral reefs sprawled beneath the surface. In the other direction, the towering skyscrapers of Sol City dominated the scene, along with the lush slopes of Mt. Iroal visible behind them. On the sand, hundreds of people — possibly thousands — had come out to lounge in the splendor of it all. It was bliss, and hard to imagine they were in the middle of a war.

Part of Riesen felt guilty that he was able to be here now, enjoying a perfect day at the beach, while so many of his people were out there putting their lives on the line. He knew he was fortunate with his placement — spoiled even — but it hadn't been his decision. All of it was entirely out of his control and he was just making the best out of the situation he'd been given.

Of course, there had been the drawbacks that came along with this cushy life. If he thought his fame brought him misery before, it was even worse now. Andersane had him delivering the Daily Update practically every other day, so there was no doubt every person in the world was very familiar with who he was. Case in point: today at the beach, at least fifty people had come up to Riesen asking him to pose with them for a Memory, the latest of which was just walking away now, no doubt bragging to their friends about how they just met the famed Riesen Ryen. Brynne loved it, probably because she could use his reputation to slingshot her own elite status, but Brandon seemed like he was getting slightly tired of it. He would try to downplay it, but Riesen knew his friend.

"You guys want to go in soon?" Brandon asked. "My Green Coast skin can only take so much sol."

"Aww, Sweety-B," Brynne said affectionately, "did you not put any ray-block on?"

"No, I did," he said. "I'm just pale as the Northern snow."

"Nahh," Riesen joked, "I see that tan. Or wait… is that red?"

Brynne doubled over laughing as if that was the funniest joke in the world. Brandon, seeing her laughing so hard, awkwardly attempted to join in as well. Riesen just stared at both of them in disbelief. At times, he was growing accustomed to Brynne, but then at other times he just wished Brandon would break up with her already. Brandon had always been so confident and self-determined, but Brynne was becoming a crutch for him. Riesen noticed the subtle changes in his best friend over the past month, and he was a little worried that he was becoming too dependent on her.

"Riesen, you're too much," Brynne gushed. Riesen didn't even so much as crack a smile in return. He did not want to reinforce this… well, whatever it was she was doing. What game was she trying to play? As if her laughter wasn't enough, she then pretended to lose her balance and reached out to steady herself by pressing her hand tenderly on Riesen's abs.

"I think Brandon's right, we probably got too much sol. Better head in," Riesen said decisively, suddenly feeling rather exposed as he leaned away, grabbing his shirt and slipping it back on.

"You guys didn't want to stay for another Sliding session?" Brynne asked, sounding rather disappointed that they were leaving.

"We probably shouldn't. Brandon does look like he got fried," Riesen remarked. It wasn't a lie — Brandon looked absolutely torched by the sol. Riesen was fortunate to have the dark Islander skin, but Brandon was Northerner through and through and much more susceptible to burns from the sol-rays. "Besides, I need to go into headquarters soon."

"I did get fried," noted Brandon, groaning as he lightly pressed his fingers against his arms. "We don't all have that perfect skin like golden boy here."

"Yeah, how does your skin never burn?" Brynne asked, lifting Riesen's shirt up as she pretended to inspect his torso for burns.

Can she knock it off, already!? he hissed silently to himself. He just ignored her, stepping over to grab his foils. That was as good as an excuse as any to walk away and pull his shirt back down.

"You guys get everything?" Riesen asked. He knew Brynne brought a lot of stuff to carry, so spurring his friends to leave might keep her hands occupied. She was being so ridiculous and it was making Riesen uncomfortable.

"Can you get my bag?" Brynne turned and asked Brandon. Sometimes she treated the poor guy like a glorified pack animal. He didn't feel too much sympathy for his friend, though — he knew that was Brandon's own fault for taking up with Brynne. Watching his friend toil for her approval was all the motivation Riesen needed to stay single.

"You hear where you're being stationed yet, Brynne?" Riesen asked, attempting to change the subject. "Weren't you supposed to find out today?"

"Oh!" she gasped. "Thanks for reminding me! I've had my Ut off this whole time. Ummm, let me see..."

She squeezed the sides of her coin-like Ut and then scrunched her eyebrows up as a look of concentration settled over her. She brushed a strand of long, brown hair out of her face, and after a few seconds, her eyes lit up.

"YES!" she exclaimed as she jumped up and down, sending sand flying through the air around her. She reached over and threw her arms around Brandon in celebration. Riesen was supremely relieved that she threw herself around her *actual boyfriend* for once. "Sol City! I'm stationed here!"

"Seriously?!" Brandon lifted her off the ground, whirling around in a circle as he joined in her excitement. "What are the odds all three of us got stationed here?!"

"Nice," Riesen offered her a friendly smile and a nod of the head, but on the inside he grimaced. He was really hoping she'd be sent somewhere else. He knew it was mean of him to wish for that, but it would make things way less awkward, and not just because his friend's girlfriend continuously tried to flirt with him. For the longest time, it was just him and Brandon. They were partners in crime, the dynamic duo. Now it felt like it was Brynne and Brandon that were the duo, and Riesen was just the third wheel.

"I'm *so* happy!" she simpered with her fake-sounding, high-pitched chirp. "This is *so* awesome!"

She reached around Brandon's neck and kissed him deeply. As they were in the middle of their embrace, which was way too over-the-top for public display as far as Riesen was concerned, Brynne opened her eyes and made direct eye contact with Riesen. He immediately turned away, scanning the ocean to look back at the waves.

Eughhh. Everything she did found a way to make him so uncomfortable. *How does Brandon not see it??*

Finally, after way too long, the couple disengaged from one another.

"I love you, Sweety-B."

"Love you too, Babe."

Riesen refused to look over at the nauseating display of affection from his companions. Brandon had fallen so far as to be content with someone calling him '*Sweety-B*'. That was not the Brandon that Riesen knew. It would've been one thing if his friend was smitten with someone solid — relaxed, easy to be around, the kind of girl everyone liked. Instead, he'd fallen for someone who Riesen thought was very fake, with wandering eyes unbecoming of someone who was supposed to be in a relationship. He had doubts that she was even in love with Brandon at all. After these last several weeks, he now saw why Niko had always hated this girl. He just shook his head in disgust as he started walking back to the rail station.

"Riesen!" he heard Brynne shout. "Wait up! Give us a chance to grab our stuff?"

"Sheesh..." Brandon chimed in. "Where's he off to?"

"Sorry," Riesen said, summoning all the good will he could muster. He supposed he shouldn't act like an ass, but why was he being blamed for them wasting time? They could've been grabbing their stuff this whole time instead of making out at a public beach.

"Someone's in a hurry all of a sudden," Brynne huffed, her fake smiles now turned to fake scolding.

"He probably wants to get out of here before he has to pose for anymore Memories," Brandon teased.

"You're not wrong about that," Riesen admitted.

"I never understood why so many people do that," Brandon laughed, shaking his head. "Ask for Memories with a random stranger. Even famous people are just trying to live their lives for blazes sake."

"Well, I think it's cute," Brynne contested. "He makes people feel special when he does it."

"Yeah, but it's also annoying," Brandon said. "It's like we can't even enjoy a day at the beach together."

"You didn't have fun today?" Brynne asked, her eyes widening in a dramatic show of sadness as she looked up at her boyfriend.

"No, of course I had fun!" Brandon corrected with exaggerated enthusiasm as he snuggled his nose up to Brynne's. Riesen knew that his friend had to feign this excitement, or else he'd have to deal with a lot of attitude from Brynne later.

"So much fun." Riesen's remark was sarcastic to the maximum, but neither Brynne nor Brandon heard him, which was probably for the best.

He perked up, startled, when he heard his name shouted from across the grassy field that flanked the beach.

"Ryen!"

He assumed it was some stranger that wanted a Memory with him, but after looking over to where he heard the voice, he realized he knew this person. It was Rush Fils. Riesen wasn't going to shout back — he didn't want to draw any unnecessary attention to himself — so he just flashed the Crescent 'C' to Rush from afar.

"Hey, man," Riesen said once they got closer, greeting with a forearm clap.

It was strange to think that just two months ago, Rush Fils had been a full-on nemesis — not just to Riesen, but to any North Territories Field fan. Before, Riesen saw him as nothing more than a privileged pretty boy with an ego to match. Sure, Rush definitely had a cocky streak, but he wasn't actually all that bad. In fact, Riesen now considered him a pretty good friend.

"Waves look good today," Rush said, also arm clapping Brandon and hugging Brynne. "You guys go out there today?"

"Yeah, this morning," responded Riesen. "Wasn't bad."

"Nice," Rush said. "I'm going out for a bit. Rangar is supposed to meet me out there."

"I'd go back out with you guys, but pale man here got pretty burnt," Riesen joked, cruelly slapping Brandon on his pink, sol-burnt back, as only a longtime friend would do. "Plus, I gotta go into headquarters this afternoon."

"I heard you're working with my dad?" Rush asked, grinning at the banter between Riesen and Brandon.

"Yeah," Riesen replied. "He's a tough boss. Absolutely brutal."

"Actually?" Rush asked surprisedly.

"Nah, just kidding," Riesen smirked. "He's actually really chill. And I like the work lot."

"Huh," Rush contemplated. "He hates the work."

"The thing Riesen likes about it is that he gets to be broadcast out to the world every day," Brandon joked.

"Well, it's kind of boring sometimes," Riesen admitted. "And I blazes *hate* being on broadcast. But it feels like what we do makes a difference at least."

"If you say so," Rush said, shrugging nonchalantly.

"You guys should stay out with themmm," Brynne pleaded with longing eyes, no doubt trying to steer the conversation back to them staying at the beach.

"I gotta go back in," Riesen said, shaking his head. "It's later than I thought it would be."

She looked disappointed, but didn't protest any further. She turned to Brandon and whispered, "wanna stay, Sweety-B?"

Thank you, Riesen thought. He would be most grateful if she could keep her attentions toward Brandon like this all the time.

"But I'm *so* fried..." Brandon pleaded. "I think I'm done for the day. I can put some stuff on and we can come back tomorrow. I promise we'll come back tomorrow."

"Okay..." she said, obviously displeased for not getting her way. "But I'm gonna hold you to that, mister. Tomorrow."

"Alright, no worries. I'll catch you guys later," Rush said, arm clapping them once more, then flashed a quick 'C' as he jogged off toward the water.

"Sorry, babe," Brandon apologized to Brynne.

"It's okay," she said sweetly, grabbing Brandon's arm and wrapping it around her as the trio walked off to the rail station once more.

"Oh," Riesen said, abruptly stopping again almost as soon as they started. "I'll catch you guys back at the place. I need to go talk to them." He gestured over to where he saw his three siblings walking toward the beach.

"You sure?" Brandon asked. "We can go say hi also."

"Nah," Riesen said, shooing them off. "It's okay. I'll be back in a few minutes."

"Alright, suit yourself. Come on, babe."

Brandon and Brynne continued on to the rail station by themselves while Riesen took a sharp left turn and walked back across the grass to where Keran, Kate, and Mack were headed. He felt guilty because he hadn't been spending enough time with his family. He'd gone over a week ago for dinner upon Kate's invitation, but had been so preoccupied by his own work ever since.

'That's just what happens when you grow up,' he remembered Keran telling him a few years ago, when he had ironically been accusing his older brother for not being around enough. Riesen supposed he understood now. There were so many responsibilities and not enough time in the day for everything or everyone. Especially for him. He imagined he had duties somewhat more important than most people. After all, the whole war effort hinged on his efforts to raise worldwide morale.

"Hey guys!" Riesen said as he came within earshot of his siblings.

"Riesen!" Kate rushed toward him and enveloped him in a tight hug. How typical.

"Little brother!" Keran greeted Riesen with a hand clap and a hug. It was always funny how Keran called him 'little brother' when Riesen stood at least ten centimeters taller than him.

"Mack, what's up, dude?" Riesen asked, ruffling his little brother's light brown hair. Mack just smiled back at him without saying anything. Riesen would have sworn that kid was mute, except for the fact that he would talk up a storm with Kyler about machines. Riesen never saw the appeal of that stuff. He much preferred to be outside and active.

Bunch of nerds, Riesen thought fondly.

"You guys going Sliding, or what?" Riesen asked.

"Nah, just gonna hang out at the beach," Keran replied. "Mom and Dad begged us to get Mack out of the house. He was spending too much time on that machine of his."

"Never too late to get into Sliding," Riesen said enthusiastically, trying to encourage Mack to give it a try. He knew he wouldn't, though.

"You go out this morning?" Keran asked.

Riesen nodded. "Me and Brandon."

"Pretty good?"

"Yeah, it was actually."

"You're welcome to stay and hang out with us," Kate invited.

"I would, but I have to get back into headquarters pretty soon," Riesen said.

"Ohhh, that's right. Gotta go spread that propaganda, huh?" Keran taunted him, albeit good-naturedly.

Riesen just play punched him. "You know it's important work."

"Right," said Kate, as Riesen caught the roll of her eyes through her sol-shades. He knew she never agreed with what they were doing — she even told him as much last month when they'd been abducted by the An-Mara — but he just ignored her for the most part. He was happy to leave it be, and was just glad that High Command never pressed him about any of his siblings' business other than Niko.

"So what are they saying about the embarkments for today?" Keran asked him.

"Oh, yeah," Kate jumped in. "Anything?"

Riesen just shrugged. "What embarkments? I haven't heard anything. I haven't been in today, yet."

"I got a Communication from Jen today," Kate said. "She said their company was being sent to Nevaly."

"Ohhh, hmm," Riesen contemplated. "They've been working up a storm in headquarters the last few days. Heard a lot of talk about Nevaly from High Command, but they haven't said anything official just yet. Maybe today. I'll let you know if I hear anything when I go in later."

It was weird how Nevaly became all the talk of the town among High Command the last few days. They usually paid little mind to anything on North Continent. The Meridians still manned a few stations in Anterg, but other than that, they'd completely abandoned the entire North to the An-Mara. For the time being, at least.

This was part of the reason Riesen was so antsy to get out and fight. He wanted to be out there to take his home territory back. He couldn't stand the fact that those smug An-Mara chums were sitting and enjoying themselves on *his* home turf while they bombarded the entire planet with completely unjustified attacks. Just thinking of Green Coast made his skin crawl. He wanted to be back so badly, but he knew he couldn't until those damned terrorists were driven back from whence they came.

"From what it sounded like," Kate continued, "Jen thinks they're leaving tomorrow."

"Oh," Riesen responded. "Yeah, I haven't heard anything just yet. I'm sure I will when I go in."

"So you haven't heard *anything* about Nevaly?" Keran mused.

"No." Riesen shook his head.

"Very weird," Keran said.

"Yeah," Riesen agreed.

"I thought the information man might have some information, but oh well," Keran kidded.

"Please," Riesen said. "They don't tell me anything. I'm still the low man on the hierarchy."

"Well, at least they didn't send you out and about into the meat grinder," Kate said, smothering Riesen with yet another hug.

"Meh." Although he did understand the importance of his work, part of him still very much wished he'd been sent out to the field. He would always feel like he held no credibility without any combat experience. He did *not* have the energy or will to explain to Kate why he wished he was sent out, though.

"Mom and Dad are really happy, that's for sure," Keran said. "You should really stop by their place more often."

"Yeahhh," Riesen admitted. "I know. I just get so busy all the time."

"Believe me, I get it," Keran commiserated. "Still, it would be nice for their sake. They're *really* struggling with you know... *Niko* and everything. I think it would be really good for them to see you more."

Keran was right. Riesen needed to be there for them. He was *so* angry at what Niko had done. She had been *so* selfish! How could she make that decision knowing what it would do to their parents? As far as they were concerned, she was either lost, kidnapped by An-Mara again, or even dead. At Cryo and Ravenna's behest, he still hadn't told anyone the specifics of their leave-taking, but he had been very tempted to at least tell his parents, if only to maybe ease their mind. Riesen figured Niko was likely still alive, especially after he saw that projection of Ajane last week. When he next saw her, though, he would throttle her thoroughly for all she put her family through!

"Yeah, you're right. Should we do a dinner for them tonight?" Riesen suggested.

"That would be really awesome actually!" Kate said excitedly. "I can send you a list of stuff to pick up on your way home?"

"Sounds good," said Riesen. "I gotta head off right now, though. It's later than I thought it was and I don't want to be late. Especially if I want to get off in time for dinner."

"Alright, love you brother," Keran said as he hand clapped Riesen farewell. Kate offered him one more hug, and Mack... Wait, where was Mack?

Oh, of course... Riesen smiled to himself. He was over underneath the shade of a palm making shapes out of little blades of grass...

———

After briefly touching up, Riesen made the quick journey to headquarters from his new place he shared with Brandon on the outskirts of Sol City. He was glad to get out of there quickly, because just a few minutes ago, Brynne had asked if she would be able to move in with them now that she was stationed in Sol City. Of course, Brandon had seemed all too agreeable with that suggestion — why wouldn't he be eager for his girlfriend to move in? There was no way Riesen was going to live with that girl, though. *No way.* He needed to have a serious conversation with Brandon later, but that was something that he did *not* want to think about right now.

Unfortunately, his bad mood followed him into headquarters. It was as if every tiny frustration was magnified right now. The excessive bustle that boomed just the other day continued still. People were running all over the place like frantic groundbirds, the small ones Riesen remembered from near Green Coast that would zoom around like they had no idea where they were going. The only thing Riesen wanted to do now was get to his work quarters.

A woman had just crashed into him, sending binders that she was carrying flying across the floor. He saw it coming well in advance and gave her ample time to dodge him, but she had been so tunnel-visioned in her mission that she didn't deviate one centimeter from the doomed trajectory. She tried apologizing as she scrambled to pick her binders up, but Riesen just shook his head in annoyance and continued briskly on his way. He knew he should've been a little nicer, but he was just not in the right mindset.

Finally, after what seemed like way longer than usual, he arrived onto his floor and into his workstation. He sat down in a huff and flipped on his screens, almost choking on the water he was sipping upon seeing the massive to-do list that was front and center.

What in the blazes? he thought to himself.

Riesen Ryen,

The material for the Daily Update is in the normal location. I will be performing the announcement this evening. I do request, however, that you formulate messages regarding Embarkments to the following citizens:

Micah Aarons
Millister Aarons
Filip Abarand
Raenile Abarand
Brendon Acho
Austin Ada
Danver Ada
Danyka Ada

...

The list went on and on. Riesen scrolled down, and scrolled down, and scrolled down...

Blazes! How many names is this?? He scrolled all the way down and performed the query to see how many names were listed. *3,058!? What the...*

He couldn't believe this. He slumped back and just stared at the screen for a solid minute. He had to construct 3,058 separate messages?! This was practically half of the service. One of his major instructions had been to always create a personal message when writing to those in the Meridian service, but there was no way he was going to be able to put full effort into personal messages to all these people being Re-Embarked.

There were so many people in the Communications office — surely there was someone else they could've designated to split the load with him? His mind raced, frantically reaching for any solution his brain could come up with to make this go quickly. He had to find some way to get it all done. After all, he promised Kate and Keran that he would be over for dinner tonight.

He took a deep breath to calm himself. He knew he'd be able to think of something, but he wasn't in the right head space for clear thought just yet. Maybe some of the meditation that he learned in training might help?

Nah, to the blazes with meditation, he thought angrily to himself. *Maybe I'll just go back out Sliding.* He knew that wasn't actually an option, but it was nice to think about. The waves were very good out today, after all…

He pulled out his Ut and projected some wave videos onto the wall. Sometimes that helped him think. He sat and stared unproductively for a few minutes and allowed his mind to wander. He first thought about Sliding, but then began to wonder about all the sudden Embarkments. And they weren't all being sent to Nevaly like he would have assumed, based on the current buzz about that place. At a rough glance, it looked like perhaps only one company was being sent to Nevaly. Strange.

Snapping himself back into focus-mode, he straightened up. There was no magic solution… he just needed to crank this out. He moved himself into a position that he could get some work done as he pulled the screens closer toward the edge of the desk. At least he was comfortable, because he was likely going to be in for an all-nighter.

———————————

PART FOUR

Nevaly

22

The An-Mara Directive

THE clear, blue horizon tilted as the whole ocean seemed to move underneath, as if a great avalanche had swept up the entirety of existence, sending everything sliding down towards the valley below. There was no turning back now. This was a big one!

The cold wind whipped at Niko's face as she picked up speed, the sensation of levitation now in effect as the hydrofoils on her arms and legs caught the water. The green of the coast was in full view, but that wasn't where her attention was focused. She was now at the bottom of the wave, sprawled out in the plank position and completely concentrated on the towering wall of water above her. She tightened her core and dug in with both her forearm and her leg, and as if defying physics, she zipped back into the vertical face that loomed over her. Before she was consumed by the white jaws of the breaking wave, though, she expertly reversed the pressure and went airborne for a short second.

The rush was otherworldly! It was as if she had no control and all of the control at the same time. She landed hard after a timeless moment in the air, but maintained buoyancy by tightening every muscle in her body, arching her back to keep from getting pummeled by the aggressive ocean behind her. After the wave's energy largely dissipated, she dove down and burrowed her way underneath the tumbling whitewater. Once above the surface again, she gritted her teeth to fend off the impending brainfreeze and paddled hard to get back to where the others were.

The clash of temperatures always felt surreal to Niko. Every time she ducked under the crashing waves, the icy northern waters squeezed her skull with a frozen grip that felt like an all-consuming stabbing sensation. In addition, her hands and feet — the only other parts of her body left uncovered by the cold-water full-suit — were almost completely numb. In sharp contrast, the rest of her was practically overheating from exertion, protected by a layer of impenetrable insulation.

"I saw that whole thing!" Jack shouted as Niko neared the group again. "That was awesome!! You're making me look so bad. I swear I'll never get this."

"No, you will!" she encouraged him, unable to hide her beaming pride. If Jack Sehs thought she was awesome, then there was honestly nothing in this world that would wipe that dumb smile off her face. Unpleasantly cold as it was, she didn't want to be anywhere else on Arhanda right now.

"Not a chance," Jack laughed. "I can't turn back up the waves like you guys."

"Here, I'll show you," Niko offered. "We can take the next wave together." She was surprised at her newfound confidence, which was in stark contrast from when she first met Jack. What a great day this was!

"Okay, show me," Jack said as he swam over to her. His swimming looked awkward, but she didn't care. It wouldn't be fair for her to judge, anyway — he hadn't grown up in the water like the rest of them had.

"Alright, let's get this smaller one coming in right now," she suggested, paddling slowly so he'd be able to keep up.

"This is a smaller one?!" Jack exclaimed, still paddling as their position in the ocean became elevated, as if they were on the slopes of a small hill.

"Paddle fast!" Niko shouted while laughing. "We got this!"

After a few more strokes, the exhilarating tug of gravity snatched her up, sending her sliding toward the bottom of that hill. At this point Jack was still right next to her.

Oh, good, he made it!

"Dig in to the left!" she yelled, but when Jack attempted to follow her instructions, all Niko saw was the lower half of his body come launching out of the water as he tumbled over in a somersault.

It was too much. Niko started uncontrollably laughing, choking on the water as she exited the wave. She looked back and saw him emerge from the depths, his thick, wet hair comically draped over his face, a few pieces of seaweed added in for extra effect.

"You good?!" she asked after catching her breath, although she was still coughing some water out.

"Yeah!" he wheezed, holding a thumbs up. "You?"

"Yes!" she half-laughed, half-choked. "I only swallowed half the ocean!"

That sent him into a frenzy, as he was not only choking on water from his wipeout, but now he was laughing, to boot. Poor guy! She swam over to him and pounded on his back. It probably did absolutely nothing to help him, but it was an excuse for her to get close. What had come over her?! Who was this girl and what did she do to Niko?!

"Phwooosh," he panted. "Okay, I think I'm good."

"Oh, good," she laughed. "I didn't want to have to perform lifesaving on you."

That was a lie; she probably *would* have liked to perform lifesaving on him, if for no other reason than to get closer to him.

"So what happened?!" he asked. "What'd I do wrong?"

"Well, you're doing a good job getting enough speed to pop out the wings on your armfoils, which is the hard part. But next time, don't let your wrist actually touch the water," she offered for advice. "You always want to make sure your wrist is higher than your elbow. Otherwise the foil will aim you down, and you wipe out." She lifted her forearm out of the water and pointed to the wings on its underside. "Gotta think of the angle always. And your armfoils are more important on the bottom turns than the legfoils. The leg ones will give you speed, but the arm ones are the ones that'll allow you to turn."

"Ahh," Jack said. "That makes sense."

"Try again on this next one?" Niko asked, spotting another smaller wave headed in their direction.

"Okay, let's do this," Jack agreed. "Wrist higher than elbow, got it."

"Yep, you got this!"

The two started paddling once again, and the whole sequence of events unfolded nearly identically as before. It was like Niko was experiencing déjà vu.

They caught the wave together. They rode the wave together. Niko turned. Jack did not.

Once again, he popped up in that same bewildered state, his shaggy hair all over the place. Niko might've even been laughing harder this time because as he swam back, Jack dramatically pretended to be drowning, swinging his head to the sky back and forth in hilarious fashion.

"I'm telling you, I'm never gonna get it," he said laughing. "It's like I can't help from slipping when I try to turn."

"I promise, you *will* get it!" Niko assured him. "It just takes practice is all. We've all been doing this for years."

As she said that, they both looked back at the main break where Tyson had just caught one of the bigger ones in the set. He dropped in and immediately swooped up to the top, adding a fancy spin before ducking through as the wave closed out, making the whole thing look effortless.

"You guys are crazy," he said. "And I've seen the Memories of your brother."

"Yeah, you should see him in person, honestly," she said. "He does all kinds of crazy airs, and he does insane vine swings."

"Vine swings?" Jack asked. "What are those?"

"Oh, that's a move where you shoot to the top like you're gonna get air, but instead you dig one armfoil back in. The rest of your body flies out in the air, but you're holding onto the wave with one arm, so it looks like you're swinging on a vine."

"Woah," Jack said. "Yeah, I don't think I'm doing any of those today. For sure tomorrow, though."

Niko laughed. She was really happy to get to know Jack, and not only because he was utterly gorgeous. He was actually really funny, and she enjoyed being able to hang out with him. She swore to herself that she'd never be one of those boy-crazy girls — and she wasn't! — but hanging out with Jack seemed to really do a number on her.

"I'll have to watch some of your brother's Memories for those," said Jack.

"It's a good way to learn," Niko agreed. "Honestly, Cryo's really good at those too. But he's really humble, so people don't realize how good he actually is. I wish he didn't go in so early today — you could've seen him."

"Yeah," Jack winced. "I feel kind of bad that I slept in so late."

"It's okay," Niko said. "It's really cold out anyway."

"Yeah, I can't believe you guys are still out here!" he remarked. "I'm about at my limit and I've only been out for what... like an hour?"

Niko nodded. She was freezing! At this point she couldn't feel any part of her hands or feet. She could barely even grip the water when she paddled. But she didn't want this to end. It was almost like what she imagined a perfect date would be like, although it was only a fantasy in her own imagination. She would *never* overstep and make things weird by suggesting anything of the sort to Jack. Sure, she might have been developing a crush on him, but there was *no* way that she was going to ruin it by admitting it to anyone. She was doing a very good job of keeping things cool right now, so she just needed to ride that wave of confidence.

"Catch one more in?"

"Sure," he grinned. "This one right here?"

Niko turned around to check it out. "Nah. That one's way too small. Look at the one coming behind it."

They waited for the first wave to pass over them, then paddled into the bigger wave that Niko spotted. As it picked them up and hurled them forward, she watched Jack to see if he had any more luck. This wave was a lot bigger than the others they'd caught, though, so he might struggle with the speed.

Sure enough, as she started to dig in for her bottom turn, she saw Jack do that same nosedive he had on the previous two waves. She just smiled and shook her head as she stalled herself just under the lip of the crashing wave, letting it curl over the top of her as she slid through the closing tube. The sensation of navigating the curl felt like a controlled fall the entire time. It was one of the greatest feelings there was in all of Sliding, if not the best. Right before the thing closed out on her, she flew out in front of the wave and rode the whitewater all the way in, looking to her right to make sure Jack was also on his way to the shore.

Once they both made it to the beach, she stumbled to her feet and attempted to help him remove his foils. It was next to impossible, though, because her hands were numbed to the point where she had zero dexterity in her fingers. She couldn't even grab her own hair to wring the water out! The wind seemed like it was picking up, and her nose and forehead ached from the biting cold. And her feet… well, they felt like nothing but a couple of ice blocks. Each and every step on the ground was jarringly painful, as if someone was taking a sledgehammer to those blocks of ice. She couldn't wait to get inside and let warm water thaw her hands and feet out.

"Wait, maybe we can grab this part with your elbows," he told her, starting to laugh. "I think we almost have it."

She started giggling hysterically as the two of them struggled epically to remove just the first of his armfoils. This was so ridiculous. She couldn't move her hands at all! She attempted what he suggested and pressed her elbows against the release mechanism for the straps wrapped around his forearms. It didn't budge at first, but she changed her angle, using both of her wrists this time instead. The position they toiled in set her head very close to his, and her heart fluttered a little. Thankfully, the thing clicked and one of the straps came undone. Now for the second strap…

"Blazes this is freezing!" he howled. "It was fun when we were out there, but how do you guys do this every day?!"

"I promise you, it's not this cold back home," she told him. "This is way more awful!"

"I can't even move my fingers a little bit!" he howled. "And they burn!"

"To the blazes with it," she decided. "Let's get back and then we can take the foils off once we can actually function as normal human beings again."

"Phwoosh," he breathed through a clenched jaw. "Good idea, let's get out of here!"

The two scrambled up the pathway that led to the trail, which was completely enclosed by the gardens that Nevaly was known for. Grasses, ferns, and flowers were completely overgrown, but that was the intended aesthetic. Niko should have known all the different species, but she was much too cold to concentrate. Walking was drying her out a little bit, but feeling still did not return to her extremities, and each step she took still felt like her feet were being hit with a hammer. At least the wind didn't feel so cold anymore now that she wasn't quite as wet.

It went without saying that this was no Amalkyne or Sol City, but it was a relatively nice day out for this area. Thin wisps high in the atmosphere — she thought she remembered Keran calling them cirrus clouds — were the only blemish on an otherwise completely clear day. Still, the temperature was very cool here on the Northern Sea, much cooler than even Green Coast was this time of the year. Funny that the weather should be so different here than Green Coast when their latitudes were not much different.

Her thoughts drifted to her home, as they frequently did. It was getting closer to summer now — her favorite season back on the Green Coast. The trademark carpeting of emerald green that gave the Coast its name would by now be dominating the landscape. The snows were likely long done for the year, and the rains would've become warmer and more sporadic. Around this time each year, the temperatures would start allowing for the comfortable wearing of shorts and t-shirts.

In contrast, along this Northern coast, the days seemed to be either clear and windy, or calm and foggy, and both variants were cold. Today was the former, but a few weeks ago, Niko got to experience the famed Northern Mists of Nevaly for the very first time. Upon stepping outside, it was as if her whole existence became enclosed inside a twenty meter sphere around herself — there was no visibility beyond that. The weirdest part was that the sound was considerably muted outside of her little bubble also, much like when it would snow. But this was something different. It was so thick and so stifling. It was a very eerie, yet magical feeling. Apparently, that hadn't even been a particularly strong event by its standards. According to what she had read, sometimes the visibility could go down to ten meters or fewer!

The current forecast called for clear skies for the next several days, however, so she would have to wait for another event like that. She wanted Jack to experience it — he hadn't been there for that one, nor had Cryo or Ravenna. Those three had just returned seven days ago from that extensive mission that Ajane had sent them on over a month ago. She had missed her friends desperately the entire time, not least because she was stuck with no one to hang out with besides Kyler and Tyson. If there were two people from the Green Coast she would *not* want to hang out with, it would be those two. By some stroke of luck, she managed to go the entire month without killing them. She even managed to tolerate them okay, although there had been a few times where she got into arguments with Kyler. Sometimes it was just impossible with that guy!

That was all manageable, though. Things only got bad for her when she started to entertain her worst fears that Cryo, Ravenna, and Jack would never return. They were in the middle of a war, after all. Ajane had tried to reassure her that they were fine, that they needed time to do what they were doing. Of course, for security reasons, she wasn't told what their mission was beforehand, but Niko did learn about their infiltration of the An-Mara after they'd returned.

This time last week, Niko had just finished some physical training when Ajane had called everyone into the briefing room. When Niko and the others walked in, she was surprised to see not only Jack, Ravenna, and Cryo — but also Riiz Alke-Tani, Setten-Lo, and Kira-Tharn. She had rushed forward to give Cryo and Ravenna big hugs, Jack a smaller awkward hug, and barely stopped herself short of hugging the An-Mara. Her better judgment told her that was something that would be frowned upon by them, and rightly so.

Regardless of odd An-Mara customs, she thought Kira-Tharn was happy to see her, in her own way. 'Greetings again, Niko Ryen,' she had said. Her way of speaking was so weird, but Niko liked her anyway.

Unfortunately, the reunion was very heavy. Although Niko was ecstatic to be reunited with her friends, their mood had been strangely somber. Even Ajane, who usually displayed a countenance of such serene harmony, showed lines of stress that spiderwebbed from the corners of her eyes. With the news they came bearing, Niko understood why.

The things she found out in that meeting still scared her now.

The An-Mara directive to destroy Arhanda. The menace out among the stars called the Machine. The Meridians' near-complete abandonment of North Continent. The further dismantling of Arhandan citizens' freedoms.

All of this had Niko rightfully terrified. Granted, she was pretty sure that not all of it was true. For one, in her experience, the An-Mara were not the mindless, bloodthirsty savages that they were painted to be. They weren't out to destroy their world! Besides, how would that even be possible? What she did know, however, was that Ajane and her friends looked very serious about it all, and that was extremely unsettling.

Ever since, things had been weird. Ajane had contacted the Meridians, of all people, and convinced them to send troops to

Nevaly, where they were currently in the process of organizing an offensive to retake Anziend Station. Apparently, that station was the key to the An-Mara's plans, so they needed to wrest it from their control. Niko didn't understand nearly any of the lingo they had used. The only word she remembered was 'Engines', which she'd only heard a couple times before — notably during that time when they'd been taken by the An-Mara last month.

"Base to Niko?"

"Sorry! What?" she said, snapping herself back to the present.

You idiot, she cursed at herself. This whole time she could've been talking to him and enjoying his company, but instead she had allowed herself to drift off into all-consuming daydreams while they'd been walking back together.

"Oh, I was asking if you've ever been to Nevaly before this trip?"

"Oh, yeah. I've been a couple times," she replied, her voice quivering from the involuntary chattering of her teeth. She would have blushed, but the cold had wrung her face pale. "Sorry for zoning out."

"Don't worry about it," he replied. "It's so blazes cold out that I can barely even think. Let alone talk."

She just shivered and nodded, picking up her pace into a borderline jog. The trail had tall grasses on either side, and even though it blocked her view of the ocean, she could hear the combination of seabirds flying overhead mixed with the purring sound of rumbling waves to the north. They both exited the trail where a paved path led to the complex that Ajane had them staying at. A large, concrete lot was bounded with grasses that grew in short stone planters. Behind the planted grasses, single-story structures formed a perimeter around the lot. They were of typical Nevalian design — grey stone walls, pointy wooden roofs, small windows, and vines and flowers running up the sides.

"Alright, thanks for teaching me how to drink the ocean water!" Jack kidded as he tiptoed over to the quarters that he shared with Tyson.

Niko just rolled her eyes. "You honestly didn't do bad!"

"Oh, don't I know it," he replied sarcastically. "I'm practically a pro now! But seriously, thanks for being sweet about it."

"See you later?" she said, somewhat phrasing it as a question in the hopes that he might want to hang out later.

"See you later," he responded as he disappeared into his hut.

Niko's heart leaped as she staggered over to her building, an involuntary smile defeating the numbness of her face. This had been the most amazing time hanging out with Jack. Why had she *ever* had feelings for Brandon when this guy was out there in the world? She scolded herself, ruing all that time that she'd been so foolish. As she stepped up the path to her quarters, she was halted by a figure that stood blockading her way.

Kira-Tharn's arms rested crossly on her hips, and her dark brown eyes that were set deeply behind bold, protruding features held Niko's gaze unblinkingly. Her black hair flittering in the rising wind was the only part of her that moved even a millimeter. She meant business.

"I do not approve of your cavalier attitude toward the events," Kira-Tharn scolded her.

Niko didn't know how to respond. She struggled to think of a way to defend herself without offending the An-Mara. Further hindering her cognitive abilities was the freezing embrace of raw cold, which surely made processing anything that much slower.

"I... I..." Niko stuttered. "I don't mean to be... cavalier."

"A critical contingency is upon us, and you spend precious time galivanting around with a male that you fancy..."

"I do not!" Niko protested, interrupting Kira-Tharn's lecture.

It was a lie, and Kira-Tharn knew as much, based on the raise of an eyebrow she gave Niko. But that was beside her point, which was that Niko wasted time having fun when she should have been preparing for whatever was ahead.

"You can't stop having fun just because there's something bad in the world," Niko insisted. "That's all the more reason to find the good in life. Go Sliding. Have fun. Live. Smile."

"We do not smile, Niko Ryen," Kira-Tharn reminded her sternly, tilting her head dangerously.

"I know that!" Niko snapped. She knew she shouldn't antagonize this woman, but she was being ridiculous. Why was Niko in the wrong for going Sliding? She didn't even have anything to do this morning, anyway. "It's just an example."

Kira-Tharn sighed. "There is much to be done. I was searching for you earlier, and you were not anywhere to be found."

"Oh, sorry," Niko apologized. "A couple of us figured we'd go Sliding."

"I will never understand your peoples' obsession with such trivialities," Kira-Tharn muttered, shaking her head.

"It's something *fun* that we do," Niko said defensively. "You should try that word sometime. *Fun*, f-u-n."

Seriously, what is coming over me? First, I find a way to comfortably talk to a boy... now I'm arguing with a blazes An-Mara! She never knew she had it in her... For either of those!

Kira-Tharn just stood there unmoving, still blocking Niko's path with unwavering posture. She did not say anything to Niko in reply, though.

"In fact," Niko continued, fueled by her newfound confidence, "you should come with us next time we go out. I'll teach you how. Or better yet, let's go into town. Even though there's no people, I can show you around Nevaly and you can see our ways. Or we can go to..."

"Have you had quite enough?" Kira-Tharn interrupted icily.

Niko abruptly trailed off, suddenly feeling quite small. This woman was very intimidating when she wanted to be.

"As I was saying, I was searching for you this morning," Kira-Tharn repeated. "The one called Ajane Solase tasked me with collecting you and your companions. She would like to meet with all of us."

"Oh," Niko said sheepishly. "Sorry."

"Go get dressed quickly and meet in the briefing room," Kira-Tharn commanded. "I will report to the one called Ajane Solase and alert her that you will be joining in fifteen minutes."

"Okay..." Niko stammered. Fifteen minutes was hardly enough time to get ready, but Kira-Tharn had sure told her off. "What about Jack? He probably doesn't..."

"You may relay the message to the one called Jack Sehs," said Kira-Tharn. Niko knew it wasn't a request. "I am sure he would be more than excited to hear anything from *you*. Fifteen minutes."

With that, Kira-Tharn turned around and vacated her position blocking Niko from entering her quarters. Niko stared after her, wondering what she meant by that.

Why would Jack be more than excited to hear anything from me??

Niko's heart jumped, but a shiver reminded her how cold she was. She let out an exasperated sigh, then scrambled up the steps to her quarters. The An-Mara were *so* odd. Although the conversation had been very tense, Niko thought that Kira-Tharn probably wasn't even that angry. This was just how she was.

With her full-suit and foils still on, Niko quickly scurried over to the washroom and turned the water on. She now had the habit of checking the temperature before plunging in, thanks to that one time not long ago when she practically boiled herself alive at the Farm. After feeling a comfortably warm stream run over her hands, she eagerly stepped all the way in. Her hands and feet burned as they thawed out, but it wasn't an unbearable burn. She knew she looked utterly ridiculous, standing in the shower in her jet-black full-suit with all of her foils still attached to her arms and legs, but she didn't care. She was way too cold to care.

A dumb smile spread across her face. *Does Kira-Tharn really think Jack might be happy to hear from me?*

She closed her eyes and stood there, enjoying the warmth as feeling slowly returned to her limbs.

"This perversion of the Time is something that we cannot abide by," Riiz said, tapping his hands on the central table.

"Is he mad at us?" Tyson mouthed to Niko.

She turned her face down as she succeeded in suppressing the burst of laughter that threatened to escape. A tight-lipped smile spread across her face as she subtly shook her head at him. Tyson had probably felt personally attacked by these An-Mara when they would get worked up into their monologues. Riiz sounded angry, and maybe he was, but at least it wasn't directed at the rest of them.

Tyson wasn't used to the An-Mara; he hadn't been with the rest of them during their encounter last month. They took a lot of getting used to, these An-Mara did. Although they didn't laugh, didn't have fun, spoke like they were from another planet — well, they *were* from another planet — dressed funny, and seemed perpetually angry at the world, Niko still found them to be decent company, as strange as it was. Tyson just returned a look that was the epitome of sheer confusion.

He'll get used to them soon enough, she told herself, still amused at Tyson's display of bafflement.

"If you three have reservations about…" Ajane hesitated as she spoke to Riiz and the other two An-Mara, deciding to rephrase her statement. "If you do not wish to be in that situation, it would be perfectly understandable if you didn't participate."

"I speak for myself when I say that I will perform what duties I must. The reach of the directive against the people of Arhanda must have a limit," Riiz said. He then turned toward his comrades. "I leave that decision up to each individual."

"I am with the one called Riiz Alke-Tani," Setten-Lo assented, nodding his head respectfully toward Ajane.

"As am I," joined Kira-Tharn. "This perversion of the Time must not stand."

"I do appreciate any support," Ajane thanked them. "But if you have reservations, please let me know."

"We have made our decision," Riiz said firmly.

"Very well," Ajane replied. "Ah… it looks like our friends from down south have arrived." She turned to walk out the door and stood looking out over the open lot in between all the buildings.

Just then, Niko thought she heard the familiar buzzing sound of an approaching aircraft. It began as a low hum, but then turned into a rumble as Niko looked to the south and saw them. One. Two. Wait… not two. Just… one? Where were the others? Was that it?? From the way Ajane had been talking the last few days, she was convinced there would be a whole fleet arriving. Maybe Niko had misunderstood. She wasn't familiar with all that military lingo, and had no clue what the difference between a squad and a company was, or a battalion versus a legion.

The transport swooped in, its roar deafening to those on the ground. Niko's hair would've blown all over the place, but Ravenna had helped her cut it into a bob only yesterday. Shorter hair definitely had its perks. Niko determinedly told herself that it was very cute, even if Ravenna hadn't given her a single compliment about it. That didn't count, because Ravenna was not one to give out compliments for anything.

The lone Meridian craft landed with a thud onto the concrete plaza, which was in profound contrast to those An-Mara vessels that she'd flown around in recently. Those things had been so smooth, and much quieter than this Meridian one! If the technological capabilities of their respective aircraft carried any indications, it was no wonder the Meridians were losing stations to the An-Mara left and right.

As the transport powered down, she saw a familiar figure emerge. A surge of joy shot through her almost as much as it had when Cryo, Ravenna, and Jack returned last week.

"Well, look who the forest cat dragged in," Tyson said with a huge grin.

"It's about blazes time," Kyler added.

"Daren!" Niko yelled out loud, although the transports were way too loud for him to hear her. She hadn't seen him since he'd been recalled into service when they first arrived in Amalkyne.

"Did you know he was the one coming?" Tyson asked Cryo.

Cryo shook his head, a smile forming on his face also.

After Daren exited, the rest of the troops in the transport filed out after him. Six. Seven. Eight. Wait… *Jen??*

Niko fought off the urge to go run over and give her the biggest hug, seeing as though she and the other soldiers looked like they were all about formalities right now. She had plenty of time to go squeeze the life out of her longtime friend later. The ten troops that followed Daren out stood at attention and saluted him.

"Look at this big shot!" Tyson teased. Was Daren actually the commander of this outfit? It sure looked like it to Niko.

After they were done saluting, or whatever nonsense it was they were doing, all eleven of the Meridian reinforcements marched over to where Ajane and the others were waiting. Niko looked to her side and saw that Tyson had finally recognized Jen from among the bunch. He tried to rush forward, but Cryo held him back, reminding him that she was on duty.

How cute! Niko thought. She was certain he was now very happy about his decision to tag along with their little swim last month.

"Welcome," Ajane said, patting Daren on the shoulder. "You are all most welcome here."

"Thank you," Daren replied with his trademark calm smile. "It's good to see you again."

"Likewise," she replied. "Do you know how many more transports are on their way?"

Daren winced. "This is it, unfortunately."

Her look of pleasant serenity never faded, but Niko could feel her disappointment from where she stood. Niko herself was alarmed at the revelation. What were they to do? Ajane was planning a huge operation to take back that station at Anziend. Would they even be able to anymore?

"I see," Ajane said calmly as ever. "Well, we have cleared out all the quarters, so you all may take what you wish. These ones back here are the only ones we're using." She pointed over to the row where Niko and her friends had been staying.

"So my unit may get unpacked and settled?" he asked.

"Yes, of course."

"Thank you," he said. "And I'm sorry we don't have more coming."

"It's no matter," Ajane responded. "We will make do with what we have."

Daren nodded and turned to his troops, huddling in. After a short talk, they saluted him one last time, then all dispersed to presumably go grab their gear. At this point, Niko saw Tyson and Jen rush forward to embrace each other in their reunion, but the rest of the troops just walked by, giving the three An-Mara defectors some very dirty looks.

"Daren, if you're able to stick around for a moment, we were in the middle of discussing a few things," Ajane caught him before he walked away.

Daren nodded and made his way over, using the opportunity to greet his fellow Green Coasters with the typical hand claps. Everyone except for Tyson, of course, who was completely wrapped up with Jen over to the side. Niko just rolled her eyes. They were so cute together, but right now Niko just wished they would go get a room!

"Daren, I believe you know Riiz Alke-Tani, Setten-Lo, and Kira-Tharn?" Ajane said.

Daren looked at them warily and nodded. He hadn't been around for the turn of events that Niko and the others had experienced. The last he saw of these An-Mara was when he was their captive.

"Much has transpired over the last weeks," Ajane said. "These three have defected to our cause."

"Oh?" he asked.

"Yes, there has been a... development," she said.

"There has been a shift in the policy of directives decreed by the Heads of Knowledge," Riiz jumped in. "We see it as an egregious perversion of the Time, and will no longer be complicit in its enforcement."

"What shift?" Daren asked.

"A directive has been issued straight from the Heads of Knowledge that the Engines are to be engaged simultaneously," Riiz said.

"It starts with Anziend," Ajane added. "That's where the master controls are located. They know this now and have been taking steps to turn on the Engines."

"I'm… a little confused," Daren said. "I never learned what the Engines are."

"Leftover terraforming machines from the days of the Nel-Mara, long ago," Cryo added. "And yes, before you ask, it's real."

To his credit, Daren remained calm, although that's just who he was. When Niko heard this news and realized that her friends were dead serious about it, she broke into a panic. She didn't quite have a meltdown like she had in Amalkyne, but she felt like she was about to.

"So, what does that mean?" Daren asked.

"They turn on the Engines and our planet becomes unlivable," Ravenna said bluntly. "Or so the An-Mara say."

"As well do I, unfortunately," Ajane added. "I am very well aware of how they work. I apologize I never told you about them. I was trying to keep their function a secret, but somehow the An-Mara found out."

"And why would they want to do this?" Daren asked, still strangely calm. "It sounds like a whole lot of people could die. The An-Mara are weird — no offense — but they don't seem like psychopathic murderers."

"The Machine is on its way," Riiz said. "That much is not debatable. What we do not agree with is the notion that traces of this civilization must be hidden from its scour, no matter the cost."

"And what is the Machine?" Daren asked. Niko remembered when she, Tyson, and Kyler had asked pretty much the same questions. Their delivery had just been a little more emotional and hectic, with a lot more swear words. Daren was being so calm! Niko could feel her blood pressure rising just by hearing all of this again.

"The Machine has been a topic of the Legends," Riiz said. "Its authenticity has been debated thoroughly, but the return of the one called Kezane has claimed it to be existent."

"Nobody truly knows what it is, if it does prove to be real," Ajane said. "But the fact is, the An-Mara *do* believe that it's real and they will do whatever it takes to complete their directive to protect their civilization from it."

"So, by destroying Arhanda?" Daren laughed.

"Apparently," Ravenna glowered.

"We do not approve of this directive," Riiz assured Daren, in case he forgot that they were on his side.

"How long do we have?" Daren asked.

"That is difficult to assess," replied Ajane. "Best guess… maybe a matter of weeks, which is why we need to take that station back immediately."

Daren nodded, as did the rest of them.

"Now, did Andersane give any clarity about receiving my follow up messages?" asked Ajane.

"Oh, he got your messages, alright," Daren said, "but he has decided against sending anyone else."

Niko could tell that Ajane looked bitterly disappointed, but she wasn't short or snappy about it. She wasn't even vocal about it. Rather, she looked like she felt… *sorry*… for all of them. It was their planet on the line after all. Thinking about that still felt weird, but Niko had become so accustomed to bad news over the past few months that she didn't feel each hit as much as she used to. This was either very good, or very bad. She didn't want to become someone completely calloused to life.

"Well," Ajane said. "I suppose I'll continue to beg him once more. They must see the importance of this operation!"

"I would try to reinforce your case, but I was given a strict 'reminder' to never question him again," Daren said, his unblinking gaze staring into the distance.

"It's okay, I've got this," Ajane assured him. "Now, you must be exhausted from your journey. Go get comfortable, all of you. I will summon you when I have more news."

Niko was glad to get out of there. She didn't know why she was required to be there. Sure, it was great to see Daren, but she didn't need to be reminded of how dire their situation was right now. If all of that was even true. Her mother always told her to 'make the best of a bad situation' when she and her siblings were growing up, so she made up her mind that she wouldn't think about this right now.

"You holding up okay, Niko?" Daren asked after Ajane and the three An-Mara had dispersed.

"Yeah, I'm doing alright," she said. "As good as I can be, I guess."

"That's good," he replied.

"It's good to see you," Niko said. "What are the odds they sent you here, of all people?!"

"I don't think it was odds," Daren said. "It's because of my association with you guys. They're probably just trying to get rid of a thorn in their side."

"Oh." It did make sense that they sent Daren if they knew he was in league with Ajane. By sending him, Andersane could kill two problems with one solution. In one move, he would get rid of someone sympathetic to Ajane's cause, *and* at the same time it would look like he was taking the fight to the An-Mara on North Continent. Everything was optics with him. "Wouldn't they send Kate, though, too?"

"Riesen is in tight with command," Daren shook his head. "They want to keep him happy by keeping his family around."

"Of course that little chum is in tight with command," Ravenna scoffed.

"Do you know how he's doing?" Niko asked Daren, ignoring Ravenna's dig on her brother. She obviously still held a grudge with Riesen from their parting over a month ago. "Do you know how any of them are doing?"

Daren shook his head. "Sorry. I've been stationed at Eastport this whole time."

"Oh, that's okay," Niko said. She missed her family so much. She wished there was some way she could contact them, but Ajane had said the only way to contact anyone was via the dreams, and that was still too dangerous and out of the question unless she had vetted the setting ahead of time. Besides, none of her family members other than Riesen had any sensitivity to that manner of contact. The one thing she didn't understand, though, was how Ajane managed to contact Andersane if all of the Meridian communications were restricted.

Niko sighed to herself.

"Well, I'm gonna go get settled," Daren announced. "I need to brief my unit on everything. Some of them are not going to respond well."

"Good thing you're their boss, right?" Kyler reminded him.

"Just smack them upside the head if they give you any attitude."

"And that right there, Kyler," Ravenna chirped in, "is why you always get beat to blazes."

"Who gets beat to blazes?" he said, acting out his version of incredulity. "I don't recall any time I've ever been *beat to blazes*."

"You want me to show you right now?" she threatened.

"Oh, so now you're gonna get violent for no reason at all?" he taunted.

"I don't need a reason with you," she said. "Your face is reason enough."

Niko smiled as her friends' banter continued. At least her Green Coast crew was still the same old Green Coast crew they'd always been…

———

23

Bridge to Anziend Station

SHE tried to speak, but nothing came out the way she intended. It was more like she… *spilled?*… a flowing river of… *cloth?*… onto the ether around her.

Blazes!

She willed herself to disappear. At least that worked. She gathered her intentions and tried once again.

Same result.

Why can't I get this!?

This was Niko's tenth attempt tonight, and it wasn't getting any better. Worse, in fact. This was also the fourth time she'd been able to connect with Riesen in her dreams, and during none of those four times had she actually been able to communicate with him. She sensed that he was aware of her, but he would've almost certainly attributed that to just… well, what *would* he even attribute that to?

This is pointless, she sighed to herself.

Ajane had been working with her for the better part of the last month on how to connect to other people via dreams. She said Riesen was the perfect candidate to practice on because he himself had psychic potential. He even experienced that same dream Niko had where Ajane appeared to them back in Amalkyne. Furthermore,

Ajane said it was safe to try to contact him because he'd been aware of their plans before and hadn't snitched so far. Unfortunately, she hadn't been able to master even a small portion of the training Ajane attempted to impart upon her. Her only progress had been in controlling her own presence. Ajane told her she'd been doing a great job with that, but that she needed more development before she'd be able to reliably communicate with others.

'*What even makes this possible?*' she remembered asking Ajane during one of their training sessions. The only response she got back was '*echoes of the Nel-Mara*', which made absolutely zero sense. Ajane had gotten way better about telling her things now, but she could still be so cryptic sometimes. Niko still wasn't exactly sure what a 'Nel-Mara' was. She had tried to press Ajane further on it, but Ajane just told her that she would talk about it later and that she needed to return to her training. Of course, she never told her about it later.

Niko always had a more curious, practical mind, one that was common among engineers. She always needed to know how things worked. What made them run. What made them tick. She loved working with her father on such matters, and would love to have his input now on this whole psychic potential phenomenon. Ajane, though a great and patient teacher, did not seem to indulge Niko's attempts at understanding the physics behind anything. All she could do for now was practice in the manner that she'd been instructed.

One more try.

She concentrated on the essence of her brother and unveiled herself from the haze of the dream once more. She couldn't see him in the sense of an image before her, but she knew he was there. It was more a sort of feeling that she had, like she was aware of his presence. Niko also knew that he was vaguely aware of hers.

Now that she knew they were both aware of each other, she concentrated on the space between them and tried to compress waves, as if there was a medium for them to propagate. She pictured the sound reaching him, but it did not. There weren't even ripples. There was no medium. She concentrated for a little bit longer, then ceased her attempts at communication, disappearing from his dream in frustration.

She opened her eyes and lay straight on her back, staring up at the ceiling made of rough stone. It was still dark out, but Niko didn't bother asking her Ut for the time. She didn't really care what time it was. She was much too frustrated from her failure to make the connection. After sitting up and looking around to catch her bearings for a few seconds, Niko then stood up and began to pace around her room, racking her brain on how she was supposed to create a medium between spaces in those dreams.

What the blazes am I doing wrong? she wondered. There had to be something. Ajane had told her that she needed more rest... maybe that was the problem.

She should've been sleepy from all the Sliding yesterday, but she wasn't in the slightest. As she expanded her pacing route into the common room, her heart skipped a beat as she was startled from the broken silence.

"Couldn't sleep?" she heard Ravenna say. Like a Northern nightraptor hunting from the shadows, Ravenna always seemed to lurk where no one would expect her. She had always reminded Niko a little bit of a nightraptor, or maybe even a forest cat. Sneaky, athletic, solitary, temperamental...

"No," Niko replied, pretending Ravenna hadn't just actually scared the life out of her. "I don't know why."

"I could probably tell you a dozen reasons why," Ravenna said matter-of-factly.

"Hah!" Niko snorted. "Yeah, you're probably right."

Niko knew there were plenty more than a dozen reasons why she couldn't sleep: the dreams, Riesen, her parents, Kate, the war, this new An-Mara directive, the Meridians, the Machine... she just sighed recalling even a few of these. She could've kept going with that list for a while, too.

"You can't sleep, either?" she asked Ravenna.

"I can never sleep," Ravenna replied.

Oh, that's right, Niko realized. She'd forgotten that Ravenna was a quintessential insomniac ever since she'd known her.

"Hmph," Niko grunted, forcing a low laugh as she slumped into a chair opposite the room from Ravenna, praying that she wouldn't mind the company. "Hey... I got a question..."

"Shoot," said Ravenna.

"Have you been able to control the dreams ever?" Niko asked. "Or has Cryo? Ajane's been trying to teach me to... how does she say it... fill in the space between consciousnesses? But I can't seem to do that."

"Sorry, can't help you there," Ravenna said. "Maybe Cryo can?

He never really talks that much about the dreams though."

"Oh, that's okay," said Niko. "It was a long shot. Thought I'd maybe ask just in case."

She really wanted to figure this out, but the more she practiced, the more it looked like an impossibility. How did Ajane do it with them that one time? Niko really wanted to talk to her brother; she missed him. She missed all of her family.

"What were your mom and sister like?" Niko didn't know what demon in all of the blazes possessed her to ask the question. Her rational mind would have told her that's a question you *don't* ask Ravenna, but it came out before she had a chance to think.

Ravenna looked up at Niko, her unreadable features illuminated by a stray trace of reflected moonlight. "They were nice." Niko thought that might've been all she would say, but to her surprise she continued. "My mom's name was Valentina. The only thing I remember of her now is this image of her trying to keep this wide-brimmed hat on during a windy day at the beach. So random. I don't even remember when that was. I had to have been so young."

"I've seen a Memory of her," Niko confessed. "She was really pretty."

"Mmhmm," Ravenna replied absently. "I don't remember much of my sister, either. Jackie was twelve years older than me, so I only remember what she looks like because of the Memories my dad showed me."

Niko wished she would've been able to meet Ravenna's family. She missed her own family dearly and had only been separated for not even two months — she couldn't imagine what not having a family around anymore must have felt like for Ravenna. The two sat in silence for an awkward minute, until Ravenna suddenly spoke up.

"Wanna go on a run?" she asked.

Niko at first didn't respond; she only laughed.

"Now??" she asked, after Ravenna didn't laugh back.

"Yes," Ravenna said plainly, as if a run in the middle of the night was the most normal thing in the world. Maybe that's why she was in such good shape...

"Ummm," hesitated Niko. She didn't really want to go — she was so comfortable in the nice, warm building — but she also didn't want to disappoint Ravenna. "Sure."

"Cool. Go get some shoes on."

Caught off guard by Ravenna's impromptu invitation, Niko

didn't even give herself a chance to second guess her commitment. She sprang up to fetch her shoes, as well as some warmer clothes considering they were going out into the frigid Northern air. At least the sky was clear — no rain, no snow, just crisp cold. Both moons were out, though, casting a soft, white glow over everything. Maybe it would even be kind of pretty out.

"Didn't you want to stretch or anything?!" Niko groaned, as she had barely put her shoes on when Ravenna opened the door to head out into the night.

"I'm ready to go now," Ravenna said. "Did you need any time to stretch?"

"Umm, well…" Niko started. "… I guess I'm fine."

She really should stretch, but she could feel the unspoken pressure from Ravenna, as if she did not want to sit around and wait.

Niko stood up and followed Ravenna out to the path, where she didn't even wait before setting off. Niko chased, praying that they wouldn't be setting too blistering a pace.

"We can fit more people than that," Daren remarked.

"Yes," Ajane said. "But we need to keep the illusion that we are still amassed here. You allowed your vehicle to be tracked here like I asked, correct?"

"Yes, of course," Daren replied.

"Good," said Ajane. "Then the An-Mara know we're here. No doubt they will be monitoring our presence, which is why most of us must remain."

Niko yawned. She was listening, but she was *so* tired! Even though it had been fun in its own way, the run she and Ravenna had gone on last night was *way* longer than she was in shape for. They were probably gone for two hours, at least. How many kilometers had they done?! Even before the run, she was already tired from Sliding for so long the day before.

Blazes, that was so stupid to go on that run…

Standing here now was a double-edged sword. On one hand, standing kept her awake — she would have definitely fallen asleep had she been in a chair right now. On the other hand, her feet and legs were begging her for some respite. The thought of plopping down right here on the floor had crossed her mind several times, but that would've only served to reinforce the whole 'kid' image if she did that. The thought of Kyler or Tyson teasing her was pressure enough to keep her standing for two lifetimes.

The entire group, including all of Daren's Meridian unit, was gathered in attendance to review the plan that Ajane had concocted. They were in the small, stone briefing room — the same one they had all their meetings in lately — and sadly, everyone fit in here today. There were only twenty-one people in total: the eleven in Daren's unit, the three An-Mara defectors, and the seven who were with Niko before. She knew Ajane had been hoping for three times that number, at minimum. However, the plan had been amended, and Ajane sounded confident with it.

"If we really want to take the station, don't we want as many people as possible in that group?" Daren pushed.

He was being very vocal, something Niko wasn't used to. She probably heard him talk more in the last two days than in the entire history of their acquaintance. He was normally a man of so few words, so it was crazy seeing him in this leadership role. It really suited him, though. He obviously was very patient by nature, but he also had this really intense look about him that demanded attention and respect. Niko always knew the leader was in there somewhere, but his position as an officer really highlighted it. No wonder the Meridians had promoted him to... well, whatever the rank was. Niko forgot what it was called.

"With this plan, we actually don't want any more than six on the assault, plus one pilot," Ajane said. "Here, I'll show you why."

She walked over to the other side of the large, stone table in the middle and cleared the holographic basin. Niko loved how those worked. A big concave depression sat centered on the tabletop, and an invisible gas would be released above it. Once a Ut was hooked up to the basin, its display would project onto the vapor, rendering a three-dimensional presentation.

When Ajane pulled up a projection of what Niko thought looked like some sort of map, she was instantly reminded of the time when she and her friends visited that station in the White Mountains by the Green Coast. It seemed like a lifetime ago. So much had happened since then.

"The station is up here." Ajane moved her hand across the projection, specifically pointing to one side of it. "The main entrance is right here, and this is where most forces are amassed. The An-Mara did assault this station twice, and both times they went through this main entrance. They will very likely shore up defenses here.

"However," Ajane continued, moving to another area on the other side of the map, "if you look over here, there is an entrance to a service bunker. It doesn't connect directly to where we need access, but there is a spot where the two facilities share very close proximity."

She angled the schematic for everyone to see. Indeed, it appeared that the walls of the bunker looked no more than two or three meters from one of the rooms in the main station. Very convenient.

"The team will drill through the rock, which should be relatively easy considering it's primarily sandstone. I imagine it will be completed in a matter of minutes, maybe fewer. Once inside the station proper, you will overrun any forces patrolling."

Overrun...? That sounded ominous, but Ajane didn't dwell on that detail.

"Unfortunately, we do not have real time schematics any longer, but from what our An-Mara friends here have said, there will be a maximum of two troops posted in each of these areas."

Ajane pointed to a long hallway, and then over to the two connected rooms.

"Two of us will clear each room, and two more will hold the hallway," she said, tapping her fingers for emphasis. "The rooms are corner-point entries, so that's why we only need six total. Any more than six will be sloppy and inefficient."

She looked up to make sure everyone was following her, then moved her hand across to another room, one adjacent to those she was just talking about.

"Once we have taken this room here, we can lock the An-Mara out of their own station, plus we'll have Engine shutdown control. We hunker down, and wait for the Meridians to back us up."

"Okay," Daren said. "Seems like a solid plan. Do you have confirmation from High Command? I have not been given it yet..."

"Yes, I spoke with Andersane this morning," she confirmed. "He assured me that he will be sending a full company to the main entrance as soon as we make initial contact."

"Good," Daren nodded. "So what does our entry look like?"

"That will be the tricky part," Ajane said. "You may recall hearing of the Anziend Mountain ruins before?"

Niko perked up. She did remember learning about those ruins just last year. They were a series of statues and tunnels built into the sandstone thousands of years ago by the ancient Antergians. Ruins had always fascinated her — one of her nerdy hobbies that her dad helped foster.

"We'll be infiltrating from those ruins. They are a protected archaeological site, so the Antergians were *very* vocal about *never* stationing troops there." Ajane chuckled softly. "At this point, we're desperate, so we have no choice but to trespass onto the ruins. Try not to break any statues." The others around her cracked a laugh.

"Once we traverse the ruins, you will come to this bridge here, which was originally built in the days of Old Anterg as a road to transport artifacts from the tunnels to their vaults. The vaults are where the station now resides." Ajane zoomed out, revealing the bridge.

All of Niko's senses prickled at once.

No.

Her breath caught, unable to take in any air, even though her mouth dropped wipe open. Heat coursed through her, and the intense burning feeling that emanated from within threatened to overcome her entirely. It never escaped — only pooled in her stomach, which was now twisted into knots. Sweat formed on clammy palms and her vision blurred at the edges.

NO.

She must have unknowingly stepped forward because all eyes had turned away from Ajane's briefing and toward her.

"Niko?" Ajane prodded gently. "Did you have a question?"

Niko just stood there dumbfounded, unable to articulate her thoughts.

"I... it's... when... we... we..." she stumbled over her words.

She just stood pointing at the hologram for a few seconds until she was able to form two coherent words.

"We can't!" she finally managed to shout.

The frown she expected from Ajane never came; she only cocked her head to the side as if imploring Niko to explain her outburst.

"It's... it's..." Niko didn't know how to explain it herself without sounding utterly ridiculous.

"The bridge?" Ajane finished her thoughts for her. She knew very well what Niko was afraid of.

Niko hadn't thought about that dream in some time. With all of the progress she'd been making, she didn't think there was anything to worry about any longer. Working with Ajane made her feel way less fearful about everything coming true. After this briefing, however, all of that worry came flooding back.

"Yes," she managed to croak.

"It's okay," Ajane said soothingly. "I assure you the events that you have seen should not come to pass. There are too many dependencies that render the dream highly unlikely."

Everyone in attendance looked entirely confused. They must have thought Niko had lost her mind. Or her nerve. Maybe both... and maybe she had? No one had any idea about this dream of hers. She hadn't told anyone about it — not even Cryo.

"The blazes?" Kyler blurted out. "What's Niko gotten into now?"

Of course Kyler would be a jerk in a situation like this. She wasn't in any mood to deal with him right now. Did Ajane really just out her psychic potential to *all* these people? And in front of Jack Sehs, too! Blazes, this was a hundred times worse than anything Kate had done.

"It's alright, Niko." Ajane *had* to have sensed her anger and was probably attempting to mend the mood. "Your concerns are legitimate ones."

"What concerns?" Kyler pushed.

"None of yours," Niko snapped. She was much too tired to be tactful with him right now.

Kyler didn't say anything back. He just shrugged his hands to the sides and looked wide-eyed around at the others in the attempt to play that innocent card. Niko just could *not* deal...

Aghhhh!! She could have screamed.

"Kyler, Niko. It's okay." Ajane sounded rather like Niko's mother when she'd scold her and Riesen after a fight.

"I didn't do anything!" Kyler protested.

"Niko, may I share your... intel... that you have gathered?" Ajane spoke quickly, ignoring Kyler in the attempt to diffuse any altercation. Niko was glad that Ajane at least asked her this time before blabbing her secret to everyone. And at least she disguised it with the word '*intel*', as ridiculous as that notion was. She might as well just call it for what it was at this point — a nonsensical dream.

Niko just shook her head. "Fine." The damage was already done — she'd already made a fool of herself in front of all these people.

"Thank you," Ajane said. "So Niko here is a very fortunate individual, and is able to have small glimpses into the real world via the incredible psychic potential that she possesses."

Gasps and murmurs echoed throughout the room. All faces turned toward Niko once again, and she tried not to look at any of them right now. This was completely and utterly humiliating. She steeled herself, preparing for the onslaught of heckling that was sure to follow. But it didn't come. The only thing that ensued was silence until Tyson, of all people, spoke up.

"That's badass!" he shouted.

"Actually, Niko?" Jack added. "That's rad as blazes."

"Niko… you never told any of us that you're a blazes genius!" Jen exclaimed.

A few more people added their compliments, and when Niko looked up, she saw the opposite from what she was expecting. It looked as if all these people were eyeing her with… *respect*? Even the An-Mara seemed taken aback by this revelation, and not in a bad way. Niko was so confused. She had been embarrassed and frightened by her affinity for the dreams ever since she first started having them. Were they actually a good thing that she had going for her?

"So, Niko did have a dream about a skirmish on this bridge," Ajane said carefully, "but she and I have talked at length about it. I am convinced that our operation is safe to proceed with. There were a number of contingencies in this dream that will not come to pass."

Niko was very curious to hear her say what these contingencies were. She still felt deep in her gut that this was truly a terrible idea. They should absolutely, under no circumstances, be going ahead with this assault. This was *exactly* the dream that she had, and merely dreaming it had been one of the worst experiences of her life.

"First off, *you* will not be going, Niko," Ajane said. "You will be staying here safe and sound."

That brought some relief to Niko. If she wasn't on the bridge, then she didn't have to die there. It still did nothing to protect her friends though…

"Second, it was daytime in the dream. We will be pursuing a nighttime assault across the bridge."

Okay, well that's good.

"Third, Riesen Ryen is not with us, nor will he be. He was one of the principal people Niko identified in her dream."

Niko had forgotten about that. She did see Riesen in her dream, although he had been kind of fuzzy. It made her feel better, but not entirely. Just the fact that she had this dream at all made her extremely nervous about sending *any* of her friends there.

"Niko's dream should serve as a beacon of caution to us, though," Ajane said. "In her dream, there *was* resistance on this bridge. The six that are going must be extremely careful so as not to arouse any alerts until they are inside the station."

"Can't we just fly across the bridge?" Niko asked. "And land at the back entrance?"

"I'm afraid not," Ajane said. "We do not possess superior numbers, so this is a stealth mission. We can fly into the ruins without being detected, but no closer. We'll need to traverse by foot from the ruins. The terrain is very mountainous, so this bridge is quite literally the only way to reach the service bunker's entrance."

"It's a bad idea," Niko muttered under her breath. No one appeared to have heard her, but she wasn't feeling confident to speak out any more than she already had.

"Now," continued Ajane, "for the matter of selecting who is to go on this mission, and who is to stay here..."

"I will go," Tyson interrupted without any hesitation. Niko knew he definitely was trying to impress Jen.

What a dumb way to impress a girl.

"Are you sure?" Ajane asked. "It has been some time since your service with the Meridians."

"Absolutely, ma'am," he responded.

"Very well, thank you Tyson Ander," she responded gently. "And I have already spoken with Cryo, Ravenna, and Jack. They will be going on this mission. They are very well experienced in this type of operation. That leaves two more spots."

Niko instantly felt that much worse, if that was possible. Luckily, Ravenna was not in her dream, but Cryo and Jack both were. Besides, she didn't want any of them to leave again. They had only just returned after having been gone for several weeks, and Niko struggled with not having her friends around.

"I should go," Daren announced.

Great. Of course he would volunteer. Each person from Niko's dream that volunteered made the pit in her stomach deepen that much more.

"I know Meridian units are supposed to stay together under command of a superior officer," Daren continued. "But I can transfer the command of my unit onto you, Commander Solase. I believe I'm well suited to the demands of the mission."

Niko had never heard Ajane referred to as 'Commander'. Maybe she'd been a commander before she was labeled a deserter and a traitor by the Meridians? Niko doubted that Daren's troops would be happy to assume her as their commander, though, even if it was only temporary. Still, it was all perfectly permitted in the Meridian military, from what Niko knew. She remembered the elders talking about how much freedom Meridian officers were given and how it was completely different from the pre-Arrival days of the world wars.

"I do think you would be a great benefit to the mission," Ajane agreed. "I accept temporary command of your unit until you get back. Now, we need one more. Any takers?"

Niko looked to her side and saw Jen start to step forward, but Riiz Alke-Tani beat her to it.

Riiz. Of course.

"I would be one to join this operation, Ajane Solase," he said in his proper, measured tone. "I know the tactics of those defending this station, and I believe you will need my expertise."

"Agreed," said Ajane. "Thank you very much. And I believe that is a sufficient crew! Plus our esteemed pilot over here."

The pilot held his arm up in acknowledgement and everyone laughed and cheered for him. Niko clapped herself, just because everyone else was, but she didn't even remember what his name was. She looked around the room and thought that everyone looked *way* too happy about all of this. Was she the only one here with bad vibes??

Niko looked to her side, noticing that Jen looked slightly disappointed, also. If Tyson was going to go off and be an idiot, she surely wanted to go with him. It was not to be, though; she'd have to wait until they all got back.

"Are there any voices of dissent as for the constitution of this crew?" Ajane asked. Niko expected some of Daren's troops to speak their minds here, but no one did. Maybe they all respected him for his decision to leave. After all, it kept them safe and out of harm's way, and they all must've been more than a little beleaguered from the war by now.

If no one else would speak up, then Niko had been considering voicing her concern once more. Something about this whole mission just did not sit right with her. Not right at all. In the end, she just stayed quiet, mainly because she didn't want to draw any more attention to herself. It was going to be what it was going to be at this point. If they were all content with the mission, then who was she to be the negative voice. She had no experience in matters of combat missions.

"None?" Ajane asked, looking around the grey stone room one more time. "Very well. It is set. I would then excuse everyone except for the seven going on this mission. Thank you all."

Niko was still agitated, but she really shouldn't have been angry with Ajane for spilling her secret to everyone. They all seemed so legitimately impressed with her. Even Jack had called her... what was it... *rad as blazes*? She smiled at that thought. He had such funny little phrases sometimes. *Rad as blazes*, or what was the other one he always said? *Phwoosh*?

I wonder where he grew up? She realized she never actually asked him. She would make a point to find out if he returned from the mission.

When he returned from the mission, she corrected herself.

"Whatchu smiling at, girl?" she heard Jen ask from beside her.

"Oh, nothing." Niko pretended to tuck her hair behind her ears, embarrassedly rubbing her face as if it was going to wipe the smile off. "What a knucklehead Tyson is for volunteering, am I right?"

"Oooh, that little..." Jen started, taking the bait at Niko's changing of the conversation. "I swear I'm going to wring his neck when he gets back!"

Niko managed a short laugh. "You two are too cute."

Niko saw Jen smile and look back at Tyson fondly as he and the others filed in closer for a more thorough mission briefing from Ajane. Just as they were looking over at him, it was as if he knew because he turned around and shot Jen that charismatic, mischievous grin everyone knew all too well. With his hair cut shorter, he really did look so much like Riesen.

"They'll be back soon," Niko encouraged her.

"Yeah. At least we had one nigh... err... day together," Jen quickly corrected herself, her face tinged with pink. Niko did not want to know what that was about. "Then he decides to up and run off to war like an idiot..."

"I'm sorry," Niko offered, seeing Jen's happiness fade once more. "I'm sure they'll be fine. Ajane said the Magistrate personally guaranteed that he'd send a whole company to back them up."

It was hard to mask her own doubts, but she had to for Jen's sake. She wasn't going to ruin that hope for Jen, but she knew the real character of the Magistrate. Shouldn't Ajane have been more terrified that Andersane would renege on his promise?

Ajane had sounded strangely optimistic that the Meridians were dead set on sending reinforcements. She probably had no other choice than to be optimistic, though. This was a must-win situation, at least according to Riiz Alke-Tani. She tried her best to throw it all out of her mind, wrapping her arms around Jen and giving her the biggest Kate-style hug she could. After the two embraced for longer than a few seconds, she disengaged, only to find Kira-Tharn standing in front of them, looking rather bothered by the show of affection.

"Oh, Kira-Tharn!" Niko said excitedly, trying to appease her just in case she was still angry with her from yesterday. "Have you met Jen yet?"

"I have not," Kira-Tharn responded.

"Well, this is Jen," Niko said. "Jen, this is Kira-Tharn."

"Nice to meet you," Jen said politely, eyeing Kira-Tharn with a hint of distrust.

Kira-Tharn didn't respond verbally, but offered Jen a slight nod of approval. Niko hoped Jen would understand that was only the An-Mara way, that she wasn't trying to be rude at all.

"Would you want to walk with us back to the domiciles?" Niko asked.

"Is that a destination that requires walking together to?" Kira-Tharn asked with what Niko thought might be An-Mara sarcasm. Maybe they did have humor after all... just in the oddest way possible.

"Yes it is," Niko replied, beating Kira-Tharn at her own game and giving her no way out. "Let's go."

"So, Jen," Niko asked as they started walking back together, "have you heard from Kate at all?"

"We communicate every once in a while, but only via Ut when it's permitted," Jen said. "She misses you a lot."

"I miss her so much, too."

"She knows you do," Jen said sympathetically. "She's stationed in the Islands and living her best life there. Your whole family's there, she says."

"Blazes, I miss all of them," Niko said dejectedly.

"Were you able to reconvene with your family after our parting thirty-eight days ago, Niko Ryen?" Kira-Tharn asked. Niko was surprised to hear her join in this conversation.

Blazes, how does she remember the exact number of days that was??

"No, I never got the chance, unfortunately," Niko said. "That was when the war broke out and we got separated."

"I would convey a deep..." Kira-Tharn paused. "I am... sorry... for that."

Did she just try to talk like... a normal person? Niko thought in amazement. Kira-Tharn's delivery sounded weird, but Niko thought she was attempting to make a real connection with her!

"It's okay," said Niko. "Not your fault."

"It was, in a way," Kira-Tharn insisted. "I would not apologize if I did not participate in the cause of the outcome."

"Kira-Tharn, it's fine," Niko assured her. "There were other people that played a way bigger part in me not seeing my family."

Kira-Tharn just grunted in reply.

"But thank you for the apology anyway."

"I forgot you never got to see them," Jen said. "When was the last time?"

"The Anniversary. The night we went to the Farm."

"Blazes!" Jen exclaimed, reaching out to touch Niko's arm in comfort. "That was *so* long ago! I'm so sorry, Niko."

"Now that is an apology for something where there was no participation in the cause of the outcome," Kira-Tharn muttered.

"Huh?" Jen looked confused. Niko knew what she meant, though, and just ignored it, only reacting with the slightest shake of her head.

"So..." Niko turned to Kira-Tharn, searching for the first thing that came to mind to change the subject. "Why do you think the Meridians are called the Meridians?"

Kira-Tharn growled, at first not responding.

Uh, oh, Niko thought. *Did I strike a nerve?*

"Only *you* would ask a random question like that," Jen laughed in her high-pitched tone. She really must've thought that was funny, because she tripped and nearly stumbled into the grasses off to the side of the raised, wood-planked path.

Kira-Tharn just shook her head, clearly not happy with the flagrant display of amusement. Jen had no idea how sacrilegious laughing was to the An-Mara. Niko wasn't about to stop her friend, though. Jen needed something good right now.

"I just was curious," Niko said, trying her hardest to keep a straight face. Jen's laugh was *very* contagious, after all.

"The ones called Meridians," Kira-Tharn began to explain, "call themselves that because they are the most pretentious lot to have ever existed."

That made zero sense to Niko. How was the word 'Meridian' equivalent to pretentiousness?

Jen, on the other hand, thought it was something even more hilarious, and only fell deeper into her pit of hysteria. Kira-Tharn looked at Jen with such a look of indignation, but Jen was too far gone to pay any mind.

"What do you mean by that?" Niko asked.

"They call themselves Meridians because they just so happen to think they own the entire Meridian," Kira-Tharn clarified, although it was hardly a clarification for Niko or Jen.

"Entire Meridian?" Niko asked.

"Yes," Kira-Tharn repeated, as if Niko should know what this meant.

"We're from Arhanda... Remember?" Niko reminded her. "Ignorant, backwater people from an ignorant, backwater planet..."

"The Prime Meridian," Kira-Tharn sighed. "I do forget how little you people know."

"Not our fault, so I'm not gonna apologize," Niko cleverly shot back.

"I suppose that is a very true statement you make, Niko Ryen," Kira-Tharn conceded. "What I should explain is that the Galactic Prime Meridian passes straight through our sector of the galaxy. Technically, the An-Mara should also be considered Meridians, as well as you people from Arhanda. It is a very pretentious move by the '*Meridians*' to claim rights to the entire Prime Meridian."

Huh, thought Niko. *I guess that makes sense.* She'd never seen a map of the galaxy before, other than in her rudimentary astronomical charts. She would love to see more detailed maps that these more advanced civilizations surely possessed.

"Well, thanks for the explanation," Jen said, finally recovered from her bout of hilarity. "You learn something new each day…"

The trio walked a little bit further before arriving at their respective quarters. All three of them were in separate buildings, so they bade each other farewell on the path. Kira-Tharn was the first to part ways, and did so quite abruptly, just walking away without saying much in the way of goodbyes. Jen thought she somehow offended Kira-Tharn, but Niko just assured her that it was typical An-Mara behavior and held no malice. Jen had another good laugh over that, and Niko was happy to see her friend's mood had brightened a little. Niko gave her one last, long hug and assured her they would hang out later tonight.

After Niko was alone, her mind became embroiled in thought once again. She really was worried about her friends that were being sent off to that blazes-accursed bridge from her dreams, but she was determined to not let that fear control her. She would wish each of them off before they left, and would simply remind them to be careful.

Niko did not pay any notice to the fact that she subconsciously entered her domicile, and she definitely didn't notice when she collapsed down into her bed. Soon, exhaustion got the better of her, capturing her into the deep clutches of slumber before she got the chance to see her friends off.

CHAPTER TWENTY-FOUR

24

The Northern Mists of Nevaly

NIKO decided that was her last ride. She had been out in the ocean for several hours now, and the massive fog bank that rolled in had made it way too difficult to see any waves coming. At first, she enjoyed the arrival of the mists. It had been an ethereal, ghostly experience out there — supremely quiet and strangely peaceful. However, the clouds had gotten thicker, and thicker, and thicker. It wasn't long before Niko realized this event seemed even crazier than the one she'd experienced a few weeks back.

After riding the whitewater all the way to shore, Niko stood and looked back. The mists were still tethered to the sea, so she was able to see the silver wall in its entirety. It was as if a giant displacement wave was towering over Nevaly, ready to devour all of civilization. Soon, the veil of fog would advance to inundate the land, but for now it was an awe-inspiring sight. Niko wished she could've snapped a Memory to her Ut, but everyone's Ut had been down since the other day. Her friends would love to have seen this sight when they got back.

If they ever returned…

In her heart, she so desperately wished they were still alive, but her rational mind told her it was unlikely. It had been six days since all contact had been lost with the team that was sent to recapture Anziend Station. In the first hours, Ajane only thought it to be a technical malfunction. She said it was likely some sort of communications jamming from either the An-Mara, the Meridians, or both. However, as more days went by without a trace of contact, more and more hope was lost.

Niko had tried to think of anything that might help. She even tried reaching out to Cryo in the dreams, but to no avail. Of course, connecting with the dreams only worked if both parties were asleep.

Maybe we just weren't asleep at the same time? That was the excuse she used, at least — one that only served to give her the tiniest sliver of optimism.

However, almost all hopes were completely dashed just this morning, when the Meridian forces in Daren's unit were contacted by High Command. The Meridians had issued a proclamation recalling the entire unit back to Sol City. Daren's second in command — the pilot who had not gone on the Anziend mission — had relayed her concerns to High Command about that mission to Anziend. The only response she'd received was that the Meridians had decided *not* to send reinforcements to help Ajane's mission, and that they were to embark to Sol City by the end of the day.

Upon hearing that news, Niko became numb. She'd only just made it out of earshot of others before breaking down. Her mind flailed about, reaching for anything, any*one*, to blame. Of course, she at first cursed the An-Mara for doing what they were doing, and then blamed the Meridians for abandoning them. But then she had turned her greatest ire toward Ajane. Why wouldn't she have heeded Niko's warnings about her dream on that damned bridge? Ajane seemed to be avoiding her this past week, so Niko knew she felt guilty over it all.

She should *feel guilty*, Niko thought contemptuously. *If only she'd listened to me… they might all still be alive.*

The what-if's had been killing Niko this morning. What if Ajane had listened? What if none of her friends went to Anziend? What if the Meridians had sent reinforcements? What if the An-Mara could be reasoned with? What if…

She was completely spiraling, and that's when the fog had rolled in. She didn't know what possessed her to go Sliding, but it was probably the best thing she could've done for herself.

Experiencing the Northern Mists of Nevaly from the water had been an incredible sort of meditation therapy. It allowed her the time and calm she needed to slow down and process everything. She knew it was a possibility that her friends were indeed gone, but that hadn't stopped her from enjoying her time out in the water.

As if the experience couldn't have gotten any more surreal, the weirdest thing happened toward the end. Just a few minutes ago, she got the strangest feeling that her friends might actually still be alive. There was no rational proof, and she couldn't explain it — it was just a gut feeling that had washed over her like a wave.

As she walked back to the base, still cold and wet in her full-suit, she decided she was going to plead her case to Ajane: a rescue mission must be sent to Anziend. If they had indeed survived whatever happened, they would surely need help. That possibility had been discussed before, but Ajane seemed reluctant to divert any more people than they already had. She said the An-Mara likely were still monitoring their presence at Nevaly and that they needed everyone here, especially since Ut communication was down.

The Uts being nonfunctional only added to the growing complexity of their situation. What unsettled Niko most was that it seemed to bother Ajane. That lady was usually pretty calm about everything — even the status of the Anziend mission hadn't rattled her all that much — but this clearly had her on edge. To make matters worse, she reverted back to her cryptic nature and wouldn't reveal much of anything.

Niko shivered as she neared her quarters. She hadn't stayed out so long as to where her hands and feet turned completely numb, but she was still quite cold, nonetheless. There was no breeze, but the air temperature was plummeting, heralding the advancement of the fog into the city. She scurried up the path to her hut, unlatching her foils and shaking them free from her legs and forearms.

Once inside, she was quick about washing up and getting something to eat, because her main focus was on going to see Ajane to convince her that they needed to send that rescue mission.

Ajane owed her. She *had* to approve a mission of the sort, even if it was only two or three people that were sent. If she was forced to plead her case, Niko would have been all too happy to tell her she had a *feeling*, much like the ones she would get during her dreams. Ajane wouldn't be able to refute *that*, would she?

When she left her quarters, surprise stopped her in her tracks — the fog had already enveloped everything around her! That was so fast! She couldn't have been inside for more than twenty minutes. Wisps of solid grey swirled about as the visibility started to erase the landscape around her. Niko figured that it would only be a matter of minutes before everything was obscured to the point it had been when she was out on the water.

Her hair was still wet when she set off to the briefing room where she would likely find Ajane. It wouldn't be drying any further in this weather, but Niko didn't care. All of her thoughts were focused on getting her friends back. If they were still alive.

No! she scolded herself. *They* will *be alive. They have to be.*

For her own stability, she needed to believe that. This whole past week had felt like a slow descent into insanity for her. She needed a win.

She walked briskly along the path and reached the briefing room in no time. Luckily, she knew the path by heart, otherwise it might've been hard to navigate with the visibility being so low. She burst through the doors and looked around the room.

It was strangely empty; Ajane was nowhere to be found. The only people inside were two members of Daren's team, who were conversing with each other animatedly. It looked like an important conversation, so she didn't want to butt in.

She waited and waited for an opening to ask them where Ajane might be, but the two men were completely oblivious to her. She didn't know their names, and she was positive they didn't really care who she was, so she just stood awkwardly off to the side, waiting for them to finish.

"Excuse me," she asked timidly, finally capitalizing on a split-second opening. She tried not to come across as rude or pushy. She didn't mean to interrupt their conversation — she just really wanted to get to Ajane, and quickly. "I need to speak to Ajane. Do you know where I can find her?"

"She's at the transport with our pilot," one of them replied. Niko had no clue what this guy's name was.

"Thanks," she said. "The Meridian transport, right?"

"Yes?..." The guy looked annoyed, and Niko understood why. That was a stupid question for her to ask. What other transport would he be talking about?

"Thank you." Niko said it with more conviction this time.

Freshly embarrassed, she quickly exited the room and headed out to the path that would take her to the open lot with the Meridian transport. It was so hard to see anything, though. This Mists event was *way* stronger than the last one she experienced. If she had to guess, she would probably say the visibility was even lower than ten meters at this point, and probably closer to five. It was neat to experience, but not when she had business to go about. How was she going to find Ajane in this weather? Especially now since the Uts were down…

She stepped onto the path, and nearly collided with Kira-Tharn.

"Sorry!" she exclaimed. "I'm so sorry!"

"Niko Ryen," Kira-Tharn began, "you do not apologize if you did not participate in the cause of an unfavorable outcome. We already discussed this."

"I'm sorry!" Niko said. "I mean…"

Ughhh! The An-Mara were *so* infuriating sometimes. She was just trying to be polite…

"Do you know where the one called Ajane Solase is?" Kira-Tharn asked.

"Oh, what a coincidence," Niko remarked. "I'm actually headed to find her right now. Care to come along?"

"I will accompany you," Kira-Tharn accepted.

"Cool. She's over at the Meridian shuttle, apparently."

The two headed along the path, but the fog had gotten so thick that Niko didn't even know if they were on the correct one.

"I am not used to these clouds," Kira-Tharn said. "Groundheim does not have weather like this. Nor does my home."

"Yeah, neither does mine," Niko said. "Not this heavy, at least."

"The only mists anywhere on my home planet are the ones by the river," Kira-Tharn said. "The one that flows beside the Grand Terrace."

"Where is your home, anyway?" she asked Kira-Tharn.

"A long journey away. It is a world called Aktun."

"Do you think you'll go back someday?" Niko asked.

"I do."

"Maybe I can come with you?" Niko mused.

"I do not think that would be likely," Kira-Tharn said plainly. Niko shook her head at the bluntness of the An-Mara. She almost certainly wouldn't ever go there, but at least Kira-Tharn could've given her false hope. A 'maybe' was all Niko needed to hear right now.

The two walked in silence for another minute or two when suddenly, the path split into three directions. Niko was pretty sure they were supposed to follow along the center, but she wasn't one-hundred percent sure.

"I could really use my Ut right now…" she complained.

"It is not good to become dependent on that machine," Kira-Tharn told her.

"Well, I know *that*," Niko said indignantly. "I'm not dependent on it. I just have no idea where we're going right now."

"I believe we are on the correct path," Kira-Tharn said.

"Okay, I thought so, too," Niko agreed.

Just then, the path split into three once more. Niko mindlessly led the way and took the center path again. The cobblestone path they walked on was bounded by thick green ferns, with pink and blue flowers integrated into the arrangement. The addition of the enchanting fog made it look like something straight out of an ancient Northern legend. They walked a little bit further when…

Nope. This was a dead end.

Niko and Kira-Tharn shrugged at each other, then walked back. Where were they?? Niko could've sworn that was the correct way. They tried one of the other paths, the one that ran south, and ended up in another dead end where the buildings formed a loop.

They walked back once more and then tried the third path, but after about thirty meters, that one faded off into grass.

Were they in that one courtyard with the well? That would mean the path would resume just beyond that point. Niko took two steps over where the well should be and sure enough, there it was. The circular stone arrangement sprang into view, its vines and flowers looking mystical against the grey backdrop. She scurried back over to where Kira-Tharn waited, then the two continued past.

Okay, this is the right way.

As they neared the concrete lot where the Meridian transport would be, Niko thought she heard voices. Was that *shouting*? Everything was so quiet and muffled that it was hard to tell. The mists were so heavy at this point that she and Kira-Tharn had to walk side by side to keep from getting separated. They moved into the lot — at least Niko thought that's where they were — but there was no transport anywhere. They even did a few laps around the perimeter, but there was nothing there. No Ajane. No transport.

"Ajane!" Niko called out. "Ajane?!"

No response.

"Are we in the wrong place?" Niko asked Kira-Tharn.

"I do not know," she replied. "I believe we are in the correct location."

"Yeah," Niko said. "I thought so, too."

More noises sounded to the east. It sounded like rocks falling, followed by shouting. Niko couldn't tell if that was fifty meters away or two hundred meters away. The whole city was so completely socked in with this fog that it was impossible to tell.

"Is that them over there?" Niko asked.

"Let us go and discover for ourselves," responded Kira-Tharn.

As they walked closer to the sounds, they became clearer and more intense. Was there construction going on or something? That was the best way Niko could describe it. Without being able to see or hear very well, she only had guesses. What construction would there be, though? All of Nevaly's residents were long evacuated to the south.

She saw a shadow whoosh by to the left, barely on the edge of her vision.

"Hey!" Niko shouted. "Hey!"

Whoever it was didn't respond. Niko and Kira-Tharn both scampered over to where they saw the shadow run off to. There was no one there, though. *What the blazes?* It was just a dead end, two stone buildings converging into a corner. This was becoming very strange. Why was nobody answering them?

"Hellooo?" Niko called out.

Another shadow moved just at the edge of their visibility to the right. Niko tried to peer through the all-enveloping mists around her, but she couldn't make out much. There was definitely someone there, though.

"Ajane?" Niko called out again.

After walking a few steps closer, she saw that it wasn't Ajane, but rather Jen.

Thank the heavens! Niko breathed a sigh of relief. At least it was someone familiar. Niko had been starting to feel spooked.

"Jen Jen!" Niko called to her, even though she was only a few meters away.

Jen didn't respond, though; she only held up a finger over her lips. She made brief eye contact with Niko, but her wide green eyes immediately scanned around, as if she were looking for something else.

Niko thought she heard the echo of a pop as she stepped over to talk to her friend. In that same brief millisecond that Niko could process, she saw a tangled mass of red in the cavity where Jen's heart had been one second earlier. Gravity did its work an instant later, and Jen flopped to the ground. Time paused for Niko.

This didn't just happen.

She couldn't believe it. She *wouldn't* believe it.

That same petite, youthful figure that Niko had always been envious of still looked beautiful, even lying broken and bloodied on the cobblestone surface. An elegant arbor of green vines and pink flowers flowing overhead created a starkly handsome backdrop to the mess of white-blonde hair draped over the body, as if someone had delicately organized it all into some cruel painting. This was the last image Niko ever saw of Jen. She couldn't even feel herself stumble backwards as the Northern Mists of Nevaly erased all memory of her friend that lay dead on the ground.

"Niko! We must move."

Jen. No...

What just happened? She wanted to will this nightmare out of existence. Niko knew this was not a dream, though — she was well versed enough in the world of dreams by now to know the difference between real and not. But that didn't stop her from reaching for her training as if she could change reality itself. That's not how it worked, unfortunately.

She knew someone else was there — they might've even been holding on to her — but her brain could not process much of anything right now. She was still locked in that same timeless moment from before. It was an odd feeling where she didn't know when or where she was. Niko knew something urgent and terrible was going on, and that she needed to be aware of her surroundings, but she just wasn't. How was she supposed to feel? What was she supposed to do? Suddenly, an instinctive urge beset her as she attempted to rush forward.

"We need to get her!" Niko protested to no one in particular. "She can't just stay there! She needs us! Someone can fix her, I know they can!"

A strong hand cupped over her mouth and pulled her further through the mists. Her subconscious mind thought she heard wisps of air buzzing by her. Her brown hair fluttered with the breeze, but she was probably imagining it. There would be no breeze when the mists were this thick. Apparently, her feet had been moving, but everything was so disorienting. She didn't even feel herself falling until her knees and palms slammed into the ground.

"Will you move please?!" She recognized the familiar, sharp voice of Kira-Tharn. Niko felt a choke from the collar of her shirt as Kira-Tharn dragged her across the ground.

Awareness started to return slowly as she felt the register of pain in her fingers, knees, and the side of her face. She realized that she hadn't tripped, but had rather been aggressively shoved to the ground by Kira-Tharn. The whizzing overhead grew more frequent. Were there people *shooting* at them?

Shooting??

Suddenly it dawned on her.

Jen. No...

In an instant, Niko was brought back to her dream on the bridge. That was the most similar feeling to what was happening now. All her senses were active — she could hear the soft rumble of waves in the distance, smell the smoke around her, and feel the thickness of condensing water droplets. The cold of everything wrapped around her face, like an icy phantom had set its clutches upon her, pulling her to the depths. Her heart was frozen with fear, but she didn't have time to second guess any actions.

As she crawled across the ground, chaperoned by the deceptively strong hands of Kira-Tharn, panic started to take over. She instinctively twitched and cowered when the ground beside her exploded into a shower of dust. She couldn't see anything beyond about five meters, but she knew it was close because small chips of concrete and stone rained down upon them.

"Niko Ryen!" she heard Kira-Tharn aggressively prompt once more. "Stay with me! Stop stumbling!"

"Sorry," she croaked.

"Do not be sorry!" Kira-Tharn admonished her. "Be focused."

Kira-Tharn yanked her to her feet, and the two sprinted around the side of a building that miraculously materialized into their five-meter globe of visibility. The near-supernatural mists had muffled the sounds, but it was becoming clearer and clearer to Niko what was happening — she could hear the distinct pacing of gunshots. She had heard them before, albeit much more clearly, when Andersane had shot those poor An-Mara in front of her.

"Are we… under attack?" Niko asked.

"Is that a sincere question, Niko Ryen?" Kira-Tharn hissed at her, her expression dark with an intense scowl.

"But… why?" she stammered.

"That is a question to answer at a later time!" Kira-Tharn snapped. "Follow!"

Kira-Tharn darted forward, almost leaving Niko's radius of visibility entirely. Niko ran as fast as she could in order to keep up. She could still hear the intermittent sounds of explosions, but they seemed to fade further and further away. Kira-Tharn still kept running, though, so Niko just stayed as close to her trail as she could. She felt like she could run at this pace forever — the fact that she was exhausted from Sliding earlier was of no consequence right now. Was this what adrenaline felt like?

After running for a minute or two — Niko didn't really know how long — another building sprouted into view out of thin air. It was the briefing hall that Ajane had made into her makeshift command center.

Thank the heavens!

Ajane would be able to get them out of this.

As the two burst into the building, however, a familiar man cloaked in a tan, hooded outfit stood over the dead bodies of Setten-Lo and the two Meridian troops she talked to just a few minutes ago. Niko only had but a moment to register what she saw when the man whirled around at their entry.

"You?!" he shouted, his face contorted into some combination of surprise and hatred as he stared straight at Kira-Tharn.

He raised his weapon at them and Kira-Tharn tackled Niko back outside the doorway. The wooden doorframe shattered overhead as the two of them rolled down a grassy embankment, becoming invisible in the mists once again.

"You will submit to the will of the Time!" Niko heard the distinct voice of Var Ashal-Han pierce through the endless grey, bullets whizzing through the air all around her as he fired indiscriminately in the direction he supposed they had gone.

"You will be Recycled into Oblivion!" he bellowed. Blazes, he was still so close! And so angry. "You will *never* become Tel-Mara!"

Niko could not fathom why the man held such hatred. He'd always struck Niko as some pompous, insecure power-freak, but this was rage on another level. He sounded like he wanted to kill them with every fiber of his being right now. She scrambled away on all fours with Kira-Tharn, praying that she was not hit by any stray bullets.

"I have spotted the one called Kira-Tharn," she could hear him say. Blazes, were there more of them right here?! They were uncomfortably close, but at least they were protected by the sheet of thick fog. "She disappeared that way. She is not far. You will engage in pursuit."

It hit Niko all at once.

This was the *An-Mara* that was attacking them?? Why would they be doing this? Before now, they'd never bothered attacking anything other than the stations. She knew Var Ashal-Han was a nasty character, but the An-Mara as a whole seemed more reasonable in her previous experience.

She didn't have any time to dwell on the thought, however, as Kira-Tharn pulled her to her feet, and the two of them ran like the blazes. Niko didn't know where they were sprinting, but she guessed it was further inland since the sound of the crashing waves faded as they continued.

It was so odd running through these mists. Buildings, walkways, and plants would pop up in front of them and come into focus. Then, a mere second later, those objects would disappear behind them into the void.

After running for about a minute, Niko might've thought that it was getting easier to see the ground around her. The thick, dark grey they had been miring through started to turn to a more piercing, lighter shade. The air became less stifling and she was able to see objects coming into focus from much further away. They were leaving the cover of the mists.

"Kira-Tharn!" Niko urgently whispered, reaching forward to tug on her Garment.

"We must get to the transport, Niko Ryen," Kira-Tharn responded.

Niko couldn't argue. Even if she had wanted to, she was breathing too heavily and would've needed to speak too loudly. She did *not* want to chance alerting anyone who might have been chasing them.

Just then, her fears were compounded when the mists suddenly opened up into a patchy, wispy haze that became infinitely brighter. They were virtually out into the open. She could even see the yellow of the sol as it was breaking through the clouds around them. They took a couple more steps forward when Niko saw a large object that stood about fifty meters ahead.

The transport!

In front of the transport, however, prowled four armed An-Mara. It looked like they were searching for something. Both Kira-Tharn and Niko froze, but it was too late.

They had been seen.

The An-Mara paused in surprise, and that hesitation appeared to spell their doom. All four An-Mara were mowed down by some unseen terror. Niko didn't know what was happening. She heard whistling through the air once more, so she hit the ground instinctively, crawling toward a bush, which was the only nearby object she could find. Both Niko and Kira-Tharn ducked and covered their heads, cowering for a few seconds as the chaotic sounds of gunfire and explosions echoed around them. To her surprise — and great relief — the An-Mara hot on their trail were not firing at them, but rather were hiding behind cover of their own. Something, or someone, was firing back at them.

Four more An-Mara who foolishly took cover behind two barrels of reserve fuel were thrown back in an intense, fiery blast that made Niko flinch, even from a distance. Two of the unfortunate An-Mara who survived the immediate blast stumbled forward, but slumped to the ground two seconds later as they were cut down by the mystery gunfire. The other two caught in the blast looked like they were already dead, or unconscious. Niko didn't know the difference, and didn't really care. She just wanted to know who was fighting them and where they were. Would they know she was on their side? She just hid under her bush, crushing its stalk in her grip. She would *not* risk emerging into the open.

She spared a glance behind her, and she saw Var Ashal-Han along with five or six other An-Mara taking cover behind a building. He made a hand gesture, as if directing one of his troops to another location. Sure enough, one of those An-Mara darted out to run across the opening, but died in less than a second. Whoever was fighting the An-Mara had them completely pinned behind that building. Var Ashal-Han, seeing that he was in no position to pursue Niko or Kira-Tharn any further, made another gesture, this one a clear sign to retreat back into the fog.

"Are they leaving?" Niko whispered to Kira-Tharn.

"They will be," Kira-Tharn replied. "It is generally advised in the Record that a commander must order a retreat when sustaining multiple losses if they were the instigators of a surprise engagement such as this."

"Oh," Niko replied. It was a long-winded explanation — a simple 'yes' would have been sufficient — but she was relieved to hear they were likely retreating.

"I think we can make it to the transport," Kira-Tharn said, starting to stand up.

"Wait!" Niko pulled her back down. "Shouldn't we wait another minute? Just to be sure?"

"We are safe to proceed, Niko Ryen," Kira-Tharn assured her. "Let us go."

Kira-Tharn stood up and strode confidently forward. Niko grabbed ahold of her Garment to follow closely, praying that whoever hunted these An-Mara knew the difference between the grey of Kira-Tharn's Garment and the tan of the ones trying to kill them. As they neared the transport, Niko saw Ajane slide off from the roof, armed with a small handgun. She must have been the one that was driving the An-Mara back!

"Niko!" Ajane breathed in relief. "And Kira-Tharn! I am glad you two are alright. Get on the transport. We are searching for any others, then we'll get to a more fortified location."

"Was that you?" Niko asked.

"Was what me?" Ajane asked pleasantly, tilting her head to the side.

"One of the ones that fought off the An-Mara."

"No," she shook her head. "That was my colleague. He is searching for the others now. He'll meet us back here when he's done."

Colleague? As in just *one* person? That felt like it had to have been at least four or five people battling the An-Mara...

"Where is the..." Niko started.

"Niko!" Ajane interrupted. "Get on the transport. I will answer your questions later."

Still wide-eyed from fear, Niko nodded and obeyed as she made her way over to the transport.

"Would you require my assistance?" Kira-Tharn asked Ajane before following Niko.

"Yes. There are weapons in the understorage," Ajane said. "You and I will defend this transport, just in case."

Kira-Tharn nodded and disappeared under the aircraft. She emerged into sight moments later armed with a huge rifle and crouched behind one of the wings. She looked so natural with that weapon, and Niko was glad to have her on her side.

She didn't want to think about what would have happened if Kira-Tharn hadn't been looking out for her today. Right from the very first confusing moments of the An-Mara attack, she had pulled Niko out of there and gotten her to safety. She would absolutely not be alive right now if not for that lady.

An overwhelming flood of emotion came over Niko. It was a combination of gratitude toward Kira-Tharn mixed with shocked devastation from what had just happened, and tears involuntarily streamed down her face. At least no one else was here to see her like this.

Oh, Jen...

Niko cried for her friend, whom she would never be able to laugh with again, dance with again, cry with again. They'd never be able to waste anymore nights away together, talking about what they wanted to do the next day, or about random topics that made no sense. She thought of the countless outings she had with Kate and Jen, of the dinners with the Ryens and the Jenaeis, of the Field games they played and watched. She thought of how much love Jen had for Tyson. Now Jen was dead, and Tyson might've been also.

She cried for all her friends. She cried for her family, who she hadn't seen in two months. She even cried for Setten-Lo, who had proven himself a loyal friend to all of them. And she cried for herself. What had her life come to?

She hadn't even had a chance to say goodbye to her friends that left on the mission last week. She'd fallen asleep like a blazes chum and hadn't seen any of them off. Now, unless by some miracle they'd somehow survived, she might never get to talk to any of them ever again, and that was something she would *never* forgive herself for.

She cried for Cryo and Ravenna, who had taken her under their wing because she was a loner and didn't have many friends her own age. She cried for Daren, the quiet friend who had allowed her to hijack his name without a single complaint. She cried for Tyson, whose mischievous antics had brought her so many laughs. She cried for Riiz Alke-Tani, who had sacrificed so much in order to help the people of Arhanda. And she cried for Jack… well, Jack… All she wanted to do was spend more time with him. He was too nice, too funny, too beautiful to be dead.

After letting all her emotions drain out for what had to have been a good ten minutes at least, she looked up. In the distance she saw two people heading toward the transport from the mists, which had largely dissipated. The crying stopped, and she instantly felt her stomach tighten in anxiety once more. Were the An-Mara attacking again? She glanced down at Kira-Tharn, but rather than taking aim to fire, she appeared to relax, standing from her position. Niko also saw Ajane emerge from her fortification in the shadows.

Niko looked closer at the two figures and realized she recognized one of them.

Kyler!

Niko never knew she would be so happy to see Kyler in her life. She rushed off the craft and practically ran Kira-Tharn over as she did so.

"You should stay close to the transport, Niko Ryen," Kira-Tharn advised her, barring her way with an outstretched arm.

She was right. What if the An-Mara weren't gone for good? What if they were going to attack again?

Kyler had already rushed over though, blindsiding Niko with an unexpectedly genuine hug. She had never known him to display any sort of affections for his friends, so she was surprised at his initiative, yet was wholly comforted.

"I didn't know who else had made it out!" he exclaimed, breathing heavily in exhaustion. "I'm glad you're okay."

"Me too," she said, the stain of tears still streaking down her face.

He disengaged slightly from the hug, looking around. "Where's Jen?"

Niko felt as if a train had knocked the wind out of her once more. Her teeth chattered as the only response she could muster was a quick shake of her head, simply pulling him back in as she buried her head into his shoulder. She couldn't admit that Jen was dead out loud. Not yet.

As the two Green Coast friends hugged each other tightly, Niko could feel Kyler's lungs deflate, his breathing becoming shallower as he started to shake. Neither of them said anymore words to each other, and that was fine. Their embrace shared all it needed to.

After a long, solacing hold, they released. Niko offered him one more sad glance, then found her attention drawn to the man Kyler had walked in with. He stood in a black, skin-tight outfit reminiscent of a cold-water full-suit, except there was an elaborate hood over his head with some sort of fancy goggles, along with boots and gloves. In his arms, which were now relaxed, he held a short rifle. It looked like he was built for a stealth mission in the shadows, which in hindsight was exactly what this seemed to be, considering how thick the fog had been.

He removed his headgear, revealing a weathered and distinguished face, patchy grey sprinkled throughout his otherwise light brown hair. He had a sharp jawline from what was visible through his neatly trimmed beard, which was kept at roughly the same length as his uniformly short hair. He stepped with an air of quiet confidence, which made sense considering he had single-handedly dispatched all those An-Mara forces with relative quickness. Something about his dark green eyes seemed... familiar... to Niko, although she was quite certain she had never seen this man before in her life.

He walked straight up to Ajane and the two gripped forearms in typical Meridian fashion.

"Are they in retreat?" Ajane asked him.

"They are," he responded in a gravelly, masculine voice. "Their commander and one other escaped to the marshes. The rest are dead."

"That is good news," she sighed in relief. "Any other survivors?"

He shook his head. "I'm afraid not."

"Well..." Ajane trailed off in disappointment, shaking her head. "Thank you for coming when you did. Your presence is most timely."

"Who *is* this guy??" Niko must have subconsciously whispered it to Kira-Tharn, for the man seemed to have heard her.

"I am Callum," he said, turning to where Niko stood. "Callum Sehs."

25

The Dead

THE afternoon sol-light shone through the small windows cut into the stone at an angle, illuminating the side of Kyler's face. It was no surprise that he sat with a glower in the corner of the room — he never liked to do any sort of work. Niko, on the other hand, usually tried to be helpful when she could, but right now she couldn't bring herself to help with this task. She only joined Kyler in blank stares.

The fog had completely faded away, and the day that was unveiled when the mists had lifted would have been a beautiful one in Nevaly. The *most* beautiful day.

It was by far the warmest weather Niko had experienced since she'd arrived here from the Northposte Mountains several weeks ago. However, there was no enjoyment to be had, even in the little things. She didn't want to stew around inside, but nor did she want to be outside. She wouldn't have even wanted to go Sliding right now, as perfect as it was.

The only thing she wanted to do was collapse into her bed back home on the Green Coast and curl up into a little ball. Her emotions were completely tapped, and she was in no mood for anything else.

Even Kira-Tharn had not said one word to Niko in the aftermath of the An-Mara surprise attack. She simply nodded her head in mindfulness toward Niko, then walked off to go help Ajane and Callum collect their dead. Niko didn't know how long they'd been gone, but surely they'd return soon. At least she hoped they would...

They assured her there was no danger anymore — Callum had decimated the An-Mara forces. He destroyed both their transports and killed all but two assailants. Unfortunately, that chum Var Ashal-Han had escaped, but he was of no consequence right now. They had said that he and one of his lackeys were plodding through the marshes to the northwest of the city, and would be for some time. There was a station the An-Mara took about a hundred kilometers into the marshes, and they would have to tread on foot to that location with no communications.

Still, Niko was scared about being left alone without Callum, Ajane, or Kira-Tharn to protect her. Kyler was here, but what was he going to do? Give him a machine to tinker with and he was a wizard, but put him in a life or death situation and Niko had no problem admitting that he was worthless.

So am I, apparently, Niko thought miserably to herself.

The feeling of intense fear that rang through her body earlier had been the worst feeling of her life, bar none. Worse than being taken by the An-Mara two months ago. Worse than watching Andersane kill those defenseless An-Mara before her eyes. Even worse than the dream where she had experienced dying firsthand.

As she sat recalling the events of the day, she buried her head into her knees and broke down into tears once more. She couldn't shake the image of Jen crumpled on the ground, her flesh torn apart as easily as paper. She thought of her sister and wondered how Kate was going to take this news.

Not well, obviously.

Kate was even more emotional than she was. And then there was Roger, Lizzy, and Brandon. Just thinking of Jen's family broke Niko's heart anew, as if it hadn't already been ripped into a thousand pieces.

She sat crying for a few minutes in silence, then pulled herself up on wobbly legs and staggered over to the washroom. She got up way too quickly, though, for a wave of dizziness hit her so hard that she was afraid she might collapse. Stars crept into her vision from the corners of her eyes, and her head was constricted with throbbing pain.

Kyler looked up at her, but he wisely refrained from saying

anything. Niko gritted her teeth, braced herself against the wall, and managed to stumble to her destination. She flung the door open and the first thing she saw was puffy, red eyes staring back at her from the mirror above the sink. She took a few shaky, deep breaths and dried her eyes with her palms.

Blazes, I am a mess.

Her face was stained with sweat and dirt, and her new haircut, which she had thought was so cute the other day, looked disheveled and ugly.

She walked up to the sink and submerged her entire head beneath a running stream of cold water, leaving it under for a solid thirty seconds. When she pulled her head back up, water ran down her face and drenched the thick, cold-weather clothes she had been wearing this whole time. The discomfort didn't matter. Nothing did. How could it?

She stood and stared blankly at the mirror for several more minutes until she heard chatter coming from the main room. She took a couple more deep breaths, dried herself with a washcloth, then returned outside to find Kira-Tharn, Ajane, and Callum waiting in the conference room.

"Niko," Ajane said sympathetically. "Are you alright?"

How was she supposed to respond? Of course she wasn't alright.

"I'm okay," she lied.

"I am so very sorry," Ajane offered. "I know you were close with your friend. She seemed like such a sweet young lady."

"She did seem very kind," Kira-Tharn added. "And... pretty."

The attempted gesture of kindness was unnatural from the An-Mara woman, like forcing a baby to give up their toys, but Niko supposed she was grateful.

"Thank you," she squeaked. "I'm sorry about Riiz Alke-Tani and Setten-Lo, as well."

Kira-Tharn didn't say anything, but nodded. How was she so good at masking her emotions? She must've been devastated at losing her companions, but she didn't show it if she was.

"If you would like to visit her to say your farewells..." Ajane delicately suggested.

Niko shook her head. "I'm sorry. I'd just prefer to not talk about Jen right now, if that's okay. I'm sorry..."

"Of course," Ajane said, bowing her head.

Ordinarily, Kira-Tharn would've admonished her for apologizing when she 'did not participate in the cause of an unfavorable outcome', but her mood must have been really bad if even Kira-Tharn knew not to push her. Niko could feel everyone watching her, but she just sat back down and stared vacantly ahead.

After a few seconds, Callum broke the silence.

"I don't mean to be uncaring, but there is the matter of where we shall take refuge," he said. "We should *not* overstay our welcome."

"Agreed," Ajane concurred. "If they really are heading to the station at the Northern Marshes, I would say we have one day — two maximum — to vacate this place."

"Kira-Tharn, do you know what An-Mara protocol dictates as a response if a team loses contact?" Callum asked.

"I do not have access to the Record," she responded straightforwardly. "But I do know that commanders are required to communicate directly with the Heads of Knowledge before pursuing any other courses of action."

"So, you don't think it's possible they're sending any reinforcements as we speak?" Callum asked.

"I believe that would be unlikely," she replied. "The one called *Var Ashal-Han* must debrief with the Heads of Knowledge themselves. That would be considered standard."

Niko noticed the way she said his name — it carried the obvious taint of unmasked, outright malice.

Good. She felt the same way about that blazes-accursed coward.

"I see." Callum nodded thoughtfully, apparently willing to trust Kira-Tharn's expertise in the ways of the An-Mara. "Then we should plan accordingly."

This made Niko feel better. If what Kira-Tharn said was correct, then the An-Mara were probably not on their way to attack again. For now, at least. But who really knew how they functioned? She gave up trying to anticipate An-Mara intentions long ago.

Besides, it seemed to Niko that waiting for an in-person debrief with the Heads of Knowledge before making a decision seemed highly inefficient, especially when that person was missing. What if they were dead? Would they just never make a decision at that point? Not that she was complaining — she was happy that the An-Mara were likely not on their way to attack again. It just seemed that with protocols like that, it was odd that the An-Mara should be winning this war. If the scenario were flipped around, the Meridians would not hesitate to throw more fuel onto the fire, especially if they were trying to execute a surprise attack.

But what did she know? She was no expert in battle tactics.

"For now, let's stay here," Ajane decided. "But we need to be ready to embark at a moment's notice. I will reach out to Andersane one more time and notify him of the situation."

"I..." Callum hesitated, raising his eyes toward Ajane. "I... believe that may be impossible."

Ajane raised an eyebrow and shot him a questioning glance, one where it seemed as if they were conversing silently. This was a look Niko had gotten quite used to over the last few months. Without thinking, she reached her mind into that imagined conversation, and she was flooded with feelings. They were nothing she could decipher, but it was a very strange sensation she had never experienced before. It was eerily similar to the training in her dreams, but yet very different at the same time.

"They are going through with the Operation?" Ajane asked quietly.

Callum nodded. "I'm afraid so. All the preparations were being made on the *Dawnletter*."

"You saw this?" she asked.

"Yes," Callum nodded again.

"Well," Ajane hummed. "That is not g..." Ajane paused after seeing the others looking at her in question. "Let me try to contact Andersane, just in case. In the meantime, let's get the shuttle loaded."

"Well, that doesn't sound ominous..." Kyler muttered under his breath.

"Did you have a question, Kyler?" Ajane asked kindly, as if she didn't hear the sharpness in his tone.

"No," he grumbled. "I said that doesn't sound like anything good. And since you haven't been telling us what the blazes is going on, I guess we'll just have to sit here and stew in panic."

Ajane and Callum looked at each other.

"And where the blazes did you come from?!" Kyler whirled around toward Callum in surprise, as if he hadn't been here all afternoon. Kyler had been uncharacteristically quiet so far, and Niko knew it was only a matter of time before he started brashly speaking before thinking.

For once, she welcomed that sort of candid speak from Kyler. She was tired of all the cryptic Meridian half-truths, too. She and the rest of her people were constantly kept in the dark about everything by these damn Meridians, and they deserved some full-truths after what they'd suffered.

"I have been off-world," Callum said levelly. "I only returned recently and stumbled into this mess."

"Off-world?" Kyler asked skeptically? "Like… in *space*?"

"Yes, on a critical mission back to the Capital system," Callum responded, as if they should all know what that was.

"I contacted Callum Sehs as soon as the conflict started," Ajane said. "By the grace of the Nel-Mara, he was on his way back and close enough to be in SGL."

Whatever that meant…

"And just where the blazes is the Capital system?" Kyler asked.

"Somewhere much too far," Callum's voice trailed off. He almost sounded… *sad*.

"You know those bright stars in the summer months?" Ajane filled in for Callum. "We call the brightest, yellowish one Providence, and its solar system is the Capital system. It's where several of our worlds lie."

Kyler just stared back at them dumbfounded for a few seconds. "And you just went there and back on a *joyride*? How long does that even blazes take?!"

"I have been gone for ten years," Callum said, striding over to the window. "It was no *joyride*."

Ajane walked over to him and put a hand on his arm. He looked like a statue, unmoving, his steel jaw silhouetted against the sol-light flooding through the window.

"I am sorry," Niko heard Ajane say quietly to him. Callum still didn't move a muscle, and continued to stand there looking out at nothing.

It suddenly dawned on Niko.

Sehs.

She must've been too distraught earlier for it to register, but this must be Jack's *dad*. That's where she recognized those dark green eyes from! It all made sense now. That's why he looked so sad — Ajane surely told him the news of the mission Jack had been sent on. If he'd been gone for ten years, that meant that Jack hadn't seen his father since he was a young kid. Suddenly her own woes seemed trivial in comparison.

"And did you return with a fleet, I hope? Because if not, that seems like it was a waste of a trip back…" Leave it to Kyler to ruin the mood. That guy had zero sense of decency sometimes. Niko became angry at him on Callum's behalf.

"Kyler!" she hissed.

"What?!"

"That's Jack's dad!" she whispered, trying to be quiet enough so Callum didn't hear.

"Oh, actually?? Sorry," Kyler apologized sheepishly.

"It is quite alright, Kyler Pierson," Callum said. "It's not your fault. I knew that this could always be a possibility."

"I… actually was going to ask you something earlier," Niko piped up, looking toward Ajane. "Before we were attacked."

"Of course," Ajane said, returning her voice to a pleasant, warm tone. "What is it, Niko?"

"This morning when I was by myself," she started, "I got a feeling that maybe the people that were sent to Anziend last week might not all be dead."

"We've already gone over this," Ajane said consolingly.

"No, this was different!" Niko pushed. "It felt like something from my dreams."

"Before Callum got to Nevaly, he scoured everywhere between here and Anziend looking for survivors," Ajane said.

"There was nothing," Callum stated, still staring out at the ocean from his window. "Just trees, mountains, rivers, and the sea."

"Besides, I've been reaching out to them in the dreams every day," Ajane added.

"I don't know, it seemed like a real *feeling*," Niko insisted. "I really think they may be ali…"

"I don't mean to quash your hopes, Niko Ryen," Ajane interrupted. "But we do have to be realistic at this point."

"I wish you would take my feelings seriously," Niko pushed harder, starting to feel enough confidence to become argumentative. "I feel like you owe me that much."

"I assure you, I do take your feelings quite ser…"

"Like you did with the bridge?" Niko interrupted, her frustration boiling over. "Because if I remember correctly, I was pushing for us *NOT* to go on that mission. You brushed me aside then. Please don't do that now."

The room was quiet for a few seconds. Ajane and Callum briefly eyed Niko, then glanced at each other. Kira-Tharn peered at her with what looked like respect, and even Kyler stood dumbstruck, mouth slightly agape.

"Please." The fire in Niko's voice vanished, replaced by her normal meek tone.

"You are correct," Ajane admitted. "I should have paid your dream much more attention when planning our mission to Anziend. But it was a mission that was absolutely necessary. We would've had to proceed with it, regardless of the risks."

She was right. What if they hadn't sent the mission? Then they would just be handing Anziend station to the An-Mara. Although, the outcome was not any different the way it turned out…

"What's going to happen now that the An-Mara have that place under control?" Kyler asked.

"We have already spoken about this," Ajane said.

Kyler sighed. "I don't really believe that's possible. It's gotta be embellishment, right?"

"I assure you, it is not." Ajane looked dead serious.

Kyler opened his mouth, ready to say something else, but Ajane quickly spoke before he got the chance.

"We can discuss the stations later. As for our friends on the mission," she carefully continued, "we can look for them one more time, but we do have to assume a realistic possibility that they are gone. We never want to give up hope, but we also don't want that hope to be the *only* thing that keeps us going."

"All I ask is that we try," Niko pleaded.

"If we do search for them, we run the risk of being intercepted by any An-Mara that adhere to the corrupted interpretation of the Time," Kira-Tharn spoke up. "I do not wish for them to be gone either, Niko Ryen, but the one called Ajane Solase speaks the truth."

"I really think I'm right about this," Niko insisted, her voice cracking under the strain of the effort to hold back tears.

Ajane's poring grey eyes locked Niko's gaze for several seconds.

"When we leave," she said, "we can make one more pass over their logical path of return. Other than that, I cannot promise anything."

"Thank you." Niko supposed that was better than nothing, but she was very bothered that Ajane still didn't trust her gut feelings. What would it take for that woman to have faith in her?!

"So, when the blazes are we actually leaving?" Kyler asked. Niko didn't know if he felt uncomfortable with this dialogue and wanted to change the subject, or if he was just being typical Kyler saying whatever the blazes came to his mind.

"As we said, Kyler Pierson," Callum reiterated, "start loading up the shuttle now with anything we need. If we have to leave, we will leave."

"And where will we be leaving to?" Kyler asked. "And why did you say earlier that we can't contact the Meridians?"

"Because they are leaving," Callum responded.

"Okayyy… And where the blazes are they leaving to??"

"They are leaving Arhanda, presumably to return to the Capital system," Callum said plainly.

What? Leaving Arhanda???

"Uhhh… what the blazes??" Kyler may have been more blunt than Niko, but she did have to admit that sometimes his thoughts mirrored her own. "Leaving Arhanda? As in… leaving leaving?"

"Yes, as in leaving leaving," Callum repeated.

"Just like temporarily, right?" Niko chimed in. "To bring back reinforcements?"

She needed to know that this was only temporary. As much as she distrusted the Meridians at this point, it was hard to imagine a world without them. Their whole way of life was tied to them.

"I don't know," Callum said. "All I know is they were making preparations to board their long-range vessel."

Before she or Kyler could ask anything else, Kira-Tharn jumped into the conversation.

"I can attempt to make contact with those among the An-Mara who have not become corrupted by the perversion of the Time," Kira-Tharn offered. "You may choose to believe it or not, but there are still some that sympathize with the people of Arhanda. They might be able to provide information about the An-Mara progress with the Engines, or possibly assist us with a departure."

"Do you have a way to contact them?" Callum asked.

"I do not have the option to immediately contact them," Kira-Tharn acknowledged. "There may be a way, but it would require several hours. Perhaps a day. And a shuttle."

"That may be an option to consider," Ajane said. "But let me retire to my quarters to think on the matter. To think on all these matters. This is a lot, and I do require rest, just like all of you surely do. After Callum and I have had time to think, let's reconvene to discuss our path forward. And don't forget to begin loading the shuttle."

Niko and Kyler looked at each other, obviously disappointed that they weren't getting all the answers they wanted.

Meridians not giving us answers? Nothing new there...

"This is blazes unbelievable," Kyler said, visibly exasperated. Without waiting for the rest of them, he threw his arms up in despair and stormed out of the room. Why did he always have to be so dramatic?

"I apologize if you are frustrated, Niko," Ajane said. "I promise I will think on everything you have said. We will discuss it all once we're presented with more clarity."

"Okay," was all Niko said. She was not sure that walking away and pushing conversations off to a later time would yield any more *clarity*, but whatever.

"Until later," Ajane said, bidding Niko farewell as she glided regally out of the room. Callum had already disappeared, so it was now just Kira-Tharn and Niko left standing together.

"I need some fresh air," Niko declared, suddenly getting an urge to walk out to the beach. As long as there would be no dead lying around... "Will you walk with me?"

"To where would we be walking?"

"The beach."

"What is the objective to be met by walking to the beach?" Kira-Tharn asked.

"You don't always need to meet a blazes objective!" Niko exhaled. "Just come with me. I could use the company."

"Very well," Kira-Tharn replied. "I shall accompany you."

Niko strode out of the stone building and onto the cobblestone path, Kira-Tharn in tow. She tried not to recall the events of earlier in the day, but it was next to impossible. Nevaly had always been such a beautiful, mystical city, but now it would forever be associated with feelings of dread and sorrow in Niko's heart. All she could do was focus on the beach in the distance. At least the ocean would always bring her feelings of tranquility and renewal, wherever she was in the world.

After covering about half the distance to the shoreline, Kira-

Tharn had finally caught up to walk side by side with Niko. The two walked in silence, but Niko was just glad to have someone there with her. She didn't really feel a pressing need to have any conversation right now; she just didn't want to be alone.

The path carved its way through stone buildings, lush gardens, and grassy courtyards, eventually finding its way onto the sand. They now stood looking out at the expanse of blue water until it met a grey wall of mists about a kilometer offshore. The Northern Mists of Nevaly looked terrifyingly gloomy, but they had been what saved her life just this morning. Niko and Kira-Tharn stood there admiring the scene for no longer than thirty seconds when the silence was broken.

"That is the one called Riiz Alke-Tani," Kira-Tharn announced calmly.

"What?" Niko didn't immediately understand what she had said. Why was Kira-Tharn bringing up the dead now?

She looked to where Kira-Tharn's gaze had swept, and what she saw almost knocked her soul out of her body.

No way...

Niko had been feeling weak and jittery ever since this morning, but she practically leaped forward with unbridled energy now. How was Kira-Tharn being so calm?!

Along the shore, in the distance to the east, she could see several figures wearily dragging themselves from the water, hauling what looked to be a big piece of wood onto the sand. Kira-Tharn was *not* seeing things — the tall guy with the ragged beard on the far right was none other than Riiz Alke-Tani.

———————

PART FIVE

Orbit

26

Operation Exodus

"HELLO? Base to Riesen..."

Riesen didn't respond. He didn't even move. He only smirked and raised his eyes to meet Rangar Thomson's.

"So... what's your take?" Rangar asked, waiting for his answer. He must've said something else before, but Riesen didn't know what it was. He hadn't been paying attention.

"Take on what?" he asked.

Rangar rolled his blue, Islander eyes. "Did you even listen to anything we were saying?"

"The boy's zoned out," Brandon chaffed. "Daydreaming like his sister probably."

Riesen just shrugged. It was odd Brandon should mention Niko, because his mind was in fact preoccupied with that dream he had last night, the one where Niko... *appeared*... to him once again. She had been in several of his dreams a few weeks ago, but he hadn't thought of her since then.

He was still super frustrated with how foolish she had been, of course, but as time passed, that frustration had faded into concern. The poor girl *had* to be struggling. Riesen hoped that she was doing okay... as well as she could be, at least, given the circumstances.

How did it come to this? he wondered.

Not only was he worried for Niko, but the war had taken a turn for the worse in the last few weeks. The Meridians had rapidly been losing stations, and after all contact had been lost with that unit sent to Nevaly, they no longer had any presence on the North Continent at all. Worse yet, High Command had been in a state of complete turmoil the last few days. The typical chaotic atmosphere at headquarters had been compounded tenfold. There'd also been an unusual amount of traffic going in and out of orbit from the airfields outside Sol City, and the fact that High Command was keeping everything hush-hush was slightly disconcerting to Riesen. With his post inside the Communications office, he'd been enjoying increased involvement in matters of security and information, but this was one thing they were keeping intentionally elusive.

"Hello? Taking bets on ideas of what the mission's gonna be?" Rangar repeated. "So what's yours?"

"Mission?" Riesen asked. He really hadn't been paying attention to anything. The others looked both annoyed and amused at the same time at how oblivious he was to their conversation.

"Blazes, Ryen," Rush Fils blurted out. "For someone that's good at everything, you're pretty terrible at conversation."

"Guilty," Riesen responded with a smug grin, while he tried to piece together what they were talking about. They were waiting for the Magistrate to make some sweeping announcement about something — that much, he knew.

Just now, he and some of the other elite Arhandans had all been mingling in the lounge when Andersane walked by and requested all of them attend a briefing in the small theater. Were they all being sent on a mission? Was that what this was?

"Umm, I think they're gonna send us into orbit," Riesen mindlessly conjectured.

The others looked around at each other before breaking into a fit of laughter at his suggestion, but he was actually dead serious. He had learned long ago to trust his intuition — he had this uncanny knack for sensing what was coming before it happened. He didn't know why, but right now it told him that the Meridians were hiding something in orbit. A weapon, most likely. Something powerful enough to turn the tide against the An-Mara. What else could explain all that space traffic?

"No, seriously," Rangar pried. "What do you think?"

"I *am* ser…"

Riesen was interrupted by the entry of Magistrate Andersane and two of his generals. Riesen and the others immediately shot out of their seats and stood at attention, 'C's held to their chests in salute.

"Good afternoon," Andersane thundered, his powerful voice reaching every centimeter of the room without the need for a sound enhancer. "Please, be seated. The reason you're all here is because you've been selected for Operation Exodus, a critical move against the An-Mara, who are intent on taking away the very heart of this world."

Andersane paused, probably to accentuate the drama. Riesen liked Andersane well enough, but he thought he tended to overdo the theatrics when delivering speeches. Although, that was Andersane's whole goal, after all. He even told him as much. It was he who coached Riesen to speak with much more passion and authority during his Daily Update addresses.

"I will not lie to you," Andersane continued, "this mission is an extensive one. You will be away from your homes for no shorter than a month, but I assure you that you'll all be able to exact righteous justice upon these An-Mara wretches. This plan is well designed, and we have utmost confidence that these sorry excuses for humans will be thrown back to the heap of trash they call home."

Rush Fils started the cheering, and everyone else joined in ovation. They all hated the An-Mara, as every citizen of Arhanda surely did. Anyone who thought otherwise was a traitor, as far as Riesen was concerned. They needed to just be *gone*. How could anyone be sympathetic to these guys? The An-Mara had killed indiscriminately, for a reason that nobody knew.

Whatever.

He was just relieved that he was finally being called to action for some operation that sounded like it actually might make a difference. He'd been enjoying his work in headquarters, but it was no secret that he was itching for some action in the field.

"This mission is highly, *highly* classified, however," Andersane added sternly. "We will not be briefing you on full details until you return tonight, but the little that we tell you now must stay in this room."

He paused again, looking each of the attendees in the eyes personally. There weren't many in attendance — fewer than fifteen in total. Riesen, Rangar, Rush, Brandon, Brynne, Kate, and Pira had all been together in the lounge when the summons came. Joining them were a handful of Arhandan officers serving in the Meridian ranks, including Rush's parents, Anson and Alana. Much to Riesen's chagrin, even Willer Brooks and Brody Felleter were in attendance.

Riesen could see why *maybe* Brooks would fit in here — after all he was a competent officer — but he had no clue why Felleter was here. The guy was a complete chum! At least Riesen now outclassed him by two full ranks. He was so far above him in every way, so he didn't spend too much brainpower thinking about that little cretin.

Even if Felleter weren't among them, though, it was strange that Andersane wanted so many young, relatively inexperienced people for a mission he claimed was of such importance. Wouldn't he want a more experienced group? Riesen wasn't about to complain, though.

"We have a large vessel in orbit above Arhanda right now," Andersane continued, satisfied that everyone knew this mission was to be kept entirely confidential. "And you will be part of the team sent to operate it. I regret there hasn't been much time for space training for many of you, so it will have to be a crash course that is very hands on and immersive."

Eyes lit up as the attendees all looked eagerly around at each other.

I knew it! Riesen thought. *And they all laughed at me when I said we'd be going into space...*

He was very satisfied that he was always right, but he wished his friends would trust what the blazes he had to say more often.

"This is very short notice, as we will be departing tonight," Andersane added. "I apologize for the inconvenience, but we do what we must. Besides, we have all become accustomed to sacrifices and changes of plans over the past few months."

This took Riesen by surprise — that *was* short notice. But he knew Andersane was right — they *had* been accustomed to dealing with last minute changes. For example, just the other day, the Meridians issued landmark proclamations relocating thousands of Sol City inhabitants to the South Continent. Of course there had been a little grumbling here and there among citizens, but most of their anger had been directed toward the An-Mara, not the Meridians. The Meridians were just doing what was best for everyone.

"You are all to report back to Bay Seven at the airfields tonight at 20:00," Andersane said. "Until then, you may take time as you see fit. If you wish to deliver farewells, that is acceptable. Just remember you must not tell anyone where you are going."

"What *are* we allowed to say, Magistrate?" Brynne asked.

Riesen rolled his eyes. *Was that really a necessary question??*

"As for *any* classified mission, just tell them that you are embarking as per the direction of High Command," Andersane replied gruffly. "No specifics."

"Yes, Magistrate," she replied in that same high pitch simper that had been annoying the blazes out of Riesen lately. He felt bad admitting it, but literally every little thing about her grated on him. He could not stand being around her any longer. He swore he was going to have a real chat with Brandon to encourage him to break up with her — he just hadn't worked up the nerve to tell his friend just yet. He knew Brandon would be crushed to know he felt that way.

"Are there any other questions before we adjourn?" Andersane asked.

There was only silence around the room. The rest of them, at least, knew when to shut up. Even though Andersane invited questions, everyone knew that it was best that you didn't ask them.

"Very good," he boomed, abruptly shifting from a stern demeanor to a more pleasant one. "I will see you all tonight." He stepped off the stage at the front of the room and exited, followed closely by his generals.

Riesen was suddenly so invigorated and intrigued. There hadn't been many Arhandans before him that had ever traveled to space. Pride surged through him, as it surely did with the others in the room. Everyone looked around at each other, wide-eyed with excitement about this opportunity they'd all been afforded.

Of course, none of them knew the details — not even Riesen had heard anything about this — but it sure sounded promising. The fact that the Meridians were going to such great lengths to keep it quiet encouraged Riesen that it would be a very effective tool against the An-Mara.

"Well," Rush said after Andersane had left, "Riesen takes the prize. We're going to space, boys and girls!"

"I'm always right," Riesen said mater-of-factly, grinning with swagger.

"Yeah, yeah," Kate said, rolling her eyes. "Whatever."

"New bet," Rangar proposed. "What do you think is up there that's so important?"

"Communications blocker, for sure," Pira said.

Riesen was glad Pira was going to be with them during this mission. She had been stationed down in Nowhere, that town in the middle of the Far Desert, but she was recalled to Sol City just the other day, which she was surely grateful for, considering she was a native of Sol City, after all. Sometimes he forgot she was Islander — her thick, black hair and brown eyes were in contrast from the typical golden hair and blue eyes. Besides, she was way more modest and far less arrogant than most Islanders he knew.

"Communication blocker? No way!" Rush exclaimed. He, unlike Pira, exhibited every stereotype of the Islanders — both in looks and in arrogance. "It's one hundred percent a weapon. Probably to blast stations from orbit. Now that we lost so many, it doesn't matter if we blow 'em up or not."

"Not a chance. I'm with Pira on this one," said Kate. "I think it has something to do with communications."

"I think we might be a diversion, honestly," Brandon chimed in. "If we get the An-Mara to spend all their resources to compete with us in space, then we can retake stations on the ground."

Hmmm, he might be on to something, Riesen thought. That actually made sense, considering they were taking a young and inexperienced crew.

"You are *so* smart, Sweety-B!" Brynne showered Brandon with kisses as she offered her praises.

"*Sweety-B* might be right," Riesen said, pinching Brandon's cheek as Brynne tried to bat him away. "But I'm also not ruling out weapon. Or communications."

"So, basically you don't have any idea, is what you're saying?" Rush hassled him. "So *spineless*, Ryen."

"Pretty much," Riesen laughed, flashing Rush his best come-and-get-me grin. "What about you, Rangar?"

"I think it's weapon testing, one hundred percent."

"Could be," Riesen shrugged.

Weapon or no, he hoped it was something that would make the An-Mara regret they ever set foot on Arhanda. A small lull in the conversation followed, but Rush spoke up quickly, powering it right along.

"Soooo," he said. "20:00. I'm gonna head home and take a

short nap before we gotta report back."

"Ooooh, that sounds nice," Rangar said. "But I probably should hang out with my family if we're gonna be gone for a month."

"Yeah, same," Kate said. "And Riesen, too."

She glared at Riesen, as if he wouldn't have gone over on his own. He didn't want to quarrel with her now, but he thought that was ridiculous. Of course he was gonna go over and hang with the family! He didn't like how she always acted like his mom, even though he was far more independent than she was.

"Same," Brandon said. He then turned to Brynne. "Babe, you going to your parents' first? You wanna come over after?"

"Sure!" she gushed. "I *love* your family so much! And I miss Jen. I just *love* her to pieces. She is the sweetest thing."

Riesen had to turn away before becoming nauseated.

"You got family here Pira?" he asked, steering the conversation away from Brynne.

"Of course," she replied. "I am from here, you know…"

"Oh, right, I knew that" Riesen said sheepishly. "You're always welcome at our place if you didn't have anywhere to go."

"Appreciated," she said. "But yeah, my family lives over by the Fraton Quarter."

"Oh, sweet," he said. "I guess I'll see you tonight then."

"Yep! See you at 20:00."

As she walked off, Kate nudged Riesen and gave him a knowing look with big eyes and a dumb smirk. She must have thought he was crushing on Pira… He just side-eyed her and shook his head. He had a great amount of respect for Pira and enjoyed hanging out with her, but she wasn't really his type. He wasn't about to protest to Kate, though, because that would only make him look more guilty.

Whatever.

Riesen started to walk back with his sister, but he noticed Andersane lingering, half hidden behind a doorway that led into the sweltering Islands sol-light.

"Wait, I need to ask the Magistrate something real quick," he told Kate. "I'll catch you back at Mom and Dad's."

"Okay, you better be there," she warned, shooting him that same glare from before.

He didn't respond. She was being way too bossy and Riesen wasn't going to reward her with any sort of acknowledgement.

He walked across the theater and over to where Andersane was. Riesen wanted to ask him about the Daily Update. Though he hated to admit it, he was becoming attached to that job and wanted to make sure it was in good hands while he was away on this Operation Exodus.

Before he even reached the doorway, however, he stopped in his tracks when he overheard General Oto speaking to Andersane. He'd been further around the corner and Riesen hadn't seen him.

"Are you certain these are the ones?" Oto asked Andersane. "What about those other Northerners."

"No one has heard from them in some time," Andersane replied. "According to my best intel, they may be dead. Besides, *he* told me that I had discretion to choose the bunch. Just no families."

Oto grunted. "And Fils?"

"That is one exception. They have all proven themselves invaluable," Andersane responded.

"Hmph, well, I hope you are right."

"As do I. We have only to forge the path ahead. It has been set in motion for years, and it's much too late to be second guessing now."

Oto nodded and gripped forearms with Andersane. "Very well, until tonight."

"Until tonight."

Riesen had already barely avoided detection while eavesdropping on those two once before; he was not about to chance it again. He stepped back, turned around, and walked away. He had *no* idea what they were talking about, and he honestly didn't care to know. He already had plenty to think about with this upcoming mission.

He could talk to Andersane later. It wasn't that big a deal that he know who they planned to take over duties for the Daily Update — he was certain they had it under control. The Meridians *always* had things under control.

He walked back to join Kate, his thoughts occupied with excitement over the prospect of going to *space*. How cool was this going to be!

It was one long marathon task, an insane scramble that had tested everyone to their limits. Initially, Niko had been ordered to stay out of the way, but after the first few minutes, it was clear that this was going to be an all-hands-on-deck situation. From there on out, Niko had been mainly appointed as a gatherer that was sent running up and down the halls, along with Daren, to scavenge any materials that Callum had asked for. Even when she wasn't needed, it still felt as if her heart was beating two hundred times per minute.

At this point, sixteen hours later, she was exhausted and could probably fall asleep at any moment. She'd now been up for more than twenty-four hours straight — easily the most trying twenty-four hours of her life. Things had only just now settled down for the first time since the others made their miraculous return yesterday.

Finally, she breathed.

By some stroke of luck that Niko thanked the heavens for, Ravenna was still alive. She likely had been minutes from death, or was perhaps even on borrowed time. Technically, her heart *had* stopped on two separate occasions, but against all odds, she'd recovered from each of those episodes.

'The universe must have some purpose for her and did not want to let go,' Callum had said about the matter.

None of them had extensive training in any health care setting, but fortunately, the hospital in Nevaly was well-equipped with surgical machines that Kyler managed to get up and running. Callum was probably the most knowledgeable in medical matters, so he had become the de facto leader that everyone deferred to.

Just a few minutes ago, everybody had been crowded into the room to watch over Ravenna, but Callum had cleared them out. He assured everyone that the machines were doing their job and that she just needed time. Niko wondered how much time they actually had, though. Weren't they supposed to be fleeing from another possible An-Mara attack?

She voiced her concerns to Ajane, but she was only met with a shake of the head. 'It will be fine, Niko,' she had been told. Niko hoped it would be, but hope alone did little to put her mind at ease.

As she shuffled away from the window looking into the room where Ravenna lay unconscious, Niko's vision started to go blurry. She needed somewhere to sit down before she passed out, otherwise she might find herself on the bed right next to Ravenna, the next patient to be operated on. She braced herself against the wall and slumped onto a bench that lined the edge of the clean, white corridor. With a sigh, she kicked her legs out, leaned back, and shut her eyes, allowing her thoughts to drift through the events that led to this point.

It would be impossible to shake the image of when she first saw Ravenna's dire condition yesterday afternoon: the wrapped torso, the blood soaking through, the pale of her skin… Niko shuddered at that memory burned into her brain.

She now basked in an overwhelming sense of relief since they had succeeded in stabilizing their friend, but because of all Niko had been through recently, any real sense of peace or happiness was still a long way off.

She didn't know if she'd fully fallen asleep just now, but she was startled back to the present when someone sat down on the bench next to her.

Ugh, can't I get a moment's rest? she complained to herself irritably. She looked up, and her annoyance fleeted when she saw Cryo.

"Hey," she said, sitting up straight.

"Hey. How you holding up?"

Niko shrugged. "I don't know."

"Yeah. Same."

Cryo stared forward at the ground, not saying anything for a few seconds. Niko was about to end the silence when finally, he spoke up.

"I'm really sorry for not doing more to speak up for you about the dream," he apologized.

Niko shook her head. "No, I'm sorry. It was my fault I never told you about it in the first place. I'd been meaning to for months, and I never did."

"Not your fault," he assured her. "Your dream didn't control the outcome of anything. That was always something that was going to happen."

Niko sat up. "What *did* happen?"

"Hmph," he grunted with a forced laugh. "What *didn't* happen? That's the better question."

Niko wasn't able to force a laugh, but she did her best to curl her lips into a smirk.

"Well, let's see," Cryo started. "As soon as we left, our pilot got a transmission from the Meridians. They requested he fly a pick-up for some of their troops they were recalling back to Sol City, so he had to drop us off on the south side of Anziend. It took us forever to sneak though the city without being detected, so we didn't end up making it to the bridge until the next morning."

"Ooof." Niko winced. "My dream of it being daytime?"

"Yep," he said. "Then we got pinned down. We were never going to make it into that place. At that point we were just trying to survive."

Niko whirled around when someone else sat down beside her on the other side of the bench. It was Ajane. She hadn't been feeling angry since yesterday, but a pang of hot rage surged through her toward the lady now.

"Niko Ryen, I owe you an apology," Ajane said earnestly, as if sensing Niko's resentment and immediately attempting to diffuse it. "I didn't consider the possibility that you had dreamt through someone else's eyes other than your own."

"Huh?" Niko was confused by what she meant.

"Yes," Ajane continued. "I incorrectly under-qualified your psychic potential, and that put lives at risk. Having the dreams through other people's eyes has been documented, and I should have considered that as a possibility, but it is incredibly rare, even among the Valanses of my world."

Niko stared back at her for several seconds before finding the words to respond.

"What's a Val…"

Niko gasped, interrupting herself.

"Oh the blazes! That was *Ravenna*!"

Cryo shot a questioning glance to Niko.

"In my dream," she clarified, "I'd been stabbed through the chest with something. I felt like I was dying, but it wasn't me! It was *Ravenna*!"

"Yes," Ajane said calmly. "The one thing that still confuses me is why your brother was in that dream."

"Hmmm. Yeah, I don't know why, either," Niko stated.

"Riesen wasn't anywhere with you guys, was he?" Ajane asked Cryo.

"Nope. Haven't seen him since we left Amalkyne."

"And you are certain that was Riesen in the dream?" Ajane

narrowed her eyes in concentration at Niko, as if she would siphon all her thoughts out through one stare.

"Pretty sure," Niko said. "I mean he was mainly faced away from me, so I didn't really get to see his face that well. But I mean who else would it be?…"

Tyson.

It hit her like an avalanche. She realized she had dreamt of *Tyson*, not Riesen! The two looked so similar, especially now since Tyson had his hair in the same style that Riesen had.

"Well, blazes," Niko conceded. "It could've been Tyson. It probably was."

"I see," Ajane hummed, nodding her head in quiet contemplation. "Well, it seems that we all have quite a bit to learn about the dreams, myself included."

Niko was now cursing herself for not paying more attention to detail. Had she caught these details, she might've been able to provide Ajane more guidance to make the mission go better. Maybe Ravenna wouldn't have been hurt, and maybe they would have succeeded in capturing the station back.

"Do not beat yourself up over what-ifs, Niko," Ajane said, as if she knew exactly what was going through Niko's head right now. "What's done is done and we have only to move forward."

Ajane offered Niko a respectful nod and stood up from the bench. Before she left, though, Niko spoke up.

"How long are we gonna be here?"

"I cannot say," Ajane replied. "Kira-Tharn and Riiz Alke-Tani should be back any minute. Once they are, we'll find out if we're able to transport Ravenna to a more advanced facility."

"Okay," Niko said.

"I'll let you know as soon as I find out," Ajane assured her as she turned to float away.

Niko turned back to Cryo after Ajane disappeared into Ravenna's room. "Blazes, that dream was *so* obvious to read in hindsight. I feel so stupid!"

"Nothing you could've done," he reassured her.

"Maybe," she responded with a sigh. "So I take it you guys experienced everything I saw? Did you really have to *jump* off the bridge?"

"Yeah," he laughed. "That was… intense."

"How did any of you guys live? Let alone Ravenna?!"

"It was a long drop…" he said. "But luckily there was a deep pool in the river right below where we landed."

"And Ravenna?" Niko asked. "She had to go through everything with that *wound*?"

Cryo nodded. "She's the toughest person I know. Anyone else would be dead, but to be honest I'm not even surprised she made it through."

Niko exhaled through puffed cheeks. "But for a whole *week* like that? How'd you guys get back anyway?"

"We floated down the rapids until the river calmed down a bit, then we found a cave to camp out in and stayed there for about a day and a half. We tried to keep her wound clean, as best we could, and then we set out after we made a raft from a fallen tree. Then we just took the river all the way to the Northern Sound."

"Woah."

"Yeah. It might've even been a fun excursion — if we weren't busy caring for our *dying* friend or dealing with frigid water temps. I don't think any of us has slept more than an hour here and there the entire last week."

"And here I thought my twenty-four hours without sleep was bad… I have nothing to complain about."

Cryo looked over at her for a few seconds before offering her some comfort. "I'm sorry to hear about what happened yesterday," he said. "So unfair."

Niko felt her eyes tear up, but she didn't break. She reached over and hugged Cryo.

"How's Tyson?" she whispered.

"Not great," Cryo said earnestly. "Really bad, in fact. I saw him heading out to go Sliding. That might be the best thing for him, actually. He needs some type of outlet."

"Yeah," Niko said. "I know the feeling. I had to go Sliding to make myself feel better when I thought you guys were dead. Except with Jen it's so final. Like she's not coming back. *Ever*."

Cryo just looked at Niko and offered her a tight, sympathetic smile. Niko knew he didn't know how to respond. How *would* anyone respond to that?

"At least there's one good story among all of this," Cryo said, gesturing over to a window across the hall. Inside the room, Callum and Jack were seated facing each other in deep conversation. She couldn't hear anything, nor would she want to butt in on a family reunion, but she was happy to see laughs from both of them.

"Yeah," she remarked. "And I thought *I* had it bad to be away from my parents for two months."

"Well… you were both separated from your parents," Cryo said. "You both had a rough go. At least he has his dad now, and I'm sure you'll see your family soon enough."

"Where's his mom?" Niko asked.

Cryo frowned. "She's dead."

"Ohhh, I'm sorry."

"It was a long time ago," Cryo said. "Around the same time Ravenna's family was killed. And same thing — Andersane had his mom killed."

"Blazes!" Niko said. "That's awful!"

"Very."

"Did you know her?" Niko asked.

"I remember her a little bit," Cryo said. "Her name was Sienna. Sienna Sehs. She was Antergian."

"His dad looks Antergian too, a little bit," Niko commented.

Cryo shook his head. "His dad is Meridian, like Ajane."

"Woah, really?" she asked.

"Yep, those two were working together to keep the 'Meridians' here in check for all these years."

"Oh, that's right," Niko mused. "I remember you saying something about that. So he went back to his home for the last ten years?"

"Well, kind of," Cryo said. "He needed to go back for what he said was a sensitive matter. So I think it was all business."

"Hmm. Well I'm glad he's back now for Jack's sake. Jack deserves to be happy."

Niko thought she saw a small smile form at the edge of Cryo's face —one that was barely detectable. Just then, the door at the end of the corridor flew open with a bang, and Kira-Tharn and Riiz Alke-Tani came marching in. Ajane popped her head outside of Ravenna's room, alerted to their arrival by the ruckus.

"Any news?" she called from across the hall. Even Callum and Jack both heard the commotion, as they seemed to have temporarily abandoned their private family moment.

"We do have news," Riiz Alke-Tani announced.

"Will he take her?" Ajane asked.

"He will," Riiz replied. "However, we are to transport her very soon."

"Oh?" Ajane asked. "How soon?"

"He is here now."

Ajane looked to Callum. "How long does she need on the machines?"

"Hard to say," Callum replied. "I would say a minimum of three days."

Rizz shook his head. "The one called Breva Taxa-Lon insists that we must depart immediately."

"Immediately?!" Kyler asked incredulously. "Why?"

"The An-Mara are leaving," Riiz responded flatly.

"They are leaving now?" Ajane asked, a hint of worry crossing her face.

"They are," confirmed Riiz.

"Where the blazes are they lea…"

"How many can you take?" Ajane interrupted Kyler. "Can you fit all of us?"

"That would be something that you would need to ask him directly," Riiz said.

"On the matter of Breva Taxa-Lon… You vouch for this man?" Callum asked.

"I do," Riiz said.

"As do I," Kira-Tharn added. "He is very honorable."

"Many of our brothers and sisters have acted with ultimate dishonor," Riiz explained, "but the one called Breva Taxa-Lon is someone that can be trusted to make correct judgments."

"Very well," Callum said. "Is he coming in?"

"He is landing the shuttle," Riiz said. "He should be arriving any moment."

Just then, as if he was waiting for an introduction, a man strode through the doors at the end of the hallway. He was a little shorter and looked a little less athletic than Riiz, but he was about the same age and wore that same ragged beard. Niko recognized him. He'd been with them when they left Groundheim nearly two months ago.

"May I introduce the one called Breva Taxa-Lon," Riiz said properly.

"Well met!" Kyler jumped in sarcastically. "I'm Kyler Pierson!"

Riiz ignored Kyler and turned back to Breva Taxa-Lon. "These are the ones called Ajane Solase, Callum Sehs, Jack Sehs, Niko

Ryen, Cryo Siriar, Daren Amibar, and Kyler Pierson. Ravenna Night is incapacitated in the other room."

Niko's jaw dropped open. How did he remember their names so well? First and last too! It reminded her of how Kira-Tharn had remembered exactly how many days it had been since they had first met. Maybe the An-Mara placed a huge emphasis on memory recall?

Breva Taxa-Lon nodded at all of them in greeting.

"Where is the one called Tyson Ander?" Riiz asked.

"He went out Sliding, we think," Cryo said. "Would you like me to go get him? If we're leaving?"

"Yes, I think that would be prudent," Ajane said. "And be quick about it. We are leaving in… how soon?"

"We should attempt to be airborne as soon as possible," Breva said. His voice was very deep and Niko thought it reminded her of an even lower version of Andersane's, albeit quieter.

"That's going to be difficult with Ravenna's condition…" Callum said, as Cryo hustled out to go retrieve Tyson. "We just got the machines working on her less than an hour ago."

"May I take a look at her?" Breva asked.

"Yes, of course," Ajane said. "She's in here."

Ajane ushered Breva Taxa-Lon into the room, and everyone else instinctively followed. Niko was shocked to see Ravenna already looked better than even from mere minutes ago. She'd still not awakened, obviously, but her coloration and complexion were massively improved. Niko's only worry was about the wound, though. It had pierced through her breast and into her lung. Would they be able to move her without making things worse?

Breva looked her over, moving to the monitor screens and swiping through some data that Niko had no idea existed. His brows were furled, and he appeared deep in concentration. Or worry. Hopefully the former.

"This is not ideal to move her, I do agree," he announced. "But I believe we do not have a choice. I have been discussing a plan with the ones called Riiz Alke-Tani and Kira-Tharn, and we believe that we can transport all of you to the station. There are much better facilities on board the ships docked there."

"And we are leaving today?" Ajane asked.

"Yes," Breva replied. "And soon. It is most necessary."

Ajane took one look at Ravenna, then locked gazes with Callum for a few seconds before responding. "Very well. What do you need from us?"

"We have the Garments on the shuttle. If you keep your heads down and do not speak, there will be no problems."

"What the blazes?!" Kyler blurted out. "We have to wear An-Mara clothes?!"

"I know putting your head down and not speaking is *not* your strong suit, Kyler Pierson," Ajane scolded him, "but for the love of the Mara, do what you're told for once."

Kyler didn't respond. He just took a step back and spread his hands in his typical show of innocence. Niko wished he would shut up; it would make this whole process a lot easier. They needed to keep Ravenna healthy — did he not understand that?

The door at the end of the hallway must not have completely shut after Breva had entered, because suddenly, a sharp gust of wind slammed it open with a deafening crack, causing everyone to jump a little. Other than being startled by the noise, Niko wasn't too concerned.

Then she looked at Ajane.

For the first time since she'd met the lady, the serene, unshakable mask Ajane always wore had vanished, replaced by a look of what Niko knew to be *panic*.

27

The Wind

A storm is coming.

The fleeting memory of Ajane's cryptic words, spoken several months ago atop the cliffs at the Farm, suddenly felt very relevant today.

"It is starting," Kira-Tharn said.

"Yes," Ajane agreed. "We need to be on our way. *Now.* And you are certain there is room on the ship?"

"There is," Breva Taxa-Lon said. "And you will be most welcome as long as you follow our lead."

"Very good," Ajane said. "Daren, Kyler. Help Jack and Callum with Ravenna. Niko, take these bandages." Ajane handed a huge roll of gauze and a stack of pads to Niko. "Take them to the shuttle, then return straight back here. Do not go anywhere else. Understand?"

Niko nodded. What was Ajane so afraid of? The last twenty-four hours had been plenty stressful, but seeing Ajane freaked like this may have been the most worrisome thing of the whole day.

Niko carried the stack of supplies down the hall, and as soon as she opened the door, it flew open with sharp force once again, practically yanking her shoulder out of its socket. Niko let out a small yelp, though it was more from the surprise than from any real pain. She shuffled outside, gripping hard onto the bandages lest they be ripped out of her arms and thrown into the sky by the seemingly spontaneous gale.

What is the deal with this wind? she wondered.

It had been windy earlier in the week, but not *this* windy. Besides, it was usually calm on the days when the mists socked the city in. Even after the mists would lift, the days were usually quite still. She wondered if it had anything to do with Ajane's strange attitude right now. She tried to push away any nagging thoughts that whispered of the Engines — or the supposed An-Mara plans to destroy the planet.

There was no way that was real. Exaggerated, at best.

She stifled a shiver, then tightened her muscles so as to be able to walk in a straight line to the shuttle. The transport was the same recognizable, metallic An-Mara model she had ridden several times before, which she was thankful for. Those were a *lot* smoother than the Meridian ones she'd ridden in.

She scampered up the ramp, dumped the supplies toward the front, then returned back to the hospital entrance. This time, she braced herself before opening the door so it wouldn't slam open and take her with it. It did try, but she was well-prepared and succeeded in controlling it without a slam. Her second victory came when she then proceeded to wrestle it back shut.

Small wins, she whispered to herself smugly.

She walked down the hall toward the others breathing hard, as if she had just done battle in a Field match. She may as well have — that wind was nasty! As she neared the group, she thought she heard arguing coming from Ravenna's room.

"Shouldn't we try to take one of the machines with us?" Kyler said. "I *know* I can hook it up to the shuttle."

"We cannot," Breva Taxa-Lon contested. "It will be too heavy, and we especially cannot take it onto the larger ship. It would not be compatible even if there was room."

"But that's what I'm saying!" Kyler protested. "You're not hearing me. I *know* I can hook it up. It *is* compatible…"

"You are the one not hearing me, Kyler Pierson," Breva shot back. "It is not a matter of compatibility, but one of propriety."

"Propriety?!" Kyler shouted. "What the blazes does a damn machine have to do with propriety?"

"Kyler!" Ajane snapped. "Right now, Breva Taxa-Lon is the

one in charge. You better obey him or I swear by the Emperor that I will leave you here."

Niko had *definitely* never seen Ajane like this. Something had seriously rattled her. On a normal day, she would've loved to have seen Kyler get told off by Ajane like that, but not today. This was becoming stressful.

"If the ride is relatively short," Callum stepped in, "I think she should be alright."

"Yes," Breva agreed. "None of this is ideal, but this is our only option. Let us stop conflicting and work together to transfer her into the shuttle."

Kyler sulked off to the side, but didn't argue any further.

"We can take her on this wheeled bed to the shuttle," Breva resumed, "but we will need to disconnect her — along with all her supplemental fluids — before placing her into the shuttle."

"Okay," Callum said. "Jack! Daren! Be ready to help prep her for the shuttle. I will disconnect the machines. Niko, can you grab these extra blankets?"

"No blankets," Breva said. "We cannot take anything with us. Garments are in the shuttle, and I fear those are the only items we may possess."

"I see," Callum said. "Can we get someone to go grab the Garments then?"

"I'll go," Niko volunteered.

"Great," Ajane said. "Kyler, go with her please." He grumbled in reply, but didn't refuse.

"I know where the Garments are and how to apply them," said Kira-Tharn. "Let us go."

Thank the heavens she didn't have to be alone with a cranky Kyler, even for a task this small.

Kira-Tharn strode down the hall, Niko scurrying after her, with Kyler trailing reluctantly behind. As Kira-Tharn reached for the door, Niko opened her mouth to warn her about the wind. Before she could speak, though, Kira-Tharn pulled it open and controlled it effortlessly without letting it slam.

Ugh! Niko thought. She was slightly annoyed at how difficult that door had been for her, and how easy Kira-Tharn made it look. She followed outside when...

Blazes!

It hadn't even been *five* minutes since she was last outside and the wind already seemed crazier than before. What was going on?!

In addition, thick clouds had formed on the horizon over the marshes to the northwest. This was too weird. She hadn't seen these cloud patterns the entire time she'd been here at Nevaly. In the other direction, over the bay far to the east, she saw the same pattern forming. This was the oddest weather she'd ever seen. Anywhere.

She would have prayed that this had nothing to do with that An-Mara directive discussed last week, but she did *not* want to even entertain that idea. She tried humming songs, thinking about Sliding, even thinking about Ravenna — anything besides the possibility that the An-Mara had found a way to do something harmful to the planet.

"We need to hurry," Kira-Tharn said, seeing Niko staring at the horizon.

"What are the clouds from?" Niko asked tentatively.

"I am not an expert in atmospheric physics," Kira-Tharn said.

Niko thought she maybe knew something, but she left it at that. Niko probably did know more about weather phenomenon than Kira-Tharn did, anyway, because of what her brother Keran had taught her.

"Come aboard," Kira-Tharn instructed.

Niko obeyed, all too happy to get out of the wind.

"Here are the Garments," she said, tossing both of them what looked to be nothing more than big piles of cloth. "To put them on, you must completely unwind them. Once they are extended, start at the shoulders and wrap under one arm, then over the other. Then over that other arm, then under the other. Wrap twice around the chest, then the large section goes around the torso loosely once. Wrap once around one leg, then the large section around your hips. Then wrap around the other leg once. Skip the knees then wrap each section around the calves. The lacing on the footwear will be placed over the calves and tightened. After all the rest is completed, you may pull the larger Garment over your head and shoulders."

Of all the blazes, Niko sighed to herself. How was she supposed to remember even half of that?! There was no way... She would surely have to ask Kira-Tharn to help her, as embarrassing as it would be.

Making sure Kyler was not watching, she removed her bulky cold-weather outfit and attempted what Kira-Tharn had said. Upon beginning the wrapping sequence, she actually found the process to be strangely intuitive. The outfit was even... dare she say...

comfortable? She actually thought she rather liked these Garments.

Niko had always thought the traditional An-Mara dress to be a little odd, but they were handsome in their own way. She felt weird wearing it — like an imposter who didn't quite belong — but she supposed it could've been way worse. After finishing, she turned to Kira-Tharn for approval.

Kira-Tharn sized her up and down with a slight frown.

"It will do."

It will do!? Ugh! Niko thought she did it perfectly!

"Where did I mess up?!"

"It just looks…" Kira-Tharn started. "It is fine."

"No, tell me! Where is it messed up?!"

"It just looks… off."

Niko sighed and stared down at her outfit. It looked fine to her…

"At least yours appears much better than that of the one called Kyler Pierson."

Niko looked over at Kyler and had to stifle a laugh. He looked utterly ridiculous. She couldn't tell exactly where he went wrong, but it looked… just… *off*.

"It will have to do," Kira-Tharn announced. "Now let us bring the Garments to the rest of your lot."

She dumped a pile of the tan fabrics into each of Niko's and Kyler's arms, then proceeded back into the brewing storm outside. Niko didn't want to admit it, but the cloud systems had grown considerably, even from two minutes ago. The pit in her stomach grew with the clouds, and she tried to distract herself in any way possible.

La lala la lala la la, she sang. *Two times five is ten… Eighteen divided by three is six…* Niko rattled through math problems, songs, facts, and anything else she could think of besides what the blazes was going on outside. She charged into the hospital after Kira-Tharn held the door open for her, then hurried down the hall.

"Well, look at you," she heard Jack say. He stood there against the wall with arms folded, a tilted smile settled on his beautiful face. "I could've sworn you were an An-Mara."

Niko just rolled her eyes and smiled back. "Here you go. They say we need to wear these." She dumped one of the Garments into his arms.

"How the blazes am I supposed to put this on?" he asked with wide eyes, staring at the fabrics confusedly.

"Start at the shoulder and do one arm at a time. After that wrap it around your chest twice, your stomach once, then go to one leg. Then you go back up to the hips and back down the other leg. Then you do the calves, and finally the footwear. After you're all done, pull the poncho thingy over your head."

After she was done explaining a very abridged version of what Kira-Tharn had taught her, she realized Jack continued staring at her, completely befuddled.

"Uhmm… what?" he asked.

"Here, I'll show you," Niko offered. She dropped the other Garments onto the floor and stepped over to press the Garment wrappings to his shoulders. She went through the whole process with him step by step, then stood back to admire the handywork. He'd obviously have to redo it himself without his clothes underneath, but at least he now knew how to…

"You may not have your attire from Arhanda underneath the Garments, Jack Sehs," Kira-Tharn said, levelling a stern look to both Jack and Niko. "That is a good way to earn the ire of the An-Mara when we walk among them." She walked away in a whirlwind as soon as she had admonished the both of them.

Niko and Jack looked at each other in surprise for a second, then burst out in nervous laughter. Niko hoped that Kira-Tharn did not hear their amusement, but it was funny. "Well, I guess you better do what she says," Niko told him.

"I guess so," he said. Niko stood there for a second longer, expecting him to say something else, but Jack just hemmed and hawed.

"Oh, sorry!" Niko was aghast in embarrassment as she wheeled around, realizing he was waiting for her to walk away before getting undressed. Feeling the heat rise in her cheeks, she picked up the other Garments and hurried away.

As soon as she left, however, the dread inside her returned once more. It was amazing how talking with Jack had put all of her ill feelings on hold, even if it was only for a minute. Maybe that was the key to getting through all of this — she just needed to spend more time with Jack. *If only that were so…*

"Niko!" she heard Ajane call from across the hallway. "We need two more Garments over here."

Niko walked over and handed them to Ajane. "Did you need

me to show you how to put them on?" she asked.

"No, no," Ajane said. "I've had to wear them before. I am quite familiar with their application."

Good. Niko did not want to have to go through the process with anyone else, because she thought she did such a poor job explaining to Jack. She nodded to Ajane, then walked over to Ravenna to see how her friend was doing.

Niko had *no* idea how she was alive. Ravenna was so utterly beautiful that not even her current condition could mar her good looks, but she still seemed to be in awful shape. The discoloration and bruising was not only visible around her wound, but on her face, as well. Niko placed a hand onto her forehead.

Get well. Please... she begged her friend, as if she could hear her.

"Niko?"

Niko looked up. She at first thought it was one of the An-Mara, but she realized it was Daren, dressed in the Garments.

"We need to take her now," he said, gesturing toward Ravenna.

"Oh, sorry," she apologized, stepping back away.

Daren, Jack, Callum, and Riiz each grabbed a corner of the gurney, wheeling Ravenna out of the room forcefully enough to send a pang of worry through Niko. Should they be moving her that roughly? Ajane, Breva, and Kira-Tharn followed without a word, so it was probably fine. They knew best, right? Niko stood still for but a moment longer before darting after them. The whole procession filed out of the hospital and...

"Blazes!!!"

She could not suppress the involuntary curse that escaped her. The wind had gotten even worse! If that was possible. The clouds had now enveloped the entire sky, and she could even see debris swirling around in the air in the distance.

A stick here, a leaf there. Ferns and flowers from Nevaly's picturesque gardens had been ripped out and were now part of the storm. Niko didn't think it was possible for cyclones to strike this part of the world, but could this be one? It was *way* too cold, right?

"Let us go!" she heard Breva yelling through the tempest, standing at the ramp to the shuttle as he ushered people inside. "Disconnect your Ut and leave it here!"

Kyler started to argue.

Of course he would... Niko thought indignantly.

One stern look from Ajane, though, and he was quick to comply. He tossed his Ut to the side and disappeared into the shuttle in front of her, waving his arms in the dramatic fashion of a toddler not getting his way.

Niko hesitated before stepping forward. She'd just gotten her Ut back not long ago, and now she had to part with it again?! How annoying. However, if Kyler could do it, then she could also. She severed the mental connection, then ran back to the hospital and placed it on a desk in there, despite Breva yelling at her to get back to the shuttle. When they got back from wherever they were going, she didn't want the wind to have carried it to blazes knew where. There were so many Memories she wouldn't want to lose...

She then sprinted back out into the wind, staying low so it didn't blow her around as much. Breva had already boarded, but Ajane was still outside, holding onto the side of the shuttle for support as she stared into the distance toward the west. As Niko reached Ajane, she saw what the lady's intense grey eyes had spotted. It was Cryo, ducking low and sprinting toward them.

"And Tyson?!" Ajane shouted to him.

"He's not coming." Cryo shook his head as he made it to where Ajane and Niko stood, his expression blank and unreadable. "I tried. I tried hard."

What? What does he mean 'he's not coming'!?

The storm was roaring, but it was strangely silent in the shadow of the shuttle. Ajane stared at Cryo for a short moment, then placed a sympathetic hand on his shoulder.

"We need to go!" Callum shouted. "Like five minutes ago!"

Niko remained frozen for a second, but was startled into action when Ajane shoved her forward. She launched herself into one of the seats and looked out the window. Cryo stood still, looking out to the ocean where Niko could see a small dot paddling around in the messy surf.

That must be Tyson. What was that *idiot* doing?! The waves weren't even *good*... She knew he had to be devastated losing Jen —they all were — but the storm was making the surf increasingly perilous. Even if he didn't manage to get himself lost, he would still be left here by himself for who knew how long until they returned.

He better not get lost... or worse...

She couldn't stand losing anyone else.

Finally, after way too long, Cryo turned around and followed

Ajane into the shuttle, the look on his face still expressionless.

"Good to go!" Callum shouted to Breva.

"You will all do well to secure yourselves with the belts," Breva announced from the front. "This will be a turbulent flight."

Wonderful... thought Niko, as she tightened the straps around her torso.

Breva gave them a few seconds to buckle up, then fired up the engines. Every other time she had ridden on this type of An-Mara transport, it had been so smooth that she could barely even tell when they became airborne. This was going to be much different, though, because Niko immediately felt the wind pick up the shuttle and toss it around like a ragdoll. Breva corrected against the motion of the wind, but not before Niko let out a small shriek. The nose dipped forward and they accelerated toward the ground, pulling up only meters before crashing.

Niko gripped the handholds on the side of her chair, something she'd never done on a flight before. She pressed her back into the seat as far as she could go, and Breva angled the transport upward into a steep climb, the engines roaring loudly as they did combat with the wind.

She looked outside and could no longer see the ground; only the abyss of the sky and streaks of rain that pummeled the windows. The endless grey of the clouds combined with the similarly colored interior of the shuttle made for a singularly disorienting experience. Even though she couldn't see anything, she stared out the window anyway.

The sky flashed white.

Did she just imagine that?? Or was that *lightning*?

Another flash. Definitely lightning.

With every passing second, the shaking increased. This was *not* normal. Was it?

The whole craft seemed to quiver with fury, as if some mythical giant had grabbed ahold, slinging them around for entertainment. The shuttle heaved to the right and Niko became weightless for an indeterminate amount of time.

One second passed.

Two.

Three.

Are we crashing!?!

She groaned through clenched teeth and closed her eyes until her weight pressed against her seat once more, although her face drooped as if she was about three times as heavy as normal. She managed to crack one eye open, only to see streaks of clouds rushing by at breakneck speeds, along with the alarming sight of the whitecapped ocean beneath them.

The flashes of lightning continued, and the shuttle dipped into a fall once more.

There were gasps throughout the cabin, but nobody screamed. Niko didn't want to be that one person who did, so she stayed deliberately silent, praying to the gods that she supposed her ancestors prayed to.

She had been squeezing the handles so hard this entire time that her hands had become slick with sweat. Her forearms, biceps, and shoulders all cramped at once, but that didn't stop her from continuing to hold on as tightly as ever.

She didn't know what happened next, but it was as if a Field defender had blindsided her and sent her sprawling. She did let out a yell this time, and there were even utterings from the normally unshakable friends around her.

"Callum! Hold her!" she heard someone shout.

Niko was completely disoriented, but it felt as if someone or something was pulling her upward up to the ceiling. She opened her eyes in panic.

The first thing she saw was Ajane's hair reaching into the sky as she was desperately holding onto Ravenna's bed with Callum, even though it was clamped to the floor. Were they *upside down*?? Before she had a chance to process, the shuttle was slammed by another unseen force. After the ensuing barrel roll, she was pressed into her seat once more, a sign that they were right-side-up again.

Please stop. Please stop. Please stop…

Her knee now throbbed — she must have banged it against the seat when the shuttle was sent into the spin, but she didn't remember hitting it. She had never been afraid to fly, but this was sure to ruin her for life. If she even survived this…

"Hold on!" Breva yelled from the front. "We need to get out of this!"

Almost immediately, Niko was once again forced against the back of her seat strongly, this time for a prolonged duration. After a few seconds, her vision started to go starry at the edges. She gritted her teeth, but that didn't seem to help.

After a few more seconds, she couldn't see anything at all. She was blacking out, but she was still strangely aware of everything.

She *felt* the uncontrollable shaking of the shuttle, the wind menacingly trying to grab hold and drag them down to the depths, and the thrashing sensations of alternating forces.

And she *heard* Callum and Ajane urgently shouting something to each other from the front, the thunderous roar of the shuttle's engines, and the raging beast of a storm clawing at them from outside.

She could *hear* and *feel*…

Until she couldn't.

———

Niko didn't know how long she was out for, but it was as if her panic didn't skip a beat when she came to. Her heart froze and she grasped onto the handles as she attempted to regain her bearings. It was still too difficult to move — that dreadfully strong force continued to press against every centimeter of her body.

The engines continued to rumble deafeningly, but the transport seemed like it might've been shaking a little less than before. Her vision returned to the point where it was only starry on the edges, and she could even see vague outlines once again. She shook her head and blinked a few times, but everything was still far too blurry.

"Where are we?" she managed to croak.

"I think we're above the storm," Cryo replied.

Niko realized she had been squeezing his hand, not the seat handles. She let go in embarrassment. The poor guy probably had an imprint from her fingernails digging into his flesh.

"Sorry!" she blushed.

"You're fine," he said in good sport. "You okay?"

"I'm alive," she responded. "I think."

"I'm glad this thing's external dampeners were working," Callum chuckled in relief from up near the front. "That was one bumpy storm."

One bumpy storm?? That's all he has to say about it!?

Niko couldn't believe his composure. Here she'd been thinking she was dead for sure…

She was still fighting quite a bit of strain from the acceleration, so she kept her eyes closed, her jaw tightened, and her muscles flexed. That seemed to be all she could do to make things more manageable.

"How much longer until we can slow down?" Niko asked no one in particular.

"We will be maintaining this acceleration for about four more minutes until we reach orbital velocity," Breva announced.

"Orbital velocity?!" she asked Cryo, lowering her voice. "As in… *space?*"

"Yes," Cryo said calmly.

"Wha…" Niko was shellshocked. "Why? Why are going to *space?*"

There were only a handful of Arhandans to ever go to space — in all of history! Why were they going now? This was unbelievable.

Instead of answering, Cryo just breathed deeply, a hint of sorrow on the sound. She couldn't see him, but it was as if she could feel him shaking his head.

That was fine with Niko if he wasn't going to answer. It was getting harder and harder for her to think, as well. She would ask questions later. For now, she focused on flexing her muscles, as tired as they were, and rode out the acceleration as best she could, praying that she wouldn't pass out again…

After several minutes, which went by surprisingly quickly, she suddenly felt herself released. The closest feeling she could compare it to would be an air maneuver while Sliding. There was no pressure on her seat anymore — there was no pressure anywhere on her body, actually.

Woahhhh…

"We have achieved orbital velocity," Breva declared. "You may release your belts if you wish. We will be docking in approximately two hours."

Niko's vision started to return, although she still was seeing stars in her periphery. She looked around as her companions started to release their belts one by one, their hair floating around them in an odd manner that could only be seen to be believed.

She was in *space.*

She unstrapped from her seat and stepped onto the floor. When she did, there was almost no pressure on her foot and she drifted up to the ceiling.

What a weird feeling!

Her worries suddenly evaporated, replaced by a rush of exhilaration at this sensation of weightlessness. It was unlike anything she could describe — not even Sliding came close. This was something else entirely. She locked eyes with Jack and offered a genuinely excited grin, but he only returned a half-smile that struck her as sad. Glancing around, she noticed all her friends wore similarly grim expressions.

What's their deal?

"It's… it's… gone…" she heard Kyler whisper to no one in particular.

What is he talking about..? What's gone?

By now, the stars at the edge of her vision had subsided for the most part, so she floated over to where Kyler was looking out the window. Far below, she saw a sight so awesome that it was beyond description.

It was their planet Arhanda in all its splendor.

However, what she saw was not what she ever recalled depicted in images or on globes. Instead of grand continents and sweeping oceans, she saw what appeared to be a quilted pattern of white swirls dotting the horizon as far as she could see. In between their seams, glowing orange seeped from beneath the cloud cover.

What in the world…? What is happening down there?

"Just look away," Kira-Tharn encouraged her, seeing her crane her neck to peer out the window. "And do not look back."

"What do you me…"

"*Do. Not. Look. Back.*" Kira-Tharn cut her off sharply, grabbing her by the Garment and pulling her in closely. Her fierce, dark eyes locked onto Niko's. With a quick shake of her head, she commanded, low and firm, "do not *ever* look back, Niko Ryen."

28

Malaise

"**WE** will require everyone to secure themselves with the belts once more," Breva Taxa-Lon said from the cockpit.

It barely registered in Niko's consciousness.

She was numb, detached from reality. The two-and-a-half-hour flight from Nevaly had felt like two minutes. Or two years. Or both at the same time. Time was irrelevant. None of it mattered.

"Niko," Cryo whispered.

"Oh," she acknowledged despondently. "Sorry."

"It's okay, I'll get you," he said, grabbing her arm and pulling her through the air back into her seat, fastening her belt for her.

Over the last month and a half, she had grown conditioned to accept hardship and disappointment, but all of that was a droplet on a lake compared to this. In one moment — one glance outside a window — her entire life had been broken.

Shattered.

Truthfully, there was no word that could sufficiently describe her devastation. If they'd been on board two and a half hours, then she must have spent a solid ninety minutes wailing uncontrollably, the most terrible shrieks that cut right to the very soul. Her meltdown at Amalkyne was laughably insignificant compared to what she now felt.

And after there were no more tears left, she sunk into complete despair.

What she felt was beyond grief. It was *nothingness*. She was too stunned, too tired, too exhausted to feel any sort of grief in the traditional sense. Her family, her friends, her home, her... *planet*. They were all gone.

Gone.

Green Coast. Green Valley. The Farm. Sliding. Nevaly. Amalkyne. Groundheim. Sol City. Everything she had ever experienced.

Gone.

Did her family manage to get out? Or were they consumed by the innards of the planet as Arhanda turned itself inside out?

Even Kyler, seated behind her, held his head in his hands, trembling without composure. If Niko could feel anything at all, she would have felt bad for him. He was an ass, but he was her friend, now bonded by heartbreak that was indescribable by words.

Callum had attempted to reassure them all that the Meridians had evacuated the day before, but he didn't know how many Arhandans they took with them... That uncertainty haunted Niko the most. Did they even have enough ships for everyone? Callum had steered away from answering that question, so she assumed that they did not.

It felt like she had wept a puddle, each drop carrying the weight of someone she feared she'd lost. Her mom. Her dad. Kate. Riesen. Keran. Mack. Brandon. The Jenaeis. Tyson. *Everyone*.

It was too much. After a while, she simply *stopped*. It wasn't that she stopped caring exactly — she just lost the will to fight against it all.

Sensing the apathy starting to creep in, Kira-Tharn had encouraged her to fight, to be angry at the An-Mara who were responsible — the ones who she claimed 'perverted the Time', whatever that meant. She said that anger was an acceptable emotion that would keep her going.

She intentionally tried to goad Niko into that anger, telling her of the Heads of Knowledge — the ones who proposed that the Engines be unleashed at the maximum levels in order to bury the evidence of Meridian civilization, to bury evidence of a Child of the Nel-Mara. She told her to be *angry* at Var Ashal-Han, who was the hand of enforcement for the An-Mara's vile decree. She reminded Niko how he had stormed Nevaly and murdered their friends, including Jen and Setten-Lo. And she told her to be *angry* at the Meridians, who had manipulated them for years, ultimately abandoning them all to their fate.

Kira-Tharn was right, and Niko *was* angry, but she needed time to just feel nothing. She wished this was all some wicked dream, but it wasn't. This was reality, ever cruel as it was, and she needed time to reconcile with that truth.

Kira-Tharn had not given her that time, however, as she had literally slapped her out of her funk. Actually *slapped* her! Across the face, and hard. Niko had lashed back out in anger, and Kira-Tharn seemed satisfied when she did. She supposed Kira-Tharn's intent was to get any sort of reaction that showed signs of life, which on that front, she succeeded. Niko was still a little upset with the slap, and could still feel her left cheek burning, but she did feel a little more alive, at least.

"...will not stand for that, so do you all understand the protocols?"

Riiz Alke-Tani had been explaining to the group how to fit in among the An-Mara, but Niko had stopped listening.

It's easy, all I have to do is commit mass murder and give up laughter for the rest of my life, Niko thought with snarky detachment. At least the last part wouldn't be an issue — she didn't think she would ever laugh again.

"Yeah, whatever," Kyler mumbled, his eyes red with grief.

"No, not *whatever*, Kyler Pierson," Riiz snapped. "It is critical that you understand your roles if you are to travel among the An-Mara."

"He understands," Cryo said softly, shooting Kyler a glance that told him to shut up. "Right, Kyler?"

Kyler didn't respond verbally, but his look of acquiescence was as if he were a little kid that had just been scolded hard by his parents. Cryo sure had a way to get his point across to Kyler without ever having to raise his voice or resort to threats.

"That is acceptable," Breva said, shifting his eyes between Cryo and Kyler. "We will be commencing docking now. Remember, follow us, be respectful, and do not say a word."

It seemed like easy enough instructions for Niko. She was in no mood to talk. It was going to be difficult to be respectful toward these An-Mara, though. Sure, there were probably some good ones, but she didn't know how many of them were good and how many of them were bad. How would she tell which ones were responsible for the destruction of her home? And as angry as she was at them, she was also *scared* of them. After all, they had just committed mass murder on a scale that was incomprehensible.

She let her fears trail off as she looked out the window. Although Arhanda still illuminated the horizon, the contrast between its glow and the black of space was more striking up here than Niko could've imagined. Up ahead in the darkness, she could make out what appeared to be a massive spinning wheel. It looked shoddily put together, with inconsistently spaced protrusions that resembled needles sticking out from it. As they neared closer and closer, she realized it had to be several hundred meters in diameter at least, and she now identified those 'needles' as what she assumed were large ships. It looked like there were five of them, and each of them boasted a huge cylindrical extension at one end, with six smaller cylinders wrapped around their midsection in a hexagonal pattern, all of which looked similar to the engines on the shuttle she was on now, only a hundred times bigger.

How had she never even heard of this place before? She had no idea there was a station like this out here. Not even rumors, not even whispers.

As if reading her thoughts, Ajane leaned over and whispered to her, "this was the station the Meridians had constructed many years ago. The An-Mara took it last month, at the same time when they were storming all the stations on the ground."

Niko simply nodded, still staring ahead.

They soon drifted past the colossal ships, each easily two hundred meters long, then approached the outer ring section. What had looked like bumps from a distance now revealed themselves to be dozens of shuttles identical to their own, all docked onto the station. Their own transport gave a sudden jerk as the guidance system aligned them with the spinning wheel of the giant space station, simulating the feeling of gravity once more.

Their motion felt agonizingly slow, but the docking process didn't take long. Within minutes, there was a soft jolt as they lurched forward and made contact with the station. Breva powered the shuttle down as all of Niko's companions unfastened their belts once more.

Niko stood up to stretch her legs, as she'd gone without Arhanda-like gravity for too long. The thought that she might never again feel her planet's ground beneath her feet brought a fresh wave of sorrow, as if she weren't already drowning in it. When she turned to look at her friends, a powerful surge of dizziness swept over her. She had been crying for some time, after all, and she needed to give her head a moment to calm itself before trying to stand up too fast.

"Careful to not move too quickly," Ajane said, noticing Niko holding onto the back of one of the seats. "This is not the acceleration, but rather the rotation."

Ok... whatever that means... Niko thought to herself. She just nodded at Ajane as if she knew exactly what she meant. After so many years as a student, she had perfected the art of nodding along as if she always understood what the teachers were saying. Everyone knew that was the best way to go about being unnoticed in the classroom.

She swung her head around to walk back to her friends and another wave of dizziness hit her. The ground seemed to pitch beneath her feet, so she tensed her body to counteract the fall, suppressing an involuntary reflex to vomit.

What was happening?

She knew she was already lightheaded from all the crying, but this felt weird. It must have had something to do with being in space. Maybe that's what Ajane was talking about? She decided just to sit back down for the moment; she would get up again when her head stopped spinning.

"Again, once we are inside, follow us to the central terminals," Riiz reminded them. Niko didn't even realize he'd been talking. "From there we will seek passage to An-Terino."

What the blazes is An-Terino? Niko wondered to herself, suddenly curious and terrified at the same time.

Before she had time to ask Cryo, the door to the shuttle opened up, revealing a short, dark tunnel. Beyond that tunnel was a dimly lit walkway where she saw many people bustling past in both directions. They were all An-Mara, dressed in the traditional Garments that she herself was wearing.

Her companions all filed out of the shuttle, so she dragged herself to her feet once again, bracing against the seats before stepping forward into the tunnel. Fortunately, there was railing along the sides, which she was not embarrassed to make use of.

Embarrassment was not something that even registered to her right now. She was still much too numb to care about something as trivial as that.

Once she emerged onto the main walkway, she carefully turned her body forward to follow her friends.

There it was again.

Any time she turned, a slight bout of vertigo threatened to empty her stomach.

"It's the Coriolis effect," Cryo whispered from behind her. Her pause must have been obvious.

"The *what*?" she asked without turning around.

It sounded familiar, but she wasn't sure where she'd heard it before. Just another stupid name that the stupid Meridians introduced, she supposed.

"Coriolis effect," he repeated. "It's when the surface you're on is rotating and it feels like you're being pushed in a direction. It's how weather works on the planet."

"Oh, yeah," she remembered. "I think Keran told me about that before."

Thinking of her brother brought her more tears, as if she had any left. It seemed that every little thing she thought of was a harsh reminder of what she'd lost. Would she *ever* be able to get over this? Probably not.

After looking up and seeing all the An-Mara around her, she quickly moved to wipe her eyes.

"I'm sorry," she said sheepishly.

"Don't feel bad for that," Cryo comforted. "You're allowed to have your emotions. Just try to hold on to them in front of these An-Mara as best you can. We'll all hug it out once we get to where we're going. Promise."

Niko forced a smile, fake as it was, and nodded at him. He was always so understanding, and she loved him so much for it. He had to be experiencing that same sorrow that she was — how was he keeping it together so well? She wished she could do the same and put on a strong front for those around her.

For now, she simply followed the rest of the group through the hallway that curved upward along the outer ring of the spinning wheel. It was a strange sensation, like climbing uphill without there ever being a downhill. She stayed near the wall just in case she became dizzy again, but fortunately she was fairly steady while walking straight in one direction. The corridor was lit by dim yellow lights running along the low ceiling's corners. There weren't many windows, and the only breaks in monotony were from tunnels that led to the shuttles. Eventually, the hallway widened into a central chamber, where a kiosk attended by several armed An-Mara stood at the center.

Breva Taxa-Lon, who walked at the front of the group, approached the kiosk and quietly conversed with the An-Mara there. Niko couldn't hear what they were saying, so she took the time to look around at her surroundings. In any other situation, Niko would've been absolutely awestruck by the fact that she was on a literal *space* station. After all, how many Arhandans ever had an opportunity like this? In a way, she was awed by it all, but she was still so numbed from the sadness that she couldn't appreciate much of anything.

If there was something that piqued her mind, it was the surprise of how many people were here. She had no idea there could be so many An-Mara in one place, let alone on a space station. She watched a group of three men and a woman walk by and wondered where they were from and where they were going to. Another group passed in the other direction, this one of six women. A man and a woman followed just behind the group of women.

Where were they all bound? Were any of these the ones that destroyed her home, killed her friends and family? Or were they the good ones?

Each of these people that passed Niko had lives that were so different from her own, but maybe not so different as she once thought. Was Niko going to be living among these people now? She had so many questions, but no energy to ask them.

After a few minutes of peoplewatching, she turned back to her friends, just as Breva returned back to them. He stopped just in front of Ravenna, who still lay unconscious on the gurney.

"We have been found fit to satisfy the previous arrangement in passage to An-Terino," he announced in his deep voice, loudly enough for Niko and all her friends to hear, but quietly enough to not draw attention.

"Very good," Ajane said, her once vivid eyes now appearing tired.

"When can we board?" Callum asked, gesturing toward Ravenna. "She really needs advanced medical attention."

"We will be alerted when we are cleared to proceed," Breva replied. "I would venture to guess that we will be required to wait no more than ten or twenty minutes."

That was good news. Niko didn't want to wait here any longer in the presence of Arhanda, which she could now see through a small window on the side of this larger room they waited in. Tears threatened to burst down the dam holding them back, but her fear of the An-Mara that surrounded her in every direction kept that dam intact for the time being.

"Isn't there a way we can get her there early?" Callum pushed.

"I am afraid not," Riiz said. "Do not worry, it will not be long. The one called Ravenna Night is stronger than any I have ever seen. Ten minutes will not kill her now."

Niko supposed that was the truth. If Ravenna could survive a piece of shrapnel piercing through her lung, being heaved off a bridge, then rafting down a river in the freezing cold elements for six days, nothing was going to kill her.

"I agree with the one called Riiz Alke-Tani," Kira-Tharn added. "It will not be long now."

"Just a reminder," Breva said, lowering his voice, "keep your heads down until our ship has departed. There are some among us in the station that will not take kindly to the ones called Riiz Alke-Tani and Kira-Tharn."

"What about us?" Kyler asked. "Are they gonna try to finish us off since they already killed our planet?"

Breva shook his head. "We have already reviewed this, Kyler Pierson. It is not about you as a people, but about your planet. I remind you that the An-Mara came here to evacuate *all* Arhandans before activating the Engines, but the stubbornness of your people was more than any of us expected. You were insistent on following the Meridians to the point of Oblivion."

Niko didn't exactly like what he said — he made it sound like the genocide was *their* fault. Talk about victim blaming...

There was no way any of them would leave Arhanda just because the An-Mara told them to. The Meridians had worked to gain their trust over six decades, whereas the An-Mara had only been there for a few years. The An-Mara were outsiders, weird and strange. Their customs were completely different, while the Meridians enjoyed the same lifestyle as the people of Arhanda. There was no realistic way to convince the people to ditch the

Meridians and follow the An-Mara off planet.

"Do not mistake me," Breva continued, "I was one to disagree with the directive decreed by the Heads of Knowledge on this matter, which is why I help you now."

"You could've helped us by not destroying our home," Kyler muttered under his breath.

Niko heard him, but she didn't think anyone else did. Kyler was extra crabby, but Niko could hardly fault him. In fact, she would have been more worried if he *wasn't* grouchy. Still, it wasn't fair for him to blame Breva Taxa-Lon for their plight. The man had genuinely saved their lives.

"As soon as we are given the clearance to proceed to the ship bound for An-Terino, I will take my leave," Breva said.

"Wait, you're not coming with us?" Jack asked.

"I am not," he confirmed. "I am required to report to Aktun."

"Where's that?" Jack asked. "Why aren't we going there?"

"Aktun is the heart of the An-Mara civilization," Breva responded. "Outsiders are not strictly forbidden, but you will find An-Terino far more welcoming for your kind than Aktun."

"Oh."

"There will be none that seek retribution upon you there," Breva added, quieting his voice even further. "The one called Var Ashal-Han, in particular. He and all the other dishonorable ones are bound for Aktun."

Good, thought Niko. The sooner she could be away from that menace the better. She hoped to never see him again.

But wait, did that mean that he was here on this station now?

"I saw five ships when we arrived," Callum said. "Where are the others bound, if I may ask?"

"Four are bound for Aktun and one is bound for An-Terino," Breva answered. "There are only the two choices."

"The other matter of relevance," Kira-Tharn chipped in, "is that passage to Meridian systems is far easier to procure at Alashadar than it is on Aktun."

"I would imagine that is quite so," Ajane agreed. She turned to Niko and the others. "We would eventually like to end up in Meridian systems. To live among the *real* Meridians, that is — not the pretenders that have doomed your entire world."

"Will our families be there?" Niko asked quietly. She had not said one word in the conversation so far, but she needed to know her family was somewhere safe. She needed anyone to tell her, even if it wasn't true.

"If your families made it off-world with the Meridians, they will likely be headed straight for the Capital system," Callum said. "We can be there in a matter of a few years."

A few years!? Niko knew that shouldn't have surprised her — her knowledge of astronomy told her that the distances between stars, even in this cluster they lived in, was on the order of trillions of kilometers. Still, hearing that she wouldn't be able to be reunited with her family for a few years, at minimum, hit hard. That was if they even survived at all...

There was some side chatter among her friends, no doubt people surprised that this was real and happening. They were going to the stars... and they were leaving Arhanda. It looked like Jack was asking his dad and Ajane something. Cryo, Daren, and Kyler turned to talk to each other, and even Riiz and Breva were quietly discussing something on their own.

"Are you going to Aktun, also?" Niko took the opportunity to ask Kira-Tharn, who was the only other one not engaged in a side conversation.

"I am not," she replied. "I will be traveling to An-Terino with you."

Niko's heart wasn't exactly in a state to leap, but the feeling she got was probably the closest to it. For so much bad that had happened, she was relieved that Kira-Tharn would be there with her, at the very least. Kira-Tharn would surely be invaluable in helping them navigate through a new An-Mara world. Besides, Niko had come to know her as a friend, someone who she'd been through a lot with.

"That makes me glad," Niko said.

Kira-Tharn just grunted in reply, nodding a half-nod. Such a typical An-Mara response...

"And thank you for snapping me out of my funk earlier," Niko said. "I needed that."

"Yes, you did," Kira-Tharn agreed.

"I'm still sad," Niko said. "I don't think I'll ever not be sad. But you're right, I do want to live."

"That is acceptable to hear, Niko Ryen."

"So, what is this place called An-Terino like?" Niko asked.

"Hmph," Kira-Tharn grunted. "I have never been there. But it is a nasty place according to the stories of my companions."

"A… *nasty* place?" Niko hesitantly asked. "How… do you mean?"

"They say the color is dreary," Kira-Tharn replied. "A place not meant for humans."

"Oh." This did not sound promising. Niko's stomach twisted into knots, and not from the malaise she'd been feeling from this Coriolis effect. Would it really be as bad as Kira-Tharn was describing?

Oh well, Niko thought. *Ajane says we won't be there long.*

"It is not entirely an An-Mara world, either," Kira-Tharn added, as if that was a bad thing. "There are many expatriates from the Meridian Empire that have chosen to reside there, as well. Too many people crammed into one ugly city, from what I know of the place. I do believe I will be eager to get off-world as soon as possible once we arrive."

Kira-Tharn really wasn't selling this place. Niko was already extremely apprehensive to have been exiled from her home, but this was tipping the scales. She could not shake the increasing sense of dread building up in her chest. How had her life turned so bad so quickly?

"How far is it?" she asked.

"I do not precisely know that answer. I would venture to say…"

Kira-Tharn was cut off as Breva Taxa-Lon ushered everyone to huddle back up. Niko stood up to oblige, and when she turned to walk, she couldn't hold back the reflex that caused her to uncontrollably retch.

She put a hand over her mouth, but that did little to stymy the stream of vomit that ensued. She crouched down and supported her weight with hands on knees, riding out the storm of sickness. When it finally abated, she looked up and saw her companions staring at her, along with half of the An-Mara walking by. So much for not drawing attention…

At first, her friends just gaped at her unbelievingly, but after a short second of inaction, Ajane rushed over to her. "Oh, Niko," she consoled her in that all too pleasant tone. "You're okay. Let's get you cleaned up."

"Do we have anything to clean this up?" Callum asked Breva.

"Yes, we do," he said curtly, clearly annoyed that she'd drawn so much attention. He disappeared into an alcove and returned with a metal box that resembled a briefcase. With a click, he released a hose-like attachment and unfolded it. The thing was like a cross between a vacuum cleaner and a power washer, spraying a thick solution of cleaning material as he passed the hose over the floor. After no more than thirty seconds, the area was spotless, as if she hadn't just thrown up all over the place. At least she didn't get any on her Garments…

"Do try to mind the quick motions, Niko Ryen," Kira-Tharn said to her. "The rotation causes sensations that are unlike those on your world."

"So I've been told," she grumbled. She felt embarrassed and angry for losing control of herself like that. Although, she was slightly relieved that she even felt anything at all. Kira-Tharn told her those were good emotions to carry with her.

Breva hurried back around the corner to put that cleaning machine back, and Niko was happy to notice that all the An-Mara were no longer staring at her. They seemed to have just returned back to their own business at hand, probably making their way to whatever ships they were departing on.

"What I was going to say," Breva started as he returned back to the group, "was that we are cleared to proceed to the ship departing for An-Terino. You may follow the ones called Riiz Alke-Tani and Kira-Tharn to your destination. I now take my leave to depart on my own ship to Aktun. I wish you well."

With that, he wheeled around and treaded off into the upward curving corridor. The An-Mara were always so short and to the point, never ones for grand exits. Niko was a little sad to see Breva Taxa-Lon leave so abruptly because she never even got a chance to thank him. After all, he had saved all their lives. Excessive outward gratitude was something that was considered inappropriate in An-Mara society, though. Another one of those oddities among their culture…

"I'll be right back," Daren said as he ran after Breva. Niko had forgotten he was even there, as she did occasionally. Maybe he was going to thank Breva for everyone? Niko was content to stay put, not about to run anywhere.

"You may follow me and the one called Kira-Tharn," Riiz announced, snapping Niko's attention away from watching Daren chase after Breva.

She turned to follow Riiz, but immediately regretted moving

too quickly, as that same lurch of vertigo gripped her once again. She slammed her eyes shut and prayed that she wouldn't turn her stomach inside out again, if there was even anything left to throw up.

Fortunately, she did not. She really needed to remember to turn slowly right now, though…

As soon as she opened her eyes, Kyler doubled over with no warning and unloaded his stomach all over the floor, also. The sight of the vomit alone nearly caused her to lose control, but she locked her eyes shut once again. She also felt no shame in plugging her ears to keep from hearing that awful splashing sound as chunks splayed across the deck. Niko felt bad for Kyler, but part of her was selfishly glad that she wasn't the only one making a scene.

Kira-Tharn looked extremely annoyed. She muttered something unintelligible under her breath as she stormed over to retrieve that same vacuum device and cleaned Kyler's mess up. After returning the device, Kira-Tharn strode aggressively up the main thoroughfare in the direction they were headed, prompting the rest of the group to follow.

Kyler seemed super embarrassed as he scurried to follow Callum and Kira-Tharn at the front. Niko pressed forward cautiously, but after seeing how Kyler could manage to walk quickly in that straight direction, she picked up her pace, feeling much better.

That is until she saw something that caught her attention from the corner of her eye. Niko looked back in a double take, making sure to turn cautiously to avoid that impending wall of malaise. Her heart stopped when she saw an An-Mara man fling his cloak over his shoulders in a very familiar and very pretentious manner.

Niko froze as she made eye contact with the man. She stopped walking, stopped moving, stopped breathing. He looked away for one moment, as if he didn't recognize her, but then stopped and swung his attention back to her. His eyes widened in recognition as the two of them exchanged glances. She wanted to scream for her friends, but she simply stood there, locked into immobility.

What happened next unfolded in slow motion for Niko.

The man raised his weapon at the same time she felt a strong tug on her Garments. Ajane had somehow seen him also, and hurled herself and Niko around a corner. The dizziness hit Niko strongly, although she didn't vomit this time. Instead, she crashed hard to the ground as stars formed at the edges of her vision.

"Get to the ship! Go!" she heard Ajane yell to the others.

Before Niko knew what was happening, she saw Ajane dart out from their cover and charge toward Var Ashal-Han. He had closed the distance so rapidly that he had no time to react as Ajane slid into his legs. The impact sent him head over heels into a flip. Ajane disarmed him in the same motion and flung his weapon across the ground. Her blitz offensive was so quick that he had no time to react to any of it. She launched herself back to her feet and sprinted gracefully over to where Niko still lay on the ground. She paid no mind to Niko's attempts to avoid the sickness, pulling her upright and charging down the corridor with her in tow.

"Run, Niko!" she panted.

Niko obeyed, even though she started retching once again. There wasn't nearly as much vomit as there was a minute ago, but what little there was trickled down her chin. She shut her eyes, allowing Ajane to guide them forward while she focused on putting one foot in front of the other.

"Come on, Niko!" Ajane urged. "Faster!"

Niko was already running about as fast as she could, but she could hear the shouting of Var Ashal-Han behind her, so she ran just a little faster. It was impossible to tell how far back he was, but she prayed he was out of her line of sight. He surely had his weapon back by now...

She worried for Daren, who was now completely separated from the group, but her focus was on her own steps, one after the other. The two of them kept racing to their destination, An-Mara jumping out of the way to avoid being trampled. She could hear their startled gasps as sounds started to become clearer. Her focus felt like it was sharpening. She was in survival mode, which was good considering she might not have had this instinct an hour ago.

"That's us up ahead!" Ajane shouted to her.

Just as the hallway expanded into a larger room, Niko looked up and saw Jack, Riiz, and Cryo disappear as they wheeled Ravenna's gurney around a corner. They just had to make it a little further! Ajane had let go of her at this point and both of them sprinted as fast as they could.

The shouting of Var Ashal-Han was growing louder, and she could even make out what he was saying. It was mostly "STOP THEM!" and "OUT OF THE WAY!", but she even heard some of his taunts, such as "YOU WILL BE RECYCLED WITH YOUR

PLANET!"

She wished Ajane had taken his weapon and killed him instead of simply discarding it to slow him down. Though she supposed if they killed an An-Mara here, they would be in huge trouble. Were they not already, though? Did Var Ashal-Han have the authority to stop their ship? None of these thoughts slowed her pace, however, as she dashed around the corner where Cryo, Jack, and Riiz had been a few seconds ago.

She failed to suppress another wave of malaise that caused her to throw up, but she paid it little mind. At the end of this hallway was a small tunnel, very similar to the one that they had crossed when exiting from their shuttle to the station. That must be the airlock bridge.

They were almost there!

She was very relieved to see Cryo, Jack, and Riiz wheel Ravenna across the tunnel and into what she supposed was the ship. Ajane and Niko were not far behind, sprinting as fast as they could. She *would* make it, vomit or no.

They still had to deal with Var Ashal-Han, though. There was no way he was going to allow them to leave. Not in this state of frenzied bloodlust he appeared to be in. The man had gone crazy. Even others were now resisting him. She could hear armed An-Mara shouting at him to stop and drop his weapon. The yelling mostly had something to do with the Time and directives. A bunch of An-Mara jargon that she didn't quite understand.

Then she heard shots.

Niko and Ajane had just made it to the tunnel when suddenly she became disoriented. This was something else entirely from the feelings of vertigo from the Coriolis effect. She lost track of which way was up or down, could barely see, and couldn't hear. There was a scraping against her skin that felt like burning. Or freezing? Both? She knew she was on that airlock bridge, but the only other thing she was aware of was the flashing of lights around her. Other than that, she couldn't see a thing.

But she also felt…

Ajane!

She was still there! And holding Niko inside the airlock bridge with a single outstretched leg. How an aged lady such as Ajane was strong enough to hold her there with one leg, Niko did not know. But she felt herself being pressed further into the airlock.

Niko flailed desperately, trying to reach out to grab anything. Her eyeballs and tongue felt as if they were boiling, and her vision started to black out. She tried to gasp, but there was no air. There was nothing.

What the blazes? Did she remember correctly? Did Var Ashal-Han *actually* throw an explosive that tore a hole in the side of the station? Was she *actually* being sucked out to space?!

Niko barely had time to panic when suddenly, she experienced a feeling that she couldn't describe.

She could breathe once again, but it was so painful! It felt as if someone was squeezing every centimeter of her body unbearably tight. A burning sensation enveloped her entire being, then the ground thudded up against her to add insult to injury. Vision started to return, and she nearly vomited yet again when she turned around to see a severed human leg right in front of her. She frantically tried to scoot back, but she was intercepted by someone behind her.

"Niko!" she heard Jack shout.

He and Riiz aggressively grabbed her by the arms and yanked her off the ground. She tried to protest, but she didn't have time before the two of them hurled her onto the ship. She desperately scrambled to resist, with the attempt to keep the door open for Ajane.

But it was already closed.

What she didn't know was that Ajane had hit the override to slam the door shut, keeping Niko safe, but separating her from the ship and severing her leg in the process. A second later, Niko saw a bright flash where she and Ajane had just been moments ago. A secondary explosion ripped through the bridge just beyond the closed airlock door, a tremendous shockwave sending a shudder through the floor on which she stood. Then, in an instant, she felt weightlessness.

Flashing yellow lights illuminated the room where she, Jack, and Riiz were now floating, and an automated An-Mara voice echoed through the halls.

"Attention: all individuals must proceed to the equilibrium

seating. Attention: all individuals must proceed to the equilibrium seating."

One day, far in the past, she might have thought this automated An-Mara voice to sound funny, but there was nothing funny about anything anymore. It was too much. Niko had enough loss for one day.

For one *lifetime*...

For a *thousand* lifetimes...

She floated into a wall, then let her body go limp. Riiz and Jack took over and pushed her wherever they were going — the equilibrium seating, she supposed. Niko didn't really care where she was going. She just wanted away. Anywhere.

She squeezed her eyes shut and refused to look back, afraid she would see the legless body of Ajane disappearing into the frozen vacuum beyond, gasping for air that would never come.

CHAPTER TWENTY-NINE

29

The Fleetness

THE last several hours had been spent wallowing in the aftermath of the 'unfortunate events' at the space station, as the An-Mara aboard her ship had referred to them. 'Unfortunate' was a light word — Niko thought 'disastrous' or 'catastrophic' would have been better fitting. Or even 'apocalyptic', if they expanded their query to include the events they suffered before arriving at that station.

At least the An-Mara aboard weren't the murderous type. In fact, they even seemed *supportive* of the Arhandan refugees, helping them with whatever they needed aboard this new ship. It wasn't what Niko was expecting, but she welcomed their help.

They assured her that Daren was alive and well, and had boarded a ship bound for Aktun with Breva Taxa-Lon. She was glad he was alive, but he was now just one more person that she was separated from. How long would it be before she would ever see him again? Would he even survive on Aktun?

She also found out that Var Ashal-Han had been apprehended aboard the station and had been summoned by the Heads of Knowledge for his actions. Niko didn't trust the Heads of Knowledge anymore, though. As far as she was concerned, they lost all credibility when they'd decreed the destruction of her homeland.

Still, she was glad they appeared to be trying to hold Var Ashal-Han accountable for all the terror he'd sowed. She would have much preferred if the man was dead, though. The fact that Ajane met such a grisly end while that repulsive excuse of a being walked away healthy flooded Niko with rage.

Kira-Tharn had told her the rage was a good thing, but no amount of it would bring Ajane back, nor would it bring back Arhanda. She didn't like the overwhelming sadness, though, either. Her emotions primarily ranged between those two, and if she had to choose, she may have preferred rage.

Unfortunately, it had swung back to sadness at the moment. She was currently standing on one of the central decks, waiting for one of the elevators after having gone on a walk around the ship to clear her head. The walk was a good idea in theory, but it didn't really do the trick. She couldn't shake free any of the day's events from her mind, no matter how hard she tried. Her characteristic daydreaming had now become her greatest curse.

She should have been more concerned with all the people, so Niko didn't know why she was so sad about the damn forest cats. A random image popped into her head of the poor beasts racing through a forest with nowhere to run and nowhere to hide. They were so innocent, yet they suffered just as much as all the people did. Maybe that's what made her so sad. They had been her favorite animals, after all.

Not anymore, she sighed. They didn't exist anymore.

Against Kira-Tharn's advice, she allowed herself one last look at Arhanda far in the distance below. The planet was unrecognizable. The entire husk of a sphere — that's all it was at this point — was enveloped in a thick, yellow-orange cloud cover. None of her companions would describe exactly what happened, but Niko had a pretty good idea. The Engines would have released all the pressure from the interior of the planet, spewing superheated gases into the atmosphere. The temperatures would have been high enough to evaporate the oceans, and an avalanche of pyroclastic flows would sweep over every centimeter of the entire world. It was almost too awful a fate to imagine, and Niko shuddered just thinking of how many of her fellow Arhandans were left to endure it.

She had spent many minutes since they departed the station thinking about all of it, and she had become numb once again. She hadn't cried in several hours; she only harbored a deep, profound sorrow that transcended any physical display of emotions.

Niko took a deep breath, then turned away from the window. She didn't know if that would be the last time she ever gazed upon her homeworld, but she certainly didn't care right now. The way she saw it, it wasn't even her home anymore. It was definitely not one that she recognized, anyhow. Without looking back, she walked into the center of the room where the elevator car arrived and stepped in.

This glorified metal prison is my new home, she thought to herself miserably. Some of the skyscrapers in Sol City were bigger than this ship she was on now…

Sighing to herself, she rode the elevator down a few levels, hearing an announcement boom through enhancers once more. It had been echoing throughout the ship's levels for several minutes now, requesting that everyone report to the pods so they could enter the 'Fleetness'. She had asked Kira-Tharn what the Fleetness was earlier, but she just shrugged and told her it was how they traveled quickly from system to system. Niko liked Kira-Tharn, but trying to extract any technical answers from her was like asking a stone wall what the meaning of life was.

Riiz, on the other hand, had offered her much more insight. He said that the Fleetness, also called the Greater Acceleration by the Meridians, was when they would be achieving maximum accelerations during their journey. He said there would be several intermittent Fleetnesses followed by periods of Recuperations, or Standard Gravity Levels as the Meridians called them — which they were technically in right now. Niko was pretty sure that's what he called all those terms, at least.

Even though she'd been languishing around in melancholy, it wasn't enough to completely kill her curiosity of the marvels of space travel. She was slightly terrified to learn how fast they would be going — Riiz said they would be reaching nearly thirty percent of the speed of light! What if they hit a rock at those speeds? She thought they would for sure be toast, but he assured her 'the angular momentum of their outer spinning Shell would be enough to keep them safe from such collisions'. Whatever that meant…

She was also curious how they were able to generate enough energy to go so fast. He was happy to explain that they used a nuclear fuel, then its waste would be annihilated in a process she didn't understand. Something about 'opposite particles', maybe? Whatever those were…

Maybe it was the way the An-Mara explained things, but it was much more difficult to understand than when the Meridians told her how things worked. The An-Mara had all these weird terms that made no sense, and it was hard to keep track of them all. At least he took the time to explain all of it to her, even if it was only because he felt guilty for what had happened to her.

When Niko had questioned the necessity of the pods, she learned that the Fleetness would be too great an acceleration for humans to withstand for an extended period of time. The liquid suspension served as a dampener to the forces exerted on the body. It was interesting, but she was a little anxious that they would be cooped up in those pods for so long. Riiz had said that during this first Fleetness, they would be in the pods for about two weeks straight! She was going to go crazy being stuck in there for so long…

She desperately wished she could've discussed all this with her father, but she would never get the chance to anymore… Thinking of him manifested a new wave of sorrow, one she attempted to dispel by thinking more of the engineering of this ship. The sooner she could bury all those feelings of despair, the better.

Finally, the elevator door opened up onto her level, and she looked up. Thick, vertical columns of water bounded by glass were splayed out in a grid across the room. Directly to her left was Ravenna, who was already in one of the pods, and had been since they first boarded the ship. She was dressed in a sort of full-suit, with a mask over her face and a hose running out of the tank. She was still unconscious now, but the An-Mara had said she should wake during the first Recuperation.

Niko imagined Ravenna was going to freak out when she woke up. As far as she knew, the last thing she'd been conscious for was jumping off the bridge with Cryo. Even if someone would manage to calm her down, they'd still have to explain what had happened to Arhanda, and where they were now. Niko sure hoped that wouldn't be her job. It would probably fall to Cryo, in all realism.

After pausing for a few seconds to check on Ravenna, Niko continued across the grated, metallic floor toward her pod in the back. This deck had twelve pods total, and she and her seven companions had all claimed spots here. In fact, they were the only ones on this level, which gave her some comfort.

But the thought lingered — were they *really* the only Arhandans who'd made it off the planet? Daren made it out, which she was very glad of, but he was gone now, headed for a completely different system. The only ones here now were Ravenna, Cryo, Jack, Kyler, and Callum. Kira-Tharn and Riiz Alke-Tani were with them too, but they weren't Arhandan. Technically, neither was Callum. So really, it was just six of them. Six Arhandans… out of how many millions?

The thought hit her like a blow. The prospects were truly horrific.

Her head drooped as she joined her friends, who were each prepping for the Fleetness. They were discussing plans for when they arrived to An-Terino, their voices strained as they adjusted the full-suits over the top of their Garments.

"There is talk of one who has come back from the precipice," she heard Riiz say as she stepped up to her pod.

"And what the blazes is that supposed to mean?" Kyler demanded. "The precipice of what?"

"I speak of the one that is said to have made contact with the Machine and returned from the precipice of certain death," he clarified. "That one is said to be skulking around on An-Terino."

Kyler frowned, obviously frustrated at the crypticity of Riiz's statement. Niko shared his sentiments completely. His clarification did not make things any clearer. What the blazes did this even mean? And why would they care about this guy?

"Skulking?" Jack asked.

Riiz shrugged. "He is one that is wanted by the Meridians, apparently."

"I thought you said the Meridians weren't on An-Terino?" Jack narrowed his eyes.

"They do not hold sway upon the world like they do in other systems, but there are some Meridians there," Riiz replied.

"So that's why you're traveling to An-Terino?" Kyler asked. "To find some dude that doesn't want to be found?"

"Yes," Riiz replied. "I must make contact with him. *We* must make contact with him."

"Speak for yourself," Kyler said. "My only goal is to find passage to this Capital place that Ajane was talking about."

"We are in this together, Kyler Pierson," Riiz reminded him.

Kyler shook his head, stubborn as ever. "I've had enough of all this Machine business, and Engine business, and blazes Minedyne, and An-Mara…" Kyler paused, trailing off with a huge sigh. "No offense."

"Offense is not taken, Kyler Pierson," Riiz said. "But perhaps you will reconsider. We have plenty of time until we reach An-Terino."

"Doubt I'll reconsider," Kyler muttered.

Riiz heard him, but didn't push the subject any further. He knew as well as any of them how obstinate Kyler could be sometimes.

"Well," Jack whispered to Niko with a grin, "at least we won't have to put up with Kyler for two weeks."

Jack had been trying hard to cheer Niko up. Normally, Niko would have been flattered by the attention he'd been giving her, but all of her enthusiasm was dulled. She still enjoyed his company, of course, but pursuing any crushes was about the last thing on her mind.

"Two weeks… That's so long," she replied. "Do we really just sit there submerged underwater the whole time?"

"Yes," Kira-Tharn answered. She had already climbed up onto her pod, which was situated on the opposite side of Niko from Jack.

Niko muscled the full-suit over her head and set about tightening the cinches around her ankles and wrists. "Is it even possible to sleep at least?"

"Of course it is," Kira-Tharn replied. "The Garments and Podsuits will regulate your metabolism."

Niko was shocked to hear anything technical coming from Kira-Tharn. "What does that have to do with sleeping?"

"Each of us has access to sleeping controls," Kira-Tharn stated, as if Niko was foolish for not knowing. "You may choose when you sleep and for how long."

"Actually?" Jack said in surprise. "That's rad as blazes!"

Sure enough, when Niko looked more closely inside her pod, she spotted a translucent screen about halfway down. Across the room, Callum and Cryo were already in their pods, tapping at their own screens, probably using those controls to put themselves to sleep.

"Yes," Kira-Tharn replied. "I shall take my leave now."

Niko shook her head. *The An-Mara and their abrupt exits…*

Kira-Tharn dropped into her pod with a splash, nodded at Niko from underwater, and swiped at her screen. After the top of her pod sealed shut, Niko couldn't help but think she looked a little silly in the Podsuit, mask and all. Honestly, they all did. She swallowed her pride, strapped on her own mask, and climbed the short ladder atop her pod.

"See you on the flip side," Jack said, flashing a grin before setting his mask in place. He really was gorgeous.

Before she got the chance to bid him farewell, though, he performed a small leap into the water and was completely submerged in an instant. Niko took one more look around the room and realized that she was the last one to enter. The lights even began to dim, a subtle last call for all the stragglers to enter their pods.

She breathed deeply through the mask, then plunged into the water, which was surprisingly warm. Though she'd spent much of her life in the water, this felt different. She was suspended halfway between the bottom and the surface, able to control her buoyancy with her lungs, but she still moved less freely than she would in normal waters. The suit she wore felt similar to her cold-water full-suits, but it must have been made of a different material — more dense, perhaps.

She also felt sort of… *claustrophobic* in this pod. She'd never really had that feeling before, but the thought that she wouldn't be getting out of this thing for two weeks was a little panic-inducing, to say the least. Hopefully the sleep controls worked as Kira-Tharn said they would…

As soon as she settled into place, Niko looked around the room and almost smiled. *Almost.* She still wasn't in the mood for such gleeful displays of emotion, but it was funny to look around at the others. She could see several of her friends in their pods, and all their images were so refracted that they looked weird — they were skinny, wide, and distorted all at the same time.

As she adjusted to her new surroundings, her thoughts started to wander yet again. What would two weeks in here feel like? Was this trip going to be dangerous? How far away was this An-Terino place exactly? What was it like? Kira-Tharn had mentioned a big city… would it be like Sol City? What were the people like there? How long would this voyage actually take?

All these questions swirled around in her brain, but she became distracted when she looked down at the screen in front of her. It displayed statuses of all the other passengers aboard, and even had an option where she could open communications with any of them. Everyone was currently marked as sleeping, though. Everyone except for Jack, who was waving at her from underwater. Her heart felt strangely light as she waved back, even though her soul was still impossibly burdened by the thoughts of all she'd lost.

Jack performed some swipes on his screen and would probably be asleep in a few seconds now, also. Maybe she'd talk to him when he woke up. At least she wouldn't have to be completely isolated this entire time…

She moved her hand to explore the options on her controls, her attention drawn to a detailed scan of her own body. All the vitals were displayed, which was neat, but she really only cared to find the option to set a sleep schedule. She swiped to the right until she found it, then wasted no time to tap the option to begin sleep immediately. She set the duration to…

Oh wow, nice. That's… rad as blazes, she thought to herself as she set the duration to *one hundred and fifty hours*! She managed to eke out an imperceptible smile, proud of her homage to Jack's funny quips, at the same time as being relieved that she could knock herself out of her misery for an extended period of time. One hundred and fifty hours would last the better part of a week, and that's exactly what she needed. She just wanted out of this reality. Maybe life wasn't all bad, but that appreciation would have to wait for another day. She was only too eager to be done with this one.

It's all just… I just… She sighed deeply into her mask, and that was the last muddled thought she had before dozing off into nothingness, never to wake in Arhandan space again.

New Beginnings

RIESEN knew he was pacing. He wanted to scream, but that was not something he did. Nor was crying. He was above that. Stoic was his style, so he settled for a subtle clenching of the jaw, a gnashing of the teeth, and just… *walked*. Anywhere.

He wasn't even paying attention to where he had gone, but somehow he ended up on an ornately paved terrace, one with lush tropical foliage neatly surrounding him on every side, and a view that was overlooking the most beautiful ocean he'd ever seen.

Such cruel irony.

The sol, Providence as it was called, hung in a clear blue sky over the shimmering waters to the… East? West? South? Riesen didn't know the compass directions of this place just yet, if they even used them here at all. He still had a lot to learn about this place. After all, he'd only arrived just a few days ago.

The striking beauty was something to behold, but right now all he could think about was the news that High Commander Silvane had delivered only hours ago.

His home was *gone*.

Destroyed.

By the damned An-Mara he so desperately wished he had the opportunity to go back and kill. He would do *anything* to fight for his home, but there was nothing he could do. There was no home anymore.

This place, he supposed, was his new one — and if he was being honest, it wasn't such a bad place to end up. Silvane himself promised that they would exact retribution upon the An-Mara, and Riesen vowed he would be there to participate in that. Still, that would not bring back the world that his entire life was built on. He yearned to see his family one more time, to go Sliding out at Green Coast one more time, to play Field in the great stadium at Sol City one more time.

Riesen didn't know what it was that made him think of the man now — he hadn't thought about Brody Felleter in years. He had *hated* that guy, but now he only felt regret and guilt over how he'd treated him when they departed. Felleter had deserved Riesen's full wrath, but looking back, Riesen knew it wasn't the right thing to do. He didn't need to kick him out. There was plenty of extra room on the ship, after all.

At the time, it was supremely satisfying seeing Felleter's face as he got rank pulled on him. Funnier yet was when High Commander Daaz had been livid with Felleter for *'missing'* the departure. The last thing Riesen remembered of the guy was seeing him walking away from the departing shuttle with the slumped shoulders of defeat. Of course, theirs was the last shuttle that made it to the *Dawnletter*, so Daaz would never find out that it was Riesen's fault that Felleter was left behind. He bore no ill will toward the man anymore, and he hoped that by some miracle he made it off-world by other means.

Suddenly, another wave of anger washed over Riesen so completely that he saw red. His vision shook at the edges and his hands subconsciously gripped the smooth white railing of the balcony. Thinking of how the An-Mara had sabotaged Operation Exodus four years ago had always triggered him, but now that anger took on a whole new form. A few stray thoughts of taking revenge upon those responsible for his world's ruin satisfied him for a few short moments. What he wouldn't do to get his hands on the murderers of his family and friends...

Were they really all dead? He found it almost unbelievable that an entire planet could be destroyed so completely, but he knew in his gut what the Meridians explained to be true. As soon as the Engines had been activated and left to run rampant, the atmosphere would have been cooked and the terrain covered in lava flows, probably within days. From what he learned, the Engines were the mechanism for the terraforming of all the planets under the Nel-Mara in the first place, but in the wrong hands, they could just as easily be used as a tool for obliteration.

Looking to the sky, he tried his best to process everything, but it was too much. In addition to the raging emotions within, he was also *so* tired. The one-way voyage to Trevi Nali had already taken a few years from him, especially since a chunk of that was spent in the pods during the Greater Accelerations. Thinking about time was often too difficult — his entire perception of it was completely messed up after this journey. To be fair, they warned him it would be. Not having the regular rotations of day and night had been very confusing for his body to get used to.

He closed his eyes and basked in the warmth of Providence, currents of anger and fatigue still alternating through him. He would've tried to sleep, but there was no chance he would be able to now. Not after he knew about his home.

At least he stopped pacing for the time being… And just at the right time, too, because he suddenly sensed someone coming down the garden path toward him.

Riesen turned around casually and saw three people approaching. Front and center was a fancy-looking girl about his own age, flanked on the sides by two men with masterfully crafted armor. The first impression that crossed his mind was that they were some sort of security detail for this girl, whoever she was.

She raised a commanding hand and the cloaked guards stepped one pace back. She peered at Riesen appraisingly for a few seconds, but said no words. Her wavy, blonde hair seemed out of place for a Meridian, as did her light blue eyes. Most Meridians he'd ever seen had darker hair, and either brown, green, or grey eyes. Her flowing white and pink robes looked crafted out of a dream — very ceremonious and definitely not practical.

The girl slowly floated three steps nearer to him, but still stood with her arms behind her back and chin held high.

Who is this? he thought to himself. *And what the blazes does she want?*

"You are one who just arrived from afar?" she asked. Her voice was kind, but oozed with confidence and power. Riesen had never seen such an aura of self-assuredness around anyone that he ever met. This girl was magnetic.

Riesen nodded, not sure what else to respond with.

"I am Morgan," she introduced herself.

Morgan? The name sounded familiar. Should he know her?

Wait... he thought to himself in disbelief. *THE Morgan!? As in Morgan Ostreodase?*

"Riesen Ryen," he replied, barely nodding his head in deference. He didn't know if he should bow, or kneel, or what. Instead, he just stood there, hoping that his jaw hadn't dropped open.

"Well met," she said, returning the head nod. "Silvane told me I might find you out here. It was my intention to deliver the most heartfelt sympathies for you and your people. We all heard about what those An-Mara did to your home."

The way she said the word '*An-Mara*' with such disdain made Riesen feel better. At least the Meridians were on his side. And these weren't just the lesser Meridians that were on Arhanda... These were the actual *Meridians*.

"Thank you," Riesen said. "I... just was out to clear my head. I only found out about my home a few minutes ago."

Riesen thanked the Mara, as the Meridians say, that he was not one to outwardly show his emotions. This girl was intimidating enough as it is — he would have felt so embarrassed if he was a blubbery wreck like Kate.

"Oh," Morgan replied, carefully placing a hand on his shoulder, "I am so very sorry."

Riesen felt a little uncomfortable with her being so close. He didn't have to look at the two guards behind her to know that they were ready to cut him down in less than a split second if he made some move to endanger her.

"I'm okay," he lied, careful to not budge even a centimeter to incur their suspicions. "I just need some time, y'know."

"Of course," she said, finally removing her hand.

Her touch strangely put him at ease, at least more than he had been. He figured it had something to do with this Valanse training he had learned about on the long spaceflight to Trevi Nali. It was a strange phenomenon, but it would explain a lot — especially what that Ajane lady had been capable of. He still thought about that one dream from time to time — the one they all had together where she appeared to them. Back then, he hadn't been able to make sense of it at all.

And then there were the other dreams where he could've sworn Niko had been there. His only conclusion now was that she must've been receiving some of that Valanse training from Ajane, too. He hadn't had any more of those dreams since he'd fled Arhanda, though, so it made sense that his sister had perished in its destruction. He always had a soft spot for Niko. She was pig-headedly stubborn half of the time — and she always acted like she had something to prove — but she was one of the smartest people he knew, and he admired that about her.

"I guess this is my new home?" Riesen had to say something to break the silence before he became too emotional thinking of those he'd lost.

"Yes, I suppose so," Morgan agreed. "We are most happy to accommodate you and your people after what happened."

"I'm grateful," Riesen said. "We all are."

She nodded in acknowledgement, yet her gaze lingered. He could *feel* the internal calculation, like she was studying him with every word he said.

"Your accents are so similar to our own," she remarked after a moment.

Riesen shrugged. He didn't think they were *that* similar.

"I guess so," he said. "Meridians were the ones who set up our entire society back on Arhanda."

"So I have heard," she said tenderly. "You must be missing your own world terribly right now. I do hope this one is satisfactory?"

He barely bit back a snort. 'Satisfactory' was hardly a word to describe this place. "This world is... *incredible*."

"Good, I'm glad you like it," she said, regally tilting her head to the side. "I am curious, though... what was your world like?"

"Compared to this?" Riesen scoffed softly. "I'm not sure it can be compared. Most of my planet was small villages, more or less. Or just wilderness. A lot of deserts, too."

"We also have much wilderness here," Morgan said.

Riesen gave a faint nod and scanned the distance. He supposed it was true — there was a lot of jungle that was intertwined naturally with the city. It was just so much different, though.

"It's hard to make comparisons because I've only seen such a small part of this place so far."

"I see. Perhaps I can show you more of the planet someday,"

Morgan suggested.

Riesen was so lost in conversation that he forgot just who it was he was talking to… This was Morgan Ostreodase, the Princess Imperial of the Meridian Empire itself! And she was offering to show *Riesen* all around Trevi Nali someday?? Was he asleep and dreaming? This just wasn't something that happened to normal people.

But it was real. For better or worse, it was all real.

"I'd be honored," he said with a polite smile.

"Excellent. Then I will make preparations for it to happen," she said. "I'm afraid I must take my leave now, though. It was lovely to meet you, Riesen Ryen. Do not hesitate to call for me should you or your people ever need anything."

"Thank you," Riesen replied. He was thinking of something more flowery and grand to say, but he was a man of few words. He just offered her his best smile and bowed his head.

Without saying anything more, she pivoted gracefully and glided away with her head held high, her flowing gown trailing like wisps of air as she floated back up the ramp. Riesen had never seen such excellent posture, such elegance, such commanding presence.

Wow… he thought, as his eyes followed her out of view. That was royalty if he'd ever seen it. What a striking woman…

He'd gotten used to being a huge celebrity on his homeworld, but suddenly he felt so small. That was *the* Morgan Ostreodase! He was completely starstruck. He didn't even realize, but that encounter had lifted his spirits just enough for him to at least relax his clenched fists.

He turned back to the ocean and gazed out at the clear expanse before him. Everything felt like a dream, but this was his new normal. He was now in an entirely alien place. It was only a few days ago when he stood atop the decks of the *Dawnletter*, staring down at the planet below, immensely proud that he was among the first Arhandans to ever visit another world.

From space, Trevi Nali had looked much like Arhanda did — clouds, water, and land all coexisting tranquilly, sweeping across the horizon in breathtaking magnificence. He could even see the haze of the atmosphere, highlighted with that same distinct hue that he'd noticed above his own planet. But this place was different — there were more dark greens and fewer yellows, and the land masses were none that he had ever seen before. Finger-like peninsulas separated by narrow seas seemed to span much of what was visible from his celestial perch.

It had been an amazing moment in history, not only for him, but for all his people. Now, though, he was overcome with the emotion of a different sort — an overwhelming sadness that he would never see his family again. Thoughts of them had weighed heavily upon his heart for years, but now there was such a finality about it that was soul-crushing.

He closed his eyes and breathed deeply. After counting to thirty to calm his thoughts, he opened them again, restoring his view of this next chapter of his life. This was his new home; he was now Meridian.

He stood calmly, unmoving for several more minutes, until he heard footsteps approaching. Turning his head casually, he was relieved to see that it was only Kate.

She walked up to him and hooked her arm through his, leaning all of her weight into his rigid frame. He'd always found her physical affection a bit excessive, but right now, her presence was a comfort. Besides, she was emotional by nature, and he wasn't about to turn his sister away. Not now when she needed him most.

Her eyes were red and puffy — no doubt she'd been bawling for hours. He should've gone to her sooner, but he just needed some time to himself. No matter, she was here now, and they could grieve together.

For many silent minutes, the two shared the dichotomy of the beautiful vista and the sorrow that threatened to consume them.

Riesen, aware that he would never return to his homeworld again, stood hand in hand with his sister, watching as Providence dipped lower to the horizon. Kate grasped his arm firmly, a single tear brimming from the corner of her eye — one that held a plethora of emotions: sadness, love, hope, and everything in between.

"New beginnings", she whispered as she leaned her head on his shoulder. "New beginnings."

MERIDIAN

APPENDIX

GLOSSARY OF CHARACTERS
(in alphabetical order)

Abel Night: father of Ravenna; worked alongside Ajane to monitor Minedyne

Ajane Solase (uh-JAYN soh-LAYZ): Meridian who traveled to Arhanda in the years after the Arrival

Alana Fils (uh-LAW-nuh FILLS): woman from the Islands Territory on Arhanda; mother of Rush

Andersane (ANN-durr-sayn): Magistrate of the Meridians on Arhanda; known for his booming voice and intimidating nature

Anson Fils (ANN-sun FILLS): communications officer for Andersane; father of Rush

Beriph Nel-Arana (buh-REEF NELL-uh-RAW-nuh): the last Nel-Mara before the Scuttling; in the Legends, was said to have a human child called the Child of the Nel-Mara

Brandon Jenaei (JEH-nye): best friends with Riesen; brother of Jen

Breva Taxa-Lon (BRAY-vuh TAX-uh-lawn): An-Mara trooper on Arhanda

Brody Felleter (FELL-it-err): officer in the Meridian service on Arhanda

Bryce: Candidate assigned to training at Sol City with Riesen

Brynne Delilah (BRINN de-LYE-luh): teenager from Green Valley; used to play on Niko's Field team

Callum Sehs (CAL-lum SEIS): Meridian who traveled to Arhanda with Ajane Solase in the years after the Arrival

Cryo Siriar (CRY-oh SEAR-ee-arr): young adult from the Green Coast; known for being calm, cool, and collected

Den-So (DEN-SO): An-Mara trooper on Arhanda

Falare (fuh-LARR): Meridian Valanse; tried to assassinate Kezane aboard the *Duskletter*

Firsin (FEAR-sinn): engineer aboard the *Duskletter* under Kezane's command

Galen Anstraes (ANN-strayss): First Officer in the Meridian Contingent

Jack Sehs (SEIS): teenager from Arhanda; friends with Cryo and Ravenna

Jacqueline Night: sister of Ravenna

Jame Ryen (JAYM RYE-inn): adopted father of Niko; engineer

Jen Jenaei (JEH-nye): best friends with Kate and Niko; sister of Brandon

John Maksolhoff (MACK-sole-HOFF): owner of The Farm on the Green Coast

Kate Ryen (RYE-inn): Niko's sister, two years older than her; known for being an empath

Keran Ryen (KEER-inn RYE-inn): Niko's eldest brother; known for his work in the weather service

Kezane Pfase (kuh-ZAYN FAYZ): Meridian Valanse commander; notable for being the most powerful Valanse in an age

Kira-Tharn (KEER-uh-THARN): An-Mara trooper on Arhanda; from Aktun

Kyler Pierson: young adult from the Green Coast; notable for his exceptional machine tinkering skills

Lizzy Jenaei (JEH-nye): mother of Brandon and Jen

Mack Ryen (RYE-inn): Niko's younger brother

Marius Silvane (sill-VAYN): Meridian Valanse commander; serves as head of the Tricouncil

Masa (MAW-suh): Meridian Valanse; tried to assassinate Kezane aboard the *Duskletter*

Maxime Oto (MAX-imm oh-toh): High General in the Meridian High Command on Arhanda

Michele Aragase (mish-ELL ARE-uh-gayz): Second Officer in the Meridian Contingent

Mora Nant-Zern (MORE-ruh NANT-zern): An-Mara trooper on Arhanda

Morgan Ostreodase (OSS-tree-oh-DAYZ): Princess Imperial of the Meridian Empire

Nicodaren Amibar (NEE-koh-dare-rin A-mih-barr): called 'Daren' by his friends from the Green Coast, not to be confused with 'Niko' Ryen; known for being exceptionally quiet

Niko Ryen (NEE-koh RYE-inn): teenager from the Green Coast; primary protagonist

Nolane (no-LAYN): Meridian Valanse; tried to assassinate Kezane aboard the *Duskletter*

Noralie Mose (NOR-ruh-lee MOHZ): Flight Deck Engineer in the Meridian Contingent

Pira Moran (PEER-ruh more-RAWN): Candidate assigned to training at Sol City with Riesen

Ralane (ruh-LAYN): Vice Magistrate of the Meridians on Arhanda

Ramen Ostreodase (RAW-men OSS-tree-oh-DAYZ): Emperor of the Meridian Empire

Rangar Thomson (RAYN-gurr TOM-sinn): world class Field competitor from the Islands; officer in the Meridian Service on Arhanda

Ravenna Night (ruh-VEN-nuh): young adult from the Green Coast; notable for her naturally multicolored hair, purple eyes, and fiery temperament

Riesen Ryen (REE-sinn RYE-inn): Niko's brother, one year older than her; notable for being of exceptional skill in multiple areas

Riiz Alke-Tani (REEZ al-keh-TAW-nee): An-Mara trooper on Arhanda

Ritose (RYE-tose): Meridian Valanse; tried to assassinate Kezane aboard the *Duskletter*

Roger Jenaei (JEH-nye): father of Brandon and Jen

Rush Fils (FILLS): world class Field competitor from the Islands; officer in the Meridian Service on Arhanda; known for his arrogant, 'pretty-boy' reputation

Setten-Lo (SEH-ten-LOH): An-Mara trooper on Arhanda

Shol Vera-Nim (SHOAL VEER-ruh-nimm): An-Mara trooper on Arhanda

Sienna Sehs (SEIS): woman from Anterg; mother of Jack

Trienne Ryen (tree-ENN RYE-inn): mother of Niko; expatriate from the Islands

Tyson Ander (TYE-sun ANN-durr): young adult from the Green Coast; known for his joking, boisterous nature

Valentina Night: mother of Ravenna

Var Ashal-Han (VARR ASH-uhl-HAHN): An-Mara senior commander on Arhanda; known for his pretentious antics

Willer Brooks (WILL-lurr): Major in the Meridian Service on Arhanda

Williame Daaz (WILL-lee-uhm DAWZ): Major Commander in the Meridian High Command on Arhanda

Zazise (ZAY-ZEESS): Major Commander in the Meridian High Command on Arhanda

GLOSSARY OF TERMS AND PLACES
(in alphabetical order)

Aktun (ock-TOON): homeworld of the An-Mara

Alashadar (AL-uh-shuh-DARR): city on An-Terino

Amalkyne (AHM-all-KYNE): resort city on the southeast coast of Poste Territory; known for hot, desert climate

An-Mara (ANN-MARR-uh): civilization that shares the Local Sector with the Meridians; split from the Meridians shortly after the disappearance of the Nel-Mara; seen by the Meridians as zealots clinging to a long-gone past

Anniversary of Arrival: the week of celebrations held each year to commemorate the Arrival on Arhanda

Anterg Territory (ANN-turg): the territory encompassing the lands on the north and east sides of North Continent; home to the Eastern Range, the highest mountains on Arhanda; the Antergians were the main aggressors in the pre-Arrival world wars

An-Terino (ANN-tear-EE-no): planet home to a mix of peoples

Anziend (ANN-zee-end): port city in central Anterg along the North River; known for the ancient Anziend ruins

Arhanda (arr-AWN-duh): planet in the Local Sector encompassing the eight Territories; was visited first by the Meridians and then later the An-Mara

Arrival, the: the event when the Meridians landed on Arhanda sixty-three years before current events, pulling them out of decades' long worldwide conflicts and transforming society from industrial to postindustrial

AutoNav: Auto Navigation; during space travel, AutoNav is used to plot courses for the ships

Boatah Island (BOH-uh-TAH): an island off the coast of South Territory

Candidate: after Induction, prospective troops are called Candidates

Capital System: star system at the heart of the Meridian Empire; includes the capital city of Trevi Nali and the star Providence

Celean Sea (SELL-ee-enn): body of water in between the Islands and North Continent

Child of the Nel-Mara (NELL-MARR-uh): in the Prophecy of the Stewards, purported to be the child of Beriph Nel-Arana

Collections: Meridian communal marketplaces where personal items are dispersed to citizens

Crescent "C" Sign: hand gesture with the thumb and forefinger forming a "C" in the shape of the Meridian Crescent, with the other three fingers tucked into a ball to signify the star Providence

Crown Lake: large lake in central South Continent

Dawnletter: Meridian long-range vessel; used by the faction of Meridians that traveled to Arhanda

Duskletter: Meridian long-range vessel; sent on a mission to the *Marina* under the command of Kezane Pfase

Eastern Range: mountain range in eastern Anterg; highest mountains on Arhanda

Engines: the terraforming engines on each of the planets; constructed long ago during the days of the Nel-Mara

Equatorial Territory: the Territory encompassing the northernmost lands of South Continent; characterized by tropical climate and dense, mountainous rainforest

Far Desert: extensive desert in the eastern portion of South Continent

Far Territory: the Territory encompassing the easternmost lands of South Continent; characterized by warm climate in the north, cooler in the south; rugged coastlines

Fennemol Outpost (FEN-neh-mole): outpost in Poste Territory, in the Great Poste Salt Flats between Groundheim and Amalkyne

Field: a team sport where the objective is to score goals, allowing for both kicking and throwing of the ball; the most popular sport on Arhanda; see Appendix: Field Rule Book

Flatlands Territory: the Territory encompassing the central lands of South Continent; characterized by vast deserts and plains; dry climate

Fleetness: the An-Mara term for the maximum acceleration during space travel, allowing ships to reach great speeds; also called the Greater Acceleration by the Meridians

Galactic Dark Patch: a large part of the galactic disk that appears dark due to increased debris and dust obscuring the light

Garments: the traditional dress of the An-Mara; there are several variations depending on occasion

Great Poste Flats (poast): flat desert in southeastern Post Territory

Greater Acceleration: the Meridian term for the maximum acceleration during space travel, allowing ships to reach great speeds; also called the Fleetness by the An-Mara

Green Coast: town in northwestern North Territory on Arhanda

Green Valley: a city in the northwest corner of North Territory

Groundheim: largest city in Poste Territory; base of operations for the An-Mara; known for its extensive tunnels and caverns; second largest city on Arhanda

Hall of Knowledge: chamber where Heads of Knowledge perform their decrees; room is designed in a manner where it is easiest for them to read their subjects

Heads of Knowledge: An-Mara judiciary; rigorous mental conditioning program to become a Head of Knowledge

High Command: the decision-making military body of the Meridians on Arhanda; also a High Command among the Meridian Empire, which has a much different structure

Hole, the: Meridian slang term for the black hole in the center of the galaxy

Induction: the ceremonious entry of new recruits into service with the Meridians

Intrusion: technique by which Valanses can read people's thoughts or intentions

Islands Territory: the Territory encompassing the Islands between the North Continent and the South Continent; smallest territory by land area

Legends: literature detailing the history of the Nel-Mara

Local Sector: the collective of inhabited worlds within the local star cluster at the edge of the Galactic Prime Meridian; includes the Meridian and An-Mara civilizations, as well as neutral planets like An-Terino or Arhanda

Machine: any piece of technology that can perform tasks for humans; see 'Machine, the' regarding the purported artificial intelligence threat

Machine, the: according to the Legends, an alleged artificial intelligence that is sweeping through the galaxy

Mainquarters: the base of operations for the An-Mara on Arhanda; located in Groundheim

Mara (MARR-uh): all the people and places of the Nel-Mara civilization prior to the disappearance of the Nel-Mara

Marina: one of millions of Nel-Mara vessels whose objective after the Scuttling was to aimlessly transmit signals to stall the spread of the Machine

Meridian Empire: the governing entity of the majority of the systems in the Local Sector

Minedyne: organization set up by the Meridians on Arhanda to focus on materials acquisitions for their empire

Mount Iroal (EER-oh-all): tallest mountain in the Islands Territory; dormant stratovolcano

Nel-Mara (NELL-MARR-uh): mythical beings of the past that possessed technologies far beyond those of any current civilizations in the Local Sector

Nevaly (NEH-vull-ee): capital city of North Territory; known for old-style stone architecture, lush gardens, and the famed Northern Mists of Nevaly

North Continent: the large land mass in the northern hemisphere of Arhanda; home to North Territory, Anterg Territory, and Poste Territory

North Territory: the Territory encompassing the lands on the north and west sides of North Continent

Northern Marshes: marshlands to the northwest of Nevaly

Northern Ocean: ocean to the north of North Continent

Northern Sea: the sea saddled between North Territory and Anterg

Northern Sound: a long bay that extends from Nevaly eastward into Anterg

Northposte Mountains (NORTH-poast): lower elevation mountain range extending east to west that runs along the border between North Territory and Poste Territory

Nowhere: town in Far Desert

Oblivion: An-Mara term for the warping of space-time beyond the event horizon of a black hole

Podsuits: the full-suits that are worn in liquid suspension pods to regulate metabolism

Poste Territory (POAST): the Territory encompassing the lands on and around the peninsula on the south end of North Continent; known for its resistance to Meridian administration; base of the An-Mara

Primary School: also called School for short; the education system that all citizens of Arhanda pass through, consisting of eleven grades before passing through Induction

Prophecy of the Stewards: the word spread primarily by the An-Mara about the return of the Nel-Mara through a human child

Providence: the name of the star in the Capital system; G-type main sequence star

Record, the: the log of all directives from all Heads of Knowledge, current and past; all An-Mara commanders are tasked with having access to this at all times

Recuperation: the An-Mara term for simulated gravity at normal levels by linear acceleration, particularly when alternated with Fleetnesses

Recycling: An-Mara penalty system characterized by progressive demotions

Scuttling, the: the moment when the Nel-Mara vanished 60,000 years ago; no trace was left of certain technologies, such as galactic-scale travel and machines that were able to process near infinite amounts of information

Shatter Industries: organization that oversaw Meridian energy projects in the past; banned from Meridian contracts after a period of corruption in the organization, along with the Meridian shift to socialism

Shell: a feature on ships during periods of high-speed travel that is used to protect against micrometeoroid impacts; upon such an impact, the angular momentum of the rapidly spinning outer shell of particles acts as an external dampener

Sliding: a sport in which Sliders use small hydrofoils attached to their forearms and legs to slide headfirst along ocean waves; see Appendix: A Look at Sliding Foils

Sol City: capital city of the Islands Territory and the largest city on Arhanda; seat of the Meridian government on Arhanda

Sol: the name that Arhandans have given to their star; G-type main sequence star

South Continent: the large land mass in the southern hemisphere of Arhanda; home to Equatorial Territory, Far Territory, Flatlands Territory, and South Territory

South Territory: the Territory encompassing the lands of southwestern South Continent; characterized by desert climate; cool and mountainous in the south

Southern Ocean: the ocean to the south of South Continent

Standard Gravity Level (SGL): the Meridian term for simulated gravity by linear acceleration

Stewards: the remnant searching for the Child of the Nel-Mara

Switching Decks: at the midway point of journeys through space, linear acceleration is reversed and all tables, furnishings, etc. are switched to the ceilings; all floors are in such ships are constructed in a mirrored and minimalistic manner to conveniently accommodate the Switches

Tel-Mara (TELL-MARR-uh): the people presided over by the Nel-Mara before the time of the Scuttling

Tenets of Broadcast Information: four ways to increase the effectiveness of broadcasts employed by certain Meridian factions: optimize audience, simplicity and repetition, activate emotion, and demonize the opposition

Time, the: a set of values and traditions observed by the An-Mara; refers to the time that will be spent awaiting the return of the Nel-Mara

Trevi Nali (TRE-vee NAH-lee): capital of the Meridian Empire

Tricouncil: the three heads of the Meridian Valanse Academy

Universal Common: the standardized language that both Meridians and An-Mara use

Ut (YOOT): short for 'Utility Machine'; small device that performs many functions; features an implant that allows users to exert minor thought processes over certain utilities; see Appendix: A Look at the Ut

Valanse (vuh-LANCE): an elite officer in the Meridian Empire that specializes in mental conditioning to perform extrasensory abilities

Waxing Crescent: the symbol of the Meridian Empire

White Mountains: mountain range just south of the Green Coast, extending south to the border between North and Poste Territories

A LOOK AT THE UT

The Ut is comprised of two parts. The main part of the machine is a small coinlike object that houses the central processing system, the Illumin and Sound Enhancer. The second part is a microchip implanted into the central nervous system that improves the interface between thought and action. Once the system is set up, the amount of time saved by thought processes is tremendous.

Communicator: opens a channel of communication to others with Uts connected on the network, or to other consoles and machines that the user can connect to. Can be video, audio, or text communication.

Cycling: the process of using thoughts to execute commands

Illumin: lighting tool on the Ute that will light up the entire room. The light is directed as the user commands. Also provides light for a screen that can be projected onto any surface; there is also a smaller built-in screen that can unfold if no other surfaces are available. In addition, the Ut can be synced with a holographic basin to project a three-dimensional image by scattering its light onto gas hovering over the basin.

Link: the chip is inserted into the central nervous system and syncs the Ut to the user's brain functions. When calibrating the Ut, the user must create certain links to commands with very specific and prominent thoughts. For example, if they wanted to contact someone, they would need to think of their name and imagine an image of the person. Some people find saying the name out loud enhances that command. In addition, the link can help to find a Ut that has been lost.

Memory: a captured moment in time. Can be presented as a three-dimensional hologram, a two-dimensional image, a sound recording, or the recalling of an emotional response felt by the user at the time of the recording.

Sound Enhancer: a utility used to project sounds. Useful for playing music, or for enhancing one's voice while presenting to a large crowd. Very useful in sports venues such as a packed Field stadium.

Virtual Reality (VR): the Ut can create a virtual environment that encroaches on the user's vision. This is primarily used for gaming, artwork, and entertainment

FIELD RULE BOOK

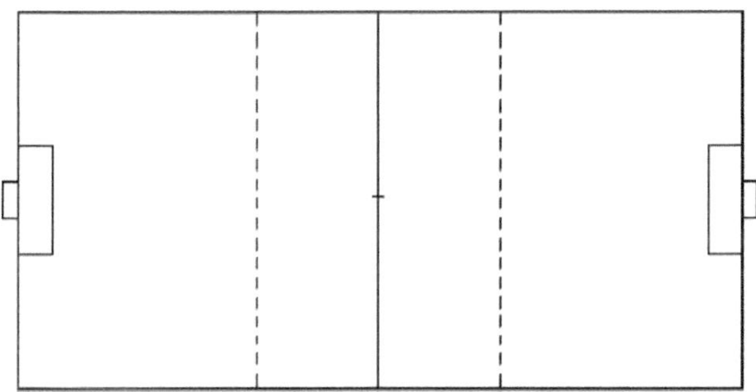

<u>Offense</u>
-Can only throw or kick the ball to a teammate with forward progress until you reach half
-Once past half, attackers can only make forward progress with the ball by running or dribbling with the ball; only lateral or backward passes to teammates. The difference between a dribble and an intentional forward pass to oneself is at the discretion of the referee.
-Can throw or kick the ball in an attempted shot. A goal is scored when every part of the ball has crossed the goal line.
-A shot may only be taken inside the final one-third of the opponent's territory. The difference between a shot and an intentional forward pass is at the discretion of the referee.
-The ball turns over if an offensive player is brought to the ground with the ball in possession.
-The ball turns over if a single offensive player holds the ball for longer than four seconds without making four meters of forward progress. This time limit is removed if the attacking team progresses the ball into the final one-third of the opponent's territory.
-No stationary picks.
-A pick is allowed if an offensive teammate creates the pick in a continuous motion.
-No part of the attacker may touch the ground anywhere inside the goal box unless the ball crosses the goal box line.

<u>Defense</u>
-No holding an opponent who does not have possession of the ball for longer than two full seconds.
-No part of the defender may touch the ground anywhere inside the goal box unless the ball crosses the goal box line.

<u>Penalties</u>
-An attacker that has committed an infraction will result in the ball being turned over.
-The first infraction committed by a defender that has committed an infraction during a possession will result in a free throw for the offense. A second infraction committed on the same possession will result in a two second freeze order for the defense. A third infraction committed on the same possession will result in a penalty attempt awarded to the offense.

<u>Penalty Attempts</u>
-During a penalty attempt, the attacker is awarded the ball at the 28m line and gets a one vs one attempt to score against a defender within an eight second time limit. During this time, there are no restrictions concerning the attacker's forward progress. The goal box rule still stands. All other players must remain behind the 28m line until the eight seconds are up.
-An attacker that commits an infraction during this time will result in the ball being turned over.
-A defender that commits an infraction during this time will result in the penalty attempt being restarted, this time with a one second freeze order for the defender.

<u>Substitutions</u>
-Player substitutions may be performed at any time on the side of the field that they are defending.
-Once a player is substituted, they may not re-enter the game. The only exception is if that substitution was deemed a medical substitution by the officials.

<u>Additional Rules</u>
-Eight players on each team.
-The field is 84m long x 42m wide. Any ball played out of bounds will be fielded inbounds by the opposite team that last had

possession.

-Goal is a square that is 4m wide x 2m tall

-Goal box is 4m outside the goal posts and 4m in front.

-The ball should weigh between 430 and 450 grams.

-No striking opponents with a closed fist.

-No striking opponents with the intention to cause harm.

-No sliding into players with cleat studs facing them.

-Two 30-minute halves.

-At the start of each half, the ball is placed onto the center of the half-marker and a sprint from the goal line will determine possession.

-There is one on-field referee that makes discretionary decisions. All boundary infractions and time limits are enforced with Ut assistance.

A LOOK AT SLIDING FOILS

Four foils are worn by the Slider, one around each forearm (armfoils) and thigh (legfoils). Initially, the foils are retracted, allowing the Slider to maneuver efficiently through the water. When the Slider catches the wave, the foils will be extended, and with enough core strength, this allows the Slider to be elevated to the surface of the water, greatly reducing drag.

The top of the foil has more surface area than the bottom, so as more fluid passes over the foil per unit time, the pressure difference between the top and the bottom becomes greater, increasing the lift force.

Armfoils:
The armfoils extend from a command via Ut. They are retracted the entire time during paddling and are only engaged voluntarily by the Slider once they have committed to the wave.

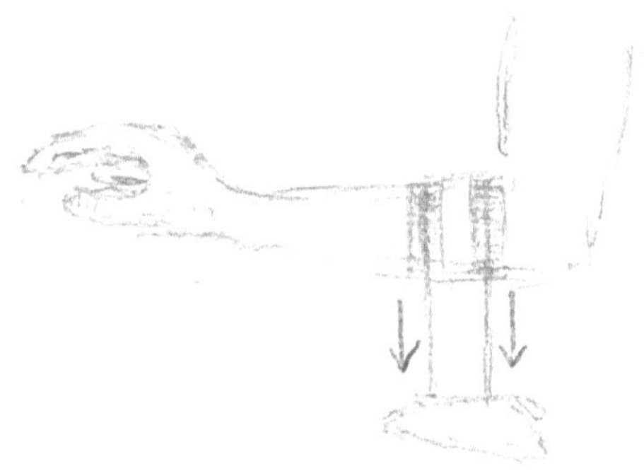

Legfoils:
As the speed of the Slider becomes sufficient to catch the wave, the respective drag force automatically extends the legfoils.

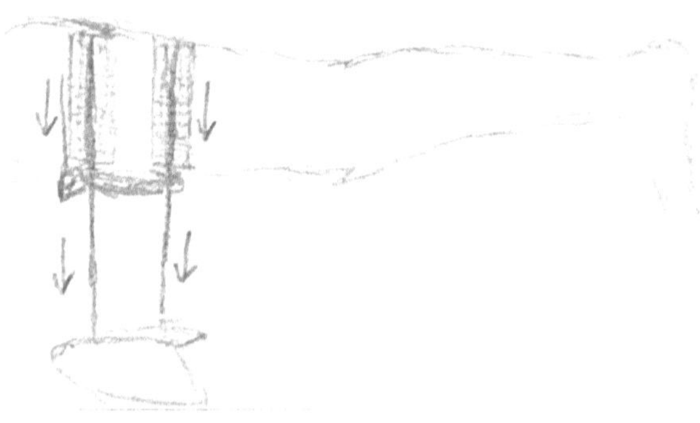

A CONFIDENTIAL CORRESPONDENCE

Confidential Meridian Ut transmission correspondence recovered by Abel Night, auto-redacted:

High Commander ██████ *,*

Behold, Arhanda. Everything is set up as you have designed. Like you surmised, there is significant potential here. We can all feel it. It shouldn't be long until they are manifested.

On another matter, there have been… complications. Two of your own have arrived — ████████ *and* ████████ *. I'm sure you know them? None of us on this mission was aware that they'd be joining. Please advise best recourse in due time.*

On a bonus note, the planet is rich in the Lanthanides, so we will be providing shipments within the decade… Project this map to monitor progress.

██████████

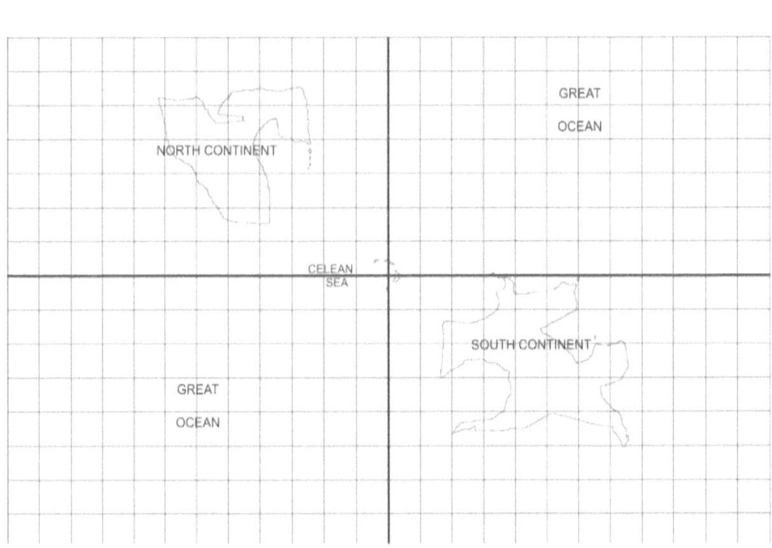

ACKNOWLEDGEMENTS & AUTHOR'S NOTES

I would first like to thank everyone who took the time to read this first installment of the *Meridian* series. I hope you enjoyed it as much as I did in making it.

Huge thank you beyond words to Natalie for not only putting up with me being shut away like a hermit for inordinate amounts of time, but also for reading the drafts and providing invaluable edits to the characters.

Thank you to all of my family, especially my parents, who have been unconditionally supportive from day one. Also, thank you to my brother and his family for being super excited about this endeavor and taking a look at my endless revisions to the prologue. Hopefully you all can go Sliding someday!

I would also like to give a shoutout to Dandan. An engineer by trade and an inventor by hobby, he provided the foundation for my interest in science and astronomy when I was a kid, which persists as strongly as ever today. He was an amazing person and continues to inspire.

Finally, I would dedicate this book to Courtney. She was the one who I first approached with the idea to put my imaginary world onto paper many years ago. She was a voracious reader and was so excited for this project, even taking a look at my early, early drafts of the first chapters. It was Courtney who was my biggest motivator in starting and finishing this book.

This first installment was just an introduction and barely scratches the surface. If you are eager to learn more about the *Meridian* story, continue to the end for a preview of the next book in the series, *Machine Row*! Also, feel free to reach out or follow:

cjyee.books@gmail.com
instagram.com/cjyee.books

―――――――

READ ON FOR A PREVIEW OF

THE FIRST TWO CHAPTERS:

Book Two in the **MERIDIAN** SERIES

1

Preview

THEY told her that this place was somewhere people went to get lost. After living and toiling here for over a year, Niko had no more doubts about those claims — time and desolation had trodden her into utter insignificance. If it weren't for her own desire to live, it would've made zero difference if she just faded into Oblivion, taking with her all hopes and dreams she may have once had. She supposed Kira-Tharn would not have stood for that, so toil it was.

Today was Niko's twenty-first birthday, but nobody cared. Not the men beside her excavating the tunnels and Rifts. Not the An-Mara she lived with in squalor. Certainly not the powers that be on this Mara-forsaken world. Niko herself barely cared. Birthday celebrations were a thing of the past, just one more backwater tradition that she had no choice but to leave behind.

Arhanda was no more, and neither were birthdays, apparently.

That's why it was so weird that Ravenna had contacted her today, of all days. 'Come over tonight,' she had said. 'Oh yeah, and Cryo says we need some nutrient mix, so stop by the market please.'

Typical Ravenna, blunt and straight to the point. She was never one for pleasantries, even when she hadn't spoken with her friend in months. Not that it mattered — Niko didn't take it personally. Her sixteen-year-old self might have, but that sensitive version of her was long gone.

"Watch the line!" Armond-Dei yelled to the workers from atop the Rift that Niko was perched within. "It is your pay that will be docked if it is damaged in any way."

What an ass, Niko thought. Armond-Dei was a washed up An-Mara sellout, a foreman that seemed to relish in ordering underlings about. He did have a point, though — it looked like Maro Del-Fiiz was getting awfully close to the line as he was dragging the gear into position.

Niko watched with an open mouth as Kira-Tharn stormed over to the crane he was operating. "Watch it!" she hissed. Leave it to her to take matters into her own hands.

Maro looked offended, holding up his hands as if to question what the blazes the woman was on about. He simply shook his head and continued, paying her cautions no mind.

Niko held her breath, half expecting an accident to unfold. The line sat very exposed on the dark reddish dirt as the crane's load inched ever closer.

Two meters. One meter. Half a meter…

She closed one eye, but to her relief, the gear swung wide — maybe only by centimeters — leaving the precious line that drew water up from the reservoir below unscathed.

She exhaled in silent gratitude, carefully lifting her helmet and removing her mask. She instinctively took a deep breath, accidentally gulping in scorching hot air. She immediately realized her mistake, hurriedly wiping away the sweat and grime that were plastered to her face before resecuring the seal.

After all this time, she still hadn't gotten used to wearing all this gear in such sweltering heat. She had once thought Sol City was hot, but that was a refrigerator compared to this oven. Even venturing this far away from the Twilight was brutal. Dangerous even. She couldn't imagine what conditions would be like further into the daylight. The things she did to make ends meet…

This whole currency thing was such a weird way of life to her. She had been raised in a Meridian system — whatever was needed was always provided. It was plain and simple. Now, it seemed like the hardest work was often rewarded with the least compensation, while those corrupt gangsters that ruled over the city hoarded all the wealth. Hopefully she'd have enough Terion credit to be able to pick up the nutrient mix like Ravenna asked her to.

"I shall throttle the one called Maro Del-Fiiz if he insists on putting all our positions in jeopardy," Kira-Tharn huffed.

"Do it," Niko managed to whisper, her throat now hoarse from inhaling the unthinkably hot, dry air.

"Our shift is almost over, and yet he insists on taking such risks," Kira-Tharn continued.

Niko hadn't often seen Kira-Tharn in such a fuss. What was her deal? Niko just nodded back at her as she reached for the time via her Ut. It *had* to be almost quitting time…

Idiot, she scolded herself. Of course there was no Ut — it had been years since she had the damn thing, but she still found herself reaching for it often.

"That one needs a swift education in the manners of proper behavior," Kira-Tharn ranted.

Blazes, was she still going on about Maro Del-Fiiz? Sure, it had been a close call with the line, but all turned out okay. Kira-Tharn hadn't been in a particularly bad mood today, so what was her big issue now?

"And I shall be the one to deliver that education if no one else will."

"Give it a rest," Niko sighed. The old Niko would've never talked back to Kira-Tharn like that, but she was far too confident for her own good these days. Or she just didn't care. After all, they did live together now, and had for over half a year.

Kira-Tharn turned to glower at Niko, although it was so hard to see through her mask because of all the dirt caked on the visor.

"I'm just saying…" Niko started.

"If he cuts the line, then I shall take your pay cut, Niko Ryen." Kira-Tharn leveled the threat at Niko in a way that left zero doubt that she would follow through.

Niko didn't bother to respond. She didn't know what was going on with Kira-Tharn right now. Maro must have really struck a nerve…

"What time is it?" she asked, changing the subject for her own peace of mind. Back on Arhanda, she could've made a rough guess as to what time it was, but here on An-Terino there were no rotating nights and days. Only regions of permanent night, permanent day, and permanent twilight.

"Our shift is completed," Kira-Tharn responded.

They would have to finish connecting the gear to the line of course, but after that, they'd be free to go. Niko was very glad to be done with the day. The work was exceptionally brutal today, and her stupid mistake of breathing in the daylight air made everything feel so much worse.

"Thank the Mara," Niko half-heartedly exclaimed.

"You should not use such expressions," Kira-Tharn cautioned her.

"Sorry," Niko said. "I forget."

"You have been living among the An-Mara for six months now, Niko Ryen," she continued. "That is more than just simply forgetting."

Niko threw up her arms in exasperation. She would say sorry again, but Kira-Tharn would probably get mad at her for that, too. It was best just to shut up and focus on connecting the gear to the line.

"If you insist on work of that quality, nobody may leave tonight," Armond-Dei yelled down to the laborers. "If I have to come down there and perform your tasks for you, it will not go well for any of you!"

Niko was tempted to yell at him to do just that — come down there and actually work. That lazy, lazy man was truly awful at times. He seemed like he was going to be nice when she had first become employed here, but after only a few days on the job, she had come to despise the guy.

She sensed Kira-Tharn tense up, as if she could feel the bristling of hairs on her friend's neck. She knew Kira-Tharn hated the guy, also. Actually, pretty much every single Rift worker in the company hated him, but there was nothing anyone could do. He was the foreman and they all had to follow his word if they wished to remain employed. There was no justice in this place. No fairness at all. This world was devoid of it.

After a few minutes of struggling to connect the gear to the line, they were finished. Even Armond-Dei seemed satisfied, because he simply turned around, stepped onto his buggy, and drove off to the rail station. The rest of the workers would have to walk, of course.

Recently, the long walk back was the worst part of the entire day. Not only was she exhausted from an entire day of manual labor, but they had progressed the line so far along the Rift that it was now about five kilometers back to base camp. And this was all decked out in full protective gear under the oppressive heat of daylight!

Niko settled next to Kira-Tharn as they both silently trudged back. Her feet dragged through the dirt one laborious step after another, each made more difficult as she looked toward the hazy orange glow of the sol — Bucon, it was called. How had her life come to this?

'Welcome to the bleakness'. That's what one of the transit clerks had told her when she first arrived, and prophetically, that was her existence now.

At one point, she desperately wished she could've gotten off this blazes Hole of a planet, but it was not to be so. Pretty much as soon as they arrived last year, it became clear that there was no way to book passage to the Capital system unless they had an insane amount of Terion credit. At the time, the entire group had a grand total of zero, so they were all conscripted into working grueling shifts just to scrape by, let alone secure transport off-world. Ever since, Niko had more or less given up looking for a way off.

Originally, she was living with Cryo, Ravenna, and Kyler in Machine Row, but those three had begun to spend inordinate hours working on very technical machine work, something she knew very little about. As the days went by, they had become so bogged down in their work that Niko started to drift away. Instead, she found herself spending more and more time with the An-Mara of all people, and now lived among them. The good ones, though — not the ones who destroyed her world.

Meanwhile, Jack and Callum, bless their hearts, had infiltrated a small contingent of Meridians here in order to find a way off-planet. She had grown so close with Jack on the long voyage to An-Terino, yet she now cursed him — and herself, she supposed — for never making a move to progress past anything other than friends. Circumstances had now separated them for close to a year, so she didn't know when she'd have the chance to tell him how she felt.

She lamented her misfortunes to herself. Her bad romantic luck would continue forever, it seemed. She thought it laughable that she was now *twenty-one* years old and had never been in a single relationship in her life. She'd never even kissed anyone.

How embarrassing.

Kira-Tharn shot her a look that was unmistakable, even through her bulky, dirtied mask. She knew Kira-Tharn was well aware of what — or *who* — she was thinking about. Niko must have been making the *face*. Every time she thought of Jack, her heart constricted and her hands grew clammy, and as Kira-Tharn claimed, she bit the inside of her lower lip. How Kira-Tharn even noticed *any* of that was a mystery… She should've just left her mask dirty so her face wouldn't be visible.

"You have only yourself to hold responsible for your own happiness," Kira-Tharn lectured her. "If you fancy a male, then it lies upon you to take action. Regretting inaction is not the way of the An-Mara."

Niko sighed. She knew Kira-Tharn was right, but it still did little to ease her regrets. She averted the judging gaze of her friend, instead focusing on not collapsing under the weight of all her protective gear.

"And do you have a *male* you fancy," Niko asked flippantly.

"That is none of your concern," Kira-Tharn replied.

Of course it wasn't.

"Yeah, and so neither is it of yours," Niko defiantly replied. Why was she so irritable today? It being her birthday surely had something to do with it. Last year, when she turned twenty, she had also been in a very strange mood.

"I only offer you advice," Kira-Tharn responded.

"Yeah, well I can't do anything about it now, can I?" Niko started to raise her voice.

"Is the one called Jack Sehs dead?" Kira-Tharn asked.

"Well… no."

"Then you very much can do something about it."

"There's no way for me to reach him!" Niko protested.

Kira-Tharn just glared back at her.

"I'm serious! I have no way to contact him! We've been over this!" Niko doubled down.

"You know who he is working with, do you not?" Kira-Tharn asked.

"Umm, well… yes," Niko admitted.

"And you know in what district he is located?"

"Maybe." Her eyes were now facing the ground in embarrassment.

"Then there is a way, Niko Ryen. You are just being obstinate."

Niko fumed, but she couldn't put words together to defend herself. Kira-Tharn had won this argument, but Niko refused to let her have that satisfaction.

She admitted there *was* a possible way to contact Jack, but it would require her to travel all the way to the other side of Alashadar, and she wasn't about to do that. Besides, what if Jack needed to maintain his cover? She blushed at the thought of her bursting in on one of his clandestine operations and professing her feelings to him. Now that would be a sure-fire way to *lose* a man forever… Not to mention, it might jeopardize their one chance to get off this hellhole of a planet.

"Just… nevermind. You don't get it."

"I *do* get it," Kira-Tharn pushed. "Better than you know. You are the one refusing to understand."

Niko just shook her head and continued on in silence. She was over this argument. How stupid was this? They were arguing over a *guy*…

No, not even that. They were arguing over Niko's *failed love life*…

After walking the remainder of the thirty-minute trek without speaking, the two roommates finally arrived at the base camp, and it wasn't a pretty sight to behold. Dusty hoses and ducts ran chaotically between makeshift tents that were arranged haphazardly. Discarded debris littered the ground and trash bins overflowed from careless use, or a lack thereof altogether. Niko stopped caring about what the place looked like long ago. It wasn't worth taking the time to clean because every few weeks, the camp would shift as they progressed the Rift further and further. What was leftover unfortunately became part of an endless trail of rubbish as far as the eye could see, which, fittingly, wasn't very far because of the perpetual haze of this place.

After walking through the base camp, Niko and Kira-Tharn wordlessly piled into the back of a transport truck that would take them about ten more kilometers to the rail depot. During this bumpy ride through excavated dirt, Niko let her mind wander to her friends from Arhanda. She hadn't heard from them in months — so what was it that Ravenna wanted today? It couldn't be that they wanted to celebrate her birthday… right? That would be a foolish notion. It was more likely that they needed something from her — an errand of some sorts, or maybe even some correspondence with the An-Mara, whom she was now very well-acquainted with.

After sitting in the back of the truck without saying a single word to Kira-Tharn, they finally arrived at the rail depot. Dozens of transport trucks all arrived simultaneously, with dozens more departing, taking new shifts of workers to the many parallel Rifts that fed Alashadar its water. The truck came to a rough halt, and the passengers jumped out quickly as a new set of workhands jumped in without missing a beat.

"I would convey an apology, Kira-Tharn."

Niko turned around and Maro Del-Fiiz stood behind them with his head bowed. Niko didn't even think his stunt a few minutes ago was that big of a deal. Why was Kira-Tharn so upset about it? And why was he being so apologetic? The An-Mara never ceased to confuse the blazes out of her.

"It was not my intention to cause alarm at the site," he continued. "I was confident that I had the matter well under control."

Kira-Tharn didn't respond — she only nodded her head slightly. Niko waited for a split second for Kira-Tharn to continue walking with her, but she remained stopped, glaring at Maro.

Niko rolled her eyes and walked on, hoping that Kira-Tharn would join her and leave the poor guy alone. It really wasn't that big of a deal…

She entered the locker room, but Kira-Tharn never joined her. She probably stayed to lambast Maro, and Niko wasn't about to wait around to watch the unfortunate wretch deal with the wrath of Kira-Tharn.

Sweat and mud were caked to her face as she peeled off her mask, and heaps of dirt shook off onto the ground as she removed the several layers' worth of heavy daylight protection. As filthy as she was, Niko opted to not take a shower there. She'd do it later; she just wanted to get home right now. Kira-Tharn was a grown woman and could find her own way back. They would almost certainly continue their argument later, but that was a worry for future Niko.

She quickly got dressed and made her way into the bustling rail depot, which was filled with mostly An-Mara, as they tended to be the poorer, more desperate class that took the jobs on the Rifts. It was important work and paid decently, but it was demanding labor. Every day, the rail that Niko rode would pass through the agricultural fields, and every day she would question whether or not to take a job there instead. That wasn't easy work, either, but those laborers at least had better hours than the Rift workers.

Niko mindlessly slogged over to a train that was loading, plugged her Terion badge into the console to allow her on board, and slumped into a seat that was farthest from anyone else. She laid her head back and allowed herself to become comfortable as she closed her eyes for a few minutes.

She would've loved to have napped the whole way back, but she sat up sharply when they slowed down for a stop as they passed through the fields, ready to pick up agricultural laborers also on their way home from work. Niko looked out the window to see inclined hills forming the waves on an endless sea of black plants that stretched all the way to the horizon.

She really *should* find work here instead... Anything seemed better than toiling her life away at the Rifts day in and day out. The weather would be cooler, the work less brutal on her body, and the commute a little shorter. Plus, the field workers always seemed just a little happier than the Rift workers did.

I will *talk to Kira-Tharn about it,* she vowed. She was very serious about doing it if Kira-Tharn would do it with her, but that was another discussion future Niko would have to deal with. Something to worry about later.

As the train came to a complete stop, the doors opened up and field workers piled in by the dozen. Niko scooted over to make room for a girl with orange hair that she'd seen before. She was a petite young woman about her own age, but Niko always felt bad for the girl — she had heavy, disfiguring scars that marred her entire face. Whatever caused that must have been horribly painful.

Niko nodded to her, offering a contrite but genuine smile. She never opened conversation, though, so Niko never knew her name or her story, as curious as she was. Nobody really talked to anybody on the trains, other than their own company they kept, so it wouldn't have been proper to talk to her now.

A few minutes after the train left the station, twilight had almost completely set in. The atmosphere faded from a light, hazy orange to a darker reddish-purple. Soon, Niko could see the glow of Alashadar on the horizon. After the track turned around a low mountain, towering buildings came into view far ahead in the distance.

Alashadar was a *massive* metropolis that dwarfed even Sol City, but Niko always thought it to be a bit dreadful the way it was enveloped in perpetual twilight. It stretched for kilometers and kilometers along the narrow strip of sol-set that banded the planet. For people who loved nightlife, it was a playground and a haven. But for those who preferred daylight and the outdoors, it was a hellish nightmare, an eternal purgatory that offered no more than the tiniest sliver of dark red sol-light from the setting Bucon.

As the rail sped forward at a blistering pace, the buildings resolved into towering structures that dominated the skyline as far as she could see in both directions, the only depression being that of the Machine Row district. There, smoke still poured from a few factories that gave the district its name, but in recent months, construction had been turning it into a tech manufacturing center, driven primarily by an influx of Meridians.

Niko hadn't actually been there in months and, truth be told, was a little nervous to go visit with all the Meridian activity about. She rarely saw her friends from Arhanda anymore, though, and it would be nice to see them, even if she had to make the long trek over from the An-Mara quarter. Machine Row was no Oldcity or NewCen, but it was a far cry nicer than the slums she was used to living in.

The train finally slowed down as it entered the central terminal, doors opening to reveal the busiest station in the whole city. Thousands of people bustled about, some loading onto several other rails that ran parallel to the city's orientation, others loading onto the trains that took laborers out to their respective workplaces radially. Though most of the major rails were at ground level, escalators and elevators rose a hundred meters into the air, connecting the terminal to adjacent trams and towers.

Alashadar was a very vertical city, most of the skyscrapers packed densely along one major artery. The outlying areas, including the An-Mara quarter where she lived, were much flatter and far less luxurious, although they were just as densely packed, if not more.

As everyone filed off the train, Niko mindlessly followed, then blended into the stream of people that were making their way over to the train that would take them to the An-Mara quarter. She'd been ground down to nothing more than a drone, a single cog in a vast machine. Her daily routine had become automatic:

Wake up.

Eat breakfast.

Walk from living quarters to the rail station.

Ride the train into the heart of Alashadar.

Transfer to the train that goes to the Rifts.

Ride the transport trucks to base camp and walk to the

excavation sites.

Work until lunch.

Eat lunch.

Work some more until quitting time.

Walk back to base camp and ride the transport trucks back to the rail depot.

Ride the train back to Alashadar.

Transfer to the train to the An-Mara quarter.

Walk back to living quarters.

Clean up.

Eat dinner.

Sleep.

Repeat.

Every single day was the exact same now for over six months, with no end in sight. She really did need a change. She had decided on the train ride back that she was serious about switching to the agricultural fields. She would speak with Kira-Tharn tonight about it. For now, though, she needed to hurry home and clean herself up before going over to visit her friends. Aside from being happy to see them, she was very eager to hear if they'd made any more progress on getting off this Mara-forsaken rock.

2

Preview

AS ugly as Niko's tiny living quarters looked from the outside, they were somehow worse on the inside. Unwashed dishes lined what little countertop space was available, and some even found their way onto the floors, which had been un-mopped for the entire time Niko had been living here. Had this place been on Arhanda, critters of filth would have abounded, but alas, life was sparse on this planet, the incomplete terraforming from eons ago too big an obstacle for native species to evolve and flourish.

Probably for the best.

Niko looked around ashamedly. She'd always been a clean freak when she was younger, someone who paid close attention to detail. At one point, she'd even been a conscientious gardener and had once aspired to turn her Green Coast home into a second Nevaly.

Now she couldn't care less about those details. Neither she nor Kira-Tharn had the time, energy, or interest to beautify their home. The only thing that mattered was having enough food for meals and a pillow to sleep on. Water for a shower was a bonus, a luxury they could barely afford. Nevermind that it was cold water…

Niko's hair was now wrapped in a towel to dry — she let it

grow long during the voyage to An-Terino and had now grown comfortable with it being at least mid-back length. It was slightly annoying to deal with, but she did like how it looked. Not that it really mattered — she always had to keep it up while she was at work anyway. But still, it was a pleasure she allowed for herself. One of the few.

As her hair dried, she considered doing a small amount of long-overdue tidying, but just the sight of the clutter was too overwhelming. She wouldn't even know where to start! Besides, her stomach grumbled in hunger, and even though she assumed they were going to have dinner tonight, she was so starving after working all day that she had to refuel with something small for now. She unwrapped a small protein packet to eat, throwing the wrapper onto the ground. Maybe she should empty trash first…

After reluctantly scooping up a few piles of garbage that had been haphazardly thrown onto the dirty floors, she walked to empty their trash bin into the community pile outside. She wondered when Kira-Tharn would get in; it was strange that she still wasn't back. Niko started to worry because it was so unlike her, but she also knew Kira-Tharn was quite capable of taking care of herself. She must have been going to the markets or something.

Niko realized she forgot to tell Kira-Tharn that *she* would be the one going shopping tonight — she had to go anyway since Ravenna had asked her to. Now it didn't make sense for her to get anything else besides what Ravenna wanted, in case Kira-Tharn did go to the markets. They sure didn't have any Terion credit to waste… Oh well.

She dumped the trash onto the pile and was a little disappointed it hadn't been cleared out to the incinerators yet. It should've been taken out days ago. What was going on?? The whole block smelled so bad that Niko nearly had to pull her Garments over her nose. Still, she was much too tired to spend time tracking down the services to make it happen. She'd rather just deal with the smell.

"I do wish that the refuse services would complete their duties."

Niko whirled around to find Riiz Alke-Tani carrying his own trash bin to the pile. He was surely just as annoyed as Niko about the situation.

"Yep," Niko agreed. "Lazy chums."

"I do believe I may pay a visit to their offices in Machine Row and request immediate relief," he said. "Would you care to accompany me?"

Niko shook her head. "I can't today. I'm visiting Cryo, Ravenna, and Kyler in a few minutes."

"Very well," he said. "Please do wish them greetings from me."

"Of course." Niko nodded respectfully, then retreated back into her quarters. Riiz was a better person than she was. She could have very well stopped by the refuse service's office in Machine Row on her way to her friends' place — she just didn't want to.

After returning inside, she replaced the empty trash bin into its corner by the kitchen, satisfied that their place was just a little bit cleaner than before. However, the smell of the community refuse pile wafted into the room when she opened the door, etching its stink into every surface. Whatever.

She finished her 'cleaning' by wiping her hair towel over the kitchen counter, then threw a jacket on before heading out into the night. The hazy purple-orange glow in the sky didn't really scream *night* by any meaning of the word, but her timepiece read 20:04. Hence, nighttime.

Niko felt ridiculous without a Ut. Having to look at the time on a clunky band around her wrist felt so *primitive*, but she supposed it was better than nothing. She was so used to time being tied to the sol's position in the sky, but here on An-Terino, the position of the sol only indicated how far you were away from the Terminator. The lighting never wavered in this place, so it was nearly impossible to tell the time without looking at her timepiece.

She walked through the An-Mara ghetto to the nearest rail station, which was a couple kilometers away. After a long day at the Rifts, she just wanted off her feet. At least she'd grown accustomed to walking many kilometers daily, so it wasn't exactly *painful*. Just inconvenient.

The sights and sounds in the neighborhood were enjoyable enough for Niko, though. A mother cooking a meal outside for all the kids on one block. Two men rebuilding a door across the street. A girl about her own age gathering water from the well on the next block. She didn't know any of them by name, but their faces were familiar. They all currently existed in the same unfortunate walk of life that she did, and she therefore felt a strong kinship with them.

A few years ago, the An-Mara had been such a mystery at best, with Niko feeling confusion, fear, and even hostility toward them after what happened to her home. But after getting to know the contingent of them here on An-Terino — especially after *living* among them — Niko had developed a great respect for their culture. True, the group living on this planet were the more progressive of the bunch, but even the social restrictions on laughing and entertainment weren't as bad as she once thought. It was just a part of the way they lived their lives, and they were humans just like anybody else.

When she first made the decision to live here, her friends told her that this ghetto was dangerous. Shantytowns always had a bad reputation, but she actually felt *safer* here than she did whenever she went into the heart of the city. Alashadar was a lawless place, one not safe for people to just walk around by themselves. Especially not young women.

Even in Machine Row she felt way out of her element, which was where she was headed now. At least her friends lived on the outskirts, away from the nightlife and the crime that came with it. She'd be quick about this whole trip, and if her friends gave her any grief about it, she would have words for them — it was their own fault she was out here walking by herself, anyway.

With a huff, she continued on through the impoverished streets of the An-Mara slums.

Upon reaching the rail station forty-five minutes later, Niko clicked her Terion badge into the console and boarded the train that was due to depart next. The ride was short, only about five minutes, but soon after it departed, she realized that she forgot to visit the market by the An-Mara quarter before getting on the train.

How stupid!

She sighed to herself, but there was nothing she could do now. She'd just have to visit one of the markets in Machine Row. It was for situations like this that she wished Kira-Tharn was with her. That lady was so confident and unapologetic in everything she did. She never got worked over in a haggle the way Niko seemed to. That's why she was responsible for buying their groceries most of the time, while Niko got to do dishes and empty trash bins. Sometimes.

After a short ride, she exited the train at the Machine Row station and looked around. Where *was* the nearest market? To her left was a cluster of factories, and to her right was the busy center of the district, even if it was a little bit further away from her friends' place.

She headed right. Surely there would be a marketplace in this direction before long. She hurriedly passed along a dark, quiet part of the street, trying her best to stay in the lamplight. A few men walked past her, and suddenly she felt very vulnerable. She smiled nervously at them, and was all too happy when none of them paid her any mind. As soon as she was out of sight of the rail station, she broke into a light jog, just so she didn't have to spend any more time in this place than was necessary. Her antics drew a few stares from passersby, but she didn't care. The fatigue in her legs held stronger protest than any strangers' side-eyes, anyway.

After about a minute of jogging through the dark neighborhood, she saw the telltale glow from large-scale neon lights in the distance. To her relief, the sights and sounds indicated a busy marketplace, so she resumed her walking pace, even if it was a little more brisk than normal. Before she stepped into the illuminated part of the street, however, her eyes were drawn to a cluster of boxes that lay in an empty yard behind a very tall fence to her left.

She stopped and looked closely. She'd seen that emblem before. Sure enough, upon further inspection, she saw that it was the Meridian Crescent. What was in these boxes? And why were they just lying about outside? Some even had the lids halfway opened. She stepped forward a few paces and saw another logo on the side.

Shatter Industries.

She knew of that company. It was one of the larger players here on An-Terino. It wasn't the company that she worked for, but they did control some of the Rifts, as well as most of the high-tech factories that were popping up here in Machine Row.

What would they *be doing in league with the Meridians?*

From what she'd learned over the past few years, Meridian civilization was based off a form of socialism, a system where goods were provided and shared. This was all she'd ever known growing up on Arhanda, so it seemed natural to her. The one caveat was that there were no private businesses that hoarded goods and currency the way that companies like Shatter did.

Her curious nature got the better of her and she looked for a way past the fence that separated her from the boxes. She followed around a corner to look for any breaks when she came upon a locked gate halfway down a dark alleyway. She walked forward slowly, just to investigate.

Should I be doing this? she wondered, almost pausing.

The fact that she even had to ask herself probably told her that no, she should *not* be doing this.

Just one look inside the boxes, she promised herself.

She tiptoed to the gate and pressed against it. A heavy, chain lock wrapped around the two fences that joined together at the gate. There was no way it would budge, but perhaps…

Yes! she congratulated herself as she slipped through the narrow crack, underneath the lock. *Finally, a benefit to being so scrawny…*

Though she had filled out a little bit in the last couple years, she was still quite slim and was able to fit through this gate, which was clearly meant to keep people out. She brushed the rust from the fence off her hands and snooped across the empty lot toward the building where some open boxes were perched. As she got close, she stood over them.

Nothing. Maybe the other ones in the front had something in them?

She turned to walk around to the front, but stopped dead in her tracks when she heard voices. She silenced her breathing and tensed her muscles as she crept to the corner of the building in the back, where some discarded wood provided a hiding place. Once there, she peered through an opening and saw two men with rifles patrol by. They were wearing Shatter uniforms.

Afraid to move a centimeter, she put a hand over her mouth, as if that would make her breathing any quieter.

"That reminds me, have you gone in to place your bet yet?" one of the men asked.

"Of course I have," the other one responded. "Have you *not?*"

"I don't know who I'm pulling for!"

"Brother, come on."

"I mean obviously the safe bet is Delmatic, but I'm really tempted to go with Jon Wilhe."

"Wilhe's a Ripper, for sure. But are you really willing to put down Terion against Delmatic?"

"I don't know, I need to think about it."

"Deadline is coming up…"

"I know! I'll put it in tomorrow."

"You better! The race is in two days, my man."

"Three, actually. But I got this. I'll put it in tomorrow for sure."

"Well, as long as your guy doesn't *die* this time, I'll consider it a win for you."

"Yeah, yeah. Laugh it up…"

As if an invitation was given, the other guard started cackling so hard he wheezed. Niko didn't exactly think it was funny. As dangerous as Trackripping was, it wasn't funny when racers got hurt.

"You know, I think I'm gonna choose Wilhe. There's no way he crashes, and if he wins, that's a *huge* odds payout. Plus, you can eat your words when he beats Delmatic."

"No chance."

"I don't know… It's possible. I've seen him on NewCen before and he rips."

"Oh I know he does! I admitted as much. There's just no way he beats Delmatic."

One of the two men's Uts suddenly made a loud, beeping noise, and Niko jumped. She clenched her teeth and pressed her palms to the ground, praying that she didn't make any sound. She was trespassing on the grounds of a Meridian warehouse wearing An-Mara Garments, and the two armed Shatter guards were stopped only a meter away from her. Not a great situation to be in…

How could she have been so stupid to think this was a good idea? And why did they have to stop right in front of her?!

Go! she commanded, as if the guards would heed her wishes. *Walk! Leave! Begone!*

"This Mara-accursed posting will be the death of me," the man whose Ut beeped complained. "They yank us around, expecting us to do this and that and everything."

"And?.. What do they want now?"

The men were *still* standing in the same spot, much to Niko's chagrin. She held her breath as she continued to will them to move on.

"They want us back at the docks for another shipment."

"*Another* one? We just finished unloading *this* one!"

"I know! It's unbelievable. Bunch of Minedyne stuff, also. I don't know why they are transferring that stuff here. They should've let it all burn with that other dump of a world."

Niko's breath caught.

Minedyne.

Were they talking about *Arhanda*? Slight anger coursed through her veins, but she stayed as silent as a field mouse avoiding a nightraptor on the hunt.

One of the men glared at the other. "You know we aren't supposed to be talking about that out here. Only behind closed doors."

"Oh, give it a rest. We're in an abandoned warehouse out in the middle of nowhere. As if there would be Terion Sight anywhere outside of NewCen or Oldcity. Maybe the nicer part of Machine Row, but this place is a load of scrap that nobody cares about."

"I guess so... But still. We should be careful."

"Grow a spine, brother," the one man chided the other. "Anyway, what I was going to say... the worst part is that I heard Andersane is being transferred here."

"Seriously? That hardass? When does he get in?"

"Not sure. Hopefully not anytime soon. Let's get back to the docks and see what they want, though..."

Not moving a muscle was torturous for Niko. She wanted to explode. Andersane?! Coming here?! And what was the connection to Minedyne?

She always made it a point to not spend much time dwelling on the events of her past, but this shoved everything that happened a few years ago back into her face, front and center. Her skin heated and she could feel sweat start to condense on her forehead. It was as if every thought she felt when her home was destroyed was rolled up into a tiny ball and forced down her throat now, finding a way to lump up in her chest.

She coughed.

Time slowed down to a near stop, and Niko didn't even have time to second guess her actions as she raced across the yard for that hole in the gate. Fortunately, the Shatter soldiers had ambled back around the corner, giving her just enough time to pull herself clumsily through the gate before she heard the shouts of the men after her.

Run! She told herself.

And she ran.

"STOP!" one of the men bellowed.

She didn't stop.

"What do we do?! Shoot?"

"Of course!! Don't let her get away!" The answer came roaring back, just as she raced around the corner.

Soon thereafter, the ricochet of bullets sounded on the wall to her left.

———————

ABOUT THE AUTHOR

C. J. Yee was born, raised, and currently resides in Santa Barbara County, California. Yee has a degree in the earth sciences, but has many interests, with special passions for astronomy, history, and anything to do with the natural world.

Reach out or follow Yee at:

cjyee.books@gmail.com
instagram.com/cjyee.books